Richard Laymon wrote over th [illegible] n May 2001, *The Travelling Vampi* [illegible] r Best Horror Novel, a prize fo [illegible] shortlisted with *Flesh*, *Funland*, [illegible] and *A Writer's Tale* (Best Non- [illegible] include the books of the Beast House Chron [illegible] *Cellar*, *The Beast House* and *The Midnight Tour*. Some of his recent novels have been *Night in the Lonesome October*, *No Sanctuary* and *Amara*.

A native of Chicago, Laymon attended Willamette University in Salem, Oregon, and took an MA in English Literature from Loyola University, Los Angeles. In 2000, he was elected President of the Horror Writers' Association. He died in February 2001.

Laymon's fiction is published in the United Kingdom by Headline, and in the United States by Leisure Books and Cemetery Dance Publications. To learn more, visit the Laymon website at: http://rlk.cjb.net

'This author knows how to sock it to the reader' *The Times*

'A brilliant writer' *Sunday Express*

'No one writes like Laymon and you're going to have a good time with anything he writes' Dean Koontz

'In Laymon's books, blood doesn't so much as drip as explode, splatter and coagulate' *Independent*

'Stephen King without a conscience' Dan Marlowe

'Incapable of writing a disappointing book' *New York Review of Science Fiction*

'A gut-crunching writer' *Time Out*

'This is an author that does not pull his punches . . . A gripping, and at times genuinely shocking, read' *SFX Magazine*

Also in the Richard Laymon Collection published by Headline

The Beast House Trilogy:
The Cellar
The Beast House
The Midnight Tour

Beware!
Dark Mountain
The Woods are Dark
Out are the Lights
Night Show
Allhallow's Eve
Flesh
Resurrection Dreams
Alarums
Blood Games
Endless Night
Midnight's Lair*
Savage
In The Dark
Island
Quake
Body Rides
Bite
Fiends
After Midnight
Among the Missing
Come Out Tonight
The Travelling Vampire Show
Dreadful Tales
Night in the Lonesome October
No Sanctuary
Amara
The Lake
The Glory Bus
Funland
The Stake

*previously published under the pseudonym of Richard Kelly

Darkness, Tell Us

and

One Rainy Night

headline

DARKNESS, TELL US first published in Great Britain in 1991
by HEADLINE BOOK PUBLISHING

ONE RAINY NIGHT first published in Great Britain in 1991
by HEADLINE BOOK PUBLISHING

First published in this omnibus edition in 2006
by HEADLINE BOOK PUBLISHING

A HEADLINE paperback

2

0 7553 3174 5 (ISBN-10)
978 0 7553 3174 1 (ISBN-13)

Typeset in Janson by Avon DataSet Ltd, Bidford on Avon, Warwickshire

Printed and bound in Great Britain by
Mackays of Chatham plc, Chatham, Kent

Headline's policy is to use papers that are natural, renewable and recyclable
products and made from wood grown in sustainable forests. The logging and
manufacturing processes are expected to conform to the environmental
regulations of the country of origin.

HEADLINE PUBLISHING GROUP
A division of Hodder Headline
338 Euston Road
London NW1 3BH

www.headline.co.uk
www.hodderheadline.com

Darkness, Tell Us

THIS BOOK IS DEDICATED TO
OUR GREAT FRIENDS
CHRIS & DICK BOYANSKI
ADVENTURERS IN MIXOLOGY AND THE
SUPERNATURAL
TO KARA & KYLE
AND OF COURSE
TO TIMMY
WHEREVER YOU ARE
WHATEVER YOU ARE

But ’tis strange:
And oftentimes, to win us to our harm,
The instruments of darkness tell us truths,
Win us with honest trifles, to betray ’s
In deepest consequence.

Macbeth, Act I, scene iii.

Chapter One

'I don't think that's such a good idea,' Dr Dalton said.

'Oh, come on. It'll be kicks.' Lana, standing on tiptoes, continued to pull the flat box of the Ouija off the bookshelf. The games stacked on top of it teetered. Monopoly and Careers, high above her, started sliding.

'Look out!' Keith warned.

She flung up a hand and blocked the boxes. But a leather dice cup, out of sight until now, slid down the tilted ramp of the Monopoly box and fell. It bounced off her forehead. She flinched, muttered, 'Shit!' and plucked out the Ouija. The rest of the games dropped, jolting the shelf.

Howard grinned. Served Lana right for going against the professor's wishes. Some of the other students were laughing.

Dr Dalton neither grinned nor laughed, but Howard saw a glimmer of amusement in her eyes. 'I *told* you it wasn't a good idea.'

'I didn't know you had booby-traps,' Lana said.

'Every so often I get lucky and trap a booby.'

'Funny,' Lana muttered. Bending down with the Ouija box under one arm, she picked up the dice cup and set it on a shelf. She turned around and met the professor's eyes. 'You don't really mind if we give this thing a try, do you? I've never seen a Ouija board in action.'

'You're better off that way.'

Keith went, 'Oooooo, ominous.'

Lana gave him a quick look as if she didn't appreciate his

interference. To Dr Dalton, with a smile and a shrug of her shoulders, she said, 'It's just a game, Corie.'

'So is Russian roulette.'

'Woooo,' said Keith.

What a scrote, Howard thought. But he kept the opinion to himself. He was no dummy. Keith, who looked and acted like a jock in spite of being an English major, could probably demolish him with a single blow.

From a padded chair in a corner of the den, Doris said, 'The analogy seems somewhat inflated, if you ask me.'

'Nobody asked,' Keith pointed out.

Lana, on tiptoes, studied the stack of games. 'Have you got a revolver up there, Corie?'

'Of course not.'

'Then why a Ouija board, if it's just as dangerous?'

'It's sort of a keepsake. Obviously, I *should've* gotten rid of it.'

'What's the big deal?' Keith asked.

'One must beware of tampering with the unknown,' Doris said, her voice full of menace. She widened her eyes at Keith, though he wasn't even looking in her direction. Then she swung her thick legs off the foot rest, bounded up and pranced toward the group.

Here she comes, Howard thought. Our fat Puck. Our spritely, pedantic gnome.

She raised a warning finger. 'There are forces lurking in the shadowy corners of the universe that . . .'

'Stuff it,' Keith suggested.

'That's enough,' Dr Dalton told him. She said to Lana, 'Hey, we're here to have a good time. If your heart's set on fooling around with that thing, be my guest. But just keep me out of it. A deal?'

'Sure! Great! OK, who's going to do it with me?'

'I'll do it with you any chance I get,' Keith said.

He probably *does*, Howard thought.

Ignoring the remark, Lana asked Dr Dalton, 'How many can play at a time?'

'Up to four, I guess. More than that, it would get awfully crowded around the board.'

'OK. We need two more hearty volunteers.'

'Include me in,' Doris said.

Keith looked as if he would rather 'include in' a wad of used toilet paper, but he made no protest.

'That's three,' Lana said. 'One more. Any takers?'

Howard looked around. Professor Dalton was shaking her head. He saw Glen over in a corner, stuffing potato chips into his mouth. Angela was sitting at the far end of the sofa, hands folded on her lap, gazing into space.

I probably ought to go over and sit with her, he thought. He hadn't really spent much time with Angela tonight. She might think he was trying to ignore her.

But God, she was so weird. As if she were from a different planet, or something, and longed for home.

Keith slapped Howard on the shoulder. Harder than necessary. 'Join the fun, Howitzer. You can play kneesies with Doris.'

He looked at Lana. 'Is it OK with you?'

'Sure. Why wouldn't it be?'

He shrugged, feeling a little dumb for asking Lana's permission.

'So, Corie, how do we play?'

Before she could answer, Doris said, 'I've done it before.'

'Where'd you find a blind guy?' Keith asked.

'Oh, that's rich, Mr Harris. It's wonderful that you've achieved the capability of amusing yourself with quips of such startling inanity.'

'Oink,' he said.

Lana swung her arm out. The back of her fist whapped

Keith's chest. It struck his left pectoral, a solid mound under his clinging shirt, with a sound like a mallet smacking raw beef. 'Knock it off,' she said.

Dr Dalton raised her eyebrows. Her lips, pressed together tightly, were turned down at the corners. Howard had seen that expression before. She was delighted that Lana had given Keith a thump. Delighted, but determined to keep her grin in check.

'I have a card table in the kitchen,' she said. 'Why don't we bring it out here so the rest of us can keep an eye on you.'

They went into the small, tidy kitchen. Dr Dalton scooted chairs away from the table. She folded one of them. As she handed it to Howard, she gave him the special look. A look she never gave anyone but him. He returned his version of it. Not a wink, but it seemed to hold the meaning of a wink: they were secretly sharing a wry amusement at the antics of the others. *What are a couple of folks like us doing in the midst of all this?*

He felt himself blush. He supposed he always blushed when she looked at him that way.

She handed chairs to Doris and Lana, then squatted down and tugged at a metal cuff to release one of the table's folding legs.

Howard saw the way her white shorts were drawn taut against the smooth curves of her rump. Her blouse was stretched across her back. Through its fabric, he could see the pink hue of her skin and the bands of her bra.

His throat tightened. His heart pounded faster and he felt a tight pressure in his groin.

Turning away, he carried his chair toward the den.

He'd taken this special summer session class for only one reason: to be in Dr Dalton's presence. He'd taken so many of her classes during his three years at Belmore University. But they were never enough. Ever since she'd stepped to the lectern on his first morning of freshman English, he'd been captivated by her. She was just so beautiful, so smart and funny, so caring.

She liked him a lot, too. He knew that.

But he also knew that she didn't think of him as a possible lover. Never would. A, he'd been born nine years too late. Not an overwhelming age difference, but still a barrier. B, he was only a rung or two up the ladder from being a nerd. C, Dr Dalton was a loner who didn't seem interested in any men, much less wimpy twenty-one-year-olds.

Just be glad she's your friend, he told himself.

But an awful feeling of loss swept through him as he set the chair down in the den. Dr Dalton's party tonight marked the end of the summer session. Howard would be packing tomorrow, flying home the day after. He wouldn't be seeing her again until the fall semester, nearly two months away.

As the others came in with chairs and the table, he found himself regretting that he'd agreed to join in. Dr Dalton had no intention of messing with the Ouija. If he'd refused, he could be spending the time with her.

Keith held the table steady on its edge while Dr Dalton snapped its legs into place. He flipped it upright, and she directed him to position it near the center of the living room.

Keith sat across from Lana, Howard across from Doris.

Lana was shaking open the box when Glen came over, a heap of potato chips cupped in his hand. The floor stopped shaking when he halted behind Doris. He gazed down at the Ouija and poked a chip into his mouth.

'Would you like to take my place?' Howard asked.

'When they're ice skating in hell, pal.'

'Very sensible,' Dr Dalton said.

Does she think I'm *not* sensible? Howard wondered. No, she understands. She realizes I was pushed into this.

Maybe he could get Angela to take his place.

He looked toward the sofa. Angela was staring at him with those big, gloomy eyes.

'Angela?' he called. 'Wouldn't you like to play?'

'Thank you, no.'

'Quit trying to squirm out, Howitzer.'

'I think you guys are nuts,' Glen said. A wet fleck of chip flew from his mouth, sailed over Doris's head and landed on the Ouija. On the Y of the YES in its upper left-hand corner. Only Howard seemed to notice. 'Didn't any of you read *The Exorcist*?'

'Get real,' Keith said.

'That's how that little twerp got possessed, fuh . . . messing around with her Ouija board.'

Doris said in her menacing voice, 'No good can come of it.' Then she chuckled.

Lana looked up from the back of the box. 'It says here we put our fingers lightly on the message indicator and just start asking questions.' She set the box on the floor, then placed the heart-shaped plastic pointer in the middle of the board and rested two fingers of her right hand on it.

'Atmosphere!' Keith said. 'We oughta be doing this in the dark, don't you think?'

'How would we read the messages?' Lana asked.

'A flashlight. Have you got a flashlight, Prof?'

'I'll get one,' she told him. 'You'll probably want a pen and some paper, too.'

Lana looked up at her. 'Is this thing really going to *say* something?'

'I wouldn't be at all surprised,' Dr Dalton said, and walked off.

'I'll get the lights,' Glen said.

As he started away, Angela reached up and turned off the lamp at her end of the sofa. She sat in the gloom for a few moments, gazing toward Howard and the others. Then she got up and came over. In her soft, hesitant voice, she said, 'If it's all right with everyone, I'll record the messages.'

'Thata girl,' Keith said.

Howard suspected that she just didn't want to be left sitting alone in the dark.

'I like all this confidence,' Lana said. 'God, it'd be cool if the thing actually does come through.'

'The spirits of the dead are always eager for human contact,' Doris said, this time using her normal voice.

Could she be serious? 'Spirits of the dead?' Howard asked.

'Who else?'

'Us? I mean, I've studied a little about this kind of thing. From what I've read, the consensus seems to be that the pointer's movements are probably controlled by the subconscious mind of one of the participants.'

'Which, in itself, could be interesting,' Lana said.

'A nice theory,' Doris said. 'Nice in its Elizabethan sense – meaning simple, naive, and ignorant.'

Keith nodded, grinning. 'Right. All the *smart* people know it's dead folks talking.'

'You may mock me now, but . . .' Her head turned as Dr Dalton came into the room. 'Hey, Professor, do Ouija messages come from the subconscious of someone guiding the pointer? Or from discarnate entities?'

'I'm no expert,' she said.

'But you've used this board, am I right?'

'I've used it. That's why I want nothing to do with all this. Who wants the light?'

'Me,' Angela said. 'I'll be taking the notes.'

Dr Dalton gave her the flashlight, a ballpoint and a pad of paper.

'OK?' Lana asked. 'Let's give it a try.'

As those at the table reached out and rested their fingers on the pointer, Dr Dalton said, 'Remember what I told you.

Don't mention my name while you're fooling around with that thing.'

'Mine either,' Glen said, taking up his position behind Doris. 'Can't be too careful when it comes to fooling around with spooks. Not that I believe in any of this.'

'We won't mention anyone, OK? Let's get started.'

'Just one of us should ask it questions,' Doris whispered.

'I'll do it,' Lana said. 'OK. Here goes.' Then she spoke in a clear, steady voice. 'Oh, great spirit of the Ouija board, we your humble servants ask that you address us. Hello? Hello? Anyone out there? Yoo-hoo. Calling all ghosts, calling all ghosts . . .'

'Don't be frivolous,' Doris muttered.

'Spirits of the netherworld, we beseech you to communicate with us. Denizens of the other side. Ghoulies, ghosties, long-leggity beasties . . .'

'Damn it, Lana.'

'Speak to us. Oh great subconscious, oh great id, get this mysterious message indicator moving. Come on, we're losing patience.'

The platform under their fingers suddenly began to slide.

'All right!' Keith whispered.

'Shhhh.'

It made loops, jerked from side to side.

'Is somebody doing this?' Lana asked.

It stopped near Howard, at the end of the top row of the alphabet. Angela's hip brushed against his upper arm. She leaned over and turned on the flashlight. 'M,' she whispered, and kept the light on the pointer as it slid away and stopped. 'E.'

It remained motionless.

'Me,' she said.

'Ooo, boy,' Keith muttered.

'It made sense,' Lana said. 'Jesus. I asked who was . . .'

The plastic heart darted for a corner of the board. It stopped on NO.

'Not Jesus,' Doris said.

'Thing's got a sense of humor,' Keith said. He sounded nervous.

'You pushed it over there,' Lana said.

'No way. I swear.'

'Howard?'

'I didn't. Honest.'

'Doris?'

The pointer moved. But not the way it had moved before. This time, it didn't glide lightly over the surface of the board. It felt weighted down, sluggish, *pushed*. 'That,' Doris said, 'is how it feels if one of us steers it.'

Lana pulled her hand back. She brought it up to her chest. Fingering a button at the top of her blouse, she stared at the board.

'Problem?' Doris asked. Her voice reeked of sarcasm.

'Shut up,' Lana said.

'We aren't feeling quite so frivolous now, are we?'

'Let's ask it something,' Keith said.

Lana tapped the button with her fingernail. 'I don't know about this.'

'*This* is what a Ouija board is supposed to do,' Doris informed her.

'Come on, Lana.'

'OK, OK.' She lowered her hand to the pointer. 'Who are you?' she asked.

It moved slowly across the alphabet, stopping long enough at each letter for Angela to check with the flashlight, speak the letter, and copy it on her pad. 'F-R-I-E-N-D.'

'Friend,' Lana said. 'Glad to hear it. Where are you?'

'N-E-A-R.'

'Ask if it's a ghost,' Keith whispered.

'Are you a ghost?'

The pointer sped toward the crescent moon in a corner of the board near Howard.

'No,' Angela said.

'Not a ghost. That's a relief. What are you?'

'S-E-R-V-A-N-T.'

'Whose servant?'

'U.'

Lana let out a quick laugh. 'Well, terrific. What're you going to do for me, servant?'

'G-I-V.'

'You're going to give me something? What?'

'U-G-I-V.'

'Me? I'm supposed to give something?'

'K-I-S-S-K-H.'

'Hey,' Keith blurted, 'that's me. It wants you to kiss me.'

'Bull.'

'I'm the only K.H. around here. Keith Harris.'

'Am I supposed to kiss Keith?'

The pointer slid toward the sun in the upper corner and stopped on the YES.

'I'm starting to like this,' Keith said.

'Who does the guy think he is, Cupid?'

'Just go ahead and do it,' Doris said.

Keith took his hand off the pointer, stood up and leaned over the table. He pursed his lips.

Lana frowned at him.

Howard wondered why she was hesitating. He knew for a fact that she was going with Keith. They'd probably done a lot more than kiss.

'This is insane,' she muttered.

'You don't have to do it,' Dr Dalton said. 'If I were you, I wouldn't do *anything* it asked.'

'Come on, honey.'

Lana sighed, stood up, bent forward, and kissed Keith on the mouth. She dropped back onto her chair. Sounding a little miffed, she said, 'OK, Ouija, I did it. Now what?'

When she and Keith returned their fingers to the pointer, it began moving rapidly.

'M-Y-T-U-R-N.'

Chapter Two

'*His* turn?' Keith whispered.

'No way,' Lana gasped. The beam of the flashlight glared on her face. A chill squirmed through Howard when he saw her lips squeeze together – as if they were being mashed by an invisible mouth.

She's doing that herself, he realized. *Afraid* it's going to kiss her.

She suddenly grimaced and turned away from the harsh beam of the flashlight. 'Cut it out!'

'Sorry.' Angela lowered the light.

'Are you OK?' Keith asked.

'Except for the fact that I've been blinded . . .'

'Did you feel anything?'

'No, of course not. Don't be ridiculous.'

'I thought for a second . . .' Keith went silent as the pointer suddenly darted sideways. Howard caught his breath, startled by the sudden movement.

When it stopped, Angela leaned over the board. She aimed the flashlight at the indicator. 'I,' she said. The pointer kept moving, stopping, moving again.

'G-I-V.'

'See?' Keith asked. 'He didn't want a kiss, after all. "My turn to give," that's what he meant.'

Lana let out a long breath. She seemed to slump forward a little. After a few moments, she said, 'OK, Ouija. What are you going to give?'

'L-O-O-T.'

'Loot? What do you mean? Money?'

The pointer slid toward the smiling face of the sun and came to a stop on YES.

'You're going to give money?'

The plastic heart under their fingertips remained motionless.

'Does that mean another yes?' Lana asked.

'I imagine so,' Doris told her.

'I *really* like this game,' Keith said. 'We split the take, right?'

Lana didn't answer him. Staring down at the board, she asked, 'Where is the money?'

The pointer darted over the curved rows of the alphabet, pausing while Angela read out each letter, then moving on. 'C-U-S-H-U-N.'

'Cushion? Under a cushion?'

'C-O-U-C-H.'

'I'll check,' Glen said. He rushed to the sofa, turned on the lamp at its far end, tossed aside the three seat cushions and started searching.

'Anything you find in there is mine,' Dr Dalton called to him.

'This guy's a real genius,' Keith said. 'Revealing the great secret of loot lost in the couch.'

'They like to play games,' Doris explained.

'Here we go.' Glen held up a penny.

'Riches beyond our wildest dreams,' Keith said.

'Maybe there's more.' Glen got down on his knees and shoved a hand deep into the crevice at the rear of the seat springs. 'Oh, yuck. Hang on. Hmmm. Anybody lose a comb?' He pulled it out, then resumed his search. 'Some more coins,' he announced. He fished them out, counted them in his palm. 'Forty-six cents, so far.'

'This is my lucky night,' Dr Dalton said.

Glen thrust his arm into the gap again. He swept it back and forth. 'There's . . . some kind of . . . Got it.' He drew out his arm and opened his hand. 'Woops.'

Nothing but a foil wrapper, Howard thought. Like the kind that Alka-Seltzer tablets come in, only red.

'Uh – oh. Sorry, Professor.'

'Just throw it away,' she said. She sounded embarrassed, defensive.

Keith and Lana both started laughing.

'I don't even know how it got there.'

'Oh, sure,' Keith said. 'Right.'

'It's nothing to be ashamed of, Corie.'

A condom wrapper, Howard suddenly realized. Somebody'd done it to Dr Dalton right there on the sofa. He saw her sprawled out naked, squirming and gasping as a strange man plunged into her. How could she *let* . . .?

What'd you think, she's a virgin? She's thirty years old. She's probably done it with lots of guys.

No! She said she didn't know how it got there. She wouldn't lie.

'Quit digging around in there, Glen,' she said.

'Just a . . .' He pulled his arm out of the crack, then lowered his head and inspected a new find. 'What the hell?'

It looked like a chunk of paper.

'Another clue to Professor Dalton's secret, tempestuous life?' Doris asked.

'Give it a break,' Dr Dalton muttered.

Keith tittered.

Glen used both hands to pluck open the tightly wadded paper. It appeared to be green.

'A whole buck?' Keith asked.

Glen spread the bill apart, stretched it taut and held it up toward the lamp. 'Holy smokin' Judas! A hundred-dollar bill!'

'You're shitting us.'

He hurried toward the table. Stepping between Doris and Keith, he placed the crumpled bill on the Ouija board. Angela lit it with her flashlight.

'That's a hundred bucks, all right.' Keith grinned up at Dr Dalton. 'I suppose you don't know how *that* got there, either.'

She moved closer to the table. 'I've never even *had* a hundred-dollar bill.'

Lana gazed up at her. 'How'd it get there?'

'It's a used sofa,' Dr Dalton said. 'I bought it second-hand a couple of years ago. Some of this stuff might've been inside the thing when I got it.'

'A likely story,' Keith said.

'*How* the money got into the sofa is irrelevant,' Doris said. 'The fact is, he led us to it. He knew it was there, and . . .'

'Doesn't take any mental giant to figure out somebody might've lost some cash down the back of a sofa.'

'But a hundred-dollar bill,' Lana muttered. 'This *has* to be some kind of a trick. I mean, it's weird enough that this Ouija thing is making any sense at all, but . . .' She looked at Glen. 'The hundred bucks came out of your pocket, right? You figured you'd put one over on us, get us all worked up . . .'

'I found it where I found it.'

'Swear to God?'

'I swear.'

'Angela, you were sitting over there.'

She took a quick step backward, retreating from the accusation. Howard twisted sideways and looked up at her.

She was shaking her head. Her mouth opened, but she didn't speak.

I ought to say something, he thought. She's too timid to defend herself.

'I don't think . . .' he started.

Dr Dalton interrupted. 'Angela hasn't been anywhere near the sofa since you started this nonsense. So, unless she's psychic, she couldn't have known that the Ouija would suggest searching for lost treasures in the sofa. Speaking of which . . .' She stepped up beside Lana, stretched out her arm, and retrieved the bill. 'Thank you very much,' she said. 'My house, friends.'

'Don't we even get a cut?'

'You got plenty of laughs at my expense, Keith. That should be reward enough.'

'Are you going to let her keep it, Glen?' Lana asked.

'Like she says, it's her house.'

'That's really not your bill?'

'I already told you. Hey, I wish it was, but it's not.'

As Dr Dalton backed away from the table, Keith put his fingers on the pointer. 'Come on, let's see what else it has to say.'

'Maybe this would be a good time to quit,' the professor said.

'What about the rest of us? You struck it rich. We haven't gotten zip so far.'

'I suppose I'd be willing to split the take with you folks. What the heck. It wasn't mine to begin with.'

'Now you're talking.'

'That wouldn't be fair,' Howard said.

'I don't mind. If it'll keep everyone happy . . .'

Doris reached out and rested her fingers on the pointer. 'Come on, people. We're in contact with a benevolent spirit here. Let's find out what else it has to tell us.'

'I wouldn't be so sure it's benevolent,' Dr Dalton said.

'Seems mighty benevolent to me,' Keith said. 'Coughing up a hundred bucks.'

He placed his fingers on the plastic heart. Lana hesitated for a moment, then did the same.

'Join the fun, Howitzer.'

'If Dr Dalton thinks we should stop . . .'

'That's OK,' she told him. 'Maybe this wouldn't be such a great time to quit, after all.'

'Are you sure?'

'I'm sure if you quit now you'll all leave here thinking the Ouija is some kind of terrific oracle. Keep at it for a while. I'm sure you'll decide otherwise in fairly short order.'

Howard rested his fingers on the pointer.

'OK,' Lana said. 'Ouija, we found the loot in the couch. Is there more?'

'4-T-U-N-E.'

'Huh? Four tunes? Songs? What are you . . .?'

'He means a fortune,' Angela explained.

'A fortune? Where?'

The pointer slid lightly over the board. Each time it stopped, Angela read the letter aloud. 'A-W-A-Y.'

'A way for us to get it?' Lana asked.

'That might be a single word,' Doris said. 'Away.'

'As in "away from here"? Far away?'

The indicator carried their fingers toward the smiling sun.

'Yes,' Angela said.

'Where? Where's the fortune?'

'4-M-E-2-N-O.'

'Huh?'

Angela finished copying the message. She frowned as she stared at what she had written.

'I don't get it,' Keith said.

'For me to know,' Angela explained.

'For me to know, and for you to find out. What is this guy, a bratty kid?'

'Games,' Doris said. 'He's playing more games with us.'

Lana frowned at the board. 'What do you want?'

'2-B-W-I-T-H-U.'

'To be with you,' Angela said.

'Oh, great,' Keith muttered.

'Tell it no,' Dr Dalton said.

Ignoring the advice, Lana asked, 'Where are you?'

'A-W-A-Y.'

'Are you dead?'

The pointer drifted around, forming spirals.

'I don't think he's going to answer,' Doris whispered.

It kept moving aimlessly.

'OK,' Lana said. 'Forget I asked. Who are you?'

'B-U-T-L-E-R.'

'Your name is Butler?'

'YES.'

'Nice to meet you, Butler.'

'P-L-E-A-S-U.'

'Please you?' Keith said as the pointer continued to move.

'R-E-I-S-M-I-N-E.'

'Please you? Are e is mine?'

'That doesn't make sense,' Lana said.

'Pleasure is mine,' Angela read from her note pad.

'Ah. Butler's a polite fellow.'

'Depends on how you look at it,' Doris said.

'Is Butler your first name or last?' Lana asked.

'I-M-B-U-T-L-E-R.'

'I am Butler.'

'Maybe I.M. are his initials.'

'Butler might be his profession,' Keith suggested. 'He already told us he's a servant.'

'But he said it's his name. So, Butler, let's get back to this fortune you mentioned earlier.'

'Y.'

'Why?' Angela said.

'You're the one who brought it up in the first place, Butler. You must want to tell us more about it. What do you want to tell us?'

'M-I-N-E.'

'It's in a mine?'

'Maybe he just means that it's his,' Keith said.

'Is the fortune in a mine?'

'YES.'

'Where's the mine?'

'4-M-E-2-N-O.'

Lana sighed. 'I don't enjoy being teased, Butler. I'm tired of your games. Maybe we should just let you go back to whatever you were doing when we interrupted. Is that what you want?'

The pointer darted to a corner of the board and stopped beside the crescent moon.

'No? Well, Butler, either you tell us where to find this fortune, or it's *adios*.'

The pointer remained motionless over the NO.

'I don't think it's a good idea to threaten him,' Doris said.

'Screw him,' Lana muttered. She pulled back her hand. 'Let's put this thing away.'

Howard took his hand off the pointer. Keith and Doris did the same.

Lana folded her arms across her chest. A corner of her mouth turned up. 'See what happens, Butler, when you don't cooperate? It's a two-way street, my friend.'

The pointer began to move.

'Oh, my God,' she murmured.

Angela flinched, her hip bumping Howard's arm.

He gasped for breath as he watched the heart slide. The beam of the flashlight followed its slow course over the board. When it stopped, Angela whispered, 'U.'

'This isn't happening,' Keith said.

'Shhhh.'

'G.'

Howard looked up as Dr Dalton took a step closer to the table and bent over it.

'I.'

She clutched her thighs. She was frowning down at the board, gnawing her lower lip.

'V.'

'You give,' Angela said.

'Who?' Lana asked.

'A-L.'

'Al?' Keith asked. 'Who's Al?'

'Maybe it means "all" of us,' Lana said.

'Someone's initials?' Doris suggested.

'Angela Logan,' Angela whispered. 'Me. He means me.'

'Butler, do you want Angela to give?'

The pointer swooped up the board and settled on YES.

'What do you want her to give?'

'B-L.'

'Who's B.L.?' Keith asked. But the indicator continued to move.

'O-U.'

'Oh you?'

'Shut up, Keith.'

'S-E-2-H-C.'

The pointer stopped, and Angela finished copying the message.

'What does it say?' Lana asked her.

'I'm not sure. Maybe "below use to H.C."'

'H.C. might be me,' Howard said. 'Howard Clark.'

'It still doesn't make any sense.'

'I don't know,' Angela's voice trembled. 'This is silly, anyway. He's not going to tell us where to find his treasure.'

'He might,' Lana said. 'If we do what he asks. Let Howard take a look at what you wrote.'

Howard turned. Angela stared down at him. Her mouth opened slightly, then closed. She handed the pad to him, and shone her light on it.

The message made immediate, perfect sense to Howard. It wrenched his breath away and started his heart thudding. 'Well . . .'

'Cough it up, Howitzer.'

'It says, "blouse to H.C."'

'All right! Shuck it off, babe!'

'Keith!' Lana snapped.

'Let's put this thing away right now,' Dr Dalton said. 'I knew it'd start pulling some kind of crap.'

As she reached for the pointer, Lana grabbed her hand. 'Just hold it a second, Corie. Hold it! We might be talking about a fortune here.'

'Bullshit. There's no fortune. This Butler – whoever the hell he is – is just messing with your heads. He's using you for his own cheap amusement.'

'Maybe, maybe not. But let's give him a chance. Let's just play this thing out, OK? All he asked was for Angela to give her blouse to Howard. It's no big deal.'

'I'm sure it's a big deal to Angela.'

'She's not a child, Corie. Why don't we let her make up her own mind. OK?' Lana released Dr Dalton's hand.

The professor stared at the board for a moment, then thrust her hands into the pockets of her shorts. 'It's just toying with you all,' she said. 'If you think this thing is going to make you rich, you're out of your gourds.'

Lana raised her eyes to the girl. 'You're wearing a bra, aren't you?'

Angela nodded.

'OK, so what's the big deal? It's not as if he's asking you to strip naked. You probably wear less when you go to the beach.'

'But he's . . . a spook or something.'

'A rich spook,' Keith said. 'Come on, Angie. Part of the treasure'll be yours, you know. We'll split it up equally.'

'Why *me*?'

'Maybe he knows you're the most likely to refuse,' Doris suggested. 'He made the demand of you because he thinks you won't do it, and then he won't have to give his information.'

'It'll be on your head,' Keith said.

'Don't do it, Angela,' Dr Dalton told her. 'Don't ever let anyone talk you into doing anything against your better judgement.'

'But they'll all blame me . . .'

'Right.'

'Keith,' Dr Dalton snapped. 'Shut your damn mouth.'

'Maybe this will help.' Lana unbuttoned her own blouse and pulled it off. 'See? It's no big deal.' She dropped her blouse to the floor and sat up straight, her torso dusky except for the white of her strapless bra.

It covers as much as a bikini would, Howard told himself. But the sight of her breasts, bare along their tops, seemed to suck his breath away. He gazed at the smooth slopes, the valley between them, and felt an erection begin to push against his pants.

'You too, Doris,' Lana said.

'Hey, Butler isn't interested in . . .'

'Just go ahead and do it.'

Doris sighed, crossed her arms against her bulging belly, grabbed the bottom of her sweatshirt, and lifted. She peeled the shirt up over breasts encased in a mammoth bra. She folded it, and placed it on her lap.

'They did it,' Keith said. 'You can do it.'

'All right,' Angela murmured.

'For Godsake.'

'It's all right, Professor.'

'Nothing about this is all right.'

Angela switched off the flashlight. She reached down and set it on the card table close to Howard's arm. Glancing sideways, he saw her tug the ends of her blouse out of her skirt.

He fixed his eyes on Lana, wanting to spare Angela the embarrassment of being watched by him. If he looked at her, it would be so obvious. She was standing right next to him. He would have to twist around on his chair and . . .

Besides, Lana was so much more beautiful than Angela. He found himself gazing at her breasts. The bra curled over their fronts just enough to hide the nipples. A little pull, and the clasp would come undone.

'Quit staring, Howitzer.'

Keith's words made him suddenly feel dirty. He murmured, 'Sorry,' and turned his head away.

Turned it toward Angela.

She had started with the lowest button. Her blouse hung open from the chest down. As Howard watched, she unfastened the button between her breasts. Then the one just below her throat, the last. She spread her blouse. She was gazing into space, not looking at Howard, so he studied her as she slipped it off her shoulders and down her arms.

She was skinny and her breasts were small. But heat pulsed through Howard's groin. Even though the single lamp was behind Angela, it gave off enough light for him to see right through her bra. Its cups were flimsy transparent pouches, stretched tight over breasts shaped like cones. Her nipples were dark and erect. They looked huge. They looked like fingertips trying to poke through the wispy bra.

She turned toward Howard. The lamplight found her left breast. So close above his face.

Howard had never been this close to a breast.

She had a tiny freckle beneath her nipple.

If he stood up just a little bit, he would be able to feel the fabric against his cheek, as smooth and soft as a breeze. Hardly there at all. The skin beneath it silken, warm. He could press his face into it, feeling the springy softness. The nipple would push against his eyelid.

'Here,' she whispered.

Her voice startled him.

He lowered his eyes. Angela offered the blouse to him. He set the note pad and pen on the table, accepted the blouse from her and folded it slowly, wondering at the strange magic that made the garment feel electric. It seemed to send warm vibrations through his fingertips, up his arms.

It's just Angela's blouse, he thought.

But it had been next to her skin. It had caressed her breasts through the bra. It had been tucked deep into her skirt, down against her panties.

He freed his hands from the garment, and felt its gentle weight against his lap. A heaviness there, pushing down on his erection.

Cut it out, he told himself. Angela's not so hot. I don't even like her.

Not much, anyway.

'Come on, Howitzer.'

'Huh?'

He saw that Keith, Lana and Doris had already placed their fingers on the pointer. He reached out. As his fingertips met the warm plastic, he looked sideways at Angela.

She had taken a few steps back from the table. She was

standing rigid. She seemed to be trembling. Her arms were crossed, hands cupping her breasts. When she saw him looking, a corner of her mouth twitched as if she were trying to smile.

'OK, Butler,' Lana said. 'We kept our part of the bargain. Your turn to give.'

The pointer slid, stopped on YES.

'Terrific,' Keith whispered.

'Tell us where the fortune is.'

The heart carried their fingers to the top row of the alphabet. Keith leaned over the dark board. He shook his head. 'Need the flashlight.'

Howard picked it up with his left hand. He turned it on and aimed its beam at the pointer.

'I,' Keith read.

Howard tracked the gliding pointer with the flashlight as Keith spoke the letters.

'M-E-E-T-U.'

'I meet you,' Doris said.

'Where?' Lana asked.

The doorbell rang. Howard's heart kicked. Lana's hand jerked away from the pointer.

'Jumpin' Judas!' Glen gasped.

It rang again.

'Just calm down, everyone,' Dr Dalton said. 'I'll see who's there.'

'I got a feeling,' Keith said, 'it ain't Jehovah's Witnesses.'

Chapter Three

'I'll go with you,' Glen said as the doorbell rang again.

'Thanks. I appreciate it.' Oh, how *much* I appreciate it, Corie thought.

'Whatever they're selling, we don't want any,' Keith said as she stepped around the table.

'Knock it off,' Lana told him.

Angela hurried toward Howard, holding out her hand. He gave the blouse to her.

The poor thing, Corie thought. Wearing that nothing of a bra. Why didn't I put my foot down?

At least no one made any cracks about it.

But God, she must've been mortified.

The bell rang again, and a fresh surge of dread pushed away her concerns about Angela. It was close to midnight. Who could be showing up at this hour?

Butler.

If it's Butler, I'm going to drop dead on the spot.

In the foyer, she flicked on a light. She halted and gazed at the door.

Glen put a hand on her arm. She jumped.

'It can't be *him*,' Glen whispered. 'No way. You know what I mean? Relax. Just relax.'

She nodded. She took a deep breath and called out, 'Who's there?'

'Coreen?'

She gasped.

'What's wrong?' Glen blurted.

She lurched forward, pulling away from Glen's hold. Her strength seemed to fall away. She slumped against the door, unlocked it and staggered backward, pulling it open.

'Chad!' The name was out of her mouth before she realized the man on the stoop wasn't him.

A wild, bearded stranger stared in at her.

Some kind of derelict in a shabby hat, a filthy shirt and jeans. He wore a backpack, and carried a wooden staff.

But he had Chad's voice!

'What do you want?' she blurted.

He grimaced, lips and mustache twisting away from his teeth. 'I guess I'm not so sure anymore,' he said. 'I just wanted to see you, Coreen. I know it's awfully late and you weren't expecting me, but . . .'

'Chad? It *is* you?'

'Well, sure.'

'Oh, my God.'

'So I guess you know him, huh?' Glen murmured.

She squeezed Glen's arm, nodding as tears made her eyes sting. 'Go on in with the others.' He started away. 'Get in here, Chad.'

'Are you sure it's OK?'

'What do you think?' She sniffed and wiped her eyes as he entered the house.

He shut the door and locked it. He propped his walking stick against the wall, lowered his pack to the floor and put down his hat. When he straightened up, Corie wrapped her arms around him. He hugged her. His beard was scratchy against her face. He smelled of sweat and wood smoke.

'You look like the Wild Man of Borneo,' she said, stepping back from him.

'Been in the mountains a while. Playing Thoreau.'

'My God, it's good to see you.'

'You look great, Coreen.'

'You, too. You lost a lot of weight. I honestly didn't recognize you.'

'Well, it's been a long time.'

'A very long time,' she said, feeling a stir of the old, familiar anger. 'You could've at least kept in touch.'

'I know. I . . .' He shook his head. The look of sorrow in his eyes made Corie's throat go tight.

'But hey,' she said, 'you're here now. That's the important thing. You're going to stay, aren't you?'

'Well . . . You've got guests.'

'Just a few of my summer-session kids. I threw a little party to celebrate the last day of class. I'll send them packing pretty soon. They've had enough fun for one night.'

Chad grinned. 'A rowdy bunch?'

'I wouldn't say rowdy.' She took his hand. 'They've been monkeying around with the Ouija board, and it hasn't exactly been a picnic.'

'Jake's old board?'

She squeezed his hand as memories started to come. 'The very same.'

He sighed. 'We used to have some good times with that thing.'

'Yeah. And some bad times.'

She led him into the den. It was brightly lighted. She saw that the girls had put their clothes back on. Even better, Lana was fitting the lid onto the Ouija board's box. They were done with the damn thing.

Lana looked up and grinned. 'Who's the hunk?'

'I'd like you all to meet my old friend, Chad Dalton.'

'Dalton?' Lana asked.

'He's my brother-in-law, actually.' Seeing the looks of confusion and surprise on their faces, she realized that none of them knew she'd been married. 'Chad's brother was my husband,' she explained. A hollow feeling spread through her. 'He passed away a few years ago.' She quickly added, 'Anyway, Chad and I are old buddies. Chad, this is my motley crew of students.'

She introduced them, and Chad gave each a cheerful greeting.

When she finished, he nodded toward the closed box. 'So, did the Ouija board keep you properly mystified?'

Angela's face went red.

'It was pretty strange,' Lana said. 'I can't believe the thing actually communicated with us.'

'That's what it's for.'

'Did it tell?' Corie asked.

She saw Lana glance at Keith. 'You mean about the treasure?'

'A treasure?' Chad asked.

'It hinted around about a hidden fortune,' Corie explained.

'No fooling?'

'You showed up just as they were trying to find out where to lay their hands on it. So, did Butler come through with his end of the deal? What did he have to say after I left?'

Lana grinned. 'For us to know.'

'Hey, whose Ouija board is it, anyway?'

'I thought you didn't want to get involved.'

'Calamity Peak,' Howard said.

'I was *going* to tell her.'

'Sorry,' he muttered.

'So was that all? Calamity Peak?'

'Right after it said that, the pointer went off the board. Do you have a map?' Lana asked. 'Might be interesting just to see if there is such a place.'

'Oh, there is,' Chad said. 'Calamity Peak's in the Shadow Canyon Wild Area. About eighty, ninety miles east of Red Bluff.'

'Red Bluff?'

'Down in California.'

'You've *been* there?' Lana asked.

'Close by. I've seen Calamity Peak from across a valley.'

'Man, this is weird,' Glen said.

'Weird?' Lana's eyebrows climbed her forehead. 'What's weird? Butler tells us the fortune's at Calamity Peak just as who should walk in but a guy who's *been* there. What's weird about that?'

'Coincidence?' Doris asked in an ominous tone. 'Or fate?'

Keith turned to Chad. 'How long would it take us to get there?'

'You can't be serious,' Corie said.

'Just curious.'

'It's probably over four hundred miles,' Chad said. 'But I have to warn you, the area isn't very accessible. The base of the mountain's at least a day's hike from the nearest roadhead.'

'So it would take what – two days at most?'

'About.'

'Keith, no,' Corie said. 'I can tell you right now that you won't find any fortune at Calamity Peak. You won't find anything but trouble. I don't know what the deal is with Ouija boards – what makes them work or who or what Butler might be. But I do know that you can't trust the things. Butler is screwing around with you. He's playing with you. He's jerking you around. For Godsake, look what he made you do.'

Keith glanced toward Angela, then met Corie's eyes. 'He didn't *make* us do anything. Nobody forced Angela to . . .'

'That's right,' Lana said. 'She did it of her own free will.'

'Oh, come off it. You people forced her into it, and you know it. Butler said, "Jump," and you said, "How high?"'

'I don't know what went on here,' Chad said, 'but Coreen's right about the Ouija board. It's a sly thing. It'll trick you. You'd be wasting your time if you went searching for that treasure.'

Lana nodded. 'I'm not real keen on the idea, myself. The way Chad talks, we'd have to hike all day and maybe even camp out.'

'No maybe about it,' Chad said.

'You can count me out.'

'Me, too,' Doris said.

Keith raised his eyes to Glen. 'How about it, my man? Up for an adventure?'

'Butler gives me the creeps.'

'Woos.'

'That's me.'

Keith glanced from Howard to Angela. 'I don't suppose either of *you'd* be interested.'

'No thanks,' Howard said.

Angela shook her head.

'Professor? Chad?'

'I've had enough of the wilds to last me a while,' Chad told him.

'I guess you're on your own,' Corie said. 'And if you have any sense at all, you'll give up the idea.'

'Don't worry,' Lana said. 'I know Keith. He's not about to do something like that all by his lonesome.' She scooted her chair back and stood up. 'Anyway, it's getting awfully late. About time we hit the road.'

As she carried the Ouija board's box to the bookshelf and shoved it into place beneath the stack of games, the others got up from their seats.

She returned to the table. 'Let's put this stuff back where we got it.'

'Oh, that's OK,' Corie said.

'No, we'll take care of it.'

She folded her chair. Keith flipped the card table onto its side to collapse its legs.

'Somebody want to get my chair?' he asked, glancing at Corie.

She folded it and picked it up.

Starting toward the kitchen, Lana looked over her shoulder at Chad. 'You spooked us all pretty good when you showed up like that. Butler had just said, "I meet you," and suddenly, whammo, there goes the doorbell.'

'Lousy timing,' he said, and walked along with the group.

'It was great timing,' Corie said. 'Four o'clock in the morning would've been fine, as far as I'm concerned. I'm just glad you're here.'

They entered the kitchen. In the breakfast nook, Keith set down the table. He snapped one of its legs into place, then grimaced at Howard. 'You want to take care of this? I've gotta hit the john.'

'Sure.'

Keith hurried away. Howard set up his chair, then crouched to open the rest of the table's legs.

'So, Chad,' Lana said, 'were you on a camping trip?'

'You might say that. I've been pretty much living in the mountains since the spring thaw.'

'All alone?'

'Just me and mother nature.'

'What a drag.' She grinned. 'Are you some kind of a hermit?'

'That's me.'

'Sounds neat,' Glen said.

Howard set the table upright. As Lana slid her chair under it, she frowned at Corie. 'Do you think I could have a cup of coffee before we go?'

The request surprised her. Lana had seemed ready to leave.

But she wouldn't mind having some coffee, herself. 'I'll make a fresh pot,' she said.

'Oh, you don't need to go to all that trouble. A cup of instant would be . . .'

'No trouble. It'll just take a few minutes, and then there'll be plenty for everyone. Chad and I might be up half the night, anyway. Right?'

He smiled. 'More than likely.'

It'll be like old times, she thought. Sitting around the card table late into the night with Chad, drinking coffee and talking for hours the way they used to do while they waited for Jake to return from the job.

She started to remember the night of the telephone call. The night of Jake's death.

Quit it!

She hurried past Chad, opened a cupboard and took out a coffee filter. With a can of Yuban from the refrigerator, she went to the counter. 'I won't make it especially strong,' she said, scooping grounds into the filter. 'Don't want to keep everyone awake till dawn, or anything. Three scoops. Enough for plenty of flavor, but you won't be able to stand a spoon up in it. Chad, you know where I keep the mugs. Why don't you take a head count and see who's interested . . .?'

I'm babbling, she thought.

But Chad showing up like this. Though she was so happy to see him, his presence would be a constant reminder of Jake. All the great times they'd had, the three of them. And how he'd stayed on, looking after her, during the period following Jake's death. And how he'd left her, finally. Abandoned her. Disappeared from her life for five years until turning up tonight.

Corie watched coffee dribble into the pot, and felt her anger rising.

He'd better have a damn good explanation, she thought.

Hey, don't spoil it. He's back. That's what counts.

How could he *do* that to me?

Why did he suddenly come back now, after all this time?

She looked at him standing over by the table, chatting casually with Lana and Glen about the pleasures of solitude. Howard was staring at him, scowling a little as if he didn't care much for what he saw. Angela's head was down. She seemed to be gazing at the floor.

They sure put that girl through it tonight, Corie thought.

I never should've let them drag out that damn Ouija board in the first place.

Keith came in. 'The pause that refreshes,' he said.

'We're going to have some coffee,' Lana told him.

'I thought we were leaving.'

'Pretty soon.'

When they were finally done with their coffee, Corie realized she wasn't eager to see them go. But nobody wanted a refill.

'It's getting awfully late,' Lana said. 'And I bet you have a lot of catching up to do with Chad.'

Corie gave each student a quick hug at the door, then she and Chad followed them outside to Lana's car.

'Are you all going to fit in there?' she asked.

'We'll manage,' Lana said. 'We made it out here OK.'

'Well, have a great summer, everyone. See you in September.'

They waved and called out farewells through the car's open windows.

Corie stood by the curb. She watched until the car swung out of sight at the end of the block. Then she took hold of Chad's hand and smiled up at him.

It's just us, now.

'Nice bunch of kids,' Chad said.

'Yeah. They're not bad. Ready to go in and polish off the coffee?'

'Could it wait a while?' he asked as they started back toward the house. 'I'm filthy as a dog. I'd sure like to take a quick shower, if that'd be all right.'

'Oh, fine. It'll give me a chance to put some fresh sheets on your bed.'

'A bed? Fresh sheets? I don't know if I'll be able to stand it.'

'If you'd rather throw down your sleeping bag in the back yard . . .'

'Trying to get rid of me already?'

'Don't even say that joking, Chad.'

Chapter Four

'Did you get it?' Lana asked after turning the corner.

'Of course,' Keith said. 'But you'd better pull over.'

She stopped at the curb. 'Where is it?'

'Back at the Prof's.'

'You *left* it there?'

'You didn't give me the car keys. What was I supposed to do, stick it on the hood? I hid it in the bushes near her front door.'

'OK. Well, let's wait a minute. Give them time to get back inside.' She shut off the headlights and engine.

'If you want my opinion,' Angela said, 'I think what we're doing is lousy.'

That's for sure, Howard thought. He was glad Angela felt the same way.

'Nobody asked,' Keith said.

Howard felt her flinch a little against his side.

Say something, he told himself. Don't let Angela take all the heat.

But he'd gone along with it this far, and so had she. Neither of them had made any protest at the house when it might've made a real difference.

The moment the Ouija board had spelled out Calamity Peak, Lana had shoved back her chair, snatched up the board and pointer, and rushed across the living room to hide them under the sofa. Returning to her seat just as Glen came back, she'd said, 'I'll distract Corie, get her into the kitchen. Keith, you get out here quick and take the Ouija board out to my car. We're going after that treasure. The six of us. Play dumb when Corie comes in.'

By the time Dr Dalton had entered with Chad, Lana was in the process of putting the lid onto the Ouija board's empty box.

That's when one of us should've blown the whistle, Howard thought. Before it went this far.

I almost did, he reminded himself.

Damn it.

He'd really expected someone else to speak up, though, and save him from being the traitor.

'OK, Keith. Go get it. We'll wait here.'

Glen opened the passenger door. His side of the car rocked upward when he climbed out. He waited on the curb until Keith was out, then climbed back in. The car sank again under his weight. He banged the door shut.

'It's theft, you know,' Angela said. 'The Ouija board doesn't belong to us.'

Lana twisted around in her seat. 'We're just borrowing it. We'll return it to her when we're done with it.'

'It's still wrong,' Howard said. Immediately, he felt better. He wished he'd protested a long time ago.

'Corie would've flipped her lid if she thought we were planning to go for the treasure. You heard her. She thinks the whole idea's insane.'

'Maybe she's right,' Howard said. Angela's hand slipped onto his thigh, squeezed him gently, and stayed there.

'What've you got against money?' Glen asked him.

'Who says we'll find any money?'

'Butler does.'

'A spook,' Angela muttered.

'Dr Dalton thinks we shouldn't believe him.'

'He was right about the hundred dollars in the sofa,' Doris said, leaning forward and putting her hands on her knees. She spread her legs until her left knee pushed against Howard. She didn't seem to notice. 'As far as I can see, there's only one way to find out whether he's telling the truth about the fortune. *I'm* certainly willing to devote a few days to the project. If we fail, at least we'll have the satisfaction of knowing we tried.'

'Besides,' Glen said, 'it'll be a blast.'

'I thought you didn't want anything to do with the Ouija board,' Howard said, easing his leg away from Doris.

'That was before it started coming up with money, pal. Anybody starts telling me where I can lay my hands on a pile, I'm all for it. A guy can always use dough. I can, anyway. Maybe you're so rich you don't care, but . . .'

'I'm not.' He felt a rush of guilt, and told himself there was no reason for it. Why should he be ashamed of the fact that his parents could afford to pay for his education? It's not a sin, no matter what people like Glen might think. 'I just think letting ourselves be pushed around by the Ouija board isn't all that smart.'

'If Howard and Angela are so against the project,' Lana said, 'maybe they should bow out.'

'Yeah,' Glen said. 'More for the rest of us.'

'Do you two want out?' she asked.

'I don't know,' Howard muttered, and looked at Angela. 'What do you think?'

She shrugged one shoulder just slightly.

'We're not going to force you into it,' Lana said.

'Hell, no,' Glen said. 'Better for us.'

'That's not necessarily true,' Doris pointed out. 'While I don't think they should come if they prefer not to, it's conceivable that their absence would put the project in jeopardy. Item, Howard was among the four of us in contact with the message indicator. Item, Butler appears to have a special interest in Angela; i.e., he requested that she remove her blouse as a precondition to giving us the actual location of the fortune.'

'Knew she was the one wearing a see-through bra,' Glen said. 'Poor bastard's probably horny out there on the "other side".'

Angela's fingers tightened on Howard's thigh.

'Be that as it may, they've both been significant participants. If they aren't among us when we reach Calamity Peak, we might not be able to re-establish our contact with Butler.'

'That makes sense,' Lana said.

'Of course.'

'If either of you decides not to come, and Doris turns out to be right, it could screw things up for the rest of us.'

'They're coming,' Glen said.

Howard let out a soft laugh.

'What's so funny, Howie?'

'Nothing,' he muttered. No point in making the guy mad. But Glen, like Keith, had always seemed to delight in sneering at Doris's pedantry. Now, Glen was latching onto her theory as if it were gospel.

All of a sudden, she's *not* full of shit?

'We aren't going to force anyone,' Lana said.

'If there's a chance we'll find money . . .' Angela muttered.

'Thata girl,' Glen said. 'How about you, Howie?'

'Are you sure?' he asked her.

'The whole idea scares me,' she said, speaking softly and looking into his eyes. 'But . . . my scholarship only covers tuition. Even with the jobs, I never have nearly enough for . . . to buy the things I'd like to. I know there's probably not much chance of really finding the money Butler told us about, but I guess I'd better . . . you know, go along with the thing. You'll go, too, won't you?'

He sighed.

'What's it gonna be?' Glen asked.

'Don't rush him,' Lana said.

He didn't know what to do.

Going along with the group would be a betrayal of Dr Dalton. They were not only stealing her Ouija board, but they'd lied to her, pretended they had no interest in making the trip. Obviously, they had no intention of giving her a share of the money – if they found it.

He didn't trust Butler. Whatever else Butler might be, he was nasty. He'd made them *do* things.

On the other hand, he felt sorry for Angela. She was scared, only going along with the others because she needed money so badly. She'd already suffered at the hands of Butler. Instead of sticking up for her, the rest of them had goaded her on, pushed her into taking off her blouse.

A lot of help I was to her then.

If I'd told her I didn't think she should . . .

He suddenly found himself thinking about the way her breasts had looked, how he'd ached to feel them. The memories aroused him now, and her hand was still on his leg and he realized he would be with her for days if he agreed to go along. No telling what might happen.

He wouldn't exactly mind being around Lana, either. She

was hard to take, sometimes, but she was sure beautiful. She'd been awfully quick to take off her blouse. Hiking and camping with her for a few days, he was bound to see plenty more of her.

The thoughts excited him, but also made him feel guilty.

Angela needs me, he told himself. I'm the only one who gives a damn about her. That's what matters.

He met her eyes and said, 'I'll stick with you.'

'You're not going along just because of me, are you?'

'What's wrong with that?'

She didn't answer. Instead, she turned and kissed him softly on the cheek. Though her upper arm pressed against him, her breast didn't. If she'd turned a little more . . .

'Should've given him one on the mouth,' Glen said as she eased away.

'Why don't you butt out?' Howard said.

Glen laughed.

'So,' Lana said. 'We're all in. What we'll do, I'll drive us around to everyone's place, and . . .' She looked to the side as a quick scuff of footfalls approached the car.

Keith rushed up to the passenger door and flapped the Ouija board at the open window. The chest of his tight, knit shirt bulged over the heart-shaped pointer. He pulled open the door. 'Out of my way, big guy.'

Glen climbed out, and Keith got in.

'Any trouble?' Lana asked.

'Right where I left it. What'd you think, it wandered away by itself?'

'Nothing about that thing would surprise me at this point.'

'Only trouble I had was the message indicator. Stuck it down inside my shirt here, and it kept sliding around. I think it was trying to tell me something.'

'You're kidding, right?'

He laughed.

Glen slid in beside him and slammed the door. 'Probably Butler checking out your tits.'

'You're the one with tits, man.'

'And proud of them. Here, want a feelie?'

'Fag.'

'Knock it off, guys,' Lana said. She started the car, put on its headlights, and swung away from the curb. 'We've gotta figure things out. I don't think we should wait for morning.'

'You want to drive there *now*?' Keith asked.

'As soon as everybody's got their stuff. From what Chad told us, we can expect to be in the mountains three or four days. So we'll need packs, sleeping bags, clothes, mess kits.'

'Food,' Glen said.

'We'll stop in a town along the way and pick up food and whatever else we're missing. Who doesn't have camping gear?'

'*Moi*,' Doris said.

'I don't, either,' Angela said. 'All I have is a sleeping bag.'

'What about you, Howard?'

'I've got stuff.'

'I can get my hands on another sleeping bag,' Lana said. 'Doris, you can use that. We'll pick up a couple of extra packs when we stop to buy the food.'

'Who's gonna pay for all this?' Glen asked.

'I'll bankroll the whole operation,' Lana said.

'All *right*! I knew there was something I liked about you.'

'I get paid back when we find Butler's stash. OK? I'll drop all of you off, and pick you up later. But make it quick. Just throw together some clothes and whatever gear you have. It'll probably be cold at night, so don't forget to bring coats. Once we're on our way, we'll figure out what we're missing and make up a shopping list.'

'Maybe we should take two cars,' Keith said. 'I mean, we've got an eight- or ten-hour drive ahead of us, and it's kind of tight in here. Howitzer's got a car. He could take Angela and Doris, and we'd have a little room to spread out.'

'Then we'd have to keep track of each other,' Lana said.

'Besides,' Howard said, 'my car overheats.' It was a lie, but they had no way of knowing.

'Let's just take my car,' Lana said. 'I think it's best if we all stay together.'

'Let us all hang together,' Doris said, 'or we shall most assuredly each hang separately.'

'Spare us the shit,' Keith said.

Chapter Five

'Hang on a second,' Coreen said. 'I'll get you something to put on when you're done.' She stepped across the corridor and disappeared into her bedroom. When she came out, she had Jake's old, plaid bathrobe.

'You kept his clothes?' Chad asked.

'A few things. This,' she said, handing the robe to him, 'some shirts and things that I can wear around the house.'

'They must be huge on you.'

She nodded, smiling a little. 'Huge and loose and comfy. That's why I kept them, not . . . you know, because I couldn't bear to part with them. I got rid of the stuff I couldn't use. Which means I've got no pants, underwear, anything like that for you to wear. If you'd like me to throw your clothes in the washer while you shower . . .'

'Oh, don't go to the trouble. Tomorrow will be plenty

soon enough. I should probably hose everything down first.'

She smiled. 'That bad, huh?' She opened the door of the linen closet, reached up, and pulled out a neatly folded blue towel and washcloth. She carried them into the bathroom, set them on a counter beside the sink. 'Anything else?'

'That should do it. Thanks.'

'See you later, then.' She stepped out and shut the door.

As Chad draped the robe over the door knob, he thought about thumbing in the lock button.

Afraid she'll come barging in?

She never did, she won't tonight.

He went ahead and locked the door. Better to eliminate the possibility than to start dwelling on it the way he used to.

He lowered the toilet lid. He sat down and removed his scuffed, dusty boots, and sighed. Always such a pleasure to get them off. He felt as if his feet had been trapped inside them, cramped and suffocating. At last, they could breathe. He peeled off his damp, filthy socks and tucked them into the necks of the boots. The tops of his feet looked shriveled from the moisture.

He stood up, took off the rest of his clothes, and piled them in the far corner. Backing away, he saw his reflection in the full-length mirror.

The Wild Man of Borneo, she'd called him.

Not so far from the truth.

Almost three months in the mountains, and it had been longer than that since his last haircut or shave. Not much of his face was even visible through the thick tangles of hair. He rubbed his beard. An old pine needle fell out.

He stepped into the tub, drew the curtain shut, and turned on the shower. The spray splattered against him. Not as cold as he was used to. It didn't give him goosebumps, didn't squeeze his genitals like a handful of ice. But he supposed he would get accustomed to it.

Back in the old days, in this same bathroom, he used to take such hot showers that the mirrors would be all steamed over when he stepped out.

It seemed like a different person who'd done that.

A confused and tormented kid, shy and overweight, obsessed with Coreen.

He squirted a syrupy puddle of shampoo into his palm, and sniffed it. Coreen's shampoo. The same aroma he remembered so well. He started to picture her sitting in the tub, lathering her hair. He shoved the image from his mind.

OK, he thought. I haven't changed all that much.

But it'll be different this time.

He slipped into Jake's robe and knotted its cloth belt. The fabric clung to his lower back where the towel had missed a few drops of water. Its sleeves, turned up, reached only partway down his forearms.

Because Coreen has been wearing it.

I won't think about that.

Crouching, he found his comb in a front pocket of his jeans. He went to the mirror. He tugged the comb through the tangles of his hair and beard. Then he rolled his clothing into a bundle, tucked it under his arm, picked up his boots, and carried them through the house. He opened the sliding glass door and took them outside. He left them on the patio next to his pack.

The night was warm. A soft breeze stirred the robe against his legs. Turning, he saw a glow of light from the kitchen window. A squirmy sensation crawled through his bowels.

Coreen's probably sitting at the card table, waiting for me.

Maybe I shouldn't have come back.

A little late for second thoughts.

Up in the mountains when he'd made his decision to return, he'd felt sure he was ready. He had grown strong mentally and physically. He was no longer the selfconscious fat guy who saw himself as a loser. He could stand in front of Coreen as a new man.

A new man, all right. She didn't recognize me. Hell, she actually looked scared.

But that went away once she realized who I was. She seemed awfully glad to see me.

Nervous, though.

OK, we're both nervous. It's only natural.

'Listening to the call of the wild?'

Heart thumping, he turned around. Coreen stood in the doorway. Her feet were bare. She wore a red, jersey nightshirt. It reached down nearly to her knees, but Chad could see her thighs through the fabric. The way the light behind her . . .

I don't need *this*.

Why hadn't she left on the clothes she was wearing earlier? Because I'm only wearing a robe. She probably thought I'd be less self-conscious if she was dressed for bed.

'We could have our coffee on the patio, if you'd like.'

'The kitchen will be fine.'

He started toward her. When she turned away from the doorway, he got a side view. She wore a bra under the nightshirt.

Thank God.

Following her into the kitchen, he glimpsed the outline of a band just above her buttocks. So she was wearing panties, too.

He felt some of his tension subside.

He sat at the card table. Coreen brought over the coffee pot. 'I had to make some more,' she said, starting to fill his mug. Her hand trembled. She poured coffee for herself, returned the pot to the counter, and sat down across from him.

She took a sip. 'So. How does it feel, being back?'

'A little strange, I guess. Have you been OK?'

She stared into his eyes. A corner of her mouth turned up. 'Lonely.'

'I thought you might be married and have kids by now.'

'Why did you go away like that, Chad?'

So sudden. It struck him like a punch. He'd known the question would come. But he wasn't ready for it, in spite of the countless times he had rehearsed answers in his mind.

'I had to,' he said.

'That's what you said in your note. It's no explanation. Did *I* do something?'

'No, it wasn't your fault.'

'Are you sure? I know I . . . tried one on the night before you left. It seemed like we were having a good time, though. We didn't have an argument, did we? God knows, I've tried to remember everything about that night. Some of it's a little fuzzy, but . . . did I say something to upset you?'

He gazed at her, stunned. 'No! Of course not.'

'Then *why*?'

'I fell in love with you.'

Coreen's face went red. Her mouth hung open. She gazed at him, then looked down at her mug.

'I'm sorry,' Chad murmured.

Staring into her coffee, she said in a low voice, 'That's not something that usually requires an apology.'

'You were my brother's wife.'

'His widow.'

'Yeah. When I left. But I loved you for a long time before that. Almost from the first time we met. It kept getting worse and worse until I couldn't even think straight anymore.'

'Oh, man.' She looked up at him. 'I never realized.'

'You weren't supposed to. Hell, I couldn't have shown my

face around here if you or Jake had known. You certainly wouldn't have let me *live* with you guys after Mom died.'

'Might've been a little awkward.'

'And it wouldn't have accomplished anything if I'd told you. I didn't want your pity, which is about the most I could've hoped for. It was better just keeping the problem to myself.'

She shook her head, frowning. She looked troubled, bewildered. 'You were *in love* with me? You sure never did or said anything to make me suspect . . . When I think of all the times we spent together, just the two of us, and you never . . . My God, *you're* the one who convinced me not to leave Jake.'

'I wanted to break his head in. It just tore me up, the hell he was putting you through.' Thinking about it, Chad felt his throat go tight. 'I hated him then for what he was doing. He had you. He *had* you. How the hell could he even think about messing around with other women? How could he do that to you?'

Coreen reached across the table. Her hand covered his, closed around it. She looked blurry. He realized he was seeing her through tears.

'Oh, shit,' he muttered. Turning away, he rubbed his eyes dry with his other hand.

'It's all right.'

He sniffed. He tried to smile. 'Maybe we ought to knock off this kind of talk before I make even a bigger fool out of myself.'

She squeezed his hand. 'I've got a better idea. Let's forget about the coffee – it's just getting cold, anyway. I'll haul out a bottle of Scotch and we'll have a little nightcap to calm us down.'

'OK.'

Her hand went away. She scooted back her chair and

stood up. 'Why don't we move into the den? It'll be more comfortable. And there're some munchies out there. You go on out. I'll be along in a minute.'

She was crouching down, reaching into a cupboard when Chad walked past her and went into the den. He felt strange, a little dazed. He was ashamed that he'd wept. But he had actually gone through with his confession. Most of it, anyway. He'd admitted that he loved her. That was the main thing, and maybe that was all she really needed to know.

The sofa's seat cushions were on the floor. He was pushing the last of them into place when Coreen came in.

'Glen tore the thing apart looking for money,' she said.

'Any luck?'

'He came up with a hundred-dollar bill.'

'Are you serious?'

'I've got no clue as to how it got there, but it sure convinced those kids that the Ouija board was on the level.'

'I'm surprised you let them fool around with that thing.'

'Big mistake.' She sat on the sofa, leaned over the coffee table, and poured Scotch into the two glasses she'd brought from the kitchen. She lifted a glass.

Accepting it from her, Chad turned toward a nearby armchair.

'Just sit right here. I don't bite.'

'Are you sure you can trust me?'

Her fingers hooked his side pocket. The robe started to pull open as she tugged him down. He grabbed its front and dropped onto the sofa. A tongue of Scotch slopped over the brim of his glass. It splashed his robe and seeped through to his thigh.

'I'm sorry. I didn't mean to make you spill. Do you want a paper towel?'

'It'll dry.'

She turned toward him. Looking into his eyes, she took a

sip. She lowered her glass. Her tongue slid across her lips. 'I wish I'd known.'

'Known what?'

'What do you mean, what? My God, Chad.'

'It would've screwed up everything.'

'Nothing. It would've screwed up nothing. You were all I had. Even before Jake was killed. Even before I found out about his other women. It was always the job, the job. I was a widow long before he walked into that 7-Eleven. From the day he pinned on his shield. Then you moved into the house, and I wasn't alone anymore. You meant so much to me.'

'As a friend,' he said, and took a drink. The Scotch went down, spreading heat. 'If you'd known what was going on in my head . . . I was such an imposter.'

'Because you *loved* me?'

'Because I loved you and because I *wanted* you. I felt sick from wanting you so much. And it got a lot worse after Jake was shot. I couldn't get it out of my mind that you were free. And we spent so much time comforting each other, holding each other. Every time I had you in my arms, I was tempted to . . . try something. I hated myself. And it kept getting worse and worse. So I left.'

'Oh, Chad.'

'Sooner or later . . .'

'What?'

'I might've tried to rape you.'

Her eyes, deep blue and solemn, stayed fixed on him as she sipped her drink. 'Maybe you should've given it a whirl.'

'I'm not kidding.'

'Neither am I.'

'What're you saying?'

'It wouldn't have been any rape, Chad. Not the way I felt about you. I don't think it's technically possible to rape a willing partner.'

'You *wanted* me?'

'I'm pretty sure I wouldn't have tried to stop you.' A wry, sad smile formed on her mouth. 'Now, aren't you sorry you left?'

'I was always sorry I left.'

'Not as sorry as me, I'll bet.'

'Don't count on it.'

'At least *you* knew why. All I knew was that my only friend in the world had pulled a disappearing act. A day never went by that I didn't wonder what made you do it.'

'Well. Now you know.'

'Now I know. Jesus H. Christ.' She gulped down the last of her drink, turned away and lowered her glass toward the table. Suddenly, she slammed it down. She twisted sideways and faced him, glaring. 'I could just kill you! You think Jake put me through hell screwing around with those gals? Well just take a look in the mirror sometime!' Her voice cracked. Tears filled her eyes and streamed down her cheeks. 'Damn you! Selfish son-of-a-bitch! How could you do that to a *friend*, much less someone you thought you were in *love* with?'

She shoved his chest, then turned away and curled down, hugging her head with both hands.

Chad, stunned, set his glass on the table. He put a hand on Coreen's quaking back.

'Don't touch me! Just get out of here!'

'OK.'

He hurried from the living room. In the hallway, he could still hear her sobs. They felt like knife blades pounding into his chest. He shut himself into the guest room and sat down on the bed.

Dear God, what had happened?

She'd seemed to be accepting everything so well. A lot better than he'd expected. All of a sudden, WHAM! Totally bonkers. It didn't make sense.

What am I gonna do? I can't leave.

I can't stay. She told me to go.

Chad slumped forward and rubbed his face.

She couldn't have meant it.

Want to bet?

You knew it might turn out this way.

Just get dressed and get out of here. Never should've come back.

He raised his head and looked around the room for a moment before realizing that his clothes and pack were outside on the patio.

Now what?

How could he get to them without going past Coreen?

There isn't any way.

Wait a while. Maybe she'll go to bed.

He heard the faint, distant sound of running water. Probably from the bathroom.

He rushed to the door, opened it a bit, and eased his head through the gap. The bathroom door was shut.

He kept his eyes on it while he made his way through the hallway. He grimaced when the water shut off. Slowing down, he crept past the door. Three strides later, he heard it open. He kept walking. He felt sick. He ached to look back.

Don't. She told you to leave. You can't leave without your stuff.

'Chad.'

Her voice seemed to grab his heart.

He stopped and turned around.

She was puffy and red around her eyes, and the crying had given her nose a ruddy, raw look. Some strands of wet hair clung to her forehead. The way the nightshirt draped the smooth mounds of her breasts and jutted over her nipples, he realized she no longer wore her bra.

'I was just going . . . to get my pack and things.'

'No. Don't.'

'You told me to leave.'

'Do you *want* to leave?'

'No.'

She walked slowly toward him. 'I didn't mean those awful things I said.'

'I deserved them.'

'It's just that I missed you. You hurt me so much.'

Chad opened his arms. She stepped between them and pressed herself against him. 'I'll never hurt you again,' he whispered.

'You won't leave?' she asked, her warm breath tickling the side of his neck.

'Not unless you throw me out.'

She hugged him hard, then relaxed her hold and tilted back her head. He kissed her soft, open lips. Her breath went into him. She moaned and squirmed.

Chad's penis began to stiffen, lifting against her belly. He stepped away quickly and turned around. 'Why don't I help you clean up the mess from your party?'

She was suddenly warm against his back. 'It can wait till morning.' Her hands moved slowly down the front of his robe, rubbing the soft fabric against his chest, his belly, his thighs. He felt her kissing the nape of his neck through his thick hair. He felt her breasts mashed to his back. He could feel her gasping for air. He could feel the throb of her heartbeat.

'Coreen,' he gasped.

'Huh?'

'You . . . don't have to do this.'

She made no answer. Her hands continued to caress him through the robe. They came close to his groin, only to slide away. Their motions loosened his cloth belt. The robe opened a little. Wider when she slipped her hands inside and they roamed over his belly.

'You don't have to . . .'

'Do you still love me?'

'I'll always . . .'

'Then hush.' She swept the robe off his shoulders. Only the pressure of her body kept it from falling as she rubbed his chest. Her hands glided lower. Trembling, Chad reached back. He felt the hanging tail of her nightshirt. He lifted it and caressed the smooth, warm skin of her rump. He clutched the firm mounds as her fingers curled around him, slid down the length of his shaft and gently squeezed his scrotum.

Then her hand was gone and she was stepping back. The robe fell to the floor and he turned around.

Coreen pulled the nightshirt up over her head. She dropped it and stood there, staring at him. Her eyes looked frenzied. Her mouth hung open. Her breasts rose and fell as she gasped for air. Reaching out, she took hold of his wrists.

She lifted both hands to her breasts. He could feel her trembling as he caressed them. When he stroked the nipples with his thumbs, she shuddered and caught her breath and jerked his hands away. She stretched his arms out wide to either side and eased forward, stopping when her belly met the head of his penis and her nipples touched his chest. Then she swayed slowly from side to side, gazing up into his eyes as she slid herself against him.

'Is this . . . how you imagined it?' she whispered, her voice breathless and husky.

'Nothing quite like this. Whatever it is you're doing.'

She continued to sway. Chad felt himself leaving a wet, slick path across her belly.

Keeping his arms outstretched, she raised them overhead. She pressed downward and remained standing while he sank to his knees. He kissed her belly. She released his wrists, and he caressed the backs of her thighs.

Holding onto his shoulders, she spread her legs far apart and slowly squatted down. The inner sides of her thighs rubbed his chest. So did the tuft of hair between them. The hair felt wet. She slid lower, her belly tight against him. He clutched her buttocks as she descended. Then his face was between her breasts. He turned his head and kissed the side of one. It slid away from his lips.

She eased lower, taking Chad into her. She was tight and slick and deep. She kept easing down. She seemed to be sucking him into her core. Then her face was level with his. She kissed him on the mouth.

'Welcome home,' she whispered.

Chapter Six

When Howard finished packing, he went to the window of his second-floor apartment and looked down. A few cars were parked along the curb. Lana's Ford Granada wasn't among them.

The road stretched away, empty and desolate, a bleak gray under the streetlights, black in shadows cast by the trees.

He didn't want to go out there.

He didn't want to leave the safety of his room and venture into the night, not with those people, not on such a bizarre quest.

He'd given his word, though.

Angela was counting on him. He couldn't let her down.

But he had no intention of betraying Dr Dalton, either.

He should've phoned her the minute he got into his apartment. Instead, he'd only *thought* about it. Thought about it while he changed his clothes, while he packed.

Procrastinating.

You're such a chicken. Scared to blow the whistle on them.

Wait long enough, and maybe you wait too long. Lana shows up, and then you've got an excuse not to make the call at all.

Already, it was probably too late for Dr Dalton to intervene. If he'd called earlier, she might've driven over in time to intercept the group, stop the whole thing.

There still might be time.

He stepped around to the other side of his bed, picked up the photocopied invitation to the professor's party, and sat down beside his nightst and. His hands shook as he unfolded the paper. At the bottom, beneath directions to her house, was her telephone number.

Should I?

She *has* to be told.

Maybe she'll ask me to stall them. Shouldn't take her more than ten minutes to get here. I could figure out a way to slow them down. Maybe tell them I've gotta use the john. Then just stay in there and wait for her.

He checked his wrist watch: 1:35. More than an hour had passed since they'd left her house. She might be asleep by now.

So wake her.

Maybe she hasn't gone to bed yet, anyway. She'd said something about staying up to all hours, talking with that guy who'd dropped in.

Her brother-in-law.

God, she'd actually been married to someone. A widow.

Maybe that explained why she seemed to be such a loner. Maybe she's still in mourning, or something.

Howard realized his mind was wandering. He'd better make the call before it was too late. Lana could show up any minute.

He lifted the phone off the nightstand, set it on his lap, and picked up the handset. The dial tone buzzed in his ear.

He stared at the number on the invitation. His heart thundered.

Do it!

He took a deep breath, trying to calm himself. Then he punched in her number, listening to the strange, brief tune.

What'll I tell her?

Just the truth.

He heard the first ring.

I'm probably scaring the hell out of her. A call this time of night, she'll think someone died.

He pictured her at the kitchen table, flinching, maybe spilling her coffee. Now she's scooting back her chair. Getting up. Saying *Who could be calling at this hour?* to that Chad guy. Hurrying toward the telephone. Was there an extension in her kitchen? He didn't know.

How many times had it rung?

Six or seven, at least.

Eight. Nine.

Where *are* you?

Even if she was already asleep, the first couple of rings should've awakened her. She could have easily gotten to a phone by this time. Twelve.

And what about that Chad guy? Can't *he* pick up the phone?

Maybe they went out somewhere.

Maybe I've got the wrong number.

Maybe Butler isn't letting the call get through.

Don't be stupid, he told himself. I've probably got a wrong number and the phone's ringing its head off in an empty house – the owners on vacation or something.

Hang up and try again?

By now, it must've rung nineteen or twenty times.

He lowered the handset onto the cradle. He stared at the invitation. He was certain he hadn't punched in any wrong numbers: he'd watched his finger peck every key. Maybe, somehow, an incorrect number had ended up on the invitation.

But he knew she was listed in the directory. He'd called her a couple of times.

He set the telephone on the floor, got to his knees in front of the nightstand, lifted the magazines stacked on its bottom shelf, and started to pull out the directory.

The beep of a car horn stopped him.

They're here!

Shoving the phone book into place, he rushed to the window. A car was stopped on the street. But it didn't look like Lana's Granada. Hers didn't have a luggage rack.

It does now, he realized. Must be one of those clampon, removeable things.

The rack was empty except for a single backpack and a small suitcase. A suitcase?

The horn honked again.

Great going, Lana. Wake up the whole neighborhood, why don't you?

He hurried to the bed, hefted his pack and shoved his arms into its straps. On his way to the door, he patted the pockets of his jeans. Keys. Wallet. Knife. Checkbook, just in case.

Forgetting anything?

Address book?

He remembered sliding it into his pack. Sometime tomorrow, maybe when they stopped for supplies, he needed to phone home so his parents wouldn't end up waiting for him at the airport.

He'd once considered writing Dr Dalton's number in his address book. But he'd decided against it on the grounds that someone might see it there and wonder.

Feeble. Big deal if someone saw it.

He gave the telephone a final glance, then opened his door, switched off the light, and stepped into the corridor.

As he strode toward the car, its passenger door opened. Glen climbed out and came around to the near side. 'Let me have it, pal.' He took the pack and hefted it onto the luggage rack. While he was strapping it into place, Howard ducked and looked into the car.

Lana was behind the wheel, Keith sitting beside her. Doris sat alone in the backseat.

Glen slapped the pack. 'All set.' He hurried around to the other side.

Howard opened the rear door, got in, and swung it shut.

'OK,' Lana said. 'We pick up Angela, then we're off.'

'Off to see the Wizard,' Keith said.

The car shook as Glen dropped onto the front seat. His door slammed.

'Don't break it,' Lana muttered. Then she stepped on the gas.

Howard felt cold and tight in his stomach as he watched his apartment house slip out of sight. He doubted that he would've felt much worse if he were being abducted by strangers. Four other people in the car, but not a real friend or ally among them.

It'll be better once Angela's here.

Not that she was much more than an acquaintance, really. He'd rarely seen her outside classes. Their only bond, at least until tonight, seemed to be that neither of them quite fit in.

They both slinked about, cloaked in shyness. Like fugitives fearing discovery. Similar that way, recognizing it, and being drawn together – though never close enough to become real friends.

Doris was an outsider, too. But of a different kind. She considered herself superior to everyone else, and made no secret of it. Howard could barely stand her. To be trapped in the backseat beside her all night . . .

Maybe Angela will back out.

If she does, I'm not going either.

He looked out the window. They were passing the university. The sight of the old, familiar buildings, lawns and walkways should've been comforting. But tonight the campus seemed forbidding. Howard imagined figures hiding near the walkways, shadowy forms lurching through empty classrooms. He turned his gaze to the back of Lana's head.

He wished someone would talk. The silence didn't seem natural.

As the car turned onto Tenth Street and entered the town's deserted business district, he decided to break the silence himself. 'Where does Angela live?'

'You know that thrift shop over on Cherry?' Lana asked.

'Huh-uh.'

'Across from the second-hand book store,' Doris explained. 'Gabby's.'

'Oh.' He'd been to Gabby's just once. During his freshman year. And avoided that neighborhood, ever since. 'She *lives* there?'

'Up above the thrift shop,' Lana said.

'Jesus.' How could she live in an area like that? And without a car. What about those nights she worked late at the campus library? Walking home alone . . . How does she stand it?

'You should've seen the weirdos hanging around when we dropped her off,' Keith said.

'They're not weirdos,' Doris protested. 'They're merely indigents who haven't had the good fortune to . . .'

'So adopt one, why don't you? There's one now. Take him home with you.'

Howard spotted the man – a shabby, bearded specter tipping a bag-wrapped bottle to his mouth. In spite of the balmy night, he wore an overcoat. His pants looked too big. Their cuffs dragged on the sidewalk as he shambled along.

Lana turned the corner. Onto Cherry Street.

Howard saw a dark figure curled in the recessed entryway of a pawn shop.

Lana drove slowly past the sleeping derelict. She swung to the curb in front of a thrift shop. She stopped. She beeped the horn.

'Neat play,' Glen said.

'Do you want to go up and get her?'

'Thanks but no thanks.' He started cranking up his window.

The window beside Doris was already shut. She reached forward and punched down her lock button.

Keith glanced back at her. 'What'd you do that for? You aren't *scared* of these poor unfortunates, are you?'

She didn't answer.

Howard cringed as Lana honked the horn again.

'She probably heard you the first time,' Keith said.

'Along with every wino on the block,' Glen added.

'So what? They're drunks, not cannibals.'

'You hope,' Glen said.

'Just give her a few minutes,' Keith said.

They waited. Only Lana's window remained down. Howard wished she would roll it up and lock her door. Wasn't she nervous at all about being here?

She'll probably roll it up in record time if a bum comes along.

One was across the street, standing in front of the closed

liquor store next to Gabby's. He seemed to be watching them. He stood motionless except for his right hand. Every few seconds, he rapped on the side of his head.

Howard twisted around and glanced out the rear window. The area behind the car looked clear. The horn had probably awakened the wino in the doorway back there, but he wasn't coming.

'One of us had better go up and see what's keeping her,' Lana finally said.

'How about it, Howitzer?'

Lana turned and looked back at him. 'Would you mind? You know her better than we do.'

'Well . . .' He didn't want to look like a coward in front of Lana.

'Please?'

'Sure. Why not?'

'Good man,' Glen said.

Lana stretched an arm across the seatback, pointing at the thrift shop. 'There's an outside stairway over on the right. She went in the door at the top.'

'All right.'

Howard pushed open his door, glanced back to be sure no one was coming, then stepped into the street and swung the door shut.

The thrift shop was dark, its entrance and display windows caged for the night behind a folding metal gate. The second story windows glowed with murky light that seeped through stained, yellow shades.

Howard moved around the rear of the car. The stairway, just ahead, was in a narrow, dark space between the thrift shop and the pawn shop.

He crossed the sidewalk and stopped at the foot of the stairs. He peered up them. Too dark. He couldn't be sure they were clear. But he couldn't turn back.

Taking a deep breath, he started to climb. The boards creaked under his weight. His legs trembled. He dug a hand into the pocket of his jeans, and felt a little better as he gripped the smooth plastic handle of his Swiss Army knife.

Not that he would have time to pull it and get a blade out . . .

With each step, he expected to collide with a foul, dark shape.

How can Angela climb these stairs at night?

At last, he reached the small balcony at the top. He knocked on the screen door and called out softly, 'Angela, it's me. Howard.'

Nothing.

He knocked again.

What if they sent me to the wrong place? Somebody's idea of a big joke. Take the wimp for a ride to the worst part of town, make him get out and knock on a stranger's door. A laugh a minute.

No, they're too serious about going after Butler's treasure to waste time fooling around.

A latch clacked. The inner door swung open. Just a crack. A strip of light spilled out.

'Go away.' The voice was high, raspy. He couldn't tell whether it belonged to a man or a woman. It sure didn't sound like Angela.

He ached to whirl away and run down the stairs.

'Is this where Angela Logan lives?' he asked.

'No. Get the fuck outa here.'

'OK. But I thought . . .'

From somewhere beyond the opening came a rough thud. Like a wall or door being kicked.

'*Angela!*' he called.

And heard the faint cry of his name.

'Hey, what do you mean, she's not here!'

'Fuck off.'

Who is this? Her mother? Her father?

The door started to shut.

'What is she, locked up or something? I'm gonna call the cops.'

The door stopped, still open an inch.

Another thud.

'Howard?' Distant, muffled.

What the hell's going on?

Should he rush down to the car, bring back Keith and Glen? They'd tease him. *What's the trouble, Howitzer?* Besides, this might be some kind of a family thing. He didn't want to give them ammunition to use for taunting Angela.

'I just want to talk to her for a minute. If you won't let me, I swear I'll call the cops.'

'She's busy.'

'The cops, then.' Howard took a step toward the stairs.

Light flooded out as the door swung wide. The screen door was pushed open by a skinny, hunchbacked old man wearing only boxer shorts. Except for his bald head, he was furry with gray hair. His face looked greasy with sweat. His eyes were huge behind thick glasses. 'Comin' around fuckin' with me this time a night. Get in here, you slimy little bastard.'

'Why don't you . . . just have her come to the door?'

'Y'want her, come in 'n see her.'

'All right.' Howard held open the screen door, waiting while the man turned and began to hobble away. He tried not to look at the hump. It was knobby and bristling with hair.

He stepped inside. Stuffy, hot air wrapped around him. It reeked of cigar smoke.

The screen door banged shut at his back. From the appearance of the old man, he'd expected the room to be a filthy ruin. The furniture was old, but there was no mess. The place looked tidy and clean. If not for the awful heat and the stinky haze of cigar smoke, it might have been reasonably pleasant in here.

Why didn't the old creep open some windows?

'Just gonna stand there?' With a gesture of his hairy arm, he signaled Howard to follow.

Another thump. From the hallway at the other end of the room.

'Hold yer water. I'm comin'.'

They entered the hallway and stopped at a closed door. From behind it came a soft hum. Maybe from a fan. An electrical cord ran under the door and was stretched along the hallway baseboard, joining an extension that led into the front room.

'Angela?'

'Howard?' Her voice came through the door. 'You'd better . . . just go away.'

'Why?' If she didn't want help, why had she called out his name? 'What's going on?'

'Nothing. Just go. Please.'

'This the slimy bastard ya was out with tonight?'

'I told you, it was a school party.'

'Did he fuck ya?'

'No!'

'Slut.'

'Nobody did anything wrong,' Howard said, his mind reeling with confusion and anger. And shame. If this guy knew what had really happened . . .

'Howard. Please. You're just making things worse. Just go. Tell the others I'm sick.'

'Have a look 'n see what y'done to her.'

'Skerrit, no! Please!'

Chuckling, the old man knocked back the bolt and pulled the door open.

Chapter Seven

Heat gushed out. So did odors of sweat and menthol.

The closet glowed red.

Not a fan, but a space heater hummed on the floor at Angela's feet.

Howard stared at Angela.

This can't be.

She was standing near the back of the small enclosure, her outstretched arms bound at the wrists to the clothes bar. She was dressed in a sweatsuit. Maybe more than one; the garments made her thick and bulky. The gray outer layer appeared wet. Her stringy hair looked glued to her head. Her ruddy face dripped.

She turned her head aside as if embarrassed.

'Tell him to fuck off,' Skerrit said.

'Go away, Howard,' she murmured. 'Please.'

'What *is* this!'

'You heard her, get outa here.'

'I'm just being punished. It's all right.'

'All *right*?' Howard lurched forward, crouched into the awful heat and twisted the knob at the top of the heater.

'Hey!' Skerrit grabbed his shoulder.

Howard sprang up, whirled around, and rammed both hands against the man's sweaty chest. Skerrit gasped and stumbled away.

'No!' Angela blurted.

His back – his *hump* – pounded the wall. His glasses fell off. His knees folded, and he slipped down the wall until his rump met the floor.

Howard watched, shocked by what he'd done to the man.

Skerrit glared up at him.

'Stay down! Stay down, damn it!' He dug into his pocket. He pulled his knife and pried out a blade.

'Don't hurt him!'

'Y'slimy bastard, I'll . . .'

'Shut up! Don't move!' He turned away, ducking, and hurled the space heater into the hallway. Then he stepped deeper into the closet. So damned hot. 'Was he trying to kill you, or something?'

'Oh, Howard.'

The menthol in the stifling air made his nostrils sting as he started cutting through the ropes. 'What's that smell?'

'Ben-Gay.'

'Huh?'

'You know, the heating rub. An ointment. He uses it for his arthritis.'

The locker room odor. He suddenly remembered. High school. Track. Rubbing Ben-Gay on his sore legs. And how it felt like fire.

'You've got some *on* you?'

'All over.' Her voice trembled.

He finished cutting her loose. 'On your *skin*? Under those sweats?'

She sagged against him and wrapped her arms around him.

'*Skerrit* did that to you?'

She nodded.

'My God.' He turned sideways and walked her out of the closet. The fabric under his hands was wet. And thick. How many sweatshirts was she wearing?

He eased her against a wall. She sagged, but stayed up.

Skerrit was still sitting on the floor. He'd put his glasses back on. His magnified eyes looked enormous and scornful.

'Get up,' Howard said. He waved his knife toward the closet. 'Get in there.'

'Y'gonna let him, Angel?'
'Howard. Don't. Please.'
'How can you stick up for this guy?'
'I *live* with him. He lets me stay here free.'
'So he can *torture* you?'
'You don't understand.'
'I sure don't. Skerrit, get into that closet.'
The old man struggled to his feet. He turned his bulgy eyes toward Angela. 'Yer gonna be real sorry.'
Howard grabbed his slippery arm and swung him into the closet. He threw the door shut. He bolted it.
'I'll let him out when we leave.'
'I can't go anywhere.'
'You can't stay. He's a madman.'
'Not really. He's just . . . strict.'
'Strict?'
'Yeah.' Leaning forward a little, she clutched the bottom of her sweatshirt and peeled it up. It dragged a red sweatshirt and a second gray one along with it. She struggled with all three, tugged them over her head, and tossed them to the floor. She was left wearing a faded blue sweatshirt that looked as if she'd taken a shower in it.
'He's only done that to me a few times,' she said.
'Only a few times? How thoughtful of him.'
She stepped away from the wall, drew several layers of sweatpants away from her waist, and pulled down all but the blue pair. Stepping on them, she freed her bare feet.
'He's OK usually. It was just because I snuck out for the party.'
'He's a madman. You can't live with someone like him.'
'I've got nowhere else.'
'Fuckin' right, Angel.'
She grimaced. She looked at Howard with bleak, desolate eyes.

'You shut up in there.'

'He's right,' Angela whispered. 'I just can't afford to stay anywhere . . .'

'Don't worry about that. I'll help you find a place.'

She shook her head. 'Just go and tell the others I'm sick. I can't go.'

'You'll go if I have to drag you. But I'd better tell them something. They're waiting down on the street. Why don't you take a shower and I'll be back in a couple of minutes.'

She glanced at the closet door.

'Don't even think about letting him out.' Howard took her by the arm. The sleeve was drenched. 'Where's the john?'

She nodded to an open door just up the hall. He led her toward it. The sleeve slid a little on her skin. Sweat and Ben-Gay.

'Take a real good shower. I'll be sitting next to you in the car. I don't want to be smelling that stuff all the way to Calamity Peak.'

She gave him a forlorn smile that tore his heart.

He guided her into the bathroom, turned on the light, and stepped out. 'You'd better lock the door, just in case he gets out. But I'll be right back. Don't worry about anything.'

'You won't tell them about Skerrit, will you?'

'No. No way.'

He pulled the door shut. He waited for the clack of the lock, then hurried away. As he walked past the closet door, he gave it a hard punch. A gasp came from the other side. He kept on walking.

He made his way down the outside stairway, remembering how nervous he'd been on the way up. Worried about running into a wino. Ridiculous. Scared of winos, and Angela's living with a sadistic lunatic.

A man. Old and deformed, but a man. Who let her stay

without paying. Just so he could punish her whenever he got the urge? What else did he use her for?

Free room or not, how could she live with someone like that? Unless she's just as weird as he is. Or so poor and desperate that she'll accept any situation just in order to finish college.

Howard stepped off the final stair, strode past the corner of the thrift shop, and halted on the sidewalk.

Lana's car was gone.

'Oh, great,' he muttered.

He glanced up and down the street. Her car was nowhere in sight.

He saw no derelicts, though he supposed some might be lurking about, out of sight.

Where had Lana gone?

I wasn't up there all that long. Maybe ten minutes?

Did they leave without us?

The possibility seemed remote.

But if they'd really left, he was freed from having to accompany them on their crazy search for Butler's fortune. He could go back to the safety of his apartment and forget about it.

But what about Angela? Would she come with him? Spend the night with him?

The chance of that excited him, but the disappearance of Lana and the others left him feeling abandoned, tricked, humiliated – like a kid ditched by his playmates.

Maybe they never intended to take us along.

A bigger split for the rest of them.

But what about Doris's theory that Butler might *want* him and Angela . . .?

A car turned the corner at the end of the block. Squinting against the glare of its headlights, Howard made out the luggage rack.

They changed their minds?

He muttered, 'Shit.'

But in ways he felt relieved.

The car swung toward the curb and stopped in front of him.

'Where's Angie?' Glen asked.

Howard stepped up close to his open window. 'She isn't ready yet.'

'Figures,' Keith said. 'Women.'

'Well, she's a little sick. She's in the bathroom.'

'A case of the trots?' Glen asked.

'Yeah. Where'd you guys go?'

'Some asshole came across the street to visit with us. Figured it'd be less hassle if we kept moving.'

'We've been circling the block,' Lana said from the far side of the seat.

'I thought you might've left without us.'

'Wishful thinking, Howitzer.'

'Will Angela be much longer?' Lana asked.

'Maybe another ten minutes. I'm not sure. I told her I'd go back up and help her pack.'

'What a Boy Scout,' Glen said.

'OK,' Lana said. 'We'll keep circling. Try to hurry her up. We've got a lot of miles ahead of us.'

'All right. See you later.'

The car pulled away. Howard rushed back up the stairs and entered the living room. He heard water running as he went to the hallway. He checked the closet door. Still bolted shut. He supposed Skerrit was capable of bashing it open. But maybe the creep was afraid of him, preferred to stay locked up rather than risk being attacked again.

Howard felt guilty, remembering how he'd shoved the old man.

What if I'd really hurt him? Jeez, he's gotta be close to seventy.

He stepped close to the door. 'Skerrit, are you all right in there?'

'Le' me alone, y' cocksucker.'

'I'll let you out when we're ready to leave.'

'Y' take her away, I'll kill y' both.'

'You'll have to find us first, you miserable old shit.' Stupid remark, Howard thought, hurrying up the hall. Arrogant and childish. Like giving the finger to a bully who's threatened to clean your clock.

He stepped to the bathroom door. The water was still going. As long as she's in the shower, he thought, it's safe.

Feeling like a sneak, he went to the doorway across the hall and looked in. A lamp was on beside the bed. A single bed, neatly made. A bureau, a rocking chair. Everything tidy except for a pair of old loafers on the floor, trousers and a shirt tossed across the bed. Must be Skerrit's room.

Heart pounding, he hurried on. The only remaining doorway was on the left. He went to it, reached into the darkness and flicked a switch. After pausing for a moment to make sure he could still hear the shower, he entered the room.

A minty aroma of Ben-Gay lingered in the hot air.

This must be where Skerrit had put the stuff on her.

The scene of the crime. Angela's bedroom.

A mattress on the floor beneath the window. A plaid sleeping bag spread out on the mattress. On the sleeping bag, a gray stuffed kitten with a missing ear. Along one wall, a couple of cardboard boxes, clothes neatly stacked inside. In one corner, a folding chair, a card table with a portable typewriter among stacked books and binders. A doorless closet. Inside it, a few garments on hangers, a pair of shoes and a suitcase on the floor.

More a cell than a bedroom.

God, the poor girl. To be living like this.

Howard's throat tightened.

He lowered his gaze to the clothing she'd worn to the party. The garments were strewn about the floor as if they'd been flung from her: the pleated skirt, the blue blouse, the white socks and sneakers; red, bikini-style panties; the flimsy little see-through bra.

Had Skerrit stripped her naked, throwing the clothes every which way?

When he saw the kind of undergarments she wore, the old creep must've really gotten mad.

Or turned on.

Maybe he *forced* her to wear such things. Maybe he even bought them for her. No telling what might've gone on between the two of them.

Crouching, Howard picked up the bra. He stared at his fingers through the wispy fabric and remembered how her breasts had looked. Small and smooth, with such large nipples.

Had Skerrit actually rubbed them with the heating ointment?

He'd put the stuff all over. That's what Angela had said.

All over?

That dirty bastard!

The faint hissing sound of the shower went silent. Howard gasped and dropped the bra. A wave of guilt swept through him, as if he'd already been caught. He stood up fast.

She still has to dry off, he told himself as he hurried for the door.

What door?

Hinges on the frame, but there was no door at her bedroom entrance.

That fucking bastard!

Once in the hallway, he slowed down. He walked as quietly as possible past the bathroom, past the closet, and on into the living room. He sat in an armchair just as he heard a door open. Then came soft footfalls.

Angela stopped under the hallway entrance. A white towel was wrapped around her waist. She held another towel to her chest. Her black hair clung to her head, draped her shoulders. She gave him a timid smile. 'Oh, OK. I just wanted to make sure you were back.'

'Feeling any better?'

'A lot. Thanks.'

'I talked to the others. They want us to hurry.'

She looked worried. 'You didn't tell them anything, did you?'

'They think you've got the runs.'

'Oh, wonderful,' she said, and a real smile spread over her face. 'Thanks a lot.'

'Would you like some help getting your stuff together?'

'No, it's fine. You just stay there. I'll be quick.' She turned away. Howard glimpsed her bare back, the curves of her buttocks through the towel. Then she vanished up the hallway.

He took a deep, shaky breath as he pictured her walking toward her bedroom. He began to imagine himself following her, spying on her. No door.

Cut it out!

That's the kind of shit Skerrit must pull.

Howard scanned the living room, trying to distract his mind from dwelling on Angela.

And saw a telephone on a stand near the kitchen entrance.

Try Dr Dalton again? Maybe this time she'll answer.

He would have to look up her number or call directory assistance, but . . .

Are you nuts?

Thank God his last attempt to phone Dr Dalton had failed. What if he'd told her about the plan and she'd put a halt to it?

We've *got* to go after Butler's treasure, he realized. Angela can't come back and live with this maniac. Hell, I won't let her. And money's her only way out. Even if we're wasting our time on a wild-goose chase, we've got to try for it.

Finding that money is her only chance.

Not her only chance, he thought. There's me.

He heard Angela's voice. She was talking softly, and he couldn't make out the words.

He pushed himself out of the chair, took a couple of steps toward the hallway, then stopped.

It's none of my business.

'Y'can't go!' Skerrit whined. 'What'm I gonna do?'

Angela spoke some more.

'Maybe I'll just throw yer stuff out, how'd you like that? Burn it all.'

What if she lets him out?

Howard walked to the hallway entrance. Angela was leaning forward, both hands against the closet door, her head down. She wore the clothes that had been scattered around her bedroom floor. Her hair was pulled back in a pony tail. Her suitcase and the rolled bundle of her sleeping bag rested on the floor beside her. She glanced at Howard, then turned her eyes to the door. 'It'll just be a few days,' she said. 'Please. You can get along without me for a few days, can't you? It's important.'

'Y' go 'n yul be sorry! Sorry ya was ever born!'

Her open hand slapped the door. 'Skerrit!'

'All I done for ya!'

She glanced again at Howard. Her eyes were red and shiny. 'I've got to go.'

'Then go, cunt! Rot in Hell!'

She pushed herself away from the door. Bending over, she picked up her suitcase and sleeping bag. She came toward Howard, her lips pressed hard together, chin trembling.

'Are you all right?' he whispered.

She shook her head.

'It'll be better once we're on our way.'

'I never should've gone out tonight. None of this . . . He was supposed to be drunk. He's *always* drunk by ten or eleven. I figured he'd be passed out, you know? He wasn't supposed to *catch* me. I'd just sneak in and out, and . . .'

'DON'T GO!'

Angela flinched.

'Come on.' Howard lifted the suitcase from her hand. He took her gently by the elbow and led her toward the front door. 'Go on down to the street. I'll be along in a minute.'

'You're going to let him out?'

'Yes.'

'Don't hurt him.'

'I won't.'

He stepped outside with her and set down the suitcase. 'If the car isn't there, don't worry. It'll be along pretty soon.'

'Oh God, Howard. I shouldn't be doing this.'

'Everything'll work out fine. I promise.'

She looked into his eyes for a moment, then started down the stairs.

He went back inside. At the hallway entrance, he paused and pulled off his shoes. He crept silently to the closet door.

From its other side came wrenching sobs.

The old creep was blubbering.

Howard carefully slid back the bolt. Turning away, he tiptoed back to where he'd left his shoes. He pushed his feet into them, then hurried to the front door. On the balcony, he picked up the suitcase. He eased the door shut and rushed down the stairs.

Chapter Eight

When Corie woke up in the morning, she turned her head and saw Chad beside her on the bed. He lay on his side, facing the other way, the sheet covering him to the hips.

He's really here. He finally came back to me.

She felt as if her heart were swelling with joy. She resisted a sudden urge to slide over and curl herself against the smoothness of his back and hold him.

Let him sleep. He had a rough night.

Smiling, she turned her gaze to the ceiling and folded her hands behind her head. She took a deep, lazy breath. She had no sheet at all, but that was fine. The breeze from the open window rolled over her skin like soft, caressing waves. It carried aromas of grass and pines.

Maybe I'll just lie here all day. Or at least until he wakes up. We'll make love, and then we'll make breakfast.

She stretched, savoring the mild stiffness of her muscles and her knowledge of how they had gotten that way.

You really took a beating, kid. Inside and out. You'll probably spend the day walking bow-legged.

She laughed softly, but it didn't seem to disturb Chad's slumber.

Why don't I go ahead and wake him up?

Brush my teeth first.

She got up slowly, careful not to jostle the bed, and moved toward the door.

Not so bad, she thought.

In the hallway, she smiled down at her nightshirt, Chad's robe. She stared at them, and it was last night again. Chad on his knees as she sank onto him. The feel of him pushing into her. How neither of them had moved for a long time, as if stilled by astonishment that finally, finally, they were joined and they wanted it to last forever.

Then the telephone had started ringing.

'Aren't you going to get it?' Chad had murmured.

'Are you out of your mind?'

Then she had lifted herself, pushing at his shoulders and feeling him leave a long empty space in her depths, an aching hollowness that she savored for a few moments while the telephone continued to ring, that she filled by dropping down, plunging him all the way up.

The telephone.

Who the hell *had* called at that hour?

And let it ring forever?

The thing was still clamoring when she lost her footing and went down on her back and Chad thrust so hard that he scooted her over the carpet and that thrust was one too many for both of them.

When she could breathe again, she'd said, 'I don't know how it was for you, but I heard bells.'

He'd laughed, his flat belly jiggling against her, his penis twitching a little deep inside her. 'I finished fast so you could answer it,' he said.

'Very considerate, but you were a tad too late.'

'Sorry. I tried.'

'Probably just a wrong number or a crank, anyway. If it's important, they'll call back.'

Nobody had called back.

It couldn't have been anything too urgent, she told herself now as she crouched and picked up the nightshirt. If there was a real problem . . . if something had happened to Mom or Dad . . . Not likely. Somebody would've called again.

That's what she had told herself last night when worries had intruded a few times. At one point, after Chad had left her to use the bathroom, she'd considered getting out of bed and calling home. By then, however, it was after two in the morning. She didn't relish the idea of waking them up. Hell, *they'd* think some tragedy had struck.

So call them now. Just to make sure.

She slipped into her nightshirt, carried the robe into her bedroom and draped it over the end of the bed, then crept out of the room and went to the kitchen phone. She glanced at the clock. Five after nine. They were probably up by now.

She tapped in their number.

It rang only twice. 'Hello?'

'Hi, Mom. How're things?'

'Oh, dear. I'm afraid your father's already left for golf. He'll be disappointed he missed you.'

They're fine. I *knew* they would be, she thought, but she felt a tightness in her throat.

'Is everything OK?' Mom asked.

'Sure. I finished my summer-school classes yesterday, and just thought I'd call.'

'Will you be coming down?'

'Maybe in a couple of weeks. I'm not sure just when, yet.'

'Well, just let us know. We're seeing our Tiburon group the last week in August, but other than that, we're pretty much free.'

'Great. I'll give you a call in a few days.' Should I tell? 'Hey, guess who showed up last night. Chad.'

'*Chad?*'

'Yeah. He just popped in. I was throwing a party for the kids in one of my classes, the doorbell rang about midnight, and there he was.'

Silence. Shouldn't have told her.

'I hope he came equipped with a good excuse.'

'Mom.'

'I suppose you've forgotten all about the hell he put you through. Leaving you all alone at a time like that. Just when you were starting to get better, and he walks out without so much as a goodbye. I sure hope you gave that young man a piece of your mind.'

'I did,' Coreen admitted, blushing now as she remembered how she'd raved at him.

'And what did he have to say for himself?'

'He was sorry he left.'

'I'll just bet he was. Did he tell you why he did it?'

'It was just that he didn't feel right, staying any longer. With Jake gone . . . he thought he didn't belong in the house anymore. You know, like he was intruding. It was just a misunderstanding, really. He didn't realize how I felt about him.'

'That's still no excuse.'

'Maybe not. Anyway, it all happened a long time ago, and he's back now.'

'Exactly why *is* he back?'

The question surprised her. 'I don't know,' she said. I really don't. 'He got in pretty late and I never got around to asking him that.'

'Well, I should think you might want to know.'

'I do. I'll ask him. He's not up yet, but . . .'

'Well, I suggest that when he *gets* up, you make certain to find out exactly why a young man all of a sudden drops in unexpectedly in the middle of the night after all these years. For all you know, he might be in some kind of trouble. I think you should most definitely question him on that topic. That would've been the first thing out of my mouth even before I so much as let him into the house. He's been gone a long time, and he always was a little peculiar. No telling what he might've gotten himself into.'

'I'm sure he's not in any trouble, Mom. Anyway, I'd better go now. I left the bacon on the skillet. Say "Hi" to Dad for me, OK?'

'I will. And you watch yourself with Chad. You just can't be too . . .'

'I know. I've really got to go, Mom.'

'All right. I'll tell your father that you called. Goodbye now, honey.'

'Bye-bye, Mom. Talk to you soon.' She hung up and slumped against the kitchen wall.

Lord! When will I learn to keep my mouth shut? Probably never. But at least I didn't blab everything.

She went into the living room, noticed the mess from the party, and began to collect empty snack bowls, used glasses and napkins. Her buoyant mood was gone. Leave it to Mom to put a damper on things.

It's only because she worries about me. And she's right, I do need to find out why Chad decided to return.

Does it matter?

It might.

Until now, Coreen realized, she'd simply assumed that he had returned because he could no longer stand to be away from her. But maybe there was a different reason.

Suppose he'd had a woman? Maybe they'd broken up, and that was why he finally came back. On the rebound. Hoping to get lucky.

He got lucky, all right.

Coreen suddenly felt used and humiliated – and worried. The way he'd talked about his passion for her, she hadn't even considered the possibility that he might've been with other women. Stupid!

Good God, let's not jump to conclusions. And so what if there *was* someone else?

Plenty of what.

I never would've thrown myself at him like that.

We didn't even use condoms. Shit!

Protection had been the furthest thing from her mind. But if he'd been with one woman, maybe he'd been with dozens. Who knows? Maybe he picked up AIDS . . .

Don't think about it! You're letting your imagination run wild. For all you know, he never touched anyone. Just calm down. Finish cleaning up.

She returned to the living room once again and looked around. No more mess. All taken care of.

Seeing the couch, she wondered what Glen had done with the condom wrapper. Probably kept it as a souvenir.

Jeez, they all thought it was mine.

That damn Ouija board led them right to it.

Butler. Almost as if he knew the wrapper was there, and lured Glen to the sofa with a promise of money just so it would be found. A typical Ouija-board brand of mischief. Toy around with people. Humiliate them.

I sure don't want that wrapper popping up again.

Coreen got down on her knees and crawled the length of the sofa, running her hand along the gap at its bottom. She found a potato chip, but not the wrapper. She tossed the broken chip onto the table, then headed for the shelves.

If *I* was embarrassed, poor Angela probably wanted to curl up and dic.

Never should've let it go that far.

Never should've let it start.

Stretching upward on tiptoes, she reached high and grabbed the Ouija board's box. She slid it forward, along with the games stacked on top of it. When the box was halfway out, she strained higher and shoved the other games back.

'Good morning.'

She flinched a little, startled, then looked over her shoulder at Chad. 'Morning.'

'Could you use a hand?'

'I'm gonna throw this damn thing away before it causes more trouble,' she said. She pulled it out some more.

'I'll get it for you.' He started toward her.

'That's OK.' She pushed back the upper games. She almost had the Ouija box clear when he wrapped his arms around her and kissed the side of her neck. The kiss sent pleasant shivers through her. Squirming, she lost her grip on the box. It fell. Its edge bumped the tops of her toes, but didn't hurt.

She nudged it out of the way, turned around and embraced Chad. When he tried to kiss her mouth, she murmured, 'No, just a second.' Her heart was pounding, but not with excitement. She felt a little sick. And the shocked, crushed look in Chad's eyes didn't help. Not at all.

'What's wrong?'

'We . . . need to talk.'

He actually winced. 'Sure. OK.'

'Hey, it's no big thing.'

'Yes, it is. When someone says "we need to talk," it's always a big thing.' He lowered his arms as if he thought she might find his touch offensive.

Coreen kept her arms around him. He felt hot through the robe. 'It's just that . . . I'm wondering why you finally came back.'

'That's all?' Such relief in his voice.

'Pretty much.'

'I came back for you.'

'But why? After all that time . . .'

'It took me that long to grow up. I was just a kid when I left here.'

'You weren't a kid. You're only two years younger than me.'

'But I wasn't ready for you. I wasn't good enough.

I was fat, immature, an emotional wreck. You deserved a lot better.'

'That's silly. I loved you.'

'Maybe so, but I was a loser. I had to stay away until I was good enough for you. Until *I* felt I was good enough for you.'

She smiled. 'So now you think you are?'

'I came back, didn't I?'

'That you did.' She squeezed him hard, then looked again into his eyes. 'Came back all strong and hairy.'

His hands returned to her, big and warm through the nightshirt, sliding down until they curled over her bottom.

'Were there . . . very many others?' she whispered.

'Other what?'

'Women.'

He didn't answer. Coreen's heart felt as if it were trying to punch its way out of her chest.

'Chad? Were there?'

'None like you.'

'But you had lovers?'

'Does it matter?'

'Yes!'

'Good.' He sounded amused.

'Did you?'

'This really bugs you, doesn't it?'

'I just want to know.'

'How about you?'

'I asked you first.'

'It's an awfully personal question, you know.'

'Your hands on my butt are awfully personal, you know.' They gave her a firm squeeze. 'Chad? Tell me.'

'There were a few women,' he said. 'Some became very good friends. But I never went to bed with any of them.'

Relieved, she asked, 'Did you go to hallway floor with any of them?'

He laughed for a moment, then moved his hands up her back and pulled her more closely against him. 'There's been nobody else. Not since I met you.'

'Nobody? Not since we met? Not even in college? You're kidding, right?'

'I know it might seem a little crazy.'

'It sounds downright insane.'

'Well, you asked. Would you be happier if I admitted to sleeping with a dozen other women? I don't think you wanted to hear that, did you?'

'Not really. But it's the truth? You didn't sleep with anyone?'

'It's the truth.'

'Jeez. It makes me feel so . . . really special, in a way. But . . . I don't know. Being to blame for something like that . . .'

'I fell in love with sunsets, too. But that's not the sun's fault.'

'But still . . .'

'Last night made it worth all the waiting.'

She covered his mouth with a kiss, squeezed him tight to her body, felt his breath inside her, his hands caressing her through the nightshirt. After a while, she eased her mouth away. 'You're so grown-up and strong and manly now, let's see if you can carry me into the bedroom.'

He did.

Chad's stomach growled.

'I suppose that means you're hungry now. Men. All you want to do is screw and eat.'

'Got me a powerful hunger, woman. But don't you stir yourself. I'll throw together some vittles for us.'

She smiled up at him. 'You'll make breakfast? Seriously?'

'Hey, I'm a whiz-bang with a skillet.'

'That'd be great. I'll take a bath while you're getting it ready.'

'Good idea. You're a terrible mess.'

She slapped his rump. 'Anyway, everything's where it always was. What'll you make?'

'What do you want?'

'How about sausage and eggs?'

'Coming right up.' He kissed her gently on the mouth. Then he eased backward, sliding out of her. He kissed her breasts and belly as he crawled to the end of the bed. Getting to his feet, he said, 'Do you still like your eggs over easy?'

'That would be just fine.'

After he was gone, she began to gather clean clothes. She held them away from her body. She *was* a terrible mess. Chad had been teasing about that, but not wrong. Her skin was slick with sweat, in many places sticky.

As she pushed a bureau drawer shut, Chad came back into the room.

'What do you suppose *this* means?' he asked. He held the Ouija board's box, its bottom in one hand, its lid in the other.

Coreen frowned. 'Where're the board and pointer?'

'Good question. I just stopped to pick up the box. It fell open when you dropped it. Nothing inside.'

'Oh, man.'

'Guess you've been ripped off.'

'Oh, man,' she muttered again as the implications rushed through her mind. 'Those damn idiots.'

'Looks to me as if they might be planning on a treasure hunt.'

'I know, I know. *Damn* it! Well, that's their problem, isn't it? If they're such damn fools . . . I've got a bath to take.'

Chad followed her into the hallway. 'It might not be

too late to stop them,' he said. 'Do you know where they live?'

'The hell with them. They made their choice.' At the bathroom entrance, she turned to Chad. She shook her head. She was having a hard time catching her breath. 'How *could* they?'

'They're kids. The Ouija board promised them a fortune.'

'Those idiots!'

'I'll go on and make breakfast,' Chad said. He gave her shoulder a brief, gentle squeeze, then walked away.

Coreen could think of nothing but her students as she bathed.

Lana must be the culprit; she had the brains and spirit for this kind of thing. If she was involved, then so was Keith. Maybe the two of them had made off with the board and the others knew nothing about it. Keith might've swiped it. He'd gone off, supposedly to use the bathroom, while everyone else was in the kitchen. That's probably when he snatched the board.

If it's just those two, she thought, it's not so bad.

And she realized that her only real concerns were about Howard and Angela.

She ought to be worried about all of them. They were all her students, all her responsibility.

It's my Ouija board. It's my fault if something happens to them. Any of them.

But she cared more about Howard and Angela. She couldn't deny that. They were special to her. More sensitive than the rest of them. Loners, and probably lonely. Maybe a little less mature than the others, certainly more vulnerable. The idea of those two going along . . .

They're too smart.

But easily controlled.

Look at Howard. He hadn't wanted to mess with the board at all last night. But they'd easily talked him into it.

And poor Angela had actually been pushed into taking off her blouse.

If Lana wanted them to join in on her damn treasure hunt they probably wouldn't have offered much resistance.

It doesn't matter who's in on it, she finally decided, just Lana and Keith, or the whole bunch of them – they've got to be stopped. I can't have my kids rushing off into the mountains. Not with my Ouija board. Not with that damn Butler pulling the strings. Not after the way they'd *all* gone along with his whims last night.

Coreen finished her bath quickly. She climbed from the tub, dried off, brushed her hair, and hurried into her clothes.

Aromas of coffee and sausage greeted her as she entered the kitchen. Chad, standing at the stove, smiled over his shoulder at her. 'You look terrific.'

'I've got to find out what those kids are up to.'

'Anything I can do to help?'

'Not at the moment. Just finish with breakfast. I'm starving.' She lifted the handset of the wall phone, called directory assistance, and asked the operator if she had a listing for Lana Tate.

This was a girl who *must* have a telephone.

And she did.

Coreen punched in the numbers, listened to the ringing.

Chad watched her, frowning a little.

Someone picked up. 'Hello?' A female voice, but it didn't sound like Lana.

'Hello. Is Lana there?'

'Afraid not. Could I take a message?'

'This is Coreen Dalton. I'm one of Lana's . . .'

'Oh, Dr Dalton! Hi. This is Sue Hughes.'

She knew the girl, an honors student majoring in psych, who'd been in her advanced composition class last spring. 'How are you, Sue?'

'Oh, just fine. Is there something I can do for you?'

'I really need to talk with Lana. Do you know when she might be back?'

'Not for a few days, maybe longer.'

Corie felt herself sinking inside.

'I hope it's nothing too urgent.'

'No. She . . . wasn't feeling too well when she left here last night. I just wanted to find out if she's any better.'

'She seemed perfectly fine. She must be OK. I mean, I don't think anybody'd go on a camping trip if they – she? – didn't feel all right.'

'She went camping?'

'Right. She left last night. Well, this morning, to be more accurate.'

'What time did she go?'

'I'm not certain. Sometime after midnight, though. She only popped in long enough to get her gear together. Then she took off to pick up the others.'

'In the middle of the night?'

'That's Lana. You live with her a while, nothing surprises you.'

'Do you know who else was going along?'

'I'm sure Keith was. Oh, and Doris Whitney. She asked to borrow my sleeping bag for Doris, but I didn't want . . . Anyway, I let Lana take it for herself with the understanding that Doris could use *her* bag. It's not that I have anything *against* Doris, but I just thought I'd feel better if it was Lana who . . .'

'Did she mention anyone else going along?'

'Is something wrong, Professor?'

'I'm not sure. I don't know. Look, I didn't really call to find out about Lana's health. The kids had talked about a trip to the mountains. I thought I'd talked them out of it. Some of them haven't had any experience at all in wilderness living. It just didn't seem like a good idea. And the last I'd heard, they'd decided to call it off.'

'Well, they went, all right. But you shouldn't be too concerned. I've been backpacking with Lana. She's no tenderfoot, and I know for a fact that Keith has spent a lot of time camping around. So they know what they're doing. I'm sure they can take care of anyone else who might've gone along with them.'

'I hope so. And you say they started out last night?'

'Right. Maybe around one o'clock, but I'm not sure about that.'

'Well, thanks a lot, Sue. You've been a lot of help.'

'No problem. And really, you shouldn't worry about them. They'll be fine.'

'Probably so. Have a good summer, Sue.'

'You, too. What's left of it. So long, Professor.'

'Bye.' She hung up. She frowned at Chad. 'They left last night.'

'So I heard.'

'At least three of them. Probably Glen, too. Maybe the whole bunch.' She checked with directory assistance again, got Howard's number, and called. His phone rang twelve times before she hung up. 'God, I think they all went.'

'What do you want to do about it?'

'I don't know.'

'Yeah, you know.'

'Shit!'

'I'm sure you could use the services of a guide.'

'We can't go after them.'

'I don't think we have a choice.'

Chapter Nine

Howard left the others at the entrance to a sporting goods store and walked down the block, heading for a pay phone he'd noticed when they drove by.

It felt good to be out of the car. The sun was hot, but he didn't mind.

This isn't so bad, he thought.

Last night had been pretty awful.

Not that anyone caused trouble. Once Lana had filled her tank at the twenty-four-hour Mobil and they got onto the highway, most of the talking stopped. Howard sat close to Angela, leaving nearly half the backseat to Doris. Angela snuggled against him. He put his arm around her as soon as Doris fell asleep.

He remained awake for a long time, his mind a turmoil.

He thought about Dr Dalton, how they had tricked and betrayed her. He wondered why she hadn't answered the phone. For a while, he even sickened himself with worries that she hadn't picked up the phone because she couldn't. Suppose Chad had murdered her? The guy looked like a tough character, and the way he'd shown up unannounced late at night . . . but they seemed to be awfully good friends. Besides, everyone at the party could testify that he'd been there. Howard finally managed to convince himself that the notion of Dr Dalton's murder was farfetched. No point in getting himself worked up over such a remote possibility. She was probably fine.

During the long hours while sleep evaded Howard, he also thought about the Ouija board, the strangeness that it made any sense at all, much less slid around that time all by itself. He thought about Butler. A spirit? A ghost? A force projected by someone in the room? Whatever Butler might be, he had a mean streak. But he'd been right about the 'loot' in the sofa. Maybe he'd told the truth about the fortune. What would he ask them to do in return for leading them to its exact location? Something weird, probably.

Most of all, Howard thought about Angela. Over and over again, he relived the minutes he'd spent in the rooms she shared with Skerrit. Often, he found himself imagining what must've happened there when Angela returned there from the party. He dwelled on Angela at the party, too. How the others had forced her to take off her blouse. How he'd just let it happen. And the way she'd looked standing beside him, her breasts showing through the bra.

In the backseat with his arm around her, she fell asleep. But Howard remained awake, remembering and wondering and worrying about Dr Dalton, the Ouija board, and Angela. Feverish with the storm in his mind. And constantly aware of Angela's body curled against him. He was very tempted to touch her. Nobody would ever know, not even Angela – unless his touch woke her up. He imagined himself feeling her breasts through the blouse. He might even unfasten a button and slip his hand inside. He could probably get away with it. Maybe he could even sneak a hand under her skirt.

Though he ached to try such things, he struggled against his urges. To feel her while she slept would be perverted. And she'd already been violated in God knows how many ways by that bastard Skerrit.

All she needs is to wake up and find *me* pawing her.

When Howard's arm finally fell asleep, he managed to lift it over her head and bring it down in front of him. He waited for the numbness and tingling to subside, then eased Angela aside so that she slumped against the door.

Her leg still pressed against him. He stared at it, at the way the skirt draped her thigh. Closing his eyes, he continued to see it. He folded his hands on his lap. He saw his hand disappear under the skirt, felt the smooth warmth of her leg, and then it wasn't Angela beside him. It was Dr Dalton, and he touched the silken fabric of her panties and she lifted his hand away and whispered, *Howard, I'm ashamed of you. I thought you were above this kind of thing.*

I thought you were Angela.

That's no excuse. Honestly, Howard.

A sudden swerve of the car threw him against Angela. Coming out of a restless sleep, he saw that the sky was gray. He was vaguely aware of the car stopping at the side of the highway, Angela asking in a groggy voice, 'What's going on?' and Lana saying, 'Just changing drivers. No problem.' Doors had opened, letting chilly air into the car. Then, with Keith behind the wheel, the car started moving again and Howard drifted back into a world of bizarre, vivid dreams.

He jerked awake gasping for breath, his heart slamming.

Daylight. They were stopped at a gas station. Angela was frowning at him. 'That must've been an awful nightmare,' she whispered.

'Yeah.'

He settled back against the seat and shut his eyes, trying to calm down.

Skerrit, he remembered. It was Skerrit. He'd found the old man at the end of a long, black tunnel where Angela and Dr Dalton were hanging next to each other by their wrists. Their sweaty, naked bodies gleamed in the fire of Skerrit's torch. They writhed and screamed as Skerrit, giggling, pranced from one to the other, jabbing his torch against them. Howard ran and ran, shouting, 'Stop it!' and digging the Swiss Army knife out of his pocket. He pulled at the main blade, but it wouldn't come out. His thumb nail tore off.

Skerrit seemed unaware of his approach, kept on giggling and burning the women. But they had seen him. Between shrieks of agony, they cried out for him to hurry, to save them. He tried to pry out the blade with his front teeth. His teeth crumbled and he spit them out. Then he remembered that the knife was a switchblade. He pushed its button. The blade sprang up and locked into place and he hurled himself at Skerrit. The man screamed as Howard pounded the knife into his back. Into his hump. Soft, not bony. As the blade tore it open, gore slopped out. And then a pair of small hands reached out of the flabby, deflating sack, grabbed Howard's cheeks and tried to pull him in. Small hands, but so terribly strong. Tugging him closer and closer to the gaping split. In the darkness of the hump, eyes opened. A mouth spread wide, and he woke with a jolt of panic.

'Are you OK?' Angela asked.

He opened his eyes again. 'Yeah. No big deal. It was just a nightmare.'

'I had some bad ones, too. I'm sure glad it's morning.'

'Yeah.' For the first time, he looked around. Doris was still sleeping. The front seat was empty. Turning around, he saw Keith behind the car, pumping gas. 'Where are the others?'

'The bathroom.'

When Lana and Glen returned to the car, Howard followed Angela to the side of the service station and entered the men's restroom. He used the toilet. He washed his hands and face with cold water. He came out into the fresh morning sunlight.

The night was over.

The long hours of torment had finally come to an end.

He waited for Angela. When she stepped out of the women's restroom, she looked younger and prettier than ever before. And carefree. As if she didn't have a worry in the world. Smiling, she took hold of his hand.

'Isn't it just wonderful here?' she said as they walked toward the car.

'It's awfully nice.'

'I may just decide never to go back at all.'

'Here come the lovebirds,' Glen called out his window.

Howard found that he didn't mind. Angela glanced at him, blushing, and squeezed his hand.

They climbed into the backseat. Keith started the car. Glen, on the other side of Lana, grinned over his shoulder at them. 'I saw what you two were doing last night when you thought we were asleep.'

'Oh, sure,' Howard said, surprised that the teasing didn't bother him.

'You jealous, Glenny?' Angela asked.

Howard laughed, amazed to hear such a cheerful, bold retort from the girl. Especially considering that they'd done nothing. He would've expected Angela to deny they had fooled around, or simply to remain silent and lower her eyes.

What's going on with her?

Whatever it might be, he liked it.

He felt himself liking everything that morning: the ride along the quiet highway, the smell of the air, the deep green of the wooded hills all around, Angela sitting beside him seeming almost reborn, even the banter and arguments and speculations in which they both participated.

Somehow, he no longer felt like such an outsider. From the way Angela behaved, he supposed she must be feeling the same way.

It's almost as if we're suddenly a family, he realized. He didn't know how it had happened. He could remember his impression of being trapped among virtual strangers when they'd started out. Somehow, a kind of intimacy had developed overnight.

His deeper feelings about Angela were easy to understand.

But why the others? Just because they'd shared the misery of spending a night cramped in the car? Or because they were all together in unknown territory, joined in this crazy hunt?

Whatever the reason, he liked the new feeling of closeness. He liked being here.

They stopped at a cafe in Redding for breakfast. He drank coffee, ate bacon and fried eggs and hash browns, and thought that a meal had never tasted so fine. Lana, checking her map, explained that Red Bluff was only an hour's drive. She suggested that they stop there to pick up the equipment and supplies. 'After that,' she said, 'it's the boondocks.'

At the pay phone, Howard called home. His father answered. His mother joined in on the other line.

He'd already decided to tell them the truth. Part of the truth, anyway.

'I'm going to be a few days late getting home,' he said. 'If it's OK.'

'What's up?' Dad asked.

'A couple of the guys invited me to go camping with them.'

'How nice,' Mom said. She was always pleading with him to make new friends.

'We're planning to leave today and go up into the mountains for four or five days. Is it all right?'

'Fine by me,' Dad said. 'Should be fun. Are your friends familiar with the area you'll be going into?'

'Yeah. They've been there before.'

'Well, sounds good to me.'

'These are boys you know fairly well?' Mom asked.

'Sure. They've been in a few of my classes.'

'Well, that was very nice of them to invite you along.'

'Yeah. They're good guys.'

'You'll call us when you get back?' Mom asked.

'Sure.'

'What about your airline ticket?' Dad asked.

'Well, I haven't bought it yet. I was going to make my reservation today, but I guess I'll wait till I get back.'

'Fine. Let us know when you'll be arriving.'

'I will. See you soon.'

'Be careful, honey.'

'I will.'

'Have fun,' Dad said.

After hanging up, Howard grinned. He'd half expected trouble about the abrupt change of plans, but they'd both seemed happy to hear about his little adventure. It would've been a different story, he knew, if he'd told them everything. Especially about the girls. But he hadn't needed to lie very much.

Feeling good, he walked back down the block and entered the sporting goods store.

He found Keith and Glen tossing food into a shopping cart.

'How'd it go with your folks, Howitzer?'

'No problem.'

'If they didn't hassle you,' Glen said, 'you must've lied through your teeth.'

'What they don't know won't hurt them.'

'Which is why I don't tell mine anything,' Glen said, and went back to gathering food. In the cart were packets of freeze-dried meals and fruit, bacon bars, pudding desserts, trail mix, punch and cocoa and instant coffee, 'Tropical' chocolate bars and cookies. Howard wondered where the girls were, but he decided to stay with Glen and Keith for a while.

Glen did most of the picking. He seemed to know just what he wanted, but gasped 'Far out!' or 'All right!' when he discovered surprising items on the shelves. Keith went along with the choices, sometimes laughing at Glen's enthusiasm.

He told Howard to go ahead and grab anything that looked especially good.

'Oh, I think Glen's doing great,' he said, then wandered away to look for the girls.

He found them in a far corner of the store. Angela smiled as he approached. She had a red pack in each hand. Lana passed a couple of fuel bottles to Doris, who set them inside a shopping cart.

'Did it go OK?' Lana asked him.

'Fine.'

In the cart were ground cloths, plastic water bottles, mess kits and packets of eating utensils. Two of each.

Lana checked the list that they had composed during the drive from Red Bluff.

'That pretty much covers it,' she said. 'We've got everything but the t.p., soap and insect repellant.'

They started walking toward another area of the store.

'What did you decide about a tent?' Howard asked.

'The hell with it. We aren't going to be out all that long, anyway. If we run into a storm, we'll pile into mine and Glen's.'

'Let us pray for fair weather,' Doris said.

'Two should be plenty. And they're heavy suckers to lug around.'

'All the food Glen's grabbing,' Howard said, 'we probably won't have room in our packs for an extra tent, anyway.'

Lana laughed.

He'd *caused* her to laugh. It made him feel good. He tried to think of a witty remark that might make her laugh again, but decided not to press his luck.

Dropping back, he joined Angela behind the shopping cart. 'Carry those for you?'

'Sure. Thanks.'

He took the two packs. 'Have you got everything you need?' he asked.

'Well, I think so. I've never gone camping before.'

'I guess the list covers most of the necessities. Do you have something warm to wear at night?'

'My sweats.'

Her sweats. The closet. Howard's heart started hammering.

'I wonder if they're dry yet,' she said, and gave him a strange look. It seemed to be a mixture of embarrassment and regret and fondness and hope. It made Howard very glad he'd resisted his temptation to sneak feels last night in the car. He felt like hugging her.

'Did you bring a coat?'

She shook her head. 'It was too big and heavy.'

'Why don't we get you a windbreaker?'

'No, that's not really . . .'

'You might freeze in just a sweatshirt. I'll buy it for you, OK?'

'No, you don't have to do that.'

'I want to.'

She hesitated.

'If you'd feel better about it,' he said, 'you can pay me back when we find Butler's loot.'

'Well. OK.'

They wandered away from Lana and Doris. In the store's clothing section, they picked out a lightweight red windbreaker. Angela tried it on. She looked wonderful in it.

Nearby was a female mannequin wearing a pink, long-billed cap, a purple tank top and shorts. The shorts matched the top, but were made of a shiny fabric so thin that the barely moving air inside the store was enough to stir it.

'How about shorts?' Howard asked. 'Did you bring shorts?'

'Yes, I did. Howard, you don't have to buy me anything else. Really.'

'A pair like these would be great. It gets awfully hot in the mountains.'

Angela stepped up to the mannequin. She stared at the shorts. She rubbed the material between her thumb and forefinger, then looked over her shoulder at Howard. She studied his eyes for a moment. 'OK. If you're sure you want me to have them.'

She knows I just want to see her in them, he realized. And she's going along with it!

'They'll be comfortable,' he said. Could he get her to go for the tank top? Don't push it.

He waited while she searched through stacks of shorts beside the mannequin. 'Do you like the purple?' she asked.

'Whatever color you want.'

She chose white.

'You'll need a hat,' Howard said. 'Did you bring a hat?'

'No.'

'That one's neat.'

'Yeah.'

They stepped over to a rack of caps similar to the one worn by the mannequin. Angela picked a white one, put it on and faced Howard. 'Like it?'

He shifted a pack to free one of his hands, reached out and turned up the bill.

She grinned.

God, she looked happy! And so cute.

'Great. Let's get it. Do you see anything else you'd like?'

'This is plenty. We'd better go and find the others.'

'I'll go ahead and buy these.' He gave Angela the packs, took the windbreaker, cap and shorts, and hurried toward the counter while she went looking for the rest of the group.

Chapter Ten

'That might've been it,' Lana said.

'That *was* it,' Doris said.

Howard glanced out the rear window. He couldn't spot the sign, but he noted that the highway was clear behind them. 'Nobody on our tail.'

As Keith backed up the car, the sign came into view on the right. Carved in its redwood was SHADOW CANYON LAKE – 22 MI and an arrow pointing toward a dirt track that twisted into the forest.

'Twenty-two miles on *that*?' Glen said.

'Worse,' Lana said. 'My map shows it stopping a few miles short of the lake. We'll have to do some hiking before we make camp.'

'Terrific,' Keith muttered. He swung the steering wheel and started forward. They left the two-lane highway behind, the car jolting and rocking as it started along the rough road. Howard looked at Angela. She grinned as she bounced and bumped against him. She took hold of his leg. He covered her hand, then glanced at Doris. The girl's heavy cheeks were vibrating. Looking out the back window, he saw a cloud of yellow dust behind them.

'This is gonna take a while,' Keith said.

Howard checked his wristwatch. Eleven-fifteen. It was ten after one when they reached a clearing at the end of the road.

They climbed out. Howard felt unsteady on his feet as if he'd just stepped onto land after a boat ride across choppy waters. He held onto the side of the car and looked around. The clearing, large enough to allow parking for several vehicles, was deserted except for their car. The shadows of surrounding trees blocked out most of the sunlight. Only a few rays got through, slanting down and making bright patches on the carpet of pine needles, cones and twigs.

'Isn't this wonderful?' Angela said.

'Nice.'

'My ass,' Glen said, reaching up to unfasten the straps on the luggage rack. 'Bloody fucking hot.'

'But wonderful,' Angela said. She stretched, took a deep breath, and sighed.

After the car was unloaded, Keith and Glen began dividing the food and other supplies into six piles on the hood of the car. While they did that, Doris and Angela emptied their suitcases into their new packs. Howard saw that Angela had brought her stuffed, one-eared kitten along. Fortunately, nobody else seemed to notice.

He opened his own pack, added his share from the hood, closed it and strapped his sleeping bag into place. Then he helped Angela get ready. When he was about to pull down the top flap of her pack, she stopped him. 'Just a second.'

Crouching, she opened the bag from the sporting goods store. She took out her windbreaker, cap and shorts, wadded the bag and tossed it into the trunk. She folded the coat and put it into her pack. She put on the cap. Then she stepped into the shorts, pulled them up beneath her skirt, took off the skirt and stuffed it into the pack. 'Now you can shut it,' she said.

Howard finished closing the pack. He strapped her sleeping bag onto the frame at the top.

'Can I borrow your knife?' she asked.

He dug it out of his pocket. A sudden memory of the nightmare intruded as he pried open the main blade. But the memory was swept away when Angela took the knife and lifted her blouse. The skin of her belly, though fair, looked almost dusky next to the stark white of the shorts.

She knotted the front of her blouse so its tails wouldn't fall and get in her way. The tags hung from her waistband by a tough plastic thread at her hip. Twisting sideways, she pulled at the tags and cut them loose.

'Thank you,' she said, and handed the knife back to Howard. In a whisper, she added, 'Thanks for the shorts, too. They're fabulous. They're so light and cool.' She tugged at the knot, and the lower part of her blouse fell, draping the shorts.

As Howard put the knife away, he saw Lana tucking the Ouija board's plastic pointer into a side pocket of her pack. He felt a quick flutter in his stomach. He wished he hadn't seen the thing.

It's only because of the Ouija that we're here, he told himself. I should be grateful to the thing, not scared of it.

But sooner or later, probably after dark, they would gather near their campfire and place their fingers on the pointer and try to contact Butler. The six of them. Alone in all this wilderness. Surrounded by the night.

Thoughts of that made something cold squirm through Howard's bowels.

Maybe the pointer won't move. Maybe we lost Butler, left him behind at Dr Dalton's house.

The squirmy feelings faded a little.

Just don't think about the Ouija board or Butler. Maybe nothing bad will happen. Shouldn't worry about what *might* happen, anyway. It's a waste of time and it'll spoil the good stuff. This could be like a great vacation or adventure or something if you just don't screw it up worrying. It might end up being the best few days you've ever spent.

Crouching, he opened a side pocket of his pack. He pulled out his battered old gray felt hat and put it on.

Angela laughed.

'Dashing, huh?' he asked.

'You look like a moonshiner.'

Lana glanced over her shoulder at him. 'Jed Clampet.'

Doris snickered. She was tying a red bandana around her head, her armpits showing. Though her sleeves were cut off at the shoulders, she had to be awfully hot in that sweatshirt. She always wore sweatshirts, regardless of the weather. Maybe she thought she looked good in them. Howard couldn't imagine her looking good in anything.

Lana slammed the trunk lid, swung her pack onto it, and leaned back to put her arms through the straps. 'Are we all set?' she asked.

'Looks like the trail starts over there,' Keith said.

'Let's hit it,' Glen said.

Howard held Angela's pack for her. When she had it on, he saw Doris struggling. He took a step toward her. 'Could you use some help?'

'I'm perfectly capable of managing my own affairs,' she said, swinging the pack up behind her.

'You've got affairs?' Glen called. 'Where'd you find guys that hard up?'

'The Braille Institute,' Keith said.

'Such wit,' Doris said. 'I'm doubled over with hilarity.'

'Come on, children.' Lana took a few steps backward, studying her car as if wondering if she'd forgotten anything. Then she turned around and strode to the trail sign. She waited there for the others.

They gathered in front of the sign. Its two short planks both pointed at the same path. The upper board read SHADOW CANYON LAKE – 4 MI. The lower, CALAMITY PEAK – 9 MI.

'Oh, brother,' Keith muttered.

'Not so bad,' Lana said. 'Only five miles from the lake to the peak.'

'But does that mean to the peak of the peak,' Glen asked, 'or to the foot of the peak?'

'I guess we'll find out,' Lana said. 'Right now, let's just worry about making it to the lake.'

She led the way. Keith followed. After a few steps, he apparently decided that the path was wide enough for both of them. He hurried forward and joined her. Glen went next.

'Be my guests,' Doris said, gesturing for Howard and Angela to go ahead.

'Are you sure you want to take up the rear?' Howard asked.

'And why wouldn't I?'

'Stragglers get picked off.'

Angela laughed.

Doris sneered. 'For Godsake, Howard. Have you started taking quip lessons from Tweedle-Dee and Dumb-Dumb?'

'No, I just . . .'

'You're not a bad fellow. Why don't you try to keep it that way?'

'We'll go next,' Angela said. 'It's no big deal.' She pulled Howard by the arm.

They hurried up the trail, leaving Doris behind. When they rounded a bend, Glen came into sight. They slowed their pace. Angela took a few sidesteps and looked back, then turned to the front again.

'I think she likes you.'

'Yuck.'

'What's wrong with that?'

'She's miserable and sarcastic, for starters.'

'I think she's just lonely.'

'Of course she's lonely. Everybody hates her. She seems to thrive on it. It wouldn't have killed her to let us take up the rear.'

'Then *we'd* get picked off.'

Howard laughed. 'Better her than us.'

'Right. But we really should try to be nice to her. You know? I mean, we're all in this together, and she's here without any friends at all, and it's terrible the way Keith and Glen pick on her.'

'They pick on us, too.'

'Yeah, but it's not the same. I mean, we have each other.'

The words gave him a strange, warm feeling in his chest.

If she had spoken them yesterday, Howard realized, he probably would've been appalled. Though he'd always felt a certain bond with Angela, he'd never been attracted to her. In fact, he'd often gone out of his way to avoid her company. He'd thought of her as 'weird Angela', the 'space cadet' and the 'Melancholy Dame'.

Last night had sure changed him.

Starting when she took off her blouse. That was the moment when he really began to want her. And later, when he found her in Skerrit's closet, he really began to care about her. From that time on, his feelings for Angela had grown until now, hearing her say 'We have each other,' he wondered if he might actually be falling in love with her.

That's crazy, he told himself. If I'm in love with anyone, it's Dr Dalton.

If I had to pick between the two of them, it wouldn't be any contest.

That's sure likely to come up.

Looking into Angela's eyes, he suddenly realized that such a fantasy choice might not be made quite so easily. Yesterday, there would've been no contest. At this moment, however . . .

'Are you all right?' she asked.

'Yeah.'

'Is something wrong?'

'No. Huh-uh.'

'When I said that . . . you know, about how we have each

other . . .' Her face blushed furiously. 'I only meant that . . . I don't know . . . just that we're sort of friends. And Doris doesn't have any friends.'

'I'll try to be nice to her,' Howard said. He glanced back at Doris. She was slogging along, far behind them. 'Should I ask her to come up and join us?'

Angela laughed. 'You don't have to overdo it.'

They walked for a while in silence. Then he said, 'I'm really glad we're here.'

'So am I.'

Soon, the trees thinned out and the trail led upward along a rocky, glaring slope. Howard's legs began to feel heavy. The heat pushed down on him. The straps of his pack made his shoulders ache. Sweat dripped down his face. His shirt and underpants were sodden and clinging. The legs of his corduroys seemed to scorch his thighs with each step, and the heavy fabric trapped the heat inside.

He wished he had changed into shorts before starting the hike. But he wasn't about to stop now and do it. Maybe if Doris weren't back there.

At least I don't have to worry about my legs getting sunburned.

'How are you doing?' he asked Angela. Her face was dripping. She was gasping for breath. Her blouse was unbuttoned partway down, and the skin of her chest gleamed. Much of her pale blue blouse was dark with moisture. But the shorts floated around her as if they were filled with breezes, and her legs looked cool.

'Butler's . . . sure making us work for that treasure.'

'I think his whole plan is to torment us.'

'Probably.' She huffed along for a while. 'Do people do this for *fun*?'

'It feels so good when you stop.'

'If we ever do.'

At the end of a long, dusty switchback, they came upon Lana, Keith and Glen resting among the rocks with their packs off. Glen's eyes were squeezed shut as he chugged water from his plastic canteen. Keith sat cross-legged in a patch of shade cast by an outcropping. Lana sat atop a boulder, spreading suntan lotion on her arms.

'You'd better put some of this on when I'm done,' she told Angela. 'At this altitude, the sun'll really cook you.'

They took their packs off. Without the weight dragging him down, Howard felt buoyant. The breeze chilled the sweat on the back of his shirt.

'I don't think we're far from the top,' Lana said, rubbing her legs with lotion.

'Maybe someone would like to carry me the rest of the way,' Glen said.

'In your dreams,' Keith told him.

'This'll make football practice look like a picnic.'

'Just think of the great shape you'll be in,' Lana said.

'If I don't drop dead up here.'

Doris showed up, red and gasping. She flopped backward against a slab of rock.

'How are you doing?' Howard asked her.

She gave him a scowl, and said nothing.

So much for being nice to her.

Angela sat down on a small, flat rock with Lana's suntan lotion. When she leaned forward to squirt it on her legs, her left breast showed inside the shadowed opening of her blouse. She wore a bra, maybe the same one she'd had on at the party. The side that Howard could see looked like a small, transparent bag clinging to her breast. He supposed it must be wet and cool against her skin. He imagined it gone, imagined his hand there instead.

Feeling guilty, he looked away and watched her spread the lotion up and down her long, slim legs. He wished he could be the one rubbing it onto her. Then he pictured Skerrit crouching in front of her, leering as he slathered hot ointment onto her legs and up between them.

Dirty, rotten bastard!

She's got me, now. She'll never have to let that old pervert touch her again.

Maybe she *liked* being rubbed all over with the stuff. Maybe she'll want me to do it to her.

She didn't like it. Are you nuts?

But the thought excited Howard.

Get off it! That's Skerrit's shit. I would never do anything like that to her.

He turned away quickly, sat down in front of his pack, and fixed his eyes on the wooded valley below the trail.

Skerrit stayed in his mind long after they resumed their hike. He hated the man for abusing Angela. But he knew that his hatred was mixed with envy. Angela had lived with the guy. His victim. His slave.

She could've been living with me, Howard kept reminding himself. I was all alone. I wouldn't have done anything to hurt her.

Maybe after we're done up here, she *will* live with me. She can't go back to Skerrit. I'll get her a ticket and we can fly home together and she can stay in the guest room until it's time for the fall semester.

Would Mom and Dad go along with that?

I'll explain how she hasn't got anyplace else to live. Won't tell them about Skerrit, of course.

As they trudged up the mountain trail, he ached to ask Angela about Skerrit. How had she ended up living with that horrible old man? How long had they been together? What other abuses had he inflicted on her? Did he beat her? Did he spy on her when she undressed?

Did he fuck her?

That was the real question.

Howard wasn't sure he really wanted to know the answer. But he couldn't ask Angela. He found that he couldn't ask her anything at all about her relationship with Skerrit. He could only dwell on it and let it torment him during the long hike up the mountain.

Finally, the switchbacks ended. The top of the mountain still loomed above them, but the trail curved along its side and led them through a pass, then angled downward into a wooded valley.

'Can't be far, now,' Howard said.

Angela looked exhausted, but she smiled at him. 'This isn't too bad.'

'At least there's shade.'

'I just hope we don't have to climb another mountain.'

'We'll probably have to go up Calamity Peak.'

'Not today. Lana said we'd camp by the lake. I can't imagine there's actually a lake way up here.'

Soon, however, Howard spotted a glimmer beyond the trees. 'Look there,' he said.

'Fabulous!' Angela quickened her pace.

More of the lake came into view as they hurried forward. Rounding a bend, they came upon Lana, Keith and Glen waiting at a fork in the trail.

'Thar shc blows,' Glcn said, pointing at thc lakc.

Its shore was straight ahead, just beyond a clearing that looked like a regular stopping place for campers. There was a campfire area – a circle of rocks surrounded by makeshift benches of split logs. Someone had left a grille behind, and even a small pile of kindling. Patches of sunlight dappled the ground. The surface of the lake gleamed.

'Decent,' Keith said.

'Let's check around before we set up camp,' Lana said. 'We might find a better place.'

'We might find a troop of Girl Scouts,' Glen said.

Angela gave Howard an uneasy glance.

'What?' he asked.

'We might find Butler.'

They all looked at her.

'He said, "I meet you." Remember?'

'At the mine,' Keith pointed out. 'The mine's supposed to be at Calamity Peak and we're . . . what? Five miles away.'

'Yeah,' Glen said. 'Geez, don't be such a downer.'

Chapter Eleven

Coreen leaned forward and rested her forearms on the steering wheel. The wind from the open window was tossing her hair, flicking the collar and short sleeves of her blouse. The back of the blouse didn't stir; its checkered fabric looked glued to her skin.

'Getting tired?' Chad asked.

'No, I'm fine. Just cooling off.'

'I'll take over, if you'd like.'

'I'll hang in a little longer. What's it been, three hours?' She glanced at her wristwatch. 'Yug. Only three-thirty. We got away at what, one?'

'Maybe a little earlier.'

'Sure seems like longer than two and a half hours.'

'Time flies when you're having fun.'

Coreen settled back against the seat. She reached over and

gave Chad's leg a gentle squeeze. 'I guess I haven't been very good company. I'm sorry.'

'You're great company.'

'I'm pissed off, is what I am. Here you are, you've finally come back, and we've gotta go chasing after a bunch of damn kids. I could just kill those jerks.'

'It'll be great once we're out in the mountains. There's nothing like it.'

'Then why did you leave them?' She glanced at him, a teasing look in her eyes.

'You're better.'

'You may change your tune after you've been around me for a while.'

'Probably.'

She laughed and pounded his thigh. 'So tell me, aside from pining away for me all the time, what did you do with yourself out there in the wilds? Just wander around yodeling and communing with chipmunks?'

'That's about it.'

'No, really.'

'Well, I worked at ski lodges during the winter. I waited tables the first year, then spent a winter bartending, and finally I got into ski instructing. Each spring, I'd load up with supplies and take off on my own. I usually made it into early September before heading back for civilization.'

'And you liked living that way?'

'Most of the time. You know what Thoreau said.'

' "Simplify, simplify, simplify"?'

'That. And, "I never met a companion so companionable as solitude." '

'Present company excluded, right?'

'Right.'

'I think it'd drive me crazy, being alone that much.'

'I got a pretty good fill of society during the winters. And occasionally I'd run into hikers. I tried to stay clear of the main trails, but people popped up anyway, once in a while.'

'Then you'd set a spell and palaver?'

He laughed. 'Yeah, sometimes. Mostly, I did my best to avoid them. You'd think I was the boogeyman, the way some of those people got spooked when they bumped into me.'

'I can imagine. You spooked *me* last night. Mostly the beard, I guess.'

'Do I look harmless enough now?'

'It's nice to be able to see your face.'

That morning, after their decision to pursue the kids, Coreen had driven off to buy supplies. Chad had stayed at the house and thrown his clothes in the washer. While they were being cleaned, he had taken a razor to his beard and mustache. He'd been a little worried about Coreen's reaction, but when she came back her delight was obvious. 'Hey,' she'd said, grinning, 'I know you.' And she'd caressed his cheeks, and kissed him, and rubbed her face against his. 'Gee, I let myself get screwed by some wild old mountain man last night. If I'd known you'd be showing up today, I might've been able to curb my lust.'

'I saw him on his way out,' Chad had told her. 'He said you were just too hot for him to handle, and he wished me luck.'

'He was sweet in his rough and rustic way, but I prefer you.'

Then Coreen had shown him what she'd bought. In addition to food and supplies for the trip, she'd purchased clothes for him: crew socks; skimpy briefs in a variety of colors; two pairs of tan hiking shorts with deep pockets and button-down flaps; three short-sleeved shirts with epaulettes; and a hat that looked like something Indiana Jones might wear. 'No bullwhip?'

'They didn't come in your size,' she'd said, slipping the

robe off his shoulders. 'Come on, let's see how you look in this stuff.'

'I thought we were in a hurry.'

'We can't leave till you're dressed, can we?'

The memories brought a smile to Chad's face.

'What?' Coreen asked.

'Just feeling good. About everything.'

'I'd feel better if the air conditioner worked.'

'Don't you like the fresh air?'

'Fresh air's fine. Hot air I can do without.'

'You'll look back on it fondly tonight when you're freezing your tail off.'

'I'm counting on you to keep me warm.'

'Well, I'll sure . . .'

Thunkthunkthunkthunk . . .

'What the hell!'

Coreen slowed down. The car no longer shook quite so much and the pounding slacked off. *Thunk thunk thunk*.

Chad felt his alarm beginning to subside. 'Must be a flat,' he said, speaking loudly, almost shouting to be heard over the pounding noise.

'Shit!'

'Just pull over and I'll change it.'

'Who's got a spare?' she asked, riding the highway's breakdown lane.

'You haven't got a spare tire?'

'Not at the moment. I meant to get it fixed but . . . I'll try for that off-ramp.'

The ramp was no more than fifty yards ahead. Chad spotted a Mobil station at the top. But the thunking went on. It sounded like a hammer whacking the front of the car. 'Maybe you'd better not try. I'll walk up there and get help.'

'I can make it.'

'God knows what you're doing to the tire.'

'I've got a sneaky suspicion it's a gonner, anyway.'

'Your rim . . .'

She started up the off-ramp. 'I don't know. Feels like the tire's working. Sort of.'

'Well, you're almost there now.'

'Come on, baby,' she whispered.

At the end of the ramp, she turned right, clumped along the road for a short distance, then swung into the station. She stopped in front of the service bay. There was only one. A Toyota was up on the rack. The mechanic beneath it spotted them, nodded, and went back to work.

'This might be a while,' Chad said.

Coreen didn't answer. She was slumped back against the seat, hands on her thighs. Her cheeks puffed out as she slowly blew air through her pursed lips. She looked haggard and relieved. As she turned her head toward Chad, a corner of her mouth lifted. 'Boy, did we luck out.'

'If we had to have a flat,' he said, 'I guess it couldn't have happened at a much better time.'

She tipped her eyes upward. 'Somebody up there likes us.'

'If he likes us so much, how come he blew our tire?'

'Don't get technical,' she said, and shoved open her door.

Chad climbed out. It felt good to be standing again, but his legs were a little shaky. Scares always seemed to leave them that way, and he'd been damn scared for just a second there with the clamor pounding his ears and the car shuddering – before he'd had a chance to figure out what was going on.

Must've given Coreen some bad moments, too.

'Good God,' she said, bending down and gazing at the left front tire.

Chad joined her.

The tire wasn't flat, but it looked as if it had been scalped.

Most of its tread was gone. A remaining section was still attached but hanging loose, and Chad realized that it had been responsible for the pounding noise. With each revolution of the wheel, the flopping panel of tread had hammered against the car. It had dented the chrome trim at the rear of the wheel well.

'Looks like you've got a problem there,' the mechanic said. He came sauntering toward them, rubbing his hands with a dirty red rag while his mouth played with a toothpick. He was a stocky, dark man. He looked Mexican, but had no trace of a Spanish accent. 'Yep,' he said, and squatted beside the tire. 'You aren't going much farther on this one. Lucky she didn't explode on you.'

'I thought this only happened to retreads,' Coreen said.

'Nope. Happens all the time with your steel-belted radials. You gotcha a little too much wear, maybe a structural flaw, you run 'em too long in this heat, it's slam, bam, *adios*.' He looked up at Coreen. Opening his mouth wide, he turned his toothpick end over end with his tongue. 'Interested in buying a new tire?'

'I don't suppose I have much choice.'

'I could put your spare on for you, but then you'll be in mighty deep waters if another tire goes south on you.'

'I don't have a spare, anyway.'

'Well, now.' The man pushed at his knees, grunted and stood up straight. 'If you wanta go for two, I can fix you up with a couple of fine new radials every bit as good as what you've got on there. They'll run you about eighty bucks each.' He grinned. 'In fact, I'll give you a deal on 'em – two for the price of two.'

Coreen shook her head and laughed. She met Chad's eyes.

He found himself smiling. 'I don't know how we can beat an offer like that.'

'Sounds good to me.'

'What I'll do for you, I'll put both the new babies on the front, balance 'em up real fine for you, give your junk tire a toss, and throw your other tire into the trunk for your spare. That way, you'll be riding with a brand fresh pair up front where it counts.'

Coreen looked at Chad. He nodded.

'Great,' she told the mechanic. 'How long'll it take?'

'Give me an hour. Now hang on a second, we'll write this up and I'll get started.' He swaggered away, tucking the rag into a seat pocket of his coveralls.

As he entered the office, Coreen said, 'This isn't too bad. We'll only lose an hour or so.'

'It sure could have been a lot worse.'

She nodded toward a coffee shop across the road. 'Why don't we go over there? We can eat while he's putting the tires on, then we won't have to stop later for dinner. That'll save us some time.'

'We might as well not worry about the time,' Chad said. 'We got such a late start, and now this. I don't see much chance of catching up with your kids today.'

She fixed her eyes on him, a grimace baring her upper teeth. 'We have to try,' she said.

'We'll try. But it's going to be dark before we even make it off the main roads.'

The mechanic came back carrying a clipboard. 'Checked the prices for you while I was in there. The tires'll run you just sixty-nine ninety-nine each, plus ten apiece for installation and balancing.'

'Fine,' Coreen muttered. She sounded as if her spirits had taken a nosedive. Chad wondered whether she was disturbed by the cost, or brooding over what he'd told her about their chances of finding the kids today.

Probably worried about the kids, he decided.

The mechanic handed the clipboard to her. A work order

was clamped to it. 'Need your name, address and phone number.'

A ballpoint dangled at the end of a dirty string which was knotted to the eye of the metal clamp. She caught the pen and began filling out the work order.

'You folks oughta head on over to Rusty's,' he said, jabbing a thumb in the direction of the coffee shop. 'Sit down, relax, have a drink, have a bite. I'll come over and let you know when she's ready to roll.'

'Thanks,' she said, and gave him the board.

'Keys in the ignition?'

She nodded. She glanced at Chad, then took his hand. They started walking. 'I don't like this.'

'I can tell.'

'It's what you said.'

'Figured it might be. I'm sorry.'

She squeezed his hand. 'It's not your fault. You're right. It'll be dark before we're anywhere close to the kids.'

They waited on the curb for a Jeep Wrangler to speed by, then stepped down and hurried across the road.

'I'm just afraid for them,' she said.

'They'll be all right.'

'God, I hope so. But . . . This is gonna sound stupid, but what if we're not *supposed* to reach them? At least not in time, you know?'

Chad was tempted to tease her. *Yeah, sounds stupid, all right.* But she was blushing. Though obviously embarrassed by her idea, she'd trusted Chad enough to share it with him. 'It was just a bad tire,' he said. 'People have car trouble all the time.'

She tried to force a smile. 'So you don't think it was Butler's way of trying to slow us down?'

'If it was, he's not much of a manipulator. Why didn't he rip the tread off the tire when we were twenty miles from the nearest station? For that matter, why didn't he knock out the steering so we'd crash? Or just forget subtlety and blow us to smithereens?'

'I guess you're right,' Coreen said.

He opened the door of Rusty's, and they stepped into the restaurant. It was air-conditioned. Chad felt his damp clothes turn cold.

'Just take a seat anywhere, folks,' a woman called from behind the serving counter.

They walked to a front booth, and Chad sat down across from Coreen.

'I know you're right,' she said, leaning forward and resting her elbows on the table. 'We had a little car trouble. There's no reason to read anything supernatural into it.'

'No reason at all.'

'But I just can't help feeling that Butler might've been behind it. If he has the power to guide a pointer around a Ouija board, maybe he has enough power to do other stuff. And maybe he doesn't want us to interfere with his plans.'

Chapter Twelve

'Come on, you chickens,' Glen called, looking over his shoulder at Howard and Angela. He had stripped down to his boxer shorts and was knee deep in the lake.

'I'm fine right here,' Howard said.

Angela, sitting beside him on the rock slab with her bare feet dangling in the water, said, 'Me, too. Besides, I didn't bring a suit.'

'Big deal. So come in in your undies, nobody's gonna tell on you.'

'You're going to freeze,' Howard told him.

'It's not so bad.' As if to prove his point, he waded farther out from shore. The water climbed his legs, and when it reached his groin he jerked rigid and cried out, 'Yeeeeah! My balls!'

Angela laughed. 'It's not so bad,' she told Howard.

'I'm sure it's very refreshing.'

Glen shuddered and gasped for breath. He was bent over slightly at the waist, arms away from his sides, fists clenched.

'You look like you stepped in a bear trap,' Howard called.

'I'm OK. I'm OK. I'll be OK in a minute.'

'I'm glad that's him and not us,' Angela said.

'Same here.'

It was the truth. He didn't want to get into that frigid water. But going for a swim would've given him – and Angela – an excuse for stripping down to their underwear. If she'd been willing, he would've done it, too.

As soon as the subject of swimming had come up, however, she'd said, 'Not me.' Nobody had tried very hard to talk her into it. So Howard, partly relieved but mostly disappointed, had said, 'I'm not going in, either. The rest of you can freeze if you want.'

Then he and Angela had wandered down to the shore and found the boulder. It was flat and fairly smooth, and slanted downward at a mild angle toward the water. Once they were sitting down, Angela had pulled off her shoes and socks and lowered her feet into the lake.

'How is it?' Howard had asked.

'Ice cold. But kind of nice.'

'Are you sure you don't want to go in?'

'I didn't bring a suit.'

'Neither did I. I'm not sure anybody did.'

She had grinned and raised her eyebrows. 'Think they'll go skinny-dipping?'

'Maybe.'

'I wouldn't do that. Not around Keith and Glen.'

But she would *around me*? 'I wouldn't either. Not around Doris.'

She'd laughed.

About that time, Glen had trotted down to the shore in his shorts. Howard wouldn't have been surprised to see him shuck them off at the last moment and charge into the lake bare-assed, but they were still on, and now they were wet.

'Here goes!' Glen bounced up and down a few times, apparently trying to gather his courage. Then he raised his arms and flung himself forward. His big body dropped, shoving the water aside. An instant later, the water rushed back and shut over him.

'He did it,' Angela said.

'He must be crazy.'

Glen's head popped to the surface. He bellowed, 'Oh, my God!'

'How is it?' Keith called.

Glen swiveled around and answered, 'Takes a little getting used to.' His voice had a higher than usual pitch.

'If you can take it, we can.' Lana's voice.

Howard felt a quick tug of excitement. 'I guess they're going in, too,' he said. Sounded inane, he thought, but he had to say something. He forced his gaze to stay on Angela.

What would Lana be wearing? A bra and panties? Nothing at all?

'Must be masochists,' Angela said. She leaned back slightly to see past him. So Howard looked.

Keith, slim and muscular and tanned, wore cut-off jeans.

Lana wasn't naked. She wasn't in her underwear. She wore

a swimsuit. It wasn't even a bikini, but a one-piece tank suit with a high neckline.

Oh, well, Howard thought. That's the way it goes.

But he quickly noticed that the suit wasn't all bad. Its glossy fabric hugged her body, showing every detail. The sides were cut so high that they left her hipbones bare. When she waded in, he saw that the suit was backless – and almost bottomless. Its tight, gleaming seat was a slim triangle that covered very little of her buttocks.

Lana waded forward until the water reached her thighs, and then without breaking stride she bounded forward, curved, and slipped beneath the surface.

'Whatcha waiting for, Keithie?'

Keith acted as if he didn't hear Glen. He stood motionless in water up to his ankles, staring at the place where Lana had vanished. He bared his teeth. He rubbed his hands together. He muttered, 'Oh, shit.' Then he charged, yelling, smashing through the water as if it were a defensive line.

'Go for it!' Glen shouted.

Keith let out a battle cry and hurled himself down.

Laughing, Glen pumped his fist in the air. 'All right!'

Lana surfaced and stood up. She was no more than six feet from Howard. He supposed she had circled around after diving, and headed back toward shore. The water where she stood was only waist deep.

She paid no attention to him as she wiped her face with both hands.

Her hair, the color of hay after a rainstorm, was slicked down against her head. Her shoulders and arms gleamed. When she lowered her arms, Howard saw how the suit was sticking to her body like a thin sheath of skin. If it were flesh-colored instead of royal blue, she would've appeared – at least without close inspection – to be naked.

He could feel himself getting hard as he gazed at her.

The clinging fabric bulged over her breasts. It looked perfectly smooth until the very front. There, it was pushed outward by small, pointed nipples.

Howard met her eyes, hoping she hadn't caught him staring. 'How is it?' he asked.

She blew out some air, puffing a fine spray from her lips. Her chin was trembling just a bit. 'If it was any colder, you could skate on it. But I figured it'd be like this. You get used to it. You two really ought to come in.'

'I think I'll just sit here,' Angela said, 'and watch you three turn blue.'

'You know, if it's just because you don't have a suit . . .'

'Well, that's one thing.'

'There's no law that says you've got to strip down. You could jump in wearing what you've got on. Whatever.'

'Well, I'll think about it.'

'What about you, Howard?'

He shrugged. 'It's pretty nice right here.'

'Suit yourselves. You wouldn't believe how great it feels, though, once you're in.' With that, she sank down, pushed herself off the bottom, and floated on her back. Arms by her sides, she began to kick. Howard watched her glide slowly away. Her long legs gleamed sunlight. Her breasts were out of the water, shaking a bit from side to side with the rhythm of her swishing legs.

'She looks great, doesn't she?' Angela said.

'Not bad.'

'Do you want to go in? If you do, go ahead. I mean, you shouldn't stay out just on my account.'

'I'm not crazy about the idea. I'll go in if you want to, though.'

She wrinkled her nose. 'Let's not, and say we did.' Twisting around, she squinted toward the clearing where they'd left their gear.

'What is it?'

'I don't see Doris.'

Howard turned and looked back. 'Maybe she ducked into the trees to change, or something.'

'I hardly think she's planning to take a dip.'

'Could be answering a call of nature. Or maybe she's gone off to sulk.'

Angela grinned. 'You're mean.'

'I just hope, wherever she went, she doesn't come back for a while. Things are a lot nicer when she's not around. It's like she's on her toes every second, just waiting for a chance to unload on somebody.'

'I hope she's all right. That's the only thing.'

'Why wouldn't she be?'

'I don't know. But doesn't it seem funny? I mean, when was the last time you saw her?'

'It probably wasn't more than ten or fifteen minutes ago,' Howard said. Doris, he remembered, had been sitting in the shade with her back against a tree while the others had discussed whether they should pitch camp before or after taking a swim. She had still been sitting there, the debate continuing, when he and Angela had wandered down to the lake. 'She was right under that tree,' he said.

'Yeah.'

'Wherever she went, she didn't take her pack.'

Angela smiled at him. 'What does that mean?'

'It means we're not in luck. She didn't bug out on us. She's not hurrying down the mountain, burning up the trail on her way back to civilization.'

'Maybe we should go and look for her.'

'I guess we could,' Howard said. 'Why don't we wait a while, though? She'll probably show up.'

'I'm in no hurry.'

They both turned to the front. Lana, Keith and Glen were

out near the middle of the lake, splashing and laughing. Glen seemed to be swimming after Lana, chasing her while Keith fled in a different direction.

'Think they're playing tag?' Angela asked.

'Looks like it.'

We could be in the water doing that, Howard thought.

He pictured himself pursuing Lana, reaching out to tag her, his hand finding a bare cheek of her rump. The skin would feel chilly. Maybe rough with goosebumps. But warm underneath.

And he wondered why he was daydreaming about Lana when he had Angela sitting right here beside him.

Maybe because it's safe. You know Lana's out of reach.

Far out on the water, Glen caught up to her. He grabbed her ankle. They both went under. They came up together in a burst of froth. Lana, laughing, broke away from him and back-pedaled. 'Hey, you!' she gasped. 'Watch it!'

'You're it.'

'*You're* a lech!'

'What'd you do to her?' Keith called. He sounded amused.

'Tagged her, that's all.'

'Yeah? Where?'

'Never you mind,' Lana said. 'Here I come, ready or not.' She went for Glen, who bolted. After a few strokes, she broke off her pursuit and headed for Keith.

'Thought she might,' Angela said, scooting backward a bit before lifting her feet out of the water. She brought up her knees, and braced herself up with stiff arms. Her wet calves were shiny. Water trickled down them and made dark spots on the granite. 'I guess I'll take a walk around,' she said. 'Want to come along?'

'Sure.' Howard's heart quickened.

Maybe it's not just to look for Doris, he thought. Maybe she wants to get me alone.

The others were certain to stay in the lake for a while longer. Once he and Angela were away from the shore, they would have complete privacy.

Except for Doris.

Some of his nervous excitement faded. Angela probably had nothing more in mind than searching.

But if we go looking for her, we *will* be alone. As long as we don't find her.

Angela leaned forward, reached around her bent legs, and used her crew socks to wipe her feet dry. Instead of putting them on, she spread them out on the rock. Then she stretched out her legs, crossed one, and worked her bare foot into a sneaker.

Howard had taken off his own boots and socks. He'd considered soaking his feet, but given up on the idea because he didn't want his pants to get wet and he'd thought he would look like a turkey if he rolled up his cuffs.

As Angela put on her other sneaker, he plucked his wadded socks out of his boots. They were filthy and damp. He dropped them onto the rock. Without socks, he wasn't eager to shove his feet into his boots. He knew they would feel awful: not only tight on his tender feet, but dank and slimy. He had a pair of Nike's in his pack. He wondered if he should go for them barefoot. Not a good idea. He might step on something sharp. Getting a foot injury way out here in the middle of nowhere . . .

'Oh, there's Doris. Over there.' Angela pointed toward the far side of the lake.

Howard spotted her at once. She was in plain sight, making her way across the sloping jumble of rock above the lake's eastern shore.

'What the hell's she doing?' he muttered.

'Exploring?'

'Didn't she get enough exercise for one day?'

'Apparently not.'

Howard shook his head and followed Doris's progress. She walked across the face of a tilted block the size of a car. At its end, she used her hands to climb a boulder. When she reached its top, she leaped across a gap and landed on a block of granite that looked like an overturned refrigerator.

'Maybe the heat drove her buggy,' Howard said.

'She's pretty agile.'

'Wait'll she gets back, she'll probably fill us all in on expertise as a mountaineer. She probably assaulted Everest last year.'

Angela cast a glance at Howard. 'Hope she didn't hurt him.'

He laughed. Then, mimicking Doris, he said, 'You been taking wise-guy lessons from Tweedle-Dee and Dumb-Dumb?'

Her head bobbed. She was mugging like a dope, her eyes fixed on Howard, and he felt a sudden rush of affection for her so strong it seemed to blot out everything else. It was a very odd sensation. Even as it swept through him, he realized it was nothing like sexual arousal. It was like tenderness or sorrow. It made him feel almost like weeping. He reached out and curled a hand behind her head and leaned toward her until his mouth found her lips.

They were soft and warm and moist.

God! he thought. What am I doing?

Before he could pull back, Angela's hand went to his face. She caressed his cheek. Then her mouth eased away. Looking into his eyes, she whispered, 'Do you want to take that walk now?'

'Yeah.'

She turned forward. She tied one of her shoes. As she tugged at the bow, she raised her eyes. They suddenly went wide. She sucked in a quick breath. Her back stiffened.

Howard shot his gaze out across the water. He spotted

Lana, Keith and Glen. Swimming, laughing. He searched the slope for Doris. There she was, striding along a granite slab.

'Angela?'

She still stared into the distance. The alarm on her face spooked him.

'What's wrong?' he blurted. 'What is it?'

'In front of Doris,' she said. Her voice was hushed, little more than a whisper. 'Just above her. See?'

Howard found Doris again. She was almost straight across the lake, now. He moved his eyes ahead of her, and upward. And heard himself gasp. His stomach seemed to drop. He went weak and shaky. 'My God,' he murmured.

The man stood motionless on an outcropping. He was hunched over slightly. His head was down, and cocked toward Doris. He seemed to be watching her. Waiting for her.

He looked like a man who might've just stepped off the stage at the Mr Universe contest. His bronze skin, bulging with knots of muscle, had an oily sheen. He seemed to have no hair at all. The top of his head gleamed in the sun. He wore sunglasses. He wore a G-string with a shiny black pouch. In his right hand was a machete.

And Doris was scurrying over the boulders, moving closer to him, unaware of his presence.

Angela leaped to her feet, cupped her hands to the sides of her mouth, and yelled, 'DORIS!'

Doris halted and turned her head toward them.

'LOOK OUT!' Howard yelled, springing up. 'A MAN!'

'What's going on?' Keith called to them.

'A *guy's* up there!' Howard answered. 'He's got a machete! Up ahead of Doris!'

Angela flapped her hand, waving Doris back and shouting, 'GET OUT OF THERE! RUN!'

Doris shook her head as if she didn't understand.

The man began to leap from rock to rock.

'HE'S COMING FOR YOU!' Angela yelled.

'BEHIND YOU!' Lana cried out.

Howard glimpsed Keith and Glen in motion – swimming toward the far side of the lake.

Not all that far.

But they wouldn't make it in time. They wouldn't come close.

Doris, apparently getting the message at last, began to turn around. The man was above her. Rushing at her straight down a steep rock slab.

He was gleaming skin and bouncing heaps of muscle. He was a stud in his black shades. He was a gayboy in his itsy-bitsy G-string. He was a skinhead. He was a madman with a machete.

Doris didn't scream. She made no sound at all that Howard could hear when she turned around and saw what was coming down for her. She jerked and flung out her arms and scampered backward.

To the edge of the boulder she'd been crossing.

Where she tried to stop.

She teetered on the brink, windmilling her arms.

'God!' Angela gasped. She grabbed Howard's hand.

Her fingernails dug into him when Doris sprawled out into the air.

The man reached for Doris.

He didn't swing his machete at her. He stretched out his left arm and tried to grab the front of her sweatshirt.

But missed.

She flapped her arms. She kicked. She had only six or eight feet to fall, but it seemed to go on forever. Howard knew he was about to see her die. In slow motion. Her head would be first to hit the granite. It would blast open . . .

But her rump hit first.

Then her legs and back slammed the tilted plate of rock.

Her head snapped down, but it was beyond the edge and struck only air.

Howard thought he saw her bounce a little. She looked limp.

On her back, head first, she began skidding down the face of the rock.

She didn't fly off as if shooting down a slide. Her descent was too slow for that.

Her head drooped lower. Her shoulders followed. Her arms flopped off the edge and dangled toward the lake. Her back bent as if the weight of her upper body were trying to snap it. Suddenly, her legs were flung upward and she somersaulted off the slab. Accidents of gravity spread-eagled her. She looked like an obese skydiver, the slipstream flapping her sweatshirt and baggy shorts, lifting her hair.

She smacked the surface of the lake. Water exploded up.

And rained down on Keith and Glen. Lana had almost caught up to them. They all dove and disappeared.

The man with the machete gazed down from the rocks.

What if he goes in after them?

'No,' Angela whispered. 'Don't. Don't.'

Dives in with that machete and hacks them all to pieces. Nobody's left but me and Angela . . . and him.

But he didn't dive in. He turned aside. He strode along the top of the boulder, leaped a gap and landed on a tilted block. His back to the lake, he let the machete dangle from his shoulder by a strap and began to climb the wall of an outcropping.

Chapter Thirteen

Howard, trembling, lowered his gaze to the lake.

Lana was boosting herself out, climbing onto a shelf of rock that jutted into the water not far from the place where Doris had fallen in. Glen was towing Doris by her hair. She floated along on her back, neither struggling nor helping. Keith swam near her feet, his head up. He seemed to be watching for the assailant.

'Is she all right?' Angela asked, her voice little more than a whisper.

'I can't tell. Doesn't look like she's moving.'

'God.'

Howard wished they would bring her to this side of the lake, but he could see that Glen was taking her toward the place where Lana had climbed out. It made sense to get her to the nearest shore. It would've been safer to come this way, though. The guy was over there.

'I don't see him anymore,' Angela said.

Howard raced his eyes up the slope, found the cluster of rock where he'd last seen the man, and scanned the area above it. Except for a few stunted trees, he saw only pale, glaring granite and shadows where odd formations blocked the sunlight.

'Must be hiding up there.'

At the shore, Lana was crouched over the water holding onto one of Doris's arms while Glen climbed out.

'We'd better go over there,' Angela said. She glanced from side to side, apparently judging the distances. 'It'd probably take us ten or fifteen minutes if we walk.'

'Should we swim across?'

'It'd be a lot quicker. Can you swim that far?'

'Sure. You?'

'Yeah.' She held onto his arm while she shifted her weight from one foot to the other and yanked off her shoes. When she let go, Howard started taking off his shirt.

'Guess we're going in, after all,' he said.

'Suits or no suits.'

'We'll freeze, you know.'

'Just for a few minutes.'

'Jeez, I hope she's all right.'

He tugged down his corduroys and stepped out of them.

Angela kept her blouse and shorts on.

Side by side, they jumped into the lake. Howard let out a cry of pain as he met the water. It was so cold it seemed to sear his legs. He felt as if his genitals had been grabbed and crushed by a frigid hand.

Angela, waist deep beside him, gave him a stunned glance. Her lips were peeled back, her teeth gritted. But she didn't hesitate. She took a wading step or two, then plunged beneath the surface.

Howard snatched a breath into lungs that felt shriveled and tight. Then he keeled forward, leaving his feet, submerging himself. A vice clamped his temples. A scream gathered in his throat. But he stayed under and kicked. The water slid over him. It seemed to search out hidden places on his body – pockets and creases of warmth – and pry into them like a frozen blade.

We should've walked, he thought.

Too late, now.

He wondered how Angela was doing.

He wondered how Doris was doing.

What'll we do if she's dead?

She isn't. She's OK.

Who the hell was that lunatic?

Howard kicked to the surface. He dragged air into his tight lungs and saw Angela just ahead of him. She was gliding along, low and sleek against the water. The way she swam looked effortless. Her strokes and kicks sped her along, but caused hardly a splash.

He glimpsed Lana and Glen huddled over Doris's body. Keith was just climbing out of the lake.

When his teeth started to chatter, Howard hurled himself forward and resumed swimming. He kicked as hard as he could. He shot his arms out and dragged them back. He held his breath until his chest ached, then blew it out, rolled, filled his lungs and kept on swimming.

As he began to tire, he took breaths more often.

He realized he wasn't freezing anymore. The water felt cold but good.

He switched from the crawl to the breast stroke. Keeping his head up, he was able to breathe steadily and see. Angela had increased her lead. She was about thirty feet in front of him. A few more strokes took her to the shelf where the others were crouching around Doris. She boosted herself up.

Howard liked the way her blouse was pasted to her back and the straps of her bra showed through. He knew he would've been able to see through her shorts, but their seat was draped by the hanging tail of her blouse.

As she climbed out, water streamed down the gleaming backs of her legs. She took a couple of steps, then sank to her knees beside Doris. The bottoms of her feet looked ruddy, as if she had been running barefoot across a field of snow.

She swung her head around and called, 'Doris is all right.'

Thank God, he thought.

But it almost seemed like bad news. Along with his relief, he felt a little cheated, disappointed.

Get off it, he told himself. I didn't want her to die. No way!

It would've gotten us out of here, though. Loot or no loot, nobody'd be ready to stick around if Doris had been killed.

Howard grabbed the gritty rock edge. He jumped and swung himself up. He started to rise. His briefs felt heavy and clinging. But nobody was looking at him, anyway. He hurried forward and knelt beside Angela.

Doris was stretched out, forehead resting on her crossed arms, her nose almost touching the granite.

'Are you OK?' Howard asked.

'Ha ha, very funny.'

'Guess you are.'

'She's just resting,' Lana said. 'She had her wind knocked out, but we don't think she's hurt.'

'Nothing broken?'

'Just her butt,' Keith said.

'Knock it off,' Glen told him.

Glen sticking up for Doris. That was a new one.

Howard ducked low. Her eye was open. It didn't look at him. It stared at the wet surface of rock under her face. A drop of water fell off the tip of her nose. 'Are you really OK?' he asked.

'Fine and dandy.'

He pushed himself up and glanced at Angela. She shrugged. He looked at the others. They were all kneeling or crouching around Doris, watching her. Glen reached down and rubbed her back.

'Hands off,' she said.

'Don't be such a jerk,' he said, and kept his hand where it was. 'You damn near got killed.'

'Tell me about it,' she muttered.

'What'll we do now?' Howard asked.

'Just give her a few minutes,' Lana said. 'She's pretty shaken up.'

'We shouldn't stick around too long,' Keith said. 'That

crazy bastard might come back.' Straining his head around, he scanned the slope.

'He won't come back,' Lana said.

'Don't count on it.'

'If he had the guts to go up against all of us, he wouldn't have run off like that.'

'What's he up to, anyway?' Glen muttered, massaging the nape of Doris's neck.

'A fuckin' maniac,' Keith said.

'Yeah, but he had a chance to chop her. Looked like he tried to catch her, instead.'

'He did,' Angela said. 'I saw that, too.'

Keith quit searching. He scowled down at Doris. 'The guy's some kind of a pervert. So, he didn't whack her head off when he had the chance. What do you think he would've done if he'd managed to grab her and pull her back? Shake her hand and say, "Charmed to make your acquaintance"?'

'Maybe he wanted to take her with him,' Angela said.

'That's what I'm thinking,' Glen said.

'Either that,' Keith said, 'or fuck her right there on the spot. And maybe *then* slice her up.'

A hitch of breath came from Doris. It sounded like a sob.

'Let's watch what we're saying,' Lana muttered.

'What do *you* think he had in mind?'

'I don't know.'

'You saw him. Did you see what he was wearing? Nobody's gonna go running around the mountains like that unless he's lost his marbles.'

'He might've just been coming down for a swim,' Angela suggested.

'Get real.'

'Well, it's possible.'

'Come on. He's sneaking around with a machete, for Godsake.'

'I think Angela's got a point,' Howard said. It felt good to be sticking up for her. And if she was right, maybe there was no actual reason to fear the man. 'If he really was on his way down to go swimming, that would explain why he was dressed that way.'

'Sure. I know I always like to swim in my G-string.'

'We just got here,' Lana said. 'He might've thought the place was deserted. Hell, I've gone skinny-dipping in lakes like this when nobody else was around. At least he was wearing something.'

Skinny-dipping, Howard thought. She does go skinny-dipping. He looked at her kneeling there. Her bare shoulders sparkled with water drops. Her nipples were hard, jutting against the filmy fabric of her suit. Lowering his gaze, he could see the indentation of her navel. He followed the sleek blue downward. Between her legs, it was very narrow. It bulged a little over twin lips, dipping in the center.

If she didn't have the suit on . . .

Howard realized his penis was rising, pushing into the wet front of his briefs.

No! They'll all see it!

That thought was enough to make his erection begin to subside. He stared down at Doris and tried to think about her fall. He was still shrinking.

Don't look at Lana again, he warned himself.

'Maybe when he saw we were here,' Angela said, 'he decided to just watch us for a while.'

'I'll buy that part,' Keith said. 'A little wilderness voyeurism.'

'But it could've been perfectly innocent. Maybe he thought he might come down and meet us . . .'

'Sure, and have a friendly chat.'

'But then Doris came along, and we spotted him and

started yelling like we thought he was a mad slasher or something and it all got out of hand.'

'That might be how it happened,' Howard said, daring to speak up now that his erection was gone.

'It's a possibility,' Lana said. He didn't look at her.

'Bullshit,' Keith said.

'Keith is an asshole,' Doris muttered. 'But he isn't a total idiot. This time, he's right.' She pushed herself up. On her knees in the center of the group, she turned her head and looked at everyone.

Howard had heard the single sob a while ago, but he hadn't realized she'd actually been crying. He would've guessed that she didn't know how to cry. But she did. She was doing it now. Her eyes were red and flooded, and tears were trickling down her cheeks. Her nose was running. The tip of her tongue darted across the slick, and she sniffed.

'That man was no innocent, happy camper coming down for a dip,' she said. 'You people are just trying to make yourselves feel better. The functional term here is "denial". You're creating a comforting fiction because the truth terrifies you. The truth is, the man's a fucking maniac. He's demented. He's a pervert.'

'We don't know that for sure,' Lana told her.

'I do. He almost got me. I know. I could smell him. I could *hear* him.'

'What'd he say?' Glen asked.

' "*Ohhh, yes-yes-yes-yes-yes.*" Like that. Very quiet and breathy. I could hardly even make it out, but that's what he said when he came running down at me.'

Doris lifted the wet front of her sweatshirt and wiped her face with it. The drooping mound of her belly looked as if it had never been touched by sunlight.

'You think he wanted to kill you?' Lana asked. Howard

looked at her, this time. But he didn't let his eyes wander down from her face.

'I think he wanted to fuck me,' Doris said. 'Fuck me, split me open and climb in. I could *feel* it.'

Some of the color went out of Lana's face. She glanced around at the others. 'OK. Let's just say the guy *is* some kind of homicidal maniac. He might not be, but let's just say he is.'

'He is,' Doris said.

'What do we want to do about it?'

'What are the choices?' Glen said. 'We either beat it out of here or we stay. Personally, I don't relish the idea of letting some Muscle Beach freako run us off.'

'I'm with Glen,' Keith said. 'Shit, we came all this way. We came after a *treasure*.'

'If there is a treasure,' Howard said.

'Butler came through with the hundred bucks in the couch,' Glen pointed out. 'We believed him enough to drive all night and hike our butts off to get up here. The only new factor is the creep.'

'And he might be gone,' Angela said.

'Or he might sneak up on us after dark,' Doris said, 'and slaughter us all.'

'If you're scared of him, just take off,' Keith told her.

'I intend to.'

'Not by yourself,' Glen said.

'Just watch me.' With that, Doris got to her feet. She grimaced as she straightened up. She stepped past Lana, limped across the shelf and started to climb the hump of a boulder.

'Hold on,' Glen said, rising. His drooping boxer shorts left the tops of his buttocks bare. He reached back with one hand and pulled them up. 'Where are you going?'

'Back to the campsite, for starters.'

'You're planning to *walk*?'

'Indeed I am.'

'It'd be easier to swim.'

'I don't swim,' she said.

Not, I *can't* swim. I *don't* swim. As if she were stating a preference.

'Well look,' Glen said. 'I'm not wearing any shoes.'

'So what?'

'I don't want to kill my feet.'

'So swim. Do you see me requesting an escort?'

Tough words, Howard thought. Typical Doris. But he thought he saw something a little frantic about her eyes.

He stood up. So did Angela. 'I'll go with you,' he said.

'Me, too,' Angela said.

'Don't do me any favors.'

'You don't have to get snotty with us,' Angela told her. 'I wasn't planning to swim back across, anyway. That water's *awful*.'

'We'll all walk,' Lana said.

Doris scowled. 'You're just trying to make me feel like a shit.'

'You are a shit,' Keith said.

'Cut it out,' Glen warned.

'Just go on and swim across. I don't want you people to ruin your feet and blame me.'

'Let's see how it goes,' Lana said. 'We'll stay as close to the water as we can. If we run into a place that looks too rough for walking, we'll just jump in and swim around it.'

'Do whatever you want,' Doris said.

'Does that go for me?' Keith asked. ' 'Cause I want to kick your fat ass.'

That got him a sharp glance from Glen.

'What're you, suddenly her protector? Jesus, man.'

'She's been hurt.'

'Big fucking deal, it didn't improve her attitude.'

'Let's all just cool it,' Lana said. 'We've got enough problems without bickering among ourselves.'

Doris, sneering, turned away and trudged up the side of the boulder.

Glen followed her. Lana went next.

'I'll cover the rear, guys,' Keith said in a quiet voice to Howard and Angela.

'She *is* a bitch,' Angela whispered.

'You're telling me.'

'But you should try being nicer to her.'

'Who died and made you camp counselor?'

Angela blushed.

'Don't talk to her that way.'

'Fuck you, Howitzer.' Dropping to a crouch, he picked up a jagged rock.

Howard took a step backward.

'Don't flatter yourself. It's not for you.'

Angela tugged on Howard's elbow. 'Come on,' she muttered.

'Keep your eyes open,' Keith said as they started away from him.

Howard considered picking up a rock. But he didn't want to look as if he were copying Keith. Besides, he wasn't much good at throwing things. If the guy did show up, he would probably miss.

'If that nut comes back,' he said to Angela, 'we oughta hit the water.'

'Good idea.'

He wished he was in the water now. Its freezing cold might be better than walking along in nothing but his underpants. They were no longer so wet that they clung to him. Except for the elastic around his waist, they felt loose and saggy. He thought he could feel air coming up through the leg holes. His genitals were bouncing and swinging. He felt naked.

'I don't think he'll show up,' Angela said. She glanced at Howard's face and quickly looked away. 'Do you? I mean, he ran off. But Doris could be right about him sneaking back after dark. He might wait till we're asleep tonight.'

'I know. Maybe we *should* head back down to the car.'

'I guess that's what Doris is going to do.'

'We can go with her, if you want.'

Angela looked at him. 'Is that what you want?'

'It might not be a bad idea.'

'We really can't let her go by herself.'

'I wouldn't mind getting out of here.'

'What about the treasure?' she asked.

'It might not even exist. Or we might not be able to find it.'

'We've got the Ouija board,' she said. 'I imagine that's why they took it last night – so we could ask more about how to get there.'

'Yeah, but Butler's weird – whatever he is. What if he's just screwing around with us? Maybe he never intended to lead us to that loot of his. Maybe he just wanted to get us up here.' An awful thought struck Howard. He muttered, 'Oh, man.'

'What?'

'Suppose Butler lured us here just so that weirdo could nail us?'

Angela wrinkled her nose. 'That's a pretty yucky idea.'

'I know, I know. It's probably crazy.'

Angela frowned and turned away from him. They walked along in silence for a while. Howard realized that he was no longer bothered about being out here in nothing but his underwear. Probably because Angela seemed OK about it.

The hike wasn't as bad as he'd expected. When he had to jump across a gap or climb, he didn't like how the skin pulled on the bottoms of his feet. Other than that, it was all right. Walking was no problem at all when the surface was fairly level. The granite felt rough and gritty, but it had few sharp places. Though it was hot, it didn't burn him.

He and Angela were both taking care to avoid being scratched by the dry, withered branches that sometimes grew out of crevices. They stayed away from the loose rocks with jagged edges sometimes littering the way.

Could've been a lot worse, he thought.

Now, if I just don't get sunburned so bad my skin falls off . . .

'I've got an even crazier one for you,' Angela said.

'A crazier what?' he asked, trying to remember what they'd been talking about.

'Idea. Than yours that Butler sent us here so the guy could get us.'

'You have a crazier idea?'

'Maybe that guy *is* Butler.'

'Wonderful.'

She made a quiet, nervous laugh. 'Just a thought. I mean, it's pretty far-fetched. When you mess around with a Ouija board, I guess it's supposed to be *spirits* who contact you.'

'Yeah. Dead guys. Ghosts. That's the general belief, anyway.'

'The fellow looked pretty alive to me,' Angela said.

'He wasn't any ghost, that's for sure.'

'On the other hand . . .'

'How many ghosts have I met?'

'He never did touch Doris. Maybe he couldn't.'

'Because he's a spook?'

'How do we know he *isn't*?' Angela asked.

'You got me. But I sure couldn't see through him. And ghosts don't normally go running around in broad daylight, do they?'

'How should I know?'

Howard shook his head. 'I don't think I can buy it. This guy was prancing around in a G-string and shades.'

'Just because he doesn't fit our preconceptions . . .'

'I know. But still.'

'Do you think we should mention it to the others?'

'Are you kidding? They'd think we're nuts.'

'I'm not so sure of that. I mean, look at us. We're all here because of a Ouija board. They'd have a lot of nerve jumping on us about ghosts.'

'They would dump all over us.'

'If that guy *is* a ghost, you know, it wouldn't be such a bad deal. It's one thing to have a flesh-and-blood maniac running around with a machete. It's not the same at all if he's nothing but an apparition.'

'If he's a ghost, in other words, he wouldn't actually be able to chop us up.'

She grinned. 'Exactly. Or at least I don't think he could. I mean, the machete would be an apparition, too, right?'

'I suppose.'

'So we wouldn't have anything to fear.'

'Except getting the crap scared out of us.'

'But there wouldn't be any reason to leave and go running back to the car, you know?'

'That's true. *If* he's a spook.'

'So, maybe we should talk to the others about it.'

'Doris will just say it's wishful thinking or denial or something.'

'Do *you* think that's what it is?'

'When it comes right down to it, I think the guy's real. Don't you?'

Angela wrinkled her nose. 'I guess there's an awfully good chance of it.' She took a few steps without speaking, then said, 'So now we're back to him being some kind of a maniac.'

'Yeah. And I think we should get out of here. It'd be stupid to spend the night with that guy around.'

'We just forget about Butler's treasure?'

'Like I said . . .'

'I know, we might not get it anyway. But what if we can, Howard? What if it's a lot of money and we go running away because of this guy? I could use it, you know? I don't think I can go back to Skerrit after last night, and . . .'

'You *can't* go back to him.'

'I don't *want* to. *God!*'

Lana heard her outburst and looked back.

'It's OK,' Angela called to her.

Though Lana was frowning with concern, she nodded and turned away. She leaped off a rock, and Howard saw that she was clear of the boulder area. Doris and Glen, ahead of her, were on a path that curved around the end of the lake.

'I've got to stay,' Angela said. 'I've got to. No matter what Doris or any of the others decide, I have to stay and find Butler's treasure.'

'If you stay, I stay.'

'You don't have to.'

'Sure I do.'

She took his hand and squeezed it.

'Get it on!' Keith called from the rear.

They ignored him, and hopped down to the path. The earth felt cool after the heat of the granite. It was springy with brown, matted pine needles.

A few strides took them into the shade of nearby trees, and Howard could feel a mild breeze. He watched his step, being careful to avoid pebbles and twigs and cones on the path.

At the end of the lake, they waded across a rapid stream. Soon, they came to the clearing where they'd left their gear.

Doris, already wearing her pack, was standing over Glen while he pulled his pants on.

'You're going to leave for sure?' Howard asked her.

'Watch my dust.'

'I'll be going with her,' Glen said.

'We're planning to stay,' Howard said.

'It's your skin,' Doris told him.

He turned to Lana, who was squatting beside her open pack and digging into it.

'What about you?' he asked.

'I'm not leaving,' she said. 'Maybe no one is.'

'Just try to stop me,' Doris said.

Lana pulled a holster out of her pack, stood, turned around, and drew out a revolver. 'Maybe this will change your mind.'

Doris went pale. Her mouth dropped open.

'Hey,' Glen said, gazing at the weapon.

'You two can run off if you want,' Lana said. 'But I didn't come all this way to get chased off by some damn lunatic. He shows up around here, he'll catch a few bullets.'

'My kind of gal,' Keith said, grinning. 'Where'd that hummer come from, anyway?'

'I always bring it along when I go camping. You just never know.'

'Well, all right!'

'Gosh,' Glen said. He looked at Doris. 'This does change things.'

'Marvelous,' Doris muttered. 'Now I suppose you aren't coming with me.'

'Hey, look,' he said. 'I know you're shook up. But we don't have to be afraid of the guy, now. It doesn't make any sense to leave. We've got a gun.'

'Big deal. A firearm is not a panacea.'

'It's all the panacea *I* need,' Glen told her.

She stared at him, looking sad and betrayed. Then she glanced at each of the others. 'So nobody will come with me?'

'We'll stay and watch your dust,' Keith said.

'Shut the fuck up!' Glen snapped at him. To Doris, he said, 'No, I'll go with you if you *have* to leave. But we won't have the gun, you realize, and that guy could be anywhere.'

'That's right,' Keith said. 'He might jump you guys on the way down.'

'And if we do get to the car OK, we'll just have to stay there. For a couple of days, probably.'

'Maybe longer,' Lana said. 'I guess I could give you the keys so you can lock yourselves in at night.'

'Hang on, now,' Keith protested. 'What if they drive off?'

'They won't.'

'Yeah? Who says?'

'I say,' Glen told him.

'Oh, yeah. Right.'

'Never mind,' Doris said.

They all looked at her. Head down, she tugged the straps off her shoulders and let the pack fall.

'Just forget it,' she muttered. 'I'll stay. You won. All right? You won. So fuck it.' She turned away, kicked her pack, then stepped around it and walked toward the shore.

Glen, fastening his belt, hurried after her. He didn't say anything. He caught up to Doris and put a hand on her shoulder.

Whirling on him, she blurted, 'Just leave me alone!' Then she threw herself against him, pushed her face against the side of his neck, wrapped her arms around his back, and hugged him hard.

'Let's get dressed,' Lana said quietly to the others. 'We've got to start setting up camp.'

Chapter Fourteen

Corie wondered where the kids had gone. Just a minute ago, they'd been surrounding the table, all of them leaning over it with their fingers on the plastic, heart-shaped pointer. But now they weren't there.

Must've gone home, she thought.

Good. I didn't want them playing with this thing, anyway.

She reached down for the pointer. It scurried away from her hand.

'Don't pull that crap with me,' she said.

As it slowed down, she made another grab for it. The pointer darted. Her fingertips thudded against the board, shaking the table beneath it.

'Damn you! Knock it off!'

It glided in a slow circle, and stopped near the middle of the board.

It wants me to look, she thought. It has a message for me.

A message that starts with T.

'OK, T,' she said. 'Go on.'

It didn't move.

'Do you want to tell me something, or don't you?'

When it still didn't move, Corie bent down for a closer look. She peered through the pointer's clear plastic window. The T shimmered, inflated, turned blue, and suddenly it was no longer a letter. It was Jake. Jake in his police uniform, legs together, arms outstretched, a bloody hole above his left eye. Jake as he must've looked after the shooting. Jake dead.

Corie gasped and swiped at the pointer. It leaped straight up. Her hand swept under it. She cried out as she struck Jake.

The blow sent his miniature body tumbling across the Ouija board, arms and legs flopping.

The pointer came down on the back of her hand. It clutched her skin. How *can* it? She jerked her arm up close to her face. And saw. The felt pads at the bottom of its three plastic legs were gone, replaced by tiny human hands. Their fingers were hooked into her skin. Turning wet red.

With the back of her other hand, she swatted the pointer. Her blow sent it hurling away, streamers of shredded flesh trailing from its clenched hands.

She thought she was rid of the horrible thing.

But it landed on her knee.

That's impossible! she thought. I'm standing up.

She *had* been standing. Not anymore. She couldn't remember sitting down, but now she was seated on a chair and the pointer was clinging to the front of her knee.

She flinched with pain as its fingers dug in.

It began to climb.

'Damn you!' She tried to swing at it, and found that her hands were cuffed behind her back.

No!

How could she be handcuffed?

Jake? No. Impossible. He's dead.

The pointer began creeping along the top of her thigh. It took its time. With each step, it sank its needle-sharp fingertips into her skin.

It was inching slowly closer to the flap of red nightshirt that draped her lap.

I'm in my nightshirt!

No! This can't be happening!

Corie squirmed and bucked and pounded her legs together, but she couldn't dislodge the plastic heart.

Its blunt tip dipped down until it touched her skin, then

nudged its way under the edge of her nightshirt. Corie froze. Her heart pounded. She gasped for breath.

The tiny hands groped and clawed. The rest of the pointer slipped out of sight. The thing crept sideways and down the inner slope of her thigh.

She slammed her legs shut on it.

And her knees bashed together, waking her up. For just an instant, she was disappointed; she wanted to know whether she'd crushed the thing or not.

Then she realized it didn't matter. She was awake. The pointer wouldn't get her.

She found that she was sitting upright in the passenger seat of her car. Her legs were wide apart, her hands gripping her thighs. Not exactly a lady-like pose, she thought. But she was wearing her red shorts, not a nightshirt. They had loose, baggy legs that reached halfway to her knees.

She felt a trickle of drool on her chin. On the right side, so maybe Chad hadn't seen it. She ducked her head a little and rubbed the spittle off against the shoulder of her blouse.

She lifted her hands off her thighs. She must've been squeezing hard. There were ruddy fingerprints on her skin, and her nails had made tiny, crescentshaped impressions.

She looked at Chad.

He met her eyes. 'Welcome back,' he said.

'Glad to be back. Jeez.' Lifting the front of her blouse, she wiped some moisture from under her eyes.

'Must've been some dream you were having.'

'Yeah. Thanks for waking me up.'

'I figured you could use your sleep. Besides, dreams are a good release.'

'Is that so,' she muttered.

' "Dreams, that knit the tattered sleeve of care." '

'That one unraveled mine.'

'Sorry. Maybe I should've woken you up.'

'Would've appreciated it.'

'Next time.'

'Thanks. Hope there isn't one.' She rubbed the heels of her hands against the fingernail marks. 'How long was I out?'

'A couple of hours.'

She nodded. Though she felt as if she'd only been asleep for a few minutes, the look of the sun was enough to tell her that she had slept into early evening. It hung low over the hills to the west, bathing the woods in a dusty, golden hue. Slopes and valleys were masked by patches of darkness. A car in front of them cast a shadow that stretched across the entire lane beside it.

She checked her wristwatch. 'Quarter after seven,' she mumbled. 'Man, I *was* out of it.'

'What were you dreaming?'

She shook her head. 'I don't know, something about a Ouija board.' The memory made her feel squirmy. She eased her legs together, trying not to be conspicuous about it, and crossed her ankles. 'Its pointer was attacking me. It had little hands. It was *crawling* on me.'

'Hard to imagine why you might come up with something like that.'

'Isn't it, though?'

'Under attack by your Ouija board.'

'If I ever get it back from those rats, I'll burn it. I should've burnt the damn thing years ago. They sell them as *parlor games*, do you believe it? People *play* with them. As if they're toys.'

'It's our culture,' Chad said. 'We're basically pretty frivolous about the supernatural. Thomas Edison's fault.'

'Huh?'

'Oh, there was a gal I met at a ski lodge a couple of years ago. A refugee from Vietnam. She used to tell me stuff. She was just full of creepy stories. According to her, we tend to ignore the supernatural over here in the States because we have so many lights.'

'It's a clean, well-lighted place.'

'That's right, Papa. And spooks don't like the light. But over in Nam, there's plenty of darkness. If you go into dark places, they get you. Those people take it seriously. Parents over there actually warn their kids not to play hide-and-seek, because the good hiding places are where the evil things might be lurking.'

'Like the V.C.?'

'I don't think it was the V.C. they were worried about. Anne – that was her name – told me about a girl she knew who went ahead and played hide-and-seek one night. Her friends looked and looked for her, and finally gave up. She was found a few days later. She'd apparently hidden in a ditch or gully or something. Anyway, she was dead. She'd died of suffocation. Her mouth was packed with dirt. When they opened her up – I guess they autopsied her – they found that she was completely stuffed with dirt. She was full of it. Her esophagus, her stomach . . .'

'God, how weird.'

'That's what happens when you hide in dark places.'

'I guess hide-and-seek's another game to stay away from.'

'Anyway, Anne also told me that they've got a Vietnamese equivalent of the Ouija board. They don't call it that. And it didn't sound like it was put out by Parker Brothers. What they do is dig up the coffin of a virgin and use its lid. She didn't tell me what they use for a pointer . . .'

'Maybe a bone . . .'

He smiled. 'Whatever. A severed finger.'

'Oh, gross.'

'But I guess they write the alphabet or something on the coffin lid, then gather around it and start popping questions. It's a fortune-telling device, just like the Ouija.'

Corie realized she was shivering. 'God, I've got goose-bumps,' she said, and rubbed her arms. 'I don't know whether it was the hide-and-seek or the coffin lid, but . . .'

'That stuff kind of gives me the creeps, too. Just talking about it. But you ought to hear Anne tell it. That'd really shake you up. Because she believes every word of it. The way she talks, you know it scares her. But she just loves it here in this country. "Too much light for ghosts," she says. "No ghosts in United States."' Chad laughed softly. 'Sounds like so much bull, I suppose. But I think she's got a point. It's easy to be a skeptic when you don't have to confront the dark. Pretty soon, you stop believing there might be something out there – monsters or ghosts or demons. You lose those things, the next thing you lose is God.'

Corie glanced at him. 'I hope you're not gonna start quoting scriptures.'

'Are you washed in the blood of the lamb?'

'Oh, Jesus.'

'Blasphemer.'

'You and the horse you rode in on.'

He held up a hand as if signaling a halt. 'I've spent a lot of time away from the lights, that's all. And it changes you. You find out very fast that there's a lot more to life than meets the eye. It's something, I think, that a lot of people tend to forget when they live in a city.'

'Unless they fool around with a Ouija board.'

'True, true.'

'It'll remind you real quick that something's out there. It might not be something you want to *know* about, but it's there. Just waiting for your call.'

' "Reach out and touch someone."'

'Yeah.' Corie grinned. 'Maybe we should write promotional slogans for the things. "Bring a Ouija board into your home, and add a taste of darkness."' Her grin fell away. She stared at Chad. 'They really *ought* to be made out of coffin lids.'

When the house went dark, *Monday Night Football* vanished from the television screen and Jake muttered, 'Oh, shit, wouldn't you know it!'

Corie, making notes for tomorrow's lesson on *Othello*, said, ' "Put out the light, and then put out the light." '

'But for Godsake,' Chad said, 'don't put out the boob tube.'

'Hilarious,' Jake said.

Because of the rainstorm and heavy winds outside, Corie doubted that the loss of power was due to a blown fuse. But she set her book and notepad aside, climbed out of the chair, and made her way carefully across the dark room. She opened the front door. A blast of chill wind spread her robe, billowed it out behind her, fluttered her nightshirt against her skin and scurried up beneath it.

The streetlights were out. The neighboring houses were dark.

She had seen what she came out to see, but she remained on the threshold savoring the feel of the wind. It gave her goosebumps. It made her shiver. It felt like secret hands exploring her body, caressing her everywhere.

She imagined herself running out onto the front yard. Naked. The wind sliding all over her, the rain streaming down her back. She saw Jake giving chase. Tackling her. She would go sprawling onto the cool wet grass, Jake hugging her legs then scurrying up her body, mounting her as she got to her hands and knees.

Right out of *Lady Chatterley's Lover*, she thought.

And where would Chad be while this was going on? Watching from the doorway?

No, he'd be too embarrassed for that.

The poor guy wouldn't know what to do with himself.

What if Jake were on duty? she wondered. And I went running out into the rain like that? Would Chad just ignore me, pretend it isn't happening, or would he . . .?

'You nuts or something?' Jake called. 'Close the damn door.'

Reluctantly, Corie stepped backward and swung the door shut. The rushy noise of the storm faded. The still air in the house felt warm and safe. But the storm had left some of its wildness inside her.

'The whole neighborhood's dark,' she said.

'I figured as much.'

'Why don't we do something exciting?'

'What've you got in mind?' Jake asked. He still sounded miffed about missing the game, but there was a slight note of interest in his voice.

'Oh, I don't know. Let's run naked in the rain.'

'Sure thing.'

Chad, hidden somewhere in the dark, said nothing.

'We could sit around and tell ghost stories.'

'That sounds cool,' Chad said.

'Forget it,' Jake said. 'Why don't you make yourself useful and go get some candles?'

'Spoilsport.'

'I'll go with you,' Chad told her.

She heard a chair creak. Moments later, his broad shape loomed out of the darkness. 'Right here,' she said.

'I see you.'

She looked down. Her robe was still hanging open. She knew she ought to close it, but she didn't want to.

No big deal. He's seen legs before.

She reached out and took his hand. He walked along beside her into the kitchen.

'Maybe we could play cards,' he suggested.

'That's not very exciting,' she said. Letting go of his hand, she crouched and opened a cupboard. She felt around inside. 'We ought to do something . . . I don't know . . . appropriate for the darkness.'

'Like hold a seance?'

'I think you need a real medium . . .'

'Let's me out. I'm an extra large.'

She laughed, and her searching hand found the box where she kept her collection of used candles. 'I know! The Ouija board.'

'Jake's old Ouija board? You've still got it?'

'Sure. He never throws anything away.'

As she lifted out the box and stood up, Chad said, 'We used to fool around with that thing all the time when we were kids. It can really spook you out.'

'Perfect.' She set the box on the counter. Gathering up a handful of candles, she stepped aside. She stuffed all but one into a pocket of her robe. 'Go ahead and grab a few,' she said, then went over to the stove.

She turned on a burner, ignited her wick, shut it off and faced Chad. 'Want me to light your fire?'

In the fluttery glow, she saw him grimace. 'Jeez, Coreen.'

'Oh, don't get so embarrassed. I was just kidding.'

'I know, I know.' He tilted a candle toward her.

As she moved her flame up close to it, she saw how its tip was jittering. 'My God,' she whispered. 'Look at you shake. What's wrong?'

'Nothing. Just a little nervous, maybe.'

'The storm? The dark?'

He shrugged. 'Maybe both. I don't know.'

Corie held his hand steady while she lit his candle.

He's just a big kid, she thought. Like all men. They grow up, but there's always a kid hidden inside, scared of the dark and a million other things, scared most of letting it show.

She gave his hand a gentle squeeze. 'You think you're nervous now, wait till we get going with that Ouija board.'

Stepping past him, she led the way into the living room.

'We thought we'd get out the Ouija board and . . .'

Jake's easy chair in front of the television was empty.

She felt a quick little drop in her stomach.

Gone.

For just a moment, Corie imagined him truly gone. Gone from his chair, gone from the house, gone from her life forever.

That's crazy, she told herself fast to stop the rush of panic. He's fine. He probably went to the john. Or he's playing games.

A dark shape came scurrying out from beside the chair. Jake on his hands and knees. 'Beware the beast of the storm! It comes for thee!' He charged her.

'Now, don't. I'm serious. I'm holding a candle.'

Growling, he lunged at Corie. His arms wrapped around her calves. His head pushed against her legs.

'Jake!' she gasped as she teetered, about to fall.

His hands shot up the backs of her legs. They clutched her buttocks, holding her steady while his head ducked beneath the front of her nightshirt.

'Jake!'

'It's all right,' Chad said. 'I'll leave the room.'

'It's *not* all right. Jake, stop it. I mean it.' Through the bulging fabric of her nightshirt, she knuckled the top of his head.

'Ouch!'

'I said not now. Come on. Chad's watching.'

He wasn't watching, she realized. He was standing right beside her, holding his candle up and gazing in the other direction. Averting his eyes. Probably embarrassed as hell.

'You watching, Chadwick?'

'She asked you to stop,' he said. 'I think you should stop.'

'Party poopers.' He gave her buttocks a hard squeeze that hurt, then crawled backward.

Corie yanked her robe shut and tied its belt. She knew she was blushing.

Jake shouldn't have done that. Not in front of his brother.

And he had no right to hurt her.

'I'll find the game,' she said.

Stopping in front of the shelves, she searched for the Ouija board. She moved her candle slowly, illuminating books and stacks of magazines, framed photos, trophies and various knick-knacks, and several games. She found the Ouija board's box on a low shelf near the corner of the room.

When she turned around, she saw Chad with two lighted candles, Jake with two more. They were bent over the coffee table, dripping wax onto plastic coasters.

'This table all right?' Jake asked her.

It was low and they would have to sit on the floor. But Corie didn't want to play in the kitchen, and hauling the card table into the living room would be a bother. 'This is OK,' she said.

She gave some of her candles to the men. While they were busy lighting them and sticking them onto coasters, she removed the Ouija board and pointer from the box. She set the board near the end of the table.

'Why don't you grab a pen and paper before you sit down,' Jake said. 'And a flashlight.'

She took her candle, and went to get them. By the time she returned, Jake and Chad were already sitting on the floor across the table from each other. Four candles stood just beyond the far side of the board. Others had been placed on the sofa's end tables. The room shimmered with soft, golden light. But much of it was dark.

'We've sure got the atmosphere for this,' she said. The candlelit room might have seemed romantic, she thought. But instead the presence of the Ouija board made it seem eerie. She realized she had goosebumps crawling up her body.

She lowered herself onto the floor at the end of the table and crossed her legs.

'Haven't done this in years,' Chad said.

'Remember Mona?' Jake asked.

'Oh God, yeah. Scared the hell out of me.'

'You weren't scared, you were jealous 'cause she liked me better than you.'

'Can't figure that,' Corie said.

Jake lifted the pointer onto the board, and they each placed the fingers of one hand on its cool plastic. 'Mona told us she'd been murdered by her boyfriend. She died without having any kids. That was her one big regret – she never had a child.'

'And she wanted Jake to correct the situation for her.'

'You're kidding,' Corie muttered.

'He fell head over heels for her.'

'Bullshit,' Jake said.

'You did. You couldn't wait for her to show up in the flesh some night.'

'Bullshit.'

'It's true.'

'If you want to know the *real* truth, Mona didn't even exist. I made her up. It was just me pushing the pointer around, making her say that stuff. And, boy, were you gullible! You ate up the whole thing. There never was any Mona.'

'Uh-huh,' Chad said. 'Right. Then why did you pound the crap out of me when I hid the board?'

'I just enjoyed pounding the crap out of you.' He grinned at Corie. His stretched lips and bare teeth looked sinister in the fluttery light. 'Man, I really had Chad going. He was so scared he hid the board out in the garage attic, and we didn't find it again until . . .'

His voice stopped as the pointer began to slide.

'Hope this isn't Mona,' Chad muttered.

'We lost her when we moved,' Jake said in a hushed voice as the pointer glided in small circles.

'I thought you said she didn't exist,' Corie reminded him.

'Yeah, that's right. She didn't.'

'You didn't have to . . .'

The pointer halted.

'. . . lie about it.'

They all leaned forward. The row of candles at the other side of the board gave enough light to see the letter beneath the raised plastic heart. 'I,' Corie read. The pointer slid and stopped, drifting around the board, spelling out its message while Corie took notes with her right hand.

When it seemed to be done, she tilted her notepad to catch the light. 'I-B-L-O-N-L-Y,' she read. 'I be lonely?' She felt a cold knot in her stomach.

Maybe Mona's back. Why did Jake lie about her? Come on, this is just a Ouija board. A game. Calm down.

Forcing herself to chuckle, she said, 'Whoever it is won't win any English awards.'

'Who are you?' Jake asked.

She read the letters out loud as the pointer roamed and stopped. 'U-N-O-M-E. You know me.'

'Who does?' Jake asked.

'U.'

'Jeez,' Chad murmured. 'Maybe it *is* Mona.'

The cold in Corie's stomach grew and spread. 'Maybe this wasn't such a great idea,' she said.

Ignoring her, Jake said, 'Who are you?'

'W-A-N-T-U.'

'Me? What for?'

'L-O-N-L-Y.'

Voice trembling, Corie asked, 'Is this Mona?'

'Hey, I told you she wasn't . . .'

The pointer carried their hands toward the top of the board. To the moon in its corner. To the NO.

Thank God, Corie thought.

Jake let out a single huff of laughter. 'See? It's not Mona. There *isn't* any Mona. So who are you?' he asked.

The pointer began moving again. Each time it stopped, Corie spoke the letters. 'J-E-S-S-E-W-A-S-H . . .' Then her voice failed. She felt as if she'd been kicked in the stomach. She gasped for breath. Her heart slammed. She jerked her hand away from the pointer. Under the fingers of Jake and Chad, it continued to drift and halt, moving to the letters she knew would follow.

A surf seemed to be crashing in her ears. Through the noise of it, she heard Jake whisper, 'Jesse Washington.'

'Oh, shit,' Chad said. He pulled his hand back. He glanced at Corie, then at Jake. 'Let's put it away.'

Jake shook his head sharply from side to side. 'What do you want, Jesse?' he asked. Using his official voice. The one he used on the job, but rarely in front of Corie. Talking firm. As if Jesse were an actual suspect, not the spirit of an armed robber he'd shot down three months earlier.

Corie watched the pointer carry her husband's hand over the shadowy board. 'Write it down,' he told her.

'Jake.'

'Do it.'

She followed orders.

After the pointer stopped, she studied what she had written. 'U-B-D-I-N-K-W-I-K-L-I-K-A-B-U-N-N-Y. I can't make any sense out of it.'

'Let me see.'

She handed the pad to Jake. He lifted it close to one of the candles. He peered at it for a long time, frowning. Then a corner of his mouth turned up. 'I think I've got it,' he said. ' "You be dyin' quick like a bunny." ' He smirked down at the board. 'Wishful thinking, asshole.'

He gave the pad back to Corie.

'Keep track,' he said.

'Don't *do* it anymore!'

'I'm anxious to hear everything this scumbag has to say.'

The pointer darted.

'C-U-N-H-E-L-L.'

Eight days later, Jake walked into a holdup in progress at a 7-Eleven. During the exchange of gunfire, a 9 mm. slug caught him above the left eye, plowed a tunnel through his brain, and blew a chunk of skull out the back.

'If they were made out of coffin lids,' Corie said, 'people might figure out the damn things aren't toys.'

'And you could use them for surfboards.'

Chapter Fifteen

Keith hunched over and blew steam off the surface of his coffee. He took a sip. Then he looked over his shoulder into the darkness beyond the campfire's glow. 'I wonder what our pal is doing right now.'

'Changing into a fur-lined nutbag,' Glen said.

'We're not amused,' Doris muttered.

'If he's got any sense,' Lana said, 'he's all bundled up and sitting by a fire, same as us.'

'Howitzer, why don't you go and see if you can spot his fire.'

Howard started to rise.

'Don't pay him any attention,' Lana said.

'That's OK. I sort of want to take a look around, anyway.' He straddled his log seat and hopped clear of it. Away from the fire's heat. But also away from its smoke. As much as he liked the smell of wood-smoke, he'd had enough of it. Ever since they'd returned to the fire after washing their supper dishes, the smoke had been going for his face as if seeking him out, ignoring the others.

He took a deep breath, enjoying the clean night air.

'Want me to come with you?' Angela asked.

'Sure, if you want.'

While she climbed over the log, Howard rubbed the seat of his corduroys. His rump felt cold and a little numb.

'Don't go far,' Lana warned.

'If you two had any sense,' Doris said, 'you wouldn't go at all. Look around you for a second. He might be anywhere.'

Howard didn't bother. He knew that Doris was right. The man could be lurking in any direction just beyond the reach of the firelight. Maybe he was watching them from among the trees. Or hidden beside one of the tents. Or crouched among the rocks near the shore.

Angela took his hand. 'Where should we go?'

'Down to the lake?'

'Sure,' she said. They started walking. 'I'll feel better if we keep the rest of them in sight. It really gave me the creeps when we had to go looking for firewood.'

'Me, too,' he admitted. 'But the guy's probably gone for good. I bet Lana's right. He's probably sitting by a fire somewhere, trying to keep warm.'

'In his fur-lined *thing*.'

Howard laughed. His chest felt tight and shivery. 'I bet he's wearing more than that now.'

'One would hope so. I sure am glad you bought me this jacket.'

'Are you warm enough?'

'My top is, anyway. The wind feels like it's going right through my sweatpants.'

'Do you want to put something else on?'

'No. Then I'd probably be too hot when we get back to the fire. Shall we go out onto our rock?'

'Our rock. That's just what I had in mind.'

They stepped up onto the slab of granite and took a few short steps down its slope before Howard pulled Angela to a stop. 'Let's not fall in.'

'Can you imagine anything worse?'

'It wouldn't be much fun.'

She let go of his hand. As she leaned against his side, he felt her arm press gently against his back. Her hand curled over his hip. He put his own arm around her.

'It's so beautiful out here,' she said.

'Isn't it?' The night sky was sprinkled with stars. A few tufts of clouds floated along, glowing white in the light of the full moon. A silver path glinted on the surface of the water. Across the lake, the piled granite blocks looked as if they'd been dipped in milk.

It really is beautiful out here, Howard thought. But then he noticed the patches of black on the far slope. And he found himself searching for the figure of a lone man.

He turned his head slowly, scanning the valley, looking for firelight.

The only fire was the one behind him.

Amazing how distinctly he could see Lana, Keith, Glen and Doris sitting around it. Every detail was brightly lighted and clear.

Sitting ducks, he thought.

'I haven't been camping since I was a little girl,' Angela said. 'I don't remember it being like this.'

'Where was it?'

'Gosh, I have no idea. Somewhere in the mountains like this. I was only four years old.'

'That's really young. I'm surprised you can remember any of it.'

'It's all pretty hazy. But my mother was alive, then. She carried me part of the way. It's about the last thing I remember about her. Carrying me piggy-back somewhere in the mountains. Except for that, all I remember about the trip is being scared and wanting to get home where it was safe.'

'I imagine the wilderness would seem awfully strange and terrifying to a kid that age.'

'Yeah.'

He wondered if he should ask what happened to her mother. He didn't want to ask. It might upset her. On the other hand, Angela might think he was insensitive if he pretended to ignore the subject. 'Your mother passed away?' he asked.

Angela nodded. 'I guess it was a few days after we got back from that camping trip. She drove off to buy a carton of cigarettes and she was in a car accident.'

'I'm awfully sorry.'

'Thanks. So am I. The thing is, it happened when I was so young. I can hardly remember her at all. I wish I could've gotten to know her.'

'It's terrible.'

'That's the way the ball bounces, I guess.'

Howard got a lump in his throat.

She patted his hip. 'Anyway, that was my one and only wilderness experience till now. If I'd known it could be like this . . .'

'Madmen running around . . .'

'Yeah, but you can find them anywhere. I've been finding them all my life.' She spoke as if stating a simple observation. Howard detected no anger or self-pity in her voice.

'Like Skerrit, you mean?'

'Skerrit. But he's not the only one. Or the worst.' She turned to him. The moon dusted her face with white. Her smile looked lop-sided. 'I think I must attract them.'

'Maybe I'm a madman, then. You sure attract me.'

She leaned against him. As he wrapped his arms around her, she tilted back her head and closed her eyes. He pressed his mouth gently to her lips. They were soft and warm and open. Her arms tightened around him. He felt the push of her small breasts. He felt her chest rise and fall as she breathed. Her breath went into his mouth.

She was trembling. So was he.

'Cold?' he whispered against her lips.

'A little. You?'

'Yeah,' he said. But he knew it wasn't just the cold making him shiver. 'Should we go back to the fire?'

She answered by squeezing him hard and mashing her mouth against his. There was something almost desperate about the fierce way she clung to him.

My God, he thought. This is incredible. Why's she acting this way?

Why me? I'm not all that special.

But she thinks I am.

I bet she'll let me do whatever I want. Tonight, when everyone's asleep . . .

She trusts me. That's the thing. I can't take advantage of her. I can't do anything to make her start wondering about me. If she's been running into madmen all her life . . .

What the *hell* did she mean by that?

Skerrit isn't the worst?

She loosened her embrace. Her lips eased away and she turned her head toward the campsite. 'Do you think they can see us?' she whispered.

His heart slammed. His legs went weak. 'Maybe. The moon's awfully bright.'

'We could walk a little ways.'

'I don't know.' His voice came out sounding thick and shaky. 'That guy might be around. Or they might worry about us and come looking.'

'It was just an idea.'

'Maybe we'd better get back.'

'I suppose so.'

I'm *nuts*, he thought as he led her up the face of the rock. She wanted to fool around and I talked her out of it! What's the matter with me?

I'm a chicken, that's what. I'm a chicken and I blew it. Shit!

They jumped down onto the shore. He glanced at Angela. She met his eyes, managed a quick smile, and turned her face away.

Oh God, she probably thinks I backed out because I didn't want to be with her.

'It just wouldn't be safe,' he muttered.

'No, you're right. I know. It was kind of a dumb idea.'

'If it weren't for that guy . . .'

'It's OK, Howard. Really.'

It wasn't OK. Somehow, she suspected the truth. That he was scared. But not of the stranger. Scared of her.

How *could* she know? She isn't a mind reader.

She squeezed his hand as if to comfort him. Without looking up at him, she said, 'I don't bite, you know.'

She *is* a mind reader.

Howard wanted to cringe and hide. At the same time, he had an urge to hug her.

'You must think I'm such a coward.'
'I don't think any such thing.'
'Well, I am.'
'What do you think I'd do to you?'
A blush heated his face. 'I don't know.'
Hurrying ahead of him, she turned around. She walked backward. From the bounce in her step, Howard figured she must be feeling pretty cheerful. Probably grinning, but he couldn't see her face at all; the firelight behind her made it look black. 'If you don't know,' she asked, 'what are you scared of?'
'I don't know.'
'Do too.'
'No I don't.'
'Should I tell what I wanted to do?'
'OK.'
She flung her hands up. 'Gee, I don't remember. Too bad. Gosh, I knew a minute ago.'
'Angela.'
Laughing, she spun around. She stayed a few strides ahead of him, but kept glancing over her shoulder until she walked into the light of the campfire.
'See anything out there?' Lana asked.
'No.' Angela stepped over the log and sat down on it.
'We did,' Keith said. 'Right, Glen?'
'Yeah yeah yeah.'
'So cough it up.'
Howard sat down beside Angela.
'My wallet's in my pack,' Glen said. 'I'll pay you later.'
'You're just trying to worm out. Get it now.'
Mumbling, he got to his feet and trudged around the campfire.
Keith grinned. 'I'm five bucks ahead already, and we haven't even found the treasure yet.'

'They wagered on whether you two would kiss,' Doris said. 'Charming fellows, eh?'

Howard felt heat rush to his face. The rims of his ears seemed to be burning. He looked at Angela. Her face was ruddy, but that might've been due to the firelight. She couldn't be blushing, not while she wore such a big smile.

'I warned Glen he was throwing his money away,' Lana said. 'I *knew* you'd do it.'

'Great,' Howard muttered. He was surprised to find that, mixed with his annoyance and embarrassment, he felt a certain pride. Maybe Angela felt the same way, and that's why she was smiling as if so enormously pleased with herself.

She leaned back and looked past him. Howard, turning his head, watched Glen crawl out of a tent and lumber toward the fire, a bill fluttering in his hand.

'You shouldn't have bet against us,' Angela told him.

'Figured neither of you had the guts to make the first move.'

'And I quote,' Keith said. ' "They wouldn't know how to kiss if they tried." '

'Thanks a lot, Glen,' Howard said.

Angela suddenly pulled him by the nape of his neck, turned him, drew his head toward her. Searching his eyes.

Are you kidding?

Her smile went away and she pressed her open mouth against him, softly mashing his lips. He went breathless as her tongue pushed in.

Right in front of everyone.

What's gotten into her?

He was shocked, embarrassed – and dazed with the excitement of it.

'All *right*!' Keith blurted. 'Go for it!'

'The call of the wild,' Glen said.

'Go for some tit, Howitzer.'

'Cut it out, Keith,' Lana said.

'Double or nothing says he won't,' Glen blurted.

Angela's body seemed to stiffen slightly. As if she were afraid Howard might try it. But she didn't pull away.

She's letting it be my decision, he thought.

'You guys are sick,' Doris said.

'Come on, man. Are we on?'

'No way,' Keith told him. 'Howitzer hasn't got the guts. Not for that.'

He felt Angela nod slightly. For a moment, he wondered if she was agreeing with Keith that he didn't have the guts to touch her breast. Then he realized she was telling him to go ahead. *Do it if you want to, Howard. It's OK with me. Go ahead and show them you aren't a chicken.*

Not this way, he thought. Not for a bet. Not to prove myself to these guys.

He shook his head enough for Angela to get the message.

Her mouth went away. She kissed him again gently, a brief touch of her wet lips. Then her smile returned. She eased back, rubbing a sleeve of her red wind-breaker across her mouth.

Keith reached sideways and plucked the bill from Glen's hand. 'Thank you very much.'

'Not so fast,' Glen said. 'It'll cost you five bucks for your share of this.' He pulled down the zipper of his coat, reached inside the drooping pouch at the front of his sweatshirt, and pulled out a pint bottle of bourbon. 'A little something to take the chill off.'

'Oh, for Godsake,' Doris muttered, rolling her eyes upward.

'All right!' Keith, grinning and nodding, handed the five back to Glen.

'He's just paid for everyone,' Glen said.

'I don't believe this,' Doris muttered. 'Lana, are you going to let them *drink*?'

'I'm not their mother.' Putting on a heavy, Irish accent, she said, 'I wouldn't mind having a wee taste meself.'

Howard laughed. 'That's pretty good!'

'Ah, thank ye, dear boy.'

Glen uncapped the bottle, took a swig, and reached it to his right. Toward Doris, sitting alone on a stump with her back to the lake. She sneered. 'I don't care for any, thank you.'

'More for the rest of us,' Keith said.

'Just take it and pass it on to Angela.'

Nodding, Doris accepted the bottle. She leaned toward Angela and stretched out her arm.

'Thanks,' Angela said. She tilted it to her lips. A moment after swallowing, she made a face and shivered. She blew air from her pursed lips. Her eyes glimmered. They were watering. In a hoarse voice, she said, 'Good stuff.'

She handed the bottle to Howard. He took a small sip. The bourbon felt cool in his mouth, but it seemed to catch fire as it ran down his throat. He took a deep breath. His own eyes began to water.

Lana was too far away. Howard got up, stepped around the fire, and gave the bottle to her. 'Thanks,' she said, and took a sip.

By the time Howard returned to his seat, Keith was already raising the bottle.

'Very smart, drinking,' Doris said. 'God only knows where that horrible man might be. He's probably watching us right now.'

'If he is,' Keith said, 'we oughta ask him over for a sip. Hey, fella!' he called. 'Schwarzenegger, Rambo, whoever you are! Come on over and have a drink!'

For just a moment, everyone sat motionless and silent as if awaiting an answer from the darkness.

'Look at this,' Doris said. 'He's not even drunk yet, and he's already acting like an imbecile.'

He grinned and passed the bottle to Glen. 'So a little booze won't make any difference, right?'

After taking a drink, Glen frowned at her. 'Do me a favor,' he said. He sounded serious. 'I know you think I'm crude and a moron and all that. But you've got to admit, I pulled you out of the lake today. So I think you owe me one.'

'Depends.'

'Just take a drink of this. As a favor to me. It won't kill you. You'll feel better.'

'That I doubt.'

'I firmly believe,' Glen said, 'that there's a nice young woman in you.'

She smirked.

'I mean it. I've caught glimpses of her once in a while. Maybe if you have a couple of drinks, it'll help her get out.'

'Trapped inside the snotrag,' Keith said, 'is a crumb of angel food trying to get out.'

Lana elbowed him.

Doris stared at Glen. Howard remembered the way they'd embraced after her decision to stay. He suspected that Glen might be right about the nice person buried inside her.

'What you see is what you get,' Doris said. 'If you think your rosy little speech or a few drinks are going to change that, you're even a bigger fool than you appear. But you did pull me out. I grant you that.' She reached out. He handed the bottle to her. She raised it to her mouth and took a big swallow. 'There. Are you happy?'

'I'm just trying to be nice to you, for Godsake.'

'Who needs it.' She passed the bottle to Angela.

'You do,' Angela said.

'*What?*'

'You might have some friends if you'd stop being such a pain all the time.'

'I liked you a whole lot better when you were a meek little whipped twit who kept her mouth shut.'

'Let's just cut it out, everyone,' Lana said. 'Why don't we knock off all this crap and have a good time? OK?'

Angela nodded, took a gulp of bourbon that made her shudder, and gave the bottle to Howard. She had a hurt look in her eyes as if she'd been slapped. It made him want to smack Doris. He shifted the bottle to his other hand, and rubbed the back of her neck.

'Let's sing campfire songs,' Keith suggested, smirking.

'How about telling some ghost stories?' Glen said.

Howard took a drink and carried the bottle to Lana. 'I've got an idea,' she said as he returned to his log. 'We're all English majors. Why don't we make up a poem?'

'Get real,' Keith said.

'Come on. We'll publish it in next year's *Orpheus*.' She took a swig. 'I'll start.' She squeezed her eyes shut. 'Around the campfire sat the six, a bold and fearless crew.' She passed the bottle to Keith. 'Your turn.'

He was about to take a sip when Glen stopped his hand. 'Verse first, Longfellow.'

'Shit. OK. Around the campfire sat the six, a bold and fearless crew . . . while out in the dark the *fiend* kept watch, though his balls were turning blue.' Laughing, he drank and handed the bourbon to Glen.

'Great! OK!' Glen scowled at the neck of the bottle. 'He shivered and shook in the bitter cold, and he ached for the heat of the fire. But he ached even more for the flesh of the gals, burning with lust and desire.'

'Lurid,' Keith said.

Glen chuckled, drank, and gave the bottle to Doris.

She stared at it. She grinned as she spoke. 'And Doris, the fat obnoxious bitch, full of righteous ire, took the bourbon from the turds and hurled it in the fire.' With that, she flung the bottle. It shot through the flames, knocked aside a burning stick and smashed against the far side of the low rock wall. Glass exploded. Booze splashed back and flared.

Glen gaped at her.

Keith seemed stunned. Blinking, he muttered, 'Did you see that? Did you see what she did? She broke the bottle. She broke the fucking bottle. Did you see that? I don't believe it.'

While he rambled, Doris got up from her stump and walked around behind Angela and Howard.

'Doris, you don't have to go,' Lana called.

'Why would I want to stay there with such a group of cretins?'

She hefted her pack off the ground and carried it to the front of the nearer tent. There, she crouched and began to lower the zipper of the tent's fly screen.

'Hey, man, that's your tent!'

'It's OK,' Glen muttered.

'She'll stink it up for you.'

'I know who it is. She's upset. If she wants to use my tent . . .' He shook his head. 'I'd rather sleep out here by the fire, anyway.'

Doris crawled in. Her pack followed.

'My stuff's in there,' Glen said. He spoke softly as if talking to himself.

'Won't be for long.'

They watched the tent.

Glen's sleeping bag and pack didn't come flying out.

'Looks as if you're not being evicted,' Lana said.

'Wonderful,' he muttered. '*Now* what'm I gonna do?'

Howard checked his wristwatch. 'It's not even nine yet. She isn't going to stay in there all night, is she?'

'Hope she never comes out,' Keith said.

'Thanks. What am I supposed to do without my sleeping bag?'

'It's your tent. Go in and get it. Or better yet, give her the boot.'

'Maybe one of us should talk to her,' Lana said. 'We'll need her, anyway, when we try to contact Butler.'

'Who says we want to contact Butler?' Keith asked.

'Well, hell, don't you? How do you think we'll find his treasure unless he gives us some directions?'

'I thought . . . you know, maybe we could wait till morning. We're not going after the thing tonight, are we?'

'I'm with you,' Glen said. 'We've got our freak to worry about. The last thing I feel like is having a chat with a spook.'

'I think we *should* try to talk with Butler,' Angela said. 'I mean, he scares me, too. And we could go ahead and wait till tomorrow before asking him about the treasure. But maybe he knows something about that guy. He might. He sent us here. Maybe the weirdo's part of it. I think we should ask Butler about him.'

'Let's not,' Glen said.

'Butler might even *be* the freak,' Angela added.

'Oh, that's a cheerful thought,' Lana said.

'It's bull,' Keith said.

'I know it's probably crazy. But he did say he would meet us up here.'

'Quit it,' Glen said. 'You're giving me the creeps.'

Lana leaned forward and tossed a small segment of branch onto the fire. 'She's got a point. I hardly think Butler *is* that jerk, but there might be a connection. It wouldn't hurt to ask.'

'Can we do it without the happy wanderer?' Keith asked.

'I don't know. She was on the Ouija last night.'

'It was *her* theory that we might need all the same people,' Glen said.

'You want to be the one to drag her out?' Keith asked.

'Why don't we give her a while to calm down,' Lana

suggested. 'There's no big hurry. It's too early to turn in, anyway, and I'm not sure any of us will be sleeping very well tonight with that lunatic around.'

'All right!' Keith blurted. 'This must mean you plan to hit the sack eventually. You had me worried there. I thought you'd be up all night, standing guard.'

'Glen can do that,' she said. Leaning forward, she grinned at him. 'You wouldn't mind, would you? You haven't got a sleeping bag, anyway.'

'I was thinking maybe I can use yours. You won't need it. You'll be in Keith's.'

'Which is why *you've* got to stand guard,' Keith told him. 'I don't want that bare-ass bastard sneaking up on me while I'm laying pipe.'

Lana's mouth fell open. She gaped at him. 'Laying pipe?'

'Just a figure of speech.'

'Try this on for a figure of speech, pal: take your pipe and lay it where the sun don't shine.'

'Hey, I'm no contortionist.'

'I'm glad you're amused.'

Glen smiled across the fire at Howard. 'Five bucks says they get it on before morning.'

'Take the bet,' Lana said. 'A fool and his money are soon parted.'

'I don't know.'

'Smart move, Howitzer.'

Angela smiled at him. 'Should I take the bet?' he asked.

She shook her head.

'Thanks for the vote of confidence,' Lana said. 'You think I'm a pushover?'

'It's a long night,' Angela told her. 'It's cold. And we're all a little scared. When you're lying all alone in your sleeping bag, I think Keith might start looking pretty good to you.'

'Sounds to me like you're the one who might need him.'

'Keith? I don't think so.'

'That's 'cause she's got Howitzer the cannon.'

'Let's put some money on them,' Glen suggested.

Angela stood up.

'Ooo, now we've driven *two* away.'

'I'm just going over to see Doris. I'll get her to come out so we can get in touch with Butler.' She walked over to the tent, sank to her knees, and crawled through the flaps.

Chapter Sixteen

'The next time we come to a passing lane,' Chad said, 'I'm going to pull over and take another look at the map. The turnoff's gotta be around here someplace. I'd hate to miss it.'

'You don't trust your trusty navigator?' Coreen asked.

'I'd trust her more if she'd stay awake.'

'Oh.' She turned her head. Chad saw the white of her teeth, and knew she was smiling. 'That golldurned mountain man hardly let me get a wink of sleep last night.'

'You've sure made up for it today.'

Just ahead, a sign read SLOWER TRAFFIC USE PASSING LANE. Beyond the sign, the road widened. Chad checked his rearview mirror. The area behind them was dark except for the glow of moonlight. He eased to the right and stepped on the brakes. The car abruptly slowed.

When it was stopped, he turned the headlight knob. The dashboard got brighter. The courtesy light came on. Coreen leaned forward, spread her legs, searched between her thighs and under them. With a quiet 'Oh,' she doubled over. Chad saw the way her breast pushed against the top of her leg. She reached behind her left heel, picked up the map and smiled.

'Some navigator,' he said. 'Lost the map.'

'But did you catch how fast I found it again?'

'Looked like quite a hunt to me.'

'But I did find it. That's what separates the men from the boys.'

He laughed. Coreen slapped the map into his waiting hand.

'While you're busy locating us, I'll pay a visit to the trees.' She took a small plastic flashlight and a pack of tissues from the glove compartment.

'Don't go far, OK?'

'Back in a minute.' She opened her door, climbed out, threw it shut and strode into the darkness.

When she was out of sight, Chad checked the map. He found the thin, shaky line that angled to the northeast out of Red Bluff. Following it with a finger, he located its Y-shaped branch. They'd come to the branch only a few minutes ago, and taken the eastern arm.

The dotted line marking the unpaved road to Shadow Canyon Lake was about half an inch up. According to the scale, that should be about ten miles.

If we miss it, he thought, we'll know soon enough. Just another half an inch above the turnoff was the town named Purdy.

He didn't think he'd ever been there.

He wondered if it had a motel. He'd been wondering that a lot while driving the curvy road, fighting grogginess as Coreen dozed in the passenger seat. The town was bound to have at least one place. But would Coreen be willing to postpone the last leg of the trip until morning?

She climbed back into the car and pulled the door shut.

'*God*, it's cold out there.' She shivered and rubbed her arms. 'So, did you find us?'

'I've got a pretty good idea where we are. We're not far from the turnoff.' He watched her stuff the flashlight and pack of tissues into the glove compartment. She snapped it shut. 'The thing is, we'll end up on a dirt road. I have my doubts about trying it in the dark.'

'We can make it.'

'I'm not sure we should take the chance. It's some fifteen, twenty miles long. In the dark. With one lane. I've been on roads like that. We'd be lucky to do ten miles an hour. So we're talking about two hours at the least. On rough terrain. It'd be tough enough even if we could see where we're going.'

'You think we should wait for morning?'

'I know you'd rather get to the kids tonight.'

'I really would.'

'But there's a town just a little ways beyond the turnoff. We could go on to it, get a good night's sleep in a motel or something, and hit the dirt road at dawn. Then we'd be able to see what we're doing. We'd be less likely to bust up the car or get stuck.'

She sighed. 'I don't know, Chad.'

'Even if we're lucky and don't run into any trouble, it'll be midnight before we reach the roadhead. I hope it's the *right* roadhead.'

'Oh, it has to be.'

'It probably is,' Chad said. They'd already discussed the several different approaches to Shadow Canyon Lake and decided that, coming from the northwest down Highway Five, the kids would be mostly likely to settle on this one. *If* they found it on their map. *If* they didn't, for odd reasons, choose to take a less direct route that would lead them into the same general area from either the southern or the distant northeastern road.

'More than likely,' he said, 'we'll find their car – or cars – at the end of it. But I doubt that *they'll* be there.'

'These aren't Marines, you know. We figured it's what, five miles to the lake? And uphill? I can't see them going for it. I really can't. Not after they've spent all night and most of today on the road. I bet they just said, "The hell with it," and pitched camp right where they parked.'

'You know them better than I do,' Chad admitted. 'I'm just saying that, if it were me, I'd push on for the lake.'

She smiled. 'You and Jim Bridger.'

'Me and John Muir.'

That brought a chuckle.

'So what'll it be?' he asked, turning off the overhead light.

'I honestly find it surprising that you'd *want* to spend the night in a motel. Wouldn't you prefer sleeping in the great outdoors?'

'Probably,' he admitted. He started the car. Accelerating, he checked the rearview mirror and swung over. 'I guess I just want to avoid that stretch of road.'

'I'll drive it.'

'That's OK, I'll do it. But you'd better keep your eyes peeled for the turnoff.'

Coreen was silent for a few moments as Chad steered around a bend. Then she said, 'If you'd really rather go on to that town . . .'

'No, it's all right. You're worried about the kids. I understand.'

'If they were just on a camping trip, you know . . . It's the fact that they're doing this because of the damn Ouija board. You should've seen them last night. The way they pushed Angela into taking off her blouse. Just because the thing told them to do it. They're good kids, basically. But they went ahead and made her do it. What'll it ask them to do next time? What if it won't tell them where to find the "loot" unless they do something really awful?'

'If they're good kids,' Chad said, 'they won't do it. They'll draw the line.'

'I don't know. I don't know them *that* well. They did that to Angela. They swiped the Ouija board. They drove all the way out here. They're really into it. I just don't know what it might take before they'd back off.'

'Well, we'll go ahead and get to them tonight. If we can.'

'Thanks.' She made a soft laugh. 'Say, aren't you glad you showed up when you did? Just in time for all the fun.'

'I'm very glad,' he said. 'I've been thinking about that. My timing.'

'Lousy timing, huh?'

'Not the way I see it. What if I'd come a day later?'

'You would've waited for me, wouldn't you?'

'Sure.' He glanced at her. She was watching out the side window. 'You would've done this on your own, I guess.'

'Yeah.'

'Well, thank God I showed up when I did. It's almost *too* lucky.'

'That's occurred to me, too. It's as if you were meant to arrive when you did. "There is a divinity that shapes our ends, rough-hew them how we will."'

'Does make a person wonder,' he said.

She looked at him and smiled. 'God figured I could use the services of my own Natty Bumpo.'

'Yup. Case we run into Injuns.'

'Uh-oh.'

He saw it, too. The road sign, briefly illuminated by his headlights, read PURDY, 8 MILES.

'If we're that close to Purdy,' he said, 'we must've missed our road.'

'Damn.'

'No problem. It's probably tough to spot the thing even in daylight.' He took his foot off the gas pedal. 'I'll just wait until we're clear of this curve, then hang a U.'

As he came out of the turn, his lights swept across a stopped car. Stopped with its left side hanging into the narrow lane. Coreen gasped. He swerved, missed it, and eased down on the brakes.

'Jesus,' Coreen muttered. 'That was a close one.'

Chad was trembling. 'The only car we've seen the past hour, and it's blocking the damn road.'

'Somebody might hit it.'

'Somebody almost did.' He stopped. Twisting around, he peered out the rear window and started to back up.

'What are you going to do?'

'I don't know. Check it out.' He steered toward the shoulder. The passenger side dropped a bit as it left the pavement. The tires made soft crunching sounds. 'A hell of a place to leave a car.'

He stopped several yards in front of it. Coreen, also gazing out the rear window, said, 'I don't see anyone inside.'

Chad shook his head. He couldn't see anything through the dark windshield. But he'd seen nobody during the moment his headlights had flooded the car.

'Wait here.' He shifted to park and set the emergency brake, but kept the headlights on, the engine running. 'Back in a second.'

'I'm coming with you.'

'Coreen.'

She opened her door and got out.

Chad flung his door wide. He called, 'Just hold on and wait for me.'

Coreen waited for him at the edge of the road. Hunched over slightly, arms hugging her chest.

'It's warm in the car,' Chad said.

'I'm not gonna sit in there alone. In fact, I'm not so sure we should've even stopped. I don't like this.'

Though the road was flecked with moonlight, none touched the car.

'Anybody there?' Chad called.

No answer came.

Side by side, they walked closer to the car.

'If this is Christine, I'm gonna shit.'

Chad laughed. He realized he was shaking. 'We ought to put on some warmer clothes before we take off again.'

'Let's do it now and forget about the phantom Fury.'

'This isn't a Fury,' he said. 'It's a Pontiac.' He felt a sudden rush of relief when he noticed its lopsided position. 'And it's got a flat.'

'Must be an epidemic,' Coreen said.

'Well, that explains what it's doing here.'

She stayed behind him as he walked around the front bumper, paused for a moment to look at the flat, then stepped up to the driver's door. Its window was rolled up. Bending over, he peered in. The interior was black. 'Can't see a thing.'

'God, if there's someone inside there . . .'

Chad stepped back and tried the door handle. It lifted. The door unlatched. He pulled it open. A loud buzz. He flinched. Coreen gasped. But the dome light was on, the car empty. Leaning in over the steering wheel, he saw that the key was in the ignition. He plucked it out and the noise stopped.

'Weird,' Coreen muttered. 'Why would anyone go away and leave the keys in the car?'

'I don't know. Unless they just went off to take a leak, or something. Hang on, I'm gonna honk the horn.' He pressed the steering wheel's hub. The horn blared through the night like the blast of an angry bugler. He let it go on for a long time, paused to listen, then gave the horn three short toots and another long one.

Coreen tapped his back. 'I think that's plenty.'

He stopped. The silence seemed oppressive. As if the noise of the horn had deadened his ears in much the same way that a brief, brilliant flood of light would've left him blind in the returning darkness. He listened for sounds of footsteps in the woods beyond the car. But he heard nothing at all.

'I don't think anyone's around,' he whispered.

'It just doesn't make sense to leave your keys in the car and go away.'

'I know. But everybody isn't sensible.' He sat down behind the steering wheel. As he leaned sideways, reaching for the glove compartment, he noticed a leather handbag on the floor. It was tucked in close to the front of the passenger seat. 'A purse,' he said.

'You're kidding.'

He picked it up and showed it to Coreen. She shook her head.

'Should we see who it belongs to?'

'It'll be pretty embarrassing if we're caught at it.'

'Well, the horn didn't bring anyone running.'

'Go ahead,' Coreen said. 'I'll keep watch.'

'Watch out for cars, too.' He pulled the door toward him, leaving it ajar so the light would stay on, then opened the purse. He glimpsed a billfold, a checkbook, some tampons, a pack of chewing gum, a hair brush. He removed only the billfold. He unsnapped it and flipped it open.

The driver's license had a photo of an attractive brunette who appeared to be in her early twenties. 'Mary Louise Brewer,' he read. 'From Stockton.'

'You'd better put it away,' Coreen said. She sounded nervous.

'Just a second.' He spread the bill compartment. A couple of twenties, a ten, a few ones, and several credit cards. He pulled out a Visa card. It had been issued to Roger Brewer.

He put it back, returned the billfold to the purse, and wedged the purse back into position where he'd found it. 'OK, stand back. I'm going to pull off the road a bit.'

'Oh, God.'

'We can't just leave it sticking out like this.'

'OK. But hurry.'

He started the car and eased it forward, steering to the right. It moved sluggishly. The flat tire made whumping sounds. There was a slight bump as the tires on the left dropped off the pavement. He quickly shifted to park, set the emergency brake, and shut off the engine. Taking the ignition key with him, he climbed out. He threw the door shut and the car went dark.

Coreen followed him to the trunk.

He opened it. Darkness inside. Dim shapes. Bending over, he searched with his hands. He felt suitcases, some smaller luggage, and a spare tire. 'They've got a spare,' he said.

'Maybe it's no good.'

'Or Roger doesn't know how to change tires.'

'It can be tricky with these crappy jacks they give you.' She paused a moment. 'Who's Roger?'

'Mary's husband, probably. One of her credit cards is in his name.' Chad shut the trunk and turned to Coreen.

'Can we go now?' she asked.

'I'm not sure. I need to think. Something's wrong here.'

'I know. It's all pretty queer. But I'm freezing. You moved the car out of the way, which was a very good idea. What else can we do?'

'Get into something warm.'

'Now that's a terrific idea.' She followed him alongside the car and waited while he returned the key to the ignition. The buzzer sounded again, then went silent when he shut the door. She hurried ahead to her car. She came back to its rear with the keys and flashlight, and opened the trunk.

Chad held the flashlight while she searched through her backpack. She took out a windbreaker.

'They probably decided to walk to town for help,' Chad said.

Coreen zipped the front of her windbreaker. She draped a pair of dark warm-up pants over the edge of the trunk. 'No telling how long the car's been sitting there. They might *be* in town by now.'

'Eight miles. That's a pretty good distance.'

'Yeah. I suppose we ought to keep going and give them a lift if we can find them.' She unfastened her shorts, pulled them down and stepped out of them. 'Ohhhh, my God!'

'A little nippy?'

'Yes!' She tossed her shorts into the trunk and grabbed the warm-up pants. Chad braced her by the shoulder while she thrust one foot, then the other, into her pants. She pulled them up, and sighed.

'Better?'

'Much, much.'

She held the flashlight for him. He dragged a denim jacket out of his pack, put it on, and dug out a pair of corduroy pants. When he took off his shorts, the cold seeped like cold water through the skimpy briefs Coreen had bought for him. He groaned and she laughed.

She held him steady while he thrust his feet into the cords. The heel of his left sneaker got caught inside the pants. He lost his balance. Coreen hugged him from behind, keeping him up, and they staggered around for a moment before he pushed his foot through.

'Thanks.'

'My pleasure.'

Laughing, he tried to button his waistband. But Coreen's wrist blocked the way. Her hand cupped the front of his briefs. 'Warm you up a little,' she said, her breath tickling the side of his neck. She squeezed him gently, and rubbed. Chad squirmed as her touch ignited a fire in his groin.

'It's working,' he muttered.

'Warming me up, too.' She squeezed him once more. Then her hand went away. She kissed his neck. 'We'd better get while the gettin's good.'

She stepped away and shut the trunk. Chad fastened his pants. They got back into the car. With a last look at the abandoned vehicle in the rearview mirror, Chad swung onto the road.

'Maybe Mary and Roger are off in the trees making whoopy,' Coreen said.

'It's possible.'

'That would explain everything, wouldn't it? They're driving along, Mary reaches over and does something like this.' Coreen reached over and rubbed his groin. 'Roger gets all worked up, pulls over, and they both run into the woods. He doesn't bother taking the keys, she leaves her purse. We come along and honk, but they're going at it too hot and heavy to care.'

'What about the flat?'

'Forgot about that.' Her hand moved to his thigh and patted it. 'OK. They get the flat. He says, "I'd better jack up the car and change it." She says, "Jack me up first."'

Chad laughed. 'If that's the way it went, why are we looking for them?'

'Beats me.'

'Should I turn the buggy around?'

'How'll we give them a lift into town?'

After that, they went silent and watched the roadsides. They saw nobody. Once, headlights came at them from around a bend. A tow truck? As the vehicle sped by, Chad saw that it was a Jeep. No one inside but the driver.

A few minutes later, they passed a dirt road leading off into the dark trees on the left. Then they came upon a gravel driveway leading to a small house with lighted windows.

'Maybe our mysterious Roger and Mary went there,' Coreen said.

'We're almost to the town.'

A short distance farther, they passed another house. Then another dirt road winding into the forest. Then a dark cafe with boarded windows. More houses, more unpaved roads tunneling into the trees.

Chad slowed as his headlights found the city limits sign. WELCOME TO PURDY, GATEWAY TO THE HIGH COUNTRY, ELEV. 6,240 FT, POP. 310.

'A metropolis,' Coreen said.

'Should we keep going?'

'I don't see much point in it. If they got this far, they're hardly in need of a lift.'

'And you're still not interested in a motel?'

'I never said I wasn't interested. But . . .'

'I know. It's all right.' Chad made a U-turn.

'I hope they're OK.'

'The kids?'

'Them, too. But I meant Roger and Mary.'

'They must've made it into town. If they couldn't get help for the car tonight, they probably checked into a motel or something.'

'If you really *want* to stay in a motel . . .'

'Nope,' he said. 'We're gonna tackle that road.'

'Thanks. You'll be handsomely rewarded for your sacrifice.'

'In this life or the next?'

'In this life, for sure. Shortly after we reach the roadhead, I should think.'

He punched the gas pedal to the floor, and Coreen laughed. Then he settled down to normal speed.

* * *

The abandoned car was where they had left it, a dark shape hunched in the shadows like a beast hiding from the moonlight. Looking at it, Chad felt the hairs on the back of his neck crawl.

'I wonder if we should've gone to the police,' Coreen said.

'What?'

'In Purdy. Told them about it.'

He glanced at her dim face. 'They probably walked to town. They're probably in a service station or motel right now.'

'I don't know.'

'Neither do I.'

'We're just *hoping* that's how it went, aren't we?'

'I guess so.'

'Or pretending.'

'You think something happened to them?'

'Don't you?' she asked.

'Are you watching for the turnoff?'

'Yeah. But what do you think?'

'They probably had a flat tire and walked to town. They were probably too careless or preoccupied or trusting to take the car keys and purse. Probably. Logically, that's more than likely what happened. On the other hand, I don't quite . . .'

'This might be it.'

Chad slowed the car. Moments later, the headbeams met a wooden sign: SHADOW CANYON LAKE. An arrow pointed to the left. 'Yep,' he said.

Just ahead, across the road, was another sign. It faced the other way. Beyond it, Chad saw a patch of bare earth, an opening in the trees. He pulled forward and stopped adjacent to the dirt road.

'Shall we do it?' he asked.

'I don't know. What do you think?'

'The kids are your responsibility. I guess they should take

priority over a couple of strangers who may or may not be in trouble.'

He didn't wait for a response from Coreen.

He turned the steering wheel hard to the left, and stepped on the gas.

'You're right,' Coreen said.

They dropped off the edge of the pavement. Even with the windows shut, Chad could hear the tires crunching over gravel and forest debris. The car shook, bounced, trembled. Out in front, the pale probes of their headlights traced the narrow way through the trees.

Chapter Seventeen

Howard put more wood on the fire. The pile of sticks and broken branches they'd gathered after supper was dwindling, but there should be enough to keep the fire blazing for a while longer. He hoped an expedition to gather more wouldn't be needed. If they wanted to keep the fire going all night, though . . .

'Tough luck, Glen,' Keith said.

Howard looked over at the tent. The bundle of a sleeping bag, apparently shoved out, stopped rolling. The tent flap bulged, and Angela crawled out backward. She dragged a pack with her. Standing up, she lifted the pack and sleeping bag. She carried them toward the fire.

'Evicted after all,' Lana said.

'That's OK,' Glen said. 'I wasn't about to sleep in the same tent with her.'

Angela put down her load, came to the fire, and sat beside Howard. 'I couldn't talk her into coming out. She's pretty angry.'

'What else is new,' Keith muttered.

'What was it?' Glen asked. 'The poem?'

'Mostly. She thought it was pretty rotten of us, making up cutesy stuff about the guy who jumped her. She said it just goes to show how we don't have any regard for her. She also said we wouldn't be making jokes if it'd been Lana he attacked.'

Keith, grinning, shook his head. 'We're so cruel and heartless.'

'She brings it on herself,' Glen said.

'She has a point, though,' Lana said. 'It was pretty callous of us to be joking around about that guy. Especially in front of Doris. We shouldn't have done it.'

'Ah, fuck her.'

'Shut up,' Glen said.

Lana turned to Angela. 'Did you tell her we wanted to contact Butler?'

'Yeah, and she said that's another good reason to stay in the tent.'

'I guess we can try it without her.'

'Let's not bother.'

Ignoring Keith's remark, Lana got up and walked toward the other tent. She brushed off the seat of her blue jeans. She rubbed her rump as if it was sore. Then she got down on her knees and crawled into her tent. Moments later, she came out with the Ouija board and pointer.

She stopped in front of Glen's tent. Crouching, she swept open one of the flaps. Howard heard her voice, but the sounds of the wind and the popping fire interfered so he couldn't make out the words. She didn't stay long.

As she approached the fire, Keith asked, 'What'd you tell her?'

'I apologized. I think she's in there crying.'

'Awwwww,' Keith said.

'Don't be such a bastard,' Lana told him.

'If I'm supposed to feel sorry for her, forget it.'

'Anyway, Doris isn't coming.' Lana sat down on the log. She placed the Ouija board on her lap and stared at it. 'I'm not quite sure how we're going to do this.'

'Good. Let's not.'

'It might be a waste of time, anyway,' Glen said. 'We don't have Doris, so the four from last night . . .'

'Maybe the original four aren't needed.'

'Last night,' Howard said, 'it moved that time when *no one* was touching it.'

Lana nodded. 'Yeah. Well, why don't we try it different ways? Maybe start with the three of us. If that doesn't work, we'll have Glen or Angela sit in for Doris. We can't do it here, though. Right there might be a good place.' She nodded toward a clear area of ground beside the campfire, and got up.

While the others gathered around her, Glen went to his pack. He returned with a flashlight and tarp. They spread the tarp, one edge close to the campfire. Lana sat down facing the fire and placed the Ouija board in front of her crossed legs. Keith and Howard sat opposite each other, the board between them. Glen started to sit in the space near the fire, but Lana suggested that he move so he wouldn't block the light. He crawled to the other side of Keith, and knelt there. He shone his flashlight on the board. 'All set?' he asked.

'Just a minute,' Angela called. She was crouched over her pack, searching the pocket on its right side. When she stood up, she was holding a pen and a small spiral notebook. 'You need somebody to keep track, don't you?'

'If we get lucky,' Lana said.

Angela came back to the tarp. The plastic made crackling

sounds as she crawled on it. She knelt behind Howard. He felt her body press against his back. The hand on his right shoulder held the pen and pad. The other hand held only his shoulder. He felt her chin against the top of his head. It moved slightly when she said, 'Ready.'

Howard leaned forward to reach for the pointer. Angela stayed with him, blocking the cold wind and sharing her warmth.

This is so great, he thought.

Maybe the Ouija board's not such a bad thing. It sure brought us together.

Lana, Keith and Howard rested their fingertips on the pointer.

'OK, Butler,' Lana said. 'We're waiting for you. Are you here?'

The pointer didn't move.

'We're here, Butler.'

'Maybe we gotta attract his attention,' Keith said.

'Like how?'

'Maybe if you gals strip down.'

Angela's left hand tightened slightly on Howard's shoulder.

'There won't be any of that,' Lana said.

'Too cold,' Angela said, and made a soft laugh that sounded nervous.

'Just an idea.'

'Why don't we try calling out his name?' Glen suggested. 'All together. On the count of three. One . . .'

'No way,' Keith said. 'That's stupid. He isn't a deaf guy, he's a spook. Besides . . .' He went silent.

'Besides what?' Lana said.

'I just don't think we oughta be making a lot of noise, you know what I mean? It's not like we're *alone* out here.'

'You really take a prize,' Glen said. 'You're the guy that called out and invited *el creepo* to come in and have a drink with us.'

'That was different.'

'Oh yeah? How?'

Before he could answer, the pointer slid half an inch.

'OK, who did that?' Keith asked.

Lana shook her head.

'Not me,' Howard muttered.

Angela pressed herself more tightly against his back.

'Butler,' Glen whispered.

'Butler,' Lana said in a clear voice. 'Are you here?'

The pointer began to move in slow circles. But it didn't stop. The circles grew larger, carrying their hands around and around.

'What is he, confused?' Keith said.

'Butler, are you here?'

The pointer picked up speed. It made a series of figure-eights. And suddenly stopped.

'B,' Glen said.

Howard felt Angela's hands leave his shoulders, and realized she must be copying the letters as the pointer moved and halted and Glen read from the board.

'W-A-R.'

' "Be war"?' Angela whispered.

'Maybe "beware",' Glen said.

'Oh, shit,' Keith said.

'Beware of what?' Lana asked.

'M-A-N.'

'What man?'

'As if we didn't know.'

'N-E-A-R.'

'The guy we saw this afternoon?'

The pointer sped to the smiling face of the sun.

'That's a yes,' Glen said. 'Jesus. And he's *near*?'

'What does he want?' Lana asked.

'F-U-K-N-S-P-L-I-T-N-C-L-I-M-N.'

After reading off the letters, Glen shook his head. 'What the hell was that all about?'

'Starts with "fuck",' Keith said. 'Couldn't follow the rest.'

Lana looked over at Angela.

'Just a . . .'

Howard heard the gasp from above his head, felt her b'elly push against his back.

'Oh, God,' she murmured.

'What is it?'

'It looks like what Doris said.'

'Come on!'

' "Fuck and split and climb in." '

Angela's warmth wasn't enough to keep an icy tide from flowing up Howard's back.

'It's what Doris thought the guy wanted to do to her.'

'Butler's quoting Doris back at us?' Glen asked.

'Who does he wanta do it to?' Lana asked, gazing down at the pointer.

'A-N-Y-l.'

'Anyone?' Lana asked. 'Not just the women?'

'A-N-Y-1.'

'I knew the guy looked like a fag,' Keith muttered.

'He must go both ways,' Lana said. She looked up at Angela. In the fluttering glow of the firelight, Howard watched a corner of her mouth turn up. 'Better odds for us gals.'

'Very funny,' Keith said.

She returned her gaze to the board. 'Is he going to attack us?'

The pointer darted to the sun.

Angela let out a low moan, but it stopped abruptly when the pointer sped to the moon.

'Yes, no,' Glen said.

Back to the sun again.

'Must mean maybe,' Lana said. 'You don't know whether he'll attack us?'

'B-W-A-R.'

Keith huffed out a breath. 'Damn right we will.'

'We'll be careful,' Lana said in the tone of voice she used when speaking to Butler. 'Do you know this man?'

'M-A-D.'

'He's a madman? Or are *you* mad at him?'

The plastic heart slid to the sun.

'Ambiguous son-of-a-bitch,' Keith said.

'Probably means yes to both questions,' Glen told him.

'Butler, did you know he was here?'

The pointer remained on the sun.

'Either that's a yes,' Glen said, 'or he's not answering.'

'Butler, did you bring us here because of him?'

Their fingers were carried from the sun to the moon.

'That's a no.' Glen sounded relieved.

'What does he have to do with all this?' Lana asked.

'M-A-D.'

'Can't we get any straight answers from this guy?' Keith said.

'P-R-O-T-E-C-T-A-L.'

Angela flinched. 'A.L.? That's me. Protect me?'

Cold spread through Howard's bowels.

'Protect Angela?' Lana asked.

The pointer rushed to the sun.

'Oh, God,' Angela murmured, and pressed her chin against the top of Howard's head.

'Why Angela?' Lana asked.

'Butler's got the hots for her, that's why.'

'Shut up, Keith.'

'That look he got at her tits last night . . .'

'Keith!' Lana snapped. To the Ouija, she said, 'Why Angela?'

For a long time, the pointer was motionless under Howard's trembling fingers. Then it sped around the board, stopping and darting.

'S-H-E-T-A-K-E-U-2-L-O-O-T.'

'She take you to loot,' Angela whispered. 'Me? I don't know where it is.'

'Does Angela know where the loot is?'

'W-I-L.'

'She will? She doesn't know yet?'

'I-G-O.'

'I go?' Glen said.

'No! Wait! Where should we go tomorrow?'

The pointer didn't move.

'Butler! Hold it! Where are we supposed to go?'

They stared down at the still, plastic heart.

'Guess he's gone,' Glen said.

Keith took his hand away. 'Thanks a heap, Butler. Shit.'

'Let's give it a couple more . . .' The pointer glided, halted, slid and stopped.

'Up,' Glen said.

'We go up?' Lana asked.

'2-M-A-R-K-N-G-O-W-I-T-H-E-A-R-T-I-G-O-N-O-W.'

The pointer shot out from under Lana and Howard's fingers, flew off the end of the board and flipped over on the ground, its three plastic legs in the air.

Lana let out a short laugh. 'Well, I guess that's that.'

'What was that stuff at the end?' Glen asked.

'I don't know,' Angela said. 'I've got it all down, here.' Howard felt her belly push against his back as she took a deep breath. 'We go . . . let's see . . . to marking o with e art. I gone ow. I go now.'

'What the hell is "marking o with e art"?' Glen asked.

Angela moved over and sank to her haunches beside

Howard. She held the pad in front of him. The paper shimmered with ruddy light from the fire. 'What do you think?'

He studied the message. 'To mark . . . Maybe the n and g aren't connected. N might mean "and".'

' "To mark and go with . . . e art." '

'If the h belongs to the next word, it would say heart.'

'Go with heart?'

' "To mark and go with heart. I go now." '

'OK,' Lana said. 'So we're supposed to go up to the mark and go with heart. Whatever that means.'

'The bastard likes his riddles,' Keith complained. 'Why can't he just come out and say what he means?'

'He was pretty clear about warning us,' Glen said. 'Man, I'm glad Doris wasn't in on this. Would've really freaked her out.'

Lana twisted around and looked toward the tent. 'We'd better not leave her alone. Nobody'd better do *anything* alone. If Butler's right about that guy . . .'

'And who should know better than a fuckin' *spook*?'

'I wonder if he's watching us,' Angela said.

'Who? Butler or our friendly local psycho?'

'I guess we know Butler's watching us,' Glen said. 'Or listening, anyway. Who is this guy? Big Brother?'

'He seems to be looking out for us,' Lana said.

'For Angela, at least,' Keith said.

'It's not my fault,' she told him.

'No, it's not,' Howard said. 'And there's something we're forgetting.'

'Oh, yeah? Lay it on us, Howitzer.'

'How do we know he's telling the truth? About anything? We don't know what he's up to. He might have us up here for some weird reason we know nothing about. That crazy guy might even be part of his plan. Maybe the guy doesn't mean us any harm, but Butler *wants* us to be afraid of him.'

'More of that denial Doris was talking about,' Glen said.

'Well,' Lana said, 'he has a point. We probably shouldn't be so quick to take Butler at face value.'

'I think Howard's right, too,' Angela said. 'This whole Ouija board thing gives me the creeps, and I think Butler's playing some kind of a game with us. I mean, why should he bring us up here to give us his treasure?'

'He's got a generous spirit,' Keith suggested.

'He's got some kind of ulterior motive,' Angela said.

'Yeah,' Howard said. 'He wants something out of us. Either that, or he wants to *do* something to us.'

'Well, we're here.' Lana got to her knees and leaned over the board. Bracing herself with one hand, she picked up the pointer. Then she pushed herself back, lifted the board and stood. 'It's a little late to call it quits, so I think our best course of action is to be careful but go for the loot.' With that, she turned away and walked toward her tent.

'Hang on.' Keith sprang up and hurried after her. 'Nobody does anything alone, remember?'

Turning, Lana drew the revolver from her coat pocket. 'I'm the gal packing the heat, remember?'

Together, they strolled to her tent. Keith reached it first, glanced inside, then held the flap out of the way for Lana. She crawled in. He followed, and the flap dropped shut behind them.

Chapter Eighteen

'They're coming back, aren't they?' Glen muttered.

'I imagine,' Angela said.

''Cause we've gotta do something about Doris. We can't just leave her alone.'

'Maybe you should go and have a talk with her,' Howard said. 'I mean, it is your tent.'

Glen sighed.

The three of them crawled off his tarp. Howard helped him fold it. Glen carried it the few steps to the place where Angela had left his pack and sleeping bag. He dropped it to the ground. Then he turned toward Lana's tent. 'You're not turning in yet, are you?' he called.

'Don't get your shorts in a knot!' Keith shouted.

Glen faced the other tent. 'Doris?'

No answer.

He walked over to it, squatted, and swept aside the flap. He didn't go in, but he started to speak.

Howard stepped closer to the fire. He picked up a few sticks and added them to the blaze, then sat on the log. Angela sat beside him. He put an arm across her back, and she snuggled against him.

'How are you doing?' he asked.

'I'm a little scared.'

'Yeah, me too.'

'Why does Butler keep *picking* on me?'

'I don't know.'

'Maybe it's like Keith says.'

'Keith is a jerk.'

'But what if he's right? What if Butler . . . *wants* me?'

She shuddered. 'I mean, he's a ghost or something.'

'I guess he doesn't mean you any harm. He told us to protect you.'

'Protect me from the weird guy. Maybe that's only so Butler can have me for himself.'

'It might not be that at all.' He squeezed her hip. 'Besides, what can he do about it even if he does want you? He's a spirit, right?'

'Who knows what he is? Did you ever see that movie, *The Entity*?'

'I read the book.'

'Do you remember what happened in it?'

'Yeah.'

'That demon, or whatever, kept *raping* that woman.'

'It was just fiction.'

'But I heard it was based on a true story.'

'I doubt if anything like that really went on.'

'God,' she muttered. 'I couldn't take it. I'd rather have that *creep* get me, than . . .'

'Hey, you guys, come on! I've got Doris.'

Howard, looking over his shoulder, saw Glen and Doris standing between the two tents. The flap of Lana's tent bulged, and she crawled out. Keith's head appeared in the opening. 'Miracle of miracles.'

'Let's get on with it,' Doris said. Zipping the front of her jacket, she hurried toward the fire. The others followed. They all went to their former seats like theater-goers returning after intermission. 'OK,' she said. 'So what's the big urgent deal?'

'We can't have you staying alone in the tent,' Lana told her. 'We can't have *anyone* alone tonight. Not with that lunatic around.'

Her lip curled. 'I'm sure our armed guard will protect us.'

'We'll have people on watch,' Lana said. 'But that's no

guarantee. I think anyone who's alone is taking a risk. An unnecessary risk.'

'You don't really want to be alone,' Glen said.

'I'm not about to have you in the tent.'

'It's his tent,' Keith pointed out.

'Who *is* acceptable to you?' Lana asked.

Doris's tiny, porcine eyes roamed the group. 'Anyone but Glen or Keith, I suppose.'

'It should be a guy. That leaves you, Howard.'

His mouth fell open. He suddenly felt sick, persecuted. 'Ohhhh, no. No way.'

'Thanks a lot,' Doris muttered.

'It isn't fair,' he said, not looking at her, looking at Lana instead. 'It's Glen's tent. If he's gonna let her use it, that's his business. Just leave me out. It's not my fault she's got a problem with him.'

'We have to pair up,' Lana said.

'I *am* paired up. With Angela.'

'Yeah. We're together. And we already have plans to sleep by the fire.'

Howard knew of no such plan, but he nodded vigorously.

Lana sighed. Glancing from Glen to Doris, she said, 'We can't have someone alone in a tent.'

Those two stared at each other. Doris looked surly, Glen annoyed.

'I could put my sleeping bag right in front of the tent,' he finally said. 'That way, my presence wouldn't be an insult to Doris's sensibilities, but I'd be blocking the entrance and I'd be able to get inside fast if I hear anything.'

'Chivalry ain't dead,' Keith said.

'I guess that would be all right,' Doris said.

'It means he'll be your partner during guard duty,' Lana pointed out.

'OK.'

'As far as guard duty goes,' Lana said, 'I think the first shift should keep at it till one-thirty. With two shifts after that, three hours each, we'll get to seven-thirty in the morning and everybody'll end up with six hours of sleep.'

'You should've been a math major,' Keith said.

'Does that sound all right to everyone?'

Nodding, Howard glanced at Angela. 'Should we go first?' he whispered.

'Sure.'

'We volunteer for the first shift,' he said.

Nobody objected.

'Keith and I'll take it from one-thirty to four-thirty, so wake us up when it's time. Have either of you got a watch?'

'Yeah,' Howard said.

'And we'll have the gun?' Angela asked.

'Right. The sentries get the gun.'

'Know how to use it, Howitzer?'

'I think I'll be able to manage.'

'But what are we supposed to do?' Angela asked.

'Keep your eyes open,' Lana said.

'And keep the fire going,' Keith added. 'If I gotta get out of my nice warm sack in the dead pit of the night, I want a good hot fire waiting for me.'

'OK,' Howard said. He wondered if enough wood remained on the pile to last through their shift.

Maybe. If we're careful with it.

'The main thing,' Lana said, 'is to make sure that maniac doesn't sneak up on the camp. You've got a fairly good view of the tents from here. If he goes for one, shoot him.'

'Just try to miss the tent,' Keith suggested.

'Is class dismissed?' Doris asked.

'What about going to the bathroom?' Angela asked.

'Hang it out anywhere, but don't put out the fire.'

'Let's take care of that now.'

'Sounds good to me.' Keith stood up, grinning.

Lana stood, clutched his shoulder, and pressed him down to his seat. 'The guys can wait here.'

'Aw, shucks.'

Angela and Doris got up. They followed Lana to her tent. She ducked inside and came out with a flashlight and a roll of toilet paper.

'You sure you don't want us to stand guard?' Keith called. 'You don't want to get caught with your pants down.'

'We'll take our chances. And don't try sneaking around for any voyeur crap, or you might catch lead.'

'Give a lady a gun and she thinks she's Dirty Harry.'

Lana in the lead, the girls walked single-file into the trees beyond the tents. After they were out of sight, Howard still caught glimpses of the flashlight's beam.

'Why are they going so far?' Glen asked.

'They probably think we *might* sneak up on 'em.'

Howard faced the fire. 'I wouldn't dare.'

'I know. You're a woos.'

'I'm just afraid I might catch a glimpse of Doris's ass.'

Keith and Glen both laughed. Howard grinned.

'I don't want to get nightmares,' he added.

'That's pretty good, Howitzer. There's hope for you.'

'Lucky me,' Glen said. 'I get stuck with her for guard duty.'

'Do us all a favor and fuck her lights out. It might improve her attitude.'

'Yeah, sure.'

'You could put a bag over her head,' Howard suggested.

'You'd have to bag her whole body.'

Glen didn't look amused. 'Not that I would, but if I *did* try putting moves on her, she'd probably make some kind of fucking wisecracks. Who needs it, you . . .'

'NO!'

The distant, shrill outcry hit Howard like a kick. He leaped to his feet as Keith blurted 'Holy shit!' and sprang up and Glen shoved him. All three were running when more shouts came from the woods.

'*Help! It's him! It's him!*'

That was Angela.

But the first panicked shriek hadn't been her. He didn't think so.

What's happening?

Why doesn't Lana shoot?

'*Nnnooo!*'

Lana?

They raced between the tents. Keith was first to reach the edge of the clearing. He sprinted into the trees, Howard close behind him, Glen at the rear.

Howard kept his eyes on the dark shape of Keith's back. He heard nothing except the wind shuffling through the night, their own huffing breaths, their shoes pounding the matted ground.

'Let her go!' Angela again.

A blast crashed in Howard's ears. Then another. He couldn't hear the wind or anyone panting for air. The footfalls sounded faint and far away through the ringing in his head.

In front of Keith and off to the right, a pale beam sliced sideways and down.

'We're here!' Keith yelled.

The light swung toward them. 'Over here!'

Angela's voice.

She's all right.

But what about the others?

Seconds later, he found out. He glimpsed Lana on the ground, legs bare, jeans bunched around her ankles. Angela, kneeling by her head, shut off the flashlight.

'She's OK,' Doris said. She sounded breathless. She was standing behind Angela.

'I'm OK,' Lana gasped.

'Jesus, what happened?'

'He grabbed her,' Angela said.

'He took off that way,' Doris said. Raising an arm, she pointed into the trees beyond Lana's feet. She had the revolver in her hand.

'You didn't get him?' Keith blurted.

'Huh-uh.'

'Give me that!' He rushed to her and grabbed the gun.

'No,' Lana said. 'Don't go.'

'Blow his fuckin' head off.'

'Stay here!' Lana snapped.

Glen put a hand on Keith's shoulder. 'We might not find him anyway. And we shouldn't leave the girls.'

Keith whirled on Doris. 'Why didn't you shoot him, you fat ox?'

Glen shook him. 'Knock it off!'

'For Godsake,' Lana said, 'she saved me. She couldn't shoot at him without hitting me. The bastard was running off with me.'

'He dropped her when Doris fired,' Angela said.

'Oh,' Keith said.

'Yeah. Oh.' Lana sat up. Leaning forward, she began pulling at one of her shoes. 'Piss all over me,' she muttered.

'Do you want the light on?' Angela asked her.

'No thanks.' She yanked the shoe off and began tugging at the other. 'He got me right in the middle of taking my leak,' she said. 'Comes up behind me and jerks me over backwards.' With the second shoe off, she struggled to free her feet from the pants. 'Next thing I know, he's got me over his shoulder. God only knows where he was going with me. But I'd be finding out if it hadn't been for Doris.'

'Where was the gun while all this was going on?' Glen asked.

'I had it in my jacket.'

'It must've fallen out,' Doris said, 'when he picked her up.'

'It did,' Angela confirmed. 'I heard it hit the ground.'

Lana started putting her shoes back on.

'She went and tried to tackle the guy,' Doris said. 'Held onto him long enough for me to get the flashlight. I just happened to see the gun there next to it. I got hold of it just when he broke loose from Angela. He had Lana over his shoulder and I couldn't see where she left off and he started, so I didn't aim for him. I fired in the air, and he threw her down.'

'That's when you should've nailed him,' Keith said.

'You weren't there,' Lana said, getting to her feet. She brushed off her rump and made a disgusted 'Ugh' sound. Howard stared at her pale buttocks as she bent over and picked up her pants. 'Let's get back to camp,' she said. 'I'm freezing.'

Angela gave the flashlight to Keith, then stepped over to Howard and took his arm. Together, they led the way.

'I should've tried,' he heard Doris say.

'You did great,' Lana told her. 'I really owe you.'

'It was just so dark. I was afraid I might miss him, and then we'd only have three bullets left.'

'If you'd hit him,' Howard said, 'we wouldn't need to worry about saving bullets.'

'Would you please cut it out?' Lana said, a pleading tone in her voice. 'She saved my life. She and Angela both did.'

'Did the guy have his machete?' Glen asked.

'I don't think so,' Lana told him. 'He was holding onto me with both hands.'

Angela looked over her shoulder. 'It was on his belt,' she said, keeping her head turned.

Howard wanted to look back, too. Maybe he'd be able to see Lana from the front. But the others might catch on that he was trying for a peek. Besides, there wouldn't be enough light to see much. He managed to keep his eyes forward.

Through the trunks and low branches ahead, he saw the faint, distant glow of the campfire.

'Was he wearing clothes this time?' Keith asked.

'Fur,' Lana said. 'I felt fur under me. It's wet fur now.'

'And he had leather pants on,' Angela added.

'Did he? I couldn't see.'

'They felt like leather, anyway. They didn't smell too great.'

As Howard stepped into the clearing, Lana said, 'Why don't you guys hurry on ahead and build up the fire? I'm going to be an ice cube. Keith, how about getting my towel and sweatpants? Clean socks and my boots, too.'

'Sure.'

Howard heard quick footfalls behind him. Then Lana ran by, holding her jeans out to the side. She rushed between the two tents. Her rump and legs were creamy in the moonlight, golden as she raced past the campfire, dim when she was beyond its glow.

'Here.' Keith's voice. 'Stay with her. I'll be along in a minute.'

Doris jogged by with the revolver.

In the distance, Lana stopped running. She dropped her jeans.

Howard, walking toward the fire with Angela holding his arm, watched Lana's vague shape hop on one leg, then the other as she pulled off her shoes. She picked up the jeans again and walked down the gradual slope to the shore.

She suddenly jerked rigid and flung out her arms as if she'd been stabbed in the back. Her feet were out of sight, but Howard knew she had stepped into the water.

Behind him, Glen said, 'Ouch! God, I bet that's cold!'

She waded farther out. Her legs looked as if they'd been cut off at the knees. With each step, the black climbed higher. Then all that Howard could see between the surface of the lake and the dark back of her jacket was the faint, pale blur of her rump. The pale area stretched upward as she lifted her jacket and shirt.

Doris moved sideways on the shore, blocking his view.

I shouldn't be staring anyway, he told himself.

'I'll throw some wood on,' Angela said as they reached the fire. 'Maybe you and Glen could go and gather more.'

'Yeah. Come on, Howie.'

She squeezed his arm. 'Stay close by, though. OK?' She gave him the flashlight.

This is good, he thought as he wandered away from the fire with Glen. Get plenty of wood now, while everybody's around. Get enough to last through our shift.

He looked again toward the lake. Now, Doris wasn't in the way. He saw Lana wading out, the jeans held in front of her. Keith ran toward the shore with a bundle in his arms.

'Hey, man,' Glen said. 'Quit watching the show and start grabbing firewood. I don't like it out here.'

Chapter Nineteen

'What do you know?' Chad said. 'We made it.'

Corie, bouncing and rocking in the passenger seat, stared at Lana's Granada as they approached its rear. The headbeams gleamed on its bumper, made the red of its tail lights glow and lit its interior. For a moment, she thought two people were sitting in the front seat. Then she realized she was seeing headrests, not heads. 'Well,' she muttered, 'they're not in it.'

'Doesn't look that way.' Chad pulled up beside Lana's car. He shut off the engine and headlights. Dark flooded down.

Corie picked up the flashlight and climbed out. It felt good to be standing. She stretched, sighing as a pleasant weariness spread through her stiff, sore muscles.

Though breezes shifted through the trees, she was met by no strong wind. The night seemed chilly, but not frigid.

Chad waited for her beside the Granada. She shone her light through the passenger window. Just as she'd thought, nobody was inside.

'Try calling out,' Chad suggested.

With a nod, she turned toward the woods beyond the front of the car. 'Hello!' she shouted. 'Lana! Howard! Angela! Anyone! It's Corie Dalton! Hello?'

Weird, she thought. Here we are, standing beside another abandoned car, yelling, getting no more of an answer than we did at the other one.

'This is like a rerun,' she said. 'But we know *they* didn't hike into town.'

'I suspect they must've gone on to the lake.'

'Which is what you suspected from the start.'

'What do you want to do?'

Corie scanned the dark woods. She shook her head. 'I don't know.'

'It'd be a tough hike to the lake, but we could probably make it in a couple of hours. Two or three,' he added. 'If we don't stray off the trail or fall off the mountain or something.'

She smiled. 'I can tell you're just rarin' to go. Gonna have to disappoint you, though. I'm too beat, myself. I couldn't make it. I wouldn't even want to try. Not tonight.'

'Thank God.'

Laughing, she said, 'Contrary to popular opinion, I'm not a masochist.'

'Could've fooled me.'

She nudged him with her elbow, then walked past the front of the car and swept her light across the area ahead. Its beam found a wooden sign – a pair of narrow planks atop a post – off to the left.

'Must be the start of the trail,' Chad said, following her.

She stopped in front of the sign and read aloud. 'Shadow Canyon Lake, four miles. Calamity Peak, nine miles.' The points of the redwood boards were aimed at an opening in the trees, and Corie's flash-light illuminated a narrow footpath.

'Why don't we just take a little walk up that way?' she said. 'Without our packs. You never know, we might run into the kids. Maybe they just wanted to get away from where they parked.'

'Possible,' Chad said, following her onto the trail.

'We won't go far.'

'Hope not. I'm owed a certain reward for getting us here.'

'Looking forward to it.'

They walked along, Corie shining her light on the trail just ahead but peering often into the heavy woods on both sides. She looked for the glow of a campfire. She listened for voices. But she saw only darkness and flecks of moonlight among the trees, and heard only their own footfalls, the squawk and chirp of night birds, the papery sounds of the piny limbs stirred by breezes and sometimes quiet, skittery sounds of small animals scurrying nearby.

'I guess this is far enough,' she finally said. She called out, but no answer came.

'We'll get an early start in the morning,' Chad said.

She turned around and took his hand. Together, they walked back to the roadhead.

Chapter Twenty

Howard sat with the gun on his lap, his back to the fire. Angela, beside him on the log, faced the fire. Positioned this way, they had a full field of vision, their sides touched, and they were able to talk quietly and sometimes look at each other.

'What time is it?' Angela asked.

Howard checked his wristwatch. 'Five till twelve.'

'Only an hour and a half to go. This isn't so bad, is it?'

'I don't think I'd be able to sleep, anyway.'

'I wonder about the others.'

'I don't know.' He looked over at the tents. Earlier, he'd been able to see a faint disk of light through the front of Lana's tent. Now, it was gone. Both tents were dark. 'I bet they're all asleep.'

'Speaking of bets,' Angela said, 'do you think Keith got to lay his pipe?' She laughed softly.

'Yeah, do you?'

'Yeah. Poor Lana was freezing. If nothing else, she would've done it just to warm up.'

'You think so?'

'Sure. And it'd take her mind off what happened, too.'

It felt strange to be talking with Angela about other people having sex. It felt strange, but good. We're talking about them, Howard told himself, but we're thinking about us.

At least I am.

'What about Glen and Doris?' he asked.

'That I doubt.'

'Me, too. But she did let him into the tent.'

'She's scared, that's all.'

'But who knows, once they're together in there? I think Glen likes her.'

'It would be awfully nice if they got together.'

'Might make a new woman out of Doris,' Howard said.

'Put a smile on her face.'

'If they tried making it, though, somebody'd end up squashed flatter than a bug.'

Angela laughed and bumped against him. They both turned their heads. Her face was rosy, a little sunburned from the day's hike, ruddy from the night's cold and the glow of the fire. She had a smudge of soot on one cheek, another just above her right eyebrow.

Their eyes met. Howard was surprised to see how solemn she looked. She leaned back a little, eased sideways, and kissed his mouth. Her lips felt cold at first, then warm. Her breast was pushing against his arm. He got breathless and hard. He caressed her hair.

She moaned softly, her lips vibrating and tickling him for a moment before they went away. 'We'd better keep watch,' she whispered.

'You started it.'

A big smile bloomed. 'That's right, I did.' She sat up straight and grinned over her shoulder at him. 'Impetuous me.'

'God, Angela.'

'What?'

'You've changed so much. And so fast. It's almost as if you're a different person. Ever since last night . . .'

'Last night you finally noticed me.' Her smile slipped a bit. 'I think it had something to do with the removal of a certain garment.'

'Well . . . maybe.'

'I haven't changed all that much. Not really.'

'You used to be so . . . introverted.'

'Well, we were almost like strangers. I guess you always thought I was pretty odd.'

'I just . . . yeah. In your own world, kind of.'

'You were scared of me.' She looked over her shoulder at him and smiled. 'Still are, at least a little bit.'

'Not so much anymore. And it's not the same.'

'Not the same how?'

'Jeez.'

'Come on.'

He sighed. 'I don't know. Before, I thought you were sort of peculiar.'

'A weirdo.'

'But you're not. Not really. I mean, now that I know about . . . the way you've been living . . . I can see why you kind of kept to yourself and always seemed so . . . preoccupied.'

Angela was silent for a moment. Then she said, 'The fire's getting low.'

Howard went shaky in his stomach.

Now I've done it, he thought. Why didn't I keep my mouth shut?

He leaned over, picked up a few sticks, then straddled the log with his back to Angela, reached out sideways and added them to the fire. Flames licked around the wood. Remembering that he was supposed to be keeping watch for the creep, he looked over at the tents and scanned the darkness beyond them.

'I was all Skerrit had,' she said. 'He didn't want me to have any friends. Neither did I, for that matter. I mean, I *wanted* friends, but I couldn't have them. I was always afraid someone might find out I was living with him. How was I supposed to explain something like that? Unless I lied. I could've said he was my father, I guess. But what kind of a relationship's that, if you have to tell lies?'

Howard swung his leg over the log and sat again with his back to the fire, his side touching Angela.

'The thing about you,' she said, and hesitated. 'You know about it and you haven't . . . acted as if I've got the plague. It has to bother you, though.'

'Yeah.' His heart was thumping hard. He feared she was ready to tell him things he ached and dreaded to know. 'I don't really understand it – how you could stay with a man like him? I know you couldn't afford a place of your own, but . . .'

'It was a lot more than that. He paid my tuition, he paid for everything.'

'But why?'

'We had a deal. I agreed to live with him and take care of him, and he agreed to put me through college.'

But he messed with you! How could you let him do *stuff to you?*

Those thoughts raged through Howard's mind, but he kept silent.

'There was more to it,' she said. 'In case you hadn't already figured that out. I guess you might say I was his mistress.'

'He molested you?'

'I don't know. "Molested" kind of sounds right. But I'm not going to lie to you, Howard. He didn't actually rape me. I was with him by choice. I didn't want any sex with him, but I let him do what he wanted. Usually. He had to force me to do some of the stuff, but usually I just went along with him. It wasn't so bad.'

'God,' Howard muttered.

It was worse than he'd imagined. A lot worse. Almost beyond belief.

'I'm sorry,' Angela said.

'How could you?'

'I wanted my education. He wanted me. I guess we were using each other.'

'But . . . it's *disgusting*.'

'I know. The thing is, he wasn't all that bad to me. Most of the time, he treated me OK.'

'Well, sure he did. You were putting out for him.'

'Hey, come on.' She sounded hurt. Howard looked around as she hunched forward. Elbows resting on her knees, she lowered her head and seemed to gaze at the ground. 'So now I'm a whore or something,' she muttered.

'I didn't say that.'

'It's what you're thinking. I don't blame you. I guess I am. Maybe I shouldn't have told. But I don't want to have secrets from you.'

'It's all right,' he said. He put his hand on her back.

'Skerrit was so much nicer to me than the others. He loved me, he really did. And he didn't hurt me often. When he did, it was only because he cared so much. He was so afraid of losing me.' She shook her head. 'I shouldn't have left him. He must think I'm gone forever. God, I hate to think what he must be going through.'

'You're not going back to him, are you?'

'Maybe that's where I belong.'

'No!'

'It wasn't that bad. It really wasn't. Skerrit's an *angel* compared to the others.'

'What others? You keep saying that.'

'You don't want to know.'

'I do.' He rubbed her back. 'I want to know everything about you,' he added, surprising himself. He hadn't expected to speak those words, but when he heard them he knew that they were true.

She sat up straight and looked back at him. She wasn't crying, but she looked sad and weary. 'OK,' she said.

'OK.'

'But let's not forget to keep our eyes open.'

'That guy's probably long gone. Now that he knows we've got a gun . . .'

'He won't give up. I've known men like him. He won't quit till he gets what he wants.'

'What do you mean, you've known men like him?'

'My stepfather, for starters. Charlie. And his boys. He had twins, Jack and George. All three of them were . . . horrible. They kept me after Mom was killed.'

'That's when you were four?'

'Yeah. The twins must've been nine or ten.'

'They were your brothers?'

Angela shook her head. 'They were Charlie's sons. I don't know who their mother was. Not Mom, though. And I don't know how Mom got mixed up with Charlie. Maybe she didn't have a choice. That's what I like to think, that he took her prisoner or something and she couldn't get away from him. But they got married. At least I think they did. I had his name, Carnes.'

'Carnes? I thought it was Logan.'

'I was Angela Carnes till I got away from him. Then I changed it. I'd read this book, *Logan's Run*. I liked the name, so I took it. Anyway, I'm pretty sure Mom was married to Charlie. I don't know why she'd do something like that unless he forced her into it. Unless Mom was some kind of an awful person and she actually *fell* for him. I hate to think she was that way, though.'

'If she'd lived, maybe she would've gotten me away from those guys. Or maybe not. Maybe she would've just let it all happen, anyway. I guess I'll never know.'

'Anyway, it's a long story. I was thirteen before I got away from Charlie and the twins. We lived in a van most of the time. When we weren't on the move, we'd be parked out in the middle of nowhere. In forests, in fields. Charlie didn't want people around.'

'I never went to school the whole time I was with them.'

'Never? How did you learn to read?'

She shrugged. '*They* sure didn't teach me. I must've learned how from Mom. At least enough to get me started. I read everything I could get my hands on while I was with those bastards. It was great. It's probably what kept me from going crazy. When I was reading, I was living other people's lives. Theirs were always better than my own – even when they were in hot water. Books were really what kept me going, I think. Books, and my daydreams.'

'We'd drive past schools, sometimes, and I'd see all those kids . . . The thing I wanted most in the world, I think, was to go to school. I used to dream about how it might be. But I couldn't go to school like other kids, so I was determined to grow up and be a teacher. That got to be the most important thing to me – to be a teacher. And to teach about books. I knew it would happen someday if they didn't kill me first.'

'You thought they'd *kill* you?'

'It's just a miracle they didn't.'

'Jesus,' Howard muttered.

'They were madmen, crazy. They were like this guy who's been attacking us, but probably worse.'

'What did they *do* to you?'

'What *didn't* they?'

'But you were only a kid.'

She shrugged. 'That didn't stop them. But they got a lot more . . . active . . . when I hit nine or ten. And then when I started to get breasts . . . It wouldn't have been so bad, I guess, but they had to always be *hurting* me. Not because they were angry, either. They did it for kicks. It . . . turned them on. They'd get my clothes off and tie me up. Sometimes, they used handcuffs. They'd do things like hang me by my wrists from a tree limb or whatever else was handy, and whip me with their belts or sticks or electrical cords . . . God, I've been whipped with just about everything you can imagine. When they weren't doing that, they'd use pliers on me, or . . . anyway, they'd get themselves worked up into a frenzy by torturing me, and then they'd . . . you know, rape me.'

Howard felt as if his mind had been stunned numb. Men had done those things? To Angela? To the girl sitting right here beside him?

He frowned at her. 'They really *did* that stuff?'

'Yeah. It wasn't just to me, either. Plenty of times, they got strangers. They'd give a ride to a hitch-hiker, maybe, and then she'd be the one they used. Sometimes, they'd even run a car off the road if there was a woman in it.'

'My God,' Howard murmured.

'I suppose some of them must've ended up dead. But I never saw anyone get killed. I'd go into the van and hide while they did what they were doing. And I'd hear the woman's screams. And them laughing and squealing and having a great time. And I'd be glad it was her and not me.'

Angela stood up. Turning around, Howard watched her rub the seat of her pants. Then she stepped past him, picked up some wood and added it to the fire. She looked back at him. 'Want to walk around some?'

'Sure.'

'My butt's starting to hurt.' She managed a crooked smile, then turned on the flashlight.

Howard stood, loosened his belt one notch, and pushed the barrel of the revolver under his buckle.

Side by side, they walked slowly toward the tents. In a quiet voice, Angela said, 'I bet you never expected to hear a story like that.'

'It's . . . terrible. God. How could people get away with stuff like that?'

'They were always on the move, for one thing. I suppose we were usually miles away by the time cops even realized anyone was missing. We were on back roads most of the time. We stayed away from towns except when we needed supplies.'

She stopped talking as they stepped behind the tents. She flicked her light against the back of each, then swept it through the woods.

'How did you get away?' Howard asked.

She waited until they were a distance from the tents, walking along the edge of the clearing.

'They killed me.'

'What?'

'It was when I was thirteen. We were somewhere in Oregon, and they stopped to pick up this hitch-hiker. She was just fifteen or sixteen, I guess. Anyway, she was about to get into the van. I just couldn't stand the whole thing anymore. So I yelled and warned her and she ran off. She got away. So they took me to a field. They spent . . . I don't know, hours . . . working on me. They thought they'd killed me. When I woke up . . . Well, what they'd done was bury me.'

'*Buried?*'

'One of those "shallow graves" you hear about. Lucky for me, they'd put me in face down. So I could breathe. And there wasn't much on top of me – a little dirt and a few big rocks, but mostly leaves and junk. I got out. And they were gone. I've never seen them again.' She shrugged. 'For all I know, the three of them might be dead by now. Or in prison somewhere.'

'I hope they're dead,' Howard said.

She took his hand and squeezed it. 'You're not the only one.'

Their wandering had taken them along the far side of the campsite, and on toward the lake. Angela played the beam of the flashlight over the rocky shoreline. Then she turned to face the camp.

'What happened after you escaped?'

'I got to a road and some people picked me up. I spent some time in the hospital.'

'Did you tell the police about everything?'

Angela turned to him. She shook her head. 'I pretended I had amnesia.'

'What?'

'I was so scared, Howard. Charlie and the twins, they thought I was dead. I was terrified they might find out I was alive and come looking for me. So I pretended I couldn't remember anything, not even my name. And it worked. Pretty soon, the cops stopped bothering me.'

'If you'd told, they might've been caught.'

'I know. But I was just too scared to take the risk. You just can't imagine how it was. They kept me nine years, *nine years*, Howard. I lived every day of that with madmen who did whatever they wanted with me. And some of it was a lot worse than what I've told you. But suddenly I was free. Really free. Because they thought they'd killed me. I would've done anything to keep them from finding out I was alive.'

Letting go of his hand, she wrapped her arms across her chest. 'I know it was wrong not to tell the cops. But I couldn't. I just couldn't.'

'Should we go back to the fire?'

'Yeah. I'm getting the shakes.'

They returned to the campfire. Instead of sitting down, they stood side by side, close to its flames. Angela put her hands out. 'Feels good.'

'Yeah.'

'Do you want me to go on?'

'Jeez, I'm not sure.'

She let out a weary sigh. 'Well, the worst is over. I ended up in a foster home, and I finally got my wish about going to school. I stayed with the same family all through high school.'

'They treated you all right?'

'Better than Charlie and the boys, that's for sure. But it wasn't a picnic.'

'Are you kidding?'

'They weren't actually brutal. Dennis and Mindy, the pious, middle-class, all-American man and wife. They didn't want to mark us up, for one thing. Also, they had two other female wards, so the abuse got spread around. I wasn't always the target. But Mindy had a real thing for me, so I got more than my share.'

'She had a *thing* for you?'

'She thought I was cute. She liked to tie me down on her bed.' Angela let out a deep breath. 'But, hey, those two were easy after Charlie and the twins. And Skerrit – he was a really big improvement on all of them.'

'How did you wind up with him?'

'He was Mindy's father. He'd come up for visits a few times. I wanted to attend Belmore and he lived near it. A deal was made. I guess Mindy wanted to keep me in the family, come to visit on parents' weekend and that sort of thing.' Angela smiled into the fire. 'Dennis and Mindy went down in an airplane during my freshman year. They went down and stayed down.'

'God.'

'I suppose I shouldn't gloat. They weren't the worst people in the world. But I hated them.'

'You don't hate Skerrit, though?'

She shook her head. 'I feel sorry for him, mostly. He's awful in some ways. Perverted. But I can't loathe him. He's too lonely and pitiful for that.' Turning her eyes to Howard, she said, 'I guess now you see what I mean about attracting madmen, huh?'

'And women,' he muttered.

'Just Mindy.'

'But that makes six altogether.'

'You kept score, huh?'

'It's unbelievable.'

A corner of her mouth trembled. 'Maybe I'm cursed. What do you think?'

'God, I don't know.'

'And now there's the wild man of the mountains running around. He's gone after Doris and Lana. My turn next.'

'He won't get you.'

'Better him than Butler, I guess. At least he's flesh and blood. He couldn't do anything to me that hasn't been done before. Except kill me.'

'Nobody's going to kill you. Nobody's ever going to hurt you again, not while I'm around.' He pulled the revolver out of his belt and pushed its barrel down the rear of his pants. Then he took Angela into his arms.

She squeezed herself tightly against him, pressed her face to the side of his neck.

He caressed her hair, her back. He felt her soft breathing on his neck. He felt her breasts, her belly, her pelvis, her thighs. All snug and warm against him.

But he wasn't aroused.

He wanted to push her away.

Her back gave a hitch, and she made a quiet gasping sound. It happened again, then again.

What's she doing? Howard wondered.

Either laughing or sobbing.

He knew which.

'What's wrong?'

'I've ruined everything.'

'What are you talking about?'

She shook her head. Her face was wet and slippery, and her eyelashes flicked against the side of his neck.

'What?' he asked again.

'Nothing.'

'Come on.'

'You can let go of me now. You can stop pretending.'

'Pretending what?'

She pushed him away.

He clutched her shoulders. 'Angela!'

'Leave me alone.' Knocking his hands away, she lurched past him and ran from the fire. Out of its ruddy glow. Into the darkness. Toward the lake.

Chapter Twenty-one

Howard sat with the gun on his lap, his back to the fire. Sometimes, he glanced over at the tents. Most of the time, he watched Angela.

She was sitting near the shore, probably on the flat surface of the boulder she had called 'our rock.' Only her head and back were visible. They were dim blurs. Howard figured she must be awfully cold.

Awfully miserable.

When she had first run off, he'd taken a few quick steps in pursuit. Then he'd halted and returned to the fire. She didn't want him chasing her. She wanted to get away from him. That's why she'd left.

He would wait her out. He would just sit here and watch over her, make sure she didn't do something weird like jump in the lake, protect her if the crazy man should make a try.

He felt sorry for her. Sorry for himself, too. He wanted

things to be the same as they'd been before she told her awful, incredible story. But when he'd embraced her there at the end, he'd felt revulsion. As if she were tainted, spoiled. Filthy. As if she reeked of all the others, their sweat and semen.

Somehow, she had sensed his reaction.

I don't want it to be this way, he told himself. Besides, it's stupid. She's still Angela. She's no different than she was when we started talking. She didn't seem *dirty*, then. And nothing happened to change her. She spoke. Air went past her vocal chords. She made words. That was all. She didn't turn rotten and smelly. All she did was speak.

It was words. Just words.

It's just words, Howard thought, if somebody says he spit in your soup.

You might've been slopping the stuff up, enjoying the hell out of it. A few words. *Guess what, I hocked a loogie in your gumbo*. Suddenly you can smell the sweetish stench of saliva and just the idea of one more spoonful is enough to make you heave.

It's not the same thing, he told himself.

Close enough.

No. They're two different things, entirely. She's clean. Nothing's still on her from those people. Nothing's *in* her. You go to restaurants, you're always eating off dishes other people have used. You don't even think about it, just as long as they've been washed good. It doesn't matter how many people have used them.

It doesn't *matter* how many people have fucked Angela.

It shouldn't.

It's stupid for it to matter.

Howard fed the fire and scanned the campsite and watched Angela. Maybe he should've gone after her. Maybe that's what she'd wanted. It would've showed that he cared.

I *do* care, he told himself.

Then why didn't I go over there? Why have I just been sitting here like a jerk all this time?

He checked his wristwatch. One-twenty. Their turn at guard duty would be over in ten minutes.

He stood up, stuffed the revolver's barrel down the rear of his pants, and walked away from the warmth of the fire. Angela didn't turn around as he approached. He stepped onto the rock. 'It's just me,' he said.

'I know.'

'Aren't you freezing?'

'It's not so bad.'

He crouched behind her. He stroked her hair, but she continued to face the lake. 'I guess you're mad at me, huh?'

'I'm not angry with you.'

'Correcting my grammar?'

'Don't try to be funny, all right?'

'Sorry.' He stood up. 'Why don't you come back to the fire now? You must be freezing. Besides, it's almost time to wake up Lana and Keith.'

She nodded, got to her feet and turned around.

Howard led the way. They returned to the fire in silence and Angela squatted close to it. He could see that she was shivering.

'I don't know what to say,' he told her.

'It's not required that you say anything.'

'God, Angela. What'd I *do*?'

'Nothing,' she muttered.

'I thought we were friends. You know?'

'We can still be friends. But I guess it stops at that.'

'Why?'

'You know why.'

'No, I don't.'

She stared into the fire for a while. Then, without looking

up at him, she said, 'I'm not exactly what you had in mind, am I?'

He shrugged. 'God, I don't know. I never . . . expected you were a virgin. I mean, who is?'

'Probably you.'

A blush heated his skin. 'It sure isn't by choice,' he said, and let out a nervous laugh.

'It isn't by choice that I'm not.'

'I know.'

'But that doesn't count, does it. What counts is that I'm damaged goods. Damaged beyond your wildest expectations. You can't even touch me, now, without thinking about all those people who've done stuff to me. And being disgusted.'

'That's crazy.'

'Don't lie. It's true, and you know it.'

'It's not true.'

She stood up and sighed. 'Is it time to get the others up?'

Howard checked his watch. 'Yeah.'

'Do you want to get them, or should I?'

'We don't have to do it right away.'

'We might as well.'

'OK. You can stay here and keep warm, I'll wake them up.' He walked toward Lana's tent. He felt sad and confused. He wanted to make things right, but he didn't know how. If only she'd kept her mouth shut about Charlie and Skerrit and everyone. If she hadn't *told* him so much.

Spit in the soup.

Damn it!

He stopped in front of Lana's tent. 'Hey, guys,' he said. 'This is your wake-up call.'

'Get fucked,' Keith replied.

'It's one-thirty.'

'Coming,' Lana murmured, her voice groggy.

Howard heard soft rustling sounds from inside the tent. Soon, the flaps parted. Lana crawled out, the bundle of a coat clutched to her chest. She was wearing a hooded sweatshirt and sweatpants. She stood up. As she struggled into the coat, her breasts shook inside the loose, baggy sweatshirt.

No bra.

Howard felt a warm stirring in his groin.

Here I am, getting turned on, he thought. Keith probably screwed her an hour or so ago. If he didn't use a rubber, she's probably got his gunk in her. So how come *that* doesn't disgust me?

She pulled the zipper up. 'I take it nothing went wrong,' she said.

'No problems.'

'Great. The shit would've tried something by now, if he was going to.'

'You'd think so.'

Keith came out of the tent and stood up, hugging his chest and gritting his teeth. A flashlight was gripped in his hand. 'What're we standing here for?'

They hurried over to the fire. Keith hunched down close to it. Lana added some wood to the blaze. 'Why don't you guys go ahead and use our tent? You might as well. We won't be needing it for the next three hours. When it's time for the next watch, maybe Glen'll let you move over into his tent. It'd beat trying to sleep out here.'

'Just use your own sleeping bags,' Keith said. 'I don't want your cooties.'

Howard looked at Angela. She shrugged.

'OK,' he said. 'Thanks. Are you sure you don't mind?'

'I wouldn't have offered if I minded.'

'Well, great.' He handed the revolver to Keith.

Angela followed Howard away from the fire. They gathered their sleeping bags and backpacks, and went to the tent. 'This will be a lot more comfortable,' Howard said.

Leaving their packs just outside the flaps, they crawled inside. Lana and Keith had left their sleeping bags spread out, sides touching each other.

'Should we move them out of the way?' Angela asked.

'Let's just put ours on top. It'll make the ground softer.'

Angela held the flashlight while Howard unrolled their sleeping bags on top of the others. When he was done, he said, 'I guess I need to brush my teeth. Do you want to come along?'

'I think I'll wait and do it in the morning.'

She gave him the flashlight. He crawled outside and took his toothbrush and paste from a side pocket of his pack. He grabbed his canteen. Lana and Keith were sitting near the fire. Keith had his arm around her back. Howard turned away from them and stepped into the trees behind the tent.

He didn't go far. He brushed his teeth quickly, thinking about the creep.

Though he suspected that the guy was only interested in girls, Butler had said otherwise.

Done with his teeth, he wandered farther from the tent so Angela wouldn't hear him. When he thought he'd gone far enough, he tucked his brush and paste into a pocket, clamped the canteen and flashlight under one arm, and unzipped his pants. Before freeing his penis, he looked all around. He could still see the glow of the campfire. But it was way off in the distance, mostly blocked by trees.

If something happens . . .

Let's just make it quick.

He dug himself out of his underwear and started to go. The chilly air felt good down there. His splashing sounded loud, but he was sure Angela couldn't hear it. He thought about her back in the tent. She was probably taking the opportunity to change clothes – put on whatever she planned to sleep in. Sitting cross-legged on her sleeping bag, reaching up behind her back and unfastening her bra, taking it off.

The limp penis between his thumb and forefinger grew and stiffened.

Guess she's not so disgusting, after all.

He was half erect by the time he shook off the last drops. He had some trouble forcing it back inside his briefs.

Maybe I'm getting over the shock, he thought as he started back toward camp. Maybe the revulsion was just some kind of temporary reaction.

At the front of the tent, he put away the toothbrush and paste. Searching through his pack, he found his sweatsuit and a fresh pair of socks.

He hesitated, wondering if he should put them on before entering the tent.

'Is that you?' Angela asked.

'Yeah.'

'What're you doing?'

'I'm gonna change clothes.'

'Out there?'

'Well . . .'

'You'll freeze. Come on in. I won't peek.'

'Well, OK.'

Holding the canteen and clothes against his chest, he crawled inside. Angela squinted and turned her face away from the flashlight's beam. She was in her sleeping bag, braced up on her left elbow. She wore her sweatshirt. Its wide neck hung off her shoulder. Howard didn't see any strap.

He shut off the light and sat down on his sleeping bag. His back to Angela, he began to undress. She had promised not to look. The tent was dark. But he felt breathless and shaky when he drew his corduroys and underwear down. The nylon cover of the sleeping bag was cold under his bare rump. He started getting hard again.

What if she sits up and reaches around and *touches* me?

She didn't.

He pulled the sweatpants up his legs, raised himself a bit and brought them up around his waist. Quickly, he got into his clean socks, stripped off his jacket and shirt, and pulled the sweatshirt down over his head. After rolling his clothes into a bundle to use as a pillow, he got to his knees and turned around.

Angela was still propped up on her elbow. Had she been watching, after all? She said nothing as Howard scurried into his sleeping bag.

He rolled onto his side. Her face was a vague blur. Her shoulder was still uncovered. It must be cold, he thought.

'Are you warm enough?' he asked.

'Fine.'

'Nice of them to let us use their tent.'

'Yeah.'

He wondered why she was staying braced up that way instead of snuggling down into her bag. After a while, he said, 'Do you want to come over?'

'And contaminate you?'

'Jeez,' he said.

'Go to sleep, Howard.' With that, she sank down and settled on her back and turned her face away.

Later, he heard her sniffing. A runny nose? No. She was crying. Softly so he wouldn't notice.

In his mind, he eased out of his sleeping bag and crawled over to her. He kissed the tears from her cheeks, her lips. And she kissed him. Feverishly. Desperately. *Make it all right*, she whispered, and opened her sleeping bag to him. He slipped inside. They embraced, the sweatclothes soft between them. *I want you*, she gasped. *I want you so bad.* She lifted her sweatshirt, pressed his hands against her breasts. He had never touched anything so smooth. He fondled them, squeezed them, kissed them. And as he did that, Angela's hand crept down and went inside his sweatpants. Her cool fingers curled around him. *Ooo, so big*, she said. *In me. I want you in me.*

He touched himself through the front of his sweatpants. His penis felt like a hot bar of iron.

Quit thinking about her and get over there! She's crying. She's lonely. She *needs* you. Get over there and kiss her.

Right. With a hard-on?

Why not? It shows you're not turned off by her. That's what she needs to know. That's the main thing she needs to know. It'll show you don't care about all the others.

She probably won't notice, anyway.

Just crawl over there and kiss her.

Slowly, Howard began to lower the zipper on the side of his sleeping bag. He was trembling, his heart slamming. The zipper made quiet clicks.

He was still easing it down when Angela snored.

What?

He listened. She was snoring, all right. Not loudly. Just a soft, peaceful sound.

Go over anyway? he wondered.

Wake her up, she might think she's being attacked. Could give her an awful scare, especially after everything that's happened today. She'll think the creep's gotten into the tent and it's rape-time again.

Surprise, it's only me.

What'd you wake me up for?

Howard slid the zipper up, settled onto his back, and shut his eyes.

He was running through darkness, running toward screams. Need my knife, he thought. He reached down. Instead of finding his pants pocket, his hand slid over bare skin. Shit! Where are my clothes? Where's my knife?

Then he realized he had something better than his puny little Swiss Army knife. In his left hand was a machete! He brandished it and yelled, 'I'm coming!'

He was answered by shrieks of agony.

He raced around a bend. The tunnel ahead shimmered with firelight. A sweaty old hunchback smiled over his shoulder. His eyes were hidden behind sunglasses. He wore nothing but a jockstrap. In his right hand was a whip. A six-foot, living snake. He held it by its tail. The beast writhed and raised its head and bared its fangs.

'Drop it!'

Skerrit lashed out with the snake.

But not at Howard.

At the girl suspended by her hands from the tunnel's ceiling. The living whip smacked against her back. She shrieked and flinched. The fangs dug in, gouging thin bloody trails down her skin before Skerrit jerked the snake back and swung it overhead.

He grinned at Howard. 'Want to give it a try?'

'No!'

'Sure you do.' The deformed old man lumbered toward Howard, holding out the snake.

The girl strained her head sideways and looked over her shoulder.

Angela. She had tears in her eyes. She looked more beautiful than ever before.

'It's all right if you want to,' she said. 'I don't mind.'

'Besides,' Skerrit said, 'it's your turn.' He tossed the snake to Howard. It flew at him head first, mouth gaping.

A swift chop of the machete decapitated it.

'Now look what you've done!' Skerrit shouted. 'Ruined a perfectly good whipper-snapper.'

'Dirty bastard!' A downward blow split Skerrit's head and knocked his sunglasses to the ground. Howard whirled toward Angela.

She gazed over her shoulder at him. She sniffed.

'Are you all right?' Howard asked.

She nodded. 'You saved me.'

He tossed the machete onto Skerrit's corpse. He stepped up behind Angela. He caressed her back. It was slippery with sweat and blood, criss-crossed with welts and fang trails. 'Does this hurt?' he asked.

'Oh, no. It feels good.'

He kissed her wounds. He licked them. She moaned and squirmed. Moving closer, he kissed the nape of her neck and rubbed himself against her back. Her buttocks flexed, squeezing his erection.

'Make love to me,' she whispered.

'Right here? Right now?'

'Yes, yes.'

Stepping back, he swiveled her around. Snakes dangled from her breasts, fangs buried in her nipples. She stretched her mouth wide and a snake shot out and darted straight toward Howard's mouth. Another slid out of her vagina, reaching for his penis.

He gasped and jerked away and woke up breathless to find the blur of Angela's face above him. The tent was dark. His head was on her lap. She was gently stroking his hair.

'It's all right now,' she whispered. 'It's all right.'

'Oh, God,' he gasped.

'Must've been horrible for you.'

'You . . . you had snakes . . . on your breasts.'

'Snakes, huh? I wonder what Freud would have to say about that.'

'It was awful.'

'Just a nightmare. Nothing but a dream.' She lifted her sweatshirt. 'See? No snakes.'

This can't be happening, Howard thought. He wondered if he might still be dreaming. He didn't think so.

He stared up at her breasts. They looked gray in the darkness. The nipples looked black.

Angela lifted one of his hands to a breast.

He had never touched anything so smooth.

'This is all my fault,' she whispered. 'If I hadn't told you those things . . .'

'Those things don't matter,' he said. 'Maybe they do. I don't know. But . . .'

'Do you want me?'

'Oh, my God.'

She took the sweatshirt off. Still fondling the breast, Howard rubbed his cheek against the silken warmth of her belly.

She eased out from under his head. Sitting down beside him, she peeled her socks off. Howard turned onto his side. He watched as she pulled the sweatpants down her legs. He unzipped the side of his sleeping bag.

Angela slid in beside him.

She tugged his sweatshirt up. He struggled with it, got it off and tossed it aside. As Angela snuggled against him, she hooked his sweatpants down around his thighs. She worked them lower by rubbing them with her feet.

Then there were no clothes in the way and Angela was all long and slim and warm and smooth. She guided Howard onto his back. On top of him, she kissed his lips. A tongue, not a snake, slid into his mouth. He sucked it. His hands glided down her back. No welts, no blood. Only smooth, wonderful skin. He curled his hands over the small mounds of her rump, slid them down the backs of her thighs.

Her legs were resting on his, parted just a little, lightly

touching the sides of his penis. It was tight against the heat between her buttocks. She closed her legs, squeezing it. As he gasped into her mouth, her legs opened and rubbed down against his thighs. She lifted herself.

On elbows and knees above him, she caressed his mouth with her wet lips. She brushed his chest with her nipples. She stroked the tip of his penis with slippery open flesh. Then she slid down, easing him slowly into a sheath of tight, hugging heat.

Chapter Twenty-two

'Yo! How about a break?'

Chad swung around as Coreen staggered to the side of the trail. She leaned back until a boulder took the weight of her pack. Then she slipped out of the straps, made sure the pack was steady, and stepped away from it.

'Oh, man,' she muttered. She rolled her shoulders, arched her back, rubbed her neck. 'God, I hate these switchbacks. Up up up. Jeez.' She slipped the red bandanna off her head and rubbed her sweaty face with it. Chad watched her slide the wadded cloth down her neck and inside the top of her shirt. 'Why don't you take a load off? I'm sure not going anyplace for a while.'

'We won't catch up to the kids this way.'

'Tough.' She sat down on a low slab of rock and stretched out her legs.

Taking off his pack, Chad said, 'We didn't exactly get off

to an early start.' As he propped it up beside Coreen's pack, he heard a soft chuckle from behind him. 'Not that I'm complaining, or anything.'

'Better not be, buster.'

He stepped across the trail and sat down beside her. 'What a way to start the day.'

'Yes and no.'

'What's this "no" business?'

She scowled at him. 'You yucked me all up.'

He laughed. 'Comes with the territory.'

'Some of it *stays* with the territory. Not that I'm complaining, or anything.'

'Doesn't sound like it.'

'Somebody oughta dump some glue in your skivvies, see how you enjoy it.'

'Might feel good.'

Coreen smiled. 'Well, it does and it doesn't. A nice souvenir, but it's a trifle sticky.'

'There'll be a lake when we get to the top.'

'Something to strive for. How much farther, do you think?'

'Well, I'd say there's more mountain below us than above us.'

'What an optimist.' With the bandanna, she mopped away the specks of sweat under her eyes. 'I can't imagine some of those kids making it up this trail. Especially Doris.'

'Is she the chunk?' Chad asked.

'Don't be cruel. But yeah, she's the hunky one. So's Glen. But he and Keith are football players. I doubt if they had much trouble. And Lana's in good shape.'

'I'll say.'

'Jerk.' Coreen bumped him with her shoulder.

'Don't worry, she's not my type.'

'She's every guy's type.'

'Only one girl for me,' he said, and rubbed her back. Her shirt was hot and damp under his hand.

She slipped the bandanna around her head, frowned at the trail for a moment, then looked at him. 'You aren't gonna go running off on her again, are you?'

'What do you think?'

'She'd hate to wake up some morning and find you gone.'

'You don't have to worry about that.'

'I'd sure *like* to not worry about it.' She stared into his eyes. 'But I can't get it out of my head that you might be here on temporary loan. Like a library book.'

'In a way, we're all here on temporary loan.'

'I'm gonna bop you. I'm serious about this. The last time you took off, I was ruined. I felt as if I'd been abandoned by my best friend or my brother or something. But now we've gone so far beyond that.'

'There isn't a chance in hell I'll leave you again.'

'You say that now, but . . . I get this awful, empty feeling sometimes. Even when we're making love. Especially then. It's like, things won't always be this way, I'll lose you, I'll be alone again.'

'I get those same feelings.'

'Maybe they're contagious.'

He shook his head. 'They're just normal. But rare.'

'Rare for you, maybe. I've been getting them all the time since you came back.'

'Good.'

'Good, my ass. Just when I should be . . . I'm going through some of the most terrific moments in my life . . . or what *should* be . . . and then they're all messed up because I picture how it'll be without you.'

'And the same thing happens to me.'

'I didn't abandon you for five years.'

'But you'll get older. We both will. We'll die.'

'Oh, terrific. That's just what I wanted to hear. Get morbid, why don't you?'

'The thing is, it's the times when we get that sad, empty feeling that are the most precious. Because we want those times to last, to never go away, but we know they will.'

'Remember I called you an optimist? I take that back.'

'You never get that feeling when you're hungry, you know. Or cold or tired or in pain. Or when you're grieving or when you're lonely. You don't get it when you're bored or when your bank account's empty or your drain is stopped up. There are a million different ways to be miserable. And when you're that way, you never once feel any kind of ache in your heart because you know the moment is going to pass and be lost. You only get that at the best of times. It's a signal that things are going damn good.'

Coreen gazed at him. A corner of her mouth tilted upward. 'When did you turn into such a philosopher?'

'And pedant?'

'That, too.'

'Solitude. It does that to you. Living alone in the mountains. It turns you into a philosopher or a madman, one or the other. Sometimes both, maybe.'

'Let me make sure I've got this straight, OK?' Her eyebrows lifted high. 'I shouldn't be concerned about my blues. I should view them as pretty blue ribbons on my precious gifts of happiness.'

'Sums it up nicely.'

'What a crock.' With a laugh, she leaned sideways and kissed his mouth. 'But I love you, anyway. Come on, we'd better hit the trail. Life's so transitory, we may never catch up with those rats if we don't really haul some ass.'

They stood up, got into their backpacks, and resumed the hike. Chad had been leading the way, but now he slowed his pace to stay beside Coreen. They trudged up the trail in silence for a while. Then she said, 'What does the philosopher think about the institution of holy matrimony?' She gave him a playful smile, but the look in her eyes was intense.

Chad gazed at her, stunned. 'You want to get married?'

'Don't you?' she asked.

'Well . . . *sure*.'

'Me, too. Someday. When the right man comes along.'

'Huh? What about me?'

'Wouldn't want you to be left out in the cold. We'll have to find just the right gal for you. She'll have to be deep, of course – someone who can appreciate the depth of your thinking. An egghead. I don't think you'd find yourself happy, over the long run, with a mindless bimbo. However, she ought to have a certain amount of bimbotude, since you're such a sex fiend.'

'The more bimbotudinous, the better.'

'An egghead who enjoys a good fuck. What other characteristics would you want to see in your spouse?'

'I like a woman with a sense of humor.'

'A smart bimbo that cracks wise. What else?'

'She has to be beautiful.'

'Jeez, you're a tough guy to please. No wonder you're still a bachelor.'

'If I'm going to spend my life with this gal, she has to be perfect.'

'Perfect, huh? That lets out just about everyone I know. Can you think of anybody who has all that going for her?'

'Nope.'

'In that case, I guess you'll just have to go screw yourself.'

He grinned. She stuck out her tongue. 'What are you looking for in a guy?' he asked.

'Fabulous wealth.'

'Is that all?'

'Well, I like my men short, skinny, bald and dumb. Preferably at least ten years older than me.'

'I guess that leaves me out.'

'I guess that makes us even.'

'You're mean,' he said.

'Yep.'

'Do you want to marry me?'

She stopped walking. They faced each other. 'Do you mean it?' She laughed softly. 'Dumb question, huh?'

'Dumb question.'

'So this is it.'

'Yeah.'

She caught her lower lip between her teeth. Her eyes glimmered. She turned her head slowly, looking around. 'Right here on a mountainside.'

'We could wait, and I'll ask you in a nice restaurant. With soft music. And an engagement ring.'

She met his eyes. 'Here's just fine.'

'I love you.'

'I know. And I love you.'

'But?' he asked, going suddenly cold inside.

'But what?'

'I don't know. But what?'

'But we have no champagne?'

'Does that mean yes?'

'Yes. Of course it means yes.'

'Oh, man.' He stepped up close to her. They both leaned forward against the weight of their packs, and kissed.

'Dalton,' she said as they made their way up the trail. 'Coreen Dalton.'

'What are you doing?'

'Seeing what my name will sound like when we're married. Sounds good, don't you think?'

'Sounds great. Hate to mention this, though, but it's already your name.'

'Jeez, you're right. This is gonna save on a lot of paperwork. I won't have to get the name changed on my driver's license, credit cards, magazine subscriptions, letterhead . . .'

'You can't marry just anyone and get a deal like that.'

'I know, I know. This'll work out terrific.'

They came to the end of a switchback. Instead of a hairpin turn and more trail slanting up the face of the mountain, they found a level footpath that curved into a wooded pass.

'Does this mean what I hope it means?' Coreen asked.

'I think the lake should be just through those trees.'

'Fantastic.' She quickened her pace.

Chad followed, dropping back far enough to have a view of her buttocks flexing under the dirty seat of her shorts, her long slim legs striding out.

My wife, he thought. She's actually going to marry me.

It seemed unbelievable.

His first night back, when they were done making love in the hallway, he'd wondered whether she would agree to marry him. He'd told himself, then, that she probably would. And he'd grown more sure of it with every moment they spent together.

She loved him. She wanted him. If he asked her to be his wife, she would probably say yes.

Now he had asked, and she had said yes (you didn't *really* think she would), and he felt stunned and astonished.

It's too good to be true, he thought.

But it is true.

We're not married yet.

That's beside the point, he realized. What matters is that she said yes. She loves me that much. She wants to spend her life with me.

Incredible!

He followed her through the shadows. He smiled and shook his head as he walked.

Coreen's perfect. The day is perfect. Everything is perfect.

The shit has probably already been launched toward the spinning blades of the fan.

Stop it, he told himself. Everything's fine.

'Lake ahead!' Coreen called, pointing up the trail.

Chad peered into the distance and saw pale blue patches beyond the trees. 'Must be it,' he said, catching up to her.

'I almost hope the kids aren't there,' she said.

'I thought the whole point was to find them.'

'It is.'

'But you're hoping they're gone.'

'Well, we don't need to find them this instant, you know. Later today would be just fine. What would be nice for the immediate future would be a little privacy so we can have a celebration and go for a swim and things. Don't you think so?'

'Sounds great to me.'

They walked only a short distance closer to the lake before spotting a swath of red.

'What do you think that is?' Coreen asked.

'A tent, maybe.'

'Damn.'

'It might not be theirs.'

'It has to be someone's. So much for having the lake to ourselves.'

Chad took over the lead. 'Just stay close,' he said, 'and don't call out or anything. Let's find out who's here, first.'

'It must be the kids.'

'You never know till you know.'

'I'm marrying Yogi Berra.'

They approached the campsite in silence, Chad walking slowly and listening. He heard no voices, no sounds of movement. At the edge of the clearing, he halted.

Two tents, a red one and a green one. A fire circle, but no fire burning within it. Other than the tents, there was no camping gear in the area. And he saw no people.

He scanned the sparse woods around the clearing. He checked the shoreline, the surface of the lake, the wall of tumbled granite along its far side.

'What do you think?' Coreen whispered.

'Looks like you got your wish.'

'Should we check inside the tents?'

'Guess we'd better.' Gesturing for Coreen to stay behind, he hurried to the red tent. Its flaps were zippered shut. Attached by a safety pin to the zipper tab was a small sheet of paper. It looked as if it had been ripped out of a spiral notepad. 'Somebody left a message,' Chad called.

'What does it say?'

He bent closer to the paper, and read aloud. 'Dear Creep, Mess with our tents at your own risk. Their fabric has been treated with a secret substance known as KAQ, which penetrates the skin tissues and Kills Assholes Quick. That means you. Hands off or you die. Sincerely, The Bold and Fearless Six.'

'What the hell's *that* all about?' Coreen said.

'Got me. But it must've been left by your kids – "The Bold and Fearless Six".' He pulled down the zipper tab and peered between the flaps. 'Empty.' He went to the other tent and looked inside. 'This one, too.'

'No gear or anything?'

'Nothing. They must've decided it'd be easier to make the last leg of the hike without the extra weight.'

'Then they're planning to be down here again before night?'

He shook his head. 'They took their sleeping bags and everything else. I think they just figure on spending tonight under the stars.'

'Nuts. I thought maybe we could just wait for them here.'

'They'll come back eventually. All we have to do is wait long enough . . .'

'That's no good. We've gotta keep after them. But let's have some lunch first. And then I want to get cleaned up.' She swung her backpack to the ground. 'What'll it be, mister? Gorp and Kool-aid?'

'No champagne?'

'Alas.'

Chapter Twenty-three

'We found it!' Keith shouted.

'What?' Angela called up the trail to him.

'Get over here and see for yourself.'

Angela picked up her pace.

Howard hurried after her. He gasped as she stepped on a loose rock. She stumbled. Her side bumped the granite wall on her right. Though the impact didn't look like much, it was enough to make her stagger to the left. Toward the edge of the trail. Howard lurched forward, reached out and shoved the side of her pack, thrusting her away from the edge.

She leaned back against the slope. She looked stunned. She was gasping for breath. Her hands were clasped against her belly. She was shaking so hard that even the flimsy white fabric of her shorts trembled.

'Are you OK?'

She nodded.

'Jesus,' he muttered.

Bending over slightly, she rubbed her thighs. And gazed past the side of the trail. Moaning, she shut her eyes and leaned back.

'It's all right,' Howard said. 'You didn't fall.'

'So close.'

'Yeah.'

'You probably saved my life.'

'I guess so.' He looked over the edge of the trail.

No guessing about it, he thought. If she'd fallen, that would've been it.

During the past hour of their hike up Calamity Peak, the terrain had changed a lot. Before, the trail had been several feet wide, slanting gently upward in a series of switchbacks much like the trail yesterday that had taken them to Shadow Canyon Lake. It had made the hike tedious and grueling, but not especially dangerous. A fall would've been painful. Probably not fatal, though. Howard had taken comfort in the thought that if he or anyone else went over the side, the fall would be stopped fairly soon by the trail. One level down.

But they had left that area behind. Now, the trail was not much more than two feet wide. The slope below was nearly vertical, jagged with protruding rocks. He couldn't even *see* the lower level of the trail. He supposed it must be down there. Somewhere. But it certainly was no safety net like the earlier switchbacks. If Angela had fallen, that would've been it.

Feeling a little sick, he leaned back against the wall.

'Maybe that was what Butler meant about protecting A.L.,' Angela said.

'Yeah.'

'Thanks.'

Doris trudged into view around a curve in the trail. She

had her right hand against the wall to keep her steady. Her face was red and sweaty. She looked terrified.

'They found something,' Howard called to her.

'Hot damn,' she muttered.

'Thrilled as usual,' Angela whispered. 'Ready to go?'

'Are you?'

'Ready as I'll ever be.'

'Watch your step, OK?'

'You know it.'

Howard kept a hand on the side of her pack as she eased herself carefully away from the wall. She started up the trail, head down. Howard stayed far enough back to avoid tripping her, close enough to reach her – he hoped – if she should stumble again.

Suddenly, she rushed ahead.

'Angela!' he cried out. Chasing her around a bend, he realized it was fine for her to rush. The narrow trail was gone. The precipice was gone. Though the mountain loomed above them on the right, the left was now a broad, gentle slope.

You couldn't fall off it if you tried.

Howard took a deep, shaky breath, and sighed. Stepping to Angela's side, he spotted Keith and Lana near the rim of the slope. They had taken off their packs. There appeared to be a drop-off in front of them, some kind of gap with a steep rise on its other side.

Walking toward them, Howard became aware of a rushing noise. It sounded like a strong wind surging down the mountainside. But he only felt a mild breeze. By the time he and Angela joined them, the noise was a roar.

He lowered his eyes and found its source. At the bottom of the chasm, at least fifty feet below him, a stream was raging through a narrow gorge. Its water raced along, tumbling over boulders, plummeting down falls, a torrent of frothy white pounding its way downward.

Angela took hold of his hand. 'Isn't it *glorious*?'

'Yeah,' he said. He thought it look wild and dangerous. He took a step away from the edge, pulling Angela along with him.

'Is this your big discovery?' he asked Keith.

'*That* is,' Keith said. 'Over on the other side.' He pointed beyond the gap.

'What? I don't . . .'

'There! There!'

Then he saw it. Someone had left graffiti on a vertical face of a granite block above the gorge. Red paint. The big, red outline of a valentine heart speared by an arrow. Inside the heart was scrawled MARK & SUSAN.

'Mark,' Angela muttered. 'My God.'

'Butler's sign,' Keith said, grinning.

'What's the big deal?' Doris asked from behind them.

Howard turned around. Glen had caught up to Doris, and was walking at her side. 'Did Glen tell you about our session with the Ouija board last night?'

'She didn't want to hear about it,' he said. 'Or anything else.'

'Well, we got in touch with Butler,' Lana explained. 'We asked him how to find his mine, and he told us to go "up to Mark and go with heart".'

'In his usual cryptic way,' Glen said.

'It wasn't all that cryptic, after all.' Keith pointed. 'Get a load of that.'

When Glen spotted the graffiti, he said, 'I'll be damned. So where's the mine?'

'We must be close to it,' Lana said.

Doris curled her lip. 'With our luck, it's probably over there someplace.'

'If it is,' Lana told her, 'we haven't spotted it yet.'

'We're supposed to "go with heart",' Angela said. 'That

heart has an arrow through it. Maybe the arrow's pointing toward the mine.'

The shaft was piercing the heart diagonally, its tip aiming upward to the right. In that direction, the rugged wall of the mountain curved out of view. 'Over there, maybe,' Howard said.

'Good chance of it,' Lana agreed.

'Terrific,' Doris muttered.

'We'll just have to find a way to cross the stream,' Lana said. She swung up her pack. Keith held it while she slipped into its straps. Then he got into his own pack.

'We're gonna get ourselves killed,' Doris grumbled.

' "We owe God a death," ' Glen said.

'Fuck you, Falstaff.'

Lana and Keith led the way. Howard followed them, Angela close to his side, while Glen and Doris took up the rear. As they made their way along the rim of the chasm, Howard gazed over his shoulder and searched the far wall for openings. It looked very rugged on the other side. There might be a dozen mine entrances hidden among the jumbled mass of boulders. But he couldn't spot one.

'That nice, cold stream would sure feel good about now,' Glen said.

'Why don't you take a flying leap and find out?'

'Doris hasn't changed much,' Howard said, keeping his voice low. Since Doris and Glen were some distance behind him and the stream was roaring, he doubted that they would be able to make out a single word.

'She hasn't had a smile on her face all day,' Angela said.

'Guess they didn't do it.'

'Slept together, but didn't *sleep* together.'

'Too bad. Might've worked wonders on her disposition.'

'Sure improved mine,' Angela said, and smiled. 'I feel so incredible.'

Howard felt a warmth spread through his chest. 'Me, too.'

'Does it bother you that they all know?'

'I kind of like it.'

'Me, too. We don't have to hide anything, you know?'

'It was a little embarrassing at the time.'

She laughed. 'I don't think it exactly surprised them.'

'They sure surprised me.' He smiled as he remembered his shock at being awakened to find himself warm under Angela's naked body and Lana with her head inside the tent, shining her flashlight on them, saying, 'Time to rise and shine, lovebirds.'

Then Keith was sticking his head into the tent, saying, 'Thata way to go, guys. But you're gonna have to unstick yourselves and move over to Glen's tent.'

Left alone, they'd scurried out of the sleeping bag, gotten into their sweatclothes and hauled their belongings outside. Glen and Doris, bundled up, were over near the fire. 'Name the kid after me!' Glen had called.

'Don't worry about a kid,' Angela had said once they were inside Glen's tent. 'I'm on the pill.'

'I wasn't worried. But I sure wouldn't have named the kid Glen or Glenda.'

She'd laughed at that while Howard, shivering, crawled into his sleeping bag. 'Wanta come over?'

Moments later, she was inside his warm down bag, snuggling with him, hugging him tight. They were both trembling. 'How about they caught us?' she'd whispered.

'I know. God.'

'Somebody probably won five bucks.'

Angela broke into his thoughts, saying, 'It was the best night of my life.'

'Me, too,' he said, glancing over his shoulder to make sure that Glen and Doris were still out of hearing range. They were even farther back than before.

'I'm awfully glad you had that nightmare,' Angela told him. 'I heard you over there gasping and whimpering, and pretty soon I just didn't care what you thought of me. All I wanted to do was hold you. It didn't matter if you thought I was . . . damaged goods.'

'Well, I don't think that.'

'You did. And I am.'

'You're great just the way you are. And if . . . things hadn't happened to you, you wouldn't be the same person. You'd be different. You might've turned into some kind of horrible, obnoxious bitch or something.'

She shrugged. 'Could be.'

'Hell, maybe you wouldn't have ended up at Belmore, and we wouldn't even know each other.'

She took hold of his hand and squeezed it.

Lana and Keith halted, turned around and waited for the others.

'What gives?' Glen asked.

'This looks to be about as good as it gets,' Lana said. She nodded sideways at the chasm, and Howard was surprised to see how the gap had narrowed. The last time he'd looked, it had been at least fifteen feet across. Here, the space appeared to be no wider than four or five feet.

But only here. The granite flared out, extending over the gorge like half the top of a huge round table, then curved inward again. Up ahead, the gap appeared to be impassable until it bent out of sight high on the mountainside.

'You want us to jump that?' Glen asked.

'Nobody has to,' Lana told him. 'But I don't see how else we're going to get over on the other side, do you?'

Glen approached the edge and stared down. 'Shit,' he muttered, and stepped back.

'You could climb down if you want to,' Keith said.

'Get real.'

'Swim the stream, climb back up over there.'

'I guess I'd rather take my chances jumping,' Glen admitted.

'Some jump,' Keith said. 'If it was any narrower, we could *step* across.' He took a small running start, leaped, and landed well beyond the far edge. Turning around, he grinned. 'See? No sweat.'

'What do you think?' Glen asked Doris.

'I don't,' she said. She folded her arms across the bulging chest of her sweatshirt and shook her head.

Lana leaped to the other side. The weight of her pack seemed to knock her forward, and she staggered off balance for a few steps before Keith grabbed her.

With a glance at Howard, Angela said, 'Looks easy enough.'

'You want to do it?'

'I don't see much of a choice,' she said.

'There's always a choice,' Doris told her.

'It's a cinch,' Lana called from the other side.

Angela frowned toward Doris. 'What about you?'

'Don't worry about me. Nobody else does.'

'Will you be able to make it all right?'

'Why don't you stop acting all concerned and jump if you're going to?'

Sighing, Angela turned toward Howard and rolled her eyes upward. She gripped the straps of her pack. 'Too bad this isn't a parachute, huh?'

'Yeah. Hey, why don't you take it off? I'll take it across for you.'

'Chivalry in full bloom,' Doris muttered.

'I don't think it'll be a problem. And you don't need the extra weight.'

'No, really . . .'

'See you on the other side,' Angela said. She skipped away

from him, turned toward the gap, and broke into a run. Howard went sick inside as she dashed closer to the edge. Then she leaped, kicking out far with a long, slim leg.

She was airborne, dark hair streaming behind her, the shiny legs of her shorts fluttering around her thighs.

Howard saw her leading foot come down on air, saw her drop, her shorts bellowing, her hair flowing straight up. The vision of it made his stomach plummet.

No!

Her foot touched down. She stumbled. Lana and Keith grabbed her by the upper arms and steadied her. Turning around, she smiled. 'Easy,' she called.

'Not so easy to watch,' Howard called back.

Then, afraid of what might happen if he gave himself time to think about it, he dashed for the edge and jumped. *Oh Jesus, oh Jesus!* His boot pounded down on the other side, jarring his whole body. His pack slammed against him. He staggered forward into Angela's arms. She hugged him.

'You were right,' she said. 'Watching's the hard part.'

They watched Doris smirking and gesturing at Glen, apparently urging him to go first. With a shrug, he turned away from her, charged the rim of the gorge, shouted 'Geronimo!' and sprang into the air.

He made it across with plenty of room to spare, landing solidly on both feet. Turning his back to the others, he waved Doris forward. 'Just give it a good running start, you won't have any trouble at all.'

'Give my regards to Butler,' Doris called. She shrugged her pack off her shoulders, dropped it to the ground, sat down and crossed her legs.

'What are you doing?' Glen demanded.

'Getting comfortable.'

'Oh, for Godsake,' Keith muttered.

'Come on, Doris,' Glen said. 'Just jump the damn thing. You're not going to fall.'

'I *know* I'm not going to fall. I'm staying right here.'

'Why do you always have to be such a pain?'

'It's my nature,' she said, tilting her head and smiling as if performing her impression of a cherubic child.

'The hell with her,' Keith said.

Glen scowled at him. 'We can't just leave her here.'

'Why don't you stay and keep her company?'

'Oh yeah, right.'

Lana stepped past Glen and halted at the edge of the chasm. 'Look,' she said, 'we can't make you come over.'

'I think that goes without saying.'

'But do you really want to stay there by yourself?'

The girl's smile faded.

'Have you forgotten about our friendly local wildman? I mean, my God, there's no telling where he might be. What if he shows up?'

Her smile returned. It looked strained. 'I'll worry about that if it happens. Just go on and get out of here. I'm not moving.'

'Aren't you curious about the mine?' Glen asked her.

'Not in the least.'

'Christ,' he muttered. 'You've come all this way. You don't want to quit now. We're almost to the mine. We're almost *there*! Don't you want to be in on it when we find Butler's loot?'

'If you aren't there,' Keith said, 'you don't get any.'

'Cut it out,' Lana told him.

'Well, why should she?'

'Because she's one of us.'

'Not if she stays behind, she isn't.'

'And she saved my butt last night. Or doesn't that count?'

He let out a loud, hissing sigh of annoyance. 'Yeah, OK. Shit.'

Lana reached back over her shoulder. She shoved her hand in between her bedroll and the top of her pack, and pulled out the revolver.

'Good idea,' Keith said. 'Plug her.'

'I don't want it,' Doris called.

Ignoring her, Lana sprang across the chasm.

Doris looked horrified. 'Damn it! Why didn't you just *toss* the fucking thing! I don't need it anyway! What if you'd fallen? Would've been all my fault!'

If Lana said anything, Howard couldn't hear it. He watched her bend down and offer the revolver to Doris. The girl's face was red, her lips pushing out. She yanked the gun from Lana's hand.

Lana leaped once more across the gap.

'You're nuts,' Keith told her. 'She won't jump the fucking thing *once*, and you do it *twice* just to hand over our gun.'

'My gun,' Lana corrected him.

'What if *we* need it?'

Grinning, she slapped him on the shoulder. 'We've got each other.' Then she turned to face Doris. 'If there's any trouble, fire it and we'll get back here as fast as we can.'

Doris nodded. She was sitting there on the ground with her legs crossed, her head down, the revolver on her lap.

'God, she's pathetic,' Keith muttered.

'Shut up,' Lana said. 'Come on, let's find that mine.'

Chapter Twenty-four

Corie felt lazy and comfortable. She was lying on the flat surface of a rock by the shore, a towel under her back. Her eyes were shut against the glare of the sun, her knees up, her hand resting on Chad's bare hip. She didn't want to move.

But she knew they should finish here and be on their way. They'd eaten lunch. They'd made love. She still needed a quick swim to clean off before they could set off to find the kids. And if she remained this way much longer, she would probably find herself with a sunburn in places she'd never had one before.

Groaning, she sat up. Dribbles of sweat ran down her body. A thicker fluid, inside her, began to trickle slowly. She plucked the towel out from under her to keep it from getting messed.

'Ready to go in?' she asked.

'I don't think I can move.'

'You were moving pretty good a while ago.'

'I'm ruined.'

'I guess so.' She lifted his limp penis and let it fall. It flopped against his thigh. And started to grow. 'Maybe not,' she said.

'Look at my knees.'

The towel hadn't helped them much. They were red, pitted with tiny indentations from the granite.

'Poor thing.' Corie got to her own knees, wincing. 'You should've said something.'

'I'm tough.'

'Yeah.' She hovered over him and kissed each of his kneecaps. 'Better?'

'Uh-huh.'

He flinched when she kissed his penis, moaned as she tongued it into her mouth and sucked it. Corie felt a hand curl around her right breast. She felt some semen starting to roll down her thigh, tickling. She slipped her mouth off him. 'You don't seem to be ruined at all. You coming in for a swim?'

'Do I have to?' he asked, a lazy, contented smile on his face.

'Not if you don't want to.'

'I'm so comfortable. And the water's freezing.'

'That's all right. I'll just be a few minutes.' She gave his belly a gentle slap, then stood, stepped down to the shore and walked into the lake. She shuddered. The water around her feet felt like liquid ice. Gritting her teeth, she continued forward.

Chad sat up and watched her. 'How is it?' he asked.

'A wee bit chilly. Want to feel?' Grinning, she bent over, cupped up a handful of water and flung it at him. He grabbed her towel to shield himself. As she'd intended, however, the water fell short.

'Missed me.'

'Don't get cocky or I might improve my aim.'

'I wouldn't *think* of getting cocky.'

Corie waded farther out, the frigid water climbing her legs. When it was almost to her groin, she halted. Bending over slightly, she reached below the surface and rubbed her thighs clean. Then she took one more step. She hissed and flinched rigid.

'What's the matter?'

'Is steam rising?'

Chad laughed. 'I don't see any.'

Gasping and shaking, she cleaned herself. Then she took a deep breath, thought, *I don't really have to do this*, and plunged in. The jolt of cold stunned her, shot pain up the back of her neck and into her head. But as she glided through the water, the pain faded. She slipped to the surface, filled her lungs, and swam toward the middle of the lake. With every kick and stroke, she felt the chill easing its grip. Warmth seemed to be spreading down her arms and legs.

This isn't so bad, she thought. But it'll be wonderful to get out. Sprawl beside Chad on the rock and let the sun dry me.

Maybe give him a big hug, first, while I'm still wet and cold.

Breathless, she stopped swimming. She saw that she'd gone way beyond the middle of the lake. She was nearly to the far side. Treading water, she spotted a low slab of granite that jutted into the lake like a small dock.

For a moment, she considered swimming over to it. She could climb out and get warm. Give Chad something to look at.

Forget it.

Just a couple of minutes in the sun, and re-entry would be a torture.

Turning around, Corie thrust an arm high overhead and waved. She started to sink; She lowered her arm. Using it to keep herself afloat, she scanned the distant shore until she located the rock where she'd left Chad. She saw only the rock. Chad, she decided, must've gotten tired of watching and laid down flat, out of sight. Either that, or he'd wandered off.

She felt a little disappointed. She'd expected him to be watching her.

Isn't every day you get to see your fiancee skinny-dipping in an alpine lake.

With a sigh of regret, she swung herself around and leaned into the water. She arched her spine and kicked, the back of her head submerging as her torso and legs drifted to the surface. Then she went limp and floated. She closed her eyes against the sun's glare. The lake buoyed her up, lapped at her underside with slick cold tongues. It filled her ears with silence. The sun soothed her with its heat.

She felt so peaceful and languid that she didn't want to move. But she knew that she couldn't stay here.

If we didn't have to go after those damn kids . . .

We wouldn't be here at all.

We'll have to come up here again. We've got the whole summer. We'll come back to this lake, maybe spend a week or more . . .

But right now, duty calls.

Staying on her back, she began to kick. The water pushed gently against the top of her head, slid over her shoulders, flowed along her back and rump. It felt like cold silk.

We'll get there when we get there, she told herself.

Raising her head a bit, she found that she was still on course and making progress. She wondered if Chad was watching her now. She hoped so. Her body gleamed with sunlit water. The motion of the kicks was rocking her gently from side to side, swaying her breasts. In spite of the sun's warmth, her nipples were tight and jutting.

If he's watching, Corie thought, he'll probably have a boner the size of a telephone pole by the time I get to him.

Have to take care of that.

Then what, take another dip?

Problems, problems, she thought, and lowered her head again.

She continued to kick along on her back for a while, then rolled over. Still no sign of Chad. He must've dozed off, she told herself. And smiled. He would be in for a big surprise when she flopped down on top of him.

She breast-stroked toward the jutting slab. Realizing he

might hear her approach, however, she veered off to the right. She swam as silently as possible, sweeping back the water with gentle strokes, slowly spreading her legs and scissoring them together.

Don't make a sound.

She felt like a kid playing commando.

And doing a good job of it. Except for a few quiet slurping sounds, she made no noise at all as she slipped past the rock. She glanced over her shoulder. The slab was too high out of the water for her to see Chad.

Or for him to see her. Unless he sat up.

Which he didn't do.

So far, so good.

With her hands and knees, she found the rock and gravel of the lake bottom. She eased her way forward, pushing herself up. Water spilled down her body, streaming and dripping. But not very loudly. Chad still didn't sit up and look at her.

Got it made.

She crawled out of the water and made her way to the side of a small, blocky boulder. There, she rose to a squat and turned to see Chad.

He was there on the slab, all right. Sprawled out motionless on his back. Spread-eagled. He had draped the towel over his face to block out the sunlight. He looked as if he must be baking. His skin gleamed with sweat.

This is almost too cruel, Corie thought as she crept toward him. But she was grinning.

Then she rushed, eager to reach him before the sun could warm her ice-cold skin. She bounded onto the rock, dropped to her knees between his legs, and keeled forward. She thrust out her hands to catch herself so she wouldn't crush him. Much. Her wet body slapped against him.

He didn't flinch. He didn't cry out.

He just lay there motionless, his skin hot and slippery under her.

Corie felt her heart lurch.

'Chad?'

She flung the towel away from his face.

His eyes were shut, his mouth drooping open. The hair above his right ear was matted flat with blood, and a thin stream of it trickled along the granite.

'*Yes-yes-yes-yes-yes!*'

Corie gasped and thrust herself up and thought, *What's going on? This can't be! We're alone!*

Alone except for the man standing ten feet in front of her. Looked as if he'd stepped off the page of a muscle magazine. Hairless, shiny, sunglasses on his face, naked except for a thin band slanting down from his hips to a bulging black pouch. Hissing '*Yes-yes*' as he pitched a rock at Corie.

She hurled herself sideways. The rock nicked the rim of her ear. She hit the slab, rolling, and toppled off. Her back smacked the lake. Even as she submerged, she flipped herself over. She clawed the bottom. Her right hand found a clump of granite. She grabbed it and lunged up, staggering in the knee-deep water.

'*Yes-yes-yes!*'

He was charging down the shore, rushing straight at her. Instead of pumping to help him run, his arms were reaching for her. Huge arms, corded and bulging. The muscles of his mammoth body flowed and bounced.

Corie hurled the rock.

It clipped a corner of his sunglasses and tore them from his face. His pale blue eyes looked cheery and mad.

She whirled away from him and dived, hitting the water flat, kicking and stroking as hard as she could, thinking, *Gotta move! Gotta go! This is crazy! Where'd he come from? Go! Come on! What'd he do to Chad? Oh Jesus Jesus Jesus! Hope he can't swim. Some kind of fucking maniac! What does he want with me? Don't find out, don't find out. Go go go! Waiting for me. He was* waiting *for me!*

Something clutched her right ankle.

Something? His *hand!*

It started dragging Corie backward.

No!

She smashed the water with both arms. She squirmed and twisted. She tried to kick at his hand with her free foot. And he grabbed it.

Now he had both her feet, and she knew it was all over.

Just beginning.

She kept struggling, trying to jerk free, trying to grab the water and stop her swift backward slide. But the icy liquid kept rushing up her body.

He suddenly gave her a quick pull that forced water into her nostrils. As she blew it out, she realized he had let go.

Move it! Move it!

She beat the surface and kicked.

Kicked once with each leg before he caught her ankles again.

His grip felt different this time.

He'd reversed it?

Before she could wonder why, her legs were hoisted into the air. From mid-thigh to head, she swept downward through the water. She stretched her arms. Her hands jammed the bottom. She grappled among the rocks, seeking a weapon. But she was being pulled along too fast. Pulled toward shore.

The level of the lake dropped rapidly like a cold garment sliding up her body, baring more and more of her. Her lungs burned for air. But she knew she would soon be able to breathe. The surface was already halfway up her ribcage. Then she felt warm air against the undersides of her breasts.

Good enough!

She bucked hard, bending at the waist. Water surged over

her face. A moment later, she broke the surface, gasping and blinking.

He was holding her feet up higher than his shoulders, grinning down at her like a crazed bully hoping to shake coins from the pockets of a kid who had no pockets.

Still lunging upward, Corie clamped her fingernails into the solid flesh of his rump. She tugged herself at him, driving her forehead toward his groin.

His knee shot up and smashed against her shoulder. The blow knocked her swinging backward. Her head went under. And stayed under. He was holding her just high enough so that the surface of the lake lapped against the tops of her shoulders. Corie held her breath.

He isn't going to drown me, she told herself. He'll let me up pretty soon.

She began to ache for air.

She remained completely motionless, waiting, staring at the man's blurred, sunlit body through several inches of water.

I'll kill him!

Her heart felt like a sledge hammer pounding thunder through her body. She had fire in her lungs.

Let me up, you bastard!

Enough!

She curled herself toward the surface. The man drove her straight down by the ankles, ramming her at the bottom. She flung her arms across the top of her head. Just in time. Something near the bottom struck her right forearm.

A moment later, she was hoisted high.

'You tried to hurt me,' the man said. Frowning, he gave her a shake. 'Don't ever try to hurt me or I'll make you dead.'

Corie sucked air into her lungs, wheezing.

'I don't want to make you dead. You wouldn't stay pretty.'

He turned around. Carrying Corie upside-down in front of him, he waded ashore.

Chapter Twenty-five

Howard was sitting on a throne of granite, feet dangling, Angela leaning back between his knees while he massaged her shoulders.

'I sure hope nobody's in there,' she said.

He looked at the mine entrance a few yards in front of them, and felt a mixture of excitement and dread. 'Me, too. Just a fabulous treasure.'

'Butter *said* he'd meet us at the mine. Remember? Just before Dr Dalton's friend showed up at the door.'

'Don't worry about it. I'll protect you.'

Howard hunched over, pressing his lips against her soft damp hair and sliding his hands down until they cupped her breasts. He squeezed them gently through her T-shirt.

Squirming, she murmured, 'Not right now, OK?'

'Nobody's here.'

'Maybe and maybe not.'

Howard returned his hands to her shoulders. Twisting around, he spotted Glen at the top of the out cropping, his back to them as he kept watch for Lana and Keith. 'Glen's looking the other way. And even if he turns around, he won't be able to see much.'

'All the same . . .'

'Afraid Butler might be peering out at us?'

As he felt Angela shrug, he wished he hadn't said that. He lifted his gaze to the door-sized hole in the granite wall. The light from outside reached only a few feet into the mine, revealing a rough gray floor of rock. Someone *might* be lurking inside, just beyond the dim spill of light. Staring out at them.

A chill crawled up his back. The skin on the nape of his neck went tight and prickly.

'Nobody's in there,' he said.

'Don't count on it.'

'Hey, come on. I'm starting to get the creeps.'

Angela patted his shins, then stroked them. He saw her head lower. 'You do have goosebumps, did you know that?'

'I had a sneaky suspicion.'

She rubbed his legs more vigorously. 'I'll make them go away,' she said. 'It's too bad we don't have the gun. Maybe they'll come back with it. For that matter, maybe Doris'll be with them.'

'I don't think they would've gone all the way back there.'

'It isn't really so far. Not from where we left the packs.'

'Yeah, but they're not going to bother with her. They want to get back here and explore the mine. They'll just grab their flashlights and . . .'

'Here they come,' Glen called from his perch on the outcropping. He started to climb down.

Angela gave Howard's legs a quick squeeze, then stepped away. He hopped to the ground. They watched Glen descend into the shadows of the narrow gorge. Near the bottom, he leaped from a boulder and landed with a jolt. 'All set for fun and games?' he asked.

'Maybe Doris had the right idea,' Angela said.

'You're not gonna woos out on us, are you?'

She shook her head. 'I've come this far.'

'Good gal. Besides, we might need you in there. Butler says you're the one who'll lead us to the loot.'

'She got us to the mine,' Howard pointed out.

Glen reared back his head, doubling his chin. 'Hey, I'm the guy that found it.'

'It was Angela's idea to go in the direction of that arrow.'

'Yeah.' Nodding, Glen said, 'Think that was all Butler meant?'

'Who knows what he ever means?'

'True. The bastard talks in riddles.'

A corner of Angela's mouth turned up. 'You'd better be careful what you say about him. We might be meeting him in a few minutes.'

Glen laughed, but it sounded a little nervous. He eyed the mine entrance. 'If he's in there, he's dead. Right? He's been communicating with a Ouija board, so he's gotta be dead.'

'Who knows?' Howard said.

'Come on, man. It's common knowledge. You use the damn things for talking with spirits. Butler's beyond the veil, over there on the other side, all that crap.'

'Hope so.'

'He said he'd meet us at the mine,' Angela said.

'He probably meant it figuratively. Anyway, if he *is* in there and he's not a stiff, there's five of us and one of him.' Glen patted the knife sheathed on his hip. 'He'd better not try anything unless he likes the taste of cold . . .'

'Ready to do some exploring?' Lana asked, striding through the gap at the end of the broad passageway. Keith was hurrying along behind her. They both looked breathless and sweaty.

Lana carried a flashlight in one hand. Looped over her right shoulder was a coil of rope – the line that she'd stretched from tree to tree, back at camp that morning, to dry her clothes in the sunlight while they prepared breakfast. The coil pulled at her shirt, spreading its front enough for Howard to see the top of her breast, a dusky sheen against the stark white of her bra. The shirt was unbuttoned, held together by a loose knot just below her breasts, leaving her bare to the waistband of her shorts. The shorts hung lower on one hip than the other, dragged down by the weight of the hatchet dangling from her belt.

'Planning to chop some wood?' Glen asked.

'Thought we . . . might need a weapon.' Howard watched her chest rise and fall as she gasped for air. 'Never know . . . what we might run into. Brought some rope, too.' She patted the coil, sending a little shimmer down the slope of her breast. 'Just in case,' she added.

'You didn't happen to pick up the gun?' Angela asked.

She shook her head. 'I saw Doris, though. She's still sitting there. Reading a book.' Lana pointed the flash-light at her face and thumbed its switch. A faint disk of brightness lit her chin, moved up her lips and nose, and swept from eye to eye. She switched it off. 'I'd like to've gotten the gun back from her. Couldn't do it, though. She'd be defenseless.'

'She'd have her mouth,' Keith pointed out.

'Quit it,' Lana said. She took a deep breath. 'OK, I guess I'm ready. Everyone else ready?'

They all looked at each other.

'I'll take the lead,' Lana said.

'Good idea,' Keith said. 'Ladies first.'

'You stick close to me.' She pulled the hatchet out of her belt and handed it to him. 'Stay ready with that, but make sure you don't whack any of *us*.'

'Who, me?'

'Just be careful with it. Glen, why don't you take up the rear? Give him your flashlight,' she told Keith.

They followed her to the mouth of the mine. There, she halted and turned on her flashlight again. Howard watched its beam sweep through the darkness. The tunnel looked as if it had been chiseled straight into the mountainside. But only for about thirty feet.

'I don't see any loot,' Keith muttered.

Neither did Howard. All he saw were the rough walls and ceiling, some rubble on the floor, and what appeared to be a dead end. There were no support beams, but he supposed that a mine bored into solid rock didn't need them.

'Maybe we'll have to dig for it,' Lana said.

'Right. A buried treasure. Shit. Maybe it's still in the *walls* – like a vein of gold – and we're supposed to whack it out a piece at a time. Butler should've warned us to bring along our picks and shovels.'

'We might have the wrong mine,' Glen said. 'If prospectors were working this area, there could be some others nearby . . .'

'Let's check it out, anyway,' Lana said.

Crouching slightly, she stepped through the opening. Keith followed, holding the hatchet low at his side. Though Angela had plenty of headroom, she ducked as she entered. Howard went in after her.

The mine wasn't chilly, as he'd expected. Instead, its stale air was hot and dry. Heavy. Stifling.

He took only a few steps before the light from outside faded. He could see nothing except the dim, pale back of Angela's T-shirt. He reached forward and put a hand on it.

'Who turned off the fuckin' air-conditioning?' Keith said.

Behind Howard, Glen's flashlight came on. Its beam shifted from wall to wall, then lowered, casting its glow along the rough gray floor. It skidded from side to side as if searching for a way past Howard's legs to light the area ahead for Angela. 'Is that helping?' he whispered.

'A lot,' Angela said. 'Thanks.'

'Looks like we're in luck,' Lana said. Her voice reverberated through the tunnel. 'It doesn't stop, it turns.'

'Terrific,' Glen muttered.

'Hey, daylight.' Keith's voice.

A moment later, Lana said, 'Uh-oh.'

'What the hell?' From Keith.

'I'll be . . . *shit*!' Lana.

'Oh, man!' Keith.

Glen's beam shot to the side, lighting the corner of the wall just in front of Angela. She took another step, then turned her head toward the passageway, gasped and lurched back against Howard's hand.

'What *is* it?' Glen blurted. He shoved against Howard, trying to squeeze by.

'Quit it!'

'Let me . . .' He shouldered Howard out of the way, sidestepped past Angela, and lunged around the bend. 'Oh, my *God*! Let's get out of here!'

'Cool it,' Lana said. 'Just cool it.'

'Never seen a stiff before?' Keith asked.

Howard's stomach went cold. He wrapped an arm across Angela's shoulders, swung his head to the right, and saw the others. Glen, just beyond the turn, stood rigid in a gray spill of light from above. At his feet were the remains of a campfire: a pile of ashes and charred wood and bones. Someone, Howard realized, must've been living here – and eating small animals.

Lana and Keith stood close together a few yards farther up the tunnel. On the other side of a rumpled blue sleeping bag that was spread out beside the dead fire. On the other side of the skeleton sitting upright beside the bag.

Lana and Glen both had their flashlights aimed at it.

The skeleton sat with its back and head resting against the wall, hands folded over its pelvis, fleshless legs stretched out.

At least it's not gross, Howard thought, fighting the cold numbness that seemed to be flowing outward from his stomach. Could've been worse. Not a rotting corpse. Just a skeleton.

A dead person.

'Jesus,' he muttered.

'It must be Butler,' Angela whispered.

Glen stepped over the legs, apparently in a hurry to join

up with Lana and Keith. 'Hey, what?' He kept his flashlight aimed at the space between their bodies. They moved farther apart.

'It's the rest of his stuff,' Lana explained, shining her own light onto the scattered gear behind her.

'Who's stuff?' Glen asked. 'The dead guy's?'

'Who knows?' Keith said.

'Come on,' Howard said. Taking Angela's hand, he led her around the campfire. He stepped on the sleeping bag. Its thickness was springy under his shoes. A down-filled mummy bag. 'Pretty good stuff,' he said.

'Maybe this is our big jackpot,' Keith said.

'Butler's loot?' Lana asked.

'We oughta go through all this,' Glen said.

'Yeah,' Keith said. 'Might be a million bucks in the backpack.'

'Could you shine one of those flashlights our way?' Howard asked.

'Sorry.' Lana turned around and trained her light on the skeleton's legs.

'Thanks,' Howard said, stepping over them. When he was clear, he looked back.

Angela halted, let go of his hand and crouched beside the legs. 'Did you notice this?'

'What?' Howard asked.

'Lana? Everyone? Come here. Look at this.'

The others returned, gathering close to the skeleton and shining the flashlights on it. Angela pointed at its knees. They were wrapped with strips of leather.

'Yeah, so?' Keith asked.

'And here, and here.' Angela pointed to the wrists and elbows. They were bound the same as the knees. 'And look.' On both sides of the mandible were shoelaces that tied it to the skull.

'Oh, man,' Glen muttered.

'It didn't do this to itself,' Lana said. She lighted one of the hands as Angela picked it up by the wrist. The collection of bones rattled quietly. From what Howard could see, the hand was complete.

He grimaced as Angela lifted it close to her face. She gazed at it, her nose wrinkling. 'All these finger bones and . . . they're tied together with hair.' She set the hand down gently, got to her feet, and rubbed her hand across the belly of her T-shirt.

'We're looking at somebody's hobby,' Keith said.

'And his sleeping bag is right beside it,' Lana pointed out.

'Yeah. Speaks highly of his state of mind, huh?'

'I wonder if he's the creep who's been jumping us,' Angela said.

Howard felt his bowels squirm.

'I wouldn't be at all surprised,' Lana said.

'Sounds like just his speed,' Keith said. 'The nut lives with a stiff in an abandoned mine and makes forays down the mountain to attack campers. A wild and crazy guy.'

'This is probably one of his victims,' Glen muttered.

'It looks like it's been here for years,' Lana said.

'Maybe he's *been* here for years,' Keith said.

'He didn't look much older than twenty. I don't know that he's old enough to have killed this person.'

'Who knows? How long does it take to turn into a skeleton?'

'You got me.'

'It could've been here when he moved in,' Glen suggested.

Keith let out a nervous chuckle. 'Yeah, and he liked the idea of having a buddy. Maybe the two of them decided it'd be nicer around here if they had a babe.'

'If this is Butler . . .' Angela began.

'Yeah. He's the one who lured us up here.'

'But he said he didn't bring us here because of the guy,' Howard pointed out.

'He might've lied,' Angela said. 'Maybe there never was any loot, and he just used it as bait so they could lay their hands on us.'

'Let's get out of here,' Glen said.

'Not till we've checked the place out.' Lana turned around and aimed her light at the heaps of clothes and gear. 'We'll go through his stuff, then search the rest of the mine. I came here for Butler's loot. The least I'm gonna do is *look* for it.'

'It's not worth dying for.'

'Nobody's keeping you here.'

'Like I'm *sure* I want to stay by myself.'

'You could go back and stay with *el chubbo*,' Keith told him.

'Fuck you.'

'Fuck *you*.'

'Cut it out!' Lana snapped. 'Look, we've been in here for five minutes or something. The bastard hasn't attacked us yet. That means one of two things. Either he's not around, or he's decided to leave us alone.'

'Either way could change damn fast,' Glen said.

'So let's look through his stuff fast.' Lana hurried over to it, and the others followed. She gave her flashlight and the coil of rope to Keith. 'Keep watch,' she told him. She toed a bundle, knocking a wadded blanket off the top, revealing a mound of gray fur. She crouched, poked the fur, and picked it up. A coat. It looked like a patchwork of animal skins: squirrels and coyotes. She sniffed it. 'This is what he was wearing last night when he grabbed me.'

'Are you sure?'

'Yes, I'm sure.' She tossed it aside and lifted a pair of pants. Their tops appeared to be regular blue-jeans. But the denim legs were gone. In their place were bulky legs of skin attached to the fabric with leather thongs. Lana stuck her arm into one of them. 'Fur-lined,' she said. 'These must be the leather pants you told us about,' she said, looking over her shoulder at Angela.

'Probably are.'

She flung them. Upright on the rock floor was a pair of high-top hiking boots. She turned them upside-down and shook them. Nothing fell out.

She crawled over to the backpack, pulled it toward her and up-ended it. Out tumbled a towel, a bar of soap, an injector razor, a pair of leather sandals, a leather belt, several pieces of rope and a plastic bottle of insect repellant, followed by an avalanche of brassieres and panties that buried the other items. 'What the hell?' Lana muttered.

'This is one weird puppy,' Keith said. He nudged the colorful array of undergarments with the toe of his boot. 'Anything of yours in there?'

'I think he's gone beyond panty raids,' Lana said.

'Yeah. Nowadays, he's after what's *in* the suckers.'

She set the pack down on top of the pile, opened one of its side pockets, and reached in.

'Careful what you touch,' Keith said.

She brought out a handful of matchbooks, dropped them, and dug deeper into the pocket. She withdrew a Band-Aid tin and a toothbrush. She flipped up the lid of the tin. 'Just bandages.' She emptied her hand, reached again into the pocket, and came out with a leather billfold.

'All right!'

'This might be interesting,' she said. Keith bent over, holding the flashlight close to the top of the wallet as Lana opened it. She spread the bill compartment.

'By God, it's our loot!'

'Knock it off,' Glen said.

Lana flicked through the bills. There weren't many of them. 'Twenty-six bucks,' she announced.

'We're filthy rich. Thank you, Butler!'

'You're a riot,' Glen said.

'Here's his driver's license.'

'No shit.' Keith squatted down beside Lana. 'He had hair then.'

Looking over her shoulder, Howard saw the card inside a clear plastic holder. The small, color photo showed a man with a broad face and curly blond hair. After a glimpse of the license, his eyes were drawn to the glossy slopes of Lana's breasts. He watched a trickle of sweat slide down the side of one and melt into the edge of her bra. Then a drop of sweat fell off his nose and splashed the top of her other breast. 'Sorry,' he muttered. Apparently unconcerned, she brushed it away with her free hand. Howard stepped back.

'It might not be him,' Lana said a few moments later.

'It's him, all right. Look at that neck.'

'Hubert Orson Elliot.'

'Name like that, no wonder he became a hermit.'

'A San Francisco address.'

Howard lifted his shirt. As he used its front to wipe the sweat from his face, Angela reached around behind him and caressed the bare skin above his hip. He wondered if this was the same hand that had held the wrist of the skeleton. And he realized it was.

And he realized he didn't really care.

Her hand felt good on his side.

She's mine. She'll still be mine after we're out of here, after all this scary mess is just a memory.

If we get out of here alive.

He let his shirt fall. Her hand stayed under it, roaming slowly up and down. He put his arm across her back and rubbed her side and wished he hadn't snuck those peeks at Lana's breasts.

'Look there,' Keith said. 'The thing expired last year.'

'Maybe he got an extension.' Lana turned the card over. 'Nope. And you have to renew every four years, so . . .'

'He apparently hasn't been a crazy panty-snatching hermit forever. That's good to know, huh?'

Lana looked through the rest of the wallet, then dropped it.

'Hey, let's at least grab the money.'

'Forget it. I'm not a thief.'

'Well, shit. The fucker jumped you last night.'

'That doesn't make it right to steal from him.'

'It isn't enough to bother with, anyway,' Glen said.

'You're just scared it'll piss him off. Tell you what. Us guys'll split the cash, and you gals help yourself to some nice bras and panties.'

'Hilarious,' Glen said.

Keith picked up the wallet.

'Don't!' Lana snapped. 'I mean it.'

'Hey, we came up here for loot. This is loot. Right where Butler said we'd find it.'

'This isn't what he meant,' Angela said, her fingers pressing into Howard's side.

'Well, it sure ain't much, but . . .'

'Butler said I'm the one who would lead us to it, didn't he? Well, I'm telling you, this isn't it.'

Keith tossed the wallet into the pack and stood up. 'OK, where is it?'

'I don't know yet.'

'Great.'

'But I think we should search the rest of the mine.'

'Yeah,' Howard said. 'The treasure might be farther in. We need to explore the whole place.'

'We're not done here, yet,' Lana said, reaching into the pocket on the other side of the pack. 'Glen, why don't you go over and make sure there's nothing in the sleeping bag? The rest of you, help me out. There's plenty of junk right here that needs to be checked before we do any more exploring.'

'My hands are full,' Keith said. He held them out as if displaying the flashlight and hatchet, the coil of rope looped over his left wrist. 'If it's all the same to you, I'll stand guard and give Hubert Orson Elliot forty whacks if he comes bopping along.'

Chapter Twenty-six

Chad opened his eyes. Sunlight came in, stabbing his brain. Groaning, he squeezed them shut.

He didn't know where he was, but he wondered if he'd been drinking last night. Must've gotten really smashed to have a hangover this bad.

His pounding head felt as if it might explode. Maybe it already had.

He raised his arms, planning to squeeze it. And flinched when his right hand met a raw lump above his ear. He jerked his hand away, then brought it back carefully. The knob, matted over with stiff, gooey hair, felt the size of a golf ball. Fingering his way through the hair, he touched a small gouge. Then he brought the hand in front of his face and opened his eyes enough to squint. His fingertips were stained red, speckled with rust-colored specks. Blood. Some dry, the rest nearly dry.

Did I fall? What . . .?

He started to sit up. Swirling with dizziness, he saw that he was lying naked on top of a rock. Before he could wonder much about it, his stomach turned. He flung himself over and got to his hands and knees. The vomit erupted. He heaved, spasms jolting his body, jamming his head with pain.

When he was done, he sank back onto his haunches and gasped for breath. He saw a towel on the rock just beyond the spreading mess. Bracing himself up with one hand, he reached out and grabbed it.

Pink.

Isn't mine.

Whose is it?

As he settled back and rubbed his face with it, he realized that the towel must belong to Coreen.

Coreen.

I was here with Coreen. Looking for her students. We camped out last night, and today we. . .

Chad's heart started sledging, pumping agony into his head.

. . . made love here, that's why I'm . . .

A clump of ice seemed to drop into his stomach.

. . . *Where is she?*

The lake. Went in to clean up, to swim.

Chad flung the towel down and struggled to his feet. As he turned toward the lake, he lost his balance. He staggered, flapping his arms, and managed to steady himself before stumbling off the edge of the granite slab.

Shading his eyes with both hands, he scanned the ruffled blue surface of the lake. It glinted specks of sunlight that hurt his head. He felt himself swaying a little. But he kept studying the lake and its desolate rocky shores.

Any second, he would spot Coreen swimming in the distance.

Or maybe perched on a boulder on the other side, sunning herself.

But he didn't spot her.

And he pictured her down below, turning slowly in the currents, her skin pale blue in the cold rays of sunlight slanting down through the water, her hair flowing lazily around her face.

'Coreen!' he shouted, blasting pain through his head. 'Coreen!'

No answer came. He heard only the hiss of the mountain breezes, bird cries and the soft lapping of the lake as it washed against his stone platform.

I was out cold, he told himself. Maybe she went to get help for me.

Why was I out cold? What hit me?

I stood up to watch her, and slipped?

Or somebody clobbered me? Who? There's nobody . . . nobody we *saw*.

Coreen wouldn't have hit me. No. Not on purpose, anyway. Some kind of accident?

He called out her name three more times, cringing with pain at each shout. Then he turned his back to the lake. He scanned the shoreline, the campsite, the shadowed woods around the clearing. Nothing moved.

He made his way carefully to the edge of the rock, stepped down, and trudged up the gradual slope to the campsite. Both backpacks were still propped against a log by the fire circle. As he walked toward them, he saw that his clothes were draped over the top of his pack. Coreen's clothes were gone.

She hadn't drowned! She must've come back here and gotten dressed and . . .

No. He remembered, and his elation died. He was the one who had stripped down here by the fire and left his clothing on the pack. Coreen had gone into the red tent. She'd come out wearing nothing but the towel wrapped around her waist.

Chad ran to the tent, wincing as each footfall pounded pain into his head. He swept a flap aside. The tent was crimson inside with tinted sunlight. On the floor were her boots and socks, her shorts with a corner of black panties hanging out through the waist hole, her bra draped across her rumpled plaid blouse. Her red bandanna, still knotted to form a headband, formed a hoop around one of the bra's flimsy, collapsed cups.

At the sight of her bandanna, Chad felt his throat go tight.

She's OK, he told himself. She's gotta be OK.

She's gone.

She wouldn't have wandered away naked.

She has extra clothes in her pack. Maybe . . .

God, what happened *to her?*

Chad ducked into the tent. The trapped air was hot. Squatting, he picked up Coreen's bandanna. It still felt a little damp. He squeezed it tight, and some moisture dribbled between his fingers. Her sweat. He pressed his fist to his mouth as his vision went blurry with tears.

'I'll find you,' he murmured. 'Damn it, I'll find you.'

He took the bandanna outside with him. He wiped his eyes with it. After the heat inside the tent, the breeze chilled his wet skin. He stood motionless, listening, gazing through the shadows at the sunlit lake. Trembling. Thinking.

She went swimming. She didn't come back here for her clothes. Even if she put on some fresh things from her pack, she would've gotten into her boots if she planned to hike any distance. So . . .

Maybe she was swimming around, got too cold, and climbed ashore somewhere to rest. And fell asleep. She might be sleeping right now. Stretched out on a sunny rock. She just didn't hear me yelling for her.

She'll show up any minute.

No she won't, he thought. She isn't just taking a snooze.

Whatever happened to her, it *has* to be connected somehow with what happened to me, Too much of a coincidence, otherwise.

He suddenly realized that she hadn't drowned, either.

Again, that would've been too much of a coincidence.

I fall and knock myself out, Coreen just happens to get a cramp or something and go down?

No way.

Chad felt a little relief. But not much.

Because, if Coreen hadn't found him unconscious and rushed off to seek help (and that seemed awfully unlikely), he could think of only one way to connect his injury with her disappearance.

He hadn't fallen down. Someone had crept up on him while he sat on the rock watching her swim. Crept up and bludgeoned him. To take him out of the picture. So the attacker could go after Coreen.

He realized that his hands had worked open the bandanna's knot. He stretched the cloth taut, wrapped it around his head, and tied it.

Then he raced for his pack.

A guy, he thought. Had to be a guy. Maybe more than one. Spied on us. Wanted her. Wanted to grab her, rape her.

Maybe she got away.

She isn't *here*, that's for damn sure.

As fast as he could move, Chad got dressed and into his boots. With fluttering hands, he opened a side pocket of his pack. He found his first-aid kit, dug out a tin of aspirin, and downed four pills with water from his canteen. From the pocket on the other side, he removed his sheath knife. He slipped it onto his belt, and took off running as he fastened the buckle.

They didn't get her here.

(Unless her body's just out of sight in the trees – or in the green tent. No!)

They didn't get her.

She made a break for it. Maybe hit the lake. That'd be the smart thing to do. If they can't swim, she's got it made. If they *can* swim, she's probably faster. She's a hell of a swimmer.

Chad halted at the edge of the lake. Swiveled his head. Nobody in the water. Nobody along the far shore. But portions of the lake and shoreline were out of sight along the near side, and there might be hidden coves or inlets.

He went to the right. Though tempted to run, he forced himself to hold back. He walked fast. He scurried up the mounds and blocks of rock as he encountered them. But never too quickly. As he moved along, he peered down at the shallows of the lake. He searched nooks and recesses along the shore. He gazed into the shadowy woods.

He imagined finding her crouched in the water, hiding among rocks close to shore, looking up at him with terror in her eyes, then sighing, saying, 'Thank God it's you. Are they gone? Where are they?'

He imagined finding her sprawled face down in a sheltered and sunny space among the boulders, himself rushing to her side, turning her over. And waking up, Coreen smiles at him and says, 'Did I fall asleep?'

He also imagined turning her over and finding a horrible slash across her throat.

He imagined finding her among the trees, barely visible in the distance, half buried as if she'd sunken into the soft mat of pine needles, the skin of her back ghastly white in the shadows.

He imagined finding her among the trees, struggling as one man held her down and another tried to mount her and Chad raced at them silently, drawing his knife.

He did not imagine finding Coreen partway up the side of the mountain beyond the other end of the lake, trudging up a switchback, followed by a giant of a man who appeared to be as naked as she was. A giant hanging onto her hair with one hand. A giant with a long, gleaming blade in the other.

But that was what Chad found after he climbed to the top of a high outcropping near the end of the lake. Though he'd known the climb would be exhausting and painful and time-consuming, he'd realized that the summit would provide him with a full view of the lake and its surroundings. And so, full of hope and dread, he'd made his way up.

From his perch at the top, he had looked down into the lake. He had scanned its shores, its little coves, the steep slope of jumbled granite that he would have to cross when he continued his way around the lake, the wooded area surrounding the campsite on the other side. He'd seen the red and green of the tents. He'd seen the low slab of rock where he and Coreen had made love, where he'd found himself unconscious. And near the far end of that shore, he'd seen a stream partially hidden by the trees, a stream emptying its run-off from Calamity Peak into the lake.

He had gazed at the mountain. That's where her students must've gone. Searching for their damn treasure.

Frowning at the rugged wall of the mountain, Chad had wondered if he should go up there and try to find the kids. Get them back down, and they could help him search for . . .

Coreen.

There she is!

Someone. It *must* be her!

Trudging up a switchback, followed by a giant.

Chapter Twenty-seven

Following Angela, Howard stumbled out of the dense heat and darkness. Though the area in front of the mine entrance was now in shadow, the daylight stung his eyes and made him squint. The air felt cool, fresh, wonderful.

Glen, who'd been in the lead, flopped onto his back.

Angela stayed on her feet, but bent over and clasped her knees. Her black hair was matted to her head, and hung in strings past her face. Her T-shirt, pasted to her back, was nearly transparent. Her skin looked pink through the fabric. The thin straps of her bra showed. So did the bumps of her spine and the curving bones of her ribcage.

Seeing the bones reminded Howard of the skeleton.

He felt very glad he had left *that* behind. With any luck, he would never have to see it again.

He staggered past Angela, sank to his knees, turned around and leaned back against the base of the rocks across from the mine entrance. He stretched out his legs.

And realized he was sitting in a position much like the skeleton.

He crossed his ankles to take away the similarity. His legs felt greasy and hot inside his corduroy pants.

Keith stepped out of the mine. He still carried the hatchet. He had looped the coil of rope over his head, and it hung like a necklace against his bare chest. His shirt, tucked under his belt, draped the front of his jeans like a loincloth. He plucked it out and mopped his face with it. After a couple of sidesteps away from the entrance, he settled back until his rump met the nearly vertical slope.

Lana came out, switching off her flashlight. Her face was

dripping. Her blonde hair clung to the sides of her head in tight, dark curls. She had followed Keith's example and removed her blouse during their long search through the tunnels. It hung at her side, its collar tucked under her belt at the hip. Her bra was very white against her tanned skin. She was dripping with sweat. Though the bra looked sodden, Howard found that he couldn't see through it. He liked what he could see, however, and watched as she joined Keith, leaning against the slope. She tilted back her head and shut her eyes. She was gasping for air. She licked her lips. 'Should've brought some water along,' she said.

'I'd like to be down at the lake right now,' Glen said. He was still stretched out on his back, but his head was lifted, hands cupped behind it, apparently so he could enjoy his view of Lana. 'Wouldn't you just love to jump in right now?'

'The stream's a lot closer,' Keith said.

'Getting down to it would be a trick.'

'There's probably an easy way down. It must be where Hubert gets his water.'

'We've got plenty down at the packs,' Lana said. She stuffed the flashlight into a front pocket of her shorts. 'Maybe one of us . . . oughta go down for a couple of canteens. Then we can look around for another mine.'

'I don't think there *is* another mine,' Angela said. She was standing up straight, now, hands on her hips. 'I mean, I think this is the one Butler meant.' She stretched, bending herself backward like a bow. 'Don't you think so?' She looked around at the others.

'We didn't find anything,' Glen pointed out.

'Shit,' Keith said, 'we *found* plenty.'

'Gimme a break.' Glen grimaced, then sat up.

'There wasn't any treasure,' Lana said. 'Or if it's there, it's too well hidden. If that's the right mine, it's a bust.'

'But don't you think the skeleton was probably Butler?' Angela asked.

'Who knows?' Glen said. 'Who cares? There wasn't any loot.'

'If that's Butler,' Keith said, 'I oughta go back in and give him a kick in the chops. Put us through all this shit for nothing.'

Angela wandered over to Howard. She sat down beside him and crossed her legs.

'What does everyone think we should do?' Lana asked.

'What we *don't* want to do,' Glen said, 'is be here when Hubie shows up.'

'I'll second that,' Keith said.

'So . . . should we just give it up and go back down to the lake?'

'Sounds good to me,' Glen said.

'We'll have come all this way for nothing.'

'Oh,' Keith said, 'but it's sure been fun.'

Glen suddenly turned his head, frowning at Angela. 'He said *you'd* know where the loot is.'

'Don't go blaming her,' Howard said.

'What's . . . the bastard's been lying to us all along?'

'There was always a good chance of that,' Lana said. 'Corie warned us, remember?'

'But he told us where to find the hundred bucks!'

'He must've had a reason for bringing us here,' Howard said.

'Yeah. So we could get nailed by his buddy, Hubie the Hermit.'

'Maybe the whole point,' Keith said, 'was to add some underthings to the collection. Either of you babes care to donate?'

Lana, frowning, elbowed him hard in the arm.

'Hey!' He kept his smirk as he rubbed his arm and said, 'I

mean it. Look at the facts. Butler got all three of you gals to show off your bras at Dalton's party. Right? He wanted to check them out. Obviously, he liked what he saw so he tricked us into coming up here. He wants your bras, babes. That was the whole point. The be-all and the end-all, the Alpha and Omega, the *raison d'être* of our pilgrimage to this scenic locale.'

'Eat shit and die,' Lana told him. She pushed herself off the wall. Striding away from Keith, she tugged her blouse out of her belt, thrust her arms into its sleeves, and started to button the front.

'Now look what you made her do,' Glen said.

'Don't you start in,' Lana warned him.

He blushed and lowered his head.

Lana finished fastening her buttons. 'We might as well get out of here.'

'Hasn't it occurred to anyone,' Angela said, 'that maybe we should ask *Butler* about the loot? I mean, we've got the Ouija board with us. It's in your pack, isn't it?' she asked Lana.

'Yeah.' Lana seemed to be frowning and smiling at the same time. 'Yeah, it is. I should've thought of that. Who wants to come along?'

'Why don't we all go?' Howard suggested. 'We might not have to come back. And it's safer if we stay together.'

Nobody disagreed.

They followed Keith out of the recess and into the sunlight, then began making their way along the rough slope, moving gradually lower. Soon, Howard could hear the rush of the stream. Pausing, he turned his head to the left and looked for Doris. Though he could see both rims of the gorge, the narrow place where they'd leaped across was blocked from view by high clusters of rock on their side.

He hoped she was all right.

She has the gun, he reminded himself. She's probably safer than the rest of us.

He moved on, following Angela down the face of a tilted granite sheet. At its bottom, they hopped from boulder to boulder. Howard saw the painted heart just ahead. They'd left their packs in a flat area below it – their starting place for the search.

He looked back again. And saw Doris in the distance, sitting cross-legged a few yards from the rim of the gorge, her head down. She seemed to be reading, though Howard couldn't make out the book.

For a moment, he envied her. She'd just been sitting there the whole time, probably enjoying herself. Not climbing around on a mountainside, not wandering through the suffocating heat and darkness of a mine, not having to see the bones of a dead person. Hell, she was even blissfully unaware that she was sitting no more than a hundred yards from the camp of the lunatic who'd attacked her yesterday.

Howard almost wished *he* had been the one to chicken out and stay behind.

But he wouldn't have liked being alone. She looked awfully lonely, awfully vulnerable sitting there by herself.

Turning away, he saw Angela scurry down to the broad ledge where they had left the gear. The others had arrived ahead of her and were already bending over their packs. By the time Howard joined them, they were gulping from their canteens and water bottles. His own canteen hung against the side of his pack. He untied its strap, twisted off its top, and drank. The water had been ice cold when he'd filled up that morning at the stream at the end of the lake. Now it was warm, but still delicious. He stopped for air, then drank more before knotting the canteen's strap to his pack.

He had left his hat here so it wouldn't get in his way while climbing around to search for the mine. It was stuffed under one of the cords that bound his sleeping bag to the top of his pack. He pulled it free, shook it open, and put it on. The big, floppy brim cast a soothing shadow onto his face.

Angela took the spiral notebook and pen from her pack.

Lana sat down, her back to the rim of the gorge. Legs crossed, she leaned forward and set the Ouija board in front of her. She placed the pointer on the board. 'Let's do it,' she said.

Glen, Keith and Howard took their positions on the other sides of the board. Angela sat beside Howard. She brought up one knee and held the notepad against it, ready to write. The rest of them leaned closer to the board and placed their fingertips on the plastic, heartshaped pointer.

In a firm clear voice, Lana said, 'It's us.'

'Again,' Keith muttered.

'Butler, are you here? Butler? We found a mine where you said it'd be. Where's the loot you told us about?'

The pointer trembled and began to glide. It stopped over the I, then slid sideways down the curving letters and halted at the M. It kept on moving slowly and pausing, and Glen spoke each letter aloud.

'I-M-B-O-N-E-S.'

'I am bones,' Angela said.

'The skeleton? You're the skeleton?'

The pointer slid upward from the S to the YES beside the smiling sun.

'You were right,' Howard said, glancing at Angela.

'We oughta make sure this is Butler,' Glen said.

'Are you Butler?' Lana asked.

'I-M.'

'I am,' Angela said.

But the pointer didn't stop. It drifted from letter to letter.

'A-N-N-A-B-E-L-L-E-B-U-T-L-E-R.'

Angela frowned at her notepad. 'Ann a bell e Butler. Annabelle Butler?'

'A gal?' Glen said.

'Are you the same Butler who brought us up here?'

The pointer carried their hands upward to YES.

'Butler's a *woman*,' Howard said.

'Looks that way.'

'So that skeleton up there's a babe?' Keith sounded astonished.

'Must be.'

'Could've fooled me.'

Howard looked at Angela. She was making odd, gasping sounds. Her left hand fell away from her upraised knee, taking the notepad with it. The pad slapped against the thigh of her other leg. She gazed at the Ouija board. Her mouth hung open.

'What's wrong?'

She, shook her head. 'It's . . . I don't know . . . Annabelle.'

'Yeah?' Keith asked. 'So?'

'It was my mother's name.'

'Where's your mother?' Lana asked.

'She died. A long time ago.'

'This isn't your mother,' Keith said. 'This is Annabelle Butler, not Logan.'

'My name isn't Logan.'

'What?' Glen blurted.

'It was Carnes.' She spoke softly, staring at the board. 'Mom was married to Charlie Carnes.'

She's telling.

Howard wondered if Angela was even aware that she was revealing parts of her awful secret. She seemed dazed, almost as if in a trance.

'Well, Carnes isn't Butler,' Lana said.

The pointer began jerking across the face of the board,

stopping only for an instant at each letter. Angela watched it move, but wrote nothing. The pad remained on the upturned side of her thigh. The fingers holding it there trembled.

'M-A-I-D-E-N-A-M-E,' Glen read aloud. 'Maiden name?'

'Holy shit,' Keith said.

'Is that right?' Lana asked, gaping at Angela.

'I . . . I don't know. I don't know *what* her maiden name was.'

'How could you not know something like that?' Glen said.

'She was just a little kid when her mother died,' Howard explained.

'Are you Angela's mother?' Lana asked the Ouija board.

The pointer glided up to the YES.

Angela dropped her pen. She curled her hand across her mouth.

'Oh, this is too fucking weird.'

Lana cast a sharp look at Keith.

Howard took his hand off the pointer. He laid it on Angela's back and rubbed her gently through the damp fabric of her T-shirt.

'What's her body doing in the mine?' Glen asked.

The pointer began to carry the remaining three hands over the alphabet.

'M-U-R-D-E-R-E-D.'

Angela made a quick, startled whimper.

'Did Hubert do it?' Lana asked.

'C-H-A-R-L-I-E.'

'Her husband,' Keith whispered.

'And Charlie left your body in the mine?'

'T-A-K-E-M-E.'

'Take you where?'

'A-W-A-Y.'

'Maybe she wants a decent burial,' Howard said.

He eased Angela close against his side as she began to sob.

'Is that what you want? To be taken out of the mountains and buried?'

The heart started moving again. 'H,' Glen read. 'E. M.'

Angela, weeping softly, snatched the pad off her leg and found the pen and began to write.

'A-D-U-K-I-L-L-N-G-E-T-M-E-A-W-A-Y.'

When the message seemed to be over, she sniffed and wiped her eyes. She held the pad up so that she and Howard could both study the string of letters.

' "He mad" . . .?' she said, her voice trembling.

'Or "Hubert Elliot mad." '

'Yeah.'

'Maybe not "mad". What about "made a duke"?'

'That doesn't make sense,' Lana said.

' "Hubert Elliot mad." ' Angela nodded as if sure of herself. ' "You kill and get me away." '

Glen moaned. 'She wants us to *kill* him?'

'Why do you want us to kill him?' Lana asked.

'4-M-Y-S-A-K-E.'

' "For my sake?" But he isn't the one who murdered you.'

'D-E-F-I-L-E-S.'

'Shit,' Keith said. 'What does she mean by that?'

'Use your imagination,' Lana told him. 'God Almighty. Look, Annabelle, we aren't going to murder anyone. Is that the reason you brought us up here? So we could kill this Hubert guy and take your bones back to civilization?'

'A-N-G-E-L-A.'

Her back went rigid under Howard's hand.

'What about Angela?'

'M-I-S-S.'

She shuddered with a sob.

'L-O-V-E.'

Lana raised her solemn eyes to Angela. 'Do you want to talk with her?'

'I . . . Mom? I . . . I love you. Oh, God, this is so . . . I'll take you with me.'

'Fun and games,' Keith muttered.

'Shut up,' Lana said.

'Look, ask her about the fucking loot. Or was that just a lie?'

'Annabelle, you told us there would be loot if we came to the mine. Was that just a trick to get us here?'

'U-G-E-T.'

'Where is it?'

'G-O-2-B-U-S.'

' "Go to bus"?'

'What is this shit?' Keith demanded. 'What bus? There's no damn bus up here?'

'We'll find the loot in a bus?' Lana asked.

'2-M-O-R-R-O-W.'

'Where?'

'O-F-F-P-U-R-D-Y-R-D.'

' "Off pretty RD"?' Keith said. 'Who's RD?' He looked around the group.

'Could be the abbreviation for "road",' Glen said.

'So we've got to find a pretty road? Terrific.'

'A-L-F-I-N-D-S.'

'I'll find it,' Angela said.

'Where is it?' Lana asked, staring at the board. 'Where do we look?'

The pointer didn't move.

'Annabelle?'

It glided slowly downward, past the numbers below the alphabet, and swept across GOOD BYE. Then it stopped.

'Shit!'

'Annabelle? Come on, you've got to tell us more.'

The pointer remained motionless.

'That's all we're gonna get,' Glen said, and pulled his hand back.

'Looks that way.' Lana leaned back, bracing herself up on stiff arms, and looked at Angela. 'Do you know what this is all about?'

'No. Not . . . it's so confusing.'

'You don't have to talk about it,' Howard told her.

She sniffed and wiped her eyes. 'Charlie . . . he said Mom was killed in a car accident. That was right after we got home.'

'They'd been on a camping trip,' Howard explained.

'Where?' Glen asked. 'Here?'

'I don't know,' Angela said. 'I guess it's possible this is where we were. It was in mountains *some*where. But I'd always thought Mom got home with us.'

'You don't *know*?' Keith asked.

Angela shook her head.

'She was only four years old,' Howard said.

'Hell,' Keith said, 'I remember stuff when I was nothing but a baby.'

'It's normal to forget nearly everything that happened before you were about five,' Lana pointed out. 'And there's also a tendency to block out traumatic events.'

'But to forget what happened to your own mother . . .'

Angela rubbed her face. She sighed. 'I always *thought* she made it back home with us. Charlie said she did. He said she went out for cigarettes and got killed in a car accident.'

'Was there a funeral or anything?' Lana asked.

'I don't remember one.'

'Did you ever see her actual grave?' Glen asked.

'Huh-uh. We . . . we'd been living in a trailer park.'

'Where was that?'

'I don't know. Maybe somewhere near Sacramento? I'm not sure. But right after Mom died, we left and started living in a van. Traveling around. And one time when I was older? I started really missing Mom, you know? So I threw these fits. You know, crying and everything. I wanted them to take me to her and I wouldn't quit bugging them about it.'

'Who's *them*?'

'Charlie and his sons. The twins. So anyway, I guess they got tired of putting up with all the tantrums I was throwing, and they said they'd take me to the cemetery so I could visit her grave. I thought they meant it. I was really happy for a while. That's where I thought we were going and pretty soon I'd get to be with her. So one night they woke me up? And we were in a cemetery, all right. Out in the country somewhere. It was a horrible place. It looked like nobody'd been there for years. It was all overgrown. Some of the tombstones were knocked over. And I got led around in the dark while they pretended they couldn't remember where Mom's grave was. But it wasn't there at all. The whole thing was just a trick. They wanted to teach me a lesson.'

'What kind of bastards . . .?' Keith muttered.

'I started getting really scared, you know? The place was *spooky*. And they were acting weird. You know, laughing and stuff. Tripping me all the time. They made me get down on top of a grave, and . . .' She shook her head roughly. She was silent for a few moments, then went on. 'They ended up leaving me tied to a tree right in the middle of the graveyard. Just left me there and drove away. And they didn't come back all night. They came back in the morning and I remember Charlie . . . While he untied me, he was laughing. And he said, "Did you have a nice visit with your Mama?" '

'Anyway, after that I pretty much kept my mouth shut about Mom.'

Everyone sat there, staring at Angela. Finally, Glen murmured, 'Jesus.'

Lana had a look of revulsion on her face. She said,

'You grew up with guys who would do something like that to you?'

'Yeah. They were sweethearts.'

'God, that's horrible.'

'So I guess now I know what happened to Mom. It was all a lie about the car accident and . . .' Lifting her head, she gazed up the mountainside in the direction of the mine. 'Will somebody come with me?'

'Sure,' Howard said.

'We all will,' Lana said.

Keith and Glen nodded.

Angela got up and went to her pack. The others followed. They stood around her as she removed her sleeping bag and opened the top of the pack. She began to take out her clothes and equipment and her share of the group's food.

Nobody asked questions. Nobody made remarks.

In silence, they picked up her things and found room for them in their own packs.

'That's all,' she finally said.

Howard glanced down into the pack. A small, stuffed kitten remained at the bottom. 'Aren't you gonna . . .?'

'That's Puffy. She doesn't take up much room. Mom gave her to me and . . . I don't know . . . I think I want to leave her in.'

Angela closed the flap. She picked up the nearly empty pack, swung it onto her back and slipped her arms through the straps.

'Let's just leave everything here except the flashlights,' Lana said.

'And this.' Keith snatched up the hatchet. 'In case Hubert shows up.'

'Let's get it done,' Glen said.

'Hey, all of you.'

They faced Angela. She was frowning. Her lower lip was

pressed between her teeth. She glanced at Howard, then turned her eyes to Glen, to Keith, and finally to Lana. In a shaky voice, she said, 'You're all really terrific.'

'That's us,' Keith said.

'Well, you are. And Mom promised we'd find the loot tomorrow, and we will.'

Chapter Twenty-eight

'Could you let go of my hair?' Corie asked. 'You're giving me a headache.'

'You'll run away,' the man said.

'Here? Are you kidding?' This section of the trail was so narrow that an attempt to run would probably send her off its edge. 'Besides, where would I go? You've got me, all right? I won't try anything. I promise.'

'You might jump.'

'I'm not going to jump,' she said.

He didn't release her hair, so Corie dropped the matter.

She had decided – it seemed like hours ago – to cooperate with this man. He was just too quick and powerful. And he was obviously crazy. If he lost his temper, he could kill her in an instant with his bare hands. Or with the machete he'd picked up after taking her out of the lake.

Corie was fairly sure that he wanted to keep her alive. Hell, he'd *said* he didn't want to kill her. And once she'd stopped struggling, he had quit hurting her. He'd hardly touched her at all, except for the hand clenching her hair.

That was an annoyance, a mild lingering torment, nothing that would damage her.

The only real damage had been done to her feet by walking.

'Where are you taking me?' she'd asked when he first began to steer her away from the campsite.

'Up the mountain.'

'Let me get dressed, OK?'

'You're too pretty for clothes.'

'But the sun'll cook me.'

'The sun is good for you. It'll turn you to gold like me.'

'At least let me put my boots on. My feet'll get torn up.'

'It'll make them strong like mine.'

'Please!'

'Don't beg. Be strong.'

He wants me to be like him. All right. Maybe that means he isn't going to hurt me unless I do something wrong. He's after a companion. A mate. And I'm it. I can live through this. If I'm smart.

She had tried to look back for a final glimpse of Chad, but the man had twisted her hair, forcing her head forward. As they made their way along the shore, she'd prayed that Chad would rush to her rescue. Then she hoped he wouldn't.

Just be alive. Be alive but stay where you are. Don't come after us. He'd kill you for sure.

I'll be OK.

I'll be OK till he decides to fuck me.

He could've done it right away, but he hadn't.

What's he waiting for?

During their trek along the lakeshore and as they'd waded across the icy stream and for a while after they'd started up the mountain trail, Corie had expected to be thrown down at any moment and raped.

When that didn't happen, she'd begun to wonder why not.

He wants to get where we're going, first?

That was the only explanation that made any sense.

She'd tried to tell herself that he was gay. After all, he was obviously a body-builder. But she knew that the stereotype was false. Plenty of those men were straight. Besides, he'd left Chad behind. He'd taken her. And he hadn't allowed her to get dressed. He wasn't gay.

Maybe his reasons for wanting her had nothing to do with sex. He might just be lonely.

In your dreams, she thought. You don't get off that easily.

He's violent. He's crazy. If he didn't grab me for sex, there's no telling *what* he's got in mind.

He wants me to stay pretty, that's the thing to remember. He wants me to get tanned the way he is. And he wants my feet to get tough like his. That doesn't sound like someone who wants to eat me or torture me or do God-knows-what. Just stay calm and play along with him.

We might even run into the kids.

This was the Calamity Peak trail. It must be the way they'd gone. Though they undoubtedly had a huge head-start, the weight of their backpacks would slow them down. They couldn't make very good time, not with someone like Doris along. And Angela probably wasn't strong enough to keep up a quick pace.

Sooner or later, Corie thought, we might overtake them.

Six of them. They'd sure have this guy outnumbered. If we all attack him at once . . .

Someone was sure to get hurt, though. Maybe even killed.

Unless they took him by surprise.

On the other hand, if he suddenly found himself facing so many opponents, maybe he wouldn't even try to fight them. He might just run off and leave her. It could happen that way.

But what if he chose to fight? With that machete . . .

He must already know about the kids, Corie realized. He'd

been at their campsite, seen their tents. Maybe he'd even been waiting for them to return, hoping to grab one of the girls, when she and Chad had shown up.

She suddenly remembered the note on the tent flap. A warning of some kind. The kids had left it. The message had started, 'Dear Creep.' It must've meant *him*.

What did he *do* to them?

Shocked and alarmed, Corie had come very close to blurting out questions, demanding to know if he'd hurt any of her students. Before she could speak, however, it dawned on her that he hadn't hurt them. Not seriously, at least.

There'd been a frivolous, mocking tone to the note they'd left behind. He'd obviously given them some kind of trouble, but he hadn't seriously injured or killed any of them.

Besides, they were hardly likely to have continued on their stupid, damn search for Butler's loot if the creep had done real damage to any of them. Or even if they considered him a serious threat.

What if he got them after they left the note?

No. That didn't seem likely. If he'd slaughtered them, where were their bodies? Where was their gear? Except for the tents, Corie had seen no trace of the kids. Besides, the creep wouldn't have killed them all. He would've kept one of the girls alive. Lana, probably. He would've grabbed Lana for his companion or mate or whatever . . . and she'd be the one he's taking with him.

It's better this way, Corie told herself. Better that he has me.

Not better for Chad.

She felt a quick surge of agony – guilt and sorrow that tightened her throat and brought tears to her eyes. She'd looked down the mountainside. She could see the lake far below, but the woods surrounding the campsite blocked any view of the rock slab where she'd last seen Chad.

It's all my fault. I got him into this. If he's dead . . .

No, he's not dead. He can't be.

He might be.

No! He'll wake up with a headache and wonder what happened to me. Will he think I drowned? What'll he do?

He'll look for me. He won't stop looking until he finds me.

And then what? He gets his head chopped?

She hurt too much, thinking about what might happen.

Think about the kids, she told herself. They're all right. They must be. And Chad's all right, too. Everything'll turn out fine.

I've just got to play along with this bastard and stay alive no matter what and eventually I'll either get away or be rescued.

But as the afternoon wore on, with the heat bearing down on her, the rough trail scraping her feet raw, her plan to cooperate seemed like less and less of a good idea.

With each painful step, she was moving closer to the place where the creep was taking her. With each step, her dread grew like a ball of ice forming in her stomach. Whatever he intended to do with her, it was going to happen when they reached their destination.

She didn't want to get there.

Even if it meant risking a fall.

And so she had asked him to let go of her hair, promised that she wouldn't try to escape, and been told that she might jump.

I wouldn't jump, she thought. He's crazy if he thinks I'm going to jump.

Crazy.

She heard herself let out a soft huff of laughter.

'What's funny?' he asked.

'You are. You said I might jump if you let go of my hair.'

'That's funny?'

'I'm not the type. But look, could I sit down or something? I can't jump if I'm sitting down. My feet are killing me. I'm worn out. If we don't rest, I might just pass out and *fall*. You wouldn't like that, would you?'

'I won't let you fall. Keep moving. We're almost there.'

Just what Corie didn't want to hear.

She let her knees buckle. She started to sink forward, arms out to catch herself. The man jerked her hair. She cried out. But she stayed limp. He held her up for a moment, then lowered her slowly until her knees met the trail. 'Let go, damn it!'

He released her hair.

She hunched over. On elbows and knees, she clasped the top of her head and rubbed her aching scalp.

She heard nothing from behind her. She knew the kind of view she was giving him. Maybe he was too interested in that to give her trouble about the delay.

I'm really asking for it.

So what?

Let him try it right here if that's what he wants. Get it over with. And maybe somebody'll take a nose-dive off the mountain. And maybe it'll be him.

'Up,' he said.

Corie didn't move. 'Where are you taking me?' she asked.

'To my home.'

'What for?'

'You're mine.'

'The hell I am. I'm not yours. I'll never be yours. I'm *mine*. And part of me belongs to that man I was with at the lake, and if he's dead so are you.'

For a few moments, he said nothing. Then he asked, 'What's your name?'

'Me Jane.'

'Get to your feet, Jane.'

She scurried forward on her elbows until she was stretched out flat on the trail.

'Get up now.'

'Do whatever you want. I'm not going anywhere.'

'Do you want to die right here?'

'If you kill me, I'll stop being pretty.' Carefully, aware that the trail was not much wider than her body, she rolled onto her back. She propped herself up on her elbows.

The man was standing just beyond her feet. His sunglasses, frames bent by the blow from the stone she'd thrown at him, rested slightly askew across his eyes. His mouth was a tight, straight line. His sweaty skin glimmered in the sunlight. The blade of his machete flashed as he raised it.

'Get up,' he said.

Though her heart was thundering and she felt as if she couldn't catch her breath, she managed to say, 'What if I don't?'

The machete slashed, whipping through the air above her legs. She knew it was missing her. But she flinched and gasped anyway.

Squatting, he grabbed her right ankle and jerked it up. With the flat of his machete, he smacked the bottom of her foot.

Corie bucked and cried out.

He flung her leg sideways. Past the edge of the trail. It dropped. Corie sucked air, shocked. Her whole leg was going down. The rim scraped the back of her thigh, dug into her buttock. She twisted away, kicking up, and he caught her ankle.

It was all, suddenly, too much. She had kept herself under tight control, she'd used her head, she'd tried to be brave. She'd pushed on, though the sun had seared her naked body and the rocky trail had bloodied her feet and the steep climb had stolen all her strength. She'd fought against her sorrow, her guilt, her terror. But the slap of the machete had hurt too much. The sudden drop of her leg had scared her too much. She broke. She bawled.

She lay flat on the trail, hands pressed to her face, spasms shaking her body as she sobbed and blubbered.

'Stop it,' he said.

'Go to hell.'

He rose from his crouch and stepped between her thighs. He slipped the leather sling of the machete over his right shoulder so that the weapon hung behind his back. Then he bent down, grabbed her wrists and yanked her up. As she stumbled forward, he threw his arms around her and jerked her hard against him. Their wet bodies slapped together. She felt herself being mashed breathless against his massive chest.

'You will walk,' he said. He squeezed her so hard she thought her ribs might snap.

When the awful hug loosened, Corie found that her legs wouldn't support her. She began to slip down his body. He grabbed her under the armpits and held her upright while she sobbed and struggled for air. Every now and then, he gave her a rough shake that wobbled her head, set her limp arms swinging and jiggled her breasts. She thought he was doing it to punish her.

But then he lifted her off her feet, raised her straight up until she was looking down at the top of his shiny, hairless head. Until her breasts were level with his face. She watched them bounce and sway as he shook her some more. He held her still for a few moments, then brought her closer. He rubbed a bristly cheek against the side of her right breast. Turning his head, he opened his mouth. He licked her nipple. Licked it like a kid with a lollipop.

Corie slammed her open hands against his ears. Roaring with pain, he hurled her away. She saw the sky, the steep slope looming above her. She wanted to reach out and grab the slope, but feared that any contact might throw her away from it and send her plummeting down the mountain. Her heels struck rock. An instant later, her rump hit. She kept her head up as her elbows and back crashed against the trail. A brief skid scorched the skin of her back and buttocks. When she stopped, she let out a shuddering whimper. She hurt all over. But she hadn't gone over the edge!

As fast as she could, she pushed herself up.

The creep was down on his knees, hunched over, clutching his ears, bellowing.

Corie scurried to her feet. She winced and wept. She wiped her eyes. She knew she ought to attack. Right now. Before the bastard could recover enough to defend himself.

Smash his head with a rock. Or grab the machete dangling by his side and chop him. Or even try to shove him off the edge.

One way or another, finish him off.

But she didn't dare. She couldn't force herself to take even a single step towards him. If she got within his reach, he just might . . .

He raised his head. '*You!*'

Corie squatted, snatched up a chunk of rock and threw it at him. Though she'd aimed for his face, it struck him just below the collar bone. It gouged some skin and bounced away. She grabbed another chunk as he got to his feet. He took a step toward her and she pitched it. This one slammed his mouth. It knocked his head back. His sunglasses fell off. He blinked his eyes, shook his head, licked his mashed lips, spat out a spray of blood, and lurched toward her.

Corie whirled around. She hurried up the thin strip of trail, jogging at first, sick with the idea of falling. But she heard the man gaining on her. He grunted. Sometimes, he gasped, 'Yes!' And the sounds were getting closer.

She knew she would rather fall than let him catch her.

So she dashed. She pumped her arms. She shot her legs out far and quick. The trail was a jolting blur through her tears. Though she could hear him, she couldn't tell how far behind he was. She wanted to look back, but she didn't dare. With the turn of her head, she might mis-step. And if he was still closing in, she didn't want to see it.

She half expected to feel a blade slice down her back. Or maybe he would simply shove her sideways, sending her in a long dive to oblivion.

She slowed a little as the trail curved to the right.

Maybe he'll take the turn too fast, she thought. He's so much bigger, so much heavier. If he tries it full speed . . .

She pictured him sprinting into space like Wile E. Coyote, running on air, OK till he looked down and saw his predicament, then plummeting.

When she rounded the bend, her stomach dropped. Confusion numbed her mind.

A few strides in front of Corie, two hands were gripping the rim of the trail.

Impossible! How did he get ahead *of me?*

Then she thought, *Now I've got him!*

Adios, asshole!

A stride away, she braked her rush. She dropped to her knees and scurried toward the edge, eager to tear the fingers from their hold.

And found herself staring down into the eyes of Chad.

With a snap of her head, she glanced over her shoulder. Just in time to see the bulk of her mad assailant rush around the bend.

'No!' she shrieked.

'Go!' Chad gasped. 'Run! Now!'

She scuttled past him, thrust herself to her feet, but

couldn't run away. Turning around, she watched Chad lunge up alongside the trail. He pulled a knife.

The creep was moving too fast to stop. He had a look of puzzlement on his face. Chad dropped across the trail, blocking his path, and he tumbled over Chad's body. His right shoulder pounded the wall. The blow knocked him sideways, but not far enough. Chest first, he slammed the trail, his head at Corie's feet. His left arm dropped over the edge.

'Get *out* of here!' Chad blurted, struggling out from under the legs.

Corie dropped to her knees. She clamped the broad, slick head between her thighs. Squeezing it as hard as she could, she leaned forward and shoved down against the man's back. 'Kill him!' she gasped. 'Gotta kill him!'

His left arm was no longer hanging. It was on the trail. He started pushing himself up as Chad straddled his buttocks. His head slid up between Corie's thighs. It pushed against her groin. It lifted her knees into the air as Chad raised the knife. The blade flashed downward.

With a quick twisting buck, he threw Chad.

The knife swept across his back, missing him as Chad tumbled away. Corie cried out, 'No!' She glimpsed Chad flinging the knife into space, clawing and kicking at the air beside the trail. He was there for an instant, and then he was gone and Corie, thrown toward the edge herself by the sudden buck, only kept safe by the grip of her thighs on the bastard's head, slammed herself down against his back.

He was on his hands and knees. She wrapped her arms around his torso and clung to him.

He started crawling up the trail.

She rode him.

He didn't try to shake her off.

This is mad! It's insane!

Playing horsey. Chad's dead. Oh, God, Chad! Dead.

She knew she could squirm off the man's back and cast herself down the mountainside. She wanted to. Better to be dead, like Chad. Better to put an end to all this. What was the point in living, now? Chad wouldn't be coming back to her. Her future had been wiped out. Why not die, and stop the pain?

And cheat this fucking creep out of *having* me!

But Corie couldn't force herself to do it. She hugged him fiercely, terrified of falling.

And felt ashamed. She had no right to go on living. No reason to, and no right. She'd gotten Chad killed. She didn't deserve to survive.

He tried to save me, she told herself. He wouldn't want me to kill myself.

He loved me. He'd want me to live.

I've got to live, she suddenly realized.

Long enough to kill this murdering piece of shit.

She heard the blade of the machete clinking and clanging as it dragged along the trail beside him. Somehow, through everything, the sling had stayed on his right shoulder. If she let go of him with one arm, she might be able to reach the weapon. And do what with it? Attached as it was, how could she get any leverage into a swing?

Besides, he wouldn't *let* her get a hand on it. The moment he felt her starting to let go, he would know she was up to something. She wouldn't stand a chance.

Corie had kept her eyes shut ever since fastening herself onto the man. Now, she opened them. Her right cheek was pressed against his back. She raised her head.

The movement didn't seem to bother him. He continued crawling along slowly.

His black waistband was just in front of Corie's eyes. A strip in its center passed between his buttocks. She realized that his rump was not only flexing, but swaying slightly from side to side. He was making himself squirm so that his back would slide against her. His head, trapped between her trembling thighs, was rubbing her groin.

You killed my Chad, you bastard, and now you're doing this *to me*?

She felt used and dirty. As much as she hated him, she hated herself more for riding him and giving him pleasure.

You'll pay for this, she thought as he carried her around a bend in the trail. You'll pay for everything.

Then she saw the wall of the mountain recede. Perplexed, she looked the other way. Where the edge of the trail had been, there was now a gradual slope.

No more narrow trail.

They had reached a level area, a place where it would be safe for him to remove Corie from his back. But still he crawled along.

Enjoying himself too much to stop now.

Maybe he wasn't even aware that they'd left the hazardous strip of trail behind.

But Corie was aware. She felt like a tightrope walker who had finally stepped onto a solid platform. Released from the fear of falling, she began to caress the man.

He didn't seem to mind. He kept on crawling.

She writhed on his back. She eased the grip of her legs. Her hands roamed up his chest, down his sides and belly. When she fingered the band at his waist, he stopped moving. She traced its path up his hips. Curled her hands over the hard mounds of his rump, slid them down the backs of his thighs, stretching as she reached. She felt him begin to tremble under her body. She brought her hands up again, over his rump to his hips. She hooked her thumbs under the thin band. She drew it down halfway to his knees.

Doesn't he even suspect? she wondered. Is he too far gone to care?

Or is he just so damn confident that he doesn't think I'd try something?

A trick?

Maybe he plans to stop me at the last moment. Let me think I'm getting away with it. All the time, he's just using me, enjoying himself, waiting for the right moment to throw me off and nail me.

I don't care.

This is my move and I'm making it.

His belly flinched a bit when Corie touched it this time. He shuddered and moaned when she wrapped her left hand around the thick post of his erection. She slid her fingers lightly down the length of it, and up again.

Got him, she thought. He won't stop me now.

Her right hand cupped his scrotum.

You're history, asshole.

But even as she clamped her hand shut, she felt her wrist being grabbed and jerked down. Her fingertips hit his testicles. Didn't squeeze them. Didn't crush them. Only tapped them, maybe bumped them together, as her hand was shoved away.

Still, he jerked and choked out a gasp. Releasing her wrist, he reared up on his knees.

Corie slid down his back. She flung her hands against the ground. Her legs flew high. She curled her back, rolled away from him with a quick somersault, and landed sitting up. As she scurried to her feet, she turned to look at him.

He was still on his knees, doubled over as if he had a bellyache.

Corie ran at him. She brought up a foot and rammed it against his lower back, slamming him to the rocky ground. But as she stooped, reaching for the machete, he rolled out of the way with such quickness that she staggered backward. The long blade swept through the air above him and clanked down. An instant later, he was clutching its handle. He shrugged the strap off his shoulder. He lurched onto his side and swung the machete at Corie. The blade hissed past her shins, missing by inches.

With a grunt of despair, she spun around and ran.

Blew it, she thought. I had him and I blew it. How did he *know*?

He can't be stopped. He's gonna get me, and . . .

Not if I can outrun him.

He's hurt. I've got a chance.

She seemed to be on a broad slope, a pass of sorts that slanted gradually upward between two bluffs. Off to the left, there seemed to be a gap. She dashed toward it. She couldn't tell how wide it might be. But if she could leap to the other side, she might have an advantage. She might be able to defend that side. At least she would have *something* between her and the madman. Maybe she could nail him when he tried to cross.

As she raced closer, she heard a rushing sound. Like a strong wind. With every stride, it grew louder. It was a roar by the time she saw that the gap was too wide. She wouldn't have a chance of jumping to the other side.

She halted at its edge and glanced down. The view of the wild stream, so far below, made her stomach drop. She jerked her head around.

The bastard was coming. Hobbling a little. His black pouch in place. His left hand cupping it, holding onto his nuts while his right hand waved the machete overhead. The area around his mouth was a bloody mess.

Corie turned her back to the gorge.

She waited for him.

Don't! Are you nuts?

You'll never outrun him anyway. Sooner or later, he'll get you.

She spread her feet, bent over slightly and opened her arms wide as if preparing herself to wrestle with him. 'Come on, you bastard!' she yelled.

So far, he wasn't slowing down.

Keep it coming!

He dashed closer and closer. All slabs and bulges of bouncing muscle. With each stride, he made sobbing, growling sounds that Corie could hear through the roar of the stream.

'You want me?' she yelled. 'You *want* me?'

He grinned, bloody lips stretching away from his teeth. He was close enough, now, for Corie to see that some of his front teeth were broken stubs.

Three strides away.

Two.

She threw herself sideways. She hit the ground, rolled onto her back, and saw that he'd braked himself at the rim of the gorge. Momentum seemed to be shoving him forward. Bending at the waist, he flapped his arms.

And found his balance.

And turned to Corie.

He sneered down at her. 'You sure sink you're tricky,' he said.

Something smacked his chest. Corie heard a blast. A gunshot? His left pectoral jumped and she glimpsed a neat round hole a few inches above his nipple. Only a glimpse before the impact twisted him sideways. He flung his right foot across his left to catch himself.

He was bent over as if studying the stream at the bottom of the gorge when the second bullet came, slicing a furrow across his back. With a squeal, he stumbled forward into space. He dropped, turning, and disappeared below the rim.

Corie rolled over. As she pushed herself up on hands and

knees, she saw a fat girl in a gray sweatshirt and shorts jogging toward her. A fat girl with a revolver.

'Doris!'

The girl's mouth dropped open. 'Dr *Dalton*?'

Corie stood up, staggered toward Doris, and threw her arms around her.

'My God!' Doris gasped. 'What're *you* doing here?'

'You got him,' Corie blurted. 'You got him. Did you get him?' She pushed herself away from Doris. She snatched the revolver out of the girl's hand and hurried back to the edge of the chasm.

She spotted the bastard.

Way down there. Floating face down in a pool of surging white water, arms stretched out as if he'd been crucified.

She took careful aim and squeezed the trigger.

The blast stung her ears. The gun jumped in her hand. She couldn't tell whether she'd hit him. She fired again.

The third time she pulled the trigger, there was no explosion. Just a hard metallic clack.

The body turned slowly in the current and began to race downstream.

Chapter Twenty-nine

Corie knelt near the edge of the gorge, set the gun down beside her, curled over and buried her face in her hands.

It's finished, she told herself. He's dead and I'm alive. It's finished. He didn't get me. He never will.

She kept seeing the bullets hit him, kept seeing him step

off the rim and drop, kept seeing him sprawled in the water down there and scooting away on the quick current.

She kept seeing Chad fall from the trail.

She couldn't stop shaking.

She felt as if she might rear up on her knees and howl with wild joy for her own survival, with agony for Chad and all that might have been.

I've got to go to him, she thought.

But she couldn't move.

She heard quiet footfalls approaching from the rear.

'God, your feet.' Doris's voice.

'I'm all right,' she murmured into her hands.

'I brought my things over. Do you want to put on some of my clothes?'

'He killed Chad.'

Silence. A hand gently stroked the back of her head.

'I'm awfully sorry,' Doris said. 'But don't you think you ought to get dressed? The others must've heard the shots. They'll be coming back any minute. You wouldn't want them to see you like this. You know Keith and Glen.'

'I've gotta find Chad.'

'I'll help you. But first you'd better put something on.'

Corie rubbed her face. Straightening up, she turned around on her knees. Surprised to find herself embarrassed after all that had happened, she pressed an arm across her breasts and dropped a hand between her legs. She was suddenly upset by the thought that Doris might have seen her on top of the man, stroking his penis.

'Did you see us . . . fighting back there?' she asked.

Doris shook her head. Turning away, she reached into her pack. 'I didn't notice anything until I heard you yell at the guy. Then I saw you down here, and him running at you with that big knife. I didn't even realize it was you. But I sure recognized him.'

'Thank God you were here,' Corie said. 'He had me . . . all afternoon. I couldn't get away from him. He would've killed me just now if you hadn't shot him.'

'He almost got *me* yesterday.' Doris dragged a big, gray sweatshirt out of the pack and handed it to her. 'He grabbed Lana last night.'

Corie pulled the sweatshirt down over her head. It was huge and baggy. Its thickness seemed to trap the heat of her skin. The abrasion on her back felt like liquid fire.

'I shot at him then, and he dropped Lana. We've been keeping an eye out for him ever since. Do you want shorts or sweatpants?'

'Shorts, I guess.'

She pulled out a wide pair of red gym trunks. 'They'll be a little big on you. I've got some safety pins here somewhere. You'll probably need one.'

While Doris searched for the pin, Corie sat down and drew the shorts up her legs. The elastic band was loose around her waist.

'Here we go.'

Doris handed a safety pin to her. She pinched in a tuck at her right hip, and fastened it there.

'He never showed up again after I shot at him,' Doris said, and started searching her pack again. 'We figured the gun must've frightened him off. Where did he get you?'

'Down at the lake. By your campsite.'

'Jesus. So he hung around. God, if only I'd hit him last night.' She lifted out a pair of white crew socks and blue sneakers. As she set them down beside Corie, she said, 'You two came looking for us?'

'What do you think?'

Doris looked at her with stricken eyes.

'I'm sorry,' Corie muttered. 'Is everyone OK?'

'Yeah.'

She put on one of the socks. It clung to the sticky bottom of her foot. 'Where are they?' she asked, pulling on the other.

'Over on the other side. Looking for Butler's mine.'

'Butler's mine,' she muttered.

'God, it's all our fault.'

'It's my fault. I let you people mess with the Ouija board. I knew better.' She put on the sneakers. They were a little too big. She laced and tied them. 'You'd better wait here for the others. I'm going down the trail. I've gotta find Chad.'

'Where . . .?'

'I don't know,' she said, her voice faltering. 'Over there someplace. Where the trail is.'

Corie stood up, wincing, wondering how she'd been able to walk at all on her ruined feet, much less run. The pain had seemed bothersome before. Now, it was torture in spite of the socks and shoes.

'Are you sure you shouldn't wait here? They must've heard the shots.'

Corie shook her head. She began to limp away, going down the gradual slope and angling toward the steep wall of the mountain. Each step sent pain shooting up from her feet. The clothing bothered her. The sweatshirt was too hot and it stuck to her back. The shorts kept slipping down her hips and rump. Every few steps, she had to pull them up.

Finally, she stopped to fix the shorts. She lifted the sweatshirt and tucked its bottom edge under her chin. The air cooled her wet skin. She sighed with relief. And thought how strange to be concerned about her physical comfort. Chad was dead, and she was worried about being too hot. But the air did feel good. It felt cool and wonderful. She unclipped the safety pin, made a larger tuck in the waistband of the shorts, and pinned it.

She realized that she was standing near the place where

she'd made her move against the man. Stroked him. The memory of it sickened her.

How could I have *done* that?

It hadn't seemed so horrible at the time. Just a . . . necessity.

That's what saved me, she told herself. That's how I got away from him.

But he would've gotten me, anyway, if Doris hadn't shot him.

Turning around, she looked for Doris. The girl was out of sight.

She didn't see me do it.

Nobody'll ever know.

Corie let the sweatshirt drop. She rubbed both hands against the front of it and wondered when she might get a chance to wash them with soap and water.

I'll have to wash a lot more than my hands, she realized.

She started walking again. The last time here, she'd been riding the bastard's back. He hadn't carried her as far beyond the end of the trail as she'd thought. Probably no more than fifteen or twenty feet. It had seemed like a hundred yards.

She stepped onto the trail, saw how narrow it was, saw the broad deep valley past its edge and felt a sickening sweep of dizziness. She placed her left hand on the granite wall to hold herself steady.

She didn't want to venture out onto that thin ledge.

That's ridiculous, she told herself. You not only walked along it before, you *ran* on parts of it.

She took a step onto it and her knees went weak.

She sank down and began to crawl.

This is better anyway, she thought. It'll help me figure the distance. *He* was crawling all the way from the place where Chad went off.

Oh, God, Chad, how could this've happened?

The stone surface of the trail hurt her knees.

She remembered the way Chad's knees had looked, not so long ago. Down by the lake. Only minutes before everything normal and good had come to such a horrible stop. They'd been red and dented from the granite slab. They'd gotten that way while he was on top of her, joined with her so wonderfully and for the last time.

We never should've come here.

The kids didn't need to be rescued. They took care of themselves. And we ended up the victims.

Corie winced as her right knee came down on a loose stone. Stopping, she lifted her head. A few yards in front of her, the trail curved out of sight.

That's where he came at us. She could see him clearly in her mind, charging around the bend. She'd just been peering over the edge, stunned to find Chad looking up at her.

She remembered, now, that her own red bandanna had been knotted around Chad's head.

He'd come for her like a gallant knight, bearing his lady's colors.

Climbed straight up the slope, scaling the mountainside to intercept them.

Only to get himself killed.

Why didn't you stay at the lake? You should've let him have me!

The trail ahead was blurry. She lifted her right arm and rubbed her eyes dry on the sweatshirt's sleeve. Then she crawled a little farther forward.

This is where it happened.

She eased down against the trail and worked her legs sideways until the wall blocked her feet. On her elbows, she squirmed to the edge. There, she lay down flat. Hands clutching the rim, she pulled herself forward and looked down and saw Chad and forgot her despair and her fear of falling and thrust herself up to her hands and knees and shouted his name.

'Coreen!' he called back. He raised an arm, then let it drop across his belly.

He was on his back on a slim shelf of rock no more than twenty feet below Corie's eyes. His left side was pressed against the sheer face of the mountain. His right leg was bent beneath him, its foot out of sight under his rump.

'Are you all right?' he called up to her.

Am *I* all right? Corie laughed and wept.

'Where's that guy?'

She couldn't answer. She shook her head.

'Hey, stop blubbering and talk to me.'

Finally, she was able to say, 'He's . . . he's dead. Doris shot him.'

Chad was silent for a moment, then said, 'Did he hurt you? Are you OK?'

'I'm . . . fine. Jesus! You're *alive*!'

'Portions of me aren't feeling too swift. Took a little fall.'

'God, Chad, quit joking around.'

'A lot of good I did you in the hero department.'

'Where are you hurt?'

'All over. But mostly my leg. It's busted pretty good. I think I'm stuck here.'

'We'll get you, don't worry.'

'Rotsa ruck.'

'Somehow,' she muttered. She realized it wouldn't be easy. The mountainside, right here, was nearly vertical and had no switchbacks.

Chad must've plummeted straight down. If he hadn't landed on that thin jutting lip, he would've dropped another hundred feet or more.

She supposed it would be possible to reach him either by climbing down or by coming up to him from below. The face of the slope was rough enough to provide handholds and footholds. It even had some other ledges and outcroppings not far from his perch. Hell, *he'd* climbed it.

But getting to him was one thing. With his broken leg, he would have to be carried. And that looked impossible.

'Just don't move,' she called.

'I appreciate the advice.'

'God, it's a miracle you landed where you did.'

'I planned it this way.'

'I'll go and get the kids. Maybe they've got a rope or something.'

'I'll be here.'

Corie crawled backward, got to her feet and hurried over the trail. She thought how ironic it would be if she fell now after finding Chad alive, but the thought didn't slow her down.

Alive. A miracle.

Chad hadn't been meant to die.

Nothing can stop us now. We'll get him off that ledge and carry him down to the lake. Maybe spend the night there. Hike out in the morning . . .

She strode off the end of the trail and stopped as she saw all six kids coming down the gentle slope, Doris in the lead. She waved both arms. She shouted, 'Over here!'

They spotted her and quickened their pace. They hardly looked like the students who'd been at her party Friday night. They seemed weary and solemn as they trudged along under the weight of their packs. Their clothes were grubby, their skin glowing with sunburn. Lana had always been so tidy and neatly groomed, but now her hair was tangled and her blouse was untucked and half unbuttoned. Keith was bare to the waist, his shirt draping the front of his pants. Glen, big Glen, appeared to have shrunken. Probably, Corie thought, because she'd seen so much of that crazy bastard who was so much larger than Glen. Howard wore a ragged, floppy hat. Its brim hid most of his face. Angela, in a T-shirt and fancy gleaming shorts, looked grim but bore little resemblance to the sheepish and pallid girl Corie remembered. Her face was ruddy, her arms and legs burnished by the sun.

They came toward her in silence.

Doris, she realized, must've told them that Chad had been killed.

'Chad's alive,' she said. 'He's got a broken leg, but he's OK.'

'That's great,' Lana said.

The others nodded and muttered agreement. They seemed a little relieved, but not overjoyed.

Why should they be? Corie asked herself. They hardly know him. They're just glad he's alive for my sake.

'How are *you*?' Howard asked.

'I've been better.'

'Did that dirty creep hurt you?'

'He made me walk barefoot. That's about the worst of it.'

'We should've hunted him down yesterday and killed him,' Keith said. 'None of this would've happened.'

'It wouldn't have happened,' Corie said, 'if you kids had stayed home.'

'We didn't know you'd come after us,' Lana told her.

'You're my responsibility. It was my Ouija board. Anyway, the hell with all that. I'm just glad everyone's OK. But Chad's stuck on a ledge. Do you have rope?'

Nodding, Lana swung her pack to the ground. As she opened it, she asked, 'How far down is he?'

'Maybe fifteen, twenty feet.'

Lana removed a coil of clothesline.

It was dirty gray, and not much more than a quarter-inch thick.

'I don't think that's gonna do it,' Corie said. 'What about the rest of you?'

The others shook their heads.

'Let's go and take a look,' Lana suggested. She swung up her pack and pushed her arms through its straps.

Corie led the way. 'Be very careful,' she warned. 'This part of the trail's treacherous.'

'We came up it earlier,' Keith said.

As she started along it, she asked, 'Did you have any luck finding Butler's loot?'

Lana, just behind her, said, 'We found the mine. It was that asshole's camp.'

'Hubert Orson Elliot,' Keith called.

'That was his name? The guy . . .?'

'Mr Universe,' Lana said.

He must've been taking me there, Corie realized. To his 'home'. A mine.

'We'll have to give Doris a prize for marksmanship,' Keith called.

'You didn't find any treasure, though?'

'Nope,' Lana said. 'Not unless you count his collection of ladies' undergarments.'

'You're kidding.'

'Nope. His backpack was full of the things. We figure he must've spent a lot of time sneaking into people's camps.'

'Maybe he took them off babes he grabbed,' Keith said.

'Damn lunatic,' Corie muttered. Then she saw the bend ahead. She took a few more steps, stopped, sank to her hands and knees, and looked over the edge of the trail. Chad smiled up at her. 'Back with the troops,' she told him.

'Everyone accounted for?' he asked.

'They're all here. You're the only casualty.'

'Lucky me.'

Lana, kneeling beside her, stuck out an arm and waved.

Keith stepped right to the rim and peered down. 'Holy shit,' he said.

Corie saw Glen on the other side of Keith. Not so brave,

he had taken off his pack and crawled to the edge. Doris stayed behind him.

Howard and Angela, also without their packs, stepped around Corie. They got down on their hands and knees and inched forward to look at Chad.

Howard, turning his head, grimaced at Corie. 'How'll we get him up here?'

'I don't know.'

'Let's just haul him up,' Keith said.

'I wonder if the rope's strong enough,' Corie said.

'Might as well give it a shot,' Lana told her. She removed the clothesline from her shoulder. Holding onto one end, she tossed the rest over the edge. The coil dropped, unlooping. Even as it fell, Corie realized it was plenty long enough to do the job. Her stomach gave a nervous flip when Chad reached up to grab it. He caught the line just above its end. Slack tumbled down on him, draping his face.

'So far so good,' Lana said.

'I don't like this,' Glen said.

You're not the only one, Corie thought.

Lana called, 'Can you tie it around yourself?'

'It's not much of a rope,' he said.

'It's all we've got.'

'This is too risky,' Corie muttered.

Chad arched his back, turning slightly away from the mountainside as he tried to shove the rope underneath his body.

Corie squirmed and gritted her teeth. She yelled, 'For Godsake, be careful!'

He twisted the other way. He shoved his right hand under his back. A moment later, his hand reappeared gripping the end of the rope. He tugged at the line, drawing more of it through the tight space between his back and the slab. Then he brought its end up. He knotted it above his chest to the vertical side of the rope. When he was done, he squirmed and worked the loop upward to his armpits.

'That oughta do it,' he said.

Lana slowly pulled in the slack. On her knees, she backed away from the edge. 'OK, guys.'

Glen took the rope from her. He stepped backward until he was leaning against the slope at the far side of the trail. He had a look on his face as if he were smelling something awful. 'If this thing breaks . . .' he muttered.

Howard moved in beside Glen. He grabbed the rope just in front of Glen's hands. Keith joined them on the other side and took hold.

'Just go easy,' Corie told them. Scooting sideways, she wrapped her hands around the rope just above the rim of the trail. She gazed down the taut line. 'Ready?' she called to Chad.

He clutched the loop. 'Have at it.'

'Go ahead,' Corie told the boys.

They started pulling. The rope went hard and vibrated in her hands. She saw Chad's head and shoulders begin to rise. The line appeared to be stretching, getting thinner.

It's gonna snap!

'Stop!' she shouted. 'Lower him.'

'What's wrong?' Keith asked.

'It won't hold him.'

'Are you sure?' Lana asked. Crouching at the edge, she stared down. 'It'll probably hold.'

'It's not worth the risk,' Corie said. 'It wasn't made for this kind of thing. What if we get him half way up and it breaks?'

Lana, frowning, looked over her shoulder and said, 'You'd better let him down.'

As the rope inched through Corie's hands, she watched Chad settle down on the ledge.

'What gives?' he called to her.

'I'm just afraid the rope won't hold you.'

'You and me both.'

'Don't worry, we'll think of something.' She backed away and got to her feet. Most of the kids' packs had a variety of belts, cords and straps used to hold their sleeping bags in place. A combination of those, plus trouser belts . . .

No. Something like that would be too flimsy. If they were all attached, there would be a dozen knots or buckles holding them together, any of which might give way.

She noticed one pack that had two sleeping bags strapped to its top, and the pack beside it had no sleeping bag at all. The cover flap of that one was stretched over a high bulge in a way that made her wonder for a moment if the kids had brought grapefruit along. If only they'd skipped the fruit, she thought, and brought a decent rope.

'What've you got in your backpacks?' she asked.

The kids exchanged odd, troubled looks. It crossed Corie's mind that they had found something, maybe in the mine, that they didn't want her to know about. Butler's loot?

She didn't care. All that mattered was getting Chad to safety.

'Just food and clothes and things,' Lana said.

'None of you has *anything* we might use to pull him up?'

'Tie some clothes together?' Howard suggested.

Corie shook her head. 'What about back at the mine? Did you see anything there?'

'Some clothes, a pack, a sleeping bag,' Lana said. 'I didn't see any rope.'

'No,' Keith said. 'And we searched the whole mine.'

'Anything in your car?' she asked Lana.

'Jumper cables. A blanket. No ropes or chains.'

'Same here,' she muttered.

'There's plenty of stuff here we could probably attach together,' Howard said.

'Whatever we attach might come apart.' Sighing, Corie stepped across the trail. She leaned back against the slope and folded her arms. 'He's OK where he is, that's the thing. If we try to pull him up . . . I just don't want to risk it unless we're a hundred per cent sure it'll work. It's a miracle he landed on that ledge in the first place. That isn't likely to happen twice.'

'So what do you want to do?' Lana asked.

'I don't know. If nobody has any better idea, I guess we should leave him where he is until we can get some real help. A mountain rescue team.'

'I was thinking the same thing,' Glen said.

'What do you have in mind, sending up smoke signals?' Keith asked.

'There's a town called Purdy only about ten miles north of the turn off,' Corie explained. 'You make a right at the end of the dirt road, and . . .'

'*Purdy?*' Keith asked.

'Yeah. It shouldn't take you more than half an hour to get there after you hit the turn-off. It's probably not much of a town, but it's bound to have a police force and they'd know what to do.'

'It's a two-day hike just getting back to the car,' Doris said.

Lana shook her head. 'It won't take that long. For one thing, we only spent a few hours hiking each day. And going back it'll all be downhill. If we really haul ass, I bet we can reach the car in five or six hours. A couple more hours to drive out to the main road.' She looked at her wristwatch. 'It's almost five, now. Figure eight or nine hours, and we'll be in Purdy. That'd make it . . . one or two in the morning.'

'So you should be able to get a rescue team out here sometime tomorrow,' Corie said. 'That's not bad.'

'Do you think Chad'll be able to make it through the night?' Lana asked. 'It'll get awfully cold.'

'I'll need some warmer clothes.'

'You're coming with us, aren't you?' Howard asked.

'I'm staying.'

'Here? All by yourself? I'll stay with you.' He looked at Angela, and she nodded. 'We'll both stay. We can help.'

'Forget it, Howitzer.'

'Do you think you'll need them?' Lana asked.

It would be nice to have the company, Corie thought. She didn't relish the idea of spending the night alone on the mountainside. 'Is there any reason they shouldn't stay with me?'

The kids all looked at each other.

'What's going on?'

'Howard can stay with you,' Lana said. 'But I think Angela would rather come with us. Wouldn't you?'

'I want to be with Howard,' she said.

'You want to be on Purdy Road tomorrow,' Keith told her. 'Don't you.' It wasn't a question.

'Well . . .'

'There's no reason to bully her,' Corie said. 'What's the problem? What's this about Purdy Road?'

'It's where we're supposed to find the treasure,' Howard explained.

'Good going, Howitzer. Shit!'

'*Angela's* supposed to find it. The Ouija board said she'll take us to it.'

'The Ouija board!' Corie blurted.

'We've come this far,' Lana said, her voice calm. 'If Angela isn't with us tomorrow on Purdy Road, we might miss our chance. Maybe we won't find it anyway. But maybe we will. If she stays here, it could ruin it for all of us. We went through a lot, trying to find Butler's loot.'

'Yeah,' Corie muttered. 'And look what Chad and I went through because of it.'

'We didn't know anybody'd get hurt.'

'When you mess around with a Ouija board, somebody *always* gets hurt.'

'Ask Angela if she's sorry we messed with it.'

'We found my mother's body,' Angela said. 'In the mine. That guy . . . he'd been *living* with it.' She stepped over to one of the packs. The one without the sleeping bag. The one with the bulging top. She unfastened the flap and pulled it back.

Corie felt her breath rush out as she found herself looking at a skull. The entire head, perched high on the stalk of its spine, protruded from the pack as if it were peering out to survey the scenery. Hairless, fleshless, eyeless, its jaw hanging.

Doris, gasping, flung a hand across her mouth.

'Jesus,' Corie murmured.

'It's my mother,' Angela explained. 'She's Butler. It was her maiden name.'

'*She's* the spirit of the Ouija board,' Lana said. 'She got us up here to find her body. And to reunite her with Angela.'

'And to nail Hubert Orson Elliot,' Keith added.

'And she's the one who says we'll find the treasure tomorrow. I don't think it's some kind of malicious Ouija board trick. I think she's sincere.'

'Your mother?' Corie asked, gazing at Angela.

The girl looked as if she might start to weep. Lips pressed tightly together, she nodded.

'We're taking her down so she can have a proper burial,' Lana said.

'My God,' Corie murmured. She stepped closer to the pack and peered down into it. From what she could see of the skeleton, it appeared to be sitting upright, intact except for its legs. The leg bones were stuffed in alongside the ribcage, the upside-down feet resting across its shoulders.

She lifted the flap forward to cover it.

Turning to Angela, she said, 'You'd better go along with the others.'

'Not if Howard's gonna stay.'

She put her arms around the girl. Angela hugged her, face pressing the side of her neck. To the others, Corie said, 'I'll be fine here by myself. Just don't go looking for that treasure until you've been to the authorities about all this. I want a rescue team up here tomorrow.'

'We'll take care of that first thing,' Lana said.

'Can you leave us a couple of sleeping bags? We'll need some food and water, too. And the rope, of course. We'll be all right.'

Chapter Thirty

They descended the mountainside into shadows. When they reached their campsite by the lake, Lana suggested they take a rest and eat.

Howard left the others and walked over to the shore. He looked for Dr Dalton. Trees were in the way. From here, he could only see the very summit of Calamity Peak. It was tipped with gold by the last of the evening sunlight, and the few scattered wisps of cloud above it were ruddy.

He supposed he had done the right thing, coming down with the rest of them. But he hated the thought of Dr Dalton up there alone on the narrow trail.

She's not alone, he told himself. She's with Chad.

And I'm with Angela. That's the way it ought to be.

But he knew that he still loved her, even though so much had changed, and he felt as if he'd left part of himself high up there on the mountainside. She was undoubtedly out of the sunlight, now. Chill winds were rushing through the valley, and they were probably stronger, colder, where she was.

He and Doris had left their packs with her. He'd taken nothing, not even a sweatshirt, leaving everything for Dr Dalton. He wondered if she had put his coat on yet. It made him feel better to imagine her wearing it. Maybe she would use his sweatpants, too. They would fit her better than whatever she might find in Doris's pack.

Angela came up behind him and wrapped her arms around his waist. 'Are you wishing you'd stayed with her?'

'Not without you.'

She squeezed him. He felt her breasts push against his back. 'I sure hope they'll be all right up there,' she said. 'This whole thing's my fault.'

'Nothing's your fault.'

'It all is. We wouldn't have come here at all except for Mom. It's like she was using everyone else, you know? Just to get me here.'

Howard turned around. Angela wore the windbreaker that he'd bought for her. Its front was open. He reached underneath it and pulled her up against him. The back of her T-shirt felt a little damp.

Off in the clearing, Lana was bent over her open pack, searching for something. Keith, nearby, was watching her. Glen was sprawled on his back, Doris sitting beside him and ripping open a package of cookies.

Nobody was watching, so he kissed Angela on the mouth. She moaned softly and rubbed herself against him. After a few moments, he eased his mouth away. 'Do you know what?' he asked.

'What?'

'I've been thinking a lot about everything. All the way coming down the mountain. This whole business is very strange.'

'You're telling me.'

'I mean particularly about Butler. Do you remember all that "you give" business at the party? Butler had you take off your blouse. Right in front of everyone. That's pretty weird when you figure she's your mother.'

'I'll say. It doesn't make sense.'

'I thought at first that she might've done it to throw off suspicion. To make it look like you're a victim, so nobody, would suspect she was on your side. But then something else occurred to me. Do you know why I think she did it?'

'Why?'

'To get me involved. So I would . . . finally notice you.'

Angela laughed softly, and he felt her shake against him. 'So you could see me in my bra?'

'Yeah. Hell, it worked. Up till then, I hadn't really thought of you as . . .' He felt himself starting to blush. ' . . someone I might want to . . . have as a girlfriend.'

'You think she was playing match-maker?'

'Yeah. I really do. I think she knew how lonely you were. Maybe she even realized I'm the guy who . . .' He shrugged. 'Maybe she knew we'd be good together, so she helped things along. And that isn't the only thing. It's all because of coming up here to look for the loot that she got you away from Skerrit.'

Howard felt her body stiffen.

'Did you have to mention him?' she muttered.

'You're not going back to him. I won't let you. From now on, you're going to be with me. No matter what. So don't worry about him, OK? This is all part of your mother's plan. She wanted us to fall in love, and I'll bet she wants you to live with me and never see Skerrit again.'

'Should we ask the Ouija board about all this?'

'What we'd better do, maybe, is go over and get something to eat.'

'OK.' She gave him a quick squeeze, then took his hand.

Together, they walked up the slope and joined the others.

'You two playing smoochie again?' Keith asked, and broke off a hunk of chocolate bar with his teeth.

'Every chance we get,' Angela said.

Lana, hopping from foot to foot as she stepped into her blue jeans, said, 'Hang on, we'll dig out some stuff for you.' Her shorts were on the ground. The hanging front of her shirt prevented Howard from seeing what she was wearing. If anything. He forced himself to look away.

'Have some cookies,' Doris said.

'Good stuff,' Glen said, crumbs flying from his mouth.

They went over to Doris and took a couple of the huge sugar cookies from the offered pack.

'What we oughta do,' Keith said, 'is break into *their* stockpile.' He poked a thumb over his shoulder as if hitching a ride. Some distance behind him, two packs were propped against the log that Howard and Angela had used as a bench last night when they sat by the campfire.

'We've got plenty,' Lana said. Howard risked a glance at her, and was glad to see that her pants were on. She was zipping the fly.

'So what? It'd be fun to see what they've got.'

'It's none of our business.'

'Shit, they've got half *our* stuff.'

'Shut up and eat,' Lana told him. She crouched over her pack and took out a plastic bag full of Tropical Chocolate bars. After taking one for herself, she tossed the bag to Howard. Then she resumed her search of the pack. 'Got some freeze-dried apricots and shit in here. Any takers?'

'No shit for me,' Glen said.

'You're already full of it,' Keith told him.

'I'll have some of them 'cots.'

Lana flipped the bag to him, then pulled out a pack of trail mix. 'Ah, the good stuff.' She turned to the others and frowned. 'You know, we *could* have a real meal. It's not as if we've gotta rush off. As it is, we won't be getting into Purdy till after midnight, and they aren't about to send out a rescue party before dawn.'

'We'd have to build a fire,' Glen said.

'Screw that,' Keith said.

'And we'd have to do *dishes*,' Doris added.

That comment won her a smile from Glen. She returned a smirk, but reached into his bag of apricots and took a handful.

Lana, still on her feet, gazed toward the lake as she tore open the trail mix. 'Its a shame we got here too late for a swim. An hour ago, I was really counting on it.'

'Go on in,' Keith told her.

'Right, and freeze my buns off. I've been *in* that lake after dark.'

'It's not dark yet.'

'Close enough. No way.'

'Man,' Glen said, 'you wouldn't get me into that lake for anything. I wouldn't jump in there if I was on fire,'

'Isn't that a trifle extreme?' Doris asked.

'How would you like to be swimming around and bump into your old friend Hubie?'

Doris stopped chewing. She looked sick.

'I hadn't thought of that,' Lana muttered, wrinkling her nose.

'I thought of it the minute Doris told us he'd taken a nose-dive into the stream. It feeds this lake. He might be floating around out there right now.' Glen glanced from Angela to Howard. 'You guys didn't happen to see him, did you?'

'They were too busy playing kissy-face,' Keith said.

'There's a good chance he didn't make it down this far,' Lana pointed out. 'He could've gotten hung up on rocks, or something, upstream.'

'Could be,' Glen said, and poked another wrinkled disk of apricot into his mouth. 'On the other hand, he might be bobbing around out there.'

'He *might* be swimming around out there,' Keith said. 'Who's to say he's dead?'

'I shot him twice,' Doris said, looking as if she'd lost her taste for food. 'And he fell all the way down there. And Dr Dalton shot at him a couple of times.'

'Did she hit him?'

'I don't know.'

'So how do we know for sure he's dead?'

'I'm sure,' Doris muttered.

Heads began to turn toward the lake.

But Howard stared at the ground in front of him. Until now, there'd been no doubt in his mind that Hubert was dead. Doris had *told* them he was dead.

If the bullets didn't kill him, the fall probably did. If he was still alive when he hit the stream, he probably drowned or got smashed to death against rocks when he went down the rapids.

He's *got* to be dead, Howard told himself.

But what if he's not?

'Come on, guys,' Lana said. 'Nobody could've survived all that.' She didn't look as if she believed her own words.

'Ever hear of Rasputin, the mad monk?' Keith asked. 'They poisoned that son of a bitch, shot him full of holes, stabbed him a couple of million times, and he still didn't go toes up.'

'Took a licking but kept on ticking,' Glen said.

A moan escaped from Howard, and the others looked at him.

'What's the trouble, Howitzer?'

'Maybe a couple of us should go back up and stay with Dr Dalton.'

'Get real,' Keith said.

'What if the guy's alive?'

'If he is,' Lana said, 'and I doubt it – he certainly isn't in any condition to climb all the way up the mountain.'

'But you can feel free to go back up there if you want to,' Keith told him. 'Angela stays with us, but you can go.'

'It would be a waste of time, anyway,' Doris said. 'The man's dead and I killed him.'

'You sound like it bothers you,' Keith said.

She scowled at him. 'I'm not in the habit of taking human life. How many people have *you* killed?'

'This guy got what he deserved,' Lana said.

'Easy for you to say; you aren't the one who shot him.'

Glen set the bag of apricots on his lap, reached over and took hold of Doris's hand. Howard expected her to jerk it away from him and make a cutting remark. But she met Glen's eyes. Her hand remained in his, and her mouth remained shut.

'You had to do it,' he said.

'I'm aware of that. It still makes me feel horrible.'

'He was a scumbag,' Keith said. 'If he's dead, you did the world a favor.'

'Yeah, sure.'

'You did the right thing,' Glen told her. 'It's just damn lucky you were there and had the gun. If you'd been with us, he probably would've killed the Proff. And then he would've gone on to his mine and run into the rest of us.'

'Then *we'd* have had to nail the bastard,' Keith said.

'But he might've gotten some of us first,' Lana added.

'I suppose.'

'We really owe you,' she said.

'Maybe we oughta vote Doris a bigger share of the loot,' Glen suggested.

'I'll go along with that.' Howard said.

Angela nodded. 'Me, too.'

'I don't want more,' Doris said. 'Not for killing a person.'

'Good thing,' Keith said. 'All this generosity makes me want to barf.'

When they finished eating, Lana got to her feet and said, 'I guess we'd better take the tents with us.'

They'll slow us down,' Keith told her.

'You don't want to leave *your* tent, do you Glen?' she asked.

'I don't suppose so.'

'We might never see them again.'

'Aren't we coming back with the rescue party?' Howard asked.

'Who knows? They might not let us. Or they might come in on a different route.'

'Maybe they'll chopper in,' Glen said.

'At any rate, they aren't going to be bothered with picking up our tents, and I'm not exactly eager to hike back in here to retrieve the things.'

'What about those?' Angela asked, nodding toward the two packs. 'If we might not be coming back, shouldn't we take them with us?'

'Forget it,' Keith muttered.

'Doris and I aren't carrying anything,' Howard pointed out.

He expected Doris to protest, but she said, 'I wouldn't mind. I'll take Dr Dalton's, if you'll take Chad's.'

He wanted to be the one with Dr Dalton's pack. It would be a pleasure to carry her load on his back, and to do the favor for her. But if he argued about it, he'd look like a jerk. 'I'll take whichever pack is heavier,' he said.

'Fair enough.'

'Let's think about this for a minute,' Lana said. 'It might not be such a good idea. What if Corie needs something out of her pack and comes down to get it?'

'We left her with plenty of stuff,' Glen said.

'Yeah, but who knows? Maybe there'll be a delay getting them out, and they run out of food. It isn't likely, but it could happen. If we leave the packs here, at least there'll be supplies and things she can get to.'

'Good point,' Keith said.

'We'd better leave them,' Angela said.

Nodding, Howard muttered, 'Yeah.' He hadn't considered the possibility of the rescue hitting a snag. But he supposed that anything was possible. A bad storm might show up out of nowhere and force a delay. Or the rescue team might be too busy with other emergencies to come in tomorrow. If it comes in by air, the helicopter might crash.

We might crash in the car on the way to Purdy. What if all of us are killed in a head-on before we even get a chance to reach help for them?

Howard knew he was letting his imagination run wild. None of that was likely to happen. But anything *could* happen.

As he got up and went to help with the tents, he imagined Dr Dalton waiting on the mountainside, waiting for help that never arrives. Finally, Chad dies of exposure. She comes down the trail, out of food by now, starving and grieving. She reaches the lake. Her pack is right here where she left it. Grateful, she sits down to rest and eat. And Hubert comes out of the lake behind her. He is dripping wet, all naked except for that little pouch. Just as he grabs her, Howard shows up and attacks Hubert with his Swiss Army knife. He slashes the bastard's throat. And Dr Dalton, sobbing with relief, throws herself into Howard's arms.

That's about as likely to happen as the car crash, he thought.

But wouldn't it be neat?

What about Angela?

He looked at her. She was crouched beside him, tugging at one of the tent stakes. She turned her head. Her eyes met his. And he knew that Dr Dalton was just for fantasies. Angela was for real life, and his.

'Hold it a minute,' Lana said. 'Somebody's been inside. The zipper's open.' She had already pulled the guy line stake. She hung onto the taut cord, keeping the tent upright. 'Howard, you want to grab this? I'll take a look.'

'Maybe Hubie's in there,' Keith called from behind the tent.

'I'll look,' Howard said.

Alarm filled Angela's eyes.

'Hubert's dead,' Lana said.

Glen and Doris stopped working on the other tent. They turned to watch Howard.

He hesitated, tempted to pull out his Swiss Army knife.

Not in front of everyone, he thought. You'll look like a dork.

Crouching, ready to lurch back, he lifted one side of the hanging flaps. And felt weak with relief.

No Hubert, crouched to pounce.

'There're some clothes,' he said.

'Well, get 'em,' Lana said.

He ducked through the opening and knelt over them.

The flaps had fallen shut behind him. The tent was nearly dark.

In spite of the deep gloom, he could see enough to send a secret thrill through him.

There were hiking boots, white socks, a plaid blouse with a flimsy black bra draped across it, and black panties hanging outside the waist of a pair of shorts as if the two garments had been pulled off together.

Dr Dalton's clothes.

Coreen's.

What were they doing here? Is this where Hubert had caught her?

He felt a rush of hatred. And envy. And guilt as he imagined himself in the tent with Coreen. Himself, not Hubert, stripping her.

Kneeling in front of her, reaching behind her back, unclasping the bra and lifting it away. But then he realized that her breasts were the same as Angela's. Small, pale globes, nipples large and jutting. He looked at the face, and it was Angela's face. His guilt faded. He was breathless and hard with desire, but somehow it seemed all right, just fine, not sneaky or dirty or any kind of betrayal now that Angela had taken Coreen's place in his mind.

As he tucked the socks into the boots and rolled the clothing into a bundle, he wondered when he would get to be alone with Angela again.

Maybe later tonight. Maybe after getting to Purdy and going to the police, they would all check into a motel. Maybe he could get a separate room, just for himself and Angela.

With the boots in one hand, the bundle of clothes hugged to his chest, he scurried out of the tent.

Chapter Thirty-one

'What're you doing?' Chad yelled up to her.

'It's visiting hour,' Corie called, lowering her legs over the side of the trail.

'Are you nuts? Stay where you are.'

'Don't worry.'

'My God, don't try it!'

She squirmed backward, the granite edge rough against her belly, rucking up the sweatshirt. The wind was cold on her back and sides, but the rock against her belly still held some of the sun's warmth. She lowered herself some more. Clinging to the rim of the trail, she swung her right leg across the face of the slope until she found the foothold that she'd spotted before starting her descent.

'Coreen, please.'

'I know what I'm doing.'

She *hoped* so, anyway.

The idea of climbing down to be with Chad had occurred to her shortly after the kids left. But the idea had frightened her. She'd pushed it to the back of her mind and busied herself with taking care of Chad.

She had asked him to untie the rope. Then she'd pulled it up and lowered a canteen to him. After drawing up the rope again, she'd prepared him a care package: trail mix, cookies, a bacon bar, chocolate bars, an assortment of freeze-dried fruit, all wrapped tightly in a shirt from Howard's pack. Once the bundle had settled safely onto Chad's chest, she'd brought up the rope and stretched out flat and talked to him while he ate.

And studied the slope, seeking a way down.

Finding possible routes.

But still reluctant to try it.

Why take the risk? She could see him from here, talk to him.

The next best thing to being there.

Not at all the same as being there.

He was twenty feet below Corie. She felt as if he were in a far-off country.

From which he might never return.

The sun had already dropped behind a distant ridge. Night would be here soon. If she kept procrastinating, darkness would kill her chance.

She knew it was foolish to climb down for a visit. Idiotic. It would accomplish nothing. But she also knew that, if she didn't, she would spend the long dark night alone on the trail regretting her lost opportunity.

And what if something happened during the night?

She didn't want to think about that. The night would pass. Dawn would come, the sun warming the mountainside. And he'd be there, alive and well – though hurting – on his narrow ledge.

But you never know.

Things happen.

She knew that she had to go down to him. Now. If only for a brief visit. Just to be *with* him for a few minutes.

Before starting down, she'd taken the precaution of rigging a safety line. She didn't trust the rope, doubted that it could bear her full weight without snapping, but figured it might be useful in case she should find herself without a handhold.

She'd secured one end to a small knob of rock a few feet up the trail from where Chad had gone over, then drawn the other end around her back, under her armpits and over her breasts. She'd tied it. To keep the rope out of her face, she'd slid the knot sideways to her right shoulder.

She'd coiled the slack and set it at the edge of the trail hoping that it would pay out slowly during her descent. If she found herself needing the rope as a handhold, she would simply pull it all down and make it taut. In the meantime, however, it wouldn't be in the way.

On her belly, she'd scooted backward and lowered her legs over the side.

And kept on working her way down the steep face of the mountain in spite of Chad's protests. The slack payed out according to plan. Until something thumped the top of her head. Startled, she gasped and hugged the slope. For just an instant, she thought that a snake had dropped onto her. It *felt* like a snake. A very long one. But then coils slipped down her head. Dirty gray rope fell past her eyes, brushed the tip of her nose, her chin, and came to rest across the tops of her breasts.

Most of it landed there.

She could feel one loop encircling her neck.

'Shit!' It wasn't her voice. It was Chad's. 'Don't move.'

'What do you mean, don't move?'

'I think some of it's wrapped around your neck.'

'Shit.' This time, it was Corie who said it.

But with so much slack piled on her chest, she figured there wouldn't be much of a problem.

She eased herself a bit lower.

'Careful!'

The rope tightened like a noose. She gasped. Her heart sledged. Every muscle in her body suddenly seemed to be shuddering. They shivered with fear. They shook with the effort of holding her spreadeagled against the mountainside.

'It's all right,' Chad said.

'Oh yeah sure it is!' Her voice came out squeaking.

'Just don't panic.'

'Who me?'

'You'll be OK if you climb *upward*.'

'I can't move.'

'Sure you can. You're scared, that's all.'

'That's all.'

'Just loosen up, calm down, you'll be fine.'

'The damn rope was supposed to keep me safe, not string me up.'

'Well, hang in there.'

'Is that supposed to be funny?'

'Just a little gallows humor.'

'Ha ha. If you ask me how it's hangin', I'm gonna come down there and brain you.'

'At least this should cure your penis envy.'

'Chad!'

'Now that you're so well hung.'

'Oh, you're a riot. You're hilarious. I know why you're doing this, you know. You're just trying to take my mind off my fucking *predicament*.'

'Is it working?'

'No!'

'Well, I might be able to reach your foot and give you a little boost.'

'Am I that close?'

'Not hardly. But I'm gonna stand up and try in about two minutes.'

'Oh Jesus.' With her right hand, she let go and reached up and grabbed the rope above her head. Pulling on the taut line, she thrust herself a little higher. The noose loosened. With some slack between her hand and neck, she dragged the rope across the back of her head and jerked it forward. It scraped and bent her ear. It scorched her cheekbone, the side of her jaw. When she yanked it past the front of her face, the rope abraded her nose and chin.

But then the noose was gone.

'It's OK,' she said. 'I got it.'

'Thank God. Now, please, climb back up to the trail before something else goes wrong.'

She didn't answer. She released the rope and clutched her solid handhold on the slope. She waited until her breathing and heartrate were no longer out of control. Then she resumed her descent.

'Coreen!'

'Loosen up,' she said.

'Why are you doing this?'

'I feel like it.'

Soon, she saw Chad over her right shoulder. His head was strained back so that he could look up at her. She was above him, her feet probably at the same level as his body. She was over to the side, though. Just as planned.

Making her way lower, she found the narrow ledge that she'd spotted from the trail. It was about a yard below the shelf that had stopped Chad's fall, and only a few inches wide. But wide enough to stand on.

She sidestepped carefully.

'You're out of your mind.'

'You looked lonely down here. And I know I was sure lonely up there.'

She found a good handhold on the wall above his face. Grabbing it with her left hand, she twisted and bent down, braced her right palm against the corner of the shelf above his shoulder, and lowered her face over his.

'You're cute upside-down,' she said.

'You're gonna fall, damn it.'

'No, I'm not.' Straining downward, she kissed him. His lips felt dry and cracked. Corie's body shook from the effort of holding herself in such a precarious and awkward position. But she felt his warm breath enter her mouth. And she was glad that she'd made the journey down to him.

She kissed the end of his nose.

She kissed his eyes, feeling the lids flutter against her lips.

Then she pushed herself upright.

'Did I make you all better?'

'My God, Coreen.'

She remembered that she had kissed his knees, down at the lake. So long ago. Only this afternoon.

She'd kissed his penis, too.

'I wish I could kiss you everywhere,' she said. 'It might be a trifle tricky, though. Short of climbing up there on top of you.'

He smiled. Or grimaced. Corie wasn't sure which. 'I was just about to suggest it.'

'Sure.'

'I'm serious.'

'Don't you think our amorous proclivities had better be postponed till . . .?'

'It's my leg.'

'Bad?'

'Doesn't hurt much. It's numb and I can't move it.'

Corie nodded. His right leg was bent at the knee, calf tight against the back of his thigh, ankle and foot trapped under his left buttock.

During earlier talks, Chad had told her that his tibia and fibula were probably broken. He'd been able to reach them with his hands and explore. 'Simple fractures,' he'd said. 'I haven't got bone ends poking out my skin, nothing like that.' Corie had assumed that the injury wasn't extremely serious except for the fact that it rendered him incapable of climbing to safety.

Now, she was worried.

'What do you want me to do?' she asked.

'Straighten it out. Get it out from under me. If you can. The way I'm on it, I'm cutting off my circulation.'

'Why didn't you tell me?'

'You might've tried to come down.'

'I should've figured it out for myself. Now, how are we gonna work this?'

'Very carefully.'

'Oh, boy.' The slack of the rope was hanging to her waist. With her right hand, she picked it up and stuffed it down the neck of her sweatshirt. She tucked it under the loose cinch made by the loop. Satisfied that it wouldn't fall out and tangle her, she leaned closer to Chad.

On each side of his head, there was room for one knee. His left shoulder and hip were flush against the vertical slope. On his right, next to his hip, she could see about two inches of flat rock.

Her right hand could go there.

'Maybe you'd better not try this,' Chad said.

'I know,' she said, and her stomach seemed to drop out from under her as she abandoned her perch and scurried onto Chad's shelf. She heard herself suck air, make a whinnying sound.

Knees on granite, she wobbled. She felt Chad grab her thighs. She ducked forward. Her left hand clutched his left hip. Her right palm thrust against the rock edge to his right.

'*Jesus Jesus Jesus!*' she gasped.

'You're OK. You're fine.'

She panted for air. She muttered, 'Holy smoke.'

'You OK?'

'I guess so. But we'd better make this quick.'

'Will it help if I raise my knee?'

'Yeah.'

'It won't hit you, will it? I can't see anything but sweatpants.'

'Just do it slowly.'

'His left knee came toward Corie's face. Letting go of his hip, she clutched his upraised thigh. She squeezed it hard. She darted her right hand from the ledge to his right ankle, grabbed hold and tugged his foot out from under his rump. He flinched and gasped. His fingers dug into the backs of her thighs.

Easing down until her shoulder met the top of his knee, she pushed at his right leg and stretched it out straight. Then she planted her right hand against the granite beside his thigh.

'That's got it,' she said. 'Should I do something else? Splint it?'

'With what?'

'I don't know. My shoes? I could use your belt . . .'

'No, don't bother. This is fine. It doesn't matter, I won't be walking on it. You'd better get back up to the trail while there's still some light.'

She raised her head. From the looks of the sky, the darkness of night was looming. Fifteen minutes, maybe, before full darkness. The mountain's wall was a deep and somber gray.

She knew that she'd better start climbing soon.

But she didn't want to leave.

If she stayed, she supposed she could manage to turn herself around and lie down flat on top of him. But if either of them rolled during the night . . . No, it was out of the question. Aside from the strong possibility of falling, there would be her weight on his broken leg. And the cold. They both needed sleeping bags, and her plan from the start had been to lower one with the rope. That had to remain the plan.

'Is there anything else I can do for you?' she asked.

'Considering our positions, there's a lot. But you'd probably fall trying to get my zipper open.'

'Probably.'

'I've been sorely tempted to try something from my end.'

'To my end?'

'You don't need the distraction.' His hands moved up the backs of her legs and gently squeezed her buttocks through the thickness of the sweatpants. She expected to feel his head rise between her thighs, to feel his mouth. But his head stayed down. 'You'd better go,' he said.

'Easier said than done.'

'Can you get your feet where your knees are, and stand up?'

'I can try.'

'Maybe hang onto my knee and your rope.'

'Yeah. Damn it.'

'What?'

'I don't want to leave you.'

'You've got to.'

'I know.'

'You go, Maria, my crop-haired one. You go and I will go with you. We will go together.'

'Cut it out.'

'Huh? You don't like my Cooper impression?'

'Robert Jordan died.'

'I'll be fine. I'll be *really* fine once you're back up there where you belong.'

'I love you.'

'I love you, too.' He gave her rump a soft pat.

'We'll be married before I've got the cast off my leg. Now go, OK?'

'OK.'

She reached high with her right hand and grabbed the robe. She pulled it tight. Not trusting it to do more than hold her steady, she pushed against Chad's upraised knee. She brought up her own right knee until the ball of her foot found purchase on the slab. Then she did the same with her left.

She came out of her squat.

Reluctantly, she let go of Chad's knee and reached for the wall. Nothing there to grab, but she pressed her hand against it, anyway, as she stood up straight.

She felt as if she were towering above Chad.

His face was far below, between her feet. He looked solemn, worried.

'I'll send a sleeping bag right down,' she said.

'Sleep tight, OK?'

'You, too. But not till we've got you tied.'

'Be careful.'

'You, too. Do you mind if I step on you?'
'My pleasure.'
On her left foot, she pivoted toward the wall of the mountain. She brought her right foot down on his shoulder, but only for a moment. Then she raised it to a crevice and began her climb.

Chapter Thirty-two

Howard sank into the backseat of the car, and sighed. It felt wonderful to be off his sore feet, off his aching legs, sitting down finally – and on a soft cushion, not on a log or the ground or a rock.

Angela slid in beside him. After she pulled the door shut, he put an arm across her shoulders.

'I didn't think we'd ever make it,' he muttered.

'It wasn't fun.'

'I guess it went pretty fast, though.'

The hike from the lake to the car had been mostly downhill, the group urged along the moonlit switchbacks by gravity. Howard had felt as if someone were pushing at his back, forcing him to take longer and quicker strides than he liked. He'd constantly needed to slow his descent. Otherwise, he would've found himself rushing down the trail and probably taking a running leap into space. The braking had taken a heavy toll on him. It had jammed his toes into the fronts of his boots. It had reduced his thigh muscles to weak, shaking jelly.

He knew that the hike must've been even worse for those with packs bouncing against their backs. Several times, he'd offered to carry Angela's, only to be turned down. Knowing what was in it, he'd been relieved. Even though the skeleton *was* Angela's mother, he got the creeps just thinking about it. But he'd felt guilty about making the descent without a burden. He had offered to take Lana's pack, but she only thanked him and said, 'I'm fine.'

Naturally, Glen and Keith had been quick to suggest he carry *their* packs. His guilt didn't go that far. Laughing, he'd told them to take a hike.

Those two had actually *run* down the final stretch of switchback to the level ground at the base of the mountain. So much for needing help. Of course, maybe they'd been too worn out, by then, to bother fighting the pull of gravity.

'Have you ever noticed,' Angela asked, 'that when you're returning from somewhere it *always* seems quicker?'

'It *was* a lot quicker.'

'Yeah. That's for sure.' She laughed softly. 'I think my toes got pushed in.'

'I wish you would've let me carry your pack.'

'It wasn't all that heavy. Besides. You know. It was my mother.'

Lana, Keith and Glen, done with loading the car, piled into the front seat. 'Let's just hope this baby starts,' Lana said. The engine grumbled and died. Then it caught. She gunned it, and it roared.

'Where's Doris?' Angela asked.

'She went off to take a leak,' Lana said.

'Here's our big chance to lose her,' Keith said.

'Fuck you, man,' Glen snapped.

'Hey, I was just kidding.'

'Well, fuck your kidding, OK? She saved Lana's butt last

night, and she saved Dalton today. She's all right. She's *better* than all right. She deserves some respect.'

'Methinks you're hot on her, that's what *me*thinks.'

'So what if I am? You got a problem with that?'

'Who, me?'

'Just lay off the cracks. From now on. You got it?'

'Sure sure sure. Christ.'

'All right, then.'

Moments later, Doris returned. She climbed in beside Howard. Even as she pulled her door shut, the car began to back up. It swung past the end of Coreen's car, then started forward and turned away.

Twisting around, Howard looked out the rear window. The car was a black, huddled shape in the darkness, not even touched by moonlight.

'They'll be all right,' Angela said.

'Some of us should've stayed,' Howard muttered.

'You had the chance, Howitzer.'

'This time tomorrow night,' Lana said, 'Chad and Corie'll be shacked up in a cozy motel somewhere getting it on.'

'Playing a little hide-the-salami,' Keith said. 'Dalton'll have to be on top, of course.'

'You're such a cretin,' Doris told him.

'Hey, Glen wants me to be nice to you. Don't make it any more difficult.'

'Then cut out the crass remarks. You're not amusing.'

'I was only attempting, in my singularly cretinous way, to allay Howitzer's concerns about the Professor's safety.'

'Yeah, well, you shouldn't talk about her that way,' Howard said.

'Screw you.'

'Screw *you*.'

'Why don't we all shut up for a while?' Lana suggested.

'You're giving me a headache. Or this road is. Something is. Let's have some peace and quiet.'

'You heard the lady,' Keith said, looking over his shoulder. 'You people quit your belly-aching back there.' He turned to the front again. Laughing softly, he settled down in his seat.

Angela squeezed Howard's leg. He looked at her. The vague blur of her face, bouncing and wobbling with the rough jostles of the car, seemed to be grinning. He pulled her closer against him. She raised her arm out of the way, put it behind him, and caressed his side. They bobbed and swayed and bumped each other.

After a while, Howard heard snoring from Doris.

Amazing. How could anyone fall asleep while being pounded and shaken this way?

He felt dead tired, himself. He wished he could sleep. But if he had to be awake, this wasn't so bad. The car was dark and warm and he was holding Angela.

They tried to kiss, but their mouths collided.

'You OK?' he whispered.

'I think so. How about you? Split lip? Broken teeth?'

'I'm all right.'

'Try here.'

She pointed. Howard brushed his lips against her cheek. The skin was smooth and warm, vibrating slightly. With a sudden lurch of the car, her cheekbone punched his nose.

'Oooo. Are you all right?'

He held his nose. His eyes were watering.

'Is it bleeding?'

He sniffed. He wiggled his nose. He fingered his nostrils. 'I don't think so.'

'We'd better stop.'

He looked away from her. Nobody was watching. Though Doris continued to snore, he wondered if anyone in the front seat had been able to hear their conversation. Maybe not.

The engine was making plenty of noise. The car squeaked and thudded as it bounced. Rocks crunched under the tires. Snaps and pops came from twigs, branches, pine cones, whatever else was being run over.

'Let's not,' he whispered.

'Let's not what?'

'Stop.'

'I don't want you to get hurt.'

'We'll be careful.'

Angela nodded. Leaning forward, she struggled to take off her windbreaker. Howard helped pull the sleeves down her arms. While he held the jacket, she reached under the back of her T-shirt. Howard realized what she was doing. His breath snagged and his heart quickened.

She brought her hands to the front, slumped back against the seat, and took the windbreaker from him. She spread it open and draped it from her shoulders.

Twisting himself sideways, Howard eased his left arm behind her head. His right hand slipped beneath the nylon cover. It met Angela's hands as they plucked the T-shirt free from the waistband of her sweatpants.

They not only untucked the shirt, they lifted it out of his way.

Howard roamed the silken, warm skin of her belly. He tried to caress it gently. Sometimes, the motions of the car made him lose the feel of her. Other times, a jolt thrust her up against his hand, or jarred him so that his hand slid abruptly across the smoothness.

Slowly, he made his way higher.

So did Angela's hand on his thigh.

Trembling and breathless, he caressed her beneath the left breast. He ached to feel the breast, but he didn't dare.

Stupid, he thought. I made love to her last night. We went *all the way*.

But the breast was like a secret treasure. He was afraid to touch it.

She wants me to, he told himself. For Godsake, she covered herself so I could do it. She even unfastened her bra. Can't be more obvious than that.

Still, he hesitated.

Until Angela's hand pressed his groin, rubbed his penis gently through the corduroy.

He squirmed and tried not to moan.

He curled his hand against the underside of her breast. So smooth. So warm. Cupping it lightly, he felt the slope jiggle. An abrupt sharp bounce of the car patted it against his palm and fingers.

This is so incredible, he thought. Doing this to each other. Right here in the car. Nobody else knowing.

Angela's hand, he noticed, was no longer rubbing him. He wondered why she'd stopped. He thought he knew why; she was too involved, just now. Distracted by her breast and his hand.

Or maybe she sensed how close he was to losing control.

Good thing.

As if reading his mind, she lifted her hand away and began to caress his thigh.

Another bounce of the car slapped her breast softly down against his palm.

Angela moaned as his thumb moved forward along the slope and met a curving ridge of firm, puckered flesh. He traced a semi-circle, following its edge, then slid his thumb up onto it. A rumpled, turgid cone rose steeply until it jutted straight out like a post. He stroked slowly upward, found the rounded top, caressed it, pushed on it, felt it bend like a rubber tube as Angela gasped and flinched and clutched his leg. A little alarmed, he stopped pushing. The nipple sprang up straight again.

'Did that hurt?' he whispered.

'No. God, no. It was wonderful.'

This is almost better than last night, he thought, bringing up his forefinger and using it along with his thumb to savor and tease the nipple.

Last night had been great. Better than great. But it had been frenzied and rushed and quickly over. This was so very different – a slow exploration of contours and textures and responses. Nothing to do *except* touch each other secretly. Not here in the car with the others present. So it might go on forever. Or at least until Doris woke up or someone in the front seat looked around. With luck, it might last until they came to the main road.

That should still be more than an hour away.

A whole hour, probably longer.

A long time. But not so long, really. He supposed he could gladly spend that much time lingering over just this single breast. But there was another. And there was the deep juicy cleft between her legs.

Would she let him slip his hand down there?

Probably.

And what would she do to him? What would she dare?

He closed his hand over the soft mound, the nipple jutting out between his open fingers. When he gently squeezed, her back arched. Her breath hissed in. Her fingertips dug into his thigh.

As the car rocked and bounced over the rough dirt tracks, Howard continued to fondle Angela's breast. He roamed it, caressed and squeezed it, held it lightly in his palm to feel its smooth weight shake and bob with the car's motions, gently pinched and pulled the nipple. Sometimes, Angela shut her eyes and sat still. Other times, she gasped and writhed. She kept her hand away from his groin as if knowing that a touch from her might be too much.

Just the feel of her breast was almost too much for Howard to bear. Every so often, nearing the brink, he took his hand away until he could calm down a little.

Aware that time was passing, he switched his attentions to her right breast. Though it felt very much like the other, its curves and textures were fresh, thrilling magic to Howard. And it was closer to him, easier to reach. He realized how heavy his arm had become, stretching across her body to the farther breast. This was much better.

He was cupping it, feeling it joggle inside his hand, when Angela reached up and drew the windbreaker aside just enough to uncover his hand and the breast beneath it. A glance toward the front seat assured him that no one was looking. Behind him, Doris continued to snore. He looked at the blur of Angela's face. He couldn't see her expression, but he saw her nod.

He lowered his gaze. Angela's T-shirt, the bra hidden inside it, formed a puffy roll just above her breast. His hand appeared very dark against her pale skin. He slid it down against the underside. There, he could feel her without obstructing his view.

He stared and stared at the creamy mound, its dark cone and pillar. He watched it jitter, felt it bounce against his palm. He watched his fingertips glide up its slope. He watched them push, felt the flesh yield but then spring up when he eased the pressure.

If only there was more light, he thought.

If only we were alone.

It's nothing but a pouch of skin filled with fatty tissue, he suddenly thought. How can it do this to me?

He didn't know how. He realized he didn't care how. All that mattered was to have it, to be holding it and seeing it, and to know that Angela cared so much about him that she was willing to let him.

Bending down, he pressed his cheek against the rumpled nest of her shirt and bra. He kissed the top of her breast. Then he turned his head and strained lower. He licked the nipple, tongued it into his mouth, squeezed his lips around it, sucked. Angela, shuddering, pushed her fingers into the hair on the back of his head. She pressed him hard against her. He took more of the breast into his mouth. It filled him. He probed it with his tongue and teeth. It was springy and warm, slick with his saliva.

He felt as if his trapped penis might throb and pump.

Not yet!

You haven't gotten *down there* yet!

He slid his hand down her belly, under the elastic band of her sweatpants. As he tried to work his fingertips under the thin band of her panties, she clutched his hair and pulled his head back and whispered, 'No, don't.' The breast came out of his mouth with a wet slopping sound.

Confused and hurt, Howard suddenly lost his agony of desire. He sat up. And watched as Angela pulled the wind-breaker sideways to cover her breast.

'What's wrong?' he whispered.

She shook her head.

'Angela?'

'I'm sorry.'

'What did I do?'

Again, she shook her head. Then she turned to him. The wind-breaker fell from her shoulders, dropped into her lap. Howard saw that she had already pulled her T-shirt down. The bra made it bulge oddly above her breasts.

She put her hand behind Howard's head and drew him closer. She pressed her cheek to his cheek. 'I'm really sorry,' she whispered, her breath tickling his ear. 'I didn't want to stop you. I loved it all. I love *you*. But . . . this is really embarrassing.'

'What?'

'I was afraid . . . I couldn't let you touch me. Not there.'

'It's OK,' he whispered.

But he felt crushed. What had gone wrong? She hadn't complained last night. They'd *made love*, for Godsake. So why, all of a sudden, was he not supposed to touch her there?

Because the others might find out?

How could that be it? She'd actually *showed* her breast. If she was afraid of Keith or Glen turning around, why did she do *that*?

'Are you awfully disappointed?' she whispered.

'No.'

'I'll make it up to you.'

'It's all right. Honest.'

'The thing is . . .' She hesitated. 'I was afraid if you . . . I've gotta pee something horrible.'

'What?'

'That's why. It's all I can do to hold it.'

Relief swept through Howard and he laughed. Angela squirmed. Her hand came up in front of his face and rubbed her ear.

'It's not funny,' she whispered.

'Let's have them stop the car.'

'I don't want to make a big deal out of it.'

'But if you've gotta go . . .'

'I can wait a while longer. We must be almost . . . it won't be so bad once we're on a smooth road. Maybe I can wait till we get to the town.'

'You oughta take care of it now.'

'The guys'd make fun of me. You know that.'

'If that's what you're worried about, I'll say I'm the one who's gotta go.'

'Let's just . . .'

A jolt bounced them. Angela groaned and held onto

Howard as they were flung up and came down so hard the seat cushions squeaked under their weight.

'Are you OK?' he asked.

'Hanging in there.'

'I'll tell them . . .' He felt the car make a right turn, felt a sudden, surprising calm. The bumps and lurches were gone. Looking over the top of Keith's head, he saw that they were riding on the smooth asphalt surface of the main road.

'Thank God,' Angela gasped.

'Do you want to try and wait for town? It's supposed to be about ten miles.'

'I think I'd rather. If I can.'

Behind him, Doris snorted. Then she let out a small gasp and murmured, 'Huh?'

Angela let go of Howard. She pulled the wind-breaker up as they both settled back against their seat. Howard looked over at Doris. She was rubbing her eyes with her fists.

Amazing, he thought. She'd slept her way through the rough part of the ride, only to wake up the moment the turbulence stopped.

She stretched, then twisted around to peer out her window.

Howard turned to Angela. The windbreaker draping her front was alive with moving bulges as she reached up beneath it and pulled her bra into place. Her hands went away. Twin mounds remained. They pushed up against the fabric while she arched and struggled to fasten the clasps behind her back. Finished, she slumped against the seat. She patted his thigh.

'I think we'd better . . .'

'Hey,' Keith said, 'there's somebody who ran shit outa luck.'

'They didn't have a trusty, indomitable vehicle like mine,' Lana said.

'Flat tire,' Glen said.

Howard looked past Doris's head as they sped past the dark shape of a car at the side of the road.

'Thank God *we* didn't get a flat,' Lana said. 'I'm surprised we have any tires left at all, after that cute piece of road.'

'Could we pull over?' Howard asked. 'My teeth are floating.'

'Hang it out the window,' Keith suggested.

'I'm serious.'

'I could use a pit-stop myself,' Lana said. The car slowed, glided to the right, and tipped slightly as its side dropped from the pavement to the ground. It crunched forward a few feet, then stopped.

'Anybody who needs to go,' Lana announced, 'should do it now. It'll probably be twenty minutes or so before we hit town.'

All four doors of her Granada swung open.

Howard climbed out behind Angela. While she thrust her arms into the sleeves of the windbreaker, he swung the door shut and saw Lana scooting across the front seat. Then Angela was pulling him by the hand, leading him in a rush toward the other side of the road.

'You don't have to watch,' she gasped. 'Just stay with me.'

'Where are you guys going?' Lana called.

Howard glanced back. She was standing beside the car, peering over its roof at them. Doris was waiting beside her. Keith and Glen, walking past the front of the car, looked over their shoulders.

'Perverts!' Keith yelled.

Glen laughed and shook his head.

'The hell with them,' Angela said. Still clutching his hand, she plunged through undergrowth beyond the edge of the road. The nearest group of trees was off to the left. She headed that way, running, Howard racing along at her side.

Almost there, they leaped over a channel of tire ruts, each landing with one foot on the center rise and bounding over the second rut.

Then Angela released his hand. She dashed to a nearby tree and ducked behind its trunk. Not quite out of sight. The trunk was narrow.

He could see her right side, gray and flecked with moonlight, as she yanked the sweatpants down to her ankles and leaned back and sank to a squat. The trunk rucked up her windbreaker. He glimpsed the pale curve of her rump, the side of her bare, bent leg. When he heard her stream start splashing the ground, he turned around.

He unzipped and pulled out his limp penis.

Though he knew Angela was close enough to see and that her pants were down, though he could hear her, he didn't feel aroused.

Too pooped, he thought, and began urinating. He aimed his stream toward the closer of the tire tracks.

It was up so long, he thought, it's all worn out.

He finished, shook off the final drops, tucked himself away and zipped up.

Angela was *still* going.

He kept his back toward her. He had no urge to look, and that seemed strange to him. Right now, he felt no sexual desire for her. Instead, there was a strong feeling of tenderness. And intimacy. As if she were his best pal, not his girlfriend. They were a couple of buddies who'd simply rushed into the woods together for a quick leak.

'All done,' she said. Howard heard her footsteps approaching. 'Boy, do *I* feel better.'

She patted his rump, and he grinned at her. 'Good thing we stopped when we did.'

'Just in the nick of time, I'd say.'

They turned to each other. Angela wrapped her arms

around him. He hugged her hard, kissed her open mouth. She was trembling.

'Cold?' he whispered.

'It's not so bad now. Do you want to . . .? You know.'

'Here?'

'Yeah.'

'Jeez.'

'If we do it fast.'

'How fast?'

'Very fast. The others, they'll start wondering about us.'

'I don't know. I want to, but . . .'

'Maybe it's not such a hot idea.'

'We'd have to really rush. It'd be nicer if we can take all the time we want.'

'In a warm place.'

'With a bed.'

'I can wait if you can.'

'Maybe we can get into a motel tonight.'

'I hope so. It's pretty late. What time is it, anyway?'

Howard released her and stepped back. He fingered a button to light the face of his wristwatch. 'Twelve-fifteen.'

'We made pretty good time.'

'And *had* a pretty good time.'

'The last couple of hours were sure great.' She took his hand and squeezed it. 'I guess we'd better go back to the car, huh?'

'Guess so.'

She took a step toward the nearer rut of the tire tracks. Howard pulled her sideways.

'Puddle,' he said.

'Oh.' She laughed softly.

He led her past the wet area.

'Safe now?'

'Probably.'

She walked down into the rut, then onto the higher ground of the center strip. Howard, staying at her side, strode along the worn path.

'Do you like me tall?' she asked. Her eyes were level with his.

'Different. But I wouldn't want anything changed about you.'

'Nothing?'

'You're perfect just the way you are.'

'My boobs are too small.'

'I love them.'

'Maybe when we find the treasure and we're rich, I could get implants. You know, get them enlarged.'

'No! Are you kidding?'

'Wouldn't you like . . . Weird.'

'Weird, all right. They're . . .'

'Not that.' Halting, she raised his hand with hers and thrust it forward as if pointing. 'Look.'

He turned his head to the front.

No more than ten feet farther ahead, the tire tracks seemed to end. Howard hadn't paid much attention to them before, but he'd thought they would lead back to the main road. Just at the edge of the woods, however, a tangle of limbs and bushes blocked the way.

'We can circle around,' he said. He pulled Angela's hand, but she resisted.

'No. Wait. Don't you think this is *strange*?'

He shrugged.

'Let's take a look.' Releasing his hand, she rushed to the obstruction. She crouched and tugged at a branch. It slid toward her feet. Leaning forward, she lifted a small bush from the pile. She tossed it aside.

'What are you doing?'

She stood up and faced him. 'I bet this is it.' Her voice was hushed, excited.

'This is what?'

'Somebody put this stuff here. To hide the way in, you know?'

'So?'

'The treasure. It's supposed to be off Purdy Road, right? Well, this is off Purdy Road.'

'Yeah, but there must be dozens of other . . .'

'Somebody took the trouble to *hide* this one.'

Angela turned her head. Howard did the same. The pair of tracks stretched away and faded into the darkness of the forest.

'If we follow it far enough,' she whispered, 'I bet we'll find the bus.'

Chapter Thirty-three

Groaning, Corie lifted her face off Doris's rolled sweatpants. The trail in front of her was so bright that, for just a moment, she thought that dawn had come.

Only moonlight.

She muttered, 'Shit.'

This had to be ranked up there as one of the longest nights of her life.

She felt as if she'd been in the sleeping bag forever.

Though it kept the cold out, it provided little relief from the hard surface of the trail in spite of the coat and other garments she'd spread out beneath it.

If she lay on her side, the ground punished her hip and

shoulder and quickly squeezed her arm numb. If she lay face down, it hurt her knees, shoved against her ribs and mashed her breasts. On her back, she might've been able to find a little comfort if not for her injuries. Her shoulder blades and buttocks cushioned her somewhat, but they'd been scraped raw when Hubert hurled her away and she'd skidded on the rocks. A few minutes on her back, and the abrasions would begin to sting.

So, over the hours, she'd adjusted her position countless times. Very carefully. Always aware of the precipice close to her side.

She wasn't sure if she had slept at all. Maybe for a few minutes now and then.

But she felt as if she'd been awake the whole time, sometimes able to think clearly, often finding her mind drifting into a nasty, surreal realm that confused and terrified her. A realm where she was being pursued over strange landscapes by Hubert. He was naked and gleaming and laughing.

Sometimes, he caught her.

Once, he had picked her up overhead and hurled her off a cliff. Plummeting down, she'd passed Chad on his narrow shelf and called out 'Good-bye' and he'd returned a forlorn last wave.

Another time, after catching her, Hubert had lifted her by the ankles. Higher and higher. Until she was looking down at his face and his mouth spread wide – too wide – and he lowered her. The top of her head went into his mouth. His teeth pressed into the flesh above her ears. Squeezed. She'd grabbed her head to stop her brains from bursting out, and that had put an end to that particular episode.

But it had soon been replaced by another, one in which he chased her over dunes that trapped her feet and slowed her down. He kept gaining on her. Glancing back in terror, she saw that he wore snow shoes. 'That's not fair,' she'd shouted.

'Yes-yes-yes!' he'd answered, and twirled his machete. Finally, trying to climb a hill of sand, she'd lost her balance, fallen backward and slid down the slope and come to a stop at Hubert's feet. The machete flashed twice. *Whiss whiss.* Lopping off her breasts.

Flinching back to reality, she'd found herself stretched out face down in the sleeping bag, her breasts mashed painfully against her chest.

Onto her back she'd turned for another try at sleep, another brief visit from Hubert. She soon was sliding down a steep wall of granite, feet first, the rough surface ripping the flesh from her rump and back. She left a wet red path as she descended. A path strewn with patches of her skin. Beyond her feet and far below, Hubert waited. His machete waited. 'Spread 'em wide, Jane! Slide right on.' She skidded closer, closer to the blade. She kicked at it, kicked at the sleeping bag, realized what she was doing and rolled over again.

And began to sob against the soft pillow of Doris's sweatpants.

He's dead. Why won't he just leave me alone?

It'll be over soon, she told herself. Dawn will come. Everything'll be all right.

Why am I even trying to sleep? Why don't I sit up, or something?

She crawled out of the sleeping bag, crawled away from it, crawled until her head bumped into bare shins and Hubert picked her up by her hair until she dangled in front of him. 'Can't get away from me that easy,' he said. 'Fuck you!' she shrieked, and stabbed her fingers into his eyes. The eyeballs popped, squirted. Both fingers went deep into his sockets. He blinked. His lids snapped shut like jaws. She screamed and jerked back her hand. The two stubs spouted blood.

'No!'

The sound of her voice broke the spell.

No is right, she thought.

Didn't happen.

She hadn't crawled out of the bag, had only thought about it.

She groaned, lifted her face off Doris's rolled sweatpants, saw the moonlit trail, muttered 'Shit,' and wondered if the night would ever end. Her eyes and cheeks itched from the tears. She rubbed them with a sleeve of her sweatshirt. Then she lowered the zipper at the side of Doris's sleeping bag, pushed herself up to her hands and knees, and crawled out.

The cold clamped her. Her sweatsuit, sodden after the series of horrible dreams or hallucinations or whatever they'd been, was clinging to her body and twisted askew. The wind chilled its moisture, passed through the heavy fabric, wrapped her skin like ice water. Clenching her teeth, shuddering, she tugged Howard's coat out from under the sleeping bag and put it on.

The coat helped a lot, but not enough. From the waist down, she was frigid. Her feet felt like clumps of ice.

With a quick search of Doris's pack, she found two more pairs of socks. She sat on top of the sleeping bag and crossed her legs. She wanted to take off the wet socks she was wearing. But they felt as if they'd been glued to the bottoms of her feet. Their white cotton, distinct in the milky moonlight, was blotched with blood. No telling what damage she might do, trying to remove them.

'Thanks for everything, Hubert,' she muttered, her voice shaking.

She pulled two fresh socks over each foot. Better. Much better.

She unrolled the sweatpants that she'd been using for a pillow, and pulled them up her legs. The extra layer blocked out most of the wind. She let out a trembling sigh.

Hands stuffed into the coat pockets, she remained on the

sleeping bag and took slow breaths, trying to calm herself and control the tremors.

'Not so bad,' she finally said.

One hell of a lot better that staying in the bag, tossing and turning, having those damn visions.

Getting to her knees, she turned herself sideways. She bent over and pressed her hands against the edge of the trail. Easing forward, she peered down the bright, moonlit slope. The rope, directly under her face, angled sideways. It looked like a solid gray rod leading down to Chad. She could only see the very top of his head. The rest of him was hidden beneath the dark oblong of Howard's mummy bag.

'And I think I've got it rough,' she muttered. 'God, Chad.'

Though he'd tied the rope securely around his chest and was probably in no great danger of falling, he had nothing but the clothes on his back to cushion him from the granite shelf. He hadn't been able to get inside the sleeping bag. Not by himself. Not without too much risk of tumbling from his perch. And he'd threatened to shove the sleeping bag into space if Corie tried to come down and help.

Must be awful, she thought, gazing down at him.

She wanted to call out, to talk with him.

For all she knew, however, he might be asleep.

It seemed unlikely. How could *anyone* fall asleep under such conditions?

But if somehow he was asleep, it would be an unforgivable cruelty to wake him.

What if he's not all right?

What if he's dying?

'Is that you?' He sounded . . . cheerful?

'How are you doing?'

'This isn't the most pleasant night I've ever spent.'

'I should think not. Are you freezing?'

'It's not too bad. I seem to be out of the wind.'

'That's wonderful. I'm not.'

'What are you doing up?'

'I couldn't sleep. How about you?'

'I just woke up a few minutes ago. And boy, was I pissed. I was right in the middle of a great dream. Starring you.'

'Lucky you.'

'Well, I was *about* to get lucky, but then I woke up.'

'Too bad. Look, is there anything I can do for you?'

'Yeah. Find someplace comfortable for yourself. You don't have to spend the night on that damn trail. You said it widens out up ahead. Why don't you move over to that area? Maybe you can find yourself some shelter. At the very least, you won't have to worry about rolling off.'

'I'd rather be here with you.'

'Frankly, it makes me nervous thinking about you up there. I'd feel a lot better if you got yourself someplace safe.'

'Well, maybe I'll check it out. Are you hungry or anything?'

'I'm fine. Really.'

'How's the leg?'

'Not so bad that it kept me awake. I'm sure glad you got it out from under me, though.'

'Glad to be of service.'

'I guess this screws up my idea of a backpacking honeymoon.'

'*What* idea of a backpacking honeymoon?'

She heard him laugh.

'Oh, I wouldn't have done that to you,' he said. 'But it did sort of run through my mind this afternoon. While I was watching you swim.'

'I hope it ran right out again.'

'Things were pretty great until that bastard showed up.'

'That's true,' she said. 'I remember thinking, myself, how nice it'd be to come back. Just the two of us. Just to have fun and not go chasing after the kids. I don't think I'd want it for the honeymoon, though.'

'Softy.'

'I'm just trying to be considerate of your knees.'

Chad was silent. Corie wondered if he was trying to think of a witty comeback. But she waited, and he said nothing.

'Chad?'

'This won't . . . that damn maniac . . . I've been all over these mountains, never had any trouble. Not till now. This was a real fluke. I just hope you won't be afraid to give it another try.'

'I don't know. We'll see.'

'It was awfully good before he got to us.'

'It couldn't have been much better.'

'And there's no such thing as being completely safe.'

'I know.'

'You could run into a guy like that anywhere. Most of them aren't in the mountains. They're out in civilization, not in places like this. They're where the people are.'

'I never said I wouldn't come up here again. But right now, it doesn't sound like the neatest idea in the world. I'm cold, tired, sore, scared . . . you name it. If it's lousy, I'm feeling it.'

'Lonely?'

She thought about that. 'Yes and no. Talking's OK. But I wish I could hold you.'

'You and me both. But don't even think about trying to come down here.'

'Can we keep on talking?'

'I'm not going anywhere.'

'Am I keeping you up?'

'You might be keeping me from a great dream, but that's OK. The real you's better, anyway.'

Chapter Thirty-four

'Shit, look at this.' Crouching over the pile of limbs and bushes, Keith lifted one end of a long two-by-four. Its length was spiked with jutting nails. 'Almost porked myself,' he muttered.

'Could've had the fun of a tetanus shot,' Lana said.

Keith picked up the rest of the board, swung it around and hurled it aside.

When they finished clearing the barricade, Lana rubbed her hands against the front of her sweatshirt and said, 'OK, let's check it out.'

'What do you mean?' Howard asked.

'Take a little ride down there and see if we can find the bus.'

'Now?'

'No time like the present.'

'We can't do that,' Doris said.

'Sure we can,' Keith said.

'It won't take long.'

'We shouldn't do *anything* until we've been to the police,' Doris protested. 'It's our obligation to Dr Dalton and . . '

Lana shrugged. 'Another half-hour or so isn't gonna make any difference to them. It's the middle of the night. Nobody's about to send out a rescue party before morning.'

Turning around, she stepped onto the pavement. Keith joined her. Together, they walked at an angle away from the abandoned car directly across the road, heading for Lana's Granada.

The others followed.

This is crazy, Howard thought.

Angela took his hand.

He looked at her and shook his head.

'I know,' she muttered. 'We shouldn't do it.'

Why did we show them the dirt road? Howard thought. That was the big mistake.

Even when they'd started clearing the debris that blocked its entrance, Howard hadn't thought that anyone would seriously consider traveling down it *tonight*. They would drive on into town, take care of reporting Coreen and Chad's situation to the authorities, then find somewhere to spend the night. A motel, if they could get into one so late. A motel where he could be alone with Angela. It would be wonderful. In the morning, they would get together again and come out here to search for the bus.

In the morning.

They climbed into Lana's car and she started the engine. But she didn't start driving. She looked over her shoulder. 'OK, everyone, what's it gonna be?'

'I already expressed my views on the matter,' Doris said. 'I'm certainly interested in finding the treasure, but our first duty is to Dr Dalton. We can always come back here tomorrow. Also, I might point out that tomorrow is when Butler told us we'd find it. Tomorrow, not tonight.'

'In case you haven't noticed,' Keith said, 'this *is* tomorrow. Butler didn't say anything about daylight.'

'I'd rather wait for daylight,' Howard said.

'Yeah, well, you always were a woos.'

'Cut it out,' Lana said.

'I'm not real eager to go down that thing in the dark, either,' Glen said. 'But I think maybe we should. I get the feeling this is when we're meant to go for it. Look at the facts. This is tomorrow. The bus is supposed to be off Purdy Road and Angela's supposed to be the one who finds it. Well, she's the one who found those tire tracks. Everything's set up just right.'

'Right on,' Keith said.

'If we weren't meant to go looking until tomorrow morning,' Glen continued, 'I think Angela wouldn't have stumbled onto the dirt road until then.'

'Excellent point,' Keith said.

'Angela, what do you think?' Lana asked.

Howard felt her shoulder lift and lower slightly against his arm. 'I don't know. I don't want to miss out on finding the treasure, but . . .'

'It might not be there in the morning,' Keith pointed out.

'It's not as important,' she went on, 'as helping Dr Dalton and Chad.'

'It's not an either/or situation,' Glen said.

'I tell you what,' Lana said. 'We'll give it five or ten minutes.' She began pulling the car forward, swinging it into a slow U-turn. 'We'll just make a short run up that road and if we don't find something quick, we'll head on into town and come back in the morning for a thorough search. How does that sound to everyone?'

'Perfect,' Keith said.

Glen nodded his approval.

'OK, I guess,' Angela said.

'All right,' Howard said.

'Bullshit,' Doris muttered.

'You're outvoted,' Keith told her.

The car rocked and bounced as Lana steered onto the dirt road. 'It's no big deal,' she said. 'Fifteen or twenty minutes, one way or the other, won't make any difference to Corie and Chad.'

Howard put his arm across Angela's back and pulled her close to his side. Together, they shook and swayed with the rough motions of the car. This seemed very much like the earlier part of the trip. But terribly different.

We shouldn't be here, he thought.

He supposed that Lana was right about Coreen and Chad. A brief delay shouldn't matter much.

But he didn't like this road.

Not at all.

Somebody had tried to conceal its entrance.

The barricade had been their clue that this was *the* road. But didn't it bother anyone that somebody had put it there? Somebody who didn't want visitors?

And what about the abandoned car?

It had a flat tire.

And there'd been that board with nails in it.

This is really bad, he thought.

Butler is Angela's mother, he reminded himself. She wouldn't be sending us into trouble.

Oh, no? What about Hubert? She ran us into him.

Maybe she doesn't care what happens to any of us but Angela.

Who knows what she's really up to?

Back there in the trunk, plotting.

In the trunk. Howard had been aware, all along, that they were riding with the skeleton of Angela's mother in the trunk. Until now, it hadn't bothered him.

Now, he found himself spooked.

The fleshless bones. The grinning skull. Jammed inside Angela's pack. Along with that tattered, stuffed kitten.

If the seatback weren't in the way, she would be near enough to touch.

A dead, horrid passenger riding along with them in silence, but leading them.

Leading them deep into the woods in the middle of the night for reasons known only to her.

'It's been more than five minutes,' Doris said.

'No place to turn around,' Lana said. 'I'm not about to *back* all the way out to the road.'

A pretty lame excuse, Howard thought. He could see past the side of Keith's head and through the windshield. Though trees bordered the twin ruts, they were far enough back for Lana to turn the car around if she wanted to.

'We're not exactly hemmed in,' Doris said.

'Give it a rest,' Keith told her.

'Just a little farther,' Lana said. 'Then we'll . . . Jesus!'

Howard glimpsed a clearing ahead. Then the bright pale beams of the headlights vanished as if sucked back into the car.

Lana jammed on the brakes. The car lurched to a stop.

'Holy shit,' Keith muttered.

Glen said, 'Oh, man.'

'That's it,' Lana said.

Howard saw it.

A bus.

He *guessed* it was a bus. At the far end of the moonlit field. Maybe a hundred yards away. But all he could see of it was a long row of rectangles that seemed to hover above the ground. Its passenger windows. Faint, glowing patches of crimson. Apparently, the windows were shrouded with red curtains.

'Looks fuckin' creepy,' Glen whispered.

'What the hell's it *doing* out here?' Lana asked.

'We've found it,' Doris said. 'Now let's turn around and leave.'

'No way,' Keith said. 'This is it. This is what it's all about. We can't quit now.'

'I don't know,' Lana muttered. 'Looks like somebody might be in there.'

'If it didn't have lights on, we couldn't have seen it. They're on for us. Right, Glen? It's all part of the same deal. Butler had to make it so we could spot the damn thing.'

'I don't like this,' Glen said.

'That shows you've retained a modicum of good sense,' Doris pointed out.

'Maybe we'd better wait for daylight,' Lana said.

'It might not *be* here. Look, let's just leave the car and sneak up on the thing. We'll check it out. We don't have to go inside, but we've gotta at least take a closer look. I mean, our treasure's supposed to be in there.'

'I guess as long as we're careful,' Lana muttered.

'*I'm* not going,' Doris said.

'Gee whiz,' Keith said, 'that comes as a mighty surprise.'

'Howard, why don't you take care of the courtesy light? We don't want it coming on when we open the doors.'

He reached up to the ceiling and tugged at the light's plastic cover. One end snapped loose. Fumbling underneath it, he twisted the bulb and plucked it free. 'Got it.' He stuffed the bulb into a pocket of his corduroys.

'Let's go,' Lana said.

Three of the doors swung open. As Howard scooted across the backseat, he glanced around at Doris. 'See you later,' he said.

'You're as big a fool as the rest of them.'

So much for being nice to her.

Climbing out, he noticed the quiet way Lana shut the driver's door. He shut his door gently, pushing until it latched. Keith, who'd followed Glen out the other side, also took care when he closed his door.

Not a single good slam, Howard thought.

We're all scared shitless.

They gathered around Lana at the rear of the car. Her keys jangled. Finding the one she wanted, she bent over the trunk and slid it into the lock.

'What're you doing?' Glen whispered.

'Flashlights and weapons.' Lana turned the key. A quiet clack. The lid of the trunk slowly rose. She leaned into the darkness, lifted a pack, turned around, and offered it to Angela. 'Just keep it for a minute.'

Angela took the pack. She stepped back, set it down at her feet, and tipped its frame so it rested upright against her legs. A milky patch of moonlight shone on its top as if for the sole purpose of illuminating the bulge for Howard's benefit. The bulge made by the top of the skull.

It's not some horrible thing, he told himself as goosebumps crawled across the nape of his neck. It's Angela's mother.

He wished it was locked away in the trunk.

The other three packs were now on the ground, being opened.

'Get your flashlights,' Lana whispered, 'but don't turn them on.'

'I'm bringing along this baby,' Keith said, pulling the hatchet out of his pack.

'Wanta trade?' Glen asked, and held a sheath knife toward him.

'Bite my shorts.'

Lana took out her revolver.

'You've gotta be kidding,' Keith said. 'The fucker's empty.'

'Nobody knows but us.'

'Can't shoot anyone with an empty gun.'

'Maybe not, but you can sure worry them.' Reaching behind her back, she lifted her sweatshirt out of the way. Howard saw a band of pale skin above her belt as she shoved the barrel down the seat of her jeans.

'I don't know about this,' Angela muttered.

'What don't you know?' Lana asked.

'Look how you're arming yourselves. If it's going to be so dangerous, shouldn't we forget about it?'

'We're just taking precautions. If I honestly believed we'd be running into trouble, I wouldn't go anywhere near that bus.'

'It can't hurt to be prepared,' Glen added.

Howard realized that his own right hand was deep in the

pocket of his corduroys, fingering his Swiss Army knife.

'If you don't like it,' Keith said, 'just stay here and keep Doris company.'

'Maybe you should,' Howard said. 'There's no reason for all of us to go. Why don't you wait here?'

'I go where you go.'

'Ain't that sweet? Just the excuse Howitzer was hoping for.'

'Get screwed,' Angela snapped.

'Ooooo, she's got a temper.'

'Knock it off, Keith,' Lana warned.

'Besides,' Angela said, 'I'm not staying here, anyway. I'm going to the bus with the rest of you. I'm the one who finds the treasure, remember?'

'Come on, let's load up and get going.' Lana finished closing her pack and hefted it into the trunk. She took Keith's pack, then Glen's, and finally Angela's. When they were all inside, she lowered the lid. Holding it down, she turned around. She bounced her rump on it, and the lock latched. 'Everybody set?'

'Let's take the suitcases,' Keith suggested. 'They might come in handy if we find the loot.'

'Couldn't hurt,' Lana said.

Keith and Glen removed the two suitcases from the car's luggage rack. Glen kept one, but Keith held out the other to Howard, saying, 'Make yourself useful.'

As Howard took the suitcase, he saw that it was Angela's and realized he wouldn't mind carrying it.

Lana and Keith led the way across the field. Howard and Angela stayed close behind them, Glen bringing up the rear.

Howard shivered as he walked. He wished he had his coat, but was glad he'd left it with Coreen. She needs it more than me, he told himself. Must be a lot colder, high up on that mountainside.

The chilly breeze seemed to pass right through the back of his shirt. He watched the way it ruffled Lana's hair. Her hair looked silvery in the moonlight. Her gray sweatshirt was pale.

It's so damn bright out here, he thought. If somebody looks out one of those windows . . .

He realized that he would probably be shivering just as much if he were bundled in a coat. Shivering because of the bus.

What's it doing here?

He could see it better, now. A dozen crimson windows. Those near the front glowed slightly brighter than those toward the rear. The driver's window, like the others, was draped with red.

He wondered if it had once been a school bus. Hard to imagine that it might've ever been such an ordinary thing – full of yelling, laughing kids. It looked so forbidding. The whole field was bathed in milky moonlight, but not the bus. It had been parked at the very edge of the forest. Overhanging limbs shrouded its bulk with shadow. Except for the red of its windows, the bus looked even darker than the woods.

Is it black?

A black bus. Christ.

Somebody must live in it.

What kind of person . . .?

Maybe it'll be empty. Empty except for Butler's loot. Wouldn't that be nice?

He wondered what the treasure would be. Money? Jewelry? It was hard to imagine finding anything of value inside that bus.

This could turn out to be a wild-goose chase.

Wild-goose chase.

How about a goose that lays golden eggs?

Fee, fi, fo, fum, I smell the blood of an Englishman.

Great. Jack and the beanstalk. That little story used to scare the hell out of him.

And here we are, three Jacks and two Jills, going for the gold.

Jack fell down and broke his crown . . .

Different Jack.

Jesus, what're we doing here?

A few strides from the side of the bus, Keith and Lana halted. They stood motionless, staring up at the windows. Listening? Howard stopped beside them. Angela took his hand. Glen's footsteps went silent.

Gazing at the covered windows, Howard held his breath and listened. He heard his own thudding heartbeat, cries of some distant birds, the wind hissing through the forest, the whisper of leaves rubbing against the roof of the bus. But no sounds at all seemed to be coming from inside.

Somebody *must* be in there, he thought.

With his hatchet, Keith gestured toward the right. He led the way. Lana followed. Angela went after Lana, and Howard stayed close to her back. He heard Glen's shaky breathing behind him.

They gathered at the rear of the bus. The windows of its emergency exit were masked with red fabric, just like all the others.

Keith looked at everyone, then turned away. Bending forward, he peered around the corner. He eased back and faced them. 'The fucking *door's* open,' he whispered. 'The front door.'

Howard went cold and crawly inside. He felt his scrotum shrivel up tight, his penis shrink as if it wanted to hide.

'Oh, man,' Glen murmured.

'I don't like this at all,' Keith said, his voice low and shaky.

'It'll make it easier for us,' Lana whispered.

'Shit,' Keith said. 'Somebody's *gotta* be in there.'

'I'm not quitting now,' Lana said. She reached under the back, of her sweatshirt and pulled out the revolver. 'We'll just take it slow and easy. Any sign of trouble, we'll get the hell out of here.'

Keith nodded. 'Here goes nothing,' he said, and stepped around the corner of the bus. Lana went after him. Angela followed her. Howard crept past the end of the bumper and saw the others just ahead. They were staying close to the side of the bus, crouching as if afraid of being seen from the windows.

These windows, like the others, were covered with red.

Beyond Keith, pale light spilled from the open front door.

When Howard crouched, his suitcase touched the ground. He lifted it higher, feeling his leg rub against it as he walked slowly behind Angela.

The forest was just to the right, some of the trees almost close enough to touch.

If anything goes wrong, he thought, we can run in there. So dark. So many trees. Plenty of good places to hide.

Just this side of the door, Keith stopped. He stood up straight and raised his left hand.

Everyone halted.

He moved into the light, turning toward the doorway, head tipped back. Then he lifted a foot onto the first stair. As he climbed out of sight, Lana entered the brightness and watched him.

After a moment, she boarded the bus.

'Must be OK,' Glen whispered.

'Guess so,' Howard said, suddenly feeling weak as tension drained out of him.

Keith was in. Lana was in. They'd obviously seen nothing alarming.

Angela was next to climb the stairs. At the top, she turned toward the aisle. She stared at something on her right, then faced Howard. Her lower lip was clamped between her teeth. She met his eyes. Looking worried, she lifted her gaze and peered into the darkness beyond his head.

'What?' he whispered.

She shook her head, pressed a finger to her lips for silence, then started down the aisle.

Howard swung the suitcase in front of him. He climbed onto the first stair and tried to see what was happening but a metal partition blocked his view. With the next step, he was able to see over it. Keith, Lana and Angela were standing in the aisle a short distance beyond the driver's seat, their backs to him. They were looking at something.

Something on a bench seat. Bundled in a filthy brown blanket.

Whatever it is, Howard thought, it must not be any big deal. They were just staring at it, not running away.

He climbed the rest of the way to the top.

Not as cold as outside. But almost. And the air smelled bad. Like a nasty bar, a dive. A mingling of stale smoke, sweat, alcohol, urine and a legion of other foul aromas.

Howard stepped past the driver's seat and stopped beside Angela.

Wrapped in the blanket was a woman. She was stretched out motionless on a bench that faced the aisle. The blanket covered her from neck to feet. Over her chest, it rose and fell slightly with the motions of her breathing.

Her brown hair was a tangled mess. Her face glowed bright red as if she'd spent far too long in the sun. Her lips were dry and cracked. A dark bruise smudged the left side of her jaw.

In spite of her condition, Howard could see that she was pretty.

And not very old. Probably in her early twenties.

He wondered if this was her home.

And did she live here alone?

Though he felt compelled to stare at her, he forced himself to turn away.

The bench on the other side of the aisle was heaped with clutter: grocery sacks; crushed beer cans; a hubcap heaped with ashes and dead cigarettes; packages of cookies and chips, some still unopened and others crumpled; piles of rags and dirty clothes.

'I'll check out the rest,' Keith whispered.

Howard glanced at the woman. She still slept.

Keith made his way toward the rear of the bus. Some of the forward rows of seats had been removed to make room for mattresses. Three mattresses piled with blankets and clothes.

Sleeping places for three more people.

Where *are* they? Howard wondered. What if they come back and find us here?

What if they're hiding, right now, among the seats?

He watched Keith pause, standing on one of the mattresses, turning his head as he looked at the two nearby steamer trunks. The tops of the trunks were littered with junk. On one was a Coleman lantern, its twin mantels hissing, filling the bus with brilliant light.

Keith moved on. He held his hatchet high as if ready to strike. He looked from side to side, checking each row of seats.

At last, he reached the emergency exit.

Thank God, Howard thought.

Keith turned around and came back.

'Anything?' Lana whispered.

He shook his head. 'We oughta have a look in the trunks. Maybe that's where . . .'

'We've gotta get out of here,' Angela said. 'Right now. We've gotta take her with us.'

'What's the . . .?'

'The stink of this place. The way it looks. And *her*.' She suddenly crouched, slapped a hand across the mouth of the sleeping woman, and hurled the blanket away.

The woman was naked. Her skin glowed scarlet as if she'd been broiled all day by the sun. She was bruised, striped with welts, seamed with shallow cuts from a knife blade or razor. She had raw crescents of bite marks on her shoulders and breasts and thighs. Her wrists were handcuffed, her ankles bound together with rope.

Howard saw all this as the woman lurched awake, eyes springing open. As she bucked, trying to sit up. As Keith gasped, 'Holy shit!' and Glen groaned and Lana muttered, 'My God.' As the woman stretched her arms down and hid her groin under crossed hands. As she settled down and lay motionless on the bench and glanced at the faces above her.

'We're here to help you,' Angela said, and lifted her hand away from the woman's mouth.

'They killed Roger!' she blurted. 'They killed him and they . . .'

'Charlie and the twins?' Angela asked.

'Yes! Yes! The old one's Charlie. Please, you've . . .'

'Where are they?'

'I don't know.'

'Charlie?' Glen sounded confused.

'Angela's stepfather,' Howard said.

'Him? My God, what's going on?'

'Where's the treasure, lady?' Keith asked.

'Forget it,' Lana said. 'We've got trouble. Let's get her and beat it.'

Angela slipped a hand under the back of the woman's neck. As she began lifting her, Howard set down his suitcase. He stepped in close to Angela and grabbed the woman's upper arm. Glen had his knife out. Crouching, he began to saw through the ropes at her ankles.

A blast slammed Howard's eardrums.

Glen's left eye exploded. A gout of red erupted from the socket and splashed the seatback in front of him.

Howard whirled away, grabbed Angela by the shoulders and threw her to the floor. A roar thundered through the bus. Keith, facing the rear, was knocked off his feet and hurled backward. Lana aimed her revolver toward a pair of red-haired men rushing up the aisle with shotguns. From behind Howard came a series of quick, sharp cracks. Lana staggered as three slugs punched through her back. Two smacked into Howard as a shotgun blast spun Lana around. The left side of her sweatshirt was blown open. She fell to her knees, a hand jerking up and clutching the red mush where her breast used to be.

The twins stopped behind her and aimed shotguns at her head.

'No!' Howard shrieked.

More fire from behind.

Chapter Thirty-five

This was a pretty good idea, Corie thought.

She spread her coat on the ground, then pulled the sleeping bag out of its nylon sack.

Here on the broad, gentle slope beyond the end of the trail, she would be in no danger of falling. And the mountain's wall sheltered her from the wind.

She'd been reluctant to leave her perch above Chad but

he'd asked her to do it and, once he'd fallen asleep, she'd decided to go along with his request. She had tucked away the sleeping bag, loaded everything she might need into one of the packs, and made her way up the narrow trail, wincing with each step though the three pairs of socks felt thick and springy under her sore feet.

Glad that she'd done it, she arranged the sleeping bag so that the coat would cushion her from waist to shoulders. She took off Doris's baggy sweatpants, rolled them up to make a pillow, slipped into the sleeping bag and pulled its zipper up.

Nice. Warm and cozy. But the ground was no softer here.

She rolled onto her belly, feeling the granite push against her thighs and ribcage and breasts. By folding her arms under the pillow, she relieved some of the pressure on her breasts.

Not so bad, she thought. I can live with it.

She just hoped she wouldn't be tormented by those horrible, vivid hallucinations.

Think about Chad, she told herself.

Think about how nice it will be when we're down from here.

But she knew that she was only a few yards from the spot where she'd made her escape from Hubert. She lay with her right cheek against the pillow. The edge of the sleeping bag, up high over her shoulder, prevented her from seeing the place. It didn't prevent her mind, however, from reliving what had happened there.

She saw herself riding his back as he crawled, felt his slick skin sliding against her, felt his head rubbing her groin. A heavy, leaden sickness settled in her belly as she remembered caressing him.

I had to do it, she told herself. It was my only chance, and it worked.

But the price.

Stroking his cock.

I still haven't washed my hand, she realized.

It was tucked under the rolled sweatpants, inches from her face.

Maybe in the morning, I can climb down to the stream.

She pictured Hubert falling off the edge of the gorge, the way he'd looked floating face down in the quiet pool.

I can't go there.

But he's gone, she reminded herself. The current had sent him shooting downstream like driftwood. Unless his body got hung up somewhere, he probably ended up in the lake. Not even the water in the pool would be the same water that touched him. It would be new, untainted, cold and clean.

She could go there. She would.

She would be hot and sweaty by the time she reached the bottom of the gorge.

She shut her eyes and imagined herself down there. Standing at the edge of the pool, the sun bright on its swirling surface, glints and sparkles hurting her eyes. The water so clear she can see her own shadow on its rocky bottom. She takes off her damp, heavy clothes, feeling the sunlight and soft breezes, then the icy shock of the water as she steps in. It would be awful at first, the terrible cold. But soon it would feel good. Cool, soothing caresses. She would float on her back and feel the sun's heat on her chilled skin.

She was floating, the water undulating, gently lifting her, lowering her, sliding like cool satin along her back and rump and legs.

'*Yes!*'

A hand slapped the top of her head, clutched her hair, jerked her head up. Pain burnt her scalp. She saw Hubert squatting in front of her, tried to tell herself this was another one of those hallucinations, knew it wasn't.

Hubert was here.

Alive.

'No!' she cried out. She clawed at the hand and forearm as he pulled her. She tried to get to her knees. Her back was stopped by the sleeping bag. She sprawled forward. Instead of throwing down her hands to catch herself, she grabbed his arm. Squirming and kicking, she was dragged from the sleeping bag. Her knees pounded the ground as she scurried forward, trying to get up.

But Hubert kept backing away.

With a twist of his arm, he flung Corie onto her back. He wrenched his arm from her grip, rushed in from the side and kicked her in the ribs. Pain erupted in her chest. Her breath gushed out. She drew up her knees and struggled to suck air.

Hubert's foot shoved her knees down. He swung a leg over her. She felt his boots tight against her hips.

He towered above her and gazed down at her.

Somewhere, he'd found clothes. The boots. Pants that were glossy in the moon's bright glow. A shaggy fur coat. He looked different in clothing. Bigger. His sunglasses were gone. Specks of moonlight flickered in the shadows of his eye sockets. His hairless head gleamed like a block of ivory.

Staring up at him as she fought to catch her breath, she wondered if this was really Hubert.

Hubert should be dead.

A twin?

But she realized he hadn't been using his left arm. It hung at his side like a dead thing. Doris's first bullet must've done that to him.

But not killed him.

And the second shot had merely creased his back. It hadn't killed him. The fall hadn't killed him. The stream hadn't killed him.

Maybe nothing could kill him.

'Don' hurd me anymore,' he said.

What?

'Don' hurd me and don' run away.' He spoke loudly, his words slurred as if his tongue had gone sluggish. 'I won' kill you if you're good. Bromise?'

'You won't hurt me?' Corie asked.

'Huh?'

In a stronger voice, she said, 'Will you promise not to hurt me?'

He shook his head. 'I can' hear you. I can' hear nothin'. You done id, hiddin' me. Now I'm shod.' He paused for a moment, then blurted, 'I'm shod 'n I hurd 'n id's all causa *your*!' Bellowing with rage, he brought up his right foot.

As he stomped down at her belly, Corie hooked a hand behind his boot and jerked it forward. Instead of smashing into her, it swept past her face. She thrust it straight upward. Hubert yelped and tumbled away.

Corie scurried to her feet. She whirled around. He was on his back, growling, pushing himself up.

Run! her mind roared.

But if she fled, he would come after her. He would chase her down.

She dashed straight at him.

He was braced on his right arm, knees high and apart, poised on his heels, about to lunge up.

Corie thrust her arms straight overhead, clenched her hands and dived between his knees. Her fists struck his face. The impact folded her elbows, drove her fists back against her own head as she pounded down on top of him, slamming him to the ground.

His head thunked the granite.

But he didn't pass out.

His right arm clamped across Corie's back. His legs squeezed her thighs together.

Crushed against him, mouth tight against his coat, she

couldn't breathe. But she punched his face, raked it with her fingernails, tried to find his eyes.

His arm went away.

Lifting her face, she sucked air.

Suddenly, he had her left wrist. He shoved her arm down against her side and yanked it up behind her. Squealing as muscles arid tendons tore, she writhed and arched her spine and threw back her head. She saw his face below her, the heel of her right hand shoving at his brow.

The eye, she thought. Gouge the eye!

Before she could go for it, he rammed her bent arm higher. She felt – *heard* – the bone pop from its shoulder socket. Along with the surge of the pain came freedom. He still had her arm up there, but it was loose, no longer restraining her.

She drove herself downward.

Slammed her forehead into his nose.

Letting out a soft grunt, he went limp. His hand fell away from her wrist. His legs stopped squeezing her.

Corie raised her head and snapped it down again. Again.

She scooted herself a little lower. With her right hand, she tore at the collar of his coat. The top button popped away. She tugged the coat toward his shoulder until she had bared the side of his neck.

A quick shove at his chin turned his head aside.

She stared at his thick, corded neck.

Don't think about it. Just do it. He's gonna come to.

She jammed her mouth down against the warm skin and bit. Sank her teeth in. Gnawed. Ripped.

Blood shot into her mouth.

Choking on it, she jerked her head back. The gusher splashed her face. She turned her head away and it spurted into her ear.

She scurried backward quickly; pushing at his body with her right hand. When her knees met the ground between his legs, she straightened up, gritting her teeth as her left arm slid down and swung from her shoulder.

She picked up the dangling wrist and pressed it tight to her belly.

And watched Hubert.

Ready to run.

He'd lived through everything else, why not this?

Blood was no longer pumping from his neck. That should mean his heart had stopped.

Still, Corie half expected him to sit up, to come for her.

He's dead, she told herself.

Not dead enough.

She went to his side and sat down. The granite was cold through the seat of her sweatpants as she scooted in close to him. Left hand resting on her lap, right arm bracing her up from behind, she planted her feet against his hip and ribcage. And shoved. His heavy body skidded over the ground.

She scooted close again, shoved again.

Again and again, pushing him slowly ahead of her.

Pushing him past the place where he'd crawled off the trail long ago in the heat of the day, bearing her on his back.

Pushing him to the edge of the slope.

With a final thrust of her legs, she sent him over.

She sat very still, listening. She heard nothing, not even the wind. As if it had ceased its rush through the mountains just for her.

Then came a faint sound like a foot, far away, being stamped in anger.

Corie eased backward. Lying flat with her knees in the air, she gazed up at the round, white face of the moon.

Chapter Thirty-six

It was a far-off chant. Not very loud, but loud enough for Howard to realize it was Angela's voice. Chanting. 'No. Please. No. Please. No. Please.' And a shrill '*Noooooooooo*' that twisted itself into a scream.

They're hurting her, he thought. Doing awful things to her. Things like she told me about.

Charlie and the twins.

They got her.

They got us all.

At least Angela's still alive. She isn't dead like the rest of us.

Interesting you can be dead and still think.

And still hurt.

'Don't. Don't. I mean it. *Pleeeeease!*'

And still hear.

And still cry.

The crying made him shake, and each spasm sent bolts of white-hot pain ripping through his head and back and side.

Maybe I'm not dead, he thought.

Whimpering, he tried to raise his right arm. It felt like lead, but it moved. He lifted it and fingered his face and knew he was dead.

Where his face should've been, his searching hand found gore: bits and pieces of skin, hard fragments of bone, all stuck in soft wet gobs. He had no eyes, no cheeks, no nose. Only sodden mush and bits of bone.

He *felt* as if he had eyes. They felt hot and stingy and wet from crying. His lids seemed to be there. But weighted down.

He fingered away a shard of bone, dug his finger into the mush, and touched his eyelid.

This isn't my stuff!

He suddenly remembered the last he'd seen of Lana. On her knees. Shot apart. Two shotguns aimed at the back of her head.

Oh, my God.

Like an echo, Angela cried out, 'Oh, my God!'

Sobbing, Howard scooped through the mess, clearing it off his eyes and forehead and cheeks and nose. He gagged a couple of times, and the spasms triggered blasts of pain.

He found no wounds on his face.

He tried to open his eyes. The lids seemed to be glued shut. With his fingertip, he carefully rubbed more gunk away. Then he got his eyes open.

Night. Trees above him.

'Noooo!' Angela again.

I've got to help her.

He pushed his elbows against the ground and nearly screamed. His left arm jerked and twitched. But that wasn't where the pain was. The pain was behind him. Back there by the shoulder blade. And lower. Lower, he felt as if his ribcage had been struck by a sledgehammer. And higher. The top of his head. And the right side of his head.

Settling down against the ground, he reached up with his right hand. The upper rim of his ear was gone. Sliced off, leaving a straight, raw edge of fire.

He wasn't sure he dared to explore the wound at the top of his head. He dreaded what he might find.

The first touch confirmed his fears. His heart lurched. But he soon realized that most of the glop and bits of bone were Lana's, not his.

His was a furrow. The bullet had plowed a gouge, maybe two inches long, through his hair and scalp. He assumed it hadn't penetrated his skull, but he wasn't ready to dig around and find out.

He lowered his arm to the ground.

He thought, I've got to get up and save Angela.

He wondered if he *could* get up.

Jesus, he thought. I've been shot four times.

Maybe more.

Me and Rasputin.

Takes a licking but keeps on ticking.

Me and Timex.

What about me and Angela? What are they *doing* to her?

He realized he hadn't heard her cry out in a while. Maybe they'd stopped hurting her. Maybe she'd passed out.

Maybe they'd killed her.

No!

Not Angela! Not her, too.

But they will.

Gotta stop them.

Howard shoved his right elbow against the ground, rolled toward it, and gasped 'Ahhhh!' as he thrust himself up into a sitting position.

What if they heard me?

Lana was sprawled across his legs. He glimpsed the dark back of her sweatshirt and quickly looked for the bus, afraid someone might be coming to finish him off.

The bus was straight ahead, maybe thirty or forty feet away. Trees blocked much of his view, but he could see the faint red glow of several windows. And its door, still open.

Nobody coming out.

They didn't hear me, he told himself.

But he kept watching the door, feeling that his gaze somehow held the killers trapped inside – and afraid of what he would see if he looked down. Lana pinning his legs. Keith and Glen. Even with his eyes fixed on the bus's door, he could see the dark shapes of their bodies: one beneath Lana's legs; the other on Howard's right, close enough to touch.

If he just kept watching the door, he wouldn't have to look at them.

His heart jumped and he flinched and let out another small cry as he heard a crunch. A footstep. Behind him.

Another footstep.

The snap of a twig.

He dropped down flat and shut his eyes and tried to hold his breath.

More footsteps, coming slowly closer.

Then a quick intake of breath.

'Oh, God.' Hushed, stricken.

'Doris?'

'Howard?'

He opened his eyes and saw her standing to his right. She looked down at him, then at the others. She pressed a hand to her mouth.

'Help me.'

She crouched at his side. She put a hand on his shoulder, and looked again at the other bodies. He heard her panting for air.

'They shot us all,' Howard said. 'We were in the bus. They came out of nowhere.'

Not out of nowhere, he thought. One must've come through the front door while the two with shotguns came in the emergency exit at the rear.

'Where's Angela?' Doris asked.

'They've still got her. I don't think she was shot, but they've got her. They're *doing* things to her. She's been screaming.'

Doris nodded. 'I know. I've been here a while. I came when I heard the shooting. Snuck through the trees. I had to find out what . . . I heard a sound over here.'

'That was me.'

'How bad are you hurt?'

'I don't know. I was hit four times. That I know of.'

'Jesus. We'd better get you to a hospital.'

'We can't leave Angela.'

Doris was silent for a moment. Then she said, 'Can you move?'

'I can sit up.' He rolled toward her and thrust his elbow into the ground. Doris pulled at the nape of his neck, helping him to rise.

As he leaned forward, she scurried around behind him. Her hands gently explored his back. He jerked when she touched his wounds. 'Can't see much,' she muttered. 'I think one got you in the shoulder blade. Another one's down lower but it's off to the side. There's a lot of blood.'

'Anything gushing?'

'No. I don't think you're bleeding a lot right now. Your lungs are OK?'

'I think so. It hurts to take a deep breath, but . . .'

'We need the car keys.'

Doris crawled past him. Kneeling on the other side of Glen's body, she grabbed Lana's ankles. She backed away, dragging her. Howard felt Lana's breast rub over his knee. He shuddered. He shut his eyes after glimpsing her head.

Its top half was gone.

A second later, she was off him.

When he heard a groan, he looked. The body was on top of Glen. Doris had turned it over. She reached into a pouch at the front of Lana's sweatshirt. 'Got 'em,' she whispered. Her hand came out clutching the car keys. 'Now we can get out of here.'

'We have to save Angela.'

Doris stared at him.

'We can't just leave her.'

'How many men are there?'

'Three.'

'They all have guns?'

'Yeah.'

'Do you think you can walk?'

'I don't know.'

'Let's find out.'

'*Yeeeeah!*' Howard shrieked. 'Oh God, it hurts, *it hurts*!'

Head propped up against the base of a tree, he glanced at Doris. She stood a little to the right, no more than a yard beyond his feet, pressing herself against a broad trunk, peering around its side toward the bus.

He turned his eyes to the open door.

Soon, a man appeared. Up near the driver's seat. One of the twins. A revolver in one hand while he struggled to shove his other arm into the sleeve of his plaid shirt. His jeans were open. After getting his arm through the sleeve, he pulled the zipper up and hurried down the stairs.

At the bottom, the wind flung his shirt out behind him and tossed his shaggy red hair. Muttering something, he hunched his shoulders. He trotted into the trees, coming straight for the bodies.

Nobody else followed him out.

It's just like we figured, Howard thought.

For the simple, annoying chore of finishing off a survivor, only one would come.

Maybe with just a knife, in which case the plan fell apart.

But he'd brought along a revolver for the job.

He stopped, looked at the three bodies, then raised his head.

'Asswipe' was all he said.

He walked toward Howard.

'No,' Howard gasped. 'Please. Don't kill me.'

'Fuck you.' He halted at Howard's feet and raised the gun.

'Wait. There's a girl. I know where you . . .'

The man fired, but he was already stumbling backward,

yanked by the hair. Howard heard the bullet chunk into the trunk above him. He saw Doris's arm reach around. Past the man's neck. It jerked back across as she tore through his throat with the Swiss Army knife.

Even as blood spurted and he fell back against Doris, she plunged the knife twice into his chest. He twitched and kicked, but he didn't cry out. Howard supposed that he couldn't. Not with his throat that way.

In seconds, he was stretched motionless on the ground at Doris's feet.

'Get up,' she whispered to Howard.

While he struggled to stand, she rolled the man and pulled off his shirt.

She brought it to him, helped him to put it on over his own shirt, and quickly fastened the buttons.

'I don't know who this is gonna fool,' he muttered.

'It doesn't have to fool anyone for long,' Doris said.

She returned to the body.

She sliced into the dead man's head. There were wet ripping sounds as she peeled off the hair.

Howard wondered how she could do such a thing. But he knew that he would've done it himself with no regrets.

She brought the scalp to him. She fitted it onto his head like a wig. It was snug. It squished and hurt his wound when she pressed against it. She fingered the dead man's hair, arranging it so locks clung to Howard's brow.

'All set,' she whispered.

He staggered forward, gritting his teeth against tides of pain, beginning his journey to the bus. Doris hurried ahead of him. As she picked up the knife and revolver, he lurched past her, afraid to stop. If he stopped, he might fall. If he fell, he might not be able to get up again.

There was a gap in front of him, a clear path between Keith's body and the remains of Lana's head. He made his way through it carefully, wobbling, dreading to step on his dead friends.

Doris rushed past him. Walking backward, she pressed the revolver into his right hand.

He took another lurching step, another.

Doris turned around. Arms out as if to keep her balance, she tiptoed toward the bus.

She got there very fast.

Howard watched her crouch beside the spill of light. She rested her hand on one knee, the blade of the knife pointing at the sky.

Then he watched the doorway. It seemed to bob and sway. And get bigger.

Then he was in it, raising a foot onto the first stair, thrusting himself up.

The partition was in his way.

Good, he thought. I can't see them, they can't see me.

Face forward, he climbed the next two stairs as fast as he could. He turned to the aisle.

The woman on the bench seat was covered again. She lay on her side facing the back cushion as if trying to hide.

'Hey, George, join the . . . What the *fuck*!'

The other twin. He was standing just beyond the first row of seats, facing Howard, Angela's face at his groin, his hands clutching the back of her head. From the waist up, he was clear. Howard thumbed back the hammer and fired. The bullet punched the center of his bare chest. His hands leaped from Angela's head.

As he stumbled backward and fell, the other man looked over his shoulder at Howard. His mouth hung open. His eyes bulged.

'Get up,' Howard said, knowing he couldn't shoot without a risk of hitting Angela in the back or head.

He pulled out of her and let go of her hips. Angela, wrists

bound to seat handles on each side of the aisle, swung down. Her knees hit the floor. She dangled there, limp, as the man got to his feet. Standing between her spread legs, he turned toward Howard.

He raised his hands.

His erection was wet and shiny.

'You're Charlie,' Howard said.

'Don't shoot. I give up. No call to . . .'

The bullet crashed through his forehead. Blood spurted from the small hole. The back of his head spat out a thick gust of red. He stood rigid for a moment, eyeballs rolling upward. Then he pitched forward and landed on a mattress.

He was in the way. Howard had to step on him. When he was standing between Angela's legs, he fired over her head. He put a second slug into the twin's chest. Then he missed and hit the floor. Then he placed one alongside the nose.

Dropping the gun, he sank to his knees. He slid his hand gently down her back, feeling the slickness of her blood, the puffed ridges of welts, the cuts. The letters C C had been carved into her skin.

Charlie Carnes.

'No,' she murmured. 'Please. No.'

'It's me,' Howard said. 'We've killed 'em all.'

Chapter Thirty-seven

They lay side by side, propped up on their elbows. The bedroom windows were open. A warm, morning breeze was sliding softly down Corie's back. It felt very good. She took a long, lazy breath. The air smelled of grass and roses.

'I think here,' Chad said, touching a fingertip to the map which was spread on the mattress under their faces. 'It's a beautiful area. I was there just last summer.'

'Where's Calamity?' Corie asked.

His finger moved down and sideways. 'It's a good thirty miles away.'

'I guess that's far enough.'

'There's a whole string of lakes. They're fantastic. And I went for a whole week in that area without running into another soul.'

'That sounds good to me.'

'Do you think you'll have any trouble carrying a pack?'

'Do you think you'll have any trouble walking?'

'Are you really sure you want to do this?'

Corie felt a squirmy tingle deep inside. 'Yeah,' she said. 'I think so. I want to and I don't, you know?'

'Same here.'

'But I think we should go ahead and do it. We've only got a week before the semester starts. If we put it off till next summer . . . I don't know. I might lose my nerve by then. It was so wonderful before . . . all the trouble. I want it to be that way again.'

'Nothing will happen this time,' Chad said.

'Promise?'

'We'll have the guns just in case, but . . .'

The ringing doorbell stopped his words.

'Great,' Corie muttered. She pushed herself up, patted Chad's rear, and crawled off the bed. 'Don't go anywhere,' she said. 'It's probably Jehovah's Witnesses or something.'

'We could pretend we're not home.'

The bell rang again.

'I'll open the door like this and watch the looks on their faces.'

'I dare you.'

Laughing softly, she walked out of the bedroom naked.

'Hey!' he called.

'A dare's a dare,' she called over her shoulder. She hurried up the hallway and into the living room, grinning. Apparently, Chad had forgotten that she'd left her robe on the sofa last night. She picked it up, slipped into it, and belted it shut on her way to the front door.

Looking through the peephole, she saw Howard Clark.

She opened the door.

Angela was standing beside him on the stoop. Pressed against her side was the Ouija board. She had its plastic, heart-shaped pointer in her hand.

'You two look great,' Corie said. The last time she'd seen them, just after Howard's release from the hospital, they'd both seemed haggard and grim. Now, they looked healthy. They were smiling. They even matched. Except for Angela's knee socks, they were dressed the same in white short-sleeved shirts, plaid shorts and white sneakers.

'Come on in,' Corie said.

They hesitated. Howard glanced at her robe and blushed. 'Is this a good time?' he asked.

'Sure. It's always a good time when friends drop by.' She waved them in, backing away. 'I'm not overjoyed to see *that* thing again, though.' She nodded toward the Ouija board.

'Well,' Howard said, 'it belongs to you. We got it back from Lana's parents. They didn't want it.'

'Neither do I.'

'We don't want it,' Angela said.

'Well, you can leave it here. I'll burn the damn thing and that'll be the end of it.' Taking the board and pointer from Angela, she led the way into the living room. 'Sit down and make yourselves comfortable,' she said. She gestured toward the sofa. 'I'll tell Chad you're here. Would you like some coffee or something?'

'Oh, no thank you,' Howard said, and Angela shook her head.

As they went to the sofa, Corie set the board and pointer on the lamp table. 'Right back,' she said.

When she reached the bedroom, she found Chad on his feet, pulling up a pair of shorts. 'It's Howard and Angela.'

'What's that I see you wearing? What happened to the dare?'

'What do you think I am, a bimbo?'

She waited while he put on a T-shirt. Together, they returned to the living room.

'Morning,' Chad said.

As the kids greeted him, he sat down on an easy chair. Corie sank to the floor in front of him and leaned back against his legs. 'They brought back the Ouija board,' she explained.

'Just what we need. So, what have you two been up to?'

Howard shrugged. He looked a little nervous. Corie realized that his hair had grown long enough to hide the missing part of his ear. 'A lot,' he said. 'We're planning to go apartment hunting today.'

'When are you gonna tie the knot?' Chad asked.

They both turned bright red.

'Mom and Dad think we should wait till after graduation.'

'That's probably not a bad idea,' Corie said.

'How was your honeymoon?' Angela asked.

'Great.'

'Painful.'

'Chad.'

'And awkward.'

'Stop it.'

Howard laughed, but he was still blushing. 'Maybe you should've waited until you were both better.'

'It wasn't as bad as he's making out. How are you two doing? You're looking just wonderful.'

'I get a lot of headaches, but . . .' He shrugged. 'No big deal.'

'He's getting better all the time,' Angela said. 'The doctors say he'll be fine.'

'What about you?'

She shrugged.

What a pair, Corie thought. Blushing and shrugging to beat the band. They were meant for each other.

'I'm OK,' she finally said.

'We've both got some nice scars.'

'But we're alive and we're together,' Angela said. 'That's what really counts. I've never been so happy. If it weren't for what happened to . . .' Her voice went husky and tears shimmered in her eyes.

'I know,' Corie murmured.

Howard put an arm across Angela's shoulders and eased her close against him.

'Doris came by a couple of days ago,' Chad said. 'Have you seen her lately?'

'No. How is she?'

'As obnoxious as ever.'

Corie laughed, and so did the kids. Angela wiped her eyes.

'Good old Doris,' Howard said.

'She's planning to sign up for my Chaucer seminar,' Corie told them. 'You two'll be taking it, right?'

'It's not an eight-o'clock, is it?' Angela asked.

'Two in the afternoon. Monday, Wednesday and Friday.'

She sniffed and smiled. 'In that case we'll be there.'

'Do you have Doris's address?' Howard asked. 'We want to drop by and give her something. We have one for you guys, too.' He leaned forward, reached into the seat pocket of his shorts, and pulled out his wallet. 'It's the main reason we came over.'

'Not just to get us out of bed?'

'Chad enjoys watching people blush.'

'Anyway,' Howard said, and took a slip of paper out of the wallet. It looked like a check. Angela squeezed his leg. Then he got up and came across the room and handed the paper to Corie.

A check made out to Chad and Coreen Dalton. From Angela's account, and signed by her. A check in the amount of $25,000.

She frowned up at Howard. He was already on his way back to the sofa. 'What's this?' she asked Angela.

'It's your share of the treasure.'

'What?'

'Let's see.'

She handed it up to Chad. 'Twenty-five grand?' He sounded astonished. 'You've gotta be kidding.'

'It's actually two shares,' Angela explained. 'Twelve-five for each of you. We're splitting it eight ways. Doris'll get a share, and we've already sent checks to . . .' She started weeping again.

'To Lana's family,' Howard said. 'And Keith's and Glen's.

Everybody gets . . .' He choked up. 'Or their survivors.'

'Where'd it come from?' Corie asked. 'What is it?'

'Butler's loot,' Howard said.

'I don't . . . there *wasn't* any loot. Was there?'

Angela nodded and sniffed.

'Yeah, there was,' Howard said. He took a deep breath. 'It's so weird. We never had to go to the mountains for it. I mean, we had to start out, but . . .'

'It was when we left,' Angela explained. 'It was taking me away from Skerrit.'

'Who?'

'Angela's uncle. She lived with him. In a second-story apartment.'

'He didn't want me to leave.'

'But we went ahead and left, anyway.'

'He was awfully upset.'

'I guess he tried to come after us,' Howard said. 'And fell. They found him the next morning at the bottom of the stairs. His neck was broken. He was dead.'

'My God,' Corie muttered. 'How awful.'

'He was old,' Angela said. 'And not very nice.'

'His life insurance was a hundred thousand dollars,' Howard explained.

Angela nodded. 'And I was named beneficiary.'

'You're telling us,' Chad said, 'that Butler's loot . . . the treasure the Ouija board promised you kids . . . was this man's life insurance?'

'That's how we figure it,' Howard said. 'All he had to do was fall and get killed. That must've happened just a minute or so after we drove away that night. It means the whole trip to the mountains . . . everything . . . was unnecessary.'

'Mom thought it was necessary.'

'Well, yeah.'

'She wanted me to find her. She wanted her body brought home. And I guess she wanted revenge.'

'She got it,' Howard muttered.

One Rainy Night

To Wren and Ida Marshall,
two of the best people I know.
May the luck of the Irish
be with you always.

The Killing Ground

This is pretty goddamn crazy, Hanson thought. But he didn't climb down.

The chainlink fence surrounding the football stadium of Lincoln High School shook as he made his way upward. Its mesh let out tinny chinging sounds that seemed terribly loud in the stillness of the November evening. But Hanson doubted that anyone would hear the noise.

The nearest houses were out of sight beyond the stands at the far side of the stadium. Behind him, an empty field stretched toward the distant classroom buildings. The stadium itself seemed deserted.

The sounds of the shaking fence would be heard by no one. Hanson knew that. Yet they unnerved him just as surely as the crunch of dry leaves underfoot might unsettle a man making his lone way through a graveyard in the dead of night. His heart pounded. Sweat seemed to run out of every pore. His arms and legs trembled.

Climbing the fence was easy. Being here was not.

At the top, he hurled himself over the rail. He dropped the nine feet to the grass, landing with his knees bent to absorb the impact. He felt the jolt mostly around his waist, where gravity tugged at his gun belt. Jostled leather groaned and creaked. Cuffs and ammunition rattled inside their cases. Standing up straight, Hanson gave the belt a couple of pulls to bring it back up where it belonged.

He rubbed his sweaty hands on the front of his shirt.

Well, he thought, you're here.

Now, if he only knew *why*.

He walked slowly over the grass, eyes on the north goal post straight in front of him.

He was kidding himself if he thought he might find anything new. The boys had gone over the area thoroughly last night, and again in daylight. They'd photographed, picked up, tagged and taken away everything: the poor bastard himself, his clothes, matches and cigarette butts, the gasoline can, candy wrappers and other shit that probably had nothing at all to do with the crime, even some of the sod surrounding the main standard where the kid had been tied. There'd been talk of taking the goalpost, as well, but the chief decided against it. They had stripped off the charred remains of the padding for evidence.

Hell, there was nothing left to find.

But Hanson, patrolling the neighborhood, had found himself circling the high school, slowing his car each time he had a view of the distant goalpost and staring out his window at the damned thing. Finally, he'd parked in front of the stadium.

And left the car without even radioing in.

Crazy.

As he crunched across the cinder track, Hanson wished he'd made the call. He could've given Lucy a phony location, claimed he was taking an early break for chow.

Would've been worse, lying to her.

He planned to marry the woman. You don't lie to someone you love.

Better this way, he thought. Besides, she'll probably cover for me if anything comes up.

The grass felt soft and springy under his shoes. He walked through the end zone, the goalpost jarring slightly in his vision. He stopped just outside the circle where the grass had been removed. He stared.

Again, he wondered why he was drawn to this place.

He'd seen murder victims before. Though not many. And only one, Jennifer Sayers, who'd met an end this brutal. She hadn't been burnt like this boy. Tortured and raped. Her mutilated body had given Hanson plenty of nightmares, but he'd never made a secret trip to the section of woods where it happened.

Somehow, this was different.

Yeah, he thought. Somehow. Maxwell Chidi was a black kid. That's the difference, right there.

When does a black guy become a nigger? When he leaves the room.

Hanson used to laugh at stuff like that. Shit, he used to *say* stuff like that.

That's why I'm here, he realized.

Guilt.

They did it to the kid because he was black. White people. They got themselves a nigger.

Hell, you're just guessing. It might've had nothing to do with that. We aren't in Alabama, here. Could've been a perfectly ordinary motive. Jealousy, greed. Maybe the kid was a pusher, could've been skimming and . . .

Right. He was black, therefore he was a pusher.

That's the kind of thinking . . .

The stadium lights came on.

Hanson flinched, sucked in a quick breath. *Oh, Jesus!* He whirled around. He scanned the stands on both sides of the field. Nobody there. But he knew he'd been caught.

Stay cool, he told himself.

Probably just a maintenance man. Might not even know I'm here. Yet.

Hell, I'm a cop. I've got business here.

He still saw no one.

Somebody turned the lights on.

Maxwell . . .

Oh, right. Sure.

But his skin prickled as he imagined the dead boy staggering through a passageway of the stadium, coming toward the field. A black shape shuffling through the dark. Rigid all over, arms sticking out, stubs of fingers hooked like claws. No face at all. Just a black, earless knot above the shoulders. With teeth.

He thought he could hear the slow shuffle of Maxwell's charred feet on the concrete, hear his crisp skin cracking as he moved, see it flaking off and drifting down from him like dead leaves.

Gonna getcha, white man.

Quit it! Hanson told himself.

Though he knew he was letting his imagination run wild, he snapped his head from side to side, eyes darting to the grandstand openings. Three on each side. Dark holes. Tunnels leading to the rear, to refreshment stands and restrooms, to exit gates in the fence.

Stop this. You're just spooking yourself. Maxwell's dead in the morgue, not . . .

Across the field, a figure emerged from the nearest passageway.

A white man in dark green coveralls. A grounds keeper? Hanson sighed. He felt as if all his strength had drained away. The effort of standing up straight made him tremble.

The guy raised an arm in greeting, then climbed over the rail and leaped down to the grass area on the far side of the track. He took all the impact with his left leg while he kept his right leg high. Then he was standing on both feet, and walking toward Hanson with a limp. 'Evening, officer,' he called.

Hanson nodded a greeting.

The top of the man's head gleamed in the stadium lights.

The hair around his ears was gray. His lean face was weathered. He looked wiry and tough. Keys jangled at his side as he hobbled closer.

'Toby Barnes,' he said, and stuck out his hand.

Hanson shook it. 'Bob Hanson.'

'Just got here, Bob. I saw your car out front. Mind if I ask how you got in?'

'I had to come over the fence.'

Toby looked relieved. 'Glad to hear it. I was afraid some idiot might've left a gate unlocked. Sorry I wasn't around to let you in.'

'No problem.'

'Anyway, I thought you might appreciate some light on the subject. I was on my way over to the school. I'm the head of maintenance, you know, gotta keep my eye on the cleaning crew. Bunch of no-good loafers, most of them.' Toby turned his eyes away from Hanson and frowned at the goalpost. 'Terrible,' he said. 'Any ideas who did it?'

'We're working on it. I just thought I'd stop by and try to get the feel of the situation.'

'I suppose you were out here last night.'

'Yeah.'

'Must've been pretty grim. I've seen my share of crispy critters, you know. Bakersfield Fire Department till a roof dropped out from under me.' He slapped his right leg. What it smacked through the trousers didn't sound like skin. 'Never a pretty sight. That's one aspect of the job I sure don't miss.'

Hanson, who'd taken a liking to the man right away, now felt a grudging admiration. 'They couldn't pay me enough to be a fireman,' he said.

Toby nodded. His eyes stayed on the goalpost. 'Think it was kids?'

'I don't know. Seems likely.'

'We haven't got any Klan here that I know of.'

'No.'

'It's the sort of thing you might expect from the Klan. Really gives this burg a black eye.'

'Did you know the boy?' Hanson asked.

'I've seen him around school.' Toby faced him, frowning slightly. 'We've only got a handful of coloreds, you know. This Chidi, he wasn't at all like the others. A tall fellow, kind of handsome, and he talked funny. I guess he came from one of those islands. Jamaica, Haiti, someplace like that. It was none of this "hey, bro, mutherfuh" stuff. He talked like he had breeding, you know?'

'How did he get along with the other students?'

'Well, from what I saw, he didn't have much to do with the other black kids. The rest of them were always hanging around together. I guess that's only natural. But I don't think I ever saw Chidi with them. When I saw him, he was always with white kids. White girls, mostly. It seems like the girls really took to him.'

Hanson felt his heart quicken. 'Anyone special?'

'Yeah, there was. I don't know the girl's name, but I could find it out for you. The past couple of weeks, they've been hanging all over each other. I wouldn't be at all surprised if she wasn't putting out for him.'

'Well, now,' Hanson muttered.

'Yeah, I can see how a thing like that might rub some folks the wrong way.'

'This is . . .'

They both jumped and threw their heads back as the sky seemed to explode. For an instant, Hanson thought a mid-air collision had occurred over the stadium. But what he saw was a searing bright flash of lightning, branched like a giant tree, ripping down through a canyon of dark, piled cloud.

The roar faded. It left his ears ringing.

'Jesus-smoking-Christ,' Toby blurted.

The rain came down.

It dropped like a shroud over the stadium lights, blocking out all but the faintest yellow glow.

A moment after the lights dimmed, the shower hit Hanson. Big, hot drops that pelted his face and shoulders. They made his skin tingle. They seemed to sink in. They warmed him. He suddenly felt a strange, wild rush of excitement.

Toby said, 'Holy shit.'

Hanson and Toby stared at each other through the faint jaundiced light, the dark shower and the mist that now drifted around them – condensation, probably caused by the hot rain sluicing through the cooler November air.

Toby looked as if someone had dumped a bucket of ink over his head. Only his eyes and teeth were white. More teeth showed as his lips curled.

Hanson popped the snap of his holster guard and snatched out his revolver as Toby lunged at him, snarling. The man's fingers clutched Hanson's neck. Thumbs dug into his throat. He rammed the muzzle of his .38 into Toby's belly and jerked the trigger three times fast. The blasts pounded his ears.

Toby staggered backward, folding at the waist.

The fourth round smacked through the crown of his bald, black head. He sat down hard, skidded on his rump, and came to a stop sitting up, drooping over his outstretched legs.

Hanson gave himself a small running start, and punted Toby's face. He hoped he might send the head soaring like a football. In spite of his power and follow-through, however, all he managed was to slam the man's back against the ground.

As Hanson's right leg reached the height of its kick, his left foot slipped on the wet grass. He flapped his arms, gasped, and flopped on his back beside Toby. Jarred by the fall, he lay motionless for a while. The rain felt very good. This was like sprawling out in his bathtub with the shower on, but this was better. He holstered his weapon, then spread out his arms and legs. Moaning, he squirmed with pleasure.

As his head turned, he saw Toby's body close beside him.

Wow, he thought. Sure wasted that son-of-a-bitch.

He laughed. Feeling the rain in his mouth, he opened up wide and stretched out his tongue. The rain felt thicker than water. It tasted, he thought, a little bit like blood.

Just a little bit. A mild coppery flavor. Very subtle.

It made him long to fill his mouth with the real thing.

Hanson rolled over, pushed himself up, and crawled. He stretched out, belly down. Elbows against the soft, wet grass, he grabbed Toby by the ears. He lifted the man's head. He clamped his mouth to the bullet wound and sucked.

A Hard Rain's Gonna Fall

1

Earlier that evening, while patrolman Bob Hanson was still cruising the streets near Lincoln High and just more than an hour before his bullets ripped out the life of Toby Barnes, Francine Walters sat down on her living room sofa. She pulled the TV tray closer as the six o'clock Eyewitness News came on. While the lead-in music played, she polished off the scotch at the bottom of her glass.

'Good evening, everyone,' said anchorwoman Chris Donner. 'At the top of our news, investigators continue to probe last night's grisly murder of seventeen-year-old Maxwell Chidi, a student at Lincoln High in the nearby valley community of Bixby. The body of the black youth was discovered in the newly completed Memorial Stadium by . . .'

'Mark my words,' Francine said, 'that boy was up to no good. He probably had it coming.'

'Shit,' Lisa muttered.

Francine snapped her head toward the girl. 'What? What did you say?'

Lisa glared at her from the rocking chair. 'I said that's shit. You don't know what you're talking about.'

'I know good and well what I'm talking about, young lady, and don't you dare speak to me that way. What's gotten into you? You haven't been fit to live with ever since you climbed out of bed this morning.'

The anger seemed to melt out of Lisa's stare. She opened her mouth as if to say something, then closed it again. Her lips mashed themselves together. Their corners trembled.

Her chin, dimpled and discolored with the effort of thrusting up her lower lip, began to shake. Her eyes filled with tears.

'Lisa?'

'Just leave me alone.' She scooted back her rocking chair. But not far enough. As she got up, her thighs bumped the edge of her dinner tray. Not hard, but the collision jostled the tray and capsized her glass, which tumbled over the edge, flinging out its contents of ice cubes and water. The glass hit the carpet with a soft thump.

'*Now* see what you've done!' Francine snapped.

Letting out an anguished sob, the girl ran from the room.

What the *hell's* the matter with her? Francine wondered. Damn it!

Carefully, she moved her own tray aside. As she stood, she heard a door slam shut. It sounded too near to be Lisa's bedroom door. Probably the bathroom, just off the foyer.

She stepped past Lisa's tray and picked up the glass. Squatting, she gathered ice cubes off the beige carpet. Thank God it was only water, she thought. She dropped the cubes into the glass. If Lisa'd been drinking milk or Pepsi . . . and you can thank your lucky stars her lasagna didn't end up on the floor.

Francine set the glass on the tray, then went looking for Lisa. She felt hot and squirmy inside. God, how she hated this kind of thing.

But this episode didn't seem like one of her daughter's typical tantrums. Something more serious. Maybe something to do with the death of that black kid.

I shouldn't have smarted off about it, she thought.

Just as she'd suspected, the bathroom door was shut.

'Honey?'

'Leave me alone.' From the girl's high, shaky voice, Francine knew she was still crying.

'Are you OK?'

'No.'

'I'm sorry I lost my temper, honey. Come on out, now, all right? You have to be at the Foxworth's in less than an hour.'

'I can't.'

'They're counting on you. Come on out and finish your dinner.'

Seconds later, the lock pinged and the door swung open. Lisa's face was red, her eyes bloodshot, her face gleaming with streams of tears. Sobbing, she rubbed her runny nose with a Kleenex.

Seeing the girl this way, Francine felt her own throat tighten. Her eyes burned as they filled with tears. 'What is it?' she asked.

'*Oh, Mom!*' She lurched forward, threw her arms around Francine and hugged her fiercely. She gasped for air. Spasms jerked her body. 'I loved him,' she blurted. 'I loved him so bad and they killed him.'

2

Denise Gunderson, done with her cheeseburger, folded the paper plate in half and dropped it into the waste container. She took a chocolate chip cookie from the freezer side of the refrigerator. Munching on it, cupping a hand under her chin in case of crumbs, she wandered into the front room.

'And what have we here?' she asked, her voice muffled by the mouthful of cookie.

She knew what she had here: a plastic bag containing the

three video tapes she'd rented that afternoon. But whenever she was alone in the house, she liked to talk to herself. It broke the silence.

She sat on the floor and crossed her legs. She poked the remains of the cookie into her mouth, then brushed her fingers against the leg of her sweatpants. The noise of her teeth crunching the frozen cookie sounded a lot louder than the soft whispery rustle made by the bag as she spread it open. She took out the tapes and examined their titles. She had *Watchers*, *Near Dark* and *The Texas Chainsaw Massacre*.

Shaking her head, she laughed softly and muttered, 'Fine, wholesome family entertainment.'

But Tom would love them. He'd probably seen them already, but that wouldn't faze him at all.

'Now, if you've just got the guts to call him.'

The clock on the VCR showed 6:11 p.m.

If you're going to call him, Denise thought, you'd better do it now. Before he goes out somewhere.

Trying to ignore the unpleasant pounding of her heart, she got to her feet. She walked back into the kitchen and stared at the wall phone.

She felt awfully shaky. Drops of sweat slid down her sides.

'Oh, man,' she muttered.

If Mom and Dad find out I had him over . . .

They had one hard and fast rule: *no boys in the house when we're not home*. So far, Denise had never broken the rule. She'd been tempted, but the fear of being caught (even innocently watching television with the guy) had always prevailed.

Tonight, however, there was no chance of her parents walking in. They were spending the night with friends in Tiburon, which was a two-hour drive from Bixby. They'd phoned at 5:30 just to make sure nothing was amiss. And Dad, who loathed driving at night, was not about to head for home before daylight. Their actual plan was to leave Tiburon in mid-afternoon.

Still, something could go wrong. A neighbor might spot Tom coming or going. His car might break down in the driveway, immovable, stuck there till Mom and Dad showed up. An earthquake might hit, trapping Tom in the house with her. 'Or caving in our beans,' she said, and chuckled. 'Screw it, call him up.'

She rubbed her clammy hands on her sweatpants. She took a deep breath. Then she reached for the phone and its sudden clamor rammed her breath out.

It's Tom, she thought. He must be psychic.

She lifted the receiver. 'Hello?'

'Is this Denise?'

Not him. A woman's voice, vaguely familiar. 'Yes, it is.'

'This is Lynn Foxworth. You sat for us a few months ago?'

'Sure.' Oh, no, she thought. But she forced herself to sound cheery as she said, 'Kara's mother.'

'I really hate to bother you with this, it's such short notice. I just feel horrible, even asking. And please, if you already have plans for tonight, that's fine, maybe you can suggest someone else. But we're in an awful bind. We have seven o'clock dinner reservations, and I just this minute got off the phone with Francine Walters. Lisa's mom? Lisa – it was all arranged for her to sit for us, but, I don't know, Francine was awfully upset. It seems she just found out that Lisa was with that murdered boy last night. There was a dance after the game? Anyway, Lisa apparently has some idea about who did it, and Francine's rushing her right over to the police department. Apparently she's afraid that, you know, somebody might try something with Lisa. To keep her from talking? Scary stuff. I guess it's just as well she *isn't* coming here. Not if *killers* might be after her, or something. Can you believe it? Anyway, now we're stuck without a sitter and I'm really at my wits' end but I thought, if you don't already have plans. Kara really likes you, and I know you only did it as a special favor last time because of your folks, but . . . can you help us out?'

Denise wished she'd let the phone keep ringing.

'I sort of had a date,' she said.

'Well, he could come over here. God, what am I saying? I'd certainly never suggest such a thing to someone like Lisa, but . . . I know how trustworthy you are. It might not be much fun for your friend, but it'd certainly be OK with us. We've got all kinds of good snacks, soft drinks.'

This, Denise thought, is one desperate woman.

'We shouldn't be very late. Maybe ten or eleven?'

'Well, I don't know about having my boyfriend there, but I'll come over. What time do you want me?'

'We should leave the house no later than ten till seven, so any time before that.'

Denise glanced at the kitchen clock. Six-fourteen.

'If you haven't eaten yet . . .'

'No, I just finished.'

'I was going to say you could eat here, but . . . Oh, Denise, you're a lifesaver. I can't tell you. This is great.'

'Glad to help. I'll see you in a while.'

'Would you like John to pick you up?'

'No, that's not necessary. But thanks.'

'Oh, don't thank me. You're a lifesaver, you really are.'

'I'd better get ready to go.'

'Right, right. Great. We'll see you in a few minutes.'

'Fine. Bye-bye.'

Denise hung up.

She thought about the rented movies. She thought about Tom. She felt cheated and sad.

'It's not the end of the world,' she muttered.

Maybe a blessing in disguise, she thought as she headed for her room to change clothes. Keeps me from breaking the 'house rule'. Keeps me and Tom from being together for hours, alone in the house, and maybe things would've gotten out of hand.

Maybe I *wanted* things to get out of hand.

God's way of saving me from temptation.

Or giving me the shaft.

3

Patterson, manning the front desk, leaned forward and smirked when Trevor Hudson entered the station. 'When are you gonna get a life, Hudson?'

'I just couldn't stay away,' Trev said. 'I know how you pine for me.'

'Your ass and my face, pal.'

'If you say so.' Trev made his way past the end of the counter, smiled a greeting to Lucy, and was almost to his desk when Patterson turned around, frowning.

'I meant that the other way around.'

'Oh? OK.' He pulled out his swivel chair and sat down.

'I mean it, though. This is Saturday night, man. *Date* night, you know? You oughta be out somewhere getting lowdown and hairy.'

'I'd rather be here with you,' he said, and winked at the burly sergeant.

Lucy, at the dispatcher station off in the corner, looked over her shoulder grinning. 'You'd better watch what you say, Trev, or you'll have Patty sitting on your lap.'

'Sit on mine, honey,' Patterson told her. 'Better still, on my face.'

'Don't you wish,' she said, then turned away as a call came in.

Trev slid open his top drawer. He took out a coupon for a dollar off a family size pizza at O'Casey's, dug his wallet out of a seat pocket of his jeans, and folded the coupon. As he tucked it into his wallet, he shook his head at the absurdity of dropping by here for a dollar-off coupon.

Nothing absurd about it, he told himself. He had to drive right past the station, anyway, on his way to O'Casey's. And a buck is a buck.

But his stomach fluttered a bit as he stuffed the wallet back into his pocket and he knew that his real reason for picking up the coupon had less to do with thrift than with procrastination.

A delaying tactic.

Maureen might not even be there. This *is* Saturday, and she'd been on the job each time Trev had gone there during the past week. It only stood to reason that she wouldn't work every night.

On the other hand, the dinner hour on a Saturday evening is probably O'Casey's busiest time. And it's a family business. She'd come to town for Mary's funeral, three weeks ago, and turned up waiting on customers when the pizzaria reopened. According to her brother, she was staying with Liam and planned to remain indefinitely, taking care of her father and helping out with the business.

So it didn't make sense for Maureen to take off Saturday night.

She would be there, all right.

And Trev planned to do more, this time, than exchange a few friendly words with her and gape at her while she made visits to other tables. He planned to ask her out. And he wasn't sure he had the nerve.

She likes me, he thought. I know she does.

It was more than her cheerful, wise-cracking banter. She talked to all the customers that way. But she didn't look at the others the way she looked at Trev. When her eyes met his, their gaze seemed to sink into him as if searching deep inside, looking for something, wondering about him, and they seemed to hold a soft challenge.

She wants me to ask her out. And she's wondering why I haven't, yet. Wondering what's wrong.

I've got to do it, Trev thought. Tonight. Now.

But he remained at his desk, staring past the deserted desks toward the door of the interrogation room.

Come on, he told himself. Get up and go. Do it.

'You all of a sudden into meditation?' Patterson asked.

Trev looked around at him. 'Just thinking,' he said. 'Try it, sometime.'

'Try eating dirt,' Patterson said. And was about to say more, but someone apparently entered the station just then, so he turned to the front.

Trev looked at the wall clock. Six twenty-five.

He'd been going into O'Casey's at eight, midway through his shift. If he showed up this early, Maureen might not be on duty yet. Maybe he should wait a couple of hours.

Don't be such a damn chicken!

He rolled back his chair. As he started to rise, he heard footsteps behind him. He stood and turned around. Patterson was striding toward him, a serious look on his face. In a hushed voice, he said, 'Since you're here anyway, maybe you'd like to handle this.'

Trev saw two females, an adult and a teenaged girl, at the other side of the reception window. 'I was just on my way out.'

'It's about the Chidi case. You're more up on it than me.'

'Well, I was there last night.'

'The girl knew Chidi. Sounds like they were going together.'

'OK, I'll talk to them.'

What the hell, he thought. I was looking for an excuse. And this might be a break. Shouldn't take long, and Maureen might not be there yet, anyway.

'You won't regret it,' Patterson said, then rolled his eyes upward and pursed his lips. 'Couple of knockouts. Maybe you'll get lucky.' Resuming a solemn expression, he turned away. He headed toward the women and said, 'Officer Hudson will see you. If you'd like to step in.' He nodded toward the opening at the far end of the counter.

Trev met them there. He sized them up quickly, decided he didn't much like what he saw, and gave them a smile that he hoped was reassuring. 'Thanks for coming by. I'm Trevor Hudson.'

The older woman, probably the girl's mother, narrowed her eyes as if she expected Trev to give her shit and rather hoped he might try. 'Francine Walters,' she said. Her raspy voice was as hard as her looks. She appeared to be about forty, but Trev had seen this type before, and they always appeared older than their years. Her hair was bleached blond. She needed to do the roots. Too much eye makeup. Lipstick too bright. A lean, drawn face with wrinkle lines in the wrong places. It was a face that hadn't smiled much, that spent too much time scowling or giving off sarcastic smirks. 'This is Lisa,' she said.

'Hi, Lisa.'

The girl didn't look up. Her head was lowered, her shoulders slumped. Her hair was the same silvery blond as her mother's, but her roots didn't show.

'Come on back here,' Trev said, 'and we'll talk.'

He led the way toward the interrogation room. 'We don't want to end up on the news,' Francine said to his back. 'We don't want it all over town.'

He opened the door and held it for them.

'Is that understood?' Francine asked.

'We'll try to keep it between the three of us,' Trev said.

The girl gave him a wary glance as she stepped by. She'd been crying, and her face looked freshly scrubbed. Trev imagined that she might be a beautiful young woman if she ever smiled. She was shorter than her mother, but had the same build – hips and breasts that seemed too prominent for her otherwise slim figure. She probably kept the high school girls in a constant state of envy and the boys in heat.

She wore a pullover sweater that might have fit her a couple of years ago. She'd probably bought it too small, just as she'd probably bought the blue jeans pre-faded and pre-slashed. The legs of her jeans, fashionably ripped and frayed, made it look as if she'd been attacked by a knife-wielding midget.

A cloying odor of perfume swept past Trev as she stepped through the doorway.

A more exotic perfume followed Francine. Not as sweet, dark and wanton, mixed with odors of whiskey and stale smoke.

Trev stepped into the room. 'Please, sit down. Could I get you some coffee? We've got a soda machine, Lisa. Would you like a Pepsi or . . .?'

'Can we just get on with it?' Francine asked.

Nodding, he closed the door. Through the glass, he saw Patterson leer at him, pump his fist, and mouth something that looked like 'Va va va voom.'

Thinks he's doing me a favor, sending me in with these two. Knockouts. Right.

I could be sitting at O'Casey's, right now. I could be talking to Maureen.

He turned to the women. They were seated facing the table, their backs to him. He stepped behind them. He picked up a legal pad from a stack at the end of the table, then swung a chair out past the corner and sat down. He wanted to keep it informal. He didn't want the table in the way. He told himself that it had nothing to do with wanting a better view of Patterson's knockouts. He crossed one leg, rested the legal pad against his upthrust knee, and said to Lisa, 'I understand that you knew Maxwell Chidi.'

'Yeah,' she said. She glanced at him, then looked the other way to check on her mother who was nearly hidden from Trev's view on her far side. She then did just what he expected. She scooted her chair away from the table, far back until it bumped the window sill and she no longer separated Trev from her mother.

Then both women turned their chairs toward him.

'They were going together,' Francine said. 'I didn't know a thing about it. The last I heard, she was still going with Buddy Gilbert.'

Trev plucked a ballpoint from his shirt pocket and wrote down the name. 'How long were you seeing Maxwell?' he asked the girl.

'A couple of weeks,' she said without looking at him. Her eyes were fixed on the knee of her jeans, where she was fingering her skin through a ragged slit. There were more gashes higher up.

'She just kept me totally in the dark,' Francine said, taking a pack of cigarettes from her purse. 'If I'd known, I would've put a quick stop to it. You'd better believe it.' She shook out a cigarette. Tapping its filter against the table, she said, 'It's not that I'm a bigot or anything.'

'Sure you aren't,' Lisa muttered.

'That's right, I'm not.' Glaring at the back of her daughter's head, she jabbed the cigarette into a corner of her mouth and fired it with a Bic. 'But I think I've been around awhile longer than you, young lady, and I think I know a few things you don't.' The cigarette jerked up and down as she talked. Lisa kept fiddling with the tear at her knee. 'One thing I know is a girl like you starts going around with a black guy, it means trouble. And I was right, wasn't I? Wasn't I?'

'I guess,' Lisa murmured.

'You guess. The boy's dead, isn't he?'

Lisa nodded.

'Think he'd be dead if he didn't start going with you?'

'Lisa,' Trev said, 'do you know who murdered him?'

'Not exactly.'

'Tell the man what you told me.'

She glanced up at Trev, then frowned at the rip in her jeans. 'I think it might've been Buddy and his friends.'

'Buddy Gilbert,' Trev said.

'Yeah. See, he didn't like it when I broke up with him. Then there was the dance after the game last night. In the gym? Buddy came in with his friends. They were all drunk, you know? Buddy tried to cut in and dance with me and I told him, you know, to get lost. And he started . . . He got real nasty. He called Maxwell . . . like every name in the book. You know?' She raised her eyes to Trev as if curious to see his reactions. 'Nigger, coon, jigaboo, spade, spearchucker, jungle bunny. That kind of thing? And he got really crude about how black people are supposed to have bigger dicks?'

'*Jesus*, Lisa!' her mother snapped.

'Well, he did. Like that was why I dumped him for Maxwell.'

'You don't have to announce it to the goddamn *world*!'

'It's all right,' Trev told the girl. 'What happened then?'

'Well, Maxwell just stood there and didn't say anything, and Mr Sherman – he's the vice principal? – he came over and kicked Buddy and his friends out.'

'Do you know the names of Buddy's friends?'

'Sure. Doug Haines and Lou Nicholson.'

4

Lou didn't want to be here. He wished he were in his own home, in bed with the pillow covering his face. But when Buddy calls and says come over, you come over.

Hell, maybe it was better not to be home. Here, at least, he wasn't alone. There were sure to be some wild times, what with the five of them together and Doug's folks over at the club. And the booze. One way or another, maybe he'd be able to forget about last night. At least for a while.

And then, as if his hopes were being answered, he *did* forget about last night. Because Sheila, his girl, chose that moment to sit down across Buddy's lap. She bounced on it playfully and fingered his left ear. 'How are we supposed to have a party when you haven't got a gal?'

'Who says I haven't got a gal?' Buddy rubbed his hand over the back of her sweatshirt.

They're just kidding around, Lou told himself. But he suddenly felt hot and squirmy inside.

Sheila smiled over her shoulder at him and said, 'I think my fella's getting jealous.'

Lou shrugged. 'Who, me?' Stupid! He wanted to grab her by the neck and throw her off Buddy's lap.

Facing Buddy again, she slipped her fingers through his hair. 'I guess Lou doesn't mind.'

'Who's talking about you?' Buddy grabbed a handful at the back of her sweatshirt. When he let go, Lou heard the bra strap whap against her skin. She flinched and yelped.

'Hey!'

Doug and Cyndi laughed from the other side of the sofa, and Lou felt a surge of relief.

Sheila scurried off his lap, being careful not to spill her rum Coke. 'Aren't *you* nice,' she said. 'I was just trying to cheer you up.'

He grinned at her as she backed away. 'That cheered me up.' He looked at Lou and raised his eyebrows. 'Did that cheer *you* up, Louie?'

Lou couldn't hold back a smile. 'Yeah, sure did.'

'What a bunch of assholes,' she said. Shaking her head and laughing, she twirled her middle finger through the air. Then she sat on the floor in front of Lou's chair. He leaned over and rubbed her back. 'Anyway, we've gotta find a gal for Buddy and get her over here.'

'I've got a gal,' he said.

'Who, Lisa?'

'That's right.'

Doug, sitting on the far side of Cyndi with one hand behind her back and the other holding a vodka tonic, hunched forward to look at Buddy. 'Guess she's all yours now, huh?'

'Yep. Now that Maxi-pad's gone to that big jungle in the sky.'

Cyndi laughed and said, 'That's terrible.'

'Sick,' agreed Sheila.

Lou wondered how the girls would react if they knew who'd *sent* Maxwell to that big jungle in the sky.

'Yeah,' Doug said. 'We should be ashamed of ourselves, joking about such a tragedy.'

'But anyway,' Cyndi said, 'I happen to know that Lisa's babysitting tonight. So she couldn't come over even if she wanted to.'

She wouldn't want to, Lou thought. Christ, Lisa *had* to know it was Buddy and us, or at least figure it might've been.

'You oughta just forget about her anyway,' Sheila advised. 'I mean, I know how you felt about her and all, but shit, she dumped you . . .'

'For a nigger,' Doug added.

'Yeah, well I'm not done with her yet.'

Uh-oh, Lou thought. Nobody spoke. The silence seemed heavy.

Buddy set his empty glass on the table. 'I don't know about the rest of you, but I'm starving.'

'Now you're talking,' Doug said.

'What've you got?' Sheila asked.

'You think I'm gonna *cook* for you slugs?'

'A couple of us could run over to McDonald's,' Lou said, 'and pick up some stuff. Me and Sheila could go.'

'I feel too comfy to move.' She leaned back against the padded front of Lou's chair, lifted an arm and rested it across his thighs. Bending her elbow, she curled her hand over his knee. He felt the side of her breast pressing against his leg.

'Yeah, shit,' Cyndi said. 'Why don't we call out for something?'

'Chink?' Doug suggested.

'Yuck,' Cyndi said.

'What about pizza?' Buddy asked.

'All *right*!' from Cyndi.

'Yeah!' Sheila.

'Fine with me,' Lou said, not quite so eager to rush off for McDonald's now that Sheila was leaning on him. He moved his leg slightly to rub it against her breast. She did nothing to stop him. In fact, she squeezed his knee.

Lou was suddenly glad to be here.

He started caressing the side of her neck.

His mind was on Sheila while the others discussed how many pizzas to order, what size, what to have on them. He was only vaguely aware of Buddy leaving the room to phone in the order.

Sheila's neck felt like warm velvet. He wished there wasn't so much clothing between her breast and his leg – the corduroy of his pants, her sweatshirt, the rather stiff fabric of her bra. Still, through all that, he could feel her breast's springy firmness.

And she wasn't giving him any grief at all.

This might get really interesting, he thought.

Then Buddy returned to his place on the sofa. 'All set,' he said. 'The pizzas'll be here in about half an hour.'

Doug checked his wristwatch. 'That'll be ten after seven,' he said. 'Don't know if my stomach can last that long.'

'Let's get some more drinks,' Buddy said.

5

Denise eased her car up against an empty stretch of curb in front of the Foxworth house. She shut off the headlights. After dropping the keys into her purse, she raised her left wrist and turned it until the face of her watch caught the faint light coming in through the windshield.

Twenty till seven.

She'd made pretty good time, she thought, considering that she'd had to change clothes and brush her hair before leaving home.

If Lynn and John don't dawdle around, they shouldn't have any trouble at all getting to the restaurant for their seven o'clock reservations.

She climbed out of the car, locked its door, and hurried toward the house thinking she really should've worn a jacket.

It's not *that* cold, she told herself. She unclenched her

teeth and tried to stop shivering, but the night air seemed to be sliding right under the hanging tails of her chamois shirt, rising like chilly water against her skin. If she wasn't going to wear a jacket or tuck in the shirt (who on earth tucks in a chamois shirt?), she could've at least worn a T-shirt under it. Too late for that now, she thought.

On the front stoop, she jabbed the doorbell, then pressed the heavy shirt against her belly to keep out some of the chill. She stood rigid, waiting.

What's taking them so long? They're supposed to be in a big rush.

She pressed her legs together. She rubbed them against each other, her corduroys making soft whissy sounds.

At last, Lynn opened the door. 'Come in, come in. Oh, you're such a lifesaver. I can't tell you.'

Denise stepped into the foyer. She managed not to sigh as the inside air wrapped its warmth around her.

'We're almost ready to step out the door,' Lynn told her. 'Let me show you a few things real quick-like-a-bunny.' To Kara, she said, 'Look who's here,' as she hurried by.

'Hi there, Kara,' Denise said.

The nine-year-old, cross-legged on the floor playing a video game, looked over her shoulder, smiled, and mouthed a silent 'Hi.' She had an amused expression that seemed to say, 'Can't interrupt Mom when she's on a roll.'

'We'll be at the Edgewood, did I tell you that?' Lynn continued as Denise followed her toward the kitchen. 'We shouldn't be very late. If you want to let Kara stay up, that's fine. Whatever. Or get rid of her. And if you want to invite your friend over, fine. The refrigerator's all stocked and we've got plenty of snacks in the cupboard. Kara can show you everything.' They reached the kitchen. She stopped just inside the entry and put a hand on the wall phone. 'Here's the phone,' she said. 'If anything comes up, you can reach us at the restaurant. The number's right here.' She tapped a long, tapering fingernail against a note pad beside the phone. 'And here are numbers for the police and fire department, just in case. God knows, you shouldn't need those.' She faced Denise, smiling. 'So, any questions? I feel like I'm forgetting something.'

You're forgetting to calm down, Denise thought. But she shook her head. 'I can't think of anything.'

'Good, good. I can't tell you how glad I am you're here. This is kind of a very big deal tonight, and . . . do you think I look all right?'

'You look terrific,' Denise assured her.

Lowering her voice, she said, 'Just between you and me and the fencepost, John thinks this dress is too . . .' She grimaced and rolled her eyes upward. 'What shall we say . . . flamboyant?' She twirled around once.

The glossy, royal blue gown had only one shoulder and sleeve. The top angled down sharply from the shoulder and didn't cover much of her right breast before it passed beneath her armpit. It slanted down the same way across her back. The hem of the skirt appeared to be cut at the same angle, descending from just above her left knee to just below her right. She wore high heels that matched the dress. No nylons, but her legs had a good tan.

The way the fabric hugged her body, Denise was pretty sure the woman didn't have a stitch on underneath it.

'I hope it's warm in the restaurant,' she said.

Lynn grimaced. 'My God. Am I indecent?'

'You look fabulous. Really.'

She lowered her head to study herself. 'It *is* awfully . . . I have a nice cable-knit shawl. I have a *stole*, for that matter. A mink stole. It's gorgeous, but John has a thing about me wearing it.'

'He's against fur?'

'He's against "conspicuous consumption". He thinks if I wear a mink somebody'll knock me on the head and run off with it. A lot of good it does, having nice things . . .' She clutched Denise by the upper arm and looked her in the eyes. 'I'll get my shawl. I should've thought of it, myself. It's just the thing. You're precious.'

'Well, thanks. You might want to wear a coat, too. It's kind of chilly out.'

'Oh, I will. I'll do that.' She laughed. 'I'm not a total flake, you know.'

She let go and hurried out of the kitchen.

Denise watched her swish away.

She couldn't blame John for having doubts about that dress.

But God, the gal looked awesome in it. Tom would climb the walls slobbering if he ever saw me in something like that. He'd never get the chance. Mom and Dad would take turns killing me.

She went into the living room and sat on the floor beside Kara. The girl pressed a button on the control device that she held on her lap. On the television screen, little Mario halted his run and Bowser the dragon froze in mid-air, a burst of fire about to leave its mouth.

'That's OK, go on,' Denise said.

'Oh, I've got it on pause.'

'It's good to see you again,' she said, and gently squeezed Kara's shoulder. 'Been a while, hasn't it?'

'Since May first. You haven't sat for me since then.'

Trust Kara to know the exact date. 'Well, I came to your birthday party, didn't I?'

'Do you want to see the video tape? It's really neat. We can watch it right now. I'll go ahead and commit.'

'Commit what?'

'Suicide. Kill off Mario. I've only got two left, anyway. I

think I'm jinxed. It's terribly difficult to concentrate with Mom running around acting crazy. She *always* acts crazy when she's going out.' Kara leaned closer and spoke softly. 'Dad doesn't even want to go. Of course, he never wants to go *anywhere*, but he really doesn't want to go to this thing tonight. I'd tell you the whole story, but I don't know it. Sometimes, they try to keep things from me. It's very annoying. I'm sure glad you're here instead of Lisa. She's OK, I guess. But she's a little weird around the edges, if you know what I mean, and she's constantly on the phone with her boyfriends. Constantly. It's very difficult to carry on conversation with her. Myself, I think maybe she hasn't got a lot of furniture in her attic.'

Denise laughed and shook her head. 'Boy, you haven't changed.'

Kara, beaming, raised her eyebrows. The fine blond hair of the brows barely showed, but the muscles above her eyes sent curved ridges and valleys climbing her forehead. 'That's good, isn't it?' she asked.

'It's terrific.'

'Well, we're off,' Lynn announced.

Denise looked around. Lynn wore a knee-length camel coat, carried a blue clutch bag in one hand and a fringed, white shawl in the other.

'How are you doing, Denise?' John asked, following his wife into the room.

'Just fine, thanks.'

'It's nice to see you again. I thought you'd retired from sitting.'

'She's just doing this tonight as a special favor,' Lynn told him.

He shook his head, smiling. He was a big, heavy-set man who always seemed friendly. Denise was glad to see him again. He wore a blue blazer and gray slacks. His necktie wasn't quite straight. It swung down as he bent over and frowned at each of Denise's arms. 'Which one did Lynn twist?'

'This one.' She raised her right arm, the hand limp and dangling.

'Better have that looked at.'

'Well, we've got to be off.' Lynn stepped past Denise, crouched and kissed Kara. 'You behave yourself,' she said.

'I will.'

John kissed her. 'Yeah,' he said. 'No torturing Denise with toothpicks.'

Kara smirked and rolled her eyes upward. 'Oh Dad, you're so weird.'

'Have fun, you two,' he said, and followed Lynn toward the door. 'We shouldn't be very late.'

Kara watched them. When they reached the foyer, she waved.

'You might want to put the chain on after we're gone,' John called. He opened the door and followed Lynn outside.

As the door began to swing shut, Kara shouted, 'THEY'RE GONE! LET'S PARTY!'

Denise heard a burst of laughter from John. Then the door bumped shut.

'I'll go ahead and commit so we can look at the tape. Or do you want to play some *Mario*?'

'Maybe later. I'll go and put on the chain.'

As she started to get up, Kara said, 'I'll do it,' leaped to her feet and ran for the door.

6

'I'm glad to see your mood's improved,' Lynn said as John backed his car out of the driveway.

'Looking forward to a good dinner.' He steered onto the street and started forward. 'We could've had that at home, of course, and without the hassle. I imagine Kara and Denise will have themselves a great time.'

'So will we.'

'We'll see.'

'This is a wonderful opportunity. I just don't know why you're so reluctant. I know one thing – if they offered to do a big write-up on *me* in a national magazine, I'd jump at the chance. Can you imagine? They may even want to put you on the cover.'

'Thrills.'

There would be no picture of him on the cover of *People Today* magazine, or inside it. John planned to make that clear, soon enough, but he figured he might as well postpone the announcement. Let the snoops make their pitch. Let Lynn enjoy herself for a while longer. Have the dinner, and then drop the bomb. She was bound to flip out.

What do you mean, you won't do it!

'Do you know what I think might happen?' Lynn asked. 'I think, when the story gets out, *everybody* will want your paintings. You'll probably even have offers to do exhibits. Wouldn't that be fabulous? Can't you just imagine walking into a gallery in Beverly Hills or San Francisco – maybe even in New York?'

'My stuff sells fine right now,' John said.

'Oh, come on.'

'And if people are going to buy my work, I'd much prefer they buy it because they like it, not because it was painted by the guy who stopped some jerk from plugging Velma.'

'Veronica.'

'Whatever. If I'd known this was gonna happen, I maybe would've looked the other way.'

'Don't say that even joking, John. You did a wonderful, heroic thing, and you deserve recognition for it. My God, the woman has *platinum* records. She's a *legend*. And you saved her life.' Lynn was silent for a moment. Then she said, 'I still can't believe you didn't tell me about it.'

'I knew you'd make a fuss.'

'You spend one day by yourself in San Francisco and save the life of a *legend* and you don't even tell your own wife. I have to find out from strangers.'

'They weren't supposed to find out, either.'

John had thought, for more than a week after returning home, that he'd gotten away clean. Then, the call came. Apparently, some damn paparazzo had followed him to the car after he broke that crazy bastard's arm and fled through the crowd. He'd never gotten a photo of John's face, but a snapshot of the car revealed its license plate number, and either the freelancer or someone at the magazine got his identity through the DMV. The call had come from an editor, who wanted to send out a staff writer and photographer to do a feature article on him. An exclusive. *Passerby Confronts Gunman, Saves Life of Rock Superstar*. John's 'Thanks, but I'm not interested' only seemed to make the editor more persistent. But John had held his ground, stuck to his refusal.

He was taking a shower half an hour later when the editor called again. This time, Lynn had answered the phone.

Thus, a dinner tonight at the Edgewood with a writer and photographer who'd come a long way for nothing.

'And I just can't *believe* you told the man you wouldn't let them do the story,' Lynn said. Then she sighed. 'Of course I believe it. Thank God he called back, or . . .'

'Why do you think that lunatic tried to shoot Veronica?' John asked, speaking softly, knowing how Lynn would freeze up if he raised his voice. 'Because she's famous. Do you think he would've gone after her with a gun if she'd been a nobody? There's a lot to be said for anonymity. John Lennon would probably still be alive today if he'd been a TV repairman.'

'Now you're being just plain ridiculous. Nobody's going to shoot you, for crying out loud, just because *People Today* does a story about you.'

'You never know. Some nut might read it and get pissed off because I interfered.' He wasn't especially worried about that, but he'd had time during the past week to think of a few matters that *really* worried him. 'There's something else. They'll want to run photos of us all. So maybe your picture turns on some pervert, and he decides to pay you a visit.'

'Oh, for God's sake.'

'Do you think such things don't happen?'

'I certainly wouldn't know, but . . .'

'I'll tell you one thing, there's no way I'm going to let them put a picture of Kara in that magazine.' Or you either, he thought. Or me. Not a chance. If they try to so much as print our names, I'll hit them with a suit for invasion of privacy.

'You're paranoid,' Lynn said. 'You're absolutely paranoid, do you know that?'

'I just don't think we should call attention to ourselves,' he pointed out, still managing to keep his voice low and calm. 'Which is why I got out of there after nailing that bastard in the first place.'

'Which is also why I'm not wearing my mink tonight and

why I can't have a Porsche and why you don't even *try* to sell your good stuff and why we'll be spending the rest of our lives living off your father's inheritance.'

Though her words hurt him, he muttered, 'That's right.' Why argue? She *was* right, and he knew it.

'Some cruds swipe a jacket off you when you're fifteen years old, and we have to spend the rest of our lives paying for it.'

'They almost killed me.'

Lynn fell silent.

'Because they wanted my leather jacket.'

'I *knooooow*.' She'd lost her spunk. Her voice came out quiet and pleading. 'But John, you don't stop buying leather jackets because of something like that.'

'You do if you're smart.'

'You don't dig yourself a hole and hide in it.'

'Come on now, honey, we aren't exactly living in a hole and hiding. There's a big difference between that and simply trying to keep a low profile.'

'We'd be living like hermits if I didn't constantly keep after you.'

'No, we wouldn't.'

'You'd probably prefer to be invisible, if you had any choice in the matter.'

He forced out a chuckle. 'Now, there's a neat idea.'

'It'd be perfect for you. The invisible man. The ultimate in anonymity.'

'Why didn't *I* think of that?'

He *had* thought of that. Often. He was sure he'd never told Lynn, though. It was his pet fantasy, being invisible, and he'd always kept it to himself. Not exactly something you share, your desire to vanish from sight.

But if he ever stumbled onto a Genie, that would be his first wish. And the only wish he would need.

He wouldn't want to be invisible all the time, of course. To be able to change at will, that'd be the thing.

He'd never again have to worry about the creeps of the world chosing him for a target. You can't hassle, rob or murder someone you can't see. That part, he knew, was cowardly. The other part of being invisible, which appealed to him just as much, had nothing to do with cowardice but seemed even more shameful.

As a teenager, his favorite daydream had involved sneaking invisible into the girls' shower room after gym class. He hadn't given up that daydream. But now his fantasies more often involved young women, not teenagers. Watching them undress and bathe.

Invisible, he could do other things, too: eavesdrop, steal anything he might want, wreck havoc on his enemies, even commit murder. Not that he would. He had no desire at all to do any of those things, and rarely gave them a thought. His fantasies included very little beyond spying on women in the shower.

But that was enough to prevent him from ever breathing a word of his secret desire to Lynn or to anyone else.

She would consider him a latent Peeping Tom, a sicko for wanting to do that. For desiring invisibility to avoid the attention of creeps, she would figure him for a paranoid coward.

She's already got that part figured, John thought as he pulled away from a stop light and realized he was only a block from the Edgewood.

He accelerated through the intersection, then swung his car to an empty space at the curb.

'Now, come on,' Lynn said. 'They've got valet parking.'

'It won't kill us to walk for two minutes.'

'God, I get so tired of this.'

'It'll save a couple of bucks.'

'That isn't it, and we both know it. For crying out loud, who'd *want* to steal this heap?'

'I just don't want some stranger driving it around.'

'Yeah, right.' She thrust open her door and climbed out.

John met her on the sidewalk. She took his hand, looked at him and sighed. 'It's not that I mind walking, you know.'

'I know.'

'It's just the way you're always trying to avoid things.'

He managed a smile. 'You should be used to it, by now.'

'Well, I'm not. It irks me more and more all the time.'

'I'm sorry.'

'And the one time in years you stand up and do something terrific, you don't even want anyone to find out about it.'

'I'm here, aren't I?'

'Under duress.'

Maybe I should let them do the article, he thought as he walked with Lynn through the chilly evening. He checked his wristwatch. Seven o'clock on the nose and the restaurant was just ahead.

It would make up for a lot in Lynn's eyes, if I go along with the damn thing. And they'll probably do some kind of story whether or not I cooperate. No threat of a lawsuit was likely to stop a powerful magazine like that.

But the consequences.

There probably won't *be* any consequences.

Beneath the restaurant's portico stood a young man wearing a red jacket and a ponytail. Waiting for customers to come along and turn over their cars. The glance he gave John made it clear he didn't appreciate people who parked on the street.

John blushed.

Can't even go out for dinner without someone giving you grief.

He pulled open one of the heavy double doors, and held it

wide for Lynn. The foyer of the Edgewood was nearly as dark as the night outside.

Lynn stopped and unbuttoned her coat. John took it from her, and she stuffed her shawl down one of the sleeves.

'Aren't you going to wear that?'

'I don't think so. It's nice and warm in here.'

Everyone in the restaurant would probably end up staring at her. Men with dreams of invisibility were likely to fantasize about watching *her* shower.

'I think you ought to wear it. That dress is awfully revealing.'

'Oh, don't be such a stick in the . . .'

A slam of thunder shut off her voice.

Downpour

Toby Barnes, gunned down at the north goalpost of Memorial Stadium by patrolman Bob Hanson, was the first to die that night when the black rain fell. He was far from the last.

The rain caught Ethel Banks while she backed away from the tailgate of her station wagon with two sacks of groceries clutched to her chest. She nearly dropped them when the thunder crashed. She did drop them when the warm rain fell on her.

'Oh dear,' she muttered.

She bent over the split bags, thinking she ought to pick them up, and was surprised to notice how dark the night suddenly seemed. Maybe the bulb in the pole lamp by the driveway had burnt out. But the two sacks and the exposed groceries grew even darker as she gazed at them.

They seemed to be turning black.

Steam swirled up around them.

'Isn't this peculiar,' she said.

Even more peculiar was the way she suddenly felt. Normally, Ethel would've been rushing for the house to get away from such a downpour. But she found herself enjoying it so much that she couldn't bring herself to move. She stayed as she was, bent over, letting the rain mat down her hair, run down her face and neck, soak through the back of her sweater, the seat of her skirt and panties.

It made her feel . . . strange.

Hot and strange and full of a restless urge that she couldn't quite focus on. She ached to do *some*thing. But what?

'Ethel?' The rain was loud, smacking the concrete, drumming on the car, pattering on the paper sacks and the plastic wrappers of toilet paper and Wonderbread that had spilled onto the driveway. But the voice was louder. 'Is that you? What's going on?'

She looked up. Through the mist and shrouds of black rain, she saw a vague figure in the doorway. 'It's me, Charlie,' she called.

'Well, don't just stand out there. You'd better get inside before you're soaked.'

'I'm coming,' she called, and stood up straight. 'I'm coming,' she repeated, striding toward the open door. 'I sure am, Charlie,' she muttered as she started to run, head tilted back, smiling into the rain. She didn't see the front stoop. The single step tripped her, sent her sprawling. She slid on her belly across the slick, painted concrete.

'My Lord!' Charlie gasped. 'Are you all . . . Why, you're as black as the ace of spades! What the devil's going on?'

Ethel scurried up, lunging forward.

Charlie yelled, 'Hey!' an instant before her head struck his groin. *That* let the wind out of him! Ethel hugged his legs, driving him backward as he doubled over her. His rump hit the marble floor of the foyer.

She shoved her face between his legs, filled her mouth with the crotch of his slacks and his pal, Mr Pete, and chomped.

Charlie jumped and shimmied as if he'd stuck his finger in a socket.

Ethel clambered up his twitching body. She sat on his chest and grabbed his ears. Using them for handles, she bounced his head off the floor. The first couple of times, it sounded like someone dropping a coconut. Then the sound softened to wet, sloppy smacks as if the back of his head might have turned into a sirloin steak. One that hadn't been broiled yet. All floppy and juicy.

* * *

Willis Yardly signed his credit card slip, tore off the top copy, and fingered the rest of it into the trough under the window. He stuffed his credit card into his wallet, then took out a dollar bill. He used that to buy a Twix candy bar for his son, Jimmy. The boy liked to come along to the filling station and make his own selection, but he had the sniffles so Mandy kept him home this time.

While Willis waited for change, he folded his copy of the slip. He stuffed that, along with the Twix, into his jacket pocket. His hand came out with a pack of cigarettes, a book of matches.

The drive home would give him time for one smoke.

Better not light up in here, he thought.

He took his change, dropped it into a pocket of his trousers, and pushed through the door. Outside, he shook the pack to jostle some cigarettes through the opening. As he raised it to his mouth and pinched out a cigarette with his lips, he noticed the woman at pump number one.

She wore a clear plastic glove so she wouldn't soil her hand with the messy job. Obviously, she didn't enjoy pumping her own gas.

Willis wondered if he should offer to do it for her.

She'd probably think I'm trying to pick her up.

She looked good, bending over like that. Her faded jeans were pulled taut against her rump. Her blue T-shirt was so tight that he could see the bumps of her spine and the outline of her bra. The bottom of it had come untucked in back, baring a strip of skin to the chilly night.

She must be freezing, Willis thought.

Maybe I *should* offer to help.

He took the unlighted cigarette from his mouth, slipped it into his pocket (it'll probably pick up pocket lint), and stepped off the walkway beside the office. He took one stride before thunder shook the night.

The woman jumped.

The rain came down, masking the bright lights of the Mobil station, splashing its heat onto Willis as he hurried toward the woman with a strange excitement.

She was dry beneath the island's roof. No longer pumping gas. Standing up straight with nozzle by her side, a look of shock on her face as Willis came out of the rain.

'Jesus!' she gasped.

'Let me help you with that,' Willis said, reaching for the nozzle.

'You're all *black*! What the hell kind of rain . . .?'

He yanked the nozzle from her grip. His other hand grabbed the front of her T-shirt. He shoved her, slamming her back against the trunk, holding her down with his fist thrust hard against her chest.

She opened her mouth to curse him or scream.

He shoved the spout inside it. He squeezed the trigger. Gasoline flooded her mouth, splashed out. She thrashed on the trunk, choking, eyes squeezed shut, hands clawing at the nozzle.

Willis pulled the spout from her mouth and hosed her face, her T-shirt. He rammed the spout into her belly. She bucked under his straight arm and gasoline exploded from her mouth.

Stepping back, he let her slide off the trunk. Her knees hit the concrete. She fell forward and caught herself with her hands.

Willis soaked her down some more.

Then he dropped the nozzle, fished his match book out of the pocket where it rested beside the Twix bar, and lit a match.

His hands and arms flamed, but he managed to toss the match.

It blew out on its way toward the woman.

So he crouched and touched her hair.

* * *

Chet Baxter was waiting in line beside his girlfriend, Christie Lord, to buy a ticket for the seven o'clock showing of *Out Are The Lights* when the thunder boomed. They both flinched. Laughing, Chet squeezed her against his side. She smiled up at him. The lights dimmed. As the hot, exciting rain pounded down on his head and shoulders, Chet watched her face go blotchy then disappear except for the whites of her eyes and teeth.

He grabbed her wet, hanging hair. Before he could yank her head back to expose her throat, her fingernails ripped open his cheek. Crying out, he clutched her wrist.

Someone smashed against them. Hanging onto Christie, Chet tumbled to the sidewalk. She came down on top of him, snarling, thrusting her head down at his face, teeth snapping.

Suddenly, she looked up.

Chet clutched her throat with both hands.

'No,' she gasped. 'Wait. Let's get *them*.'

He ached to choke the life out of the bitch, but her words made him hesitate. He relaxed his grip for a moment, and she lurched free. She scurried backward, crawling off him. 'Them,' she said again.

On her knees, the sodden black spector thrust an arm straight out and pointed. 'LET'S GET *THEM*!' she yelled.

Chet sat up, ignoring the alarmed voices and outcries of those behind him – those at whom Christie was pointing. Instead, he watched the eight or ten struggling figures beyond her back. Some were down on the sidewalk, pounding and ripping at one another. Others were still on their feet. Chet saw one man slamming the face of a teenaged boy against the top of a fire hydrant. He saw a woman clamped to a storefront wall by a man's forearm across her throat while the guy rammed a pocket knife into her belly.

'LET'S GET THE DRY ONES!' Christie shouted.

It seemed like a fine idea to Chet. It seemed fitting, somehow.

Apparently, the idea appealed to the others as well. They ceased their struggles, let go of one another. Some fell to the sidewalk. Some didn't get up. Those were left behind as the faint shapes of the others approached.

With Christie and Chet in the lead, they rushed under the marquee. The dry ones were already in flight, a few racing away, running out from under the shelter and into the rain themselves, but most seeking the safety of the theater, yelling as they pushed through the glass door, knocking aside the flustered teenaged boy whose job was to take their tickets.

One man remained in front of the ticket booth, shouting at the girl inside the glass enclosure to hurry. As he reached into the opening for his ticket, Christie smashed his head against the glass. The glass didn't break. Not that time. But Christie, Chet and a pregnant woman used the man for a battering ram, driving his head against the ticket booth until the glass disintegrated.

They hurled the man aside. The pregnant woman fell upon him.

Inside the booth, the ticket girl was turning in circles, her eyes bulging, her mouth hanging open. She looked as if she wanted to make a dash for the theater entrance, but a rain-blackened man was trying to rip open the locked door at the rear of her enclosure. And others were already rushing through the lobby.

Her back was turned when Christie leaned in, grabbed the shoulders of her blazer and wrenched her off her feet. Chet reached in to help. Together, they dragged the shrieking, kicking girl onto the counter. Her flapping arms struck the edges of the glass, slashing her sleeves and breaking off jagged shards. When she was halfway out, Chet put a headlock on her. Christie jerked the girl's blazer, popping its single fastened button away, then tore open the blouse.

Her skin was pebbled with goosebumps. Her breasts shook as she squirmed. Her nipples were visible through the black lace of her bra, pink and jutting.

Christie splite the girl's belly with a blade of glass.

Entrances

1

Maureen O'Casey, with three family-sized pizzas stacked on the passenger seat of her Jeep Cherokee, stopped beneath a street light to check her map of Bixby.

She looked for Mercer Lane. She'd set out from the pizza parlor certain that she knew where to find it. But the street had turned out to be Merced, and she realized she didn't have the foggiest notion where Mercer might be.

Her brother, Rory, would probably be able to drive there blindfolded. He'd been delivering pizzas for six years, ever since the family moved here from Modesto. Except for occasional visits, however, Maureen had spent those years in San Francisco doing graduate work and later writing books for children. Her visits had provided her with knowledge of Bixby's general layout and quite a few of its streets, but not Mercer.

Maureen found her ignorance annoying. She liked to feel in control of whatever situations presented themselves, and she was definitely not in control of this. She should've anticipated that she would be asked, sooner or later, to make deliveries. But she hadn't. Rory's illness had taken her totally by surprise, and totally unprepared to fill in for him.

'Ah-*ha*! There you are, you little bugger.'

Mercer appeared to be only three blocks from her present location.

She folded the map, tossed it onto the dashboard, and made a U-turn.

With any luck, she would make the delivery and be back at

the restaurant by seven-twenty. That would give her forty minutes to spare, but of course her father would likely ship her right off on another errand. And then another.

'Buck up,' she told herself. 'It's not the end of the world. Consider it an intermission.'

Though she wouldn't be seeing much of Trevor tonight, he would surely pop in tomorrow.

That wasn't much consolation. She'd been looking forward to tonight, had even discarded her usual jeans and blouse for a dress, all the better to attract his eye.

Well, she would find time to drop by his table no matter what. Slip off the coat, first. Have a few words with him.

Maureen made a left turn, then smiled. Suppose she invited him to come along? He's off duty tonight, isn't he?

I don't want to scare him off.

Cop or not, he's obviously a timid man. The poor blighter might go into cardiac arrest if I try to drag him off with me . . . But not if I plead for his help. After all, I'm the new girl in town and don't know my way around – who better to help me navigate the foreign streets than a policeman?

How could he possibly refuse?

She laughed softly. 'Am I brilliant, or what?'

Stopping at the next intersection, she leaned toward the windshield and peered at the corner sign.

Mercer!

She turned right and drove along, delighted with her scheme. It wouldn't be an actual date, but they'd finally have a chance to be alone with each other. Guiding her around town, Trev was bound to get over his jitters. Before long . . .

She spotted 3548 painted on the curb, and pulled over.

Just to make sure of the address, she plucked the order slip off the top box. This street was darker than the other. She turned on the overhead light.

The address was 3548 Mercer, just as she'd remembered it. The order had been placed by someone named Buddy.

This is it, all right.

Maureen shut off the lights and engine. She dropped the keys into her coat pocket, swung open her door, then lifted the three white cartons off the passenger seat. Slipping a hand under the bottom box, she felt the heat. In spite of her small detour, the pizzas hadn't cooled off.

She climbed out of the Cherokee and knocked its door shut with her rump.

As she stepped over the curb, she noticed three motorcycles parked on the driveway. She wrinkled her nose. These didn't look like the cute little bikes a family might use on weekends. These were burly machines – hogs, choppers – steel mounts for tattooed men with skulls emblazoned on the backs of their denim jackets.

Or boys who like to fancy themselves tough, Maureen thought as she strode toward the lighted front porch of the house.

She was pretty sure she wouldn't find a band of savage bikers here. Even in Bixby, where real estate was cheap by California standards, a home like this must be worth at least a hundred and fifty thousand.

More than likely, the pizzas were for the son and his friends.

If bikers *had* taken over the place, they wouldn't be ordering out for . . .

Overhead, the night seemed to explode.

Maureen cringed.

'Oh, wouldn't you just know it,' she muttered, and started to run for the porch.

The rain came down before she got there. When she felt its heat on her head, she stopped.

Hey, she thought, this is nice.

Bending over, she set the pizza boxes on the walkway at her feet. She took off her coat, stretched out her arms, and tilted back her head to feel the rain on her face. In seconds, her dress was soaked and clinging to her body.

A warm tremor spread through Maureen. She felt an urge to strip naked and roll on the grass. But a different urge was stronger.

Just ahead, to the left of the front steps, she saw the faint shapes of rocks along the border of a garden. She hurried over and tugged one loose from the soil. She felt so good, squatting in her soaked clothes, that she was reluctant to stand up again.

But she pictured herself swinging the rock, smashing a face to bloody pulp. The image of that stirred Maureen to action.

She carried the rock back to the walkway, set it on the sodden black cardboard of the top box, and lifted all three pizzas.

Grinning, she climbed the steps. At the door, she shifted the load, bracing it up with her left hand, the edges of the boxes against her chest to keep them steady. Her right hand removed the rock and used a corner of it to ring the bell. 'Pizza!' she called.

She lowered the rock. She pressed it against her right buttock, out of sight. In her eagerness, she bobbed up and down on the balls of her feet.

The door opened.

'Pizza!' she shouted into the face of the teenager. The kid, a big muscular guy with brushed up hair and a garden of raw pimples on his chin, looked glad to see her. For half a second.

'What the *fuck*!'

She swung the rock, aiming for his chin.

His arm shot up. Maureen's wrist struck it. Pain flashed up her arm. The rock flew from her numb fingers, missing him and clumping the door frame and bouncing off as the boxes of pizza hit the stoop.

She tried to duck, hoping to retrieve the rock, but the kid clutched the front of her dress. He jerked her forward. She stumbled over the threshold. Felt herself being turned and thrown off her feet. The kid's scared face was above her for a moment. Then her back slammed the floor. As her breath exploded out, the impact snapped her head down.

It made a terrible thud. In the instant before she lost consciousness, Maureen saw her brain as a grenade going off, blowing fire out her eyes and nose and ears.

2

'My *God*, what was that!' Francine blurted, hand scurrying over the table top to retrieve the cigarette that had leaped from between her fingers.

Trev himself had flinched at the sudden muffled roar. Lisa must've jumped an inch off her seat, and her breasts had bounced dramatically under the tight sweater.

'I hope it was just thunder,' Trev said.

Lisa studied the ceiling as if she expected it to come down.

'*God*,' Francine said again. She clamped the cigarette between her lips. It jiggled. She took only one pull, then crushed it in the ashtray.

'It isn't suppose to rain,' Lisa muttered, still frowning at the acoustic tiles above her.

'I'm sure there's nothing to be concerned about.' As Trev said that, he turned his head. Out in the other room, Patterson looked concerned. The man was scowling, saying something as he walked toward Lucy at the switchboard. Lucy was shaking her head and shrugging.

'Anyway,' Francine said, 'about protection for us.'

Trev faced her again.

'My daughter's a witness . . .'

'Well, she's certainly provided valuable information.' He looked at Lisa. 'Is there anything else you want to tell me about last night?'

Shrugging, the girl shook her head. She resumed her study of the frayed knee of her jeans.

Trev turned his eyes to Francine. 'Would you like to step out the door for a minute?'

'No, I would not. Lisa has nothing to say that can't be said in front of me.'

'I've already told you everything,' Lisa said, her voice pouty. 'I'm not keeping any big hot secrets, if that's what you're getting at.'

Trev glanced through the glass in time to see Patterson stride around the end of the front counter. Probably going out to make sure it *had* been nothing but thunder.

He looked again at the girl. 'Well, you've been very helpful, Lisa, and I really appreciate it.'

'I know they killed him,' she said.

'But you never saw Buddy or his friends after they were escorted from the dance?'

'That's what I told you.'

'And the last you saw of Maxwell was when you kissed him goodnight in the school parking lot. Then you left his car to go back to your own car, but didn't see . . .'

'I didn't really look around. They might've been there, and I just didn't see them. You know? They could've had their motorcycles hidden behind something. Some buses were parked over at the side.'

'You've got to give us police protection,' Francine demanded. 'We can't just walk out of here and go on our merry way. Those boys will come after Lisa. I know it.'

'I doubt if they'll have the opportunity,' Trev told her. 'We'll pick them up tonight and bring them in.'

'Oh great,' Lisa muttered. 'Then they'll *know* I blabbed.'

Trev gave her a smile, then tapped the top page of the legal tablet resting on his leg. 'I've got a whole list of people who saw those guys acting up at the dance. Buddy and his friends won't know you're the one who talked to us. I certainly won't tell them.'

'They're not stupid,' she said.

'They *are* stupid, or they wouldn't have murdered that young man. If they did it, they're going down. You can bet on it.'

Francine smirked. 'Who are you, Sergeant Preston of the Yukon?'

'No, ma'am.'

'I've got it. Joe Friday.'

'Two of my favorite cops.'

'I'll just bet.'

Standing, he slid the pad of paper onto the table. 'We'll have a talk with Buddy, Doug and Lou tonight, and see how things develop from there.'

'And you'll let us know what happens.' It wasn't a request.

'Of course.'

As Francine and Lisa got to their feet, Trev stepped past them. He opened the glass door. 'I really appreciate your taking the time to come in about this. And Lisa, if you think of anything else that might . . .'

The noise that pounded Trev's ears, this time, was not thunder.

He jerked his eyes toward the blast and saw Lucy's chair lurch backward, hurling her away from the switchboard as the base of her skull erupted, splashing a red mess at the floor.

'Down down down!' he shouted, sinking to a squat in the doorway and reaching for the off-duty revolver at his side while the black thing on the other side of the counter (is that *Patterson*?) fired a round into Lucy's chest that sent her chair flipping over. She tumbled out of it, legs flying up, and hit the floor in a backward somersault.

Then Patterson's gun was aimed at Trev. He heard himself yell 'SHIT!' as explosions smacked his eardrums and a slug whizzed by his face and some of his bullets missed but two struck Patterson high in the chest and another punched through his throat and Patterson flopped out of sight behind the counter.

Gasping for air, Trev switched the empty gun to his left hand. He grabbed the metal doorframe with his right hand and pulled at it to drag himself upward. When he was standing, he looked over his shoulder. Francine was on her hands and knees, staring up at him with wild eyes. Lisa hadn't dropped. She was frozen upright behind her mother, fists pressed to her cheeks.

'Are you both OK?' he asked. He could barely hear himself through the ringing in his ears. And he didn't need to ask the question. He could see that they hadn't been hit. 'Stay right here,' he said.

He staggered through the doorway and headed for his desk. It seemed like a great distance away. He kept glancing at the counter, though he doubted that Patterson was capable of popping up and firing (fuck, you shot his throat out).

As he walked along, he emptied his cylinder. Brass casings clattered against the floor.

From the top drawer of his desk, he removed a box of cartridges. His shaky hands dropped two of them while he tried to reload. At last, he managed to fill the cylinder and snap it shut.

Glancing back, he saw Francine in the interrogation room doorway with her arm around Lisa. They both looked dazed and sick.

He walked over to Lucy. She was sprawled facedown in a spreading swamp of blood.

The switchboard was a panel of blinking lights, a call on every line.

What's going on?

Trev leaned across the counter.

Patterson was stretched out on his back, revolver on the floor near his right hand. His eyes and teeth were still white. His throat and chest were bright red. His shield gleamed silver. Some blue showed below the knees of his uniform trousers. Otherwise, the man was black.

Wet and black. Like an oilman in the movies who has struck a gusher and stood in its downpour.

'Did you get him?' Francine called.

'I got him.'

'Who was it? Why did he shoot that woman and . . .'

'He was the desk sergeant,' Trev said. 'I don't know why he . . .'

'The man we *talked* to?'

'Yeah,' he said, and climbed over the counter. He dropped to the floor at Patterson's feet. 'Stay put. I'll be right back.'

For a moment, he considered taking Patterson's revolver or at least kicking it some distance from the body. But he didn't want to disturb the crime scene. Patterson was in no shape to use the revolver, anyway, and the gun was almost certainly out of ammunition. So he left it there and hurried toward the station doors.

'Don't go out there!' Lisa shouted.

Patterson went out, he thought. Patterson came in wet

and black and shooting. Doesn't make any sense at all.

The double doors were blue painted metal, each with a square window of bullet-proof glass at head level. From the other side came a faint hissing sound like rain striking pavement. He cupped his hands to one of the panes, and peered out.

Something was wrong with the lights. The walks, driveway and parking strip in front of the station should've been bright under the sodium arcs. Instead, they were barely visible. He could make out the faint smudges of two cars – his own and probably Francine's.

Trev released the door's catch and stepped back. With his right foot, he flung the door open. The sounds of the falling rain came in, along with a mild breeze. He sniffed, wondering if he might detect fumes, but the air smelled fresh and clean.

As the door started to swing back, Trev stopped it with his shoe.

The area of walk directly beyond the door, sheltered by an overhang, appeared to be dry. But he decided not to risk stepping outside.

Patterson went out, and look what happened. Had the black stuff *made* him act that way? Hardly seemed likely, but something had sure screwed up the man's head. He'd gone out normal, and come in homicidal and covered with black fluid.

It must, somehow, have to do with the rain.

The light spilling out through the doorway didn't reach far enough to show Trev the color of the rain.

But if the falling water wasn't black, what was that all over Patterson? And why couldn't he see the parking lot lights?

Trev toed down the metal stop to keep the door from swinging shut, then stepped outside. He took a few strides. Halting a yard from the edge of the overhang, he stared at the curtain of falling water. It looked dark, all right. But hell, the night itself was dark.

Though he couldn't be certain that the rain was black, it was obviously warm, for he saw a faint, pale mist rising off the walkway ahead of him and the grass that bordered it.

He pulled a folded white handkerchief from his pocket. He shook it open, then wadded it into a ball and tossed it underhand. The cloth unfurled. The instant it passed into the shower, it ceased to be white. Trev watched a sodden black rag drop to the walkway.

'Holy shit,' he muttered.

He rushed back inside the station.

3

Kara didn't jump, but her face pulled a contortion that made Denise laugh: eyes wide, forehead rumpled, nose wrinkled, lips twisted sideways. It was the kind of expression, Denise thought, that this particular girl might put on her face if she just happened to notice a boogeyman leering at her from the darkness of a closet – a weird mixture of fright, disbelief and amusement.

'You'd better hope it doesn't freeze that way.'

Kara didn't say a word, but Denise had no trouble at all deciphering the exaggerated motions of her lips and tongue. *What. Was. That?*

'Either thunder or the end of the world, take your pick.'

Kara screwed up her face again, then let it settle back into place and said, 'Which one would you pick?'

'Thunder, I imagine.'

'Me, too. Though I'm not especially fond of thunder, either.' She pressed the mute button on the VCR's remote and sat very still for a moment.

Denise heard the soft, windy sound of rain falling on the roof.

'It must be raining cats and dogs,' Kara said. 'I hope they don't hurt themselves. If it *really* rained cats and dogs, you know, the cats would all land on their feet. But I'm not sure the dogs would fare so well. They would probably break their necks, don't you suppose?' A smile spread across her face. Leaning toward Denise, she said, 'And just imagine the mess they'd make on the lawn. Toes-up dogs everywhere you look, not even to mention all the *elimination*.'

'Not a pretty picture,' Denise admitted.

'A gross-out of major proportions, that's what I think.'

'Probably won't happen, though.'

'Do you know what? Maybe I should round up some candles. We just might lose the juice, you know. That happened two years ago, the day after Thanks-giving.'

'Your mom and dad would have to eat in the dark.'

'Ooo, yuck, they might come home early and ruin our fun.'

'Maybe while we've still got juice we should make the popcorn.'

Kara frowned upward for a moment as if deep in thought. Then she snapped her fingers. 'Hey, I've got it! Let's make some popcorn!'

'Weird kid.'

Kara pressed a button on the remote to shut off the tape of her birthday party, and a regular show appeared on the television. She bounded off the sofa. Denise followed her through the dining room to the kitchen.

There, Kara rushed around gathering the popper, the

plastic bowl, a measuring cup, popcorn and oil and butter and salt. She arranged them all on the counter, plugged in the cord, dribbled oil into the pot, and dropped in three kernels.

'That should be enough for you,' Denise said. 'But what about me?'

'We need to wait for these to pop so we know the oil's ready and . . . Oh, right. As if you didn't know. Honestly, you're as bad as my dad. Come with me.'

'Where to?' Denise asked, following her from the kitchen.

'I've gotta ride the porcelain trolley.'

'Huh?'

'I've gotta *pee*.'

'And that requires my presence?'

'I'm not going in there alone. It's storming out. What if I'm by myself and we lose the juice?'

'While *you're* losing the juice.'

Kara laughed. 'If you were on *The Gong Show*, I'd gong you for that.'

'You're a cruel little thing.'

'Yep.'

She's not all that little, Denise thought. Her slender build probably made her look taller than she really was, but the top of the girl's head seemed to be almost level with Denise's shoulders.

It was odd, having to accompany her to the toilet.

She's only nine, Denise reminded herself. In spite of her height and rather grown-up behavior, she's still just a kid. A kid who doesn't like storms. A kid who's afraid of the dark.

At the end of the hall, Kara said, 'You don't have to come in if you don't want.'

'I appreciate that.'

Kara turned on the light, entered the bathroom, and stepped out of sight behind the open door. 'Don't go away.'

'I won't.'

She heard a rustle of clothes, then splashing sounds.

'Mom said it'd be all right if you wanted to invite your boyfriend over. Would you like to do that? I think it might be neat. What's his name?'

'Tom.'

'Is he nice?'

'He wouldn't be my boyfriend if he was a jerk.'

'Well, I should hope not. Why don't you see if he wants to come over? He could have popcorn with us, you know?'

'Well, I don't know. The storm and everything.'

'It might be nice to have a guy around, especially if the lights go off.'

'You just want to steal him from me.'

'No, I don't.' She sounded disgusted by the thought. 'Boys are a pain in the neck. All they ever talk about are P-38s and M-16s and F-17s. Guns and planes and tanks and stuff. As if I even know what they're talking about. As if I care.' Denise heard her spin the toilet paper roll. 'But I really think you ought to phone Tom and see if he wants to come over and have some popcorn. How far away does he live?'

'A few blocks.'

'Does he have a car?'

'His parents do.'

The toilet flushed. 'Well, he can drive over, then. He won't get very wet.'

'I don't know, Kara. He might just want to talk about P-38s and things.'

'If he does, we'll send him packing.' She stepped around the door, zipped her jeans and reached for the light switch.

'Aren't you going to wash your hands?'

She grinned. 'Didn't get anything on them.'

'How about washing them, anyway? You're going to be sticking your hand in the popcorn bowl.'

Kara sighed, then went to the sink. She didn't use hot water, but she did use soap. As she dried her hands, she said, 'Besides, it's not fair that you didn't get to go out with him tonight.'

'That's OK.'

'You can phone him from the kitchen. I'll take care of the popcorn.'

It would be nice, Denise thought as she walked down the hallway with Kara. Though she didn't regret her decision to babysit, she'd found her mind straying while she watched the videotape of the birthday party, found herself imagining how it would've been if she'd stayed home and Tom had come over.

With Kara here, she could spend the time with him and not have to worry about matters getting out of hand.

'Maybe I'll do it,' she said as they entered the kitchen.

'All right!'

'No harm in calling, anyway.' She lifted the handset of the wall phone. While she punched in Tom's number, Kara hurried to the popper and checked inside. As the phone rang, Kara scooped a cupful of kernels out of the jar. She dumped them into the pot.

A woman's voice said, 'Hello?'

'Hi, Mrs Carney. This is Denise.'

'Oh, how are you? Tom's right here. Hang on just a sec.'

Kara covered the popper, then turned around to watch. *Is he there*? she mouthed without speaking.

Denise nodded.

'Hey, Denny,' Tom said.

'Hey, how's it going?'

'Pretty good.'

'I'm over here sitting for Kara Foxworth. That dynamite kid I told you about?'

Kara drew her head back, giving herself a double chin and beaming.

'I was just thinking about you,' Tom said.

'Something good, I hope.'

'Wondering what you were up to. I figured you were all alone at home, you know, with the storm going on and everything. Man, did you catch that thunder?'

'Who could miss it?'

'I thought the house was going to come down.'

'Have you got an umbrella?'

'Why? What's up?'

'Well, Kara here is awfully eager to share her popcorn with you.'

Kara made a face and jammed her fists against her hips.

'You want me to come over?' Tom asked.

'Yeah. I mean, I know it's miserable out, but if you could make it over here without getting yourself drenched . . . Kara's parents are out to dinner, so they won't be very late. And they said it's all right for you to come over. We could watch some TV, have some popcorn and stuff.'

'Sounds great. Hang on a minute, I'll see if it's OK.'

Denise heard his phone clatter against something. 'He's checking with his parents,' she told Kara.

'You didn't have to say it was *my* idea.'

'It was your idea.'

'Well, stillllll.' In the pot behind her, popcorn began to burst with soft explosive sounds and a general clinking of kernels hurled against the walls and lid.

When Tom returned to the phone, he said, 'It's OK with them.'

'Really?'

'Yeah. They're not overjoyed about me going out on a night like this, but I told them we wouldn't be driving around in it. I'm supposed to go straight to your house, and come straight home afterward.'

'Nobody's there.'

'Hey, if they knew you were babysitting, there's no way they'd let me come. As far as they know, you're at home with your folks and we're just going to stay there and watch the tube.'

'Liar liar, pants on fire.'

That seemed to amuse Kara no end.

'Necessity is the mother of deception,' Tom said. 'So, what time do you want me?'

'As soon as you can make it. The popcorn's gonna be ready in about five more minutes.'

'I'll be as quick as I can.'

'Get here while it's hot.'

'I'll try. See you.'

'See you,' she said, and hung up. To Kara, she said, 'He's on his way.'

4

'What's going on?' Francine sounded more angry than frightened, as if she hadn't come to the police station in hopes of being shot at, and blamed Trev.

'I don't know,' he said. He stepped around the end of the counter. 'The rain's black out there.'

'That's ridiculous.'

'Look for yourself if you want.'

Francine shook her head. She and Lisa had come out of the interrogation room and were standing among the desks, holding hands. Lisa's gaze was fixed on Lucy's body. She looked as if she might get sick.

'You two keep an eye on the door. If someone comes in, speak up fast.' Trev moved in between Lucy's overturned chair and the switchboard.

'What are you doing?'

'I'm gonna see what some of these calls are about.' The headset lay on the floor where it had fallen when it flew off Lucy. Trev pulled it up by the cord and put it on. The earphones had a built-in microphone that curved around in front of his mouth.

He pressed a button on the switchboard. One of the lights stopped blinking and he heard a line open.

'Hello? Hello?' A woman's voice, high-pitched.

'Bixby Police Department.'

'You've gotta send a car! Quick! God, where've you been? There's a madman trying to break in. I shot at him. He tried to come in a window, but I shot at him. I don't think I hit him, but he's still out there. I'm all alone and he's trying to get me!'

'Could you describe him?'

'He's black, that's all I know.'

'A Negro?'

'No. I don't think so. He's just got black stuff on him, I don't know. What does it matter? I need help!'

'Give me your address, please.'

'4329 Larson.'

'Got it. Hang on, I'll contact a patrol car.'

'Hurry! Hurry!'

Trev picked up the radio mike and fingered the speak button. 'All units, report.' He released the button. Waited.

'Oh my God!' the woman squealed. 'Oh my Jesus! He's . . .'

Trev cringed as gunblasts hit his ears.

Then the woman was sobbing. 'There's . . . there's no hurry any more. You can . . . take your sweet time now. He's dead. I shot him dead. Oh, Jesus. Where *were* you?'

'We've got troubles here, too. Are you sure the intruder's dead?'

'Oh, yes. Oh, yes. Oh, yes.'

'OK. Now, we'll have a car there as soon as possible. In the meantime, just take it easy and try to stay calm.'

'Ho ho. Calm, yes. Jesus.'

'And don't go outside or let anyone into your place. There's something strange going on.'

'You're telling me? Oh, I think I've already noticed. Strange?'

'And don't touch the intruder. That black liquid on him . . . it may be dangerous. It may be contagious.'

'What, you think I'd *touch* him? No, I don't think so. No, I don't think so. What do you mean, contagious? He was sick?'

'I just don't know. I think the rain might be making people crazy. Look, I've got to go now.' He disconnected.

He realized he'd told the woman that he would send a patrol car and she shouldn't let anyone in. Good move, he thought.

But no response had come from the radio.

He activated the mike again. 'Anybody out there? Hanson? Yarbrough? Gonzales? Paxton?'

The crackle and hiss of white noise came from the receiver. Nothing more.

'Where are you guys? This is Hudson. Talk to me, damn it!'

Nobody answered.

He took another call, this one from a man.

'You better hustle some troops over here, pal. Man, I never seen nothing to beat it. Place is going wild.'

'Where are you calling from?'

'My shop on Third. Jiffy Locksmith? I go to leave and, man, there's a fucking riot going on in the street. Must be a dozen of 'em, yelling and running around getting soaked, bashing in windows. Shit! They're killing folks, man. Honest to God. I seen 'em run in the fucking doughnut shop across the street, and they just started tearing into the folks in there. Killed every last one of 'em, far as I could see. So, you gonna send in the army, or what?'

'I'm afraid we don't have anyone to send right now.'

'Figures. Well, don't say I didn't give you the poop.'

'Just stay in your shop and try to keep out of sight. We'll try to send help, but . . .'

The man hung up.

Trev felt numb. O'Casey's was on Third Street, just two blocks south of the Tastee Donut shop.

If I hadn't procrastinated, damn it, I'd be there right now.

Oh God, Maureen, what've I done to you?

He pulled out his wallet. His hand trembled as he removed the pizza coupon.

The dollar-off coupon gave the phone number.

All the lines were busy again, so he disconnected one and punched in O'Casey's number. He listened to the ringing.

'Come on, come on,' he muttered.

It rang fifteen times before he gave up.

He flung the headset down. Francine, on the other side of the counter, whirled around.

'I've gotta go out,' he said.

'In the rain? You can't do that.'

'Watch me.'

5

'My name's Peggy, and I'll be serving you this evening.' Peggy, John noticed, wore a frilly peasant skirt and a bodice that left her shoulders bare. Her breasts bulged over the top of the laced, corset-like garment, and it occurred to John that a deep breath might pop them right out of it. The hostess near the front door had sported a similar costume. He supposed Lynn's dress wasn't so bad, after all, with everyone running around in those outfits. But he still wished she hadn't given up her shawl to the cloak room girl. 'Would you care for something from the bar?'

'Do you think we ought to wait for the others?' he asked Lynn.

'Oh, let's just go ahead.' Smiling up at Peggy, she asked for a margarita.

'Would you prefer that with or without salt?'

'With, please.'

'And I'll have a Mai Tai,' John told her. When the waitress was gone, he said, 'Maybe we'll be lucky, and they won't show up at all.'

'Now, don't be that way.'

'Are you sure we've got the right night?'

'I wrote it on my calendar. Seven o'clock, November eleventh, the Edgewood.'

'Maybe it was supposed to be at seven *a.m.*'

'I hardly think so. I'm sure they'll be along shortly.'

'Shortly, and wet,' he said. He hoped they didn't have umbrellas. It would serve them right. If they'd been here on time, they would've missed the downpour. He didn't even know the people, but they irked him. Not only were they butting into his life, but now they were late for the dinner they'd supposedly arranged and they hadn't even bothered to make reservations.

The Edgewood was a popular restaurant, so the lack of reservations might've forced them into a long wait. No thanks to their absent hosts, they'd been spared that. Luck was with them, and there had been several empty tables.

John looked around, wondering if the pair from *People Today* had arrived on time, after all, and simply neglected to mention they were expecting him and Lynn.

We might all be here at separate tables, he thought. That'd be swift. All of us go ahead and eat our dinners thinking we got stood up.

He saw three parties of four. Wouldn't be any of those. Couples sat at four other tables. Among them, he recognized Steve and Carol Winter. That left three pairs of strangers – men sitting across from women.

'Was this Dodd character supposed to be with a man or a woman?' he asked.

'He mentioned a photographer, but I'm sure he didn't say whether it was male or female. Why?'

'I'm just wondering if they're already here.'

'I suppose that's possible, isn't it?' An eagerness seemed to come over Lynn. Her head swiveled as she scanned the diners to either side, then she twisted around in her seat. Facing John again, she said, 'I don't know. What do you think?'

'Well, I'm not about to go around asking.'

'It's pretty unlikely, I suppose. These people were all here before us. I'm sure, if one of them were Mr Dodd, he would've told someone he was expecting us.'

'You'd think so. But then, you'd also think they might've made reservations.'

Peggy arrived with the drinks. John watched the bulges at the top of her bodice while she bent over the table, and Lynn started in on her. 'You know, we're supposed to be meeting some people here. A Mr Dodd and someone else? None of us know each other from Adam, and I'm concerned there may have been some kind of a mixup. They may already be here, for all we know.'

'I'll be happy to check with the hostess for you,' Peggy said.

'Would you, please? That would be wonderful. And in case they haven't arrived yet, they'll be looking for us when they do show up. John and Lynn Foxworth? You might want to give the hostess our names, and warn her to be on the lookout for . . .'

'HEY!'

The woman's distant, alarmed voice hushed the restaurant. The quiet undertones of conversations and laughter and tinking of utensils ceased. In the silence, John heard clanks and clatters from the kitchen area and the piped-in music of an orchestra playing 'Send in the Clowns'. Waitresses halted. Diners turned in their seats. From somewhere near the front came a crash as if a heavy piece of furniture had been knocked over.

Then a sharp cry of pain that ended the shocked silence.

'My God!' Peggy blurted.

'John?'

He shook his head and gazed toward the front. The foyer and doors – and whatever might be happening – were out of sight beyond a corner of the dining area. Waitresses and a few guests started rushing that way.

'I'd better . . .' he muttered, shoving back his chair.

'No, stay here. Don't involve yourself in . . . John!'

'I'll be right back.'

He hurried along with the others, passed the corner and saw a waitress tugging at the arm of a wildman who sat astride the overturned hostess station and bounced on it, pounding the heavy wooden lectern against the chest of the young woman pinned beneath it. Her scarlet face was twisted with pain. Her breasts *had* popped out of her bodice, and they shook as she strained to shove away the punishing weight.

The man, sodden and black (it's the parking attendant who gave me the dirty look, John realized), flung the clinging waitress off his arm. As she stumbled backward, a guy in a sport coat shot his foot out, ramming the lunatic's shoulder and knocking him off the lectern. That man and two others threw themselves. onto him.

John tumbled the lectern off the hostess. He knelt beside her. Wheezing for breath, she drew up her knees and hugged her ribcage. Her teeth were bared and she whipped her head from side to side. John took off his blazer. He covered her from waist to shoulders.

'Are you all right?'

'Move out of the way,' a man said. 'I'm a doctor.'

He crawled aside. A gray-haired man crouched and swept John's blazer to the floor. 'You'll be fine,' he said in a gentle voice. 'What's your name, dear?'

'Cassy,' she gasped out.

'Cassy, I'm Dr Goodman. I'm sure you'll be just fine.' With a pocket knife, he severed the laces down her front.

She raised her head off the floor to see what he was doing.

'Nothing to be alarmed about, Cassy. I'm just going to take a look. I won't hurt you.' He spread the bodice. The girl flinched and gasped as he fingered her lower ribs where her skin was red. 'Uh-huh, uh-huh.'

John watched her breasts jiggle as she twitched. They were small and firm. The creamy skin just above her nipples was seamed with indentations left by the tight garment. Her nipples were erect. John felt heat spreading through his groin.

He was suddenly glad he'd been forced to come here, tonight.

Then he felt guilty about it and looked away.

The attacker was squirming on the floor a couple of yards away, one man sitting on his chest, others holding down his arms and legs. John realized that quite a few people were yelling, shouting questions and commands.

'Have you got him?'

'Call the police! Somebody call the police!'

'What'd he do?'

'*Look* at him!'

'How's the girl?'

'Why's he all black like that?'

'What's going on?'

'Is everybody all right?'

'Somebody fuckin' call the cops!'

'Probably just some bruised ribs,' the doctor said, his voice soft and calm through the mayhem. 'Maybe a couple of hairline fractures. Nothing to be especially concerned about, I should think, but we'd best get you to the ER for some X-rays.'

John looked again as the doctor covered her with his blazer.

'Just lie still for the time being.'

The waitress who had tried to pull the attacker off Cassy came over and squatted down. 'Are you OK, hon?'

'I'll live.'

'Christ, what got into Bill? What got *on* him?'

'I don't know. But thanks for coming to the rescue, Joyce.'

'No problem, hon.'

'Did he hurt you?'

'Naa. I'm fine. You take care of yourself,' she said, then straightened up and turned to the crowd surrounding the man.

Dr Goodman turned his head toward John. 'And you are?'

'John Foxworth. I was just eating here.'

'Why don't you watch out for her, John, while I go and phone for an ambulance?'

'I don't want an ambulance,' Cassy said. 'I'll be OK in a minute. He just . . . knocked my wind out. I'm feeling . . . a lot better.'

'Be that as it may,' Goodman said, 'I think it would be wise to have you checked over.'

'I'll stay with her,' John said.

Goodman patted his shoulder, then pushed against it as he uncrouched.

The moment he was gone, Cassy shook her head. 'I don't want any ambulance.' Holding the blazer to her chest, she started to rise.

'I'm not sure you ought to do that.'

Ignoring him, she sat up. The top of her costume slid off her back and dropped to the floor. She scowled at the man who'd attacked her.

Her scowl looked troubled and confused, not angry.

John had spoken to her briefly when he entered the restaurant, but he'd been too preoccupied to notice much about her appearance. Now, he found himself staring at her. He guessed she wasn't much older than twenty. She had a small, faint scar on her right cheekbone. Like a nick that a sculptor might've given his statue because he found it too perfect and felt the need to give it a small flaw for a touch of humanity and vulnerability. Her hair was glossy black. It was very short, cut in a style that reminded John of Peter Pan.

He imagined himself painting a portrait of her. A nude, of course. Right. When hell freezes over. A, she would never go for it. B, Lynn would pitch a fit. C, the temptation to do more than paint her picture . . .

If only he were invisible . . .

John forced himself to look away from her.

People were gathered around her assailant. Through a narrow gap, however, John saw that he was facedown. Some men were using their belts to bind his arms behind his back and lash his feet together.

'God, why did he do that to me?'

John shook his head.

'He just ran in and attacked me for no good reason. We've always been friends. It's like he went crazy or something. God! I don't get it. And what's that all over him?'

'I don't know.'

She looked at John. 'Can I keep your jacket for a while?'

'Sure. Go ahead.'

'I don't know why that man had to *cut* my costume. I'll have to get new laces and . . .' She sighed. 'I suppose everyone here got an eyeful.' Apparently, however, she didn't care much. Or figured there was no more reason for modesty. She took the blazer away from her chest. John managed not to moan as a rush of heat surged through him. He knew he should look away, but he couldn't. Cassy swept the jacket behind her, pushed her arms through the sleeves, then overlapped the front and held it shut. She smiled at him. 'Hey, this is nice and warm.'

'Well, keep it as long as you like.'

One side of her lip curled up, showing her teeth. 'I wonder what I'm supposed to do now.'

'Well, the ambulance . . .'

'Screw that. But I can't very well greet customers like this.'

'I don't think anyone would expect you to. Not after what happened.'

'I'm sort of the "acting manager" tonight.'

'This isn't exactly business as usual. Why don't you come over to our table and have a drink? Just relax until the cops show up and take that guy away. Somebody else can watch the door for you.'

'I don't know,' she said, still frowning. 'Yeah, OK.'

She started to get up. John stood quickly, took a gentle

grip of her arm, and helped her to rise. When she straightened herself, she grimaced and bent over slightly and clamped her arms against the lower part of her ribcage.

'Are you all right?'

'Maybe I *should* have those X-rays.'

Both the front doors flew open at once. The cluster of people blocked John's view, but not for long. With shouts and squeals, some dropped to the floor cowering and others scattered, fleeing toward the dining room or the cocktail bar at the other side of the restaurant. Some stayed to fight.

One man tumbled backward when a camera slammed the side of his head. The woman wielding it rushed after him, dropped her knees onto his chest as he struck the floor, and pounded his face.

John shoved Cassy toward the dining room. 'Get away from here!' he snapped.

Nobody was coming to the aid of the fallen man. The woman kept battering his face, holding her camera by its zoom lens and swinging it down like a club.

Her hair was matted down and black. Her dripping face was black. So were the shoulders of her trench coat.

As John hurried toward her, a man in a corduroy jacket staggered backward and collided with him. The impact knocked the man sideways, turning him. Blood shooting from his torn throat splashed John's shirt.

The guy who'd done it to him was still up, the waitress Joyce riding his back and twisting his head while he struck out with his fist at two men who were keeping their distance. His fist bristled with metal. Keys. Three of them squeezed between his fingers, sticking out like little daggers.

John stumbled over the feet of someone kneeling on the floor, lurched forward and almost stepped on the ruined face of the man he'd come to help. As the woman raised her camera for another blow, he kicked. The toe of his shoe smashed her throat. The camera flew from her hand. She was lifted off her knees and thrown onto her back. Choking, she clutched her throat. She bucked and twitched.

The man was down, now, Joyce still on his back. Someone stomped his key hand against the floor and he cried out. Joyce scurried off him, and the two men kicked his head until he stopped moving.

'WE'VE GOTTA LOCK THE DOORS!' John shouted. 'LET'S LOCK THE DAMN DOORS!'

He remembered that Cassy was the acting manager.

She'll know where the keys are.

He whirled around. 'CASSY!'

6

Trev didn't waste time searching the station for rain gear. It was unlikely that he would find anything useful. The weather had been dry for the past two weeks, and he knew that clear skies had been predicted for the next several days. Besides, even if he could find an umbrella or raincoat, he wouldn't have trusted them to do the job.

Whatever was wrong with the rain to make it black and apparently turn people into killers, he suspected that a single drop touching exposed skin or even seeping through clothes might be enough to contaminate him.

So he headed straight for the janitor's closet. There, he found a box of plastic garbage bags. He brought it out, and spotted Patterson's Stetson on a corner of the sergeant's desk.

He tried it on. The cowboy hat fit loosely, but it would do. He took the hat and bags to his desk.

'What *are* you doing?' Francine asked.

'Gotta make a rain suit.'

'You can't be serious about going outside.'

He rushed past Francine and Lisa. In the top drawer of Lucy's desk, he found a pair of scissors and two rolls of strapping tape. He took them back to his own desk, then pulled out a garbage bag. He shook the bag open. Hopping, he thrust his right foot to the bottom. Then he rolled his chair back, sat down on it, and stretched out his covered leg.

'You've got to be kidding,' Francine muttered.

'People are running amok out there.' With his scissors, he started to cut off the bag so it reached only as high as his groin. 'I've got a friend who might be in trouble.'

'What about us?'

'That's up to you. You can either stay here or come along.'

'Oh, fabulous.'

He wrapped the plastic around his ankle and leg. 'I can lock the doors. I'll get you some firearms.'

'Mom, we can't stay here.'

'There're *bodies*.'

'I'm well aware of that.' Trev cut off a length of tape, and cinched the bunched up bag around his ankle. He bound a yard-long strip of tape several times around his thigh, pulling it tight. Tight enough, he hoped, to prevent it from slipping down. When he finished, his right leg was encased in layers of green plastic.

'That isn't going to stay up,' Lisa said.

'I don't know,' he muttered. He pulled out a second bag and shook it open.

'If you're gonna do that, you oughta wear your pants *over* the bags.'

He looked up at Lisa.

For the first time, he saw her smile.

'That's a good idea. Thanks.' While he ripped the tape loose, Lisa squatted by his foot and tugged at the bag. She tore it down his leg and flung it aside.

Trev swung a foot up across his knee and grabbed his sneaker.

'No, leave your shoes on. You won't get them on over all the plastic. Put the bags *over* your shoes, *under* your jeans.'

'You done this before?' he asked.

'Not hardly.'

As he unfastened his belt and pants, Francine said, 'We'll have to go with you.' Something was different about her voice. She no longer sounded snotty.

The change in her, Trev thought, probably had to do with the way Lisa had suddenly decided to pitch in and help.

'Fine,' he told her. 'I can pull my car right up to the door so you won't get wet.'

When his jeans were off, both women crouched in front of his outstretched legs. He felt a little uncomfortable, sitting there in his Jockey shorts. Nothing they haven't seen before, he told himself. And neither of them made remarks. They measured the bags, cut them off, pulled them over his shoes and up his bare legs. They wound the plastic tightly around him. They bound it in place with strips of tape. The back of Francine's hand brushed against his genitals once while she taped his thigh. She murmured, 'Sorry,' and didn't do it again.

When the plastic leggings were snug, he stood up and got into his jeans. He unclipped his holster, set it on the desk, and took off his belt.

Lisa cut head and arm holes in a bag. Trev took off his shirt, put the bag on. It hung down to his knees. Francine took the scissors from her daughter and slit the sides so the bag wouldn't inhibit his leg movements.

Then they fashioned coverings for his hands and arms, wrapped them snugly, and taped them tight around his wrists and upper arms.

Lisa chopped off the bottom of another bag. She slipped the bag over his head. While Francine held it in place, the girl carefully snipped out eyeholes and a breathing slot. Then they taped it in loosely around his neck.

'All set,' Francine said. 'No way you'll get wet.'

'Course, you look like something out of a horror movie.'

'Oughta do the job,' Trev said. 'Really appreciate it.' His voice sounded muffled and strange to him. Probably because his ears were covered.

The women helped him into his shirt and buttoned it for him.

'What about his eyes?' Lisa asked.

'The hat,' he said.

The bag over his head made crinkling sounds as Francine pushed the hat down firmly over it.

'That should do it,' he said. 'Thanks.' He took a step toward his desk, picked up his belt, and fastened it around his waist. With every movement, his ears were filled with quiet noises as if someone were wadding up plastic wrappers nearby. He clipped the holster to his side. He unsnapped its guard strap, drew his revolver, then explored the trigger with his covered index finger.

It was like wearing thin, rather slippery mittens.

He supposed he could fire the gun if he had to.

He holstered it.

'Go, and get your handbag,' he told Francine, figuring she must've left it in the interrogation room.

While she went to get it, Trev stepped to the other side of the counter. He picked up Patterson's revolver, carried it into the public restroom at the far end of the reception area, and held it under the faucet. The hot water spilled over it, showing a shadow of gray as it ran into the sink. Then the water was clear against the white enamel.

Trev turned off the faucet, shook excess water from the gun, and dried it with paper towels.

Back in the main room, Francine and Lisa watched as he crouched over Lucy's body. He used her skirt to make sure that no trace of water remained on the weapon. Then he broke it open and cleared the shell casings from the cylinder. He wiped the cylinder.

'Do you know how to use a handgun?' he asked Francine.

She nodded. 'I used to go with a deputy.'

He stepped up to her and offered Patterson's .38.

She stared at it. 'I don't think . . .'

Lisa snatched it from Trev's hand.

'No!'

'It's all right. See?' She switched the gun to her left hand, and held her right hand open in front of her mother's eyes. 'See? Clean.'

'OK, give it to me.' Francine took the weapon.

'Go on and load it,' Trev told her, nodding toward the open box of cartridges on his desk. 'Then put the box in your purse. You'll have to do the reloading for both of us if things get bad.'

She started sliding rounds into the cylinder.

'I'll be back in a couple of minutes. I'm going out back. If I come in acting weird, don't be afraid to use that piece on me.'

Francine looked up at him, eyes narrow.

'Be careful, officer,' Lisa said.

'It's Trev,' he told her. Then he hurried to a cabinet behind the counter. It contained keys for three offduty patrol cars. He gathered them, and ran for the rear exit of the station.

He thrust open the door. He stepped outside, hesitated for

just a moment under the portico, then took a deep breath and held it and entered the downpour.

The rain pattered softly on the felt cowboy hat, the shoulders of his shirt. It tapped the plastic covering his hands and shoes. Though the lights of the parking lot were masked by rain, the area ahead wasn't totally dark. He could see that the rain was falling straight down, so at least he didn't need to worry about it blowing in beneath the wide brim of Patterson's hat, getting into his eyes or mouth.

He made out the faint shapes of the three patrol cars straight ahead. Over to the right were the personal cars of Lucy, Patterson, and the four cops who were out cruising (maybe wet and crazy by now and blowing away citizens).

Crouching at the rear of the nearest black and white, he tried keys until he found one that fit the trunk. The lid swung up. He felt around in the darkness of the trunk until he found the 12-gauge Ithaca riot gun. He took it out, slammed the trunk, and trotted to the next car. As he opened its trunk and lifted out the shotgun, he considered using one of these cars instead of his own.

And decided against it.

With all hell breaking loose, he sure didn't want to be driving around town in a cop car. Too damn conspicuous. The crazies might zero in on it.

Shotgun braced under each arm, Trev walked toward the station.

He resisted an urge to run.

Slip on the wet pavement, go down on your back, and in comes the rain through the face holes.

He wished he hadn't thought of that. It made him feel cold and shaky in the bowels.

But at least that cheerful scenario hadn't occurred to him until now, when he was on his way back.

I'll have to wash off these Ithacas before we go, he realized.

Shit. Another delay. Might already have waited too long. *God, Maureen, hang in there.*

He switched one of the shotguns to his other arm, pulled open the station door, stepped into the light, flinched at the sight of Francine aiming a revolver at his face, slipped on the tile floor and fell on his butt.

7

'Let's clean her up,' Buddy said, nudging the body with his toe. 'See what our tarbaby looks like under that shit.'

'I still think we should call the cops,' Sheila said.

'Get real,' Buddy told her.

'I mean it. She tried to bash your brains out.'

'No cops.'

'Yeah,' Doug said. 'Let's keep her.' Grinning at Buddy, he said, 'We were one babe short. Now we got one for you.'

'Crazy bitch,' Buddy muttered.

Lou couldn't stop staring at the young woman. She gave him the creeps, black like that. Ever since he'd come into the foyer with the others and seen her, he'd felt cold and shaky. Last night, they'd done all that to Chidi. Now, a gal brings pizza to the house and *she* shows up covered with wet stuff that makes her as black as a nigger and she tries to whack Buddy. Like she was some kind of avenging phantom, or something.

Fucking weird.

They'd checked outside and the *rain* was black. If it *was* rain.

Lou had tried to tell himself that this was just an ordinary woman who came to bring the pizza and got caught in the storm. But that didn't ease his fears. Why in hell was *black* crap coming down out there? Why in hell did she try to brain Buddy?

He couldn't rid himself of the awful feeling that, somehow, Chidi was behind it.

Buddy and Doug were spooked, too. Even though they kept joking around and stuff, he could see it in their eyes.

'Yeah,' Buddy said after a few moments of silence. 'Let's lug her into the john.'

'I don't know if we should touch her,' Sheila said.

Doug, mocking her in a trembling voice said, 'Oh, my, it might be contagious.'

'It's nothing to kid about. I mean, we don't know what that stuff is. It's *black*.'

Buddy spread his arms and smiled at her. His shirt and pants looked smudged with soot from his struggle with the woman. His hands didn't appear stained, but they'd been black before he wiped them on the legs of his trousers. Some faint, gray blotches still showed on the inner sides of his wrists.

'If it's contagious, I've got it. And I'm gonna *get* you!' He lurched forward like a zombie, reaching for Sheila.

'Stop it!' she cried out, quick-stepping away from him. 'You're not amusing.'

Baring his teeth, Buddy pivoted toward Cyndi. She stood her ground. 'Just quit it.'

He dropped his act. 'Look, gang, I got that stuff on me and it didn't do anything.'

'How do you know there isn't an incubation period?' Sheila asked.

'What kinda period's that?' Doug asked, grinning.

'That's when gals bleed from their incubators,' Buddy explained.

'I mean it, guys.'

Deciding to take some of the heat off Sheila, Lou said, 'What she means is, maybe a space of time has to go by before you show any symptoms.'

'I know what she means, asswipe,' Buddy said. 'And it's stupid. The rain only started a minute or two before this babe went berserk with her rock. It's been – what? – five or ten minutes since I nailed her.'

'Good point,' Doug told him.

'So it doesn't do shit, touching her.'

Doug seemed convinced, 'I'll help you,' he said.

Buddy looked at Lou. 'OK,' Lou said.

'You guys take her feet. Whatever you do, don't drop her, she'll fuck up the carpet.'

Lou followed Doug around to the feet of the sprawled woman. She was wearing low heels. A little bit of green still showed where the shoes weren't stained with black. She didn't wear stockings. Her shins and ankles were streaky. The damp skirt of her dress reached down just past her knees, and looked glued to her legs. Here and there, its fabric was still green.

Lou realized that Doug had already lifted her left ankle off the floor.

He didn't want to touch her.

But he wrapped both hands around her right ankle. He'd expected her skin to feel cold. It was warm, though. It felt good. Some of his dread seemed to ease.

She's just a normal woman, he told himself, and lifted. Doug brought her other leg high. Buddy, squatting, grabbed her under the armpits. He straightened up. The sudden increase in weight nearly pulled her ankle from Lou's grip.

'Heavy mother, ain't she?' Doug said.

Sure heavier than she looks, Lou thought, taking careful

steps as Buddy walked backward with her. The woman looked slim. Pretty tall, though.

'Is her skirt dragging?' Buddy asked.

'Just a little,' Cyndi said.

'Well, get it off the floor, damn it.'

Wrinkling her nose, Cyndi rushed in from the side. She reached under and pulled a handful of skirt toward her and folded it over the gal's thigh. Then she scowled at her hand.

'I told you, there's nothing to worry about.'

Buddy changed direction toward the foot of the stairs.

'We're going upstairs?' Doug asked.

'My room,' Buddy said.

Lou had figured they would carry her into the guest restroom on the ground floor. But he realized, now, that it only had a sink and toilet, no tub or shower. Buddy's bedroom, on the second floor, had its own john with a big bathtub.

And we're going to put her in it.

He wondered if they would take her clothes off. The girls won't stand for that, he thought. Maybe *they'll* strip her but make us leave.

Buddy started up the stairs. The top of the gal's head was pressed against his belly. Her shoulders were bare except for straps that looked like wide ribbons. The dress was low cut, but not *that* low. It didn't show any of her breasts or cleavage. Her breasts were there, though, making the fabric bulge. And they shook just a little as she was jostled.

Oh, man, Lou thought.

Sheila and Cyndi, behind him on the stairs, weren't saying anything.

They probably don't like this.

He suddenly wished the girls were gone. As much as he liked Sheila, she had a real prissy streak. She still wouldn't let him get into her pants, even though they'd been going together since summer. She *sure* wouldn't go along with it if they wanted to mess around with this gal.

Cyndi wasn't as big a prude as Sheila. But she was likely to throw a fit if they tried something. Especially Doug.

Shit.

This gal's our captive. She's at our *mercy*. We could do *anything* to her.

But not with Sheila and Cyndi here.

Lou was surprised when he found himself at the top of the stairway. The climb had been a cinch.

Cyndi sidestepped by, and led the way to Buddy's bedroom.

Maybe she'll be OK, Lou thought.

They followed her into the room. She hurried ahead of them and turned on the bathroom light.

Looking over his shoulder and changing course for the john, Buddy said, 'We'll put her right in the tub so this stuff doesn't get on anything.'

When they reached the tub, Buddy stepped over its side. He lowered her while Doug climbed in with her left leg. Lou leaned over the edge and put her right leg down.

'OK,' Buddy said. 'Everybody out.'

Doug's mouth fell open. 'Huh?'

'Go on downstairs, all of you. Look in the kitchen, find something to eat, have some more drinks.'

'I thought we were gonna give this babe a bath.'

'Not we. Me. She's mine.'

'Hey, man, we helped you get her up here.'

Lou, feeling robbed, nodded but didn't speak.

'Yeah, thanks,' Buddy said. 'Now get out.'

'That's not fair.'

'Come on,' Sheila said, taking hold of Lou's wrist. 'We don't want any part of this.'

Speak for yourself, he thought. But he didn't argue. He let Sheila guide him toward the bathroom door.

'Shit,' Doug said. 'This really sucks.'
'Let's go,' Cyndi told him.
'Buddy.'
'Get off it,' Cyndi said, sounding a little miffed. 'What do you want with her, anyway? You got me. Besides, she's *old*.'
'She's not that old.'
Moments later, Doug followed Cyndi out of the bathroom. His face was red. He looked as if he might either start to cry or take a swing at somebody.
'One of you shut the door,' Buddy called.
Doug turned around. He slammed it.
'Don't be such a sourpuss,' Cyndi told him, and thrust her fingers under his belt buckle and pulled him up against her.
Lou wished Sheila would do something like that to him. But dragging him toward the door, she said, 'Let's go down and find some food.'

8

Denise unplugged the cord, put aside the lid, and dumped the popcorn into the plastic bowl. When she set the popper down, Kara tossed in a chunk of butter. It met the hot metal, sizzled and started to melt.
'I'll do the butter and salt,' Kara said. 'You can get the drinks. I think I'll have a New York Seltzer. Do you know what Tom likes?'
'He's big on Pepsi, if you've got some.'
'Oh, sure we do.'

Denise went to the refrigerator. It was loaded: cans of Bud, Diet Coke and Pepsi, bottles of New York Seltzer and Michelob, a jug of white wine. She took out two Pepsis and a bottle of cherry-flavored seltzer.

'I hope he gets here pretty soon,' Kara said. 'Popcorn's best when it's hot. It's OK after it's cooled off, but I think it loses something, don't you?'

'Definitely.'

'What'll we do when he gets here?' Kara asked, looking away from the melting butter and furrowing her brow with concern. 'I really don't think we should bore him with the birthday party, do you?'

'We can put on whatever you want.' Denise took three glasses down from a cupboard, then returned to the refrigerator for ice cubes.

'I have some movies Mom taped off cable for me.'

As Kara started to name them, Denise thought about the tapes she'd rented for tonight. She wished she hadn't left them at home. They might not be suitable for Kara, but . . .

Why don't I ask Tom over to my place? Lynn said they'd be back early. He can follow me home, and maybe we can watch one or two of them. And it'll give us a chance to be alone.

The idea made her nervous and excited. She really shouldn't have him in the house with her parents gone, but it'd sure be neat. As long as they didn't get *too* carried away. And as long as nobody ever found out.

'So what do you think?' Kara asked. 'Maybe one of those? Maybe not the Disney stuff, you guys are too old for that. But maybe *Goonies* or *The Stuff*. Have you ever seen *The Stuff*?'

'I don't think so.'

'Oh, it's great.' With a potholder, Kara lifted the popper and tilted it over the bowl, dribbling butter onto the popcorn.

'See, there's this white goop kind of like marshmallow topping? Only thing is, people can't stop eating it and it turns them into these *awful* yucky monsters. It's really gross, but it's funny, too, and it's not really a kid movie. You think Tom'll like it?'

'We can give it a try. But you must've already seen it.'

'Oh, I like to watch movies over and over again if they're good.' She shook the popcorn bowl and jiggled it up and down. 'I bet I've seen *Willy Wonka* a hundred times.'

'A hundred?'

'Well, maybe just seventy-eight or eighty. I never actually counted.' She set the bowl on the counter and started to sprinkle salt onto the popcorn.

And the doorbell rang.

'He's here!'

'Made good time, didn't he?' Denise picked up the Pepsis and seltzer. 'Do you want to bring the glasses in?' She watched while Kara gathered the glasses, pinning one between her wrist and chest, holding the others in her hands. 'Now, be careful.'

'I don't drop things. I'm not like Dad.'

The girl followed her into the living room. The doorbell rang again as Denise set down the cans and bottle on the table in front of the sofa. 'Coming!' she called.

She hurried for the door, leaving Kara behind to unload the glasses.

She slid the guard chain off its track. 'What's the password?' she asked.

'C'mon, open up.'

She did.

Tom, face shiny black, lunged across the threshold thrusting the steel tip of his umbrella at Denise's midsection. She gasped and twisted away. The dull point plunged under the placket of her shirt and streaked across her skin. Half the closed umbrella rushed against her belly, slick and wet, before its tip poked a hole through the side of her shirt. As she fell, she grabbed it with both hands.

The floor pounded her shoulder and hip. Keeping her hold on the umbrella, she rolled over on it. The weapon was wrenched from Tom's grip and snapped against the tile.

He kicked the side of her thigh.

'STOP IT!' Kara shouted. 'YOU STOP THAT!'

He kicked her in the ribs.

Why's he doing this?

Clutching the shoulders of her shirt, he yanked Denise backward to her knees. Buttons flew off. She tried to squirm out of the shirt, but only managed to free one shoulder before Tom clamped an arm across her throat. He jerked her head against his belly, bending her spine back, choking her.

Denise felt her head starting to go warm and numb. Her ears rang. The lights, the furniture, Kara watching with her mouth wide – all were rimmed with flashing electric blue.

She reached behind her. Hooked the backs of Tom's knees. Jerked them forward and tried to throw her weight against him.

His knees folded.

He fell, keeping his chokehold and tumbling Denise onto him. She heard his wind blow out. With both hands, she forced his forearm away from her throat. He grabbed his wrist. She didn't have the strength to resist the power of his two arms. But she tucked her chin down to protect her throat. As his forearm shoved against it, she writhed and pushed and sank her teeth into the sleeve of his jacket and clamped down with all her might.

Crying out, Tom tore his arm from her mouth.

Denise flipped over, rolled off him.

He rolled, reaching out as she got to her hands and knees.

He jerked her arm out from under her, tugged her toward him.

And Kara, standing behind him, swung a fireplace poker like a golf club. Its brass handle struck him above the ear. The impact knocked his head sideways. His grip on Denise went loose. She fell against him as he flopped onto his back.

She pushed herself up.

Tom was sprawled out motionless, Kara raising the poker for another swing.

'No, don't!'

She lowered it.

On her knees, panting for air, Denise rubbed the front of her neck and stared down at Tom. His hair, normally the same light shade of blond as Denise's hair, was slicked down and black. Only the lids of his closed eyes and an area under his chin were unsoiled by the ebony liquid.

'Did I kill him?' Kara asked. Her voice sounded high and frightened.

The soaked front of Tom's jacket rose and fell, so he was breathing.

'No,' Denise gasped. 'You only knocked him out.' She looked up at Kara. 'Thanks.'

'Why'd he go and do that?'

'I don't know.'

'Gads.'

'I've never ever seen him fight with *anyone*. I just can't . . . it's like he lost his mind. It's crazy.'

'What *is* that all over him?'

'I don't know.'

'Is the rain *dirty* tonight? It looks dirty. I thought rain was always supposed to be clean. Do you think he got mad at you because he came over and got all dirty like that?'

'I doubt it. Maybe the rain's toxic or something, I don't know.'

'You mean like poison?'

'Maybe. I don't know.'

Kara's red face contorted and her chin began to tremble. 'Well, Denise . . .' Tears came to her eyes. 'You've got it on *you*.'

Denise looked down. Below her white bra, her skin was smeared dark gray from the umbrella. She also noticed a red mark left by the steel tip. Though the dull point hadn't broken her skin, the mark felt hot. She rubbed it gently.

Raising her eyes, she saw Kara weeping silently, her face flushed and tears running down her cheeks.

'Don't worry, OK? I feel fine. Just a little beat up. But I don't feel weird or poisoned or anything.'

'Are you sure?'

'Yeah.' She straightened her shirt and pulled it shut. All the buttons were gone except for one just below her throat, which hadn't been fastened. With shaky hands, she pushed that one into its hole.

'Maybe you'd better wash,' Kara said. 'You know? Just in case . . .'

'Can you find something we can use to tie him up? Rope or something?'

Nodding, Kara wiped a sleeve across her wet face.

'Let me have the poker.'

Kara handed her weapon to Denise, then hurried away.

Hanging onto it, she walked on her knees to Tom's feet. She set the poker down. As she pulled his legs straight and pressed them together, she watched his face closely for signs that he might be regaining consciousness.

God, she thought, what if he *doesn't* come to? What if he's in a coma, or something, and never comes out of it? Or he wakes up, eventually, but his brains are scrambled and he's nothing but a vegetable for the rest of his life?

He'll be OK, she told herself. He'll be fine. People get knocked out all the time and come out of it OK.

She took off her belt, wrapped it twice around his ankles, pulled it tight, and fastened it. The buckle was on top, so she slid the straps until it disappeared behind his ankles.

He could still get to it, but not easily.

She picked up the brass poker and watched him.

As much as she wanted Tom to regain consciousness, she hoped he wouldn't do it too soon. Not before Kara got back and they had time to tie his hands.

Maybe when he comes to he won't be crazy anymore.

But if he is . . .

God, I don't want to hit him.

But I can't let him get loose and attack us.

Kara, where are you?

She heard quick footfalls behind her, looked back, and saw the girl rushing forward with a couple of jumpropes. 'Will these be OK?'

'Fine,' Denise said, though she wished the ropes didn't have those wooden handles. She pulled Tom's arms down, crossed them over his belly, and started tying them together with one of the ropes.

'Do you think we'd better call the police?' Kara asked.

Denise shook her head. 'I don't know. I don't want to get him in trouble.'

'Yeah, but he tried to *kill* you, didn't he?'

'He can't do anything once he's all tied up.'

'He kind of scares me.'

'I know. He scares me, too. But maybe he'll be normal again when he comes to. Maybe whatever was wrong with him will go away. And even if he's still nuts, he won't be able to hurt us. We'll make sure he doesn't get loose.'

'How? You mean like bonk him on the head again?'

'If we have to.'

'Well, *you'll* have to do it, then. Not me. It's your turn.'

Nodding, Denise tugged the red wooden handles to

tighten the bundle of knots. 'He won't get out of that,' she said.

She took the second rope from Kara. She made a slip knot near one of its handles, then lifted Tom's head off the tiles and put the loop around his neck. She slid the knot up against his skin. Holding the other handle, she scooted backward to take most of the slack out of the rope, sat down on the floor and crossed her legs.

'He causes any trouble,' she said, 'I'll give him a yank.'

'Sort of like a dog?'

'Exactly.'

A reluctant smile curled up a corner of Kara's mouth. 'Neat idea.'

'Why don't you go get the popcorn and our drinks? And maybe a couple of cushions to sit on.'

'Oh, this is really weird. You mean we're going to go ahead and have our party right here?'

'Might as well. We'll watch Tom instead of the television. We'll have a guardin' party.'

'A what?'

'Garden party, guarding party. Get it?'

Kara laughed softly and shook her head. 'I think you might be even weirder than my Dad.' Then she went to get the refreshments.

Captives

1

It was like driving blind. The eyeholes in the bag killed most of Trev's peripheral vision, dark rain spattered the windshield faster than the wipers could clear it, the parking lot lights were so dim that they might've been on rheostats turned way down, and his headbeams only seemed to penetrate fifteen or twenty feet into the heavy downpour before fading out completely.

Though he couldn't see worth a damn, he drove fast and hoped for the best.

Too much time had already gone by.

Crazies might've already overrun O'Casey's, might've already gotten to Maureen.

She'll be OK, he told himself.

His wheels bumped over the curb. He drove across grass, steering closer to the hedge by the station wall until bushes squeaked against the right side of his car. He spotted the portico's nearest support post. Slowing down, he passed between it and the station's front door. His tires rolled onto the walkway's smooth pavement. Rain stopped hitting the hood, the windshield. He eased forward until it went silent above his head, then set the emergency brake and looked over his shoulder.

His back door was out of the rain and lined up with the station's door. He reached over the back of the passenger seat to unlock it. Then he beeped the horn.

Light spilled out of the station as the front door swung open. Francine and Lisa came out, each carrying a shotgun.

They had plastic bags draped over their heads and shoulders in case water should run off the car while they entered, and their arms were covered to the elbows.

Francine, in the lead, opened the back door of Trev's car. She climbed in. Lisa ducked in after her and shut the door. Trev watched them push the covers off their heads.

'Everybody OK?' he asked.

'It's insane, going out in this,' Francine said.

'Better than staying in there with a couple of stiffs,' Lisa told her.

'I'm not so sure anymore.'

Trev decided they were acting normal. Turning away from them, he shifted to reverse. He slowly backed his car out from under the shelter. When its front was clear, he started forward and headed for the parking lot.

'So where is it we're trying to go?' Francine asked.

'O'Casey's Pizza.'

'God, it's so dark out here,' Lisa said. 'Will you be able to find the place?'

'I'll find it.'

Somehow, he thought.

'It's just a straight shot up Guthrie and a left on Third,' he explained as his front tires bounced down from the curb onto the parking lot's pavement.

In normal weather, the drive shouldn't take more than five minutes. With this kind of visibility, he knew they would need some luck to make it at all.

We'll probably get creamed.

'This is really the pits,' Lisa muttered.

Trev drove straight forward until his headbeams met the bushes of the narrow strip that separated the station's parking lot from the sidewalk and Guthrie Avenue. He was tempted to plunge through the barrier. The possibility of tire damage stopped him. So he turned to the right. Stepping on the gas, he sped alongside the landscaped area to the entrance lane. There, he swung out onto Guthrie.

Nothing broadsided him.

Maybe we'll be lucky, he thought. Nobody but an idiot would be out driving in this crap.

An idiot, or somebody without any choice.

Or crazies, already wet and cruising for action.

He eased toward the middle of the road until he came to the broken yellow center line.

Keep watching the line, he thought. When you come to an intersection, there'll either be a left-hand turn pocket or the line will end.

He ran the names of the cross-streets through his mind. Should be seven before Third Street.

'Why don't you try turning on the radio?' Francine said.

The center line stopped. He looked both ways, saw no hint of approaching headlights (you won't see them anyway until it's too late), and tromped on the gas pedal to get through the intersection as fast as possible. When the line reappeared, he slowed down. He turned on the radio.

Glen Campbell was singing 'Wichita Lineman.'

'Try to get some news,' Francine said.

'This is as close as we're gonna get to a local station,' Trev told her.

'What is it, Bakersfield?' Lisa asked.

'Yeah.'

'Do you think they'd be playing music if . . .?'

'No, I doubt it. Bakersfield must be OK.'

'Maybe it's only happening . . .'

'That was good ol' Glen Campbell, and this is Bronco Bob for KLRZ, bringing you all the best in country music. We're coming up now on seven-forty in the P.M., and we've got a chilly fifty-nine degrees outside so snuggle up to your honey and stay tuned in. Waylon's coming up, along with Ronnie Milsap, The Judds, and Miss Robin Travis.'

'Nothing about any rain,' Lisa said.

'Well, we're some hundred miles from Bakersfield.'

'Maybe it's just happening here.'

Trev sped through another intersection. Two down, five to go. He eased off slightly on the gas.

'If it *is* just happening here,' Francine said, 'we ought to be grateful. I'd hate to think this was going on everywhere, wouldn't you?'

'I wonder if anyone out there even knows about it.'

Trev flinched as something pressed his shoulder. Then he realized it was Francine's hand.

'You know,' she said, 'maybe we can drive out of this if we just keep going. If it's the rain making people nuts and we get out from under the storm . . .'

He hit the brakes and jerked the wheel, shouting 'Hold on!' and they skidded and slammed the side of a station wagon blocking the lane. The force of the impact jerked him, tried to throw him over onto the passenger seat, but he kept his grip on the wheel.

Behind him, the women were gasping and moaning.

'Anyone hurt?' he asked, twisting around to look back.

Francine had been hurled against Lisa, and Lisa was hunched down against the right-hand door.

'I think I'm OK,' Lisa muttered.

'I can't believe this,' Francine said, pushing herself up. 'I just can't believe this.'

'At least we didn't break any windows,' Trev said.

'What're we *doing* out here?' Francine blurted.

Great, he thought. She's losing it.

'Just take it easy,' he said.

'Take it easy? You almost got us killed, you fucking maniac!'

'Mom, cut it out.'

'Well, he did!'

'I didn't expect there to be a goddamn car stopped *sideways* in the middle of the street.'

'If you hadn't been driving like a maniac . . .!'

'I'm sorry. I really am.'

'Lot of good sorry does.'

Trev turned his attention to the windows. His car appeared to be flush against the side of the station wagon. He couldn't see anyone inside.

But as he studied the car, he saw another in the glow of his headlights. A compact Dodge. Its rear against the front bumper of the wagon.

'Oh, man,' he muttered.

'What?'

'*Two* of them.'

'What?'

An intentional roadblock?

He stepped on the gas pedal. His car lurched forward with sounds of scraping, crunching metal. Then it parted with the side of the wagon and the noises stopped.

'What's going on?' Francine demanded.

Trev didn't answer. He backed up, watching the wagon. Parked at its rear was a pickup truck.

'Trev! Answer me!'

'It's a trap,' he said, trying to keep his voice calm.

'A what?'

'Make sure your doors are locked,' he said, and the car rocked on its shocks. He darted his eyes to the rearview mirror. Couldn't see anything but darkness. Couldn't see the man or woman scuttling over the trunk toward the back window. But the slight shaking of the car told him someone was there.

A hard thud against the rear window. He shot the car forward and heard a muffled outcry.

'What was *that*?'

'Lost a visitor,' Trev said, and wrenched the wheel, turning away from the roadblock. The sweep of his headbeams lit four black shapes rushing in. Coming at them. A man with an axe. A woman with a tire iron. A woman who seemed to have no weapon and a kid maybe twelve or thirteen from the size of him with something bigger than a softball swinging at his side.

From behind Trev came a quick, high sucking sound.

'Oh my God!' That was Francine.

It isn't a softball, Trev realized as he rammed the pedal to the floor.

It was the head of a girl, and the kid was swinging it by its long hair.

He figured he could speed through the group. Not touch any of them.

But if he tried that, the bastard with the axe might bash the windshield, let the rain in. So he steered for the axeman.

The guy didn't try to dodge clear. He met the car face on, swinging the axe down from straight overhead with both hands as if he planned to split a log. It chopped into the hood. Then its handle caught him in the belly, hoisting him off his feet.

Something whacked the windshield in front of Trev's face.

The head. Face first. The blow mashed its nose flat. Teeth broke from its open mouth. Pale blurs of eyes glanced in at him. Then the head bounced away and through his side window Trev saw the kid stumbling backward, still hanging onto the thing's hair.

'*Jesus*!' he gasped.

He realized someone was shrieking in his ears.

And he realized he hadn't lost the axeman.

He sped away from the roadblock, away from all the attackers but one.

The head of the axe was still buried in the hood. And its handle seemed to be buried in the man who'd put it there.

The center line ended. An intersection. 'Detour!' Trev yelled.

He swung a hard right. But not hard enough to lose his guest. The guy stayed put, riding through the rain like a big, limp hood ornament.

2

Maureen thought, the pizzas are getting soaked. She knew she should stop this and get up and put her clothes back on and take the pizzas to the door, but it felt so good to be sprawled on the grass with the hot rain splashing down on her. She didn't want to get up ever.

When the rain filled her mouth, she choked. She raised her head and opened her eyes.

She was in a bathtub, not on the lawn. Not her bathtub. It wasn't rain coming down, but spray from a shower nozzle. There was a curtain rod, but no curtain enclosed the right side of the tub.

And she wasn't alone.

Someone was down low, peering in at her.

She sat up fast. Too fast. The sudden motion made her head spin, her vision cloud, her stomach churn. She grabbed the rim of the tub, hunched forward, threw her legs wide and vomited between them. The spasms wracked her. Pain throbbed through her head. Tears filled her eyes.

When she was done, she stayed bent over. She gasped to catch her breath. Water pounded against her head and shoulders and back. It ran down her face. She blinked the wetness of water and tears from her eyes. While she watched her mess spread out and slide toward the drain, the dizziness faded. It left confusion, shame and fear.

I'm naked in someone's bathtub. Who is that guy? What's happening?

He's the guy I tried to smash with a rock, she realized.

Why the hell did I want to do that?

What's he doing with me?

'Hope you didn't get any on you,' he said.

Maureen didn't look at him. She stopped holding onto the side of the tub, and wrapped both hands around her upthrust knees.

'What's your name?' he asked. He sounded friendly. The friendliness seemed mocking.

'Maureen.'

'Name's Buddy,' he said. 'I'm gonna be *your* buddy.'

He touched her back. His hand moved gently, making slow circles.

'You tried to knock my brains out,' he said.

'I know. I'm sorry.'

His hand moved higher and he began to massage the nape of her neck. 'Why did you do that?'

'I don't know.'

'You don't know?'

'Huh-uh.'

'Were you mad at me?'

'I don't know you.'

'Did somebody send you?'

'I just came with the pizzas.'

'And you just suddenly got an urge to brain me?'

'Yeah.'

'Don't like my face?'

'It wasn't you. I just wanted . . . to kill whoever came to the door.'

'Real nice.'

'I'm sorry.'

'What do you think we oughta do about it?'

He didn't call the police, Maureen realized. He brought me in here and stripped me, instead.

'Maybe you should call the police,' she murmured.

'Would you like to be arrested? Would you like to go to prison? You assaulted me with a deadly weapon. That'd be a prison term for sure, wouldn't it?'

'Maybe.'

I'd rather take my chances with the police, she thought.

Trevor. Oh God, Trevor. If Rory hadn't been sick . . .

One hand continued to rub her neck. The other, his right, slipped beneath her armpit and closed gently around her right breast. Squirming, she dug her fingernails into her knees.

'No, don't,' she said. 'Please. Come on.'

'I think maybe you should be very nice to me, and maybe we won't have to bother the cops with this.'

His hand moved in a slow circle, palm stroking her nipple.

Maureen let out a shaky breath.

'You like that, don't you.'

'Come on, stop.'

'Bet it feels a lot better, now you're awake to enjoy it.' Laughing softly, he thumbed her nipple. 'Yeah, I already felt you up pretty good. This is better, though. This is a lot better.'

The hand slid down from her breast, down her chest and belly. And lower. When he fingered her pubic mound, she grabbed his wrist with her left hand and jerked it toward her hip. She rammed her right elbow back. It missed Buddy. Her upper arm collided with his face as he fell toward her, but she knew she hadn't done much damage.

And she knew she was in trouble.

The hand at the back of Maureen's neck shoved her away. She released his wrist. She flung her arm up. The far wall of the tub smacked her arm down against her side. A hand covered her face, pushed her down.

It went away. As she struggled to push herself up, Buddy rose from his crouch beside the tub. He wore nothing. He was grinning. He had a wide neck. His arms and chest were bunched with heavy muscles. His penis was erect. Big and thick and pointing high.

He climbed into the tub.

His broad body blocked the shower.

Maureen kicked at his shins until he squatted and grabbed her ankles. The water came again, splashing her face and torso. He spread her legs wide. He pulled her toward him. She twisted and bucked as her back slid over the slippery bottom of the tub.

Buddy sank to his knees. He tried to shove his hands under her rump, but she knocked them away.

'Naughty naughty,' he said, and punched her just below the navel. Right fist, then left, then right again. The blows bashed her breath out, made her guts feel hot and mushy, tore all her strength out.

She tried to struggle, but couldn't move.

Buddy stuck his hands under her rump. He clutched her buttocks and lifted.

Spine bent, arms hanging limp, the back of her shoulders and head sliding along the tub's bottom, she was dragged forward and impaled.

3

John, along with several other men, carried the bodies into the kitchen. It was Dr Goodman's suggestion.

Earlier, someone had called the police and Goodman had phoned for ambulances. While the doctor's call had at least been picked up, he'd been told that no units were available. So there would be no cops, no ambulances. Not for a while, anyway. Maybe not for a long while.

Dr Goodman thought it best, for everyone's sake, to remove the bodies from sight.

Among the dead were Andrew Dobbs, the reporter from *People Today*, and the female photographer who'd charged into the restaurant with him. She had no purse, no identification. The man she'd bludgeoned to death with her camera was Chester Benton, a local real estate agent. The man whose throat had been ripped open by Dobbs's keys was Ron Westgate, a high school teacher.

Four dead.

And John, himself, had killed the woman.

According to Goodman, she'd probably suffocated as a result of a collapsed trachea. John could've told him that, but he'd feigned ignorance. Why draw attention to himself?

Steve Winter, lugging her by the arms, knocked open the door to the kitchen. John followed him into the brightness with the woman's legs.

The savory aromas of the kitchen stirred his hunger.

After things had settled down a little, Cassy had ordered the cooks and dishwashers (who'd rushed out with knives and cleavers too late for the action) to return to their jobs. She planned to see that everyone ate.

Good for her, John thought as he followed Steve past a bank of ovens.

'I'm famished,' Steve said. Apparently, the wonderful odors were working on him, too.

'At least we don't have to worry about starving,' John told him. 'Good place to be in time of siege.'

'You going to stick around?'

'Aren't you?'

'Carol wants to go home.'

'I want to get home, too. Hell, my kid's with a sitter. I don't know about going out there, though.'

'What do you think's happening?'

'Shit if I know.'

'You think it's the rain?' Steve asked.

'I've never heard of rain making people homicidal.'

'I've never heard of rain being black.'

'Hold up,' John said.

They stopped and waited while two men came out of the freezer, looking pale and cold.

'OK. Go on ahead.'

John followed him into the walk-in freezer unit. The air felt like cold water seeping through his shirt. He wished he'd kept his blazer on. Until he remembered where it was and thought about Cassy's warm bare skin against its lining.

Looking over his shoulder, Steve stepped alongside the body of Andrew Dobbs.

They set the woman on the floor beside him.

Steve scowled down at her black face. Then he met John's eyes. 'Do you think this is it?'

'It? What do you mean?'

'You know.'

'The end of the world?'

'The Big One. World War Three. Only they didn't nuke us, they hit us with some kind of biological shit.'

That had already occurred to John. He supposed it must've occurred to everyone.

'Let's get out of here before we freeze up,' he said.

He waited for Steve. The two walked side by side toward the freezer door.

'So what do you think?' Steve asked as they stepped into the warmth of the kitchen.

'I don't know what's going on, but I don't think it's Doomsday. I sure hope not.'

Steve let out a nervous laugh. 'You and me both.'

'For godsake, don't bring up anything like that in front of the women. They're spooked enough as it is.'

They stepped aside as two men approached with the body of Chester Benton, and John wished he'd been quicker to take out the camera woman. Maybe it wouldn't have helped, anyway. For all he knew, the first blow might've been the fatal one that rammed a shard of skull into the poor guy's brain.

'If it's not the Big One,' Steve said, 'what do you think it might be?'

'Something of ours?'

'We're not supposed to be developing chemical weapons.'

'What we're supposed to be doing and what we *are* doing ain't necessarily the same thing. You know? Maybe the honchos decided to test out their new secret weapon on the citizens of Bixby.'

'No, that's . . .'

'Or maybe something just went wrong. Maybe that boom wasn't thunder. Maybe it was some kind of military transport blowing up, and it had a nasty cargo.'

'You think so?'

'Hell, I don't know. I'm a *painter*, for godsake. You're the science teacher around here.'

'I'm no great research chemist. An MA in biology, that's it. And a secondary credential.'

'You must keep up on new developments.'

'Yeah, well *Scientific American* hasn't run any articles on black shit that gives people the hots for murder.'

'Maybe you missed that issue.'

Steve suddenly burst out with laughter. His face went red and he covered his mouth. 'John, you're weird.'

'That's what my kid tells me. Come on, let's get out of here and cheer up the ladies.'

They stepped around a couple of guys carrying the last body.

'I don't know about you,' Steve said, 'but I'm going to wash my hands.'

John glanced at his own hands. There was no black on them. He'd thought there wouldn't be. He'd checked the woman's ankles before picking her up, and they'd looked clean. Apparently, the legs of her slacks had protected them.

But he'd been touching a dead woman.

'I'll go with you,' he said, and followed Steve from the kitchen.

The dining room was dimly lighted. Most of the people had returned to their tables. Lynn was now seated across from Carol at a booth near the front wall. She had a fresh margarita in front of her, and there was an additional Mai Tai on the table. Waitresses were scurrying around, most of them carrying trays of drinks.

He spotted Cassy sitting with an arm around a sobbing woman, Chester Benton's widow.

He turned away and walked with Steve to the entryway.

A couple of chairs had been brought over. Men sat in them, facing the doors and the prone body of Bill. A meat cleaver rested on the lap of one of the men. He had a croissant in one hand, a martini in the other. The second man held a carving knife and a glass of red wine. The young parking attendant was glaring at his guards, but lying still, making no attempt to free himself from the belts that bound his hands and feet.

'Behaving himself?' John asked as he stepped in front of the guards.

'I guess he knows what'll happen if he doesn't,' said the man with the martini.

'Well, keep up the good . . .'

Someone knocked on wood. John snapped his head sideways and stared at the doors. The knocking came again. Not a rough pounding, but a rather polite rap of knuckles.

The skin prickled on the back of his neck.

'Oh, shit,' Steve muttered.

John looked around at the two seated men. The one with the knife had slopped red wine onto the front of his camel jacket, but he didn't seem to be aware of that. He was gazing with wide eyes at the door. The martini man stuffed the remains of the croissant into his mouth and lifted the cleaver off his lap.

The knocking continued.

'If I were you guys,' John said, 'I wouldn't answer the door. Come on, Steve.'

Steve watched the door over his shoulder as he followed John into the cocktail lounge. Then he met John's eyes and said, 'This is really bad shit. I don't know. I don't know.'

'They seem like pretty sturdy doors. If you want to worry about something, worry about the windows.'

'Oh, thanks for mentioning it.'

'You're the guy who wants to go home.'

'I think I'll pass on that.'

John scanned the dimly lighted room. A few men and women were seated on bar stools. Small groups sat at some of the tables. 'Must be close to twenty people in here,' he said. 'Maybe about thirty others, including the help. That's a lot of manpower if the place gets stormed.'

'Stormed? Oh, Jesus. Great.'

'I'm not saying it'll happen.'

In the alcove at the far end of the room, people were lined up to use the two pay phones. John wished Lynn were among them instead of back in the dining area sopping up margaritas and chatting with Carol.

As he stepped through the group, he heard a woman at one of the phones say, 'In the nightstand drawer on your father's side of the bed. It's loaded, so be careful and don't let Terry get his hands on it. There's a box of bullets in the top dresser drawer, so make sure you get that, too.'

John groaned and kept moving.

God, he wished *he* had a gun in the house. He hated the things. He had vowed never to use one again. And he'd always felt secure in the knowledge that he rarely left Lynn and Kara by themselves. He worked at home. When he went out, they usually came with him. And he always figured he could defend them, if the need arose, without using a firearm.

Then this happens.

He rammed open the men's room door. It just missed crashing into someone about to come out.

'Sorry,' he muttered.

'Take it easy, partner,' the guy said.

Inside, a young man in a corduroy jacket was bent over, holding onto the sides of the sink and gazing at his face in the mirror. He didn't look away from his reflection when John and Steve entered.

John stepped up to the sink beside him. 'How you doing?' he asked, starting to wash his hands.

The kid kept staring into his own eyes.

He was about twenty. He sported a thin, blond mustache which was probably meant to make him look older.

'Everything'll be OK,' John said.

The kid looked at him. 'We're all gonna die.'

'It's not that bad. I know how you're feeling, but it's not that bad. What's your name?'

'Andy.'

'Andy, I'm John. This is Steve.'

Steve, at the sink to the left, leaned forward and raised a sudsy hand.

'I've been in a lot worse than this, Andy. And I'm here, all in one piece. You'll be fine. We'll all be fine. Are you here with somebody?'

'My . . . friend. Tina?' He said the name as if he expected John to know her.

'Where is she?'

'In the bar.'

'And probably scared half to death,' John said. 'Go out there and sit with her. Give her a hug. You'll both feel better.'

Andy just stared at him.

'Do it. Now.'

The kid hurried for the restroom door.

'Nice little pep-talk,' Steve said.

John rinsed the soap off his hands. 'I'm gonna get in the phone line. Would you mind telling Lynn? I'll be along as soon as I've gotten through to the house. You stay with the gals, OK?'

4

He shut off the water and climbed out of the tub. 'So,' he said, 'was it good for you?'

Maureen didn't answer.

She thought, I'm going to kill you, you rotten bastard.

'I usually don't go off so quick.' He sounded chipper. 'Guess you're just too hot for me.'

Maureen lay still, gasping and sobbing. Her knees were up. She felt Buddy's semen rolling slowly inside her. Some of it leaked out and flowed down. She clenched her buttocks together. The stuff felt like thick glue.

A big, white towel flopped onto her belly.

'Let's go,' he said. 'Dry off. I've got some friends I want you to meet.'

Holding the towel to her belly, she sat up. She wanted to stuff it down between her legs and swab away the sticky mess, but that would ruin the towel. So she shook it open and started with her hair. While she dried herself, she felt more and more of the stuff dribble out of her. It tickled a little bit. It made her anus itch.

Finally, after she'd dried her legs, she struggled up to a squatting position and tried to rub away every trace of the fluid.

'Squeaky clean?' Buddy asked.

She looked at him. He was smiling, doing a merry little dance as he rubbed an open towel across his back. His penis was red. It was sticking out straight, partly erect, bobbing and swinging as he moved.

'Want some more?' he asked.

She turned her face away, dropped the towel and stood up.

She stepped over the side of the tub. Though dry, the skin between her buttocks still felt a little tacky.

Her dress was heaped on the floor, partly covered by Buddy's discarded shirt and trousers. Crouching, she reached for it.

'No way, babe,' Buddy said.

Ignoring him, she clutched a corner of green fabric and pulled it toward her.

Buddy flicked his towel at her. There was a quiet *whap*, and the damp end of it stung Maureen's shoulder. Wincing, she grabbed her hurt.

'I'm the master,' he said. 'You're the slave. This is my whip.' He swung the towel beside his leg, the circular motion winding the towel around itself. 'Would you like another taste of the lash?'

Maureen shook her head. She stood up, leaving her dress on the floor.

'Excellent.' Turning sideways, he stretched the towel between his hands and twisted it. 'You're an excellent wench. I'm growing very fond of you.' And he snapped the towel at her again. It unfurled, striking toward her right breast. Lurching backward, Maureen jerked her arm up. The moist tip lashed her forearm.

She almost reached out to snatch the towel from his hand, but stopped herself.

He's the master, she thought. I'm the slave.

'You don't have to hit me with that,' she told him. 'Just tell me what you want. OK? I'll do whatever you want.'

His smile widened. 'Right now, I want to eat. Into the bedroom with you.'

Maureen turned to the door. She opened it. The towel smacked her rump. Her throat tightened.

Buddy followed her into the bedroom.

'Sit down.'

She sat on the side of the bed.

He went to a dresser, dropped his towel to the carpet, and opened a drawer. Looking over his shoulder, he said, 'My first command, don't try to get away. That would carry extremely severe penalties, including but not limited to torture, gang-bang and probable execution.'

He removed a white T-shirt and a pair of faded red gym shorts from the drawer.

He came toward the bed and tossed them to her.

'Get 'em on,' he said.

Maureen picked up the shorts, bent down, and slipped her feet into them.

'My second command is to do precisely what I ask of you. No questions, no delays. If you're a very good girl, you might just survive the night.'

You won't, she thought, nodding submissively as she drew the shorts up her legs.

5

Denise and Kara sat cross-legged on cushions, watching Tom. Denise kept her hold on the jumprope looped around his neck. But he hadn't moved since being struck.

'Aren't you going to eat some?' Kara asked, her voice muffled by a mouthful of popcorn.

Denise raised her right hand.

'You could always wash it.'

'I don't want to leave you alone with him.'

'I could always go with you.'

'We've got to watch him.'

'It's OK if you want to go and wash,' Kara said. 'Just don't take all night. I'll yell my head off if he moves a muscle.'

'Are you sure you don't mind?'

'I think I'd like it if you didn't have any of that stuff on you. It gives me the willies.'

'OK.' Denise slid the jumprope handle across the tiles toward the girl's knee. 'I'll be quick,' she said, stood up and rushed for the kitchen.

At the sink, she squirted liquid soap onto one hand and turned on the hot water. She worked up a lather. She rinsed. Before reaching for the roll of paper towels, she shut the water off. She listened for sounds from the front while she dried her hands.

So far, so good.

She checked her hands. Clean.

She unfastened the button at her neck and spread her shirt open. Then she wadded some fresh towels, dampened them, and rubbed the skin of her belly that had been soiled by Tom's umbrella. The stains came off as easily as if they were nothing more than muddy water. When she was done, the wet ball of paper towels was flat where it had pressed against her. It looked like a rag used to clean off a window sill that hadn't been dusted for a year.

Still, no yell of alarm from Kara.

She dropped the wad onto the counter. With a fresh handful of wet towels, she rubbed her face. The paper came away clean. But it was black when she looked at it after scrubbing her neck. She wondered if she'd gotten it all. She wished there was a mirror. The bathroom had a mirror, but that was too great a distance from Kara.

With some dry towels, she wiped her neck and belly. She fastened the button of her shirt. Then she tore off a yard of towels, moistened them, and left the kitchen.

Hurrying through the living room, she saw Tom still lying motionless near the door, Kara sitting on one of the cushions and reaching into the popcorn bowl beside her.

The girl looked over her shoulder as Denise approached. 'Did you get it all off?'

'Hope so.' On her knees beside Kara, she set down the damp towels and spread the collar of her shirt. 'Did I miss any?'

'I don't think so. There's none on your skin, anyway. Your shirt's dirty. Maybe you could borrow one of Mom's blouses or something. You want me to get one for you?'

'Not right now. I want to do this first.' Picking up the towels, she moved closer to Tom. 'Thought I might as well clean his face off.'

'Do you think that's a good idea? I mean, what if it wakes him up?'

'We've got him tied good.'

'Yeah, but still . . .'

'He won't look nearly as scary once he's cleaned up a little,' Denise said, and gently rubbed the wad of damp paper across his forehead. He didn't stir. In the wake of the towels, his skin looked clean and pale. She wiped his right cheek and jumped as the telephone rang.

'I'll get it,' Kara blurted.

'No, I will.' She lurched to her feet and dropped the towels.

'I bet it's Mom and Dad.'

'Probably. You watch him.' She ran for the kitchen. The phone rang three more times before she got to it. 'Hello?'

'Denise? It's John. Is everything all right there?'

'Yeah, fine.'

'You're both OK?'

'Sure.'

She heard him sigh into the phone. 'Well, look, I don't

know what's going on but people are going nuts outside. It apparently has something to do with the rain. The rain's black out there. We just had three people go crazy and come into the restaurant and kill some people.'

'My god,' Denise muttered.

It isn't just Tom, she thought. She'd felt sure that he wasn't to blame, but knowing that other people had also gone crazy made her feel better about him.

'Are you and Lynn OK?' she asked.

'We're fine. But we're stuck in here. I don't know when we might get out. We'll get home as soon as we can, but it might not be for hours. I just don't know. We have to stay until the rain stops.'

'Well, I'll stay here till you show up.'

'You've got to. You can't go outside. Make sure Kara doesn't go out, either. And whatever you do, don't let anyone into the house.'

'No. I won't.'

'People might try to break in,' he said, and Denise felt a squirmy coldness in her bowels. 'I just don't know. I don't want to upset you. But it's possible. I want you to round up some weapons just in case. There's a hammer in the kitchen in one of the drawers. Kara knows where to find it. And there're plenty of knives. Grab a couple of big ones. The bathroom door has a lock. It isn't much, but it's better than nothing. You can lock yourselves in if there's trouble.'

'OK,' she said, and stiffened as Kara appeared beside her.

'Is it Mom?' the girl whispered.

Denise shook her head, and waved her away.

'One more thing,' John said.

'Dad?' Kara whispered.

Nodding, Denise frowned and jabbed her finger toward the front of the house.

'I know Kara won't be thrilled by this, but I want you to turn off all the lights in the house.'

'Can I talk to him?'

Denise shook her head sharply and kept pointing, but Kara stayed.

'If the house is dark, I think there's less chance of someone trying to break in. They're after people. At least that's what I'm guessing. So they might not waste time with a house they think is deserted.'

'OK. I'll do that as soon as I hang up.'

'Fine, fine. Is Kara there?'

'She sure is. Just a second.' Denise covered the mouthpiece. 'Don't mention Tom,' she warned, then passed the handset to the girl.

'Oh, hi, Dad.' She stared at Denise while she listened. She had a nervous look in her eyes.

Don't tell him!

'Yeah, everything fine. We're having a nice party. We made some popcorn, and . . .' She fell silent. Her lower lip strained down, baring her teeth. 'Oh, gosh.'

I'd better check on Tom, Denise thought.

But she wanted to hear Kara's end of the conversation.

'I will . . . OK . . . I love you, too . . . Bye.' She reached high and hung up the phone. When she turned to Denise, she wore her spooked-by-the-boogeyman look, but there was no hint of amusement. 'What're we going to do?'

'What did your father say?'

'He said I should do whatever you tell me and not give you any argument.'

Denise gently squeezed the girl's shoulder. 'Everything will be OK.'

Her face changed. She looked as if she might be considering something that was very personal and very embarrassing. 'I hate to say this, but I think maybe we oughta hide.'

'Probably a good idea. But your dad mentioned a hammer. Do you know where it is?'

'Oh, sure.'

'Why don't you get it and pick out a good sharp knife for me? I'll be right back.'

Denise strode quickly through the dining room, into the living room.

She halted when she saw the foyer.

Tom was gone.

'Oh my God,' she muttered.

He'd left his shoes behind. Along with Denise's belt, coiled and abandoned on the tile floor beyond the cushions and popcorn bowl and soda glasses. The two jumpropes were missing. So was the fireplace poker.

Breathless, she took a few steps backward, then whirled around and raced into the kitchen. 'He got loose.'

Kara's eyes spread wide and she sucked in a quick breath. In one of her hands was a claw hammer.

Denise rushed up to her and took it. She slipped a butcher knife from the wooden block on the counter.

'What'll we do?' the girl whispered.

'I don't know.'

'I don't think I want to go around hunting for him.'

'Me neither,' Denise said. She hurried to the kitchen entrance and looked out. 'Let's just stay right here. At least he won't be able to take us by surprise.'

6

'Mom! Mom!'

Francine kept wheezing.

Trev slowed the car and looked back. Lisa was shaking her mother by the shoulders so roughly that the woman's head was flopping.

'That isn't doing any good,' Trev said. He faced the front again. 'Just try holding her or something.'

'What's *wrong* with her?'

'Does she have asthma?'

'No.'

'It's probably a panic attack.'

'Mom!'

The woman went on sucking air with high, whiny gasps.

Should've left them in the station, Trev thought. If he'd known the gal was going to lose it . . .

Hell, she has every right.

Trev himself felt as if he were hanging over a cliff by his fingertips and the slightest push might send him plunging down into a chasm of panic.

He kept seeing the four black figures coming toward his car. He kept seeing the severed head slam against the windshield. And the body speared by the axe handle, still bouncing and swaying in front of the hood, kept it all from receding into the past.

He wanted to *lose* the damn thing.

But the guy was stuck fast.

He'd considered jumping out into the rain and just yanking him off the axe. It would've been worth the risk of getting wet or being attacked by other crazies. But he'd decided it was not worth the loss of time.

The crash and detour had stolen four or five minutes from him. From Maureen.

Let the bastard have his ride.

Trev hadn't returned to Guthrie. He'd gone one block over, made another right, and now he was speeding up Flower Avenue, parallel to Guthrie. He'd lost count of the cross-streets. He'd quit slowing down for intersections. He suspected he must be getting close to Third.

We'll either crash and burn, or we'll be there pretty quick.

He wished Francine would stop making those awful gasping noises. He had half a mind to climb back there and shut her up.

The center line ended. He hit the brakes. His car fishtailed into the intersection. When it slid to a stop, he peered out the windows. His headbeams lit the side of a red Porsche. It seemed to be parked at a curb.

If his sense of direction wasn't screwed up, the skid had taken him across the northbound lane of the cross-street. This should be O'Casey's side of the street.

If this is Third.

The restaurant would be near the middle of the block.

He steered away from the Porsche, drove slowly alongside it, passed a Subaru, and came to an alley. He swung into the alley and stopped.

'Wait here.'

'You can't leave us!' Lisa blurted.

Francine kept wheezing.

'You can't get out,' Trev said. He shut off the wipers and headlights, and stuffed the keys into a front pocket of his jeans. 'I'll be back pretty soon. Just keep your eyes open. Give me one of those shotguns.'

Lisa passed an Ithaca over the seat back.

'Keep the other one handy. And your mom's got Patterson's revolver. Get it out of her purse and have it ready.'

'Please!' Lisa cried out.

'I'll hurry. Just take it easy.' He flung open the door. Clutching the forestock of the shotgun, he climbed out into the rain. He punched down the lock button and slammed the door.

He took a couple of steps toward the front of the car. Holding the shotgun by its barrel, he leaned over the hood and pressed butt plate against the dead man's shoulder. He shoved hard, thrusting the body away. The axe handle came out. The guy tumbled backward and dropped out of sight.

Trev saw no point in wasting precious time to wrench the axe out of the hood.

He walked quickly past the rear of the car, stepped out of the alley and headed up the sidewalk to his left. A nightlight illuminated the interior of the shop beside him. The place looked deserted. The sign near the top of its display window identified it as Ace Camera, and Trev's heart quickened.

This was Third, all right. Ace Camera was adjacent to O'Casey's.

Please, he thought. Please, let her be OK.

Just ahead, the overhang of O'Casey's awning blocked out the rain. Beyond the curtain of darkness, light spilled onto the sidewalk. Trev hurried toward it. He thought of Hemingway and the clean, well-lighted place. This was a dry, well-lighted place. A safe refuge from the storm.

Though he ached to get there, he also felt dread.

What if . . .?

Don't think about it.

Then he was under the awning, out of the rain, standing in the light. He gazed through the open space where O'Casey's window used to be. He felt as if his brain were squeezing itself into a cold, dark ball.

Numb, he made his way to the open door.

He entered and scanned the restaurant. Nothing moved.

He felt half blind, trying to see through the eyeholes. With one hand, he pulled off Patterson's hat and dragged the plastic hood over his head. He set them on the nearest table and breathed deeply and realized he was making wheezy noises just like Francine.

He wanted to call out for Maureen and Liam, but he knew he didn't have enough breath for that.

He moved carefully through the room. The hardwood floor was slick with patches of dark water, spilled beer and blood and slabs of pizza. It was littered with window glass, overturned benches and tables, broken steins, wine and soda glasses, pitchers and plates. There were knives and forks on the floor. Glass shakers of salt and pepper, parmesan cheese and red pepper flakes. And bodies. So many bodies.

He tried not to see the kids. He only glanced briefly at the male adults. None was stocky and red-haired. Two of the men, blood mixed with the black of their skin and clothes, must have been assailants from outside.

One of the dead women was also black.

Of the other females, one was obese. She lay on her back with a wedge of pizza still in her mouth and a wedge of glass in her throat. One, facedown, looked tall and slender like Maureen, but had blonde hair. One, curled on her side with her arms around a small boy, was pregnant.

Trev squeezed his eyes shut.

I've gotta get out of here.

But he couldn't leave, not without knowing.

One female, head out of sight under a table, wore a denim skirt that was rucked up around her waist. She had heavy legs. She wasn't Maureen.

That left a slim, long-legged female sprawled on her back across the top of the last table before the order counter. Trev knew that he'd found Maureen. He couldn't see her face or the color of her hair. The way her head hung over the far end of the table, only the underside of her chin was in sight. But he knew.

And he knew that they'd done more than murder her.

Why her?

It was obvious. Because she was so beautiful. Her looks must've turned on one or more of the invaders.

She usually wore corduroy pants or jeas. They were gone. Both her shoes were missing. She wore white socks. A torn rag of red panties dangled from her left ankle. Her thighs were mottled with gray smudges. On the table between her legs was a pizza. Her blood covered it. And blood concealed the true color of her pubic hair. Where her torso wasn't sheathed with gleaming crimson, her skin bore dark streaks and stains. A mouth-sized chunk of flesh was missing from her right breast. Most of her throat had been chewed out.

Saliva kept flooding into Trev's mouth. He knew he was about to vomit. He swallowed quickly, but more saliva poured in.

He took a few more steps, staggering past the side of the table, and saw the woman's face.

She wore a mask of blood. Her wide mouth showed broken teeth. Raw pulp remained where her nose should've been. One eye was gone, and all that remained was a sloppy red pit.

Her hair hung toward the floor in thick, matted ropes of red.

But here and there, blood had missed it.

The hair was blonde.

Blonde, not the auburn of Maureen. Thank God, Trev thought.

He threw up.

When he was done, he looked across the aisle. There were no bodies near the table there. Its surface was clear except for a glass of red wine and a stein of beer. He stepped over to it.

The stein was half full. He picked it up and began to drink. The beer was cool, but not chilly.

Maybe Maureen and Liam escaped, he thought. He knew that the kitchen had a rear door. They could've fled out into the rain. Or maybe they hid.

He was certain he would find their bodies in the kitchen area.

Please, he thought. Don't let them be dead.

He set down the empty stein. He took a deep, trembling breath, then strode to the open side of the counter and entered the kitchen.

He saw no one.

Stepping past the ovens, he felt their heat. Probably pizzas in them right now, as black as the crazies who had committed the slaughter.

He found dials, and turned the ovens off.

He considered opening them and looking in. As he reached for a handle, however, he remembered a book he'd read a few years ago. *Phantoms*. The oven of an abandoned bakery had a severed head or two inside. So he stepped away from the ovens.

'Maureen?' he called. His voice sounded high and strange, and much too loud. But he forced himself to call out Liam's name.

No response.

He found Liam on the floor behind the food preparation island. The Irishman's body was sprawled on top of a woman. Her slim, bare legs were stretched out between Liam's. Her head was out of sight beneath him.

Trev felt his mind shrivel and duarken just as it had done when he stood outside and first looked in at the massacre. A vague, shadowy image came to him of Liam throwing his body on Maureen to protect her.

But there was so much blood on the floor around them.

He tumbled Liam off the woman. The handle of a knife jutted from the middle of his chest.

The crescent blade of a two-handled pizza cutter was embedded deep in the woman's neck.

They'd killed each other.

Her black face was intact.

Not Maureen.

Her skin was stained ebony from head to toe. At first, Trev thought she was naked. Then he realized she wore a string bikini.

A bikini in November?

Changed into it, all the better to enjoy the sudden warm downpour?

Trev's dazed mind pictured a bikini-clad young woman prancing through puddles, dancing around a lamp post, singing in the rain.

Gene Killer.

He heard himself chuckle.

He thought, Fuck, don't lose it. Hang on.

And he hung on while he searched the rest of the kitchen.

7

'What's he doing?' Kara whispered.

'I don't know.'

'Maybe he left.'

Denise supposed that was possible. Since discovering that Tom had gotten loose, she and Kara hadn't seen or heard anything to suggest that he remained in the house. He *might've* gone straight out the front door.

Or he might be waiting for them just beyond the dining room entry.

'Your dad said we could lock ourselves in the bathroom,' Denise whispered.

'We can't get there.'

'We can if Tom left the house.'

'But what if he didn't?'

'I don't like waiting here,' Denise said, watching from the kitchen doorway. 'I know we'd be able to see him coming, but we've got no door at all. He can get right at us. If we could just make it into the bathroom . . .'

Kara shook her head. 'He'd get us.'

'Maybe not. Not if it's dark.'

A look of alarm filled the girl's eyes. 'Oh, I don't think I like that idea. Not even one little bit. He might just sneak right up on us.'

'I know it'd be scary, Kara. But it'd be just like we're invisible. If we don't make a sound, we might be able to creep right past him, and he'd never even know we were there. Do you know where the fuse box is?'

'Sure, but I don't think . . .' She shut her mouth, probably recalling her father's command to obey Denise. 'It's right over there,' she said. She turned from the doorway and nodded toward a closed door just beyond the stove.

'It's not outside, is it?'

'Huh-uh.'

'Where are those flashlights and candles you talked about right after we heard the thunder?'

Kara looked relieved. 'Everywhere. Well, not everywhere. I've got a couple of flashlights in my bedroom and Dad has a big red thing by his bed. It's *real* bright.'

'Is there one here in the kitchen?'

'Yeah, right where I got the hammer from.'

Why hadn't she mentioned that in the first place? Come on, Denise told herself. She's just a kid.

'OK, what about candles?'

'You mean just in the kitchen? Because we've got candles in a lot of . . .'

'Just here in the kitchen.'

'Yeah. Mom keeps some in her junk drawer.'

'Matches?'

Without saying a word, Kara turned around and reached high. She snagged a wicker basket off the top of the refrigerator and pulled it down. The basket was filled with matchbooks. 'Mom collects them. Wherever she goes, she gets matches. They're souvenirs. These are extras, though. She won't mind if we use them.'

Denise switched the butcher knife to her left hand. She reached into the basket. She lifted out a handful of matchbooks and dumped them into the breast pocket of her shirt. She took out a second handful. The right front pocket of her corduroys held the hammer, stuffed in headfirst. With her knife hand, she swept the hanging front of her shirt out of the way. She thrust the second bunch of matchbooks into the pocket on her left.

'That should do it,' she said. Kara set the basket onto the refrigerator. 'OK. I'll keep watch here. You hurry and round up the flashlight and candles.'

While the girl was away, Denise stared through the dining room, into the living room beyond its entryway.

She felt tight and sick inside. Though she hoped Tom had left the house, she couldn't bring herself to believe it. By now, he'd had plenty of time to work his hands free of the rope. He would be waiting for them. Even in a house that was pitch black, their chances of sneaking past him to the bathroom were slim.

Tom, why are you doing this to us?

She was terrified of him. At the same time, she hated the idea of being forced to hurt him. If he attacked, she would have to defend herself and Kara.

What if I kill him?

But I can't let him kill us.

Just make it to the bathroom, she thought, and we'll be safe. He can't get us there, and we won't have to fight him off.

Kara returned with the flashlight and four long, pink candles.

Denise took two of the candles and slid them into a seat pocket of her cords. 'You keep those,' she said. 'Take some matches, too, just in case we get separated.' She removed a couple of matchbooks from her shirt, and gave them to the girl. 'Do you want to keep the flashlight, too?'

Kara nodded.

'OK, turn it on and come with me.' Denise stepped past the stove. She opened the door and entered a small room. It contained a water heater, a mop, a couple of brooms, a dust pan, a yard stick, a rag bag and a collection of neatly folded grocery sacks. On the far side was a door. She pointed at it. 'What's through there?'

'The weather.'

'Not a porch or anything?' she asked.

'No. That stuff'd get us all wet if we went out.'

'Guess we don't want to do that, huh?'

'I don't think so.' Kara pointed the flashlight beam at a gray metal panel on the wall. 'There's the fuse box,' she whispered.

Denise stepped up to it. She clamped the knife between her knees so she could use both hands, slipped her fingertips under the edge of the thin overlapping door, and tugged. The door popped open with a squawk. She yanked the other open. Within the panel were two main switches and rows of clear glass circuit breakers. 'Ready?' she asked.

'I guess so.'

She flicked both switches down. The light from the kitchen vanished. The refrigerator ceased its quiet hum. 'Turn off the flashlight,' she whispered.

Kara shut off its beam.

Reaching down, Denise slipped the knife from between her knees. She pressed the flat of its blade against her belly. She decided to leave the hammer in her pocket so her right hand would remain free.

'OK,' she whispered. 'Now, stay behind me. Maybe hold onto my shirt tail.' She stepped past Kara and felt a small tug as the girl clutched her shirt.

They left the small room and slowly crossed the kitchen. Their sneakers made quiet squeaky sounds on the tile. Denise couldn't see a thing in front of her. She reached out, hand exploring the area ahead. After a few steps, her fingertips brushed the refrigerator. Keeping to its side, she moved straight forward.

The dining room carpet silenced their shoes. Denise heard nothing except rain pounding the roof, her own thudding heart and shaky breathing, and Kara's trembling breaths behind her.

She touche the back of a chair, pictured the layout of the dining room, and turned in the direction of the entryway. She half expected Tom to be waiting just inside the living room. Any second, he would jump them.

He can't see us, she told herself.

But he might be able to hear us.

She had a sudden, strong urge to whirl around and race for the kitchen.

She kept moving forward, sweeping the area ahead with her open hand.

We must be in the living room by now, she thought. So far, so good. Maybe we've already snuck past him. Hell, he might be anywhere. He might be right in front of me. One more step, and I'll touch him.

Denise took that one more step. Felt nothing. Took another. And another.

And gasped as her fingertips prodded something that felt like fabric. She lurched backward, jerking her arm away from it, and Kara bumped against her. A second later came a quiet crashing noise. A pop of glass.

The sounds of a lamp striking the carpeted floor, its bulb bursting.

You hit its shade, she thought. You knocked it over. And Tom knows right where we are.

No more point in sneaking.

She shoved the knife handle between her teeth. She fumbled a matchbook out of her shirt pocket. She flipped it open, tore out a match and struck it. A blinding bright flare, then the fire settled to an orange bloom. In its glow, she saw the lamp on the floor at her feet. She saw the sofa and much of the room beyond it. No Tom.

Thank God.

She spun around. He wasn't rushing at them from the rear.

'Turn on your flashlight,' she whispered. 'We'll make a run for it.'

The flashlight shot its beam against Denise's belly, then swung away. She shook out her match. She pulled off her shirt. Matchbooks spilled from the pocket as she wadded it. She wrapped the sleeves around the clump of fabric to hold the bundle together, knotted the sleeves once, and clamped shirt between her knees. Then she struck another match.

She lit her shirt on fire.

'You're gonna *burn* yourself.'

'Probably,' she muttered.

As flames climbed around the fabric, she grabbed the knot, pulled the shirt from between her knees, and turned away from Kara. She took the knife from her teeth. 'Go first,' she said. 'Run for the John. Don't stop for anything.'

The girl rushed past her.

Knife in her left hand, the blazing wad of shirt in her right, Denise dashed through the living room. She kept her arm high, carrying the fireball overhead like a torch.

Kara, a few strides in front of her, cut to the right at the foyer and dashed for the hallway.

No Tom. So far.

Where is he?

Denise's shoes slapped the tiles. She turned. Raced after Kara. The pale beam of the girl's flashlight skittered over the hallway carpet, the walls and dark doorways. Then the carpet was under Denise. Her torch cast orange light into the gloom ahead, fluttered against the walls and carpet. She felt heat surrounding her hand. So far, she didn't think she was being burnt.

So your hand gets burnt, she thought. You can live with it. Just get to the John.

And a dark shape lunged out through a doorway and blocked the hall and whipped the fireplace poker at Kara's face. The girl ducked under it. Her head rammed Tom in the belly. Instead of knocking him down, the blow sent Kara stumbling backward. She landed on her rump. Denise leaped over the girl. Tom swung the poker. Its brass bar whapped against her side. She shoved the blazing shirt at his face.

Dropping the poker, he lurched to the side and slammed a wall as he flung up both arms to shield his face. Denise thrust the torch against his arms. She knew his midsection was unprotected, knew she could drive the knife straight into him with her left hand. But she refused.

'KARA!' she shouted. 'GO! GO!'

The flames flapped against her face, curled hot around her fist and forearm. But she didn't stab Tom. She just kept jamming the fireball against his crossed arms.

Kara rushed by.

Made it into the bathroom.

Denise pumped her knee into Tom's groin. His breath exploded out. He spasmed against the wall. Denise lurched away from him, dashed to the bathroom, hurled the flaming remains of her shirt into the sink, swung around and drove her shoulder against the door, slamming it shut. Her thumb jabbed the lock button down.

She slumped back against the door. As she gasped, coughing on the smoky air, Kara turned on a faucet. Water splashed down. The burning shirt hissed. Its glow faded. In seconds, the bathroom was dark except for the beam of the flashlight.

Denise's right hand and forearm felt as if they were still burning. She stepped to the sink, and set down her knife, and splashed cool water against her skin.

'Are you hurt bad?' Kara whispered.

'I don't think so. How about you?'

'I'm OK. Did you stab him?'

'No.'

'How'd you get away?'

'Kneed him in the nuts.'

'Huh?'

'Never mind. Why don't you light a couple of the . . .' Densie jumped as something crashed against the door. From the sound, she guessed Tom must've struck it with the poker. She pulled her arm out from under the water, hurried to the door, and pressed her back against it.

The next blow jolted her.

That was a kick, she thought.

While she braced the door, Kara lit a candle, dripped

some paraffin onto the side of the sink, then stood the candle upright in the small puddle.

Tom struck the door again.

Kara said, 'Somebody better keep that gizmo in.' She stepped up close to Denise and clutched the doorknob. Her small thumb pushed against the lock button. 'It can get popped out real easy,' she whispered. 'It doesn't even take a key.'

She held the button in.

Denise curled a hand around the back of the girl's head. As she caressed the soft hair, Kara leaned forward, slumped a little against her, and rested a cheek against her chest.

8

'What are they *doing* up there?' Cyndi said. She studied the kitchen ceiling as if it might give her a clue.

'I don't want to know,' Sheila said.

'Maybe I oughta go up and check on 'em,' Doug offered.

Cyndi glowered at him. 'Oh, you'd like that.'

Lou sipped his vodka and tonic, then squatted down and peered through the glass of the oven's door. The frozen, fried chicken pieces spread out on the cookie sheet looked as if they might be done pretty soon. The crust, getting darker, was shiny with juice or oil that bubbled. He could hear faint sounds of sizzling and crackling.

The sounds reminded him of last night. Chidi tied to the goalpost, wrapped in flame. That kid's skin had sizzled and crackled.

The memory gave Lou a heavy, sick feeling.

I didn't do it, he told himself. I didn't do any of it.

He knew that wasn't quite true. He hadn't done the *bad* stuff, though. He hadn't cut on the kid or burnt him. He hadn't killed him.

All I did, he told himself, was help snatch the bastard and strip him and tie him up. I trashed him just a little, maybe, but nothing serious. Nothing that even would've put him in the hospital for godsake.

Buddy never should've done that stuff.

Now I'm in just as much trouble as him, and I didn't do a damn thing. Lisa's gonna spill the beans on us. We'll be fucked.

We oughta be shutting up Lisa, not having a goddamn party.

And Buddy's upstairs with the pizza gal as if he doesn't have a worry in the world.

The whole thing's crazy.

And it's storming black shit outside and the crazy bitch tried to *kill* Buddy, and we're all acting like nothing's wrong. The whole damn world's gone nuts.

'How's the chicken doing?' Sheila asked. She crouched beside Lou and looked into the oven. 'A while longer, huh? I like it good and crispy.'

You should've seen Chidi. He was good and crispy.

Sheila leaned against him. She caressed his back. He felt her breast pressing his upper arm. Breath tickling his car, she whispered, 'Do you think we can get out of here?'

'Not while it's raining,' Lou whispered. 'Or whatever it's doing out there.'

She kissed his ear. Lou knew she was doing this so Doug and Cyndi would think they were making out, whispering endearments or something. 'I don't like this. We oughta get away. I just know Buddy's raping that woman.'

'Probably.' The feel of Sheila and images of Buddy putting it to the pizza gal started to make Lou horny. He slipped a hand under the back of Sheila's sweatshirt. Normally, she wouldn't have allowed that with people around. But she didn't protest. Her skin was warm and smooth. 'It's not like we're accomplices or anything,' he whispered. 'We're down here, you know? He's up there. They might just be talking.'

'Oh, sure.'

'Besides, she tried to knock his head off.'

'That's no excuse to . . . violate her.'

'I know,' Lou whispered. He moved his hand over the cross-strap of Sheila's bra. He knew she would go ape if he tried to unhook it.

The lucky son-of-a-bitch, Buddy. Up there with the pizza gal. Bet he got the bra off *her*. Everything else, too. The bitch was in no position to argue.

Bet he violated her but good.

'Maybe Buddy's got some raincoats and umbrellas around,' Sheila whispered. 'If we covered up really good . . .'

'It's too risky.' Then Lou came up with an idea that he knew should please her. 'Besides, there's no telling what Buddy might do to the gal.'

'That's what scares me. I don't want to be around . . .'

'If we stay, we might be able to keep him in line, you know? Stop him from . . .'

'Nobody stopped him upstairs.'

You didn't, either, Lou thought. But he didn't want to say anything that might turn Sheila against him. He rubbed her shoulder, sliding the bra strap out of his way.

'I won't let Buddy do anything *really* bad,' he said.

'Oh, raping someone isn't *really* bad? What do you call *really* bad?'

'I don't know. Like if he wants to get rid of her or something.'

'That's what I thought you meant. 'Cause I'm thinking the same thing. How's he planning to keep her from going to the cops about this if he doesn't . . . like waste her?'

'Well, she *is* the one who started it.'

'I'm not gonna be here for something like that.'

'We won't let it happen.'

'Yeah, sure.'

'I mean it. I'll stop him.'

'Will you?'

'Damn right.' Just like I stopped him last night, Lou thought. 'I'm not gonna let him kill someone in front of us.'

'How's the chick-chick coming?' Doug asked, stepping up behind them.

'A few more minutes,' Sheila said. She patted Lou's back, then stood up. Lou stood up, too, keeping his hand on her shoulder.

'I wish Buddy'd get down here,' Cyndi said.

'He's probably already eaten, anyway.'

'Very funny. Maybe one of us *should* go up and . . .'

'Help him,' Doug said.

'You're really asking for it.'

'Think I'll get it?'

'Not . . .'

'Hi ho, everyone,' Buddy said, stepping into the kitchen with the pizza gal beside him. 'What's cooking?'

'We found some chicken in the freezer,' Cyndi told him. 'It's about ready.'

'Well, we're just in time.' He smiled at the pizza gal and patted her rump. 'Friends, this is Maureen.'

Lou's hand dropped out from under Sheila's sweatshirt.

Incredible, he thought.

'Turned out to be a white girl,' Buddy said.

'Holy shit,' Doug muttered.

Holy shit is right, Lou thought. She's a fucking knockout.

She was taller than Buddy, but slender. Even from across the kitchen, Lou could see the brilliant emerald of her eyes. Her hair must've been blow-dried. It seemed to float around her face, a rich curtain of brown and rust and gold. Lou couldn't recall ever seeing such a beautiful face. Not in the flesh, at least. Maybe on movie screens, in magazines, never in the same room with him.

She wore a white T-shirt. One of Buddy's undershirts? It was much too large for her. It hung down so low that it covered all but the bottom inch of her red gym shorts. It seemed to drape from her shoulders, hardly touching her body anywhere except her breasts. There, the shirt was pushed outward, smooth over the soft mounds, peaked at the very front by the thrust of her nipples. Her skin showed through the thin fabric. Pink except for the darker disks at the tips of her breasts.

Like the T-shirt, the shorts were far too big. They looked as if they might fall down. Their legs gaped around her slim thighs, so loose and baggy Lou figured there was probably room to stick your head inside either one of them.

He thought about doing just that.

Buddy, you lucky bastard.

Buddy rubbed her rump. She stood rigid, letting him. Her lips were pressed tightly together, her fabulous green eyes fixed on the floor. 'Maureen has agreed to be our servant for this evening. I'm her master, of course, but you're the guests and she will be acting accordingly.'

'What a load,' Cyndi said.

Doug stepped toward Maureen and offered his hand. 'I'm Doug. Pleased to make your acquaintance.'

She smiled at him, the corners of her mouth trembling slightly, and held out her hand. Doug gripped it. With a silly grin, he hopped up and down, pumping her arm.

'Grow up,' Cyndi muttered.

'My friend, Cyndi, doesn't find me amusing.'

'Oh, that's right. Just great. Tell her all our names, why don't you.'

'It doesn't matter if I know your names,' Maureen said, meeting Cyndi's eyes. 'I'm not about to tell on anyone. I assaulted Buddy. Now, I'm paying for it. He's my master and I'm his slave. It's fair. Besides, the way I see it, Buddy may have saved my life.'

Buddy looked surprised and pleased. 'Really?' he asked. 'How's that?'

'This oughta be a good one,' Cyndi said.

'It's simple,' Maureen said, facing Buddy. 'You cleaned me. You made me all right again.'

'I bet he made you, all right,' Doug said.

'Shut up,' Buddy told him.

'Could I have a drink?' Maureen asked.

'Sure,' Buddy said. 'Why not.'

'I'll get you one,' Lou told her, and caught Sheila giving him a sour look. 'What would you like? How about a vodka and tonic?'

'That would be nice. Thank you.'

While Lou hurried to prepare the drink for Maureen, Cyndi complained, 'I thought she was supposed to be *our* servant.'

'Dry up,' Doug said.

'Oh, real nice. Looks to me like *she's* all of a sudden ruling the fucking roost around here.'

'I only asked for a drink,' Maureen said, her voice soft and apologetic.

'Yeah, well, screw you.'

'That's already been done,' Doug said.

Lou, at the counter, looked over his shoulder and saw a blush spread over the young woman's face. 'That wasn't necessary, Doug,' she said. 'I'd like to be your friend. I know that I sort of crashed the party, and I'm sorry about that. I really had no choice in the matter. But since I'm here, I'd like to be friends with all of you.'

'You can be my friend any old time,' Doug told her.

'She's pulling your chain, you dork.'

'No, I'm not,' Maureen said.

'Fuck you.'

'I love this.' Doug grinned at Buddy. 'They're fighting over me.'

'Wouldn't be any match,' Buddy said. 'Maureen would clean her clock.'

'Up yours,' Cyndi blurted.

Buddy's face lost its smile. 'Why don't we find out?'

'Why don't we eat?' Sheila suggested. Turning around quickly, she pulled open the oven door.

9

Denise's thigh muscles shuddered from the effort of bracing the door with her back. She had taken over the job of holding the lock button down, though Tom hadn't attempted, so far, to pop it open from the other side. He seemed content with crashing against the door.

Each time he struck it, the door jolted Denise.

She knew that only her body prevented it from ripping out the latch and flying open.

Sweat streamed down her face, stinging her eyes, dripping off her nose and chin. It rolled down her chest and sides, tickling her, making her itch. It made the wood slick against her back. The knife was so slippery in her right hand that she feared she might drop it. The sweat seemed even more irritating than the soreness of her back or the tight hot throb of her spasming leg muscles.

'Get a towel and wipe me,' she gasped.

Kara whipped a towel down from a bar near the tub, hurried over to her, and started to mop her face. 'What're we going to do?' the girl whispered.

'I don't know.' She winced into the soft towel as the door hit her back. 'I can't do this much longer.'

'What about the window?' Kara asked.

'Even if we get out in time, we'd be in the rain. It'd make us like him.'

Kara was silent for a moment as she rubbed the towel over Denise's shoulders and chest. 'What if we *pretend* to go out?'

'I don't . . .' Another blow. 'TOM! QUIT IT! THIS IS DENISE. YOU DON'T WANT TO HURT ME!'

Even as she yelled, the hammer was tugged from her front pocket and Kara hurried past the bathtub toward the louvered window. She boosted herself onto the counter. With quick blows of the hammer, she smashed the slats. Glass exploded outward, bounced off the screen and clattered down on the counter at her knees.

Hissing, spattering sounds of the rain came in.

Tom hit the door again. Denise gritted her teeth.

Kara struck the frame of the screen with her hammer. Again and again until the screen dropped into the night.

She jumped down from the counter. At the sink, she grabbed the flashlight. She raced with it to the window, turned it on, and rested it on the sill so its beam was aimed at the door. Back at the sink, she pointed toward the bathtub. Then she puffed out her candle.

Tom hit the door again, pounding agony through Denise.

Kara climbed into the tub. It had sliding shower doors of clear glass. In the dim glow from the flashlight, Denise saw her crouch down at the back of the tub and beckon to her with the hammer.

It'll never work, Denise thought.

Neat idea, but it'll never work.

She let the door ram her one more time, then thrust herself away from it and raced for the tub. She stepped over the side. She brought her other leg in. She eased the shower door shut, stepped backward, and raised the knife from her side. She pressed its pommel hard against her belly, blade straight out.

Fall for it, Tom. Please. I don't want to stab you.

She flinched when the bathroom door burst open.

Tom lurched into view, stumbling. He almost fell, but got his balance and hurried alongside the tub. He still had the fireplace poker. He went straight for the window, leaned over the counter, reached to the sill and picked up the flashlight.

Then he turned away from the window.

He played the beam across the shower doors.

Denise squinted when its glare jabbed her eyes.

'I *seeeee* youuuu,' he said in a mad, cheery voice.

He strode toward the tub. Toward Kara's end of the tub. He shined his light down at the crouched girl.

'Leave us alone!' Kara blurted.

'Oh, I don't think so.' The light went out.

'OVER HERE!' Denise shouted. She threw the shower door wide, putting a double thickness between Tom and the girl, and braced it there with her knife hand.

She heard a quick *whiss*. A clink. The knife jerked and dropped from her hand. A blind, lucky swing of the poker must've struck its blade. Denise's fingers tingled, but the poker had missed her hand.

Gazing into the blackness straight ahead, she stepped

backward. Some kind of hose brushed against her left arm. As her back met the cool tile wall behind the tub, she reached up.

A clank, and the shower doors shook. He must've whipped his poker across the opening and hit the metal frames.

Denise found the shower nozzle. One of those removeable things with a handle. She tugged it from its mount, pulled it in close to her face.

She heard Tom's harsh breathing.

It came from straight ahead.

She didn't hear the poker swing, but felt a quick fiery streak across her belly.

Suddenly, a harsh rolling rumble. The shower doors. Someone thrusting them shut in front of her? For an instant, Denise thought that Tom must've gone back to the other end of the tub to get Kara. Then he grunted. The rushing doors must've caught him.

Kara, back in action.

Denise dropped to a squat, fumbled in the dark as the doors clamored. She pictured Kara at the other end, trying to keep them shut, Tom in front of her, shoving at them.

She found a faucet. She turned it on all the way. Water rushed from the faucet, pounded the bottom of the tub, splashed her. Cool, but getting warmer.

She hoped the Foxworth's kept their water heater turned up high – hot enough to scald.

Fingering the top of the spout, she found the shower knob and lifted it.

Water stopped thudding into the tub. The nozzle throbbed in her hand. She aimed it upward where Tom's face should be. Heard a few sputters, a *shhhhhhh* as the hot water shot out. Then hard drumming. The spray was hitting the shower door, not Tom. Hitting it and flying back at her and it was hot. Not scalding, maybe. But damn hot.

Whimpering with pain, she squeezed her eyes shut and turned her face away and shoved herself up to get her bare skin away from the spray.

The shower doors skidded. Kara yelped. Tom squealed. Something clattered against the floor of the tub, slid against Denise's shoes. The poker?

'You bitch!' Tom cried out.

She aimed at the sound of his voice.

Heard him splash into the tub. Heard breathless, whiny noises from him. Her hand was knocked aside. A fist struck her just below the left breast. Hooking an arm around Tom, she squeezed him hard against her. With her other hand, she clubbed his head with the plastic nozzle.

As he clutched her neck, she tried to knee him in the groin. Hit something that made him grunt – probably just his thigh – and he threw her sideways by the neck. Her feet slipped out from under her. She fell, keeping hold of the nozzle, felt a rough tug when it reached the end of its hose, heard a crack of breaking plastic.

Her back slammed against the tub but something cushioned her head as it snapped down. Kara?

Tom came down on top of her, mashing out her breath, squeezing her throat. She pounded the nozzle against the side of his head. Water no longer sprayed from it. But water was spouting down, anyway, probably from the shower arm. Not hitting Denise. Shooting against Tom. And starting to fill the tub, burning against her buttocks and back.

Dropping the nozzle, she cupped water in both hands and flung it at his face. He cried out. His stranglehold loosened. She grabbed his thumbs and tore them away from her throat. His hands plunged into the water, splashing it up against her face and shoulders, and she yelped as the droplets stung her.

'Denny?'

Tom's voice. Alarmed.

'Oh my God, Denny, what am I *doing* to you?'

'Tom?'

'God, I'm sorry. I'm so sorry.' His cheek pressed the side of her face.

10

The car's dome light came on when Trev opened the door. Francine and Lisa were still in the backseat. Francine looked as if she'd recovered from her panic. But her eyes were wide and frightened. So were Lisa's.

Lisa had Patterson's revolver pointing at his face.

'Everything OK?' he asked.

Neither of his passengers answered. Lisa said, 'Are *you* OK?'

'I didn't get wet,' he muttered, then slid his shotgun across the seat, climbed in and shut the door.

'Did you find your friend?' Lisa asked.

'No. Thank God,' he muttered. 'It was a massacre in there. Her father's dead.'

'What'll we do now?'

Trev shook his head. He wanted to sit here and do nothing at all. What *is* there to do?

Maureen had been staying at Liam's house. He'd called there from O'Casey's, and the phone had gone unanswered. She was either out somewhere, or home but unable to pick up the phone. He'd pictured her dead, sprawled out, stripped and bloody, savaged like the woman he'd found on the table top.

'I'll tell you what we'll do,' Francine said. 'We'll drive the fuck out of here. That's what we should've done in the first place, drive till we get out of this fucking rain and madness.'

'I can't leave without Maureen.'

'The hell you can't.'

The plastic crinkled and pressed against the nape of his neck. Through the thin layer of garbage bag, he felt a ring the size of a quarter.

The muzzle of a shotgun.

'Mom, for godsake!'

The muzzle jabbed him. 'Let's get moving.'

Trev didn't move a muscle.

'Now!'

'Maybe you should,' Lisa said, a pleading sound in her voice.

'I'll *shoot* you! Nobody'll even blame me. They'll think the wet people did it.'

'Lisa will know who did it,' Trev said. Though he realized that the woman was desperate enough to pull the trigger, he felt no fear. He just felt weary, a little numb. 'Besides, if you fire that thing, you'll probably blow out the windshield. How do you feel about letting the rain come in?'

'How do you feel about being dead?'

'Mom!'

'I'm doing this for you, honey. We've gotta get out of this town.'

'You can't kill Trev. That'd be murder. You'd be just as bad as the wet people. Worse, even. You know? I don't think they have any choice. I think the rain *makes* them do it. But you'd be doing it because you want to. That's a lot worse.'

'I don't want to. Shit!'

'Well, put it down.'

'No.'

Trev heard the *snick-clack* of a cocking revolver.

'If you shoot him, I'll shoot you.'

'Lisa!'

'I mean it! They murdered Maxwell last night, and it was all my fault. I'm not gonna sit here and let you murder a man right in front of me. I don't care if you *are* my mother. You just can't do it. Put the gun down!'

Trev felt the muzzle ease away from his neck.

'OK? *OK?* Are you happy now?'

Lisa didn't say anything.

After a while, Francine said, 'Are we just going to sit here?'

'How about if I take you home?' Trev suggested.

'Fine. Just fine.'

'Is there a way in that's sheltered?'

'The carport's covered,' Lisa said. 'The kitchen door's right there.'

'OK. Let's do it.'

He started the car, put on its wipers and headlights, and backed slowly out of the alley. He glimpsed the black heap of the axeman before turning his eyes to the rearview mirror.

'Will you stay with us?' Lisa asked.

'We'll see,' he said. He had no intention of staying with them.

'That means no,' Francine said.

'It means we'll see. Where do you live?'

'4823 Maple.'

'OK.' He swung out onto Third Street, started forward. Easing down on the gas, he suddenly realized that the visibility had improved. Though the rain still came down, it no longer splashed a black sheet against the windshield, no longer deadened his headlights so much or blanketed the street lights. Trev could actually see cars parked along both sides of the road, and the glow of shop windows. He felt a swelling of hope. But it dwindled when he noticed the dim shapes of people in the rain.

The dead and the living.

'Oh, my God,' Lisa muttered.

Francine sucked in a quick breath.

It was better when we couldn't see, Trev thought. He wished the rain would come down in a heavy shower like before and hide all this.

He glimpsed several bodies. Some were sprawled in the street, others on the sidewalk. He saw a man draped out the window of a pickup truck, torso split open and ropes of entrails hanging to the pavement. He saw a German Shepherd tugging at the leg of a child, trying to drag the small body over a curb. He swerved to miss the carcass of a woman in the middle of the road – a twisted jumble of broken limbs, head mashed flat. She looked as if she'd been run over many times.

The sights of the dead sickened Trev. The sights of the living terrified him.

Alone or in small groups, some skulked through the darkness like phantoms searching for prey. Others pranced around like revelers. Others raced in mad pursuit of fleeing victims. Many had discarded their clothing.

He saw a naked woman sprawled on the pavement, squirming and rubbing herself as if the rain had triggered a fit of erotic ecstasy. He saw a couple rutting on the hood of a car. The man was on top, and Trev couldn't be sure whether the woman jerking beneath him was alive or dead. At the corner, he spotted two women and a man hunched over a corpse, tearing at its clothes and flesh.

Those people, distracted from their chore, turned their heads and peered toward Trev's car. A chill prickled the back of his neck. He shoved down hard on the gas pedal.

In the back seat, Francine was wheezing again.

No sounds at all came from Lisa.

'At least we can see where we're going,' Trev muttered.

He wondered if Maureen was among those he'd seen, demented or dead.

Maybe she's safe, he told himself.

I'll drop these two off and drive to her house. Maybe she's there, safe and sound, and I can stay with her and protect her.

'What could do this to people?' Lisa asked, her voice high and shaking.

'I wish I knew. Poison in the rain? Chemicals? Germs? I've got no idea. Hell, maybe God's finally decided he's had enough crap from humanity . . .'

'God wouldn't do this,' Lisa said.

'No, you're probably right. Maybe it's the Devil.'

A teenaged kid darted into view from behind a parked van. He sped toward Trev's car on a skateboard, waving a machete overhead. He wore nothing but undershorts and a ballcap.

Trev swerved.

Not to avoid this one, to hit him.

The kid flipped high as the bumper knocked out his legs. He lost his machete. His ballcap spun away. He missed the axe handle. He bounced on the hood and tumbled. His knee thumped the windshield. Then he flew upward out of sight. Trev heard some rough bumps on the roof before the kid toppled off.

'*I can't stand it!*' Francine blurted.

And Lisa said, 'Maybe it's Maxwell's grandpa.'

'What?' Trev gasped.

'He's some kind of a witch doctor, Maybe this is his revenge, or something.'

Ridiculous, Trev thought.

But what mad, poetic justice if it were true. White boys murder a black kid. Next thing you know, down comes the rain making *everyone* black and kill-crazy. Revenge in spades.

But black magic? Come on, Trev.

'What do you know about him?'

'Just that Maxwell . . . he wouldn't ever let me meet his family. He said they wouldn't like him going out with someone like me . . . you know, someone white. But especially his grandfather. He said the old man might do something weird if he ever found out. Like put a hex on me. I told Max I wasn't afraid of any hexes, but he said I *oughta* be. He said his grandpa was really into that stuff, and it worked. He even told me some stories about how his grandpa got back at enemies, and stuff. How he'd cripple them up, or make them go crazy, or even die. Like there was a doctor back on the island they came from, and he gave Max's grandmother some drug she was allergic to and she died. So Max's grandpa put a spell on him, and the doctor went crazy and carved up his whole family, his wife and kids and everything, and when they found him he was still alive but he'd cut off both his own feet and his left hand, and even his you-know-what . . . his dick. And he'd poked out both his eyes.'

'Oh, wonderful,' Francine said, her voice high and shaky.

'I mean, Max really *believed* his grandpa made the doctor do all that. And he was afraid the guy might hurt me if he found out we were going together. It kind of scared me, you know?'

'So you never met the grandfather?' Trev asked.

'I never met anyone in his family. Except his sister. She's in the tenth grade. She promised not to tell on us.'

'Did Max ever mention black rain?'

'No. Huh-uh. I would've caught on right away, if he ever had. It was just, you know, when you said that about the Devil. I never even thought about Max's grandpa till you said that. It just sort of clicked, you know? That maybe this is all some kind of a curse and maybe the old guy's *making* it happen.'

'That's insane,' Francine said.

'What isn't?' Trev muttered.

'You don't honestly think . . .'

'It makes as much sense as anything else,' he said. 'It makes a hell of a *lot* of sense. The motive, anyway. I'm not saying a guy could actually *do* this. But if he could, it'd be a damn nifty way to get back at the town he blames for murdering his grandson.'

'Oh, for godsake.'

'I know it sounds weird, Mom. But what if he *is* doing it? You know? And what if there's a way to make him stop? Maybe the rain'll end.'

'Did the grandfather live with the family?' Trev asked.

'Yeah. He had his own room in their house.'

Trev knew that he'd seen the address on reports. Fairmont Avenue, but he couldn't recall the house number.

Near the north end of town, and he was heading south.

'Do you know the address?' he asked.

'Huh-uh.'

Trev made a U-turn.

'Our house is *that* way,' Francine protested.

'First things first,' Trev said. His headbeams swept past the tattered body of a man bound to a lamp post. Like Chidi tied to the goalpost standard. This guy was black, but hadn't been born that way. And hadn't been burnt. He had a gaping pit below his ribcage.

'You can't do this!'

'Mom!'

'Damn it! It's a waste of time, and you'll get us all killed.'

'Maybe I can end the whole mess.'

It might be too late for Maureen, he thought.

But if Chidi's grandfather was responsible, and if Trev could get to the house, there was a chance he could put a stop to the downpour and save lives.

'You can't seriously believe some damn *witch doctor's* behind all this.'

'Of course I don't,' Trev said. 'But I'm going to proceed as if I do. Lisa, do you know if they're listed in the phone directory?'

'Yeah, they are.'

'I'll have to make one more stop, then we'll head straight out to Chidi's place and see what the bastard's up to.'

11

Soon after John joined the others in the booth, Peggy brought plates of top sirloin, baked potato and green beans. She explained that the menu had been dispensed with, and the meal was complementary.

Lynn and Carol asked for fresh margaritas.

John and Steve exchanged glances. 'I'm fine,' John told the waitress. He was halfway through his second Mai Tai. A third would be nice, but it would also be enough to impair his faculties.

'I'll pass on another one, too,' Steve said. After Peggy left, he added, 'Hate to get busted for DWI on the way home.'

Lynn laughed. 'I'd say that's the least of your worries.'

'What *about* going home?' Carol asked.

'Too dangerous,' Steve said, and started cutting into his meat.

'If I could think of any way to get home,' John said, 'we wouldn't be here. I'd give anything to be with Kara right now. But I just don't see how it can be done. Maybe I'd be able to handle whoever's outside, I don't know. I don't know how many there are, or how they might be armed. But the problem's the rain. If I get wet, it's all over. I'd be just like them. Hell, I might just turn around and come in to nail *you* people.'

'We just have to wait for the rain to stop,' Steve said.

'Eat, drink and be merry,' Carol muttered. She tongued some salt off the rim of her glass. 'I hope Peggy hurries with those drinks. If I'm gonna die, I want to be good and sloshed.'

'Nobody's going to die,' Lynn told her.

'Tell that to those poor slobs in the freezer. I'm sure the news would cheer them up considerably.'

'We're all going to be fine,' Lynn persisted. John reached around her back and caressed her shoulder.

You tell them, honey.

'Before we know it,' she said, 'the rain'll let up and we'll all go on home and this'll be just like a bad dream. Isn't that right, honey?'

'Yep.'

'Bullshit,' Carol said.

'Eat your food,' Steve told her.

'We're perfectly safe in here,' Lynn said. 'Look how many of us there are. And we've got plenty of sharp cutlery if push comes to shove.' She twirled her serrated knife in front of her eyes.

'A lot of good steak knives'll be against a horde of raving lunatics.'

'What horde?' Lynn said. 'There's no point in blowing things out of proportion. One person's knocking on the door. For all we know, nobody else is out there.'

'Maybe half the town's out there,' Carol said.

'We could open the door and see,' Steve suggested.

'Oh, great. Why don't you just go and do that.'

'As long as they're making no serious effort to break in,' John said, 'it really doesn't matter a whole lot. We're safe right now. I think we should go ahead and eat, and try not to worry about it.'

'Yeah, sure.' She gave him a sullen look, then lowered her head and began to cut her meat.

Peggy showed up with the drinks.

'All quiet on the western front?' John asked her.

'Some nut's still pounding on the front door. Other than that, not much is going on. A lot of folks are getting pretty polluted. And there's a bunch in the bar I think are getting ready to abandon ship.'

'Don't they know what'll happen to them?' Steve asked.

'They just want to go home.' Peggy shrugged, then carried her tray to the next booth and set a martini in front of Chester Benton's widow. Cassy, still sitting with her, met John's gaze and smiled slightly.

He returned the smile, then looked down at his plate. Don't think about her, he told himself, and pictured her sprawled on the floor, the doctor cutting her laces, spreading her bodice.

Knock it off!

'What about those people in the bar?' Steve asked.

John took a bite of beef. 'What about them?'

'Maybe we ought to see what they're up to.'

'That's not a bad idea,' Carol said. 'What if they've figured out how to get out of here?'

'It's worth a check,' Steve said.

'Should probably try to talk them out of it,' John muttered. He didn't want to get involved. Let them do what they want, he thought. If they're fools enough to go outside . . . It's not my job to save people from their own stupidity. But they get wet, and they might be *our* problem.

He remembered the guy in the men's room. Andy. After calling home, he'd noticed Andy and the girl, Tina, holding hands across their small table in the cocktail lounge. They'd looked like a couple of kids, helpless and terrified.

What are their chances if they go outside?

He took one more bite, then looked up at Steve. 'I think I'd better go on over there and . . .'

The window beside the next table exploded. Cassy twisted away from the flying glass, squeezing her eyes shut and hurling up an arm to shield her face. The Benton woman, closer to the window, squealed and lurched sideways against her. John realized she must've looked toward the source of the sudden noise. Her face was a mask of raw rips, studded with shards. A triangle of glass jutted from her left eye.

Lynn grabbed John's sleeve and yelled 'Don't!' as he lunged from the booth and a fat bald man, shiny black, leaned through the broken window and caved in the woman's forehead with a tire iron. John pulled free. He didn't bother to dodge Steve, who was leaning out and starting to rise. He shouldered him out of the way, rushed past the empty bench and table, clutched Cassy's arm and tugged her from the booth. She came up brushing against him, gasping warm breath against his face.

The man in the window grabbed a handful of Mrs Benton's hair and dragged her limp body toward him.

At least he's not coming in, John thought.

Taking her. Taking her out with him.

John swung Cassy away. He sprang onto the cushioned bench. It was soft and springy under his shoes. He took only one step before the man hurled the tire iron at him, sidearm. He shot up a hand to block it. The bar struck his wrist. Instead of bouncing away, it took a quick flip around his wrist and smashed him across the brow.

A strobe flashed behind his eyes.

He fought to stay on his feet.

Gotta stop him!

It didn't matter that the woman was probably dead. Didn't matter much, anyway. Dead or not, John didn't want the bastard to take her.

He brought up his knife hand. The knife seemed to be missing. He stared at his empty hand. He was sure he'd had the knife a second ago.

He looked up.

He couldn't see much. The lights were just too faint. But he could see enough to realize the guy was using both hands, now. The woman's head was clamped between them, and he was pulling her toward the window.

John knew he was about to go down.

He teetered back ward.

NO!

He waved his arm, struggling against gravity and unconsciousness, and managed to correct the direction of his fall.

He tumbled forward.

Onto the moving body. It dropped, trapped against the seat and wall. Some glass in the woman's face cut John's cheek.

He wrapped his arms around her.

You won't get her now!

He was vaguely aware of commotion around him. There were shouts. The edge of the table shook against his side. More sounds of breaking glass. Then people were pulling at his legs. He held onto the woman. Together, they slid over the cushion. Her legs went out from under him. His knees followed, jabbing into them, and he murmured, 'Sorry', and tried to get off her.

He released her. Then he was carried backward and lowered to the floor.

Someone bending over him. Lynn.

'Oh, you idiot. You fool.'

'I didn't . . . let 'im get her.'

'No, you didn't. God, John.'

He tried to sit up, but she pushed him down, pinned his shoulders to the floor. 'Just stay put, honey.'

Then Cassy was on her knees beside him, patting his face with a cloth napkin.

'Are you OK?'

'He took an awful knock on the head,' Lynn said.

Lynn stopped holding him down. She stroked his hair while Cassy dabbed at the cuts.

'I keep some bandages in my purse,' Lynn said. 'Stay with him?'

'Sure.'

When she was gone, Cassy said, 'You keep coming to my rescue.'

'Glad to help,' he said. He noticed the way the blazer drooped, closed only by its two low buttons. He glimpsed her shadowy right breast, then forced his eyes away from it and watched the way her short, glossy bangs swayed above his face.

'Come away from there!' Carol snapped.

'*Jesus!*'

'Steve!'

'Where'd they all *come* from?'

'How many?' asked a voice John didn't recognize.

'I don't know. A bunch.'

'Let's block up that window.'

12

Trev parked in the alley near O'Casey's. His headbeams lit the black heap of the axeman. He shut them off, killed the engine and stuffed the keys into his jeans.

'Hurry, OK?' Lisa said.

'I'll be as fast as I can.' He grabbed the shotgun and climbed out. The rain came down on him. More of a soft shower than a downpour.

Making his way toward the street, he avoided puddles. Though he hadn't checked the bottoms of his feet, he was sure that his earlier walking must've worn holes in the plastic under his shoes. The thick rubber soles of his sneakers should keep his feet dry so long as he didn't step in anything much deeper than half an inch.

I keep wandering around in this stuff, he thought, and I'm bound to get wet.

At the front of the alley, he checked both ways. A body on the sidewalk to the right, several yards away. At the corner, someone darted by and vanished behind a parked car. But that was a good distance away. Trev didn't think he'd been seen.

He turned to the left. The sidewalk ahead looked clear. He walked quickly toward O'Casey's.

He knew what he would find in there. He didn't want to see those bodies again. Probably every shop on Third Street had a telephone directory. He could've gone into any one of them to look up Chidi's address. But he *didn't* know what he would find in other places. He didn't want surprises.

Also, the alley seemed like a good place to leave the car. The women had been safe there, last time.

He stepped under O'Casey's awning and paused, glad to be out of the rain. He took deep breaths. Though he hadn't exerted himself, he felt winded.

Something trickled down the back of his neck.

A chill crawled up his spine.

Oh, my God!

Another droplet ran down his neck.

And he realized it was only sweat. He let out a quiet, shaky laugh, and hurried into the restaurant.

He scanned the bodies. They looked the same. He headed for the kitchen, stepping around the bodies and broken glass, being careful not to slip on the wet floor. As he walked, more sweat trickled down his neck and face.

He'd probably been sweating like a hog, all along, and simply hadn't paid attention to it. The hair at the back of his head was dripping. The garbage bags felt slick and greasy against his skin. Only his socks and underwear kept him from being completely encased by the slimy, clinging plastic. And they were sodden.

He had a sudden urge to strip free of the damned wrappings. Feel the cool air on his body. Strip down to his briefs and *stay* here. Have some beer. Throw together a pizza. Forget about going back out in the rain.

The body of the woman sprawled across the rear table put a quick end to that.

She looked *so much* like Maureen.

He stopped beside her drooping head, blinked sweat out of his eyes, and studied her hair until he spotted some blonde.

What if Maureen had bleached her hair?

Trev considered getting a wet rag and cleaning the gore from her pubic hair, just to make sure *it* wasn't auburn.

Don't get crazy. That isn't her.

Stop wasting time.

He stepped into the kitchen, removed Patterson's hat and

slipped the hood off his head. The fresh air felt wonderful. He set them and the shotgun on the counter.

He glanced at Liam. His friend. Maureen's father.

The poor girl. Both her parents gone.

She might be dead, herself, by now.

Trev turned away quickly and hurried to the telephone. He threw open the directory. His plastic mitten dripped dark liquid onto the pages as he flipped to the Cs.

Chidi, Clarence was at 4538 Fairmont. He memorized the address, then searched through the Os until he found Liam's number again. He snatched up the handset, picked up the same pen he'd used before to punch in the number, and jabbed the keys.

He heard the quiet ringing.

Answer it, answer it, answer it! Come on, Maureen!

Maybe she'd been in the shower, last time.

It rang eleven times. Then it was picked up.

Oh, thank God. 'Maureen?'

No answer.

'Maureen? It's Trevor Hudson.'

'Hi, Trevor.' A woman's voice, low and husky, and not Maureen.

'Who is this?'

'Maureen.'

The skin on the back of his neck prickled.

'Come on over, honey. It's lonesome here. We'll have us a party.'

He closed his eyes. He felt as if his breath were being squeezed out. 'You're all alone there?'

'Sure am, sweetheart.'

'Have you got any bodies?'

'Mine. And it wants you, Trevor. Real bad.'

'I want dead people,' he said.

'Maybe we can go out and find some.'

'None in your house, though?'

'I wish there was. But you come on over, now. OK? We'll have us a real good time.'

'Fine,' he said. 'See you.' He set the phone down on its cradle and struggled to fill his lungs.

13

Tom held the flashlight on the fusebox, and Denise flicked the switches. They stepped out of the small room. Denise squinted when she met the brightness of the kitchen. Kara, waiting there, let out a sigh as if her world had just undergone a tremendous improvement.

Denise smiled. 'Better, huh?'

The girl bobbed her head. 'Darkness is not one of my favorite things.'

'This is better, all right,' Tom said.

His eyes shifted upward quickly to Denise's face, and she felt herself blush. In spite of the towel draped over her shoulders to cover her bra, she suddenly felt almost naked. It hadn't bothered her earlier, while they dried themselves in the bathroom and made their way through the house by flashlight. Nobody could see much, and she'd been too relieved by the change in Tom to care much about modesty.

'Maybe we should get into some dry clothes,' she said. She turned to Kara. 'You don't think your folks would mind us borrowing . . .'

'Oh, no. Let's go and change. This feels yucky.'

'Could I use the phone first?' Tom asked her. 'I want to call home and make sure my parents are OK.'

'OK, sure.'

He thanked her, then picked up the kitchen extension. He tapped in the number. He smiled nervously at Denise. His gaze dropped for a moment. He looked away fast. 'Hi, Mom, it's me . . . No, nothing's wrong. Can I talk to Dad, though?' Covering the mouthpiece, he said, 'Sounds like everything's fine over there.' He took his hand away.

'Yeah, hi Dad. Nothing weird's going on over there, is it?. . . Well, some guy tried to break in over here. The rain's black, Dad . . . No, I mean it. And it's really dangerous. It's making people into killers. I heard they broke into the Edgewood, too, and killed some people there . . . No, I'm not *on* anything. It's really true. I don't know what's going on, but I wanted to make sure you're all right and warn you and Mom. You oughta get out one of your guns and keep it around. Don't let anybody into the house . . . I don't know why there haven't been any reports on the TV. Maybe nobody knows about it . . . Look, if you don't believe me, take a look at the rain. But be careful, OK? Don't get any on you, or it'll make you want to kill people . . . You can't talk to them, they're not here . . . They're at the Edgewood. They called from there . . . Yes, I knew. I'm sorry. But jeez, it's no big deal . . . If I try to come home, *I'll* get wet. Besides, I have to stay here and take care of Denny. She's all alone, and there's no telling what might happen . . . OK, then ground me. For godsake, Dad, this is a real emergency. I'm not kidding. Something really terrible's going on, and I don't understand it, but it's sure happening . . . Just get a gun and watch out, OK? I've gotta go.' He hung up. His cheeks puffed out, and he blew air through his pursed lips.

'Guess you're in hot water,' Denise said.

He laughed. 'Well, at least they're safe. Dad might want to kill me, but they're safe.'

'Do you want to call your parents?' Kara asked Denise.

She shook her head. 'They're out of town.'

'I hope it isn't raining where they are.'

'Me, too. But it's a long way from here.'

'Can we change, now?'

'Yeah, let's.'

Kara led the way. Denise turned off the kitchen lights and followed, Tom walking close behind her. It felt good to know he was there.

So weird, she thought. A while ago, he was a raving lunatic and you were scared to death of him. Now, it's like he's your protector. All it took was enough hot water.

'Maybe we can find me some aspirin,' he said.

She looked around at him. 'Are you all right?'

'Just a headache, mostly.' In a louder voice, he said, 'You've got a mean swing, Kara.'

She looked back, contorting her face. 'I'm awful sorry.'

'Hey, I'm glad you did it. God. I just can't believe I was actually . . .'

'Don't worry about it,' Denise said. She paused in the living room to pick up the lamp she'd knocked over.

'I hate it that I hurt you.'

'I know. But you couldn't help it. And I got you pretty good, too.' At the other end of the sofa, she turned off the next lamp. 'I'm just glad you're back to normal.'

'Thank God we ended up in the bathtub.'

Denise crossed the foyer. As she reached for the switch panel, Kara frowned. 'You're not going to make it dark again, are you?'

'You can turn on the hallway light. But your dad thought we'd be safer if the house looks deserted.'

'Most people leave lights on when they're gone,' Tom pointed out.

'Yeah, you're right. OK.' She dropped her hand away from the switches.

Kara started up the hallway, then halted. 'Maybe it'd be better if somebody else goes first.'

Denise stepped forward. 'Let's go together.' She took the girl's hand.

'Can I change first?'

'Sure.' The hallway smelled smoky. Though there didn't seem to be any ashes on the beige carpeting, Denise's burning shirt had left a grimy trail along the ceiling. She wondered if soap and water might take care of it.

When they came to Kara's bedroom, Denise reached around the doorframe and turned on the light. They entered. Tom stopped in the doorway. 'Are there fresh towels somewhere?' he asked.

'Oh, that's a good idea. They're in the closet by the bathroom.'

He went to get some.

'Do you think he's OK?' Kara whispered.

'I think so.'

'Me, too. He seems really nice. Though he does tell a lot of fibs.' She sat on the edge of her bed and started to undress. 'I try never to tell a lie, especially to my Mom and Dad. I'm sure that I would never get away with it, anyway.'

'Doesn't look as if Tom's getting away with it.'

She laughed. 'He's in trouble, all right. But I'm sure glad he isn't weird anymore. Do you think it was just washing off the black water? That cured him?'

'It sure looks that way.'

'Yeah. I guess that's a good thing to know.' Leaving her underpants on, she stepped to her dresser. The panties looked damp and clinging. The backs of her legs had blotches of a faint reddish hue from the bath water.

'Do the burns hurt?' Denise asked.

'Oh, not very much.'

'Kind of like a little sunburn?'

'Yeah.'

'Me, too.'

'You got a lot more on you than I did,' the girl said. 'Should I put on my nightie, or what?'

'Might as well. I don't think we'll be going out.'

She pulled open the top drawer, took out a pink nightgown and fresh panties, and looked past Denise as Tom came into the room. Her eyes went wide. Denise whirled around. Some neatly folded towels were pressed to Tom's side. His other hand was full with the fireplace poker, hammer and knife. 'Don't worry,' he said. 'I just thought we'd better keep this stuff with us.' He stepped toward Kara. 'Do your parent shave any guns?'

'No. Dad doesn't like them.' She put on her nightgown.

'Here.'

Kara pulled a towel out from under his arm. Tom turned away as she reached under her nightgown. She took off her panties, spent a few moments drying herself from the waist down, then stepped into the dry underwear. She went to her closet. She put on a pair of Alf slippers.

Then she led them down the hall to her parents' room. 'What do you suppose you want to wear?'

'It's up to you,' Denise said.

'How about warmups? They'd be good and cozy.'

'Fine.'

Kara searched some drawers. She took out a royal blue warmup suit for Denise. The jacket had a hood, a zipper front, and white piping up the sleeves. The pants matched, with piping up the sides of the legs. 'Snazzy,' Denise said.

Kara gave her the suit, and a pair of white socks.

'Dad hasn't got anything as neat,' she told Tom.

'Whatever,' he said.

She found a gray sweatsuit and white socks for him. He dropped the weapons onto the bed, and she handed the garments to him.

'I'll change in the John,' he said.

'We ought to stay together,' Denise said. 'Why don't you just go in the closet?'

He left a towel behind for her, stepped into the roomy closet, turned on its light, and pulled the door shut.

'Don't come out till I say so,' she warned him.

'Aw.'

She laughed. She undressed in front of the closet door. It had a full-length mirror.

'You *really* got wrecked,' Kara said.

Denise nodded while she dried her hair. She looked as if she'd sunbathed in the nude and stayed out too long. And maybe as if there'd been a tree above her, a few leaves blocking out the sun so she ended up with pale blotches here and there. The red was very faint, though. She suspected it would go away entirely in an hour or so.

The discoloring across her throat was a deeper red than the burns. Where Tom had choked her. That would probably turn into a bruise. The same with the patch under her left breast. Where he'd punched her. She had two crimson streaks across her belly. One from the tip of the umbrella, a longer one from the point of the fireplace poker he'd whipped at her while she stood in the tub. The umbrella hadn't broken her skin at all, but the poker had scraped off a layer. The skin was ruffled up around the edges of the wound, leaving a strip that looked raw and juicy.

She pointed to it for Kara's benefit. 'I'll have a nice scab there.'

'I had a really bad one on my knee. I had it forever.'

'Did you pick it off and eat it?'

'Oh, gross!'

'Hey,' Tom said. 'I'm missing all the fun.'

'Just admiring the wounds you gave me.'

'You should see what you did to my arm.'

'Sorrrry.'

Kara laughed.

'Can I come out, now?'

'No way. Stay put.' Though Denise's skin wasn't very wet anymore, it seemed moist and clammy. The towel felt good. Her burns were a little tender, but didn't hurt much. She gently patted the streaks on her belly.

When she was done, she stepped into the warm-up pants and pulled them up. They were soft and clingy. They seemed to trap in the heat of her skin, making the burns feel slightly worse. Otherwise, they felt wonderful. She put on the jacket. She raised its zipper to her throat, then lowered it a few inches to let some air in.

She rapped on the mirror.

'Yo.'

'I'm dressed. Are you?'

'Yep.' He opened the door and came out. The sweatsuit came with him. Drooping and baggy. He looked like a kid lost in the clothes of a giant.

Denise laughed. Kara, grinning, shook her head.

'Your dad must be a pretty big guy,' Tom said.

'Oh, he is.'

'You aren't gonna lose your pants, are you?' Denise asked.

'If I do, you'll be the first to know.'

'I'm not sure *anyone* will know,' she said.

'Look at this,' he said, and pushed his right sleeve up to the elbow. His forearm showed a red crescent of teeth marks. But the skin wasn't broken.

Denise pursed her lips. 'I did that, huh?'

'You should see what you did to her,' Kara said.

Denise lifted the bottom of her jacket.

'Yeah, I know. You weren't wearing that before, remember?'

She blushed. That seemed to make her burns feel even hotter. She pulled the jacket down again.

She went to the bed, sat down, and put on the socks.

'What'll we do now?' Kara asked.

Tom picked up the fireplace poker. He frowned at it, and turned it slowly in his hands. 'Well, I came over here for some popcorn.'

'Yeah. Why don't we make a new batch and have a nice party and watch some TV.'

'Might as well,' Denise said. 'It might be a long night.'

Warriors

1

'Messy, messy stuff,' Buddy said. He dropped the last of his chicken bones onto the paper plate on his lap, then leaned forward and set the plate on the coffee table. He settled back against the sofa. Smiling, he raised his hands to show the others.

Lou, from his seat across the room, could see the shiny grease and flecks of chicken fat on Buddy's fingers.

'What're you trying to do,' Sheila said, 'make us sick?'

'It's just so messy. Sticky. Ick.' With that, he turned sideways and held his dripping hands in front of Maureen's face. 'Be a good girl and lick them clean for me.'

'For godsake,' Sheila muttered.

Cyndi grinned. Doug tore a chunk off his drumstick and turned his head to watch.

Maureen swallowed her mouthful. She stared at Buddy, her eyes narrow.

'Do you have a problem with that?' he asked.

She shook her head. With the back of her hand, she wiped the grease from around her lips. Buddy took the plate off her lap. She sat up straight. Then she opened up, and he slid his right thumb into her mouth.

'Suck it, honey, suck it.'

Lou's heart started thumping. Maureen shut her eyes. She was breathing hard through her nose, her breasts rising and falling under the thin shirt. Buddy plucked the thumb from her mouth. It came out with a wet slurpy sound. He stuck in his index finger.

'This is disgusting,' Sheila said.

Buddy grinned at her, then pushed against Maureen, his hand pressing her down until she was slumped against the sofa back. The breath hissed through her nostrils. She writhed a little. He took out the finger and slid his middle finger into her mouth.

'Yeah, suck it hard, baby.'

'Oh lordy,' Doug murmured.

Her legs swung apart and she pushed at the floor and one side of her shorts gaped. Lou could see up the leg hole. He gazed at the shadowy smoothness of her inner thigh. He almost had a view of her groin, but not quite. If he got down and sat on the floor . . . But Sheila would catch on.

He squirmed. It's a good thing I can't see any higher, he thought.

'When you're done with him,' Doug said, 'I could use some of that. Don't know how I got chicken grease all over my dick, but . . .'

Cyndi jabbed his arm.

'Just kidding, just kidding.'

'Shithead.'

Buddy popped his middle finger out of Maureen's mouth, and poked in his ring and pinky fingers together. 'Ooooh,' he said. 'So tight and wet. Love it. Suck, honey, suck.'

Sheila, sitting on the floor near Lou's chair, twisted her head around and scowled up at him. He knew his face was red. He knew he was panting some. He hoped Sheila didn't know the reason why, and just thought he was upset. At least his legs were crossed so she couldn't see the bulge. He shook his head to show her just how disgusting he considered Buddy's behavior.

'Thank you so much,' Buddy said. He took the fingers from her mouth, clutched her breast and squeezed it through the shirt. She gasped and her lips peeled away from her teeth.

'Just drying off,' he said. He turned his hand over and wiped its back against her shirt. Lou watched how it pushed her breast in, and how the breast came springing back when it went away.

'I don't believe you,' Sheila said.

Buddy grinned at her. 'If you don't like it, go home.'

'I don't think we should all just sit here and let him *do* stuff like this.'

'Buzz off,' Cyndi told her. 'She deserves anything she gets.'

Buddy jammed his left hand into Maureen's mouth. All four fingers at once. She choked, grabbed his wrist and shoved his hand out. As the fingertips cleared her lips, he drove his right fist into her belly. Her breath gusted out. She lurched forward, hunching over her thighs, and wheezed for air.

'You're such a bastard,' Sheila said. 'It's no wonder Lisa dumped you.'

The mention of Lisa made Lou go tight and cold inside. For a while there, he'd been able to forget about her, forget what they'd done to Chidi.

Buddy grinned at Sheila. 'She didn't dump me. She just got a hankering for some dark meat. That's all over now.'

'Done,' Doug said. '*Well* done.'

Buddy chuckled.

'That's sick,' Sheila muttered.

Lou reached to the lamp table for his drink. He picked it up. The cold, wet glass was slick in his sticky fingers. He thought about Maureen sucking his fingers clean, but the idea of it didn't turn him on. This damn talk about Lisa and Chidi.

Maureen was still bent over, huffing for breath.

'I sure hope Lisa's all right,' Buddy said. He looked at Cyndi. 'You said she's babysitting tonight?'

'Yeah.'

'You wouldn't know where, would you?'

'Oh, sure. They live just down the block from me. The Foxworths. That's where she is.'

'I think I'll give her a call and check up on her.'

'She isn't interested in you,' Sheila said.

'Oh, don't be too sure about that.' He grabbed the back of Maureen's neck and pushed, using it like a handle to help himself off the sofa, shoving her down hard against her thighs. 'Keep a sharp eye on my honey, folks. But no feelies. That means you, too, Sheila.' He winked at her.

She gave him the finger.

That's twice in one night, Lou thought. She's sure getting brave with Buddy. Any braver, and she would probably get herself stomped.

Buddy laughed and strode out of the room.

Lou finished his vodka.

'Don't you gals need to use the powder room?' Doug asked.

'Take a leap,' Cyndi told him.

'I think we've all got to stand up to Buddy,' Sheila said. 'We shouldn't just sit here and let him *do* things to this woman. It's horrible.'

Maureen raised her face. She looked at Sheila. 'Thanks,' she murmured.

'You shut up,' Cyndi said.

'Lou!' Buddy called. The faint voice came from far away. 'Get in here, would you? Lisa wants to talk to you.'

Lou's heart thumped. He felt as if he were falling. But he got up from the chair. On wobbly legs, he stepped past Sheila and headed for the kitchen.

What does she want to talk to me for? It doesn't make sense.

Thanks a lot for murdering Maxwell, you fucking bastard.

I didn't kill him. It was Buddy.

What's going on?

He entered the kitchen. Buddy was standing by the wall extension. But he didn't hold the phone. It was hanging where it belonged. Buddy had the directory open in his hands.

'Did she hang up?' Lou asked.

'I didn't call her, numbnuts. Are you kidding?'

Thank God.

'What's going on?'

'Checking out the address. We're gonna pay the cunt a visit.'

'What?'

'Are you deaf or just stupid?'

'What do you mean, pay her a visit?'

'I been thinking about her all day, man. Sooner or later, she's gonna lose it and squeal on us.'

'Yeah. I think she might.'

'You, me and Doug are gonna go over and take care of her. It's perfect, man. We tell the gals we're all done messing with Maureen and want to take her back to her place. They'll be glad to get rid of her, you know? They're both so fucking jealous you can taste it. We leave them here. They'll be our alibi, you know?'

'I'm not so sure Sheila'll lie for us.'

'Don't worry about that, man. She'll do whatever we say.'

'So we leave them here and take Maureen with us?'

'That's the idea.'

'What'll we do with Maureen?'

'Anything we want. You're both aching for her.'

Lou moaned. 'You'll let us . . .?'

'Damn right. Then we'll dump her and drop in on Lisa. Take care of her.'

'Kill her?'

'Don't worry, man. I'll do it.'

Lou leaned back against the doorframe and stared at Buddy.

He's gonna let me at Maureen.

'Then we'll all be in the clear. Neat, huh?'

'Wait. Wait. What about the rain?'

'What about it?'

'If we get wet . . .'

'So, we don't get wet. No big deal. I've got umbrellas, raincoats. Go on back and tell Doug to come here. Then keep an eye on our babe. Those gals might let her get away if they get the chance.'

'This is wild,' he muttered. His mind felt numb.

Buddy slapped him on the shoulder, and he headed for the living room.

We can't do this, he thought.

But, oh, we sure will.

2

Trev, shaken by his talk with the stranger at Maureen's house, pulled the plastic hood down over his head and put on Patterson's hat.

The way she'd talked, it was obvious that she'd been out in the rain. A crazy. A killer hoping for some action. Hoping I'll come by so she can nail me.

She might just get the chance, Trev thought. He picked up the shotgun and made his way toward the door.

She'd claimed there were no bodies in the house. She could've been lying. But he wanted to believe her. If Maureen wasn't dead in the house, then she might still be alive. Either in the house, hiding, or away somewhere.

So how do you play it? he wondered.

Maureen didn't seem like the kind of woman to run and hide if she realized someone was breaking into her house. Hell, no. She'd attack.

But who's to say the intruder went in alone? She could've been with a whole gang. Just because she'd claimed to be there by herself, lonesome . . .

They jumped him as he stepped out onto the sidewalk. One leaped onto his back and hooked an arm around his throat. Another, a skinny naked man, came in from the front driving a knife toward his chest. He rammed the muzzle of his shotgun into the knifeman's belly and pulled the trigger. As the blast slammed the guy away, he pumped a fresh shell into the chamber.

He pivoted, planning to ram backward against the doorframe, and saw a third assailant, out of sight until now because the damn hood killed his peripheral vision. This one swung a baseball bat at his face. He had no time to aim. He tugged the trigger. The shotgun bucked. Its load ripped through the man's upper arm, tore it away in a mess of flying tissue and bone, and spun him.

Staggering beneath the weight on his back, Trev turned in a full circle to make sure there were no others.

None.

Then he went blind as the arm across his throat jerked sideways, shifting the plastic bag and sliding the eyeholes away from his eyes.

He stumbled backward. Struck something that made the person on his back grunt. Sounded like a woman. Probably is a woman, he thought. Not much force in the choke hold. More like she was just trying to hold on and ride him.

He took a step forward, then threw himself back hard, pounding her against the obstruction. This time, the impact brought more than a grunt. She cried out in pain. The pressure on Trev's throat eased. Reaching up with his left hand, he yanked the arm away. She slid down his back. He pulled her sideways just enough to give himself a target, then shot his elbow into her body. A good solid blow that pounded the air out of her. He felt her start to slump, trapped between his back and the wall or whatever it was that he'd battered her against.

Lurching away from her, Trev adjusted his mask until he found the eyeholes. He was standing over the man who'd come at him with the knife. The guy wore sneakers. He had a cave just above his groin.

Trev pumped the shotgun. As he started to swing around, he saw a man standing by the curb, trying to fit his severed arm onto the gushing stump below his shoulder. Trev blasted him in the chest. The guy flopped backward and slammed against the side of a parked car.

He whirled toward the woman.

She was on her rump, legs stretched out, back against the doorframe of O'Casey's. Her arms were folded across her belly and she was gasping for air. She gleamed black in the light from the restaurant. Her eyes were squeezed shut. Her pained grimace showed the white of her teeth.

Trev pumped the shotgun and aimed at her face.

A kid. She looked no older than fifteen or sixteen.

Her bangs were pasted to her forehead. She wore a jumper over a blouse with a frilly collar. Her sodden, pleated skirt clung to her thighs. She wore knee socks and loafers.

Kid or not, Trev thought, she's a killer now. If I don't shoot her, she'll go on her merry way and maybe nail someone.

Tie her up, leave her in O'Casey's?

He didn't want to waste the time. Besides, she might get loose and end up hunting for victims again. Or other crazies might find her and kill her.

Do they kill their own?

They'd either kill her or set her free.

'Come on,' he said. Crouching, he grabbed the girl's wrist and dragged her to her feet. She tried to pull away. He tugged and she stumbled forward. With a growl, she drove her head into his stomach. Trev brought his knee up. She folded and dropped. 'Now *stop it*! I want to help you.'

He reached down. He clutched the black rope of her pony tail and pulled, trying not to hurt her but applying enough force to give her the message. She stood up. Left hand gripping the pony tail, right hand pressing the shotgun to her spine, he guided her toward the alley.

'Just stay cool,' he said. 'You'll be all right. Just keep walking. You'll be fine.'

He hoped nobody was coming up behind him.

Only once did the girl try to struggle free. Trev yanked her hair back and jabbed the muzzle into her back, and she yelped and settled down.

'It's OK,' he told her. 'It's OK. We're almost there.'

He swung her into the alley. The car was there, and he heard the rain drumming on it as he pushed the girl closer to its rear. 'Get down,' he said.

She tried to turn around, so he tugged her pony tail. She went to her knees. He nudged her with his knee until she turned sideways. Then he forced her down onto the pavement. He stepped over her. With a foot on her rump to keep her from getting up, he propped his shotgun against the bumper. He dug out his keys and unlocked the trunk.

He straddled her, jammed his hands under her armpits, and picked her up. The girl squirmed. She kicked backward, the heel of her shoe striking his shin. 'Damn it!' he gasped, and shoved her headfirst into the trunk. Then he slipped a hand under her skirt, clutched the side of her right thigh, and swung her legs up and over the side. She tumbled into the dark trunk. He slammed the lid.

Picking up his shotgun, he hurried to the driver's door. Francine unlocked it for him. He climbed in, jerked the door shut, and locked it. 'Everything OK?' he asked.

'What happened?' Francine asked. 'What did you put in the trunk?'

'A girl.'

'One of *them*?'

'Yeah. Just a kid.'

'You're taking her *with* us?'

'It was either that or kill her.'

'You should've killed her.'

'I told you, she's just a kid. She didn't ask for any of this. She's a victim, same as everyone else.'

'She's one of *them*!'

'She's one of us, now.'

'Great. Just great.'

'We heard some shots,' Lisa said.

Trev poked his key into the ignition and started the car. He turned on the headlights. 'That was me. Three of them tried to nail me when I came out of O'Casey's.'

'Are you all right?' Lisa asked him.

'I had to drop a couple.'

'And bring one along,' Francine muttered.

'They didn't hurt you?'

'I'm fine.' He started backing the car out of the alley.

'Did you find the address?' Lisa asked.

'Yeah, I got it.' Eyes on the rearview mirror, he swung the car onto Third Street. He started forward. Heading north. Toward Chidi's house. But also toward the home of Liam O'Casey, where a strange woman had answered the phone.

Both on the north side of town. Chidi's house a couple of miles closer.

Trev knew what he ought to do – hit Chidi's first. See if the grandfather's playing with magic. More important to stop the rain than to bust into Liam's on the chance Maureen might be there.

But if he could save Maureen . . .

You've got a few miles to go before you have to make up your mind, he told himself.

He told himself that. He already knew his first stop would be Liam's house.

3

Following John's instructions, Steve brought the people from the cocktail lounge into the entryway, where they joined the restaurant staff gathered by Cassy, and John's group from the dining room. John stood with his back to the double doors. For the moment, nobody was pounding on them. The only pounding was inside his head. He rubbed the lump on his brow. He hoped the aspirin would kick in soon.

'I think everyone's here,' Cassy told him.

'OK,' he muttered. Then he raised his voice. 'Could I have your attention, please?'

The murmuring faded.

'We need to get organized, here. You're probably all aware that a guy broke through a window a few minutes ago and killed Mrs Benton. Well, apparently there's quite a crowd outside.'

'Just how many are we talking about?' asked a stocky, florid man near the front of the group.

'Steve?'

'I just took a quick look out the window,' Steve said. 'I didn't have time to make an accurate head count, but I'd guess anywhere from twenty to thirty.'

'Oh, dear God,' a woman muttered.

Other people moaned, shook their heads, moved closer to their spouses or friends, whispered.

'They were scattered along the sidewalk in front,' Steve went on. 'There was a pretty good bunch right outside the doors.'

'Why are they *doing* this?' asked Tina. Her boyfriend Andy squeezed her shoulder.

'They're after the fine cuisine,' said a small guy in a plaid jacket.

'This is no time for levity,' Dr Goodman pointed out.

'Levity in the face of disaster is a hallmark of the American character.'

'Oh, shut up,' said a woman John figured must be the guy's wife.

'They're outside,' Cassy said, 'because they want to come in and kill us. That's pretty obvious, isn't it?'

'But *why*?' From Tina.

'It doesn't matter why,' John said. 'I'm sure it has something to do with the black rain. But that's not our concern, right now. What we need to do is get organized so we can protect ourselves.'

'Hey,' said a big guy with a beer mug in his hand. 'Who died and made you king shit?'

'It's all yours,' John told him. 'You can be king shit.'

The guy sneered. 'You trying to be a wiseguy?'

'I'm totally serious. You take over. I don't want this, anyway.'

Cassy frowned at him. 'Hey, John, come on.'

'I don't even want to be here, much less be the guy giving orders. Let macho man . . .'

'Look, buddy . . .'

'Hey, shove it,' Lynn told him. 'If we waste time arguing, those jerks are going to break in and God only knows what'll happen to us. So just shut up and listen to John. We've got to have a leader and I don't know most of you people, but I know my John and he's the man for it.'

John looked at her. He felt a swell of pride at the way she was taking on the bastard, but he wished she would shut up. He didn't *want* to be the leader. The only reason he'd gotten involved was because someone had to take control fast and nobody else was doing it.

'Gimme a break, lady,' the guy said. 'I know who he is. He's the fuckin' *painter*.'

I'm not so anonymous after all, he thought.

'Yes, he's a painter,' Lynn said. 'He's an *artist*.'

'We want a pansy artist running the show?'

'He also served two tours in Vietnam,' Lynn said. 'And he holds a third degree black belt in Karate.'

Thanks a lot, John thought.

But the guy who'd called him a pansy grew a sickly smile and took a step backward.

Everyone stared at John.

Now they think I'm a miracle worker. Really appreciate it, Lynn.

'OK,' he said. 'I see that quite a few of us already have weapons. After we break up here, I want everyone to get a knife.'

'Some of you got them with your dinner,' Cassy added. 'We'll bring more out from the kitchen in just a minute.'

'We should also make ourselves some clubs,' John said. 'Legs from tables and chairs, maybe. A good blow to the head'll put a man out in record time.'

'How about putting knives on the ends of the clubs?' Andy suggested.

'Whatever you can think of. Use your imaginations. Just put together the meanest weapons possible.'

'What've *they* got?' asked the red-faced man who'd asked about their numbers.

'Some of them must've gotten into a hardware store,' Steve said.

'Handyman's down at the end of the block,' Dr Goodman said.

'Figures. I only took a glimpse, but I saw knives, tire irons, hammers, hatchets and axes.'

A woman let out a quiet whimper. There were moans from several others, including men.

'I want us to split up into groups,' John said. 'Cassy's told me that the rear door opens out into the alley. It has no handle on the alley side, it's a solid door and it's locked. Our main areas of vulnerability are the windows and the front doors here.

'I want a group of men at the doors with me. Steve. You,' he said, nodding at the man who'd called him a pansy. 'You.' He indicated an oriental wearing a chef's floppy cap and holding a meat cleaver. 'And you two,' he said, giving the nod to a pair of husky men from the cocktail lounge.

'OK. The rest of you, form into two groups. One group will be stationed in the bar area, one in the dining room. Your job is to watch the windows. Anyone tries to break in, deal with him. Or her. Don't let it stop you if the invader's a female. Remember, it was a woman who killed Chester Benton.'

'Equal opportunity maniacs,' said the guy who believed in levity.

'If there's any kind of concerted assault, just call out and the rest of us'll come over to reinforce you. Any questions?'

'What about getting out of here?'

'Yeah. Some of us have kids at home.'

'So do I,' John said. 'But we won't do our kids any good if we get killed.'

'Won't do 'em any good staying here, either.'

'If you want to leave,' John said, 'be my guest. But you've got a street full of bloodthirsty nuts outside, and the rain. From all appearances, the rain'll turn you into one of them. But if you want to risk it, go on ahead. It's pretty clear to me that we stand the best chance by sticking together in here and holding down the fort.'

'They come in here with axes and shit, we're dead meat.'

'Yeah, what if they overrun us?'

Overrun.

The word sent a shock of cold through John.

'We're not going to let that happen,' he said, trying to keep his voice steady.

'Yeah, and how do we stop it? All they gotta do is bash in the doors, thirty of 'em coming pouring in with their damn hardware. We won't stand a chance in hell.'

'What'll we do then?' a woman blurted.

'We're all gonna die,' Tina muttered.

John saw panic spreading through the group like a brush fire on a windy day. Eyes widened. Faces blanched. Tina and another woman began to sob. A small, long-haired man near the back whirled around and ran off into the cocktail lounge. Men and women hugged each other and spoke in low, urgent tones.

As if sharing a silent cue, Lynn and Cassy both raised their arms at once.

'Please,' Cassy called out.

'Everyone just calm down,' Lynn snapped. 'We'll be all right.' As the group quieted down, she looked at John. 'Tell them, honey.'

Fighting his own fear, he lifted his voice. 'The guy's right. If we're overrun, we're in deep trouble.'

'John!' Lynn gasped.

'So we have to make sure that doesn't happen.'

'Good plan,' said the humorist.

'I do have a plan,' John said. 'First we arm ourselves and take our positions. Like I told you, my group mans the doors. Then we let 'em in.'

'What?'

'He's flipped.'

'That's the craziest damn thing I ever heard.'

'We let 'em in *one at a time*.'

'Oh, right. Sure.'

'One at a time, two if we can't help it. Yank 'em in, slam the door on the rest, take care of the ones we've got. Put 'em out of commission one at a time, thin out their force.'

Lynn squeezed his arm. Cassy frowned at him, nodding, her lips a tight line. Steve shook his head. 'That *is* crazy,' he said. 'Let's do it.'

4

'What's the deal with Lisa?' Cyndi asked when Buddy and Doug came back into the room.

'She's just fine,' Buddy said. 'Wants me to take her out tomorrow night. That's if things are back to normal with the rain.'

'Has she had any trouble?' Sheila asked.

'Nope.'

'Maybe everyone else is OK,' Lou said. 'Maybe it wasn't the rain that made Maureen do that.'

'It was the rain,' Maureen said.

'Why don't we turn on the TV and see if there're any reports about it?' Lou said.

'Feel free.'

He got up from his chair, went to the television and turned it on.

Buddy sat down beside Maureen. She stiffened as he reached toward her. But he frowned and drew back his hand. Looking from Cyndi to Sheila, he shook his head. 'I guess I didn't realize how much I still . . . care for Lisa.'

'Yeah,' Sheila said. 'You've really been *acting* like you care for her.'

'I know,' he muttered. 'I know. I feel like a . . . a pig.' He met Maureen's eyes. 'Look, I'm sorry. I'm sorry about all this, about everything. I just don't know what got into me.' He contorted his face to show his misery.

This is all a damned act, she thought.

'At least you had an excuse for your behavior,' he said. 'The rain got you. You couldn't help what you did. I just . . . I feel awful. Can you forgive me?'

Maureen said, 'I forgive you.'

What's going on? she wondered.

Lou, squatting in front of the television, flicked from channel to channel with the volume low.

Buddy turned and looked at the others. 'I'm going to take her home.'

'You're kidding, right?' Cyndi asked.

'No, I'm totally serious.'

'You idiot, you raped her. You can't just let her go.'

'I won't tell,' Maureen said.

'I believe her,' Buddy said. 'She tried to kill me.' To Maureen, he said, 'We're even, right?'

'Yeah.'

'You're out of your gourd,' Cyndi told him.

'I'm all for it,' Sheila said. 'I think he *should* take her home.'

'It'll be risky,' Buddy said. 'But it's the right thing to do.'

'Since when have you cared?' Sheila said.

'I never should've . . . messed with her. Talking to Lisa just now . . . God, I've never felt so rotten.' He glanced from Doug to Lou. 'You guys'll come with me, won't you?'

Maureen's stomach went cold.

'Now hold on,' Sheila said.

Lou turned off the television. 'Nothing,' he said. 'Just the regular shows.'

'So, you in with me?' Buddy asked him.

'You mean, taking Maureen home?'

'Yeah.'

'Sure.'

'I don't know,' Doug said. 'We shouldn't leave the gals here alone.'

'They'll be a lot safer here,' Buddy pointed out. 'We don't know what's going on in the streets. That's why I want you two along with me – in case we run into trouble between here and Maureen's place.'

'Just put her out the door,' Cyndi said.

'Good idea,' Sheila said.

'I can't do that.' He gave Maureen a miserable, guilty look. 'I owe her. After all this, the least I can do is make sure she gets safely home.'

'What're you trying to pull?' Cyndi asked.

'I'm not an animal, for godsake. I feel bad, OK?'

'Yeah, sure.'

'I think it's the right thing to do,' Lou said. He turned his eyes to Sheila. 'Don't you think so?'

'I guess. But what about me and Cyn?'

'You'll be fine here,' Buddy said. 'We'll be back before you know it.'

'This really sucks,' Cyndi muttered.

'What kind of car do you have?' Buddy asked Maureen.

'A Jeep. A Cherokee.'

'We'll have to take that. My folks went off in the BMW, and we can't all fit in the Austin. Where's the Jeep, out front?'

She nodded.

'Do you have the keys?'

'No.' She rubbed her face, and tried to remember what she'd done with them.

In my coat pocket.

She'd taken off the coat, thrown it down on the front lawn just after the rain got her.

'You can't even get to her Jeep,' Sheila said. 'You'll get wet.'

'I'll cover up and go after it,' Buddy told her. 'I'll pull it into the garage. That way, they won't have to worry about the rain.'

'You have it all figured out, huh?' Cyndi said. She gave Maureen a sweet smile. 'And guess what happens to you, cutie, when the three of them get you alone.'

Maureen didn't need the hint. She'd already figured it out. 'I trust them,' she said.

'We're not going to lay a finger on her,' Buddy protested.

'Who's talking about fingers?'

'*I'm* not gonna touch her,' Lou said, giving Sheila a solemn look.

'Me neither,' Doug said.

'If you do,' Cyndi told him, 'I'll know it. I'm gonna check you out when you get back.'

He laughed. 'Is that a promise?'

'Damn right. And if you think I won't know the difference, man, you've got another think coming.'

'Jeez, can't wait.'

'If they try anything,' Buddy said, 'I'll bust their heads.'

'Yeah, sure.'

'I left the car keys in the ignition,' Maureen said.

'Thanks.' He slapped her thigh, but not very hard. Then he got up and hurried from the room. Maureen saw Doug and Lou exchange glances. She heard quick thuds as Buddy raced upstairs.

Doug slipped an arm around Cyndi's back. 'How's about a little something for the road?' he asked, and pulled her closer.

'Get real. I'm sure I'm gonna get you all turned on and then you go off with *her*.'

'Oh, come on. Be nice.'

'We'll see about being nice. When you get back.'

'Please?' He put a hand on her breast. She shoved it away. 'Come on. There's no telling what might happen to me out there.'

'I know what better not happen.'

'We could all get killed.'

'Wouldn't *that* be too bad.'

'If it's that dangerous,' Sheila said, 'you shouldn't go.' She faced Lou. 'I don't think I want you going out there.'

'We'll be careful.'

'He doesn't want to miss his chance at Miss Pizza Pussy,' Cyndi said.

'That's not true,' he snapped.

Sheila stared at him. 'If you do fool around with her, you can just forget about me. I mean it. I won't have anything to do with you. Ever.'

'I promise. We're just going to drive her home. Honest. I don't even *want* to go. But I have to. They'll need me if there's trouble.'

Maureen heard Buddy rushing down the stairs. Her heartbeat quickened. It pounded so hard that she felt sick. Her lungs seemed tight, constricted. She couldn't bring in enough air to fill them. Her hands, pressed tight against her thighs, were wet and cold.

Take it easy, she told herself. Don't let them suspect anything.

Buddy came into the living room. He wore a black raincoat, heavy gloves of red leather that looked as if they were designed for snow skiing, and rubber boots that reached nearly to his knees. In one hand was an umbrella. He was grinning. 'This oughta do the trick, huh?'

'Haven't you got anything for us?' Doug asked.

'What for? No need for anyone to leave the car except Maureen.' He looked at her. 'You can use this stuff when you go to your house.'

She nodded. She knew it was a lie, like everything else he'd been saying. When they finished with her, they would just throw her out.

They won't get me *in*, she told herself.

'OK,' Buddy said. 'You folks can take her out to the garage and open the door for me. I'll be with you in a minute.'

That's about how long I've got, Maureen thought. About a minute before he gets to the Jeep, sees that the keys aren't there, and comes running back.

She got up from the sofa, 'Be careful,' she said, and squeezed Buddy's arm through the slicker. 'Don't get wet.'

He looked a little surprised. He smiled. Maureen held onto his arm, and they walked together, the others close behind. When they reached the foyer, she released his arm and stepped away. He opened the umbrella. He raised it overhead, pulled the door wide, and said, 'Here goes nothing.'

'Don't get any on you,' Doug warned.

Buddy's smile looked a little nervous. 'No way,' he said. Then he stepped out.

Maureen swung the door shut and locked it. She snatched up the dangling guard chain and fitted it into the slot before a hand yanked her arm away and spun her around.

'What the hell are you . . .' Cyndi blurted.

Maureen's fist crushed her nose. Cyndi stumbled backward, crying out, clutching her face. She bumped into Sheila. They both staggered away, Sheila grabbing the girl to keep her from falling. 'Guys!' Sheila cried out.

Lou stood there with his eyes wide, his mouth hanging open. Doug hurled himself forward, slamming Maureen's back against the door. As her breath blasted out, she wrapped her arms around him. She squeezed him tight against her body. He squirmed, trying to get loose. Until her mouth found his lips. She kissed him hard. His mouth opened. She thrust her tongue in. Then he was moaning.

'Doug!' Lou shouted.

'Look what she's *doing*!' Sheila cried out.

Maureen let go of Doug and pulled her shirt up. His hands went to her breasts.

'Make her stop!'

As Doug's greasy hands groped her breasts, Maureen tugged open his belt.

'Oh, my God,' Lou muttered.

'Lou!'

She unfastened the button at Doug's Waist, pulled his zipper down.

'Stop her, damn it!'

She slipped her hand down the front of his underwear, curled her fingers around him. Gently stroking, she eased her mouth away. Doug, writhing, sucked the side of her neck. 'Lou,' she gasped. 'I want you, too. Now. Quick.'

'Don't you . . .!' Sheila let go of Cyndi and grabbed Lou's arm. While Cyndi sank to her knees, Lou shoved Sheila hard. 'You bastard!' she shrieked.

Lou came forward. He was gasping, his face scarlet.

Maureen held Doug's penis with one hand. With the other, she pushed his pants down around his thighs. 'On your knees, honey,' she gasped. 'On your knees.'

'Buddy'll kill you!' Sheila blurted.

Cyndi looked up, but didn't move. She just knelt there, bloody hands cupped to her nose, eyes blinking.

Lou came in from the side as Doug, on his knees, pulled Maureen's shorts down. She took Lou's hands and pressed them to her breasts. They stayed there, fondling her. She felt Doug's mouth between her legs. With a hand behind Lou's head, she drew his face to hers. She kissed him.

Sheila, letting out a wild squeal, launched herself at Lou. She yanked his hair, pulling him away. Lou whirled around, swinging at her.

Maureen shot her knee up.

It caught Doug under the chin, hurling him backward.

Lou's fist missed Sheila's chin. She plowed into him, driving him back, snatching his hair again with one hand. As Sheila's other hand raked his cheek, Maureen yanked her shorts up and leaped over Doug's sprawled body. He grabbed her foot, but she jerked it free.

She ran.

Ran from the foyer, through the dining room, into the kitchen.

Heard nobody in pursuit.

Snagged the door latch down.

Tugged open the sliding glass door and rushed outside into the rain.

5

'You bastard! You bastard!' Sheila cried, driving Lou back to the wall as she punched him and clawed him and tore at his hair.

'Stop it!' He caught one of her hands. The other punched his cheek. 'She's getting away!'

'You bastard!'

Then Doug was behind Sheila, throwing his arms around her, hurling her aside. She tripped over her feet and hit the floor hard.

'Buddy's gonna kill us!' Doug yelled as they raced for the kitchen.

'We'll get her,' Lou gasped.

'We'd better!'

We're screwed, Lou thought. The bitch! Made me do that right in front of Sheila.

He knew Sheila was done with him. All Maureen's fault. And Buddy would go ape when he found out they'd let her get away.

She hasn't gotten away yet!

In the kitchen, Lou saw the open door just as Doug lurched to a stop.

She went out?

Maybe a trick.

Lou halted beside Doug. They both scanned the kitchen. No Maureen. No spaces where she might be crouched, hiding. No cupboard or pantry doors that looked large enough to conceal a person.

Their eyes met.

'We've gotta get her,' Lou gasped.

'Here goes nothing.' Doug rushed outside, Lou at his back.

The warm rain splashed Lou's face, tingled against his scalp, soaked his clothes. And he realized he'd been foolish to fear it. There was nothing bad about this rain. It felt great. He spread out his arms and tilted back his head, moaning as a strange excitement pulsed through his body.

He ached with desire.

For a moment, he didn't know what he desired. Then it came to him.

His head snapped down and he grinned at Doug.

Doug, already turning, rushed him. Grinning, too. Teeth white in his black face. Doug dropped low. He drove his head into Lou's stomach. As Lou's breath exploded out, he glimpsed Maureen.

Someone, anyway.

The black smudge of a head that seemed to be floating on the surface of Buddy's swimming pool several yards away.

But he didn't care. He cared only about the pain in his belly, the hot desire pounding through his blood. His chin hit Doug's back, crashing his teeth together. He was carried backward and down. As his rump struck the patio's concrete, he grabbed Doug's sides. The momentum slammed him down, but he kept his grip on Doug and the boy tumbled over him, landing on him, mashing his face. His teeth clamped down on the seat of Doug's jeans. Felt flesh under the heavy fabric. He bit hard and Doug yelped and flinched.

He tried to catch Doug's head between his thighs. Got it for an instant. But the head twisted free. He spread his legs, hoping to scissor it again, but the head dropped and struck his groin.

Pain blasted his body.

Through the daze of agony, he realized that Doug had scurried off him. He rolled onto his side, clutching his genitals and curling up.

6

Maureen, watching from the middle of the pool, wanted to join in.

Rip them up. Tear their flesh. Lap up their blood.

Yes!

She slipped beneath the surface and swam for the side and thought, *Am I nuts?* They're at each other. This is my chance to get away.

Her urge to savage the two boys was gone, leaving her with a heavy feeling of repugnance.

How could I even *consider* . . .?

The rain.

Oh, Jesus.

The black, warm rain. It had soaked her when she dashed from the house, and she remembered how she'd suddenly wanted to turn around and rush back inside and kill them all. But she'd been moving too fast to halt herself before plunging into the backyard pool. The water had engulfed her, and the urge had passed. It had returned when she stood up and watched the boys come out.

The same vicious impulses would take hold again if she came up for air.

Some rain on my head, I'll be just like them.

Staying underwater, Maureen turned herself around. She breast-stroked for the middle of the pool, angling downward, fighting her buoyancy that was like a balloon in her chest trying to lift her to the surface.

Gotta stay down!

Her lungs burned. They seemed to be squeezing themselves tight, wanting to force her breath out to get ready for fresh air.

Maureen let the breath slip from her mouth. As she felt herself begin to sink, she tugged the baggy gym shorts down her legs and off.

She draped them over her head.

She guided herself slowly upward and broke the surface, the shorts hanging like a big, floppy hat. She sucked air into her lungs.

She was facing the deep end of the pool.

And the diving board.

She slipped beneath the water, caught the sodden rag as it started to drift away, and swam for the board. She needed to get under it. There, she might be able to breathe without the rain touching her, making her crazy.

Her left hand touched the slick tile wall at the end of the pool. Staying below the surface, she peered up. But she saw only dark water. She pressed the shorts to the top of her head and surfaced.

A yard to the left of the board.

She plunged under, kicked and came up again directly beneath the board. She turned sideways, reached out and clutched the pool gutter. With her other hand, she plucked the shorts off her head.

She felt the cold water encasing her body. No warm rain striking her head or shoulders or outstretched arm. No urges to rend flesh or taste blood.

Satisfied that she was all right, she turned her gaze toward the patio.

Doug was standing, pulling Lou's arm. Helping him up?

A chill gripped Maureen's bowels.

Lou got to his feet. He was hunched over slightly as if hurting, but he nodded eagerly.

She knew what would happen next. They would come for her.

She heard a sharp laugh.

Then the two guys, side by side, turned away.

And Maureen saw Sheila dash through the lighted kitchen, arms stretched out, face twisted with terror. Cyndi ran into view, and for a moment Maureen thought Cyndi was chasing the girl. Then she understood.

They were racing for the door.

Doug, apparently realizing what they intended, suddenly bolted for it.

Sheila reached the door first and hurled it sideways. Over the sound of the splashing rain, Maureen heard the door rumble across its rails and thud shut.

Doug slid to a halt. He yanked the outside handle. The door didn't budge.

The girls on the other side of the glass gazed out. Sheila started backing away. Cyndi wiped blood off her lips and chin. They both jumped when Doug hammered his fists against the pane. Sheila, shaking her head, shouted at him. Cyndi darted behind her and vanished. Doug pounded the door again, then slammed his forehead against it. Maureen heard the thump. The glass held.

At the sound of a clank, Maureen looked away from the brightly lighted scene. She saw Lou over to the side, a black shape against the darkness of the wall, lifting the iron lid off a barbecue kettle. He snatched something off a nearby tray. Carrying the lid in front of him like an odd, dome-shaped battle shield, he ran toward the door.

In the kitchen, Cyndi rushed up beside Sheila. She passed a butcher knife to Sheila and kept one for herself.

Doug dodged out of the way. Lou punched the iron lid against the door. The glass shattered, blasting inward, throwing shards at the girls as they staggered backward.

Lou leaped through the opening, shield first, right hand waving a yard-long barbecue fork overhead.

7

He went for Sheila, but Cyndi lunged in from the side, shrieking like a madwoman. As she stabbed downward, he whipped her across the face with the rod of his fork. The blow turned her head. Her body followed, and the blade cut only air. Doug, diving, took her down.

Lou flung the barbecue lid to the floor. It struck with an awful, ringing clamor that made him cringe and grin. Sheila glanced around at him, then hurled herself through the doorway and into the dining room. Lou raced after her.

Great fun, he thought. Great fun!

Sheila slapped a chair, tumbling it away from the table to block his path. Lou, laughing, leaped over it.

He chased her into the living room. Gaining on her. But not too quickly. He was enjoying himself so much that he didn't want to end this. Not right away, anyhow. He watched the way her glossy hair bounced and swayed, the way her sweatshirt shook, and how her pumping legs pulled the jeans tight against the flexing mounds of her rump.

In the foyer, she turned toward the front door. She glanced back at Lou. Then she struck the door with her shoulder and reached up for the guard chain.

The door shot open. The chain snapped taut, trapping Sheila's fingers as it bumped her away. She shrieked and yanked her hand free, flesh ripping from her fingers. As she dashed for the stairs, Lou glimpsed Buddy's black face grinning at him through the gap. 'Hey, pal, let me in.'

'Busy!' Lou cried out.

'Hey!'

He took off, chasing Sheila up the stairs, closing in on her as fast as he could. No more time to waste. Buddy was back, and changed, and would try to steal the kill once he got through the door. The guard chain might keep him out for a while, but not for long.

Sheila was almost to the top when Lou thrust the barbecue fork upward. Its tines popped through the seat of her jeans. They sank into her right buttock and she squealed. He shoved. The fork slipped in deeper. Instead of stopping her, it seemed to speed her up. He felt the wooden handle twitching with the flex of her muscles. A patch of blood began to spread over the denim surrounding the twin holes.

He rammed again. She reached back and grabbed the fork as she bounded up the final stairs, but she couldn't dislodge it. Lou leaped to the top, driving her ahead of him. He steered her across the corridor. He slammed her against the wall and pulled out the fork.

Sheila whirled around, slashing at him with the knife. He lurched backward. The blade flashed across his chest, missed, but sliced through his right sleeve and nipped his upper arm. She swept it at him again. Lou took another quick step back and swung the fork at her arm and his foot came down on air.

Yelping, he flung the fork from his hand. He reached out for the banister. His fingers hooked over the rail, but the weight of his tumbling body tore his hold away. His back struck the stairs. He saw his wet, black legs fly up. His neck twisted. He felt his legs kicking high, flipping him over, coming down. His knees thumped the carpeted stairs and he slid down, treads rubbing their way up his body like the rungs of a ladder. They bumped his face. One edge caught his genitals and mashed them up against his crotch. Then another did the same, and another.

At last, he came to a stop. He lay sprawled on the stairs, pain roaring through his body.

He heard quick footfalls.

Sheila hurrying down to finish him off?

'Asshole.' Buddy's voice. 'Should've let me in when I asked you.'

The stairs on which he was lying shook a little as Buddy climbed past him.

He *is* going to steal my kill, Lou thought.

'No!' he gasped.

He tried to push himself up, whimpered as the strain sent spears of pain radiating out from his testicles, and sank back against the stairs.

8

Denise lifted the popcorn bowl off her lap, leaned forward and set it on the table beside her glass. She picked up the glass. As she drank the last of the Pepsi, Tom's hand went to her back. It moved in an easy circle, sliding the warmup jacket against her skin.

She finished drinking. She set the glass down. Instead of settling back against the sofa cushion, she rested her knees on her elbows.

Tom's hand was warm through the jacket. The fabric was very soft. Her mind seemed a little foggy from all that had happened. She felt peaceful and lazy. The good feel of his hand made her eyelids heavy.

'There you are again,' he said.

Lifting her gaze to the television screen, Denise saw herself in a sunny backyard, laughing hard and trying to dodge a water balloon hurled by Kara. As she twisted away, the balloon caught her in the hip. It burst to shreds. Clear, gleaming water exploded out, darkening her red shorts, gluing her T-shirt to her side, splashing down her leg.

Tom laughed.

Kara didn't. Not even when two of her friends charged into view and nailed Denise with more balloons, drenching her, and she cried out and snatched up the garden hose and went after them.

Denise looked over her shoulder. Kara, with her Alf slippers resting on the edge of the table, was slumped back against the sofa asleep.

'Our little friend's zonked,' she whispered.

'I know,' Tom said.

She looked at him. From his smile, she realized that Kara's dropping off had been his cue to reach for her. 'We might as well turn this off,' she said, and picked up the remote.

'Hey, I'm enjoying it.'

'Kara wouldn't like us watching it without her. She's the star.' Denise pushed the 'off' button. The birthday party vanished, replaced by a Jeep commercial.

'Aw. It was just starting to get good.'

'We can turn it back on if she wakes up.'

'Can't we at least rewind and watch you get wiped out again?'

Smiling, she shook her head and settled back against the sofa. Tom's arm was trapped for a moment. Then it worked its way up. As he curled his hand over her shoulder, she swung her legs onto the cushion and leaned against his side. She patted his thigh. 'Why do you want to watch me on the tube when the real McCoy's right here?'

'That way, I get you in stereo.'

The commercial ended, and a Clint Eastwood movie came on. One of those old spaghetti westerns. Clint looked gritty and cool, squinting as he lit the stub of a thin cigar.

'*Fistful of Dollars*,' Tom said. 'It's a great one.'

'How many times have you seen it?'

'Who knows? I never counted.'

'Kara does,' Denise said. 'She counts. She's seen *Willy Wonka* eighty-nine times, or something.'

'My kind of kid.'

'Mine, too.' Face relaxed in sleep, Kara looked so peaceful. Like an infant. As if the world's troubles had never touched her. 'God, she's so cute.'

'She's really neat. I usually can't stand the little ankle-biters, but she's something else.'

'I hope I have a kid just like her someday.'

'That wouldn't be so bad, huh?'

'It's a spooky world, though.'

'Yeah,' Tom said. 'I've noticed. Sometimes, I think I shouldn't ever have any kids. Because of that, you know? What with nuclear bombs, and all the crime, and the environment getting shot to hell. Like it wouldn't be right, bringing kids into such a mess.'

'I think there's plenty around to make it worth the risk,' Denise said. 'I'm glad *I'm* alive, even if it does get creepy.'

'Yeah. Me, too. I guess.'

'Glad to hear it.'

'But jeez, there's so much that can go wrong.'

'But we're in here, safe and sound. It's nice. It's almost as if there *isn't* the black rain out there.'

'Thanks for reminding me,' Tom said, and she felt his hand tighten on her shoulder.

'It'll end sooner or later. Everything will be fine again.'

'I sure hope so.' When he said that, Denise felt his breath stirring her hair, warm or her scalp, tickling a little. 'At least . . . I'm glad we're together.'

'Me, too.'

He gently kissed the side of her head. Then his lips went

away. Denise snuggled against him and yawned. 'I'm so wiped out,' she muttered.

'Do you feel like sleeping? I can move over to a chair so you can stretch out.'

'Don't do that. I like you just fine here.' She snuggled against him and sighed with contentment.

Tom's hand moved gently from her shoulder to her elbow, then up again. 'This is pretty nice.'

'Maybe I will take a little nap,' Denise said. 'Would you mind?'

'Heck, no.'

She scooted away and lay down, resting her head on his thigh, bringing up her knees so her feet wouldn't interfere with Kara. The movements rucked up her jacket so it bulged out from her chest. The opening at the top of the zipper was like a pyramid-shaped window. It gave her a clear view of the shadowy sides of her breasts.

She murmured, 'Woops,' and wondered if she'd said that to draw Tom's attention to the gap. His head was higher, though. He wouldn't be able to see in. Not quite so far, anyway. And she could feel that the jacket had come up enough to reveal a band of bare skin at her waist. Maybe he was looking there. Or maybe his eyes were on the Eastwood movie.

She imagined his hand slipping inside the gap, drifting over her skin, cupping one of her breasts.

He wouldn't do that in a million years, she thought.

And if he did, I probably shouldn't let him.

She gripped the elastic around the bottom of the jacket and tugged. The bulge came down. The fabric pressed snug against her. She folded her hands on her belly.

The opening was gone. But her thoughts about Tom's caresses had excited her. The mounds where her breasts pushed the jacket up were tipped with blunt peaks.

Oh, Lord, she thought.

She felt a blush spread over her skin, heating up the mild burns.

She willed her nipples to soften, to melt down flat. But they didn't obey.

Sighing, she closed her eyes.

This is just so embarrassing, she thought.

Maybe Tom hasn't noticed.

Of course he has.

He squirmed a little, shifting his position beneath Denise's head, and she wondered if he had an erection.

Maybe I should sit up and watch the movie.

But she didn't move. With each breath, she felt the soft rub of the fabric. She waited for the feel of Tom's hand.

Then it came.

But not to either breast. His warm fingertips caressed her forehead, brushing some hair aside. She felt him trace the curve of one eyebrow, then the other. His gentle touch was soothing. Heat seemed to pass from him, seep into her skin and go inside her skull and fill her head with a heavy, dark calm.

9

Lou, sitting at the bottom of the stairs, wrapped a handkerchief around his cut arm. As he pulled the knot tight with his teeth and left hand, Buddy came down.

His face was more red than black. He had Sheila's knife. Its blade was slick with blood.

'She was mine,' Lou complained.

'Guess not. She was too much for you, man.' Buddy stopped in front of him. He shifted the knife to his left hand. Lou noticed that he no longer wore the ski gloves. His right hand was crimson. It was slick and sticky when Lou grabbed it and Buddy pulled him up. The weight on his legs made him wince.

'You OK?'

'I'll live,' Lou muttered.

'Sorry you missed the fun.'

'You owe me.'

'I don't owe you shit.'

'Yes, you do.' Lou hobbled alongside the staircase. He crouched, groaning with the effort, and picked up his barbecue fork. As he straightened up, he frowned at Buddy. 'You've gotta let me have Maureen.'

'I don't gotta anything, dickhead.'

Lou waited while Buddy shut the front door. The guard chain, ripped out of its mount on the doorframe, dangled from its track.

Some lock, he thought. If it had held, Sheila would've been mine.

'So where is she?' Buddy asked, and started through the living room.

'Maureen?'

'Who do you think?'

'She's in the pool.'

'The pool? How the hell did she get away from you bozos?'

Buddy wouldn't like the truth. 'Sheila and Cyndi helped her,' Lou said.

'Figures. The bitches.'

'That's how we got wet. We went after her. Me and Doug.'

'But you didn't get her, did you.'

'Doug tried to kill me. Then we figured it'd be a good idea to come back inside and nail the gals.'

'Great. She's probably long gone by now.'

'We'll get her.'

'She lied about the fucking keys,' Buddy muttered.

'We still gonna go after Lisa?'

'You bet. We'll take the bikes. But we gotta take care of Maureen first.'

'Let me, OK? It's only fair. You got Sheila.'

Then they entered the kitchen. Lou's heart pounded, his mouth went dry and heat surged through him when he saw Doug with Cyndi. Breathless, he limped toward them. But Buddy grabbed his arm.

'Stay put,' Buddy said. 'Doug, cut it out. Come on, we got business.'

Doug paid no attention, kept wallowing.

Buddy stepped closer, slipped on the bloody floor and almost went down. But he caught his balance in time. He kicked Doug in the hip.

'Hey!' Doug looked back over his shoulder, scowling.

'Let's go!' Buddy snapped.

'Shit.'

'You dorks let Maureen get away. Now, *come on*!'

Shaking his head, Doug pushed himself up. His hands flew out from under him. He splashed down on Cyndi and laughed until Buddy grabbed the back of his collar and dragged him off. 'OK, OK,' he said. 'Let me go.'

Buddy released him. On hands and knees, Doug searched through clumps of fleshy debris beside the body. He found Cyndi's knife. Then he stood up. He stared down at her. 'She sure made a mess of your kitchen.'

Buddy punched his shoulder. 'Let's move.'

Their shoes crunched on broken glass as they walked toward the door. Lou was first to step outside. It felt good to be under the rain again. Striding toward the pool, he rolled the makeshift bandage down his arm. He peeled his sodden shirt off, and sighed with pleasure as the rain found his skin.

'OK,' Buddy said. 'So where is she?'

Lou scanned the dark surface from end to end as he pushed the knotted handkerchief back up his arm to cover the gash. No sign of Maureen.

'She supposed to be in the pool?' Doug asked.

'That's what Louie says.'

'I saw her. She was right there watching us.' He pointed toward the middle.

'Well, she ain't there now.'

'Maybe she ducked under.'

'I'll check,' Doug said, and rushed for the edge.

'Damn it, don't . . .'

Even as the words left Buddy's mouth, Doug leaped.

'Bastard! I'm gonna make *you* clean it!'

Doug, standing in shoulder-deep water, turned around and grinned. 'What, you don't want any Cyndi in the pool?'

Lou started to laugh, but suddenly realized that Doug might beat him to Maureen. 'I'll help,' he said. Before Buddy could protest, he dived in.

The water shocked him. He'd supposed it would be like the rain, but it wasn't. It was frigid. It felt like icy arms squeezing his breath out. As he kicked for the surface, he pictured Cyndi's mutilated carcass on the kitchen floor. He imagined Buddy upstairs, ripping Sheila. And horror gripped him. Freezing, suffocating horror. *What have we done?*

He burst to the surface screaming.

The warm fingers of the rain tapped his face, entered his mouth, and his scream twisted into laughter.

'What's so funny?' Doug wanted to know.

'Everything's beautiful.'

'It'll be beautiful if we find her.'

'I call first tibbies.'

'Bullshit.'

'Hey, you got Cyndi and Bud got Sheila. It's my turn.'

'Whoever finds her first,' Doug said. Turning away, he called in a sing-song, 'You-whooooo, Maureeeeen. Where *arrrre* youuuuuu?'

Lou scanned the dark surface.

No Maureen. Could she hold her breath this long? he wondered. What if she'd drowned? Better for her to drown than get away. But the idea pulled at him with disappointment. He wanted her alive. He wanted to make her blood burst out. He wanted to bury himself in her hot gore.

Lights suddenly pushed away the darkness around the pool. Peering through the black shower, Lou saw Buddy by the switch panel at the rear of the house. Then the pool lights came on. Instead of the brilliant shimmering blue that Lou remembered from summer night parties, the water looked murky. Like used dishwater. Its surface, calm except for ruffles set in motion by Doug swimming toward the deep end, was spickled with tiny geysers spashed up by the raindrops.

Lou turned in a slow circle, scanning the depths. Though the water was cloudy with gray, he could see the bottom. At least at the shallow end. When he studied the other end, he realized he couldn't make out the drain at the deepest point. So the gloom obscured the very bottom.

Maureen couldn't be that far down, he thought. Not if she's alive.

And dead, wouldn't she float to the surface?

Doug stopped beneath the diving board, reached up and grabbed its edge. 'I don't think she's in here,' he called to Lou.

'Me neither.'

Buddy walked out to the end of the board and gazed down.

'You see her?' Doug asked.

Buddy shook his head. 'Dive on down and check the bottom.'

'Thanks, but no thanks.'

'Do it.'

'You and the horse you rode in on. I went under a minute ago and it scared the shit out of me.'

'Scared of the dark?'

'You wanta check the bottom, help yourself. Have fun.'

'Fuckin' woos.'

'I don't think she's in here, anyway,' Lou called. 'She must've climbed out and run for it.'

Shivering, he waded to the side of the pool. He tossed his barbecue fork onto the concrete, then boosted himself up. At once, the rain began to soothe his chill. Twisting around, he sat on the edge and scooted backward. He stretched out. The rain poured down on him, caressing away the cold from the pool, melting his goosebumps, covering him like a warm blanket. He shut his eyes and opened his mouth.

It felt so good.

He didn't want to move.

His drifting mind imagined that the rain was blood. Maureen's blood. She was suspended above him, maybe in some kind of a harness that held her horizontal over the ground. She was naked and sobbing. Blood poured from wounds all over her body. Blood from her face spilled onto Lou's face. Blood from the severed stub of her tongue dripped into Lou's mouth. Blood from her breasts splashed against his chest. From her vagina came the blood that pattered the front of his pants and soaked through, hot against his groin. He imagined the harness lowering her slowly. Closer and closer. Soon, she would be on him.

'Get off your ass!' Buddy shouted. 'Doug, get out of there. We gotta find that bitch and put her down.'

Yanked from his fantasy, Lou groaned. But then he realized

it had only been make-believe. When we find her, he thought, it can get real.

10

Trev steered up the driveway and stopped under the carport.

'Do you want me to come with you?' Lisa asked. 'I know Maxwell's sister.'

He shut off the lights and engine. 'This isn't Chidi's house.'

'What?'

'It belongs to the man who ran the pizza parlor. I've got to see if his daughter's here.'

'Oh, for godsake,' Francine muttered.

'I won't be long. Sit tight.' He opened the car door, then hesitated, wondering whether he should leave the key in the ignition. A crazy woman had answered the phone. She might still be inside. She might not be alone. If something should happen to him . . .

But if he left the key, Francine might just drive away.

'What is it?' Lisa asked.

'Nothing. You two keep your eyes open. Don't be afraid to use those guns if there's trouble.' He pulled out the ignition key. Then he dragged the shotgun across his lap. He climbed out, locked the door, and shut it.

As he stepped past the rear of his car, he heard thumping from the trunk. His prisoner. He wondered if she had enough air.

Don't want her to suffocate, he thought.

So he propped the shotgun against the bumper and unlocked the trunk. The lid sprang up, shoved by the girl. 'Hey!' he yelled as she scurried to her knees. 'Get down!'

She snarled. Before she could leap, his fist caught the point of her chin. Her arms flew out. Her head snapped back and rang against the underside of the trunk lid. As she started to slump away from him, he reached in. With both hands, he grabbed the shoulder straps of her jumper. He tugged her forward and down so the lid wouldn't hit her, then slammed it shut.

'Damn!' he gasped. He struggled for air.

Just trying to be a nice guy, and she goes for me!

He felt angry and betrayed, but mostly he felt scared.

As if he'd offered a nice chunk of meat to a stray dog, and the damn thing had turned into Cujo.

Should've expected it, he told himself. He picked up the shotgun. Consider it a lesson. Don't trust anyone, and watch your ass or they'll take it apart for you.

Still shaken by the encounter, Trev stepped around to the passenger side of his car. He climbed two stairs, tried the knob of the house door, then peered through the glass.

Liam's kitchen. Its lights were on. He saw no one, alive or dead.

On the table were Liam's salt and pepper shakers. China Leprechauns. Trev's throat went tight. He'd spent a lot of time at that table, drinking Guinness and laughing with Liam and Mary. They'd seemed a bit like leprechauns, themselves. Full of blarney and mischief. They never tired of joking about themselves, a couple of folks from County Kerry coming to the States and opening a pizzaria. *Sure, 'n there's no accounting for the whims of a Kerryman.*

Trev's vision went blurry. He blinked his eyes clear, then stepped down to the driveway.

If the woman who'd answered the phone claiming to be

Maureen wasn't a guest, she'd broken into the house. Better to find where she entered, and go in that way, than to smash through a door or window.

Keeping his shotgun ready, Trev passed the bushes at the corner of the house. He looked over the low stucco wall of the porch. The front door – what remained of it – was shut. Light spilled out through a ragged gap above the handle.

Someone had bashed through the door.

Trev pictured a wild, axe-wielding woman bursting into the house, going after Maureen.

She would've had some warning, though. All that noise. Maybe she got out in time. If she was inside, at all. And if she didn't try to defend the place.

At the door, Trev crouched and peered through the gap. The living room lights were on. He didn't see anyone. On the carpet just inside were dark water drops and footprints, but they faded away after the intruder had gone a short distance.

Only one set of footprints. Made by sneakers. Large for the shoes of a woman, but it had been a woman who answered the phone.

A big gal. But apparently alone.

He tried the knob. It turned, and he eased the door open until it met the wall. He stepped into the house.

He closed the door. He pulled off his hat and plastic hood, and dropped them to the floor. That was a lot better. Now, his vision wasn't limited to the eyeholes. The cool air felt good on his face.

A few strides took him to the center of the living room. The sofa, easy chairs, lamp tables and television stand were flush against the walls. Nobody could be hiding behind them. Nobody seemed to be lurking in the corners. He saw no bulges in the window curtains.

Trev moved slowly toward the dining room. The

chandelier above the table was dark. The only light was that which spilled in from the living room. Stopping in the archway, he sank to a crouch. He peered through the bars of chair and table legs. Staying low, he scanned the rest of the room. Nobody.

Over to his left, the kitchen door was shut. A strip of light showed at the bottom. He had checked the kitchen from the door beside the carport, but someone might've entered after he'd headed for the front.

Leave it for last, he decided.

Beyond the kitchen door was the opening of the short hallway that led to the two guest bedrooms and the bathroom. The master bedroom was on the far side of the table, just to the right. Its door stood open. It was dark inside.

Trev rose from his crouch. He sidestepped silently to the right. As he rounded the end of the table, he could see down the hallway.

Dark. Except for a strip of light beneath the bathroom door.

His breath hitched. His heart kicked.

Easy, he told himself. The light doesn't mean she's in there. Go charging, she might just pop out of a room and plant an axe in your head.

He crept to the doorway of the master bedroom. He scanned the darkness. Nothing moved. All he heard was his thudding heartbeat. Bracing the shotgun with his left hand, he eased into the room and elbowed the light switch. Lamps came on at both sides of the bed. He studied the beige carpet and found no water stains. To the right of where he stood, the closet door was shut.

She might be in there. Or hiding at the far side of the dresser or bed.

Probably in the bathroom, he thought. But this was no time to take anything for granted.

Trev strode quickly forward, stepped up onto the bed, and walked across it. The mattress was springy under his feet. The bed creaked a little, but he doubted that the noise would carry beyond the room. Nobody beside the dresser. Nobody hiding alongside the bed. Turning around, he made sure the closet door was still shut. Then he stepped down, knelt, lifted the hanging coverlet, and checked the space beneath the boxsprings. Suitcases. He let out a trembling breath, then got to his feet.

Only the closet remained. He dreaded opening its door. But he had no choice.

He stared at it as he made his way around the end of the bed.

If the woman was in there, she'd probably heard him walking on the bed. She might even be able to hear his approach. Though his shoes were silent on the carpet, the plastic bags encasing him in their slick heat made crinkling sounds that might be picked up by keen ears behind the door.

He imagined her waiting in the darkness, the axe raised overhead.

He took a deep breath and held it. Reaching out, he closed his hand around the knob. He clamped the shotgun's stock tight against his side, hooked his mittened fingertip over the trigger, jerked the door open wide and leaped back.

Nobody lurched out at him.

He saw only rows of clothing on hangers. Liam's shirts and pants along the right side, Mary's blouses, slacks and dresses to the left.

Liam hadn't gotten rid of her things yet. Now, he wouldn't have to.

Shoes on the closet floor. Trev crouched to make sure nobody was hiding among the hanging garments.

And saw a pair of feet, legs bare to the knees where they vanished behind curtains of clothes. His breath shot out and he lurched backward. His calves struck the bed. He dropped onto the mattress.

'You in there.' His voice was high and shaking. 'Come out. Right now.'

Silence from the closet.

What if it's Maureen?

Maureen would've answered.

'Maureen?' he asked.

No answer.

'OK, lady. Come out or I'll shoot.'

'Trevor?'

A chill squirmed up his spine.

'Are you Trevor, the guy that called?' Whoever she was, she sounded scared.

'I'm Trevor.'

'You . . . you're one of *them*.'

'I pretended to be one of them when we talked. I'm a police officer. Come out of there. Now.'

'Did you get the stuff on you?'

'No. But you did.'

'Yeah, but . . . I don't wantcha killing me.'

'Just come out.'

Deep in the shadows of the closet, Mary's clothes slid toward the front. Trev heard hangers skidding on the rail. A woman squeezed her way clear, stood up straight and faced him.

'Don't you shoot me, now.'

Trev got to his feet. He kept the shotgun trained on her chest.

She stepped forward.

Trev let her stride through the doorway, then said, 'Hold it right there.'

'Yes sir.' She halted and stared at him. She looked terrified.

She was a big woman, just as her footprints had indicated.

Probably over six feet tall, with broad shoulders. Her brown hair was matted down. She looked to be in her mid-thirties. A pretty face, with hints of creases where they'd be if she grinned and laughed a lot.

She wore a faded green bathrobe. Probably Liam's. It was tight across her shoulders. The sleeves ended well above her wrists. Her chest wouldn't let the front close completely, but the edges of the robe met at her waist where the cloth belt was tied. The robe reached almost to her knees.

Trev saw no black on her skin.

'You came in from the rain,' he said.

'Yeah, I did. And I know what you're thinking. But I ain't one of them. Not any more.'

She didn't *seem* like one of them. But Trev kept his guard up and kept the muzzle pointed at her chest. Her skin looked pale and sleek between the lapels of the robe.

'I'm OK,' she said. 'Honest.'

'You didn't sound OK when we talked on the phone.'

'Well, I *weren't* OK then. I still had the black on me. But then I took me a bath and now I'm OK.'

He stared at her, confused. 'What do you mean?'

'Well, it passed. You know? I just went real wild when the rain got me. I was out for a walk and the rain got me and I just run around wild for a spell. I just didn't know what to do with myself. Then I got my hands on a hatchet out in a tool shed and I busted in here. I gotta tell you, I was all hot to bust some heads. I ain't in here but a few minutes,and you called up. You said you'd come on over, so I figured I'd knock *your* brains out.' She frowned at Trev. She nibbled her lower lip. 'I'm right sorry about that. But it was like I had a hoodoo on me? I wanted to bust your head something fierce.'

'But not now?' Trev asked.

'Not after I got clean. I stripped down and took me a hot shower. You know? The rain out there, it felt so darn good.

But I didn't want to go outside, what with you coming over. So I figured the next best thing'd be a hot shower. But it didn't feel the same, at all. And before I know it, I don't feel like bashing heads no more.'

'The shower *cured* you?'

'Well, it's like I said. All that wild feeling just leaked right out of me. All I felt then was scared. So I come in here and hid.'

'There's nobody else in the house?'

'I sure don't think so. I ain't seen anybody but you.'

'Let's have a look. You go first.'

He followed her out of the room.

'What's your name?' he asked.

'Sandy Hodges.'

'In there,' he said. Sandy stepped into the first guest room and turned on the light. 'Stand over there and don't move.' She stepped to the far wall. She watched while Trev searched. He found no blood, no body. A woman's clothes were hanging in the closet, and he supposed they must belong to Maureen.

Where *are* you?

At least she wasn't in this room.

Nor was she in the next. The second guest room had a convertible sofa that was still pulled out. Green pajamas were wadded on top of the sheets. For a moment, Trev wondered who'd been sleeping here. Then he remembered that Liam had mentioned using one of his spare rooms. The poor man hadn't been able to sleep in his own bed since Mary's death.

'Are you OK?' Sandy asked.

He shook his head. 'I knew the people who lived here.'

'Well, I hope they're OK.'

'Let's check the bathroom.'

She led the way, opening the door and stepping over the damp, black clothes heaped on the floor: socks draped over sneakers, corduroy pants, a flannel shirt with panties and a bra on top.

A moist white towel hung from the shower curtain rod. The tub was empty, its enamel still beaded here and there with clear drops of water.

Trev leaned against a wall. He felt weak with relief.

She's not in the house. Sandy didn't bash her head in. God knows, Maureen might be dead or in bad trouble, but at least she isn't here. She could be all right.

'Where's your hatchet?' he asked.

'Under my duds,' Sandy said.

Stepping away from the wall, he nudged the pile with his shoe until he spotted the wooden handle.

'You'd better get dressed,' he said.

Sandy raised her upper lip. 'I can't put them things on. They'll get me all dirty and I might go wild again.'

He supposed that was true. 'You don't want to go out in that,' he said.

'Well, I don't much wanta go out at all.'

'I can't leave you here.'

'I don't see why . . .'

'Maureen might come home.' There was a roughness in his voice that made Sandy draw her head back.

'Well, I wouldn't hurt her or nothing.'

Softening his tone, he said, 'I'm not going to leave a stranger in her house. Besides, she might come home wet. If that happens, she'll attack you. I don't want either one of you getting hurt.'

'Well, I don't wanta get wet again.'

'I've got a car just outside the kitchen. It's not in the rain.'

'Where do you aim to take me?'

'Just away from here. You won't have to leave the car. Come on.' He backed his way out of the bathroom, watching her. She stepped over the pile of clothes, taking a long stride to avoid them, the robe slipping away from her thigh. She made no attempt to snatch up the hatchet.

She's either all right, Trev thought, or she's putting on a good act.

But he didn't think he was ready to turn his back on her.

He waved her into Maureen's room, and followed her in. 'Find something to wear,' he said.

She pulled open a dresser drawer and lifted out a pair of black panties. She frowned at him. 'You don't gotta watch me, do you?'

'Put them on.'

'Well, shoot.' She turned away from him, bent over and stepped into the panties. She drew them up beneath her robe, groaned and pulled them down again. 'These little things'll cut off my dang circulation.'

'We're wasting time. Try the closet. Maybe she's got a coat or something.'

Sandy entered the closet. She pulled a string to turn on the light bulb, then searched among the hanging clothes. 'Reckon this is a pretty big gal,' she said. 'Not as big as me, but she's tall, ain't she?'

'Yeah.' The talk of Maureen made him feel empty.

'Now, here.' She pulled a tan trench coat off a hanger. 'This oughta do just fine.' Still in the closet, she faced Trev. 'You just *gotta* watch me?'

Shaking his head, he turned around.

'That's a sight better,' she said.

'Don't try anything.'

'You sure don't trust me very much.'

'I'm just trying to keep alive.'

'Well, same here.' A few moments later, she said, 'OK, I'm decent now.'

Trev turned. She came out of the closet with the robe in one hand. Maureen's coat was tight across her shoulders and chest, but the sleeves reached to her wrists and the bottom of the coat covered her to the knees. Though she hadn't been able to button it, the belt cinched it shut.

'You'll need shoes,' Trev said. 'You'll have to wear your own, I suppose.'

Nodding, she stepped to the dresser. She took out a pair of white socks. 'These'll probably fit OK. Maybe you can wash off my shoes for me. You got them bags on.'

'Let's go.' He waved her ahead, and followed her toward the bathroom.

'Maybe we can dig up some trash bags for me,' she said.

'We've already wasted too much time. We'll just get your shoes ready, and take off.'

'You're sure in a mighty rush to get out in that rain. You sure we shouldn't just oughta stay right here and be safe?'

'I've got to make one more stop. Then we'll see about finding a place.'

11

So far, the trick was working fine.

They'd taken care of three outsiders, one each time, keeping the right hand door of the restaurant latched with the steel pegs at its top and bottom, shoving open the door on the left, grabbing the first crazy to squeeze in, and taking him down while Terry and Rafe jerked the door shut again by tugging on the table cloth they'd passed through its handle.

They'd killed one intruder. He was a skinny, giggling man

who came in swinging a crowbar. As John chopped his arm, Gus jammed a steak knife into the side of the guy's neck and severed the carotid artery.

'Let's not kill them if we don't have to,' John had said while they dragged the body out of the way.

'We don't kill 'em, what'll we *do* with 'em?' Gus wanted to know. He was the one who'd called John a pansy.

'Let's try to disable them, then maybe tie them up.'

'Great. That how you handled the VC? No wonder we lost the fuckin' war.'

'This isn't a war. These people are just like us except they happened to get caught in the rain.'

'Like a mutt happens to get rabies.'

'John's right,' Steve said. 'We should try to take them alive if we can.'

'More risky that way,' said Roscoe the chef.

'Fuckin' right, more risky.'

'I'll handle the next one,' John told them.

The next one had charged into the restaurant with a knife in each hand. John broke both his arms, then his nose. The screaming man was dragged into the cocktail lounge where people huddled over him and bound his feet.

The third outsider was a teenage boy with a Mohawk haircut and a monkey wrench. John took the wrench away. Gus clobbered him with an uppercut that lifted him off his feet. The first part of the kid to hit the floor was the back of his head. From the noise it made, the stiff brush of hair hadn't been much of a cushion. He was taken into the cocktail lounge to be trussed.

'We do much more of this,' Gus said, 'folks are gonna start running low on belts.'

'Let's worry about one thing at a time,' John told him.

'This is working pretty good so far,' Steve said.

John stationed himself at the door. He glanced at Terry

and Rafe, off to the side with the table cloth. Steve stood next to him. He checked the rear. Gus and Roscoe, waiting, nodded.

'Let's do it,' he said.

Terry and Rafe let the cloth droop. John shoved the door open. This time, those outside were ready. Two of them hit the door, forcing it wide. The crowd surged forward.

'Oh shit!' Steve cried out.

The first to rush in was a woman in a nightgown. She drove a screwdriver down at John's face. He blocked it, slammed a fist into her belly, and hurled her sideways for Steve. An elderly man tried to bring down a golf club, but it was too long. Its head knocked against the top of the door-frame. John chopped both sides of his neck, grabbed the front of the man's jacket, kneed him in the groin, then swung him aside for Roscoe. A kid rammed his head against John's hip. John's elbow punched into the back of his neck. The kid flopped and two men blocked the doorway, elbowing each other as they tried to squeeze through at the same time.

John yanked the knife from his belt. He shoved it up under the ribs of the man on the right. John recognized him. Henry, the night man from the Shell station.

Damn!

He pulled the knife out and kicked high, the blow shoving Henry into the crowd. Gus crashed a chair leg down on the head of the man on the left. As that guy started to slump, John slashed his throat and shoved him. That one knocked against the pair bracing the door open. John ducked, snatched up the hanging table cloth and threw himself backward.

A woman with a clawed gardening tool leaped over Henry's body. She managed to get her arm inside. The door slammed on it. She shrieked and dropped the weapon. John gave the cloth some slack. The woman's arm jerked out of the gap.

With a quick tug, he jerked the door shut. Steve rushed in from the side and locked it.

John stepped over to the wall. He leaned back against it, gasping, and let his legs fold. He slid down the wall until his rump met the floor.

It seemed as if everyone from the restaurant had poured into the entryway. Some just stood around looking shocked. Others were gathered in small groups, probably surrounding the crazies he'd brought in. He heard quiet murmurs, weeping, voices high-pitched with alarm, the thumps of blows landing on the kid, the golfer and the woman. He thought he should get up and tell them to stop, but he just sat there.

Too close. It had been too damn close. His trick had backfired, could've gotten everyone killed.

He saw Cassy push her way into one of the groups, heard her snap, 'Quit it! That's enough.'

Then Lynn came through the crowd and sat down beside him. She slipped an arm across his shoulders.

'Pretty rough?' she asked.

'God,' he muttered.

'You're not hurt, are you?'

He shook his head. 'So much for brilliant plans.'

'You did fabulous, though. Really. The plan really *did* work. You got . . . how many of them? Six?'

'Plus two outside.'

'So eight. That's fabulous. That's really whittling them down, honey. We got eight of them and they didn't get any of us.'

He faced Lynn. She had a forced smile and a sad, rather frantic look in her eyes.

She'd led a peaceful, sheltered life and there was no reason in the world for her to understand. But she did. John could tell. She knew this wasn't pretend, knew that lives had been lost, that he had killed people whose only crime was getting caught in the black rain, and that he hated all this.

'I'm so sorry I made you come here tonight,' she said.

'We didn't know what would happen.'

'If Kara gets . . .'

'She'll be fine.' He wished he could believe that.

Lynn was silent for a while. Then she said, 'I used to have these horrible daydreams. About earthquakes and nuclear war. I always thought, what if something like that happened and we weren't all together? I'd see myself out grocery shopping or something, and I knew I couldn't get home. And that was the worst part, not being with you and Kara . . . at the end.' Sobbing quietly, Lynn lowered her head.

'This isn't the end,' John said. He put his hand on her thigh, and realized he was touching skin. He looked down. Her leg had come out of the slit side of her gown. He'd given her a rough time about wearing the outfit. Hurt her feelings. Over something as minor as a dress. They might not survive the night. Kara might . . .

Kara will be all right, he told himself.

He moved his hand up the smooth warmth of Lynn's thigh. 'It *is* a nice dress,' he said.

She sniffed. 'Oh, sure.'

'Really.'

'I wore it for you, you know.'

'I know.'

He eased his hand under the slick fabric, and felt a quick surge of desire when he realized she wore no panties. She caressed his shoulder. More of her leg came out of the slit. He touched her soft curls, slipped his hand lower and spread his fingers, opening her. She squeezed his shoulder. Breath hitching, she squirmed a little, rubbing herself against his hand. He curled a finger into her. She moaned.

With her free hand, she wiped tears from her face. She looked as if she didn't know whether to keep on crying, or laugh, or beg him to stop, or reach for his zipper. She said, 'Jeez, John.'

'Jeez yourself, lady. You got nothing on under there.'

'All these people . . .'

'I'm sorry I gave you a bad time about it. About coming here. About everything. I love you.'

'I love you, too.' She gave a loud, wet sniffle. She moved his hand away, but didn't let go of his wrist as she got to her feet. 'Come with me,' she said.

John stood up. As she led him through the foyer, he saw that people were busy with belts, binding the three he'd let in. Nobody paid attention to him or Lynn.

She hurried ahead, pulling him through the cocktail lounge. One woman was hunched over the bar, nursing a drink. Otherwise, the room was empty.

'Where are we going?' he asked.

'Not far.' Lynn glanced over her shoulder at him. Her smile was crooked and strange.

'You're kidding,' he said.

'Oh, yeah?'

'They might need me out front.'

'They can do without you for a while. Can't they?'

'They'll have to, I guess.'

Lynn pushed open the door marked Damsels and pulled John in. The restroom appeared deserted. As the door swung shut, she leaned back against it. She pulled at her single, glossy sleeve, baring her shoulder. As the sleeve descended her arm, the top of her dress peeled down from her breasts. She shook her hand free. With a funny half-smile, she used both hands to twist the dress at her hips. Its slit came to the front. She slipped the dress higher until golden hair filled the peak of the opening.

'Holy smoke,' John whispered.

Lynn said nothing. Gazing into his eyes, she pulled at the knot of his necktie. The movement made her breasts sway a little. He held them, caressing the stiff nipples with his thumbs while she opened the buttons of his shirt.

Cassy came into his mind. The way she'd looked when she stretched back to put his blazer on.

Even before he could feel any guilt for thinking of Cassy, he forgot about her as Lynn guided one of his hands down between her legs. He stroked her there. She was wet and slippery. Moaning, squirming, she unfastened his pants. They dropped around his ankles, and she pulled at his shorts, dragging them down, freeing him.

She curled her fingers around his straining penis. They glided down it, and up, and down again.

'I'm not quite sure how to go about this,' he said.

Lynn chuckled. 'You'll think of something.'

'Hope nobody comes in.'

'Then we'd better get on with it.'

'What about the floor?'

'Yuck.'

'And hard on my knees.'

She swallowed. She shook her head. She looked as if she were in pain. Her tongue darted out and licked her lips. 'Just fuck me right here against the door,' she said.

Fuck me? John had never heard her say that before. Somehow, the words didn't sound foul. Just blunt and urgent.

'Fuck me,' she said again.

And he no longer cared how, as long as he did it.

He moved forward and Lynn spread her knees wide and he went up against her feeling the firm soft push of her breasts, her arms going around him. When he tried to crouch, the door at Lynn's back stopped his knees. He pulled her away from it, clutching her buttocks through the slick dress, urging her closer.

And he slid up into her as she sank down, wet and tight and hugging.

Her legs came up around his hips. They seemed to be climbing him. The higher they climbed, the deeper he plunged.

Then he had her pinned to the door. He kissed her mouth. It got away, and his lips met her chin. Her mouth was a moving target, and he stopped trying to kiss it. He watched her eyes, and she watched his as the hard thrusts jammed her upward and she slid down against the door only to be pounded up again. She grunted and bit her lips and whimpered. She whipped her head from side to side. She let go of him with her arms. Slumped back against the door and jerking up and down against it, she rubbed and squeezed her breasts.

John had never seen her like this before.

12

'Denny?'

She awoke with a start and found herself lying crooked on the sofa, her legs hanging to the floor and her head resting on Tom's lap. Kara still slept at the other end.

'News bulletin,' he said. His hand, just above Denise's face, pointed at the television. 'They broke into the show.'

She turned her eyes to the TV and recognized Chris Donner, the Eyewitness News anchorwoman.

'. . . been receiving sketchy reports that a crisis has developed in the nearby town of Bixby. Our news staff received its initial telephone call from a citizen of Bixby shortly after seven-thirty this evening, in which we were informed that a storm was dropping rain onto the town which appeared to be black. We were further told that the caller's spouse, caught in the mysterious storm, quote "went out of her senses and attacked me for no good reason" unquote.'

'In our attempts to verify the story, we tried to make contact with various Bixby officials. Our calls to the mayor, fire department and police department have gone unanswered.'

'Since that time, we have received numerous calls from people in that area. We have determined that an emergency situation exists in Bixby, and we have notified officials in surrounding areas.'

'It appears that the storm began shortly after seven o'clock this evening, that it is generally confined to the city limits of Bixby, and that the black rain-like substance falling from the sky may be causing those who come into contact with it to commit acts of violence. We understand that affected citizens are roaming the streets, and breaking into business establishments and homes in search of victims. Though the reports we've received have been sketchy, we understand that an undetermined number of people have been killed by these roaming marauders.'

'Let me repeat that, at this time, the crisis is occurring only in Bixby and in the areas immediately surrounding its city limits. The situation is not taking place in any of the neighboring towns. If you are not a resident of Bixby, there is no cause for alarm.'

'We ask that our viewers who *are* in Bixby remain indoors. Under no circumstances should you venture outside. Also, it is imperative that you avoid contact with anyone who has been exposed to the rain. Many of those people have armed themselves, and they should all be considered extremely dangerous.'

'We take you now to Stan Fisher, live at the scene. Stan?'

'Thank you, Chris.' The screen showed a tidy, middle-aged man wearing a bow tie and an open sweater. He was standing in lights beside a van marked 'Eyewitness News.' Staring grimly into the camera, he said, 'I'm here at a roadblock set up by the CHP on Route 12, two miles south of the town of Bixby. County and local law enforcement agencies are cooperating with the Highway Patrol in an effort to seal off all roads leading into the stricken community. Nobody is being allowed to enter the area.'

The TV showed Chris at her news desk, the picture of Stan Fisher on a screen behind her as she spoke into a telephone. 'Stan,' she said, 'is anyone coming out?'

'As a matter of fact, Chris, three cars have come out just since we arrived. Unfortunately, we haven't been able to interview any of the survivors. They were immediately taken into custody. I presume that authorities are questioning them even as I speak to you.'

'In effect, they're being quarantined?'

'That seems to be the case, Chris.'

'Do you know whether they had come into contact with the rain?'

'It appears that they hadn't.' Stan again filled the TV screen and the camera pulled back, showing a man in uniform beside him. 'Chris, this is Commander Brad Corkern of the Highway Patrol. Sir, what can you tell us about the situation in Bixby?' He held his microphone toward the man.

'Well, Stan, I'm afraid we don't know a whole lot at the present time. As you've mentioned, we're doing what we can to prevent people from going into the rain area. We've had a total of eleven people come out since the time we established the roadblock here.'

'How were they?'

'Rattled. Plenty rattled. But they don't appear to be infected.'

'Infected. Is it a disease of some kind?'

'We don't know what it is. We've talked to these people, and they indicate that anyone who gets wet from the rain – or whatever it might be – takes on violent behavior. Many of them reported witnessing assaults, and they saw quite a few dead bodies before they got out of the area.'

'Do you have any idea what might be causing such violence?'

'The dope,' Tom said. 'The guy already told him . . .'

'It's like I said, Stan, we can't explain it.'

The TV showed Chris in the studio as she said, 'Ask him if it's something like acid rain.'

The camera stayed with her, showing Stan in the background as he touched a button in his ear, nodded and said to the commander, 'Could this have anything to do with acid rain?'

'This is *black* rain, Stan. I don't know from acid rain. Isn't that something to do with Canada?'

From Chris again, 'Are there chemical plants in the area?'

'Could this be caused by a problem at a local chemical plant?'

'We're looking into that, Stan. We're also looking into the possibility that some kind of biological agent has infiltrated the area.'

'By "biological agent," you're referring to a bacteria or virus that may have gotten into the rain?'

'Something like that, yes.'

'Is there a possibility that Bixby has been subjected to any kind of biological or chemical warfare weapon?'

'I'd say that's highly unlikely. I don't think it's in anyone's best interest to speculate about such things. We've got enough on our hands without folks jumping to conclusions and panicking about some kind of war breaking out. This is purely an isolated situation. Nobody who isn't in Bixby has anything to worry about.'

Chris said, 'Stan, ask if the storm is moving, and in which direction?'

'Does the storm appear to be moving toward any other populated area?'

'From all we can tell, it's stationary over Bixby. Like I said before, there's no call to alarm anyone. If it does begin moving, we'll let folks know in plenty of time to evacuate or take protective measures.'

'Stan, ask if any rescue efforts are under way.'

Stan nodded. 'Is any effort being made to send authorities into the area to restore order?'

'We're looking into the possibility. Until we've been able to determine the cause of the contamination, however, we're extremely reluctant to take that measure. If we send in armed men, not knowing what they might be up against in terms of the conditions at the root of this thing, we'd be risking the possibility that they'll become infected and turn their weapons on innocent civilians. Right now, I'm afraid, our wisest course of action lies in adopting a wait-and-see posture, preventing people from entering the town, and making sure that nobody who's been infected is allowed to get by us and possibly carry the problem to other areas.'

The camera pulled in close on Stan. 'That's the latest from Commander Brad Corkern of the Highway Patrol, here at the scene on the outskirts of Bixby. This is Stan Fisher reporting for Eyewitness News. Back to you, Chris.'

'Thank you, Stan.' She hung up the phone. The screen at her back went blank for a moment, then showed a map of central California with a black circle ringing Bixby. 'Our mobile news unit will remain at the scene, and we'll bring you further reports as the situation develops in Bixby, where a black rain of mysterious origins appears to be contaminating the residents, breeding violence and death. This is Chris Donner for Eyewitness News, returning you now to our regularly scheduled program.'

A commercial for Excedrin came on.

'Cute,' Denise muttered. 'What's this, Excedrin headache number three?'

Tom looked at her, narrowing his eyes. 'People are driving right out of this mess.'

'Some are.'

'Maybe we should give it a try.'

Her stomach went tight and cold. 'Are you kidding?'

'If we can make it to one of those roadblocks . . .'

'Tom, too much could go wrong. We're safe here.'

'Right now, we are. But God, who knows? This could go on for a long time. Sooner or later, some of those lunatics might break in. What'll we do then?'

'I'd rather take my chances here. Really.'

'I think we should get while the gettin's good.'

13

Lou, searching the alley behind Buddy's house, caught a glimpse of someone ducking behind a garbage can.

All *right*! he thought.

When Buddy had ordered them to split up and search for Maureen, picking Lou to hop the high redwood fence and check the alley, he had nearly given up hope of being the one to get her. He was sure she'd gone a different way, probably fleeing along either side of the house and escaping through a gate rather than trying to climb the fence at the rear. Buddy and Doug had taken those routes. One or the other of them would end up with Maureen, and Lou would be out of luck.

Now, he realized how wrong he'd been.

She *had* gone over the fence.

She's mine, all mine.

Lou's heart thudded wildly as he strode toward the garbage can. The rain felt great splashing against his bare skin, running down his body in hot rivulets. He thought about stopping long enough to take off his pants so he could feel the rain all over him. And feel Maureen's body and blood all over him when he took her. Too tricky, though. He knew he couldn't get his pants off without removing his shoes. Then he would have to put the shoes on again because what if she made a run for it and he had to chase her? He sure didn't want to go racing down the dark alley barefoot.

Nail her first, he decided. Get her down so she can't run. Then you can take your time stripping and doing her.

His breath came in rough gasps as he halted in front of the garbage can. The can was just off the alley blacktop, set in a strip of weeds alongside someone's fence.

She might think she was hidden just fine, but Lou could see the faint dark curve of the top of her head.

'Come on out, honey,' he said.

She didn't move. She didn't make a sound. Lou heard only his own heartbeat and ragged breathing, the rain pattering against his skin, hissing on the alley pavement, thumping the hard rubber lid of the garbage container.

He kicked the barrel aside. It skidded, tumbled over.

Maureen, beautiful Maureen in her clinging wet T-shirt and baggy shorts wasn't cowering in front of him.

Lou muttered, 'Fuck.'

Squatting in the strip of weeds was a bony, naked man who leered up at him, said, 'Hi-ya, honey,' and sprang. Lou leaped backward as the man lunged at him, driving the jagged end of a broken bottle at his stomach.

'NO!' Lou yelled.

He lashed out with his barbecue fork and sucked in his belly, expecting the glass fangs to bite deep. The man jerked his head back. The tines missed him, but the bottle jabbed short. Lou grabbed his wrist. He shoved it sideways an instant before the man smacked against him. They both went down. The bottle shattered, off to Lou's left, and then his back hit the alley and the man pounded down on top of him and pinned both his hands to the wet asphalt.

'Get *off* me!' Lou squealed. 'Get *off* me!'

'You're mine,' the man piped.

Lou twisted and bucked. The man's skin was slippery and hot against his chest and belly. Something was pushing against his groin. He realized what it was, and he whimpered.

'Get *off* me, you bastard!'

A crazy thought came to Lou's mind: he ought to be just as turned on as the filthy madman writhing on top of him. It had been that way when he fought Doug by the pool and when he'd gone for Sheila. This shouldn't be any different.

But it sure was.

He felt no lust, just terror and revulsion.

Lou opened his mouth to scream, and the man's mouth came down, slimy against his lips.

He's kissing me! Oh, my God, no!

Before Lou could twist his face away, the teeth chomped in on his lower lip and yanked, and he shrieked as his lip was ripped off. The man spat it out. It stuck to Lou's cheek and the head darted down again and he felt the man suck on the raw wound.

Lou jerked his head aside. Growling, the man clutched both sides of his face and wrenched it upward and clamped his mouth to the wound again. He sucked furiously, his growls softening to moans of pleasure. His fingernails dug into Lou's cheeks. He licked and sucked and gnawed on the open flesh. He writhed, rubbing himself against Lou's body.

And Lou, through the pain and horror, realized that the man's hands were holding onto his face. They weren't pinning his own hands to the alley. Not now. They couldn't be.

Stretching his right arm out sideways, he lifted the barbecue fork. He swung its long rod up, and eased it down until the tines were an inch from the side of his assailant's neck.

He rammed them in.

A harsh gasp blew spittle and blood into Lou's mouth. The man twitched and shuddered. Lou rolled, throwing him off and tugging the fork from his neck. The guy was on his back, mouth and eyes wide, one hand clutching his throat as if he were trying to strangle himself. His heels were shoving at the alley, thrusting his rump off the asphalt, scooting him along on the backs of his shoulders and head.

Lou crawled toward him. Past the man's head. The guy scooted closer. Lou caught the head between his knees. Holding it there, he raised the long fork overhead with both hands and drove it down. He missed his target and the tines ripped furrows in the guy's left cheek. He tried again. This time, he hit where he wanted. The bridge of the nose. One of the twin tines on each side. They punched into the corners of the eyes and went deep.

The orbs burst. The man's shriek only lasted an instant. While he flapped and bounced, Lou pressed down hard on the fork handle and shook it.

Stir him up a little.

He grinned, but winced as the pulling sensation burnt

the raw tattered flesh where his lower lip should've been.

He got me. He sure got me. But not as good as I got him, the dirty old shit.

After the man stopped moving, Lou waved the fork back and forth a few more times. Then he pulled it out. As he licked the tines clean, he remembered Maureen.

Buddy and Doug had probably gotten her by now.

They probably sent me on this wild-goose chase just so they could have her without me.

Lou got to his feet. Staring down at the dead man, he cautiously tongued his wound. Some of his lip was still there. He'd thought the whole *thing* had been ripped off, but only a thin strip, right in the middle, actually seemed to be missing. He touched his cheek where the piece had landed. It wasn't there now.

He stomped on the man's face.

Then he rushed back to Buddy's section of fence. He tossed his fork over the top, grabbed the edge, boosted himself up and dropped to the other side.

Nobody in sight. The patio and pool lights were still on. Lou picked up his fork. He studied the murky depths of the pool as he hurried around it, wishing Maureen would come to the surface and he could jump in and have her all to himself. But the pool looked empty.

'Lou!'

He spotted Doug by the corner of the house.

'Any luck?' Doug called.

He shook his head, afraid of how it might feel if he tried to speak. But he smiled and the pain came, anyway.

If Doug was asking about *his* luck, it meant they hadn't found Maureen.

He ran to meet his friend.

'Shit, man. What happened to you?'

'I ran into a guy,' he said, and realized that those particular words hadn't required him to move his jaw or mouth. No extra pain.

'You kill him?'

'Yeah.'

'Hot damn.' Doug slapped his shoulder. 'We haven't turned up Maureen or anyone else. Buddy's kicking up a shit fit. Come on.'

Lou followed him alongside the house and through the gate.

In the driveway, Buddy was sitting on his Harley. 'Did you find her?' he asked.

Lou shook his head.

'What the fuck happened to your mouth?'

'A guy got . . .' He closed his lips to form the m of 'me' and felt as if burning oil had been dumped on his wound.

'Lou murderated him.'

'Big deal. You dickbrains let Maureen get away.'

'She's gotta be somewhere,' Doug said.

'Yeah, well we can't waste the whole night looking for the bitch. Saddle up. We're gonna pay Lisa a visit.'

Lisa? Lou wanted Maureen, not Lisa. Then he remembered. Last night. That Chidi bastard. Lisa might tell on them. They really ought to kill her.

But she wasn't like Maureen. She wasn't tall and slim and beautiful. She was short and her tits were too big.

'I want N'reen,' he said.

'Tough shit. You should've thought of that before you let her get away. Now let's move it!' He kick-started his Harley. Its engine thundered.

Doug clamped his butcher knife between his teeth as if he were a pirate. Then he mounted up.

Lou stepped to his bike. He swung a leg over it, and lowered his rump against the warm puddle gathered on its seat.

He wished he could stay behind. Maybe he could find Maureen.

But he didn't want to be left alone.

There might be others around like that horrible man in the alley.

Besides, Maureen might be far away by now. Better Lisa than nobody, even if she was kind of a pig.

She's babysitting, Lou reminded himself. Won't be alone. There'll be a kid, maybe a couple of them. Maybe girls.

Yeah!

He pushed the fork under his belt so it pressed against his side like a saber, then fished out his keys.

Collision Course

1

Maureen, flat on her belly under her Jeep, head just below the front bumper, squirmed backward as the three boys swung their motorcycles around and roared down the driveway. They turned away, however, so she needn't have worried about headlamps finding her.

As the bikes sped off, she scooted herself farther back until she was clear of the tire. Then she scurried out from under the Jeep, dragging her coat beside her. Still sprawled on the road, she waited until the bikes disappeared around a corner.

Seconds later, she was sitting behind the steering wheel. She dug into a pocket of her coat, found the keys, and slid the Jeep key into the ignition.

'Now I've got you,' she muttered.

Grinning, she started the engine. She pulled away from the curb. As she picked up speed, she put on the windshield wipers. But she left the headlights off.

By the time they know I'm coming, she thought, it'll be too late.

This was working out even better than Maureen had hoped. Earlier, when she'd climbed out of the pool, she'd ached to rush straight into the house and find whatever weapons might be handy and tear the boys apart. The boys *and* their damn girlfriends. But she'd known she wouldn't stand much chance against the four of them . . . five, if Buddy should come back in after discovering she'd lied about the keys.

As much as she'd wanted their blood, caution had won

out. So instead of blundering into the house, she'd raced to the front. She'd rounded the corner just in time to see Buddy burst in through the door and slam it shut. Then she'd snatched up her coat and taken shelter under her Jeep.

To wait for them, to watch for her chance.

Waiting, she'd heard distant screams, some far-off bangs that sounded like gunshots. Somewhere, people were getting creamed. She imagined bodies being ripped by knives, blown open by bullets. She saw guts spilling from a slashed torso. She saw herself kneeling over a stranger, sucking blood and clots of flesh from a bullet wound. Thinking about such things took her breath away and made her moan and squirm against the pavement.

A couple of cars had gone by, their tires swishing over the wet road.

Then she'd heard a strange, quiet rumbling sound accompanied by clicks and clatters. Roller skates? Sure enough, when she raised her head and peered back she saw a guy on skates dancing and whirling his way up the middle of the street. He must've been well over six feet tall. He appeared to be entirely hairless. He was shiny black under the streetlights. All he wore was a long scarf wrapped around his neck. Its tails should've been flying behind him as he sped along, but when he twirled Maureen saw that they were plastered to his bare back.

He carried an assault rifle with a banana clip.

Watching his approach, Maureen had wondered about her chances of jumping him and taking the gun.

If she got her hands on that sucker, she could blast Buddy and Doug and Lou and Sheila and Cyndi. She could blow their heads off.

He'd blow off mine if I tried, she thought.

Then, fearing that he might spot her, she'd scurried deeper into the dark beneath the Jeep.

He'd pranced and twirled past her hiding place, and the sound of his roller skates had faded to silence.

Some time later came the quick smack of footfalls on the sidewalk. Maureen had pushed herself sideways, savoring the rough rub of the street against her breasts and belly and groin, and peered over the curb. Two women – fat things in hair curlers and clinging housecoats, were chasing a kid. One of the women brandished a cordless electric carving knife. The other didn't seem to be armed. Those were probably her scissors sticking out of the kid's shoulder. The kid wore pajamas. He looked no older than seven. He seemed to be outrunning the gals.

Maureen wanted the electric knife.

It was no assault rifle, but a lot better than nothing.

She started to squeeze up between the curb and the undercarriage.

But the squawk of gate hinges warned her in time, and she slid back under the Jeep moments before Buddy appeared beside the house. She watched his feet as he rushed around. Then someone joined him. Either Lou or Doug, she supposed. She heard voices, but the pounding rain and the distance prevented her from making out what was being said.

When one of the boys approached the Jeep, Maureen knew she was about to be found. More excited than frightened, she'd wondered whether to stay in the tight space, or scurry out and attack. But the kid never looked under the vehicle. Apparently, he just peered in through the windows. Then, he'd gone away and there was more talk.

Working her way toward the front, she'd seen Buddy and Doug standing by their motorcycles near the top of the driveway. After a brief conversation, Doug went through the gate. Buddy waited by his bike.

Alone.

Now, driving her Jeep in pursuit of the boys, Maureen was

glad she'd resisted her urge to go for Buddy while he was waiting by his bike. She'd been very tempted. She'd wanted to crawl out from under the Jeep and let him see her, pull off her T-shirt and shorts as he approached. The rain would feel wonderful on her bare skin. She would caress herself, tell Buddy how much she wanted him. And he would put his knife away to free his hands for touching her.

It had worked with Doug and Lou in the house. It would work with Buddy.

And just when he was so overcome with lust that he didn't care about anything else, she would strike. Crush his balls. Grab his knife. Rip him open.

It would've worked. It would've been great.

But she'd stayed under the Jeep thinking about it and was still there, savoring the fantasy, when Doug showed up with Lou.

It's probably a good thing I didn't try, she told herself. Something might've gone wrong. And this way I can get all three of them. Without any risk.

They were a block ahead of her, riding abreast up the middle of the street.

The noise of their engines should keep them from hearing her approach.

She pressed down harder on the gas pedal and felt the surge of speed press her back into the seat. The three boys on their choppers grew. Lou, on the right, didn't have a shirt on. Maureen grinned as she imagined how the pavement would shred his skin. But she steered for Buddy. The Jeep wasn't wide enough to take down all three at once, and she wanted to nail Buddy on the first pass. He rode between the other two. Smash him down. Maybe get Doug at the same time, then swerve to the right and try for Lou.

The distance closed.

Four car lengths separated Maureen from her quarry. Then three, then two.

Buddy glanced back over his shoulder.

'*Adios, bastard!*' Maureen yelled, and floored the accelerator.

As she roared down on him, lights pushed in from the left. A car. Just ahead. Speeding toward the intersection.

Oh, my God!

Maureen shoved at the steering wheel and braced herself for the impact.

2

Moments before spotting the headlights and motorcycles speeding in from a cross-street, Trev figured he was about a mile from the Chidi house. A few more minutes, and he would be there. With his carload of women.

Sandy had seemed relieved when she stepped out the kitchen door and found two other females in the backseat of his car. 'You got yourself quite a collection here,' she'd said.

'There's another in the trunk.'

'You ain't gonna put me back there, are you?'

'She's one of *them*,' Trev said, and opened the passenger door.

Sandy said, 'Howdy, ladies,' as she climbed in.

Trev hurried around to the driver's side and slid in behind the wheel. As he backed his car out of the driveway, Sandy turned around in her seat. Her knee pushed against the side of Trev's thigh.

'I'm Sandy Hodges,' she said.

'I'm Lisa Walters. This is my mom, Francine.'

Trev swung onto the street. He started forward. The knee nudged him. He looked down. Through the eyeholes in his mask, he saw that Sandy's leg was out of the trench coat, bare all the way up her thigh.

He felt a strange mixture of desire and sadness. That was Maureen's coat, but not Maureen's leg, not Maureen's groin just out of sight under the draping fabric.

He wondered if he would ever see her again.

Damn it, he shouldn't have been so timid about getting to know her. If only he'd realized that time was so short.

It's too late for regrets, he told himself. You can't go back in time and change anything. Just gotta live with your mistakes. And your losses.

'I sure am glad to meet you two,' Sandy said. 'It was getting to where I was starting to feel like there wasn't anybody else sane but me in the whole darn world.'

'I'm not sure how sane we are,' Francine said, and let out a peculiar laugh as if to prove her point.

'Well, you're sure a sight for sore eyes, I tell you that.'

'I bet you were awfully glad Trevor showed up,' Lisa said.

'Thought he aimed to kill me, is what.'

'We bundled him up real good so the rain wouldn't get to him.'

'Wish I had me an outfit like that.'

'They're garbage bags,' Lisa explained.

'And they feel horrible,' Trev said. 'Be glad you're not wearing these things.'

'Well, I feel right naked.'

'Are you and Trev . . . do you go together?' Lisa asked.

'Never seen him before tonight.'

'I thought you were his girlfriend, or something.'

'Me? Nope.' To Trev she said, 'Is Maureen your gal?'

'Not exactly. She's the daughter of a friend.'

Sounding annoyed, Francine said, 'So she wasn't even home? You took us all the way over there for nothing?'

'Mom.'

'Shit. He's been dragging us around all night on this wild-goose chase of his, looking for this woman. He's damn near gotten us killed. And he *still* hasn't found her. We could've been out of here by now.'

'You been searching around like she says, Trevor?'

'Tried a couple of places.'

'We could get out of this rain and be safe if he'd just quit this damn nonsense.'

'Mom,' Lisa said again.

'I think that's mighty noble,' Sandy said. 'Your Maureen's a lucky gal, having a fella like you searching high and low for her.'

'Noble, my ass,' Francine said. 'You'll think he's noble when he stops again to go looking and we get jumped by crazies and they kill us all.'

'You got quite a burr up your hindquarters, lady.'

Lisa laughed.

'What sort of a hick are you?' Francine snapped. 'You fall off a haywagon on your way to the rodeo?'

'Gosh, Trevor, how long you been putting up with this gal?'

'Seems like ages,' he said, smiling.

'I reckon as how I'd of given her the boot if I was you.'

'It's crossed my mind. But she's Lisa's mother. Lisa's a good companion.'

'Lisa's what got us into this mess,' Francine said. 'But you wouldn't know that, would you, Daisy May? My wonderful daughter here took up with a jungle bunny and . . .'

'I don't like your mouth one whit, lady.'

'Thank you,' Lisa murmured.

'*You* tell her,' Francine said. 'I'll bet she'd be very interested in knowing all about it, so she'll know just who to blame when one of these maniacs murders her.'

'I started going out with this guy,' Lisa said. 'And some kids killed him last night. Because I was going with him. And because he was black.'

'I'm mighty sorry,' Sandy said.

'Oh, you haven't even heard the best part yet. Tell her the best part, honey.'

'We don't even know it for sure.'

'The coon's grandpa is some kind of a witch doctor,' Francine explained. 'He's put a hex on the whole town. That's what's happening here. That's why we've got the black rain. It's grandpa's idea of payback.'

'Well, that's a load if I ever heard one.'

'It might be true,' Trev said. 'We're going over to his place right now to check on it.'

'You're telling me this *is* a hoodoo?'

'I plan to find out.'

'Well, don't that just beat all? What're you aiming to do about it?'

'Make him stop.'

'Aren't you scared he'll hex *you*?'

'I guess he might try.' Trev realized he hadn't given any thought to that possibility. But the idea of it didn't frighten him, and he wondered why.

Maybe because you don't really believe the old guy has any special powers.

If he doesn't, why are you bothering to check him out?

Just on the off-chance he *does*?

I'll find out soon enough, he thought. Can't be more than a mile from the Chidi house.

A few more minutes, and he would be there. With his carload of women.

Beyond the yard of the corner house, the headlights of

three motorcycles pushed pale beams through the night. Trev flinched and Sandy yelled, 'Look out!'

The riders were black. Crazies. For an instant, Trev considered taking them down. But he thought better of it. Those were big bikes. A collision might put Sandy through the windshield. He swerved to the right, hoping to cut behind them.

He shouted, 'Hang on!' His front tire bounced over the curb. Then the rear tire hit and the car tilted and he heard Francine squealing behind him but it was OK, he'd missed the bikes, the nearest speeding by just ahead of his bumper as he came off the corner and he waited for the jolt of his tires coming down and something hit them.

It felt like the sledgehammer of a giant bashing the rear side of the car. He heard screams, a roar of sundered metal and bursting glass.

The blow slammed his teeth together and threw him against the door, knocking Patterson's hat off his head, then hurled him back against his seat. The world outside the windshield twisted and tipped sideways. Something clipped his cheek. The shotgun? Sandy dropped onto him. Sparks flew at the windshield, tossed up by the side of the car skidding over the pavement.

He glimpsed the red brake lights of whatever had hit them. Then the spin of his car wrenched the lights out of view.

3

Maureen's quick swing to the left had almost taken her past the rear of the car that came racing in over the corner of the block, tipped up and riding on its outside wheels. Almost. Her bumper caught it just behind its back wheel.

The jolt thrust her forward, stiff arms folding at the elbows. But she was well braced. The impact wasn't as severe as she'd expected. She didn't even hit the steering wheel.

She plowed right through, bashing the car out of her way, then saw that she was speeding toward the far corner. A mail box there. A tree beyond it. She wrestled the steering wheel to the right.

And spun out.

She gasped. Her Jeep twirled. She saw the car she'd hit skidding along on its driver's side. Then it was whipped out of sight like something glimpsed from a carousel.

When she came to a stop, she couldn't believe her luck. Her Jeep was upright near the middle of the intersection, facing in the very same direction she'd been driving before the accident.

The lights of the motorcycles were specks in the distance.

Maureen stepped on the gas. Nothing happened.

She twisted the ignition key. The engine roared to life.

Far away, the bikes turned to the right and disappeared.

She jammed the gas pedal down. The tires grabbed, and she sped after her prey.

4

Trev, pinned on his side between the door and Sandy, suddenly realized he could only see with one eye. He started to panic, then remembered the bag on his head. He pulled an arm out from under Sandy and tugged the bag off. He could see again.

Sandy's head. Hanging hair hid her face as she shoved at the window of his door in an effort to push herself up.

'You OK?' he asked.

'I been better,' she gasped.

From behind Trev came moaning sounds. 'Lisa? Francine?'

'I think Mom's knocked out,' Lisa said in a squeezed, breathless voice.

'You OK?' Trev asked.

'Kind of.'

'How are the windows back there?'

Silence for a moment. Then he heard a quick, high suck of breath. 'Oh my God, Trev! The whole rear window's busted!'

The rear window, he told himself. Not the back passenger window. Otherwise, rain would be pouring down on Lisa and her mother.

'Is rain getting in?' he asked.

'I can't . . . Just some trickles.'

'For godsake, don't let any of that water touch you.'

'It's OK so far. But it's kind of starting to run.'

'Don't let it touch you!'

'I'll try.'

'Gotta do better than try.'

'This is some fix,' Sandy said. She sounded fairly calm about it.

'We'll be all right,' Trev said.

'How do you figure that?'

'Cause we're the good guys.'

'Reckon that's what they said at the Alamo?'

'If you can get off me, I'll try to get out the back window.'

'That'll do us a heap of good.'

'You'd better do something quick!' Lisa blurted.

'Try to cover up the window with those bags you've got back there.'

He heard the rustle of plastic.

'It's just kind of running in along the . . . MOM! Oh, God, Trev, Mom's face is in it! I didn't see . . . There's a *puddle*!'

'Don't touch it!' he snapped. Twisting so his back was against the door, he shoved at Sandy's shoulder and chest. She got a knee onto his hip. Then she put her other foot against the door. 'Try to stand up,' he told her. Then, to Lisa, he said, 'Your mom's still out cold, isn't she?'

'Yeah. I think so. She's moving a little, though.'

'Oh shit.'

Hanging onto the steering wheel, Sandy pulled herself up. Her weight lifted off Trev's hip. As she rose, her head bumped the passenger window. She hunched down some.

'I think Mom's starting to wake up,' Lisa said.

'The guns! You've got the revolver and shotgun back there! Get rid of them! Throw them out the window!'

'If I can find 'em.'

'Don't let your Mom get them!'

Trev struggled to sit up. He reached under the hanging tail of Sandy's coat, clutched her leg, and pulled at it. She wobbled a little, but held steady. Then she bent down. She grabbed the front of his shirt and tugged. He squirmed and kicked, and came to rest with his rump on the window. The car wobbled slightly as he slumped backward against its ceiling.

He turned his head toward the rear and found Francine close enough to touch. She was slumped against the side of the car, face against the window. She was moaning softly. The darkness hid her eyes. He couldn't tell whether they were shut or open.

Lisa was half standing, her back to Trev, right foot on the window sill below her mother's chin, left knee propped on the woman's hip. As he watched, she tossed the shotgun underhand through the high, narrow gap of the rear window. Its barrel clamored against the open lid of the trunk, bounced back toward the window and dropped out of sight.

The trunk!

Trev remembered the girl he'd left there.

He suddenly felt sick.

The right rear of the car must've taken a terrible impact to pop open the trunk that way.

She can't be alive, he thought.

A kid. Just a kid. A girl in a jumper and knee socks.

I killed her.

The revolver, tossed by Lisa, clunked against the trunk and fell.

If she's not dead, we've just given her two guns.

Francine raised her head. Trev leaned toward her and pounded it down. It struck the window with a thud, and the woman went limp.

'What'd you do?' Lisa blurted, looking around at him.

'Hit your mom. We can't have her waking up and going crazy on us.'

'Jeez.'

'I'm sorry,' he muttered.

Fingers suddenly clenched Trev's hair. 'Hey,' Sandy said. 'I got me an idea. Why don't we see we can't knock the car back down on its wheels? Get on up here.' She pulled his hair.

Trev stood up, his back rubbing along the ceiling.

Sandy maneuvered until she was standing in front of him. She pressed her body against his. 'Give me a hug,' she said.

He wrapped his arms around her.

'Lisa,' she said, 'you stand there on the back door. On the count of three, we'll hit the seats. Trevor, you just throw me backward hard as you can. Lisa, tackle your seat.' She pushed her cheek against the side of Trev's face.

'I guess I'm ready,' Lisa said.

'Here we go. One, two, *three*!'

Trev rammed Sandy backward, smashing her against the seat. Her breath gushed hot against his ear. The car rocked away beneath the impact, teetered, and started to fall.

My God, it's working!

The car seemed to drop for a long time. Then Sandy was smashed up against him, grunting. He felt the tires bounce. And heard a rip and clank and knew at once that the front axel had given out.

'We did it!' Lisa sounded as if she might cheer.

Trev grabbed the seatback and pulled himself up. Kneeling between Sandy's legs, he looked out the windshield. The wipers swept back and forth, clearing off the black raindrops.

The car had a tilt, thanks to the axel, but Trev was glad to see the world right-side up again. He smiled at Sandy. Her face was a pale oval that showed white teeth.

'I guess we're still in a fix,' he said. 'But at least we're down.'

The engine had quit. The headlights were still on, driving pale tunnels into the darkness ahead. The car had come to rest near the right corner of the intersection. He peered through the windshield, then through the windows on each side. He saw nobody.

Lisa leaned forward and crossed her arms on the back of the seat above Sandy. 'What are we going to do now?' she asked.

'We won't be driving anywhere,' he said. He crawled backward until the door stopped his shoes. Sandy raised her knees. The trench coat spread open to its belt. Trev looked away while she scooted backward and sat up. She tugged at the coat to cover herself, then leaned back against the passenger door. Smiling at Lisa, she reached up and stroked the nape of the girl's neck.

'Seems to me,' she said, 'we either stay right here or we don't. We stay put, we got water coming in the rear and we got Francine already wet. She's bound to go for us when she comes to her senses.'

'We could tie her up,' Lisa suggested.

Trev said, 'There's no telling who might come at us from the outside.'

'We *can't* leave the car,' Lisa said.

'Well now,' Sandy said, 'we can if we want to. We'd get wet and wild, but that ain't necessarily the worst thing in the world. I been there, you know. And your mom, she's already that way. Trevor, you'd have to get yourself wet along with us.'

Trev's heart suddenly felt like a fist trying to punch its way out of his chest. 'We'd turn into killers,' he said, his voice shaky.

'That don't mean we'd have to kill each other. Back when I was wet, I ran into some others in the rain. I had kind of a hankering to go for 'em, but I was plenty more interested in getting after folks that was still dry. If we was all to step out and get ourselves soaked . . .'

'Were you still able to think straight?' Trev asked.

'Pretty much. Just that I had these nasty desires, is all. Except for that, I was pretty much like normal.'

'So do you think the four of us . . .' Trev had to pause and catch his breath. 'Could we walk on over . . . to the Chidi house? And take care of business?'

'Don't see why we couldn't. After we get there and finish up whatever we've gotta do, we can shower off and be OK again.'

'Would we kill everybody there?' Lisa asked.

'I reckon we'd sure want to.'

'But if it's only the grandfather causing the trouble . . .'

'Lisa's right,' Trev said. 'Maybe the whole family's in on it with the old man. But maybe not. We might end up killing some innocent people. And not just at the Chidis. Maybe we won't be able to control ourselves and we'll stop along the way. Once we're changed, we might not even *care* about getting there. What if we just go on a rampage?'

Sandy shook her head. 'Well, we might.'

'I don't want to go around killing anyone,' Lisa said.

'OK,' Trev said. 'Look. I can go out on my own and not get wet. With any luck, I should be able to make it to the Chidi place on foot in six or seven minutes. We're only about a mile away. If it is the grandfather . . .'

The door behind Sandy flew open. The overhead light came on. Sandy gasped with surprise and flung her arms wide as she flopped backward. Her right arm swung out into the rain. Her left hand clawed at the door frame. Lisa's hand darted down and grabbed a lapel of her coat, but the coat merely pulled open and didn't stop her fall. Trev gripped her ankles.

And cried out 'NO!' as the girl from the trunk hooked an arm under Sandy's chin and tried to drag her from the car.

Not dead. The crash had freed the teenager, not killed her.

At least she hasn't got the guns, Trev thought.

He heard himself groan as he watched the raindrops splatter black against Sandy's face and coat and chest. She was stretched out straight, only her rump and legs still on the car seat, the girl tugging at her head. She writhed and kicked against Trev's restraining hands.

He let go of one ankle and reached for his revolver. Her other ankle jerked free. Her legs slid away from him. He snatched the weapon from its holster. He brought it up, hating what he had to do, feeling betrayed by the girl he'd tried to save, thinking *It's her or Sandy* but knowing it was already too late for Sandy as he pointed his .38 at the girl's chest just above the bib of her jumper and tried to find the trigger through his slippery plastic mitten and Lisa threw open her door.

'Don't!' he yelled.

Ignoring him, she leaped out into the rain at the same moment Sandy's thrashing legs dropped toward the pavement. The girl from the trunk couldn't handle a woman of Sandy's size. She fell backward, pulling Sandy down on top of her. Lisa rushed at them. Her pale sweater looked as if it were being eaten by the darkness. She dropped to her knees beside the two, and tried to tug the girl's arm away from Sandy's throat.

Trev, holstering his weapon, crawled across the seat.

Don't do it, he told himself. Get your hood on first.

But he knew he had to get wet. He had to be like them.

No!

If the rain got him, he might lose control. He might never make it to the Chidi house.

He twisted away from the open door, spotted his plastic hood crumpled on the far edge of the seat, reached back and grabbed it, then snatched Patterson's cowboy hat up off the floor. His shotgun was there. He made a quick decision to leave it. The 12-gauge would require both hands. Besides, a blast from that would almost certainly be fatal, and he didn't want to kill any of the girls.

He pulled the bag over his head, blind for a moment until he found the eyeholes, then jammed the Stetson down to hold it in place.

He crawled across the seat and climbed out.

Sandy was sprawled on top of the girl from the trunk. Lisa had one of the girl's arms pinned to the street. Sandy was trying to sit up.

Her trench coat was wide open, still on her shoulders but leaving the rest of her body naked except for her socks and sneakers as she pushed backward at the pavement. Her skin gleamed black under the streetlight. Trev stared at her, feeling an unexpected rush of heat. Then he hurried forward, careful not to step on any legs. He ducked down, grabbed Sandy's coat by the shoulders, and pulled her up.

She threw herself against him. As he staggered backward a step and braced himself, Sandy ripped open his shirt. He felt her fingernails through the thin plastic. Before they could tear it, he caught her wrists. He shoved her arms down against her sides, then forced them up behind her back. She came tight against him.

'Sandy!' he yelled in her face. 'Stop it!'

She shook her head and squirmed. Through the plastic glued to his chest, he could feel the heat of her skin, the rub of her breasts, the stiffness of her nipples.

Her head darted toward his face.

He rammed her arms up higher. She squealed and tossed back her head, rising as if going up on tiptoes, arching her spine. He felt a soft, curved ridge pressing his groin and realized he had an erection.

'Damn it!' he snapped. 'Settle down or I'll break your arms off!' He gave them an upward yank. She shrieked and tried to climb his body.

Letting go, he shoved her away. She stumbled backward and fell to her rump beside the struggling girls.

Trev pulled his revolver. He aimed it at her chest.

'Come at me again, I'll shoot you! You're gonna do what I tell you!'

She sat there, glaring up at him.

Trev kept the gun on her, and turned his eyes to the girls. They were a rolling, snarling tangle as they punched and bit and scratched one another. Trev rushed forward and kicked. His shoe caught Lisa just under the armpit and sent her tumbling off the other girl.

Standing above her, he aimed at her face. 'Get up slow or I'll kill you.'

Lisa bared her teeth.

Glancing from her to Sandy, he stepped over to the girl from the trunk. She'd obviously been no match for Lisa. She was sprawled on her back, whimpering as she gasped for breath. The bib of her jumper had been torn down. Her blouse was ripped open and pulled off one shoulder. The skin of that shoulder looked mangled. In the glow from the street light, Trev saw blood there, mixed with the running black rain water. Her pleated skirt was rucked up around her waist. A knee sock had come down and was bunched above her ankle. Trev nudged that ankle with his shoe.

'Get up,' he said.

He stepped backward, sweeping his weapon from side to side.

'I'm in command,' he told the women as they slowly rose to their feet. 'You'll do whatever I say. Anybody causes trouble, I'll shoot. If you behave yourselves, we might all get through this mess alive. Is that . . .?'

From behind him came the metalic snick-snack of someone working a pump action.

He whirled around.

Francine. She stood by the car's open door, grinning, a shotgun at her hip.

The one he'd left in the car.

Jesus!

He jerked his trigger. In the instant before the hammer dropped, he heard a clack from the shotgun and realized it was empty. He had no time to turn his muzzle away. The revolver bucked. Its blast crashed in his ears. Francine flinched. Her mouth fell open. She lowered her head and turned it as if trying to find the stain of something carelessly spilled. Dropping the shotgun, she lifted a hand and touched her sweater midway between her left shoulder and the top of her breast. She took the hand away, turned sideways and looked at her fingers in the light from the car. Then she looked at Trev. 'You shot me, you bastard,' she said. 'You . . .' She pitched forward and fell flat. Trev cringed at the sound her face made hitting the pavement.

Lisa rushed in, and he realized he'd forgotten about the women at his back.

He swung around. Sandy and the girl from the trunk, both hurrying forward, abruptly stopped.

Standing sideways, he was able to keep them covered and still watch Lisa.

He felt sick. He'd shot her mother.

The girl, on her knees, pulled Francine onto her back. She tore the sweater off the woman's shoulder, jerked the bra strap out of her way, sank down and pressed her mouth to the wound.

'Lisa!'

She ignored him. He heard sucking sounds. He rushed forward, kicked her sprawling, then crouched beside Francine. He pressed an open hand against the woman's chest, felt her rib cage rise and fall.

She was breathing.

Keeping his eyes on the other three, he holstered his revolver. He grabbed Francine under the armpits and pulled her up. Careful not to knock the Stetson off his head, he hoisted her onto his shoulder. He clamped his left arm across the backs of her legs, and stood. He drew his gun. 'OK, ladies,' he said. 'Let's go.'

5

John was waiting by a sink when the door opened and Tina, Andy's girlfriend, entered the restroom.

'Oh!' she gasped.

A blush warmed John's face. He smiled. 'Just waiting for my wife,' he said, and nodded toward a toilet stall.

'Is she all right?' Tina asked.

'Yeah, she's just fine. Thanks. Anything happening out there?'

'It's all just so awful.'

'What?'

'Well, you know.' She sighed and shook her head. Her eyes were still red from crying, her face smudged and streaked with makeup that had dried after running. 'Just everything.'

'They haven't opened the doors again, have they?'

'Oh, no. They sure haven't. Not since you did it and everybody tried to get in.' She drew her arms in close to her sides and shuddered. 'Everyone's just so scared and crazy. And they're wondering where you went off to.'

'Thought I'd better stay with Lynn,' he said. Then he called out, 'Honey, I'll wait for you right outside the door.'

'OK. I won't be much longer.'

To Tina, he said, 'Sorry if I startled you.'

'No, that's all right.'

He went out the door, noticed that no one was using the pay telephones, and stepped over to one. He dug into his pocket for change. He lifted the receiver off its hook. Its black plastic was slippery with his sweat. He realized he was suddenly trembling.

Reaching toward the coin slot, he hesitated.

What if nobody answers?

But he knew that he had to make the call. Denise would probably pick it up. He could talk to her, to Kara. If everything was all right, it would lift a terrible weight off his mind.

He took a deep, shaky breath, then dropped a quarter into the slot. He punched in his home number.

Some hissy sounds.

A ringing.

Answer it! Come on!

It rang four times. Five.

Sweat trickled down John's sides.

Six. Seven. Eight.

Damn it! Please!

A soft click and clatter. 'Hello?'

'Denise!'

'Mr Foxworth?'

'Thank God.'

'We're OK.'

'Thank God,' he said again.

'Are you and Mrs Foxworth all right?'

'Fine. We're fine. It's insane around here, but . . . we're holding on. Nothing's happened at the house?'

Silence.

'Denise?'

'Yeah?'

'Is something wrong?'

'No. But look, I have to tell you something. My boyfriend's here. Tom? I didn't mention it before, but . . . anyway, Lynn said it'd be OK if he came over.'

'Your boyfriend?'

'Yeah. Tom Carney.'

'When did he show up?'

'It was after the rain started, but . . .'

'Oh, my God. He didn't get *wet*?'

'Well, yeah. But he's OK now. Nobody got hurt. He got . . . washed off, and he was fine.'

'What?'

'Yeah. You know the rain? At least with Tom, he stopped being crazy once it was cleaned off. He was just the same as usual.'

John gazed at the phone. His mind seemed to be reeling.

They had a guy with them. He must've come in crazy, maybe even attacked them. But they were OK. They hadn't been hurt. And somehow, the black stuff had been washed off and he'd returned to normal.

It doesn't make them permanently nuts.

The implications of that . . .

'Mr Foxworth?'

'I'm here. Are you sure Tom was all right again after he got clean?'

'I'm positive.'

'Jesus,' he muttered.

'Kara's right here. Do you want to talk to her?'

'Sure.'

'But don't hang up,' Denise said. 'I want to talk to you about something.'

'Fine. OK.'

A moment later, Kara said, 'Oh, hi, Daddy.'

Oh, hi. As if it came as big news that he was on the line. Those were always her first words into a telephone, even when she was the one instigating the call.

Tears filled John's eyes. 'Honey.'

'How are you?' she asked.

'Mommy and I are just fine,' he said through the tightness in his throat. 'We're still at the restaurant. How's everything there?'

'Pretty neat. We had popcorn and I had a New York seltzer and we watched my birthday on the VCR but I fell asleep.'

'Sounds like you're having a great time.' John used his

sleeve to wipe his eyes, but more tears came. 'Wish I was there,' he said.

'Me, too. When're you and Mommy coming home?'

'I don't know, honey. I think we'll have to wait till the rain stops.'

'Can I stay up till you get home?'

'Well, stay with Denise and Tom. You don't have to go to your bedroom. Sleep on the sofa if you get tired.'

'I'm not tired now.'

'How's Tom?'

'Oh, he's real nice. I guess Denny told you what happened, didn't she?'

'A little.'

'Well, we beat up Tom real bad and knocked him out. I bonked him right on the head. But he's fine now.'

'You're a tough little monkey, huh?'

'I am not a monkey, Daddy.'

'No, you're not. I love you, honey.'

'I love you, too. Can I talk to Mommy?'

'Not right now. She's in the bathroom.'

'Oh. OK.'

'You be good, honey. Now, let me talk to Denise again.'

'OK, bye.'

A moment later, Denise said, 'Me again. What I wanted to tell you, there's been some news on the TV. They said this is only happening here in Bixby.'

'Well, that's good to know.'

'Yeah. But the thing is, Tom has this idea about the three of us trying to drive out. You know, go where it isn't raining? He's got an umbrella, and he's already found your raincoat and some galoshes. I don't know. I think we ought to stay here. What about you?'

'*Yes*. For godsake, don't leave the house. There's no telling what you might run into.'

'Yeah, that's the way I see it, too.'

'Let me talk to him.'

'Sure. Just a second.'

John heard a quiet whoosh behind him, realized it must be the restroom door opening, and turned to see if Lynn was there. She met his gaze. And suddenly went rigid. Her face lost its color. A frantic, stricken look came to her eyes.

I've been crying, he thought. Shit!

He said fast, 'Everything's fine.'

Lynn shut her eyes. She let out a breath, went a little limp, and leaned her side against the door frame.

'Mr Foxworth?' A stranger's voice.

'Hello. Tom?'

Lynn opened her eyes. She looked confused.

'Yes. Denny said you wanted to speak with me.'

Nodding, he forced himself to smile for Lynn. 'I want you to stay in the house, Tom. Forget about trying to get out of town, OK?'

'Well, you know, if we can get to one of the CHP road-blocks, we'll be safe.'

'Don't try it. Not with my daughter. And not with Denise. If you want to go by yourself, that's up to you. But what I'd really like you to do is stay in the house and take care of the girls.'

'Well . . . I wouldn't go off and leave them, sir.'

'Then you'll stay put?'

John heard nothing for a few moments. Then came a quiet sigh. Tom said, 'Yes, sir. I'll stay. I'll protect them as best I can if anything happens.'

'Good man.' Lynn pushed away from the wall and stood up straight again, frowning as she stared at John. 'Is it true what Denise said about you getting wet?' he asked.

'Yes, sir. The stuff got on me when I came to your house from my car. But I didn't hurt anyone. Denise, a little. But she's OK. I never touched Kara.'

'I'm glad to hear it. But you're all right, now?'

'Yes, sir.'

'You got clean, and then you were all right?'

'Uh-uh.'

'That's great news, Tom. It's been nice talking with you.'

'You, too, sir. And you can count on me. I'll stay right here and take care of everything.'

'I really appreciate it.' He smiled again at Lynn. 'Is Kara still there?'

'Sure,' Tom said. 'You want to talk to her?'

'Her mother does.'

'Here she is.'

John stepped aside and held the handset out for Lynn. Her eyes filled and her chin started to tremble. She rushed forward and took the phone. 'Kara?' A moment later, in a choked voice, she said, 'Oh, hi to you, too.'

While she talked, John stood next to her. He caressed her back. It shook against his hand each time she sobbed.

She's really been through it tonight, he thought. We all have.

Now she's weeping, overcome with love for Kara and relief that the girl is OK and probably despair that she might never see her again. A few minutes ago, she'd been mad with lust.

It's having death right outside the door, John thought. Death trying to get at you. Makes life so urgent and sweet.

His hand drifted down to her rump. He squeezed it gently through the slick fabric and she smiled at him and sniffed and told Kara, 'We'll be home pretty soon, honey.'

After she hung up the phone, she turned to John and held him tight. 'I want us to be home with her,' she said.

'I know. So do I.'

'What'll we do?'

'We'd better get back to the others.'

'Can't we leave?'

'You know we can't. Not yet.'

He took Lynn's hand and led her through the cocktail lounge to the foyer. Everyone seemed to be gathered near the closed doors. 'Can I have your attention?' John called out.

People turned to him. The talking faded.

'Where the hell've you been?' Gus snapped.

'I was on the phone.'

'For ten fucking minutes?'

'Shut up,' Lynn told him.

'I found out a couple of things,' John said. 'I talked with someone who saw a newscast, and Bixby's the only place where this is happening. Every place else is fine.'

Some of the people appeared relieved. He heard murmurs of 'Thank God,' and 'Well, that's something, anyway,' and 'At least we're the only ones.'

Gus muttered, 'Lot of good that does us.'

Dr Goodman said, 'Do they know what's causing the situation?'

'I don't know,' John said. 'But I think it's reassuring that it's confined to this area. Authorities are aware of it. Apparently, the Highway Patrol has set up some roadblocks nearby.'

'Will they be coming in to rescue us?' Carol Winter asked.

'I don't know.'

'We can't depend on that,' Cassy said, stepping toward the front of the group. She smiled at John, then turned to scan the others. 'We've got to take care of ourselves.'

'They haven't tried anything for a while,' said an elderly woman.

'Probably waiting for us to open the doors again,' Peggy said.

John raised a hand to regain their attention. 'I found out something else. The madness isn't permanent. Once the rain has been washed off, the people apparently become normal again. Now, we've got several of them tied up in here. Those who haven't been disabled can help us defend this place if we clean them up. So let's form a group and take them into the kitchen.'

'Throw 'em in the dishwasher,' suggested the little man who believed in levity.

'There are a couple of wash tubs,' John said. 'Let's get started.'

6

Maureen slowed her Jeep as she drove through an intersection. She glanced both ways. Cars were parked in driveways and along the curbs, but the street looked deserted.

'Where *are* they?' she muttered.

The last she'd seen of the three motorcycles was just after the collision when they'd been turning right onto a sidestreet. By the time she'd reached the corner, however, they'd been gone.

She'd headed down that road, looking for them. Maybe the bastards had reached their destination, and she would spot their bikes in front of a house.

She'd scanned the curbs, the driveways, the front lawns of the houses along the street. She'd checked both ways at the corners, peering down the crossstreets in search of their lights.

But this was the fifth, or sixth intersection she'd passed without finding any sign of them.

They'd had a big headstart. Still, if they'd gone this far,

she should've seen them when she first turned onto the road. So they must've taken one of the earlier sidestreets.

Maureen swung across the road, pulled into a driveway, reversed her way out, and started back in the direction from which she'd come.

I'll find them if I have to drive down every street in the whole damn town, she thought. Find them and waste their sorry asses.

If that car hadn't cut in front of her . . .

Snarling, she pounded the steering wheel.

For a few moments, she considered driving back to the scene of the accident and killing the ones in that car. She'd caught a glimpse of those inside. There'd been three or four in there. She could have a field day. If they were still hanging around. They're probably long gone, she thought. Unless they were hurt.

And they might be armed.

Also, they were strangers. Killing them wouldn't be half as good as killing Buddy and Doug and Lou. Those guys had messed with her. Buddy, for godsake, had raped her. She remembered how she'd wanted to kill him for it even before she escaped from the house and got herself wet again.

Her mind went back to the rape. She could feel herself sprawled on the slick bottom of the tub, the hot shower pouring down, Buddy pulling at her buttocks and thrusting into her. The memories took her breath away. She felt heat spreading outward from her center. Her nipples tingled as they pushed against the damp fabric of her T-shirt. She imagined herself reaching up for Buddy, pulling him down against her, sinking her teeth into his throat. Blood spurting down her throat while his cock twitched deep inside her, pumping her full of semen.

Trembling, she let out a sigh.

That would've been just incredible.

She remembered how she'd felt only pain and outrage and shame when Buddy had actually taken her. No thrill at all. Even the desire to kill him hadn't brought any feelings of lust.

I was sure different then.

'Weird,' she muttered.

She suddenly had an urge to feel the rain, so she cranked down her window and put her arm out. The warm drops splashed against it. How nice it would be to have a convertible, to feel the rain pouring down on her. She cupped some in her hand. As she rubbed it over her face, she glimpsed a stop sign.

I could stop and get out, she thought. Just for a minute.

No, I've got to find them.

The rain would feel good on her. But their blood would feel better.

Then she realized she had just gone through the intersection without even looking for the guys.

She stepped on the brake. The Jeep came to a stop, and she shifted to reverse. She started to back up, but changed her mind.

They'd probably gone up one of the streets closer to where they'd turned onto this road. One of the first few.

She continued driving forward while she thought about the matter.

They'd probably made a left. A right would've taken them parallel to Buddy's street, and back in the direction they'd started from. If they'd wanted to do that, they would've headed the other way when they came out of Buddy's driveway.

Maureen grinned.

It was so obvious. They'd gone left.

That means I make a right, she told herself, since I'm coming from this direction.

I'll start at the first street they could've turned onto, check it out for a while, then work my way back on the next one.

She sped up.

She'd gone two blocks when a man dashed out of a driveway. She pressed down harder on the gas pedal, hoping to hit him. But he was running too fast. He would get by her in time, and she was reluctant to make a swerve for him, fearing she might spin out and crash. He suddenly flung his arms wide and seemed to dive at the pavement. He skidded to a halt right in front of her. Maureen saw the feathered shaft of an arrow upright in the middle of his back. She looked to the side and glimpsed the man with the bow. Standing on a front lawn. Wearing a breechclout, a feathered band around his head. Drawing another arrow from his quiver. Then she bumped over the body in the street.

Moments later, something thunked her Jeep.

An arrow? The bastard shot at *me*!

She had a sudden urge to back up and go after the guy, run him down.

Hell no, she thought. Keep wasting time, and I'll never find Buddy and his pals.

7

'Does anybody want to see more of my birthday party?' Kara asked as *Fistful of Dollars* came to an end.

'I think we should keep this channel on,' Denise told her. 'They might have another news report.'

'Oh. OK.'

Denise, smiling, patted the girl's knee. And gripped it when she heard a growling rumble of engine noise. She glanced at Tom, then stared at the front door. The roar seemed to be coming from beyond it. As if a motorcycle or a souped-up car was thundering by on the street outside. She waited for the sound to fade away. But it grew louder and louder and ended abruptly.

A chill squirmed up her back.

'Uh-oh,' Tom said.

She turned to him. He was gazing at the door. He looked as if someone had just invited him to eat a worm.

'Is something the matter?' Kara asked.

Denise ducked forward, snatched the remote control off the table, and shut off the television. 'Somebody stopped in front of the house,' she whispered.

Kara's lips formed an O, then stretched away, baring her teeth as her eyebrows climbed her forehead.

'Sounded like motorcycles,' Tom whispered.

'More than one?' Denise asked.

He shook his head. 'Three or four, maybe.'

'Does that mean somebody's coming *here*?' Kara asked.

'We don't know,' Denise said. 'Let's be real quiet. If they think no one's home . . .' Her voice trailed off.

Kara snuggled up against her. Tom put a hand on her back. The three sat motionless on the sofa, gazing at the door.

They all flinched when the bell rang.

Denise glanced at the table beyond her knees. The fireplace poker was there, along with the hammer and butcher knife.

The doorbell rang again.

'Should we see who it is?' Kara whispered.

'Shhhh.'

Someone pounded on the door. Each blow shook it. Each blow felt to Denise like a punch in the stomach. She struggled to breathe. Her cheeks tickled. She rubbed them with one hand, and found the skin pebbled with goosebumps.

'Lisa!' a voice called through the door.

'Lisa?' Kara whispered, frowning up at Denise. 'She was supposed to be sitting for mc tonight.'

'Yeah. I know.'

'It's Buddy,' the voice called. 'Come on, open up.'

'Buddy Gilbert,' Denise muttered.

'Oh, great,' Tom said. 'And he thinks Lisa's here.'

'They go together,' Denise said.

'They did till she started running around with Max.'

He pounded the door again. 'Open up, Lisa! Come on, I know you're in there.'

'He's probably got Doug and Lou with him,' Tom said.

'Lisa!' Buddy shouted. 'Let me in! Right now! Or I'll bust the fucking door down!'

'The F word,' Kara whispered.

Tom leaned forward. He snatched the poker off the table and got to his feet.

'What're you doing?'

'I'd better tell him Lisa isn't here. Maybe they'll go away.'

'Fat chance.'

A hard blow rattled the door in its frame.

As Tom hurried toward the foyer, Denise picked up the hammer. She went after him, glanced back and saw Kara following, the knife in her hand.

Tom pressed his shoulder to the door. 'Buddy?'

'Who the hell are you?'

'Tom Carney.'

'What the fuck are you doing there, Carney?'

'Lisa isn't here.'

'Bullshit. Let me in.'

'It's the truth,' Denise said. 'Lisa was supposed to be here, but she canceled out.'

'Who're you?'

'Denise Gunderson.'

'Denise, huh?'

The way he said her name, she thought of how he leered at her in school. The look had always made her feel crawly.

She heard some quiet voices through the door. Then Buddy said, 'You're bluffing. I know damn well Lisa's there. She got you two for body guards, or what?'

'She's not here!' Tom shouted.

'Bullshit.' He crashed against the door.

'We've got guns!' Tom yelled. 'Now knock it off! Get out of here or I'll start shooting! I swear to God, you hit the door one more time and I'll put some bullets through it!'

Denise heard more faint conversation from outside. Then silence.

She stared at Tom. Grimacing, he shook his head as if he thought the warning about guns was a pretty lame idea, but the best he could do.

He looked surprised when the motorcycles grumbled to life. A grin spread across his face. He whispered, 'I'll be damned.'

'Get away from the door,' Denise said, suddenly fearing that Buddy might try to ram it down with his bike.

'You don't think . . .?'

'I don't know.' She rushed over to the picture window and swept the drapery out of her way. Clamping the hammer between her knees, she cupped her hands against the glass and peered out.

Far to the right, she saw the three boys mounted on their motorcycles. The bikes turned in tight circles near the end of the driveway, their headlights sweeping across the window. Then the bikes roared down to the street, swung right and sped out of sight.

Denise stepped away from the window. Tom and Kara

gazed at her, their eyes wide. 'I don't believe it,' she said. 'They really left.'

Kara beamed. 'They just didn't want to get shot to smithereens.'

Tom, with a weary smile, sagged against the door. 'God,' he muttered. 'That was a close one.'

'I wonder if they'll be back,' Denise said.

'Yeah. I wouldn't put it past those creeps. Did you see who was with Buddy?'

'Two other guys. I didn't get a very good look, but I think they were probably Doug and Lou like you thought.'

'Probably. Those three are always together.'

'I wonder what sort of plans they had for Lisa.'

Tom shook his head. 'Did you hear what happened at the dance last night?'

Denise had agreed to miss the football game and the dance that followed so her parents, being away for the weekend, wouldn't have to worry about her.

'It was on the news about Max,' she said.

'Well, that was afterward. But I saw Jim Horner today, and he said Buddy and Doug and Lou showed up drunk and really gave Lisa and Max a bad time. They got themselves booted out.'

Denise felt herself sinking inside. 'You don't think . . . you don't suppose they're the ones who *did* that to Max?'

She saw Tom's face go red. His lip curled up.

'What happened to Max?' Kara asked.

'Somebody murdered him last night,' Denise explained.

'Oooo, yuck.'

She frowned at Tom. 'Kara's mom . . . she told me on the phone that Lisa couldn't come here because her mother was taking her to the police station. It sounded like Lisa wanted to tell the cops something about the murder.'

'Oh, my God,' Tom muttered. 'I guess it'd crossed my

mind that those guys might've . . . But . . . I can't believe they'd actually do that to someone. They're real jerks but . . . I mean, to actually . . .'

'Can we change the subject?' Kara asked. Denise glanced at her, then met Tom's eyes. 'I bet they came here to kill Lisa.'

'They're wet,' he said. 'They'll kill anyone they can.'

'But if they think she's here . . .'

'Maybe they're heading for her house.'

'Or maybe they just rode away to trick us,' Denise said, 'and they'll come back on foot.'

8

Lou hadn't wanted to leave. Not with Denise there.

But he followed Buddy and Doug away down the street, hurting with disappointment.

They swung into the driveway of a house at the end of the block, only four homes away from the Foxworth place. Lou shut off his engine, kicked down the stand and climbed off.

'Why'd we stah here?' he asked, being careful not to move his lower lip, forming the words deeper inside his mouth than usual. He knew they sounded garbled, but he didn't care. 'I thought we were going to Lisa's.'

'We *are* going to Lisa's dickhead.'

Lou's heart quickened. 'Huh?'

Doug shook his head, smirking at him. 'You didn't believe that shit they handed us back there, did you?'

He hesitated. 'I guess not.'

They strode down to the sidewalk and started back.

'Those asswipes were probably lying about the guns, too,' Buddy said. 'But just in case, we're gonna go in careful. Find ourselves some windows.'

Lou nodded. He wasn't sure how going in carefully would solve the problem of being met by firearms. It wasn't likely, after all, that windows had been left unlocked. Glass would have to be broken. The noise would ruin any chance of taking them by surprise.

Lou didn't want to get shot.

But Lisa had to be killed, that was for sure.

And Denise was in the house. Denise Gunderson.

We're going back. Oh yeah, we're going back!

He'd missed his chance for Maureen, but Denise . . . whenever he saw her in school, he ached with strange feelings of desire and sadness. She was more than just beautiful. There was something fresh and innocent about her that made him hollow inside.

Lou remembered the empty feelings of loss that she always stirred in him. But they weren't here, now.

' Cause I'm going to get her, after all. Tonight.

He pictured her tied spread-eagle to a bed. He saw himself ripping her clothes off. Pushing the tines of his barbecue fork against one of her breasts. Watching the skin dent as she writhed and screamed. Seeing the points break through her skin and slide in. And that would just be the start.

Lou's heart pounded like a hammer. His breath came in shaky gasps. His penis strained against the front of his pants and he wanted to let it out but the guys would laugh at him.

Buddy halted in front of the house next door to the one where Denise waited. 'Let's go around the back,' he said. 'Find us some windows.'

'All *right*!' Doug said.

Lou grinned, and winced with pain from his torn lip. Then he slid the barbecue fork out of his belt. 'I want Denise,' he said.

'You get who you get,' Buddy told him.

9

Trev knew they weren't making good time. It slowed him down, lugging Francine around on his shoulder. And it slowed him down, keeping the others covered in front of him.

Without the women, he would've been at the Chidi house by now. But he couldn't leave Francine to die from her wound or be killed by any of the crazies he sometimes glimpsed in the distance. Nor could he allow the other three to run wild and maybe kill innocent people.

For one reason or another, all four women were here because of him. They were in his care. They were his responsibility. He planned to make sure they lived through the night.

No matter how much they slowed him down.

Only a couple more blocks to go, he told himself.

Lisa was the worst. She kept walking backward, staring at him and Francine. Trev was sure that his gun was the only thing that kept her from attacking.

The girl from the trunk behaved herself. She walked beside Sandy, her head low. Trev supposed that her injuries must've taken her spunk out.

Sandy hadn't caused much trouble, so far. She'd thrown Maureen's trench coat to the pavement soon after they began their journey, and Trev had told her to put it back on. She'd drawled, 'You aim to plug me if I don't?' and kept on walking. He had decided it wasn't worth fighting about. And he found that he didn't mind watching her stride along, naked except for her socks and sneakers. Sometimes, she turned around, grinning and rubbing herself. Trev wasn't sure whether she was trying to be seductive in hopes of getting close so she could put her teeth into him, or whether she was simply aroused by the feel of the rain.

'Why don't you turn around before you trip?' he told Lisa.

Instead of obeying, she halted, crouched, spread her arms and growled.

Trev aimed his gun at her face. 'Keep moving.'

The girl from the trunk continued walking forward, but Sandy pranced up behind Lisa and slapped the side of her head. 'Do like he tells you,' she said.

Lisa whirled around. 'You bitch!' she snapped. 'We can take him!'

'You're dumber than a dead dog's butt, girl. He'd put holes in us sure.'

'He won't shoot us.' Lisa bared her teeth at him.

'You like us, don't you.' It wasn't a question. 'You want to *save* us, don't you.'

'My own skin comes first, Lisa,' he told her.

She lurched toward Sandy and grabbed the woman's arm. 'Come on. Help me.'

'Not on your life, gal.' Sandy tugged her arm from Lisa's grip and the blast of a gunshot crashed in Trev's ears and Lisa's head jerked sideways as if it had been kicked. A mess flew out from her left temple.

'Down!' Trev shouted.

He dropped to a crouch as Lisa toppled to the pavement. Sandy threw herself flat by the curb. The girl from the trunk turned around slowly as if confused.

'Get down!' Trev yelled at her.

Another shot. A bullet kicked sparks off the hood of a parked car. The way the girl leaped backward, it must've just missed her. She squatted quickly beside the car.

Trev dumped Francine off his shoulder. He spread himself out flat on the street.

A slug whined off the pavement near his face.

He twisted his head to the left. Lost his eyeholes. With one hand, he turned the bag until he could see again.

A man in plain sight. An old, bald guy in a plaid shirt, standing some fifty feet away under the shelter of his porch roof. The porch was lighted. Even as Trev spotted him, the geezer levered his rifle and put another shot through the screen. The bullet chopped the curb near Sandy.

He's not wet!

He killed Lisa and he's not even fucking wet!

'Hold your fire, damn it!' Trev yelled. 'I'm a police officer!'

'Whoop-de-doo, fella!' He swung the barrel in Trev's direction and fired again. The bullet struck the street somewhere behind Trev's head.

'Stop it! Just let us pass. We've got no business with you.' *Except you killed Lisa*, Trev thought.

'I got business with you!' the man called. He levered another round into the chamber as Trev shoved himself up to his knees and the bag blinded him and he threw it off along with Patterson's hat and he could see again and the rain felt good on his head and he braced his aiming hand and the man sighted in on him and fired. Something stung Trev's thigh. Something else slopped against it, and Trev snapped off four shots as fast as he could pull the trigger. The old man jerked, staggered backward and fell out of sight.

Trev looked down. A mess clung to the leg of his jeans. A chunk of skull, hair still clinging to its patch of scalp, slid down the denim. It had come from Francine's head. There was a cavity above her right ear.

He set his revolver on the pavement and tugged the plastic bags off his hands.

There was a slash at the side of his jeans just above the knee.

Like one of the cuts in Lisa's jeans.

I'm a fashion plate, he thought, and chuckled softly.

His skin under the slash felt burnt. The bullet must've nicked him.

I'll live, he thought.

He touched the glop that had splashed the leg of his jeans. It felt spongy and warm. He scooped some off and stuffed it into his mouth. Moaning at the good taste of it, he shoved his fingers into Francine's head and started to dig out more.

'Trevor!'

Sandy stood in front of him. He took his fingers out of Francine's head and reached for her. He wrapped his slippery hands around her buttocks and drew her closer. When he pressed his mouth between her legs, she grabbed his hair. She yanked his head backward. He gazed up between her breasts, at her frowning black face.

'Grandpa Chidi,' she said. 'Remember him?'

Trev nodded. He remembered. But he didn't care. He strained against Sandy's grip, trying to get his mouth on her again, but she jerked his hair so hard that tears filled his eyes. He cried out.

'I reckon we gotta finish what we started,' she said.

'OK, OK.'

She released his hair and stepped back.

Trev reached down for his gun.

She stepped on his hand. Her knee crashed against his forehead. The blow knocked him backward. His hand pulled out from under her shoe. But without the gun.

He pushed himself up.

Sandy had the gun. It was aimed at his face. 'Get up off the street,' she said. 'We got us a job to do.'

10

Of those from outside the restaurant who'd been taken-alive, the kid with the Mohawk haircut remained unconscious and one man had broken arms. There was no point in washing either of them.

Four others were in good enough shape to help defend the place: Bill the parking attendant; a kid of about sixteen wearing only a T-shirt; a young woman dressed in a nightgown; and the old fellow who'd tried to strike John with his golf club.

Bound and struggling, they were carried into the kitchen and placed on the floor near the wash tubs.

The tubs were about two feet deep. Each looked large enough to permit someone to sit down or kneel. John stoppered the drain of one, and turned on the water.

'Let's do Bill first,' Cassy suggested.

Roscoe the chef dragged the young man to his feet. John held a knife on him while Roscoe removed the belts lashed around his arms and legs. Lynn and Cassy held onto his arms. He struggled against them until John pressed the blade to his throat. 'Calm down, pal.' Bill glared, but stopped resisting.

Steve and Carol kept watch on the other three as Roscoe, Lynn and Cassy stripped Bill down to his underwear. He was mostly black to his neck. From his shoulders to his feet, he looked clean except for his hands. Apparently, he hadn't been under the rain long enough for it to penetrate his clothes to the skin.

'I don't think we'll have to put him in,' Cassy said.

'Yeah,' John agreed. 'Just dunk his head and hands.'

Roscoe shoved Bill against the sink and pushed his head down into the water. Lynn and Cassy plunged his hands in. The three of them held him under, Roscoe rubbing his hair. The water turned murky gray. Then they let him up. He lurched out of the water, gasping. His hair was blond, his face red. He looked around, blinking.

Cassy gave him a dish towel. He frowned at her.

'How are you?' she asked.

He shrugged. 'OK. I guess it worked, huh?'

'Did it?' Cassy asked him.

'I guess I hurt you, huh? When I came in?'

'Yeah.'

His face flushed to a deeper shade of red. 'Jeez, I'm really sorry.'

Cassy met John's eyes. She smiled. 'It really did work,' she said. 'This is great.'

'Let's do the rest,' John said. 'Bill, you can get your clothes back on and go out to help the others.'

He scowled down at his wet, stained clothes.

'It's all right,' John told him. 'Secondary contact doesn't seem to bother anyone.'

'What do you mean by that?'

'It means the rain actually has to get you,' Cassy explained. 'You can touch someone who's black, or you can touch their clothes, and it doesn't make you weird.'

'That doesn't make any sense,' Bill said.

'Maybe not,' Cassy told him. 'But it's true.'

Bill wrinkled his nose, then crouched and picked up his clothes and moved out of the way.

'OK,' Lynn said. 'Who's next?'

'Her,' Roscoe said. He pulled the woman up by her arms, stepped behind her and began to remove the belts while Lynn and Cassy held her.

Unlike Bill, she looked as if she'd been out in the rain for a long time. Her hair was black, matted down and stringy. Her nightgown was a sodden, clinging rag. The women peeled it up and dropped it to the floor. John saw that the rain had seeped right through it. She was black from head to toe.

Steve gave the chef a hand and they lifted her into the sink. She sat down in the water, knees up.

John stepped aside to make room for the women. They went to work with dish rags, starting at her head. In seconds, her hair was blonde again. Water streamed down, sluicing through the black, leaving strips of pale skin. They scrubbed her face, her neck, her shoulders. John watched rivulets run down her breasts, drops fall from her nipples. Then Lynn blocked his view and he looked away.

Do the kid next, he thought. Probably a better fighter than the old man.

'That should just about do it,' Lynn said.

'Missed some on her shin,' Roscoe told her.

The woman in the tub began to weep.

The boom of a gunshot made John jump. Lynn's head snapped around. Her eyes were suddenly frantic.

Faint shouts of alarm came from somewhere beyond the kitchen. Screams. Another explosion.

John raced for the kitchen doors.

'No!' Lynn yelled.

'Stay here!' He slammed through a door and burst into the dining room. Men and women rushed by, some hunched low, others glancing back in panic. A few ducked under tables. Dr Goodman hurled a chair through a window. As the glass shattered, he dived out into the rain.

'My God!' It was Steve. Behind him.

'What's happening?' Carol's voice. She must've come out with Steve.

Another blast.

John ran toward the foyer, but stopped abruptly when he saw that the doors stood wide open. Crazies were already in, throwing themselves onto those who'd stayed to fight. In their midst stood a man with a short-barreled shotgun. A gunbelt laden with equipment hung around his waist. On the chest of his drenched shirt, a shield gleamed. A police badge.

As John watched, the cop shoved the muzzle of his shotgun into the belly of a waitress – Peggy – and pulled the trigger. The blast folded her in half and lifted her feet off the floor.

She was still in the air when John whirled around. He glimpsed Steve and Carol dashing for the broken window.

Planning to take their chances with the rain.

Better that, maybe, than staying to be slaughtered in the restaurant.

John rammed through the door into the kitchen. He saw Roscoe running for the alley exit, pulling the naked woman from the tub along behind him.

Lynn and Cassy were still by the tub. They both held knives. They both stared at John with terrified eyes.

'This is it,' he gasped. 'We're being overrun.'

Overrun. Like his firebase.

He'd survived that. He would survive this. The same way. But with Lynn and Cassy. This time, he wouldn't be the only one to make it.

'What'll we do?' Lynn asked.

'Get invisible,' he said.

They looked at him as if he'd lost his mind.

'Strip,' he said. He snatched the clump of black nightgown off the floor and tossed it to Lynn. 'Put it on.'

As she caught the gown, John saw the look in Cassy's eyes. She seemed to understand what he had in mind. And to understand that there was only one black nightgown, and he'd given it to his wife. She looked like a kid who hadn't been picked for a game, and was trying not to show her letdown.

She flinched at the sound of a gunshot. This blast had a hard, flat sound. Not the shotgun. A revolver.

'Get your clothes off,' John told her.

Two more shots.

In the wake of the blasts, John heard screams and shouts and wailing and giggles. Sounds of a madhouse where slaughter was in full swing.

Dropping to his knees, he cut through the belt that bound the teenaged boy's hands together. The kid started to fight him. John slashed his throat. Clamping the knife between his teeth, he tugged off the boy's wet T-shirt. It had been all black a moment ago. Now the black was mixed with red. He threw the shirt to Cassy.

She looked stunned by what he'd done. But she pulled the shirt over her head. It came down halfway to her knees.

Lynn already wore the nightgown.

Both women looked sickly pale where they weren't covered by the garments.

'Come here,' he snapped. 'Quick.'

They rushed up close to him.

John flung blood at their bare legs from the pumping throat of the boy.

'Get plenty on you. Quick!'

Crouching, they cupped blood and spread it over their hair and faces. Lynn washed her shoulders with it. John painted their legs.

Then he got up. 'The freezer!'

'Where?' Lynn asked.

He pointed at the freezer door. 'Hurry,' he gasped. 'Get in there and play dead.'

'What about you?' Lynn blurted.

'I'll be all right. Go!'

The women ran for the freezer, Lynn glancing back, her face dripping crimson, a look in her eyes as if she thought she might never see him again.

John crouched beside the body of the boy he'd killed. When he heard the heavy thud of the shutting door, he clamped the knife between his teeth and lifted the body.

11

They sat on the sofa, Kara watching while Denise and Tom fashioned their weapons.

Tom had broken off the ends of a broom and a mop they'd found by the water heater, leaving each shaft with a jagged point. Kara had fetched a ball of twine from a kitchen drawer. They'd gathered more knives and returned to the living room.

The living room, Denise thought. The heart of the house. Its center.

She supposed this wasn't precisely the center, but it was close enough. From here, they should be able to hear anyone attempting to break in, and get to the trouble spot fast.

She worked quickly, lashing the handle of a long, serrated carving knife to the blunt end of her broom handle.

Tom finished making his spear and offered it to Kara.

'Can't I just use my poker?' she asked. 'I'm pretty good at bonking people.'

Grinning, Tom rubbed the lump on his head. 'Yeah, I noticed.'

'Keep your poker,' Denise told her. 'But I want you to have a knife, too.'

'OK.'

'We'll wipe 'em out with these things,' Tom said.

'Maybe they won't show up,' Denise said. She gripped the bound handle of the knife and put some pressure on it. The twine made quiet creaky sounds. The knife didn't wobble at all. 'Decent,' she muttered.

'Sheena.'

'That's me. God, I hope we don't have to use these things.'

'I wonder if we should split up, kind of stand guard at different parts of the house.'

'We do not want to split up,' Kara said. 'They do that in all the movies, and it's absolutely silly.'

Denise smiled. 'She's right.'

'I don't know if we should just sit here. We could patrol the house.'

'Together?' Kara asked.

'I think we're better off . . .' A noise of crashing glass stopped Denise's voice. Her heart kicked.

Tom leaped up, staring toward the opening of the hallway. 'A bedroom?'

'Sounded like it.'

'Oh, gosh,' Kara muttered.

'Let's get 'em!' A knife in one hand, his makeshift spear in the other, Tom ran for the hall.

Denise leaned forward with her spear and snatched another knife off the table. She got to her feet and waited for a moment while Kara gathered up her poker and knife. Then she went after Tom. The girl was quick. Denise didn't need to hold back. Kara stayed close behind her as she ran to the foyer, cut to the right and raced up the hall.

She caught up with Tom when he stopped in the doorway of the master bedroom. He elbowed a switch. Light filled the room. Peering past him, Denise saw no broken window. She stepped aside. Tom rushed past her, and she followed him to Kara's bedroom.

Again, he flicked on a light. This time, he didn't stop in the doorway. He dashed across the room. Running in after him, Denise checked the windows but her view of the one on the left was blocked by Tom's body.

'Careful,' she gasped. Lurching sideways, she caught sight of the window. A hole near the bottom. As big as a head. Splintered edges.

Nobody was reaching in.

She saw only darkness through the break.

Tom stopped a yard from the window to avoid stepping on glass with his stocking feet. He crouched toward it and gazed out.

'See anything?'

'Huh-uh.'

Denise scanned the pale blue carpet. It was littered with shards and bits of glass. She saw nothing that might've been hurled through the window.

'The screen's still on,' Tom said.

'Maybe it was a trick,' Kara said.

'What do you mean?' Denise asked.

The girl frowned. 'You know. A division?'

Tom whirled around. 'A diversion!'

Denise felt her stomach drop. 'Oh, my God,' she muttered.

12

John dropped the dead boy to the floor beside the freezer door. Lying down, he pulled the body on top of him. He grimaced as its cheek pressed the side of his face.

It was worse last time, he told himself. Last time, he'd buried himself under three bodies. One was Lieutenant Becker, and Becker's belly had been split open and his guts were all over John. He'd been underneath the corpses so long that, by the time he finally struggled free, Becker's intestines had dried against his fatigues. They'd come with him when he got up. He'd had to peel them off.

Hours under those corpses.

This won't be as bad, he told himself.

He wondered how long Lynn and Cassy could last inside the freezer.

They shouldn't have shut themselves in, he realized. With the door shut, the cold would build up too fast. And he wasn't sure whether the door could be opened from the inside. If something happened to him, they might be trapped.

He listened. Screams and laughter and shouts still came from the other areas of the restaurant. But he didn't think anyone had entered the kitchen. Not yet.

He shoved the body off, got to his feet, took a quick look around, then tugged open the freezer door.

Among the bodies of the journalists and two men who'd been killed by them, Lynn and Cassy lay sprawled on their backs. They should pass for crazies, all right, in their soiled wet nightgown and T-shirt. But one glance convinced him that they wouldn't pass for dead. The blood in their hair, on their faces and arms and legs made them look damn gory, but hardly concealed that they lay there stiff and shivering.

He whirled around to make sure once again that no one had entered the kitchen.

'Come out of there,' he said. 'It won't work. Hurry.'

Lynn pushed herself up on her elbows. 'What's the matter?'

'Don't ask questions,' Cassy said, saving John the trouble.

Both women got to their feet. Hunched over, they rushed to the front. Lynn's teeth were gritted and she was rubbing her arms. Cassy hugged her chest for warmth. Then they were out and John threw the door shut.

'What'll we do now?' Lynn gasped.

'Stick with me.'

They followed John as he hurried to the old man who'd tried to bash him with a golf club. The guy was still bound with belts and sitting near the tub with his back against a counter. He wore a sport jacket over his knit shirt. Some of the jacket's plaid still showed, but it was mostly stained black by the rain.

John kicked him in the head. The man fell onto his side, dazed but conscious. John slashed the belt that bound his arms behind him. He tore off the jacket and struggled into it.

'Get your knives,' he said.

Lynn and Cassy searched around and found the knives where they'd dropped them before getting into the wet garments.

'Now what?' Lynn asked.

'We go out there. We act like the crazies.'

'You're kidding,' Lynn said.

'Let's go.'

As he rushed for the kitchen doors, he heard Cassy behind him say, 'Here goes nothing.'

13

Denise let Tom take the lead. She ran close behind him, Kara at her side.

They'll be in by the time we get there, she thought.

Probably smashed the window and headed for the other side of the house while we were on our way to check it out. We got into Kara's room and couldn't even hear them breaking in for real.

She raced out of the hallway. Had enough time for one quick look at the living room – long enough to see that nobody was there – and then the house went dark.

'Uh-oh,' Kara murmured.

'Hold up,' Denise gasped at Tom. She skidded to a halt near the front door. Kara brushed against her arm.

The thud of Tom's footfalls stopped. Denise saw his faint shape moving toward her. She heard him panting for breath.

'They're at the fuse box,' she whispered.

'Someone is. Or was.'

'Maybe the juice went off,' Kara suggested.

'Hang on.' Denise stepped in the direction of the door. Holding her spear upright, she reached out until she touched the wood. Then she moved sideways, running her hand over the door, its frame, the wall. Draperies brushed her knuckles. She clamped the shaft between her legs, fingered the draperies, found their drawcord and pulled.

The drapes slid open. A hazy, gray glow came in from the window. She glanced out. Through the falling rain, she saw a streetlight casting dim silver onto the top of Tom's car. Across the street, a porch light burned.

'It's not the power,' she whispered. 'They're in the house.'

'Get away from the window,' Tom said.

She wrapped her hand around the shaft of her spear and stepped backward. Turning to face the living room, she gazed into the shadows. The light from the window helped. She could make out the dim shapes of the sofa, the lamps, the television.

The entrance from the dining room was as black as the mouth of a cave.

'We oughta be able to see them coming,' Tom whispered.

His face was a faint oval blur. His gray sweatsuit was slightly less visible than his face. Though Denise couldn't see him clearly, he didn't blend in with the darkness around him. Neither did Kara in her pink nightgown. She looked down at herself. Her warmup suit was royal blue, but it appeared to be black. Her hands were dusky gray. Her white socks almost seemed to glow.

'They'll see us, too,' she said.

Tom squatted down. Denise and Kara did the same.

'Where the hell are they?' he muttered.

'They're being sneaky. They think we've got guns, remember?'

'I sure wish we did,' Kara whispered. 'Wouldn't it be neat if you could wish for something and make it come . . .?'

'Shhhhh,' Denise warned her.

From off in the distance beyond the living room came the sound of a thud. Someone muttered, 'Shit!'

'Stay with Kara,' Denise muttered.

'What're you . . .?'

'Shhhh.' She lowered her spear to the floor, shifted the knife to her right hand, and crawled toward the living room.

I'm out of my gourd, she thought. She struggled to stop breathing so loudly. Her heart wanted to pound the air from her lungs. She felt as if she might wet her pants. But she kept moving.

Away from the front door. Away from Tom and Kara. Closer to the three unseen intruders who'd come here to kill them all.

She sank to her belly and squirmed forward. She passed an end table. Made her way into the narrow gap between the coffee table and the front of the sofa. Through it and past the other end table. Across an area of open floor to the front of an easy chair close to the wall. The wall that stood between her and the dining room.

She got to her hands and knees. The chair blocked her view of the dining room entrance, but she could see the area through which the boys would have to pass when they went for Tom and Kara.

She waited. She held her breath until her lungs burned and she feared her head might explode. Then she let her air out slowly and inhaled. Sweat stung her eyes. The handle of her knife felt oily.

Come on, she thought. Let's get it over with.

She wondered if this was the dumbest thing she'd ever done. Probably was.

Putting herself out here alone.

Seemed like a good idea at the time.

It *is* a good idea. I can't let those bastards get Kara. Or Tom, for that matter.

Off beyond the chair, something moved. A low, bulky shape that was darker than the darkness. Like a black animal creeping forward.

One of the guys. Crawling.

Denise stared at his head. She couldn't make out who he was. Probably Buddy. He was the worst of the three (if it's them at all), and he would be in the lead.

She suddenly feared that he might sense he was being stared at. She tried to force herself to look away, but her eyes refused to leave him. So far, he seemed to be watching the area in front.

At last, his head disappeared behind the sofa.

Denise saw another crawling shape behind him. This one had a faint sheen on its back. Whatever light there was seemed to be gleaming off its wet, black skin.

This is them, all right, she thought. One of the three had been shirtless when she'd watched through the window and seen them ride away.

Keep moving, she willed him. Don't look over this way. Just keep your eyes on Buddy.

The third crawled into view.

Denise held her breath. She waited. The feet of the second intruder vanished behind the sofa. Number three was out in the open. Then the sofa blocked her view of his head.

Do it!

She leaped up, took four quick strides across the carpet, saw the kid look back over his shoulder. 'Shit!' he cried out. She rammed the knife down. It sank into his back. 'No!' he squealed. 'Guys!'

She jerked out the knife and stabbed him again. This time, it struck something hard. The kid, shrieking, flopped flat. Denise tugged at the knife. It didn't come out. Her hand slipped off it. The blade must've gone into bone.

The other two guys were scurrying up, coming for her.

Tom!' she yelled.

'Gotcha gotcha gotcha,' gasped the kid duckwalking toward her.

She leaped sideways, twisting in the air as she dived over the back of the sofa. Something stabbed her hip, tore skin and ripped the side of her pants. She landed on the cushions, face up.

Her knees caught the kid dropping onto her. His breath gusted out. She shoved at his bare chest, felt his weight shift, and saw him tumble away. He crashed against the edge of the coffee table and fell to the floor.

Denise flipped herself over. On hands and knees, she scuttled along the sofa. From the other side came thuds and grunts. Tom must've come to help her. Reaching out, she grabbed the table lamp. She hooked her other hand over the sofa back and pulled herself up.

Tom was there about to drive the knife end of his spear into the chest of the kid at his feet. But Kara, a running blur in her pale nightgown, came up behind him swinging her poker.

'No!' Denise blurted.

The brass handle crashed against the side of Tom's head. He dropped his spear and stumbled away, reeling.

'Kara!'

The girl chased after him and hit him again. He went down on one knee, covering his head.

'What're you doing?'

The sofa shook with a sudden jolt. A hand grabbed Denise's ankle.

'Gotcha!'

She swung the lamp off the table and twisted around. A dark arm darted up. She glimpsed a rod of some kind in the hand. Yelped as spikes jabbed deep into her right buttock. Then the base of the lamp clubbed the guy's face. His head was knocked back. He released her ankle. The spikes were yanked from her rump.

She climbed onto the sofa's back. Straddling it, she saw Buddy down on the floor. Tom, over by the wall, was on his knees, both arms over his head to protect it as Kara struck downward again with her poker. It whapped his arms and he cried out.

'Kara! Stop it!'

Buddy sat up. Denise threw herself off the sofa. She dropped both knees onto him, smashing him flat. His arm hooked around her back. He rolled, hurling her to the floor beside him. 'What're ya . . . tryin' to do to me?' he gasped.

Not Buddy's voice.

'Tom?' She ran her hands over his chest. Felt a sweatshirt. A dry sweatshirt. 'Oh God.'

That was Buddy who'd had the spear? And Tom on the floor about to be stabbed when Kara came along? Didn't seem right. But this was Tom on the floor beside her.

Denise rolled away from him as Kara yelped. Looked up. Saw Kara spin away. Her hands looked empty. Buddy – the real Buddy – had the poker. He swung it at her. Denise heard the rod hiss through the air. It missed the girl. Buddy staggered, fell to his knees.

Then hands dug into Denise's armpits and pulled her up.

'Your room, Kara!' Tom shouted. 'Run to your room.'

The girl glanced back, then ran for the front of the house.

Denise got her feet under her, stumbled as Tom thrust her forward. 'Go!' he snapped.

'We can finish 'em!'

'Go!'

She raced after Kara and heard Tom close behind her. Her buttock felt as if it were burning inside. Her pants were wet and clinging around the wound. Warm blood spilled down the back of her leg. Each time her right foot hit the floor, pain bolted through her body.

Shouldn't be running away, she thought. We almost had them.

With what?

Did we *all* lose our weapons?

Like some kind of a damn nasty joke. We go in armed to the teeth and now we've got nothing.

I got one of the bastards, she reminded herself. That's something, anyway.

Ahead of her, Kara lunged to the left and vanished into the

doorway of her bedroom. Denise rushed in. She felt a shove. As she staggered forward, the door slammed.

'Gotta block it shut,' Tom gasped. 'I'll hold it. You two, get something over here. A dresser or something.'

14

Maureen was beginning to give up hope of ever finding them. Maybe the guys hadn't stopped, at all. Maybe they'd just kept on riding and were miles away by now.

I'll get them, she told herself. I'll get them if it takes forever.

But maybe this searching was pointless. She wondered if she should return to Buddy's house. Wait for them there. Sooner or later, they would probably show up.

She saw the motorcycles.

Three Harleys standing in the driveway of a corner house. But no Buddy. No Doug or Lou.

She knew they'd gone into the house.

Grinning, she swung her Jeep onto the driveway and stepped on the gas.

This'll bring 'em running!

Three hogs, all in a row. She hit the first bike, smashing it into the second before her front tires bumped over it and she rammed the second bike into the third. The third stayed up somehow – maybe locked to the front of her Jeep – and it skidded along sideways with shrieking rubber until she crashed it through the garage door.

It came loose when she backed up. She bounced her way

over the other bikes, metal groaning and crunching, glass bursting. Then she was on smooth pavement again.

Maureen grinned at the debris.

She couldn't even see the third bike. It was somewhere in the darkness under the remains of the garage door.

She beeped her horn.

'Come on out, guys. See what happened to your hogs.'

She scanned the front of the one-story house. The porch light was off, but the draperies behind the picture window glowed. The draperies didn't stir. The front door didn't open.

Maureen honked again. This time, she kept the horn blaring for a long time.

Nobody came from the house.

'They deaf or something?' she muttered.

She shut off the engine, took the key from the ignition, and climbed out. The rain poured down on her. It felt even better, more exciting, than she remembered. She stopped at the rear of the Jeep, threw back her head and arched her spine, savoring the touch of the water as it splashed her face and soaked through the front of her T-shirt. One hand held the keys, but the other was free to peel the shirt up above her breasts. The raindrops made her bare skin tingle. They tapped against her breasts, teased her nipples, slid down her body like the tips of tongues. Trembling, she pulled the elastic band of the shorts away from her waist and let the hot little streams run down to her groin and thighs.

Take off your clothes and lie down on the grass, she thought. Forget about Buddy and his friends. Let the rain . . .

Buddy and his friends.

Maureen let the elastic snap back against her belly. She bent over the tailgate, very aware of how the rain now fingered her back, soaked through the seat of her shorts and streamed down her legs, but struggling not to let the exciting feel of it overwhelm her.

I'm gonna get those suckers, she told herself. I'm gonna roll in their blood and that'll be even better than the rain.

She held her right hand to steady it, and pushed the key into the lock. She twisted the key. She opened the tailgate. She leaned into the darkness, savoring the way her sodden shorts pulled taut against her buttocks but regretting the loss of the rain on her head and back. Soon, she found the jack. She dropped the keys, wrapped her hand around the steel bar of the tire tool, and pulled it out.

Turning away, she swung the bar through the air.

'Break their heads apart,' she muttered.

She rushed toward the house. The grass was thick and slippery. She wanted to dive onto it and roll over. But she kept running.

She pressed her way through shrubbery at the front of the big window. Leaves rubbed against her. Limbs poked and scraped her.

Then she was at the window.

She drew the tire iron back and hammered it through the glass.

15

'I think this is it,' Trev said.

'Well, is it or isn't it?' Sandy asked.

He'd checked the street sign at the corner. This was Fairmont, all right. Crouching, he looked more closely at the house number painted on the curb. 4538. Back at O'Casey's, he had memorized Chidi's address. He was pretty sure it was 4538 Fairmont.

But was that right?

He'd had to struggle so hard to remember the address. As if the rain had submerged it, hidden it at the bottom of a deep and murky pool, forcing him to go down through the dark heat and search.

'I'm pretty sure,' he said.

'Well,' Sandy said, 'I reckon we'll know soon enough.' She waved his revolver, gesturing him toward the house. 'Come on along, Rhonda,' she said to the girl from the trunk.

Trev stepped over the curb, crossed the strip of grass and then the sidewalk. Looking back, he saw Sandy and Rhonda a few strides behind him. Sandy had her left hand on the girl's good shoulder. As if Rhonda were her kid sister, or something.

Weird how she'd started acting.

She'd been like an animal in heat before the shootout. Then, all at once, she was different. She got serious. Trev didn't understand. Mostly, it pissed him off. But part of him, far down under the churning new desires, was glad she'd taken command. Down there was the memory of a mission – to stop the rain and somehow save Maureen. He knew the mission was important. He knew that he cared about it. But he also knew that too much was in the way. Hungers to rip flesh, taste blood, tear into throats and breasts and guts.

Sandy's and Rhonda's, for starters. Then, anyone else he could find.

But Sandy, gun in hand, kept all that from happening. And got him here to the Chidi house.

Under his dark heat and anger stirred a lost man who was grateful.

Walking backward over the lawn, he watched how Sandy's skin gleamed black in the light from the porch. He was pretty sure he'd fired four rounds at the man with the rifle. Before that, one into Francine. Which left only one in the revolver. Maybe Sandy would use it on the Chidis. Then he could get her.

He tripped and dropped down hard on the concrete stoop.

Sandy came closer, one hand still on Rhonda's shoulder. 'Get up,' she said.

Trev stood, climbed the two steps, and moved to the front door. There was no screen door, just a panel of dark wood with a handle and peephole.

'Want me to ring the bell?' he asked.

'Don't be a jerk, Trevor. See if it's locked.'

He tried the handle, then shook his head.

'Didn't reckon they'd make it easy for us,' Sandy said. 'OK, go on and kick it in.'

'They might be waiting and kill us,' Rhonda said.

Trev was surprised to hear her speak, though he knew she'd been talking with Sandy along the way.

'I'll go in first, honey. Trevor, get on with it.'

'You'd better hang onto me,' he said. 'The stoop's slippery. I'll end up on my ass.'

Sandy studied his eyes for a moment, then nodded. She pressed herself against his back and wrapped her left arm across his chest. Her right hand shoved the gun muzzle against his ribs.

Do it so we both fall, he thought.

Hell, it would probably happen anyway. Kicking open doors wasn't as easy as it looked on TV. His foot was likely to bounce right back at him and knock them both flat.

Of course, Sandy might pull the trigger.

But maybe she wouldn't. With a little luck, he could get the gun away from her once they hit the concrete.

'What're you waiting for?'

'Be careful with that gun,' he said. Then he raised his right leg, drew his knee in toward his chest, and drove his foot at the door. The heel of his shoe struck beside the handle.

Pain didn't streak up his leg. The door didn't throw his foot back at him.

Instead, he felt an instant of hard resistance and the door burst open and slammed the wall behind it.

He was still off balance when Sandy hurled him forward. He tripped on the threshold, staggered across some carpet, and fell to his hands and knees. Sandy rushed past him. She was crouched low, head turned away, sweeping the revolver from side to side.

Trev crawled toward her. She swung around and jabbed the muzzle against his forehead. 'Mind your manners, pal,' she said. Taking a step backward, she straightened up and looked toward the doorway. 'Come on in, Rhonda. Nothing in here's gonna hurt you.'

The girl stepped inside and shut the door. She gazed into the living room. 'Are they dead?' she asked.

Perplexed, Trev got to his feet. He looked past Sandy. A teenaged girl lay sprawled on the sofa. One arm hung toward the floor. Trev saw no blood on her tan corduroys or white blouse. She looked as if she might be asleep. But if she'd been sleeping, the clamor of their break-in should've shocked her wide awake.

An adult male was slumped in a reclining chair in a corner of the room. He wore gold-rimmed glasses, a pale blue sport shirt, dark slacks and black socks. A book lay open on his chest as if he'd dropped asleep while reading.

Nobody else was in the room.

'I reckon we got the right house,' Sandy said, her voice low.

'Yeah,' Trev said.

He'd never seen any of the Chidi family except Maxwell, the boy dead and charred, bound to the goalpost. But these two were probably his sister and father. It wasn't likely that Trev had gotten the address wrong. And there were only a few black families in town.

Not really black, he thought as he stared at the girl.

We're black.

Her hair was black, all right, but her skin was a deep, rich brown.

Sandy went to the sofa and bent over the girl. In the bright lamplight, she didn't look nearly as good as before. Her wet skin gleamed, but it was streaky and Trev liked the soft brown of the girl's skin better than the dirty black of Sandy's.

'This gal's breathing,' Sandy said.

Trev moved closer. Sandy, keeping an eye on him, stepped over to the man.

He watched the girl's chest rise slowly and sink. He could see her white bra through the blouse, pale against her dark skin. He glanced over at Sandy. She was bending over the man.

'They musta been drugged or something,' she said.

He ripped the girl's blouse open and heard the sudden click-clack of a cocking gun.

'Just leave her be.' Sandy had the revolver pointed at his face.

'Hey, come on,' he said. 'Let me have her. You take him.'

'That's just the rain talking.'

'So what? You're wet, too. What's the matter with you?'

'I got it reined in, buster.' A half smile tipped a corner of her mouth. 'You'd best rein it in, same as me. We gotta find gramps and put a stop to all this. Now I can do it by myself, or you can help me.' She straightened her arm, closed her left eye, and seemed to be sighting in on him down the entire length of her arm.

'I'm on your side,' Trev said.

With her thumb, she eased the hammer down. She lowered her arm. 'Let's have a look around,' she said, and nodded toward the dining room.

Trev went first. He glanced back at the girl on the sofa.

Get back to you, he thought.

Just need to wait for Sandy to use that last bullet.

Nobody in the dining room.

He headed for the kitchen, and suddenly grinned. There was *no need* to wait for Sandy to use the last bullet. The fool had cocked the revolver and let the hammer down on its only live round. She'd have to go through five spent shells before the cylinder would bring the good cartridge back into firing position.

I've got her!

I've got them all!

Should be a knife in the kitchen, he thought. A good sharp knife would come in handy.

He entered the kitchen. The faucet was running. On the floor in front of the sink was a shattered plate. A woman sat at the table, arms folded beneath her face.

The mother, Trev thought.

She wore white jeans and a green blouse. The hair draping her face was glossy brown with red highlights. The look of it stirred something deep inside Trev.

Can't be her natural color, he thought.

Might be.

He frowned at the thick auburn tresses.

Hair just like Maureen's, he realized.

'I spect gramps must've doped their food,' Sandy said.

Hair just like Maureen's.

Maureen.

Trev tried to focus his mind on her. He remembered her smile and the soft, amused challenge in her eyes.

Hold onto it.

He stepped to the counter and drew a long knife from its wooden holder.

'Drop it, Trev.'

He turned to Sandy. She aimed the useless revolver at his

chest. 'Pull back the hammer and let it go five times,' he said. 'That'll put a live round into position.'

One of her eyes narrowed, its lid twitching slightly.

'Try to save it for grandpa,' he said.

16

With Lynn and Cassy close beside him, John ran into the midst of the carnage. It was worse than he'd imagined. The air was dense with screams and shouts and growls, rippling with horrible giggles. It stank of excrement and urine. Everywhere he looked, people were being slashed and hacked and bludgeoned. The dead were being killed again. Clothes had been torn from bloody victims. He saw people being eaten, raped, sodomized. One man had his head completely buried inside the split torso of another like a dog searching for a hidden treat: even as he delved, a drenched woman chopped an axe into his spine and let out a wild laugh.

Shouldn't have come out here, John thought.

No, this is best. This is how we blend in.

He nudged Lynn toward a waitress scurrying nearby. The woman still wore the bodice of her costume, but her skirt was gone. The handle of a knife protruded from her shoulder blade. 'Get her,' John yelled. Lynn caught on and hurled herself onto the woman's back. Cassy, with a quick nod to John, leaped onto the two.

None of the real crazies joined in.

They were all too busy.

John scanned the crowd quickly, seeking a restaurant patron to attack.

He saw the cop.

Reloading.

The man was several strides away, standing motionless in the swamp of gore and thrashing bodies, his head down as he stuffed cartridges into the cylinder of his revolver.

John didn't want to go for him. He wanted to *blend in*, damn it, join in the fighting and be *invisible*.

I'm not a damn hero, he thought.

He just wanted to survive and make sure Lynn survived so they could get home to Kara.

He didn't want to go for the cop even as he leaped over someone squirming atop a body, elbowed a man aside, and saw the cop snap the loaded cylinder into place. He knocked the gun aside with one hand and smashed the heel of his other hand up against the underside of the cop's nose. The nose crunched, went soft and flat as John's blow drove its ridge bone up into the brain. The head flew back. The cop staggered away, stiff and twitching, and dropped to the floor.

Took him out of the picture, John thought.

That was all he'd intended – to stop the man from running amok with a loaded gun.

He suddenly felt like an idiot.

He could use the gun.

He saw a hand reaching for it. The bloody hand of a man on his knees, whose sweater was wet and black. John stomped down, popping the man's elbow. He ducked and snatched up the revolver, shot the man in the head, then looked at the cop.

He glimpsed a plastic name plate on the chest of the uniform. HANSON.

Hanson hadn't snapped his cartridges case after reloading. A dozen rounds had fallen out when he hit the floor. John dropped to his knees, scooped up a handful, and dropped the ammunition into his shirt pocket as he got to his feet.

He spotted Lynn and Cassy, still on top of the waitress. Cassy had tugged the knife out of the woman's shoulder. She held it in her teeth while she pinned the waitress down and Lynn pretended to chew on the nape of the gal's neck.

It's working. John thought.

They looked like the real article, and nobody was bothering them. Not yet.

John made his way toward them. Just get to them, he thought. Stay there, shoot anyone who tries to take them. But even with the extra bullets in his pocket, he knew he didn't have enough ammo to kill *all* the crazies.

He glimpsed someone rushing at him from the side. He whirled. A man with a steak knife. Black face grinning.

He swung the revolver up.

Steve Winter?

'No!' he yelled.

As the knife flashed down at his chest, John sidestepped and chopped Steve's wrist. The knife flipped away. He slammed the gun barrel against Steve's head. The man started to drop. John grabbed the front of his shirt and hurled him sideways, watched as he toppled over the back of a woman hunched over bloody remains, watched him roll and come to a stop near Lynn's feet.

Where's Carol?

John spotted Steve's wife near the open doors. She was on her knees, biting the face of a screaming man while a guy with a pocket knife split open the man's leg from hip to knee.

John rushed to get her. Somebody grabbed his ankle. He pulled free, leaped over a couple of struggling women, and saw the gal with the axe prance in from the right. She had the axe overhead. Maybe she wasn't going for Carol. John decided he didn't care who she was going for.

He aimed and fired.

She wore a sleeveless gown. The slug punched through her skin just under the armpit. Its impact nudged her sideways. She jogged along, knees pumping up the front of her dress, axe still raised. She angled toward the doors like a sleepwalker in a big hurry. The doorjamb at the far side stopped her. She struck it with her face, bounced off and fell back.

Rushing forward, John grabbed Carol's wet hair. He yanked, jerking her head up.

The man with the pocket knife glared up at him.

Dr Goodman.

'She's with me,' Goodman said, as if this was some kind of a damn prom and John was trying to put moves on his date.

The same knife he'd used to cut the laces of Cassy's bodice was now deep in the thigh of the man who was gasping and writhing on the floor.

Goodman tore the knife out and waved it at John. 'She stays with me!'

'No she doesn't,' John said, and shot him in the forehead.

He looked around quickly. Nobody rushing them. He jammed the revolver into a rear pocket of his slacks, chopped the edge of his hand against Carol's neck hard enough to black her out but not kill her, then hoisted her onto his shoulder and carried her toward the corner of the foyer – toward Lynn and Cassy and the waitress and Steve – where he would make his stand.

17

After searching the rambling house, Maureen returned to the living room. She saw bright red footprints on the gray carpet.

Someone had followed her into the house!

A chill spread goosebumps over her skin. She turned, watching the bloody tracks wind their way through the room toward the kitchen.

One set of tracks. One intruder.

She clamped the tire iron between her knees, rubbed her sweaty right hand on the side of her sodden shorts, then gripped the bar again.

She gazed at the tracks.

Whoever made them had been damn sneaky. She hadn't heard a sound while searching the house. She hadn't *felt* the presence of anyone.

From the feel of the house when she first came in through the window, she'd been sure it was deserted. Somehow, she'd known that nobody was here. But the Harleys had been left out front, so she'd gone ahead and searched and found nobody.

But damn it, *someone* had come in after her.

Someone awfully stealthy.

Stalking her.

That can work both ways, Maureen thought. She started to follow the bloody footprints. Her heart raced. Her stomach felt fluttery. Her skin crawled as if a basketful of spiders had been dumped on her head. With her left hand, she reached up to where her T-shirt was still bunched above her breasts. She tugged it down.

What if he's creeping up behind me?

She whirled around.
Saw *two* sets of red footprints coming toward her across the carpet.
The second set ended at her own bare feet.
She stared at them.
She sighed.
'A Woozle,' she muttered.
Winnie and Piglet go hunting and almost catch a Woozle.
She remembered that long ago she'd been a writer of children's books. Long ago, this morning.
'And now I'm reduced to Woozle hunting,' she said.
She laughed softly. Then she sat down on the carpet and crossed her legs and gazed at her lacerated feet and wept.

18

The dresser rammed Denise's back.
It's like being in the bathroom again, she thought. Trying to keep Tom out.
But now Tom was beside her, helping to hold the door shut.
The dresser wasn't much of a barricade. Too lightweight. The first smash of the door would've toppled it over if they hadn't been bracing it up. Had it been any heavier, though, she and Kara might not have been able to push it to the door in time.
She was glad they'd done it. At least the dresser put a little distance between her back and the door – and the two crazy bastards on the other side.

They hit it again. Hard. The dresser's top edge jammed against Denise's back, shoving her forward, bending her knees. A drawer slid out. It pounded her rump, hitting her wound and sending a throb of pain down her right leg. She thrust her heels into the carpet. Wincing, she drove the dresser backward.

The door slammed.

Her right leg started to jiggle. She grabbed her thigh and tried to hold it still.

'We can't keep this up,' she whispered.

'We have to,' Tom said.

'Look what I found,' Kara said. A tube of frosty light suddenly appeared in front of the girl. She waved it. The tube carved a twirl of brightness through the air. 'My *Star Wars* light sword,' she explained.

Some weapon, Denise thought. It looked like a cylinder of translucent plastic attached to a flashlight. But she was glad Kara had found it. Better than being in the dark.

'I wish it was a real laser sword like Luke Sky-walker . . .'

'See what else you can find,' Tom gasped.

As Kara vanished into the closet with her light, the door bashed the dresser forward. Denise winced and shoved herself back. Her right leg gave out. The door banged shut, and she dropped. The open drawer caught her rump. Wood splintered. The drawer broke away and she found herself sitting on a soft cushion of clothes. She flipped over, got to her knees, scurried forward and pushed her shoulder against the dresser just as the boys hit the door again.

The blow shook Denise, but she stayed on her knees. The dresser tipped for a moment before she and Tom could force it back.

'Buddy!' Tom suddenly called.

'Yeah?'

'Let's talk.'

'Nothing to talk about, dickhead.'
'Who do you really want?'
'Huh?'
'Can we make a deal?'
'Like what?'
'I can make it easy for you. I'll let you have the girls, but you've gotta promise to leave me alone.'
He's conning them, Denise told herself. Stalling for time.
Isn't he?
God, what if he means it?
'Yeah, sure, okay,' Buddy said.
'How do I know you won't try to nail me if I let you in?'
'You got my word, man.'
'Cross your heart and hope to die?'
'Yeah, fuck. Cross my heart.'
'And hope to die?'
'Yeah yeah yeah. Cut the stupid games and open up.'
'OK. Just a second.' He put a hand on Denise's head. She winced. He gently stroked her hair and whispered, 'Get ready for another hit.'
Denise turned her head as Kara came up behind her. In the glow of the sword, she saw that the girl held a small leather bag and a thick, foot-long pink pencil in her left hand. Clamped against her side was a metal baton.
'Your second's up, asshole,' Buddy said.
'Just hang on.'
Kara handed the pencil to Tom. She gave the baton to Denise. It had rubber bulbs at each end.
'He's just shitting us.' Someone else's voice. Lou?
They hit the door. The dresser rocked. Denise shoved her shoulder against it. Kara threw herself at it. Tom grunted as he pushed. The dresser dropped back and the door crashed shut.
Denise twisted the rubber bulb off one end of the baton. It popped off with a hollow, ringing sound.

'Let 'em in and try to take 'em?' she whispered.

'Jesus, I don't know.'

'I think the smart thing to do,' Kara said, 'is to go out the window.'

'We'd get wet,' Tom muttered.

'Better wet than dead,' Denise muttered.

'Maybe.'

Kara helped at the dresser as the boys struck the door again. Then she ran to her bed. She tore the top cover off, rushed past the end of the bed and threw the blanket on the floor beneath the window.

So our feet won't get cut, Denise realized.

Kara dropped her light saber onto the blanket. She stepped to the broken window, unlocked it, and shoved up the lower sash. Some glass fell off, clattering when it hit the sill.

Denise got to her feet. She dropped back against the dresser. Her right leg felt rubbery, its muscles still trembling but no longer twitching out of control.

She hoped the leg would carry her to the window.

The door jumped, slamming the dresser against her back. She dug her heels into the carpet. This time, the door didn't rebound and crash shut. Buddy and Lou were giving it all they had. She heard them grunting with effort. She felt the dresser start to scoot on the carpet.

Twisting her head around, she saw the dim shapes of fingers clenching the edge of the door. She shoved herself upward, the dresser's rim digging into her back. Then she was high enough to get her right elbow over the top. With a flick of her wrist, she whacked her baton against the fingers.

Somebody yelped. The hand jerked out of sight and the door slammed shut.

'Go!' Tom whispered.

Denise raced across the room. Ahead of her, Kara was shoving at the window screen.

19

Trev led the way through the Chidi house, Sandy and Rhonda close behind him. In the hallway, he glanced into the dark rooms until he came to a closed door.

He pressed his ear against it and heard soft mumbling sounds.

He looked over his shoulder. He nodded.

'Let's take him,' Sandy whispered.

With his left hand, Trev turned the knob and gently swung the door inward. Smoke, fanned by the opening door, rolled and swayed away in front of him. He smelled a terrible stench. He held his breath and tried not to gag.

He'd encountered the same odor last night. At the stadium. It had come from Maxwell Chidi. The reek of burnt hair and flesh. But Maxwell's stink had been mild compared to this.

What's the old bastard doing in here?

Trev could still hear the low, incoherent mumbling. It came from somewhere ahead and to his right. Through the swirling smoke, he saw the tongues of candle flames. Dozens of them. All around the room. In the direction of the voice, he saw a blur of slow movement. And a blaze too large for a candle.

He stepped silently toward it. He jerked to a halt as something brushed his arm. Turning his head, he saw Sandy beside him. She was squinting in the direction of the voice. Her eyes were red from the smoke, tears cutting pale streaks down her black face. Her left hand was clasped against her mouth, pinching her nostrils shut.

Trev blinked tears from his own stinging eyes. He looked again toward the side of the room. Though he tried to hold his breath, what he saw made him gasp.

Much of the smoke had cleared away. Probably poured out through the doorway. A murky, orange haze remained. Thin enough to let him see too much.

He gagged once, but the white-haired man didn't seem to notice. Maybe in a trance, Trev thought as he willed his throat to relax. Sandy suddenly hunched over and vomited. Still, the man paid no attention.

Trev wondered where Rhonda was. Maybe she'd stayed in the hall. Lucky her.

Grandpa was crouched, facing the wall. He was naked. His brown skin gleamed like polished wood. As he chanted softly, he ripped pages from a book that lay open on the floor. He rolled the pages into a tube, held them over a candle until they ignited, then raised his blazing torch to the charred and runny flesh of the corpse on the wall.

A female. Rather small, but not a child. Old enough to have breasts. She was nailed upside-down to the wall, her arms and legs stretched out wide. Trev could see no skin on her that hadn't been burnt. Her hair was gone.

On the floor beneath her head and shoulders was a plastic tub brimming with black fluid. Bits of gray ash floated on its surface. So did small, white globs of congealed grease.

As Trev watched, disgusted and amazed, the old man filled his mouth with something from a golden urn in his left hand. He raised the blazing roll of pages to his lips, then spewed a fine spray through the fire. A gust of burning fluid swept across the girl's crusty black midsection, spread out and streamed down. Flaming rivulets slid over her breasts and between them, down her neck and face. Trev heard sizzling, crackling sounds, saw streamers of smoke rise from the fiery streams. When they ran off her shoulders and head, their fires died. Black drops fell like rain and splashed into the tub.

Grandpa, still mumbling, crumpled the remnants of the burning pages and snuffed them in his hand. He let the ashes drift to the floor, then reached down to the book. He flipped through several pages. Trev glimpsed a color plate of Jesus surrounded by lambs.

A *Bible.*

The old man ripped the pages from their binding. He started twisting them to form another torch.

Trev turned to Sandy. She was still doubled over. Her hands were on her knees. Trev dropped his knife, reached through strings of hanging mucus and took the revolver from her right hand. She made no effort to keep it.

He walked slowly toward the squatting man, who had already lit the *Bible* pages and filled his mouth from the urn. As fire sprayed at the girl, Trev pressed the muzzle against the base of the old man's skull and pulled the trigger.

For just an instant, he wondered if Sandy had turned the cylinder to the correct position.

She had.

The blast jerked the gun in his hand. The old man's head lurched as if it had been clubbed. Still squatting, he pitched forward. The top of his head smashed against the upside-down face of the girl. His knees hit the floor. He slid down, the wound above his neck pumping blood, his head rubbing the girl's face. The charred mess came apart like a shattered jigsaw puzzle, sliding down over bloody bone, bits of it clinging to his white hair.

His head splashed into the tub.

It went under.

The girl had lost her lips. She seemed to be grinning at the old man's fate.

20

Lou rubbed his shoulder.

'Come on, man,' Buddy muttered.

'It hurts.'

'Now!'

Together, they rammed against the door. This time, it wasn't shoved back at them. Something on the other side scooted away, then crashed to the floor. Buddy squeezed between the edge of the door and the jamb. Lou followed.

Saw Buddy hurl his spear. Its dim, fleeing target dived through the window, and the spear stuck in the wall just beneath the sill.

Lou scanned the dark room. Nothing moved. Had they all managed to get out?

He caught up with Buddy. Side by side, they raced for the window. He whipped the barbecue fork from side to side, relishing his memory of stabbing its tines into Denise's firm rump, aching to sink it into her breasts.

Outside the window, a girl sprang up. Her arm shot over the sill. She flung something from a small bag, then dropped out of sight.

Buddy gasped, 'Fuck!' One of his legs flew sideways. He tumbled, crossing in front of Lou, tripping him. Lou fell over Buddy's back. His forehead bumped the shaft of the spear. The long fork in his right hand whapped the blanket spread under the window. His other hand pounded down, something like a small rock jamming its heel.

He picked the object up.

A marble!

Is that what the bitch had tossed into the room? A bunch of marbles?

Lou scurried off Buddy. He crawled onto the blanket. Beneath it, glass crunched. A tiny, hard ball dug into his knee. Another marble.

He got to the sill and pulled himself up. Poking his head out the window, he caught a glimpse of Denise, the girl and Tom dashing alongside the house.

He crawled through the window and jumped. Standing on the fallen screen, he saw the three disappear around the house's corner.

And realized that the night air was clear.

The rain had stopped.

He tipped back his head, scowling, wanting to feel the hot rain on his face, wondering where it had gone. Above him, the clouds parted. The glare of the full moon hurt his eyes and made him squint.

Buddy, spear in hand, leaped from the window. 'Let's nail 'em, man! Which way'd they go?'

Lou nodded toward the front of the house.

They ran over the slippery grass, Lou longing for the rain to come back but knowing he would soon have Denise – and that would be great.

21

John knew he'd blown it. He shouldn't have taken the cop's revolver. He shouldn't have gone on the quick rescue mission to save Carol. He'd made the crazies too damn aware of him. In spite of his bloody face and the wet, black jacket he'd taken from the old man in the kitchen, they seemed to realize he wasn't one of them.

Twelve, fifteen – maybe more – were converging on the corner of the foyer where he knelt with Lynn and Cassy.

Should've just played along. Might've made it.

Lynn and Cassy had given up their act. They were crouched on either side of him. They held their knives ready. The waitress cowered behind Lynn, hanging onto her shoulders and gazing with terror at the approaching mob.

At least the crazies were holding back.

None eager to get shot.

But John knew he only had three rounds left in the gun. He could feel the weight of the extra cartridges in his shirt pocket.

A lot of good they'd do.

He wouldn't have time to reload.

Three bullets left.

Take out the ones with the best weapons: the bearded guy with the axe; the woman in panty-hose who had the hatchet; the fat naked guy with the meat cleaver.

That would still leave people with knives, hammers, screwdrivers, crowbars and one crazy bastard with pruning shears.

They'd all be on him the instant they realized his gun was empty.

John knew he was good. In hand-to-hand combat, he could take any of them.

But not all of them.

He glanced at Lynn. 'When I start shooting, run for it.'

She shook her head. 'I'm not leaving without you.'

'You've got to. You've gotta get out of this.'

'John.'

'Just do it. Get home to Kara.' He elbowed Cassy.

'Run for it when I open fire. You and Lynn.'

'Right,' Cassy said.

John aimed at the axeman, two yards away, and fired. The bullet knocked a hole through his chest. He staggered backward a few steps, bumping into those behind him. 'GO!' John yelled.

He got to his feet, sweeping his gun from side to side. The crazies, muttering and snarling, glared at him but stayed away. A few of them flung up arms to shield their faces.

He glanced to his right. Lynn was beside him, standing there, scowling at the black faces.

'GO!' he shouted.

She shook her head.

'Damn it!'

On his left, Cassy stood hunched over, jostling the knife in her hand like some kind of fifties delinquent eager to join in a rumble.

This is mad, he thought. We'll all be killed.

Three of us against the mob. Cornered.

They're still not attacking.

Let's at least get out of the foyer. Maybe make it to a window.

He sidestepped, nudging Cassy, taking quick aim at the nearest crazy, who gasped and ducked. Lynn stayed with him. They made their way to the entryway between the foyer and the main dining room. Cassy checked the rear.

Then they backed out of the foyer. The crazies came toward them, but none was foolish enough to charge.

'We'll try for a window,' John muttered.

It felt better, being in the big, open room. A little better, anyway.

They stepped past overturned chairs and abandoned tables. Some of the tables had been swept clear in the melee. Others were still cluttered with the remains of interrupted dinners: plates, glasses, silverware and wine bottles shimmering in the soft glow of the centerpiece candles; some plates loaded with food, others nearly empty.

As John and his women (he realized the waitress was still with them) backed their way through the room, the crazies fanned out.

Can't let them circle us.

Cassy tripped over a body. Her back pounded the floor. The fat man with the cleaver, maybe pushed beyond caution by what he saw as Cassy swung her legs up to roll clear of the body, rushed at her. Bellowing. Waving his cleaver overhead.

John fired. The bullet struck him under the left eye. The eye popped from its socket. The man veered away from Cassy, his piles of flesh flopping like a bloated bag of pudding. He crashed down on a table top.

Cassy scrambled to her feet as the table overturned.

One shot left, John thought.

'Go for the window!' he yelled.

A woman with a steak knife rushed in from the right. John swept his revolver past the others and put a bullet into her chest.

That's it.

But the others held back, not realizing his gun was empty.

Lynn was still beside him. John glanced toward Cassy. Saw her squat by the fat man and snatch up his cleaver. The guy was half buried under the linen tablecloth. A pile of linguini in red sauce was sliding slowly down his back.

Flame licked up from a corner of the tablecloth that had fallen into the shattered chimney of the table's candle.

Cassy, cleaver in hand, rushed over to John's side.

He ached to reload. The weight of the cartridges in his shirt pocket pressed against him like a cruel joke. The instant he broke open the cylinder . . .

He looked past Cassy at the fire. Half the tablecloth was

blazing. The dead man's hair steamed. Flames leaped around his massive torso. His skin crackled and bubbled.

John stuffed his left hand into his pocket, clutched as many cartridges as he could, and threw them at the fire. They spread apart in the air. Some dropped into the flames, while others bounced off the body and rolled away on the hardwood floor.

A crazy yelled, 'Hey!'

'Dumb fuck!' shouted another.

Others looked surprised, others scared, some angry. A few whirled away and fled.

Cassy suddenly hurled her cleaver. It tumbled end over end, sliced off a man's ear and chopped into the chin of a woman behind him.

'Let's get 'em!' a man yelled.

Now she's done it, John thought.

Nobody charged, but the remaining ten or so crazies started moving in.

'Stop or I'll shoot!' John snapped.

Cassy threw her knife at the nearest man. He twisted away and ducked. The handle of the knife struck his side. The knife fell to the floor. He grinned.

Now Cassy had no weapon.

Had she lost her mind?

John was sure of it when she peeled the big, loose T-shirt over her head. The males among the crazies gaped at her.

'Cassy!' he shouted.

She rushed to the fire and threw her shirt into the flames. Then Lynn was beside her. Lynn yanked the nightgown up her body, and off, and flung it onto the fire.

As the flames surged high, devouring the clothes, the crazies attacked. Ignoring John's gun. Ignoring John. Apparently no longer caring about the bullets as they charged toward Lynn and Cassy.

'Run!' John yelled.

He lunged sideways. The nearest man dived for Cassy. John's kick caught him in the hip, turning him in midair. The guy dropped back-first onto the pyre and screamed. John drove his elbow into the face of a giggling lunatic. He pivoted and crashed his revolver against the forehead of an old woman.

He was hit hard in the back. Lynn shrieked and hurled herself onto someone behind him. He spun around in time to see her throw a skinny little guy to the floor. She landed on top. She pounded her knife into the guy's chest. A woman rushed in from the side, hatchet raised. She started to swing it down at Lynn's head. John's kick flung her backward.

Off to the side, two men had Cassy down. One pinned her arms to the floor. The other was sitting on her legs. She squirmed and writhed, twisted and bucked. But they had her. John saw the guy on her legs pull a screwdriver from between his teeth.

Gotta help her!

A woman dropped to her knees beside Lynn and bit the back of her thigh.

'No!' John yelled.

Before he could move to help either woman, arms grabbed him around the legs. Someone jumped on his back. He staggered, trying to stay up. An arm came down from the front, driving a knife toward his chest. He caught the wrist of the knife-hand. As he fought to hold the knife back, a blast crashed in his ears.

Blood flew from the head of the man sitting on Cassy's legs. His screwdriver was already speeding down. Its blade dented the skin below her left breast. Then the handle popped up from the man's fist. The screwdriver tilted and started to fall. He flopped down on top of her.

Another round of ammunition exploded in the fire. Then another. Something zipped past John's face.

He twisted the wrist. The knife fell from his assailant's hand. He shot his elbow backward, connected and heard a grunt through the ringing in his ears.

Then the rain came down.

Cold rain, pouring onto his head.

A woman with a hammer sprang at him from the front. His knuckles caved in her throat. Her weight struck him. He stumbled back, falling onto the one holding his legs and the one clinging to his back.

He blinked water from his eyes.

Above him, a ceiling sprinkler cast down its cold spray.

The fire, he thought. *Jesus, the fire did it.*

Cassy hadn't lost her mind, after all.

22

Denise and Tom raced over the wet grass, side by side, cutting diagonally across the front lawn, heading for the sidewalk at the end of the hedge.

And Denise suddenly wondered where Kara was. The girl had been right behind them when they'd come around the corner of the house. She heard no one back there, now. She looked over her shoulder.

Kara was gone.

She slid to a stop and whirled around.

At first, she didn't see Kara. Her stomach sank. Then she spotted the girl among the bushes near the front stoop.

'Kara!' she shouted.

Buddy and Lou came around the corner of the house, running slowly, heads turning.

They're gonna get her!

'Guys!' she yelled.

They sprinted toward Denise and Tom.

And didn't notice Kara there in the shrubbery. They ran right past her. Buddy had a spear in one hand. Lou waved some kind of long fork overhead and let out a whoop.

'Denny!' Tom gasped.

She couldn't move. She couldn't run off and leave Kara.

The boys dashed closer and closer.

Water suddenly shot up from the ground. Geysers of it, sprouting everywhere. Denise flinched as cold spray from a nearby nozzle seeped through her warmup suit.

Kara had turned on the lawn sprinklers?

Lou cried out as if he were being scalded. Buddy, laughing, leaped one of the showers. He stopped laughing when he slipped. He landed flat on his back.

Tom took hold of Denise's arm. He looked at her. In the moonlight, she saw him smile and shake his head.

'It'll be all right,' she said.

'That kid's amazing.'

'Yeah, isn't she?'

But Lou didn't stop and throw away his fork. He kept running toward them through the fountains of cold, clear water. And Buddy was already scurrying to his feet, lifting his spear.

Why aren't they quitting?

Maybe they haven't been washed clean enough yet.

Lou, bare to the waist, looked pale under the moonlight. Buddy's hair was blond again, his face white.

But the two guys acted the same as when they'd been black.

Buddy, still running, threw his spear. Tom shoved Denise

aside. She stumbled, trying to stay up. Her foot struck a sprinkler head. Crying out, she fell sprawling. As she slid to a halt, she rolled onto her side and saw Tom running from Buddy. He only took a few strides before Buddy leaped and tackled him.

Then Lou walked out of the spray beyond Denise's feet. He had the fork in his right hand. His left hand was tugging at the belt of his pants.

'Leave me alone!' she gasped. 'It's over! Lou, it's over!'

'Huh-uh.'

She squirmed away from him, shoving herself over the grass with her heels and elbows. Lou unfastened the button at his waist. He started to pull his zipper down and Kara jumped onto his back. Denise jerked the baton up from her side. She rammed it upward with both hands. Lou fell, his belly striking the end of the metal tube, driving the baton down. She yelled as the weight of Lou and Kara pounded the baton's rubber knob against her ribs.

Lou shrieked as the pipe punched into him.

Denise bucked and squirmed. The weight shifted. Lou and Kara tumbled to the left. They hit the grass. Denise saw the baton jutting out of Lou. He had dropped his fork. He grabbed the baton with both hands and pulled. Inches of it slid out of him. The end made a hollow sucking pop when it came free. Blood poured from a hole the size of a nickel.

Kara, behind his back, got to her knees. 'Are you OK?'

'Yeah.' Denise sat up. 'Thanks. You . . .' She saw the spear come flying out of the spray too late to warn Kara.

The girl yelped with surprise when it hit her.

The knife ripped through the nightgown glued to her body, ripped through her skin, glanced off, and struck Lou's back with a heavy thunk. Kara grabbed her slashed thigh. She turned to look over her shoulder.

Buddy rushed in through the moonlit, silvery shower.

'No!' Denise cried out. She jerked the baton from Lou's limp hands. As Buddy grabbed Kara from behind and hoisted her overhead, Denise scurried over Lou.

He clutched the front of her jacket. 'Gotcha.'

Her knee rammed the bleeding hole in his belly.

Someone said, 'Put the girl down easy, you bastard.'

23

Buddy turned around, holding the little girl high over his head as if she were a barbell.

'Put her down,' Maureen said.

'Where the fuck did you come from?'

Maureen stood shivering in the cold spray. The lust for killing was gone. But not the need. 'You raped me, mister.'

'Guess what? I'm about to do it again.'

Behind him and just off to the side, a girl crawled over Lou's twitching body, scampered to her feet and rushed forward. She tossed away a shiny weapon of some kind.

'All you're gonna do is die,' Maureen said.

The girl leaped, reaching up, grabbing the kid and pulling.

Buddy yelled, 'Hey!' He tried to hold onto her, and stumbled backward a step as the kid was yanked from his hands and fell into the arms of the girl. He looked over his shoulder to see what had happened.

Maureen thrust the tire tool into his belly. His breath huffed out. He doubled over. Maureen swung with all her strength. The steel bar crashed through his cheekbone, snapped his head sideway. He hit the grass and rolled, his back cutting off the spray of a sprinkler.

Maureen straddled his chest. She raised the bar over her head and swung it down with both hands, caving in the top of his skull.

Aftermath

1

Tom was sitting up when Denise and Kara got to him. 'Are you OK?' Denise asked.

He nodded and winced. His face looked battered and puffy. Blood no sooner spilled from the split skin above his eye than it was washed away by the spray.

'Buddy sort of punched my lights out,' he said.

Denise gripped one of Tom's arms. Kara took the other. They helped him up. The three of them walked over to the woman. She was sprawled on the grass beside Buddy, knees up, arms spread out, a tire iron resting across her belly. The bar went up and down, wobbling as she gasped for air. She squinted up at them through the rain of a nearby sprinkler.

'Hi,' Kara said. 'Thanks for helping us.'

'Glad to.'

'Would you like to come into the house?'

'I think so. Yeah.' She pushed herself up. The tire tool rolled down to her lap. She grabbed it, and got slowly to her feet.

Tom crouched down over Buddy. 'Jeez. What happened to him?'

'Me,' the woman said.

'Good going,' Tom told her.

'Where'd you come from?' Kara asked.

She pointed down the block. 'I'd just come out of the house over there. I saw what was happening.'

'Thank God,' Denise muttered. She stepped over to Lou and pulled the spear from his back. Looking around at the others, she said, 'We'd better keep some stuff, just in case.'

'And let's leave the sprinklers on,' Kara said. 'If anybody comes on the lawn, it'll make them good again.'

'It didn't make Buddy and Lou good,' Denise told her.

The woman made a funny sound. It was sort of a laugh, almost a sob. 'With them,' she said, 'I don't think it was just the rain. Where's the other one?'

'In the house,' Denise said. 'I stabbed him.'

'So that's it, then,' the woman said.

'Unless someone else shows up. Come on, let's get inside.'

2

With a towel wrapped around his waist, Trev stepped through the steamy bathroom. He stopped at the door. His hand hesitated on its knob.

They're still black, he thought. What if they try to nail me?

They won't.

Sandy has it 'reined in.' I hope.

He opened the door. Sandy stood in the corridor, leaning back against the wall, holding Rhonda by the shoulders. The girl was slumped against her, head resting between her breasts.

'You save some water for us, pal?'

'It's all yours.'

He stepped past them, and watched as Sandy pushed away from the wall and guided the girl into the bathroom. The door swung shut.

Trev hurried down the hallway. He averted his eyes from the closed door of the room where grandpa Chidi had worked his terrible magic.

In the master bedroom, he rid himself of the towel. He stepped into a pair of soft, dry corduroy pants belonging to the father. He put on socks and a pair of Reebok shoes that were slightly too large, then slipped into a flannel shirt.

He remembered that the woman in the kitchen was about Maureen's size. Maureen's clothes had been too small for Sandy. But the father's things should be about the right size. He gathered another pair of corduroy pants, a sweatshirt and socks. The man had a set of snake-skin cowboy boots in his closet. A smile worked its way across Trev's face as he picked them up.

They ought to suit Sandy just fine.

He carried his load through the hallway, and put it down by the bathroom door.

In another room, he found clothes for Rhonda: a pleated skirt, a white sweater, socks and white tennis shoes. He put them beside the garments he'd picked for Sandy.

He went to the living room. The father and the teenaged girl still slept.

Whatever grandpa had used to drug them, Trev hoped it kept on working. He didn't want to be here when they woke up.

He entered the kitchen. In a cupboard near the sink, he found the family's liquor supply. He took out a bottle of Irish whiskey, carried it to the table, and sat down across from the woman.

Auburn hair. Just like Maureen's.

He twisted the cap off the bottle. 'I'm sorry for your troubles, lady,' he said. And then he drank.

3

'Uh-oh,' Tom said. He turned away from the picture window. 'A car's stopping out front.'

A sick feeling made Denise's stomach sink. She went ahead and pressed the bandage across the twin punctures on her right buttock, then pulled up her soggy pants. She winced as the elastic waistband was dragged over the torn skin of her hip.

Kara rushed toward the window. She had the fire-place poker in one hand while her other hand pressed a washcloth to her lacerated thigh.

Denise picked up the spear she'd taken from Lou's back.

Maureen, with her tire iron, hobbled toward the window on her bandaged feet.

Kara got to it first. She pressed her face against the glass. 'I think it's Mom and Dad!' She dropped her poker and rushed to the front door.

'Wait!' Denise snapped.

'Someone's getting out,' Tom said.

The girl unlocked the door, threw it open and left the house.

Denise ran after her. She found Kara standing just outside the door, eyes on the big, dark shape of a man dashing through the sprinklers with a knife.

She raised her spear.

'Dad!' Kara cried out.

'Honey!' He ran closer.

Denise recognized him. John Foxworth, all right. And he didn't look black.

'I think it's OK,' she said as Tom and Maureen came out.

John threw away his knife. He opened his arms. Kara leaped from the top of the stoop. Somehow, he managed to stay on his feet when he caught her. She wrapped her arms and legs around him.

While they embraced, Denise saw a woman hurrying across the lawn. She recognized the dress first. It was the slinky, one-armed gown with the slit up its side. The dress that Lynn had felt so uncertain about wearing.

The woman rushed closer, and Denise recognized her face.

Lynn went to her husband and daughter. She wrapped her arms around both of them.

Tom put a hand on Denise's back. She leaned against him and sighed.

Then another woman came striding through the sprinklers. She wore a skirt and a dark blazer. The blazer was buttoned at her waist. She didn't seem to be wearing a thing underneath it. She suddenly smiled. 'Maureen? Is that you?'

'Cassy?'

Maureen trotted down the stairs. Moments later, those two were embracing.

'I guess they know each other,' Tom said.

'Guess so.'

'Everybody's hugging but us.'

'Looks that way.' Denise dropped her spear. She turned to Tom, slipped her arms around him, and squeezed him hard.

4

In spite of the sun's warmth, Maureen felt a chill spread over her skin when she saw a splintery gap in the front door of her house.

'I'll go in first,' said the CHP officer. One of a virtual army that poured through the streets of Bixby soon after the rain had stopped. He'd come to the Foxworth house a few hours after dawn.

His name was Jack Conroy. He'd already taken Cassy back to her apartment, and gone inside to make sure there were no lurking crazies. Then he'd driven Tom and Denise to Tom's home. He'd stayed with them, but hadn't needed to go inside because they were met on the porch by Tom's family.

Now, he drew his revolver. With his left hand, he threw the door open. He rushed into the house, crouching. 'Freeze!' he shouted.

Maureen went in behind him.

On the living-room sofa, hands in the air, sat Trevor Hudson. When he saw Maureen, he clamped his lower lip between his teeth and looked as if he might be about to cry.

'It's all right, Jack,' she said.

'I guess he looks clean.'

'I'm clean,' Trevor said, his voice trembling.

'Do you know this man?' Jack asked.

'Yeah. He's a friend. An old friend of the family.'

'So, it's OK to leave?'

Maureen nodded. 'Thanks for the ride.'

'Glad to help. Take care.'

He left.

Trevor got to his feet. 'I hope you don't mind me coming in like this.'

'It's nice to see you.'

'It's nice to see you, too. God. It was a bad night.'

'No kidding.'

'But you made it. I'm so damn glad you made it.'

'Is Dad around?'

From the look on Trevor's face, she knew. 'Oh, my God.'

'Rory's fine. I talked to him. He's worried about you.'

'But Dad . . .?'

'He didn't make it. I'm sorry.'

Maureen dropped onto the sofa. She didn't cry. She felt only stunned and weary. Trevor sat down next to her. She slumped against his side, and felt his fingers gently stroke her hair.

The Richard Laymon Collection Volume 1

Richard Laymon

RICHARD LAYMON'S ACCLAIMED BEAST HOUSE TRILOGY

THE CELLAR

The deeper the tourists go into the Beast House, the darker their nightmares become. But the worst part is beneath the haunted structure. Don't even think about going into the cellar . . .

THE BEAST HOUSE

Bestselling author Gorman Hardy is looking for ideas for his next novel. Petite Tyler and her sexy friend Nora are looking for a wild time. Maybe Malcasa Point can provide both? On the other hand, it is just the place to find pain, bestiality and death . . .

THE MIDNIGHT TOUR

Horrific events have made the Beast House infamous. For the full story, take the Midnight Tour. Saturday nights only. Limited to thirteen tourists. It begins on the stroke of midnight. You'll be lucky to get out alive . . .

'If you've missed Laymon, you've missed a treat' Stephen King

'A brilliant writer' *Sunday Express*

0 7553 3167 2

headline

The Richard Laymon Collection Volume 2

Richard Laymon

THE WOODS ARE DARK

In the woods are six dead trees. The Killing Trees. That's where they take them. Innocent travellers on the road in California. Seized and bound, stripped of their valuables and shackled to the Trees. To wait. In the woods. In the dark . . .

OUT ARE THE LIGHTS

The Vampire movie came first, then the story of the Axeman. This was the horror movie series to end them all. Cinema buffs admired the grainy, amateur camera work – it suggested the action was the real thing. But it couldn't be – could it?

'If you've missed Laymon, you've missed a treat' Stephen King

'A brilliant writer' *Sunday Express*

'This author knows how to sock it to the reader' *The Times*

0 7553 3169 9

headline